A CLASSIC MARVEL OMNIBUS

THE DARKEST HOURS OMNIBUS

MARVEL

A CLASSIC MARVEL OMNIBUS

SPIDER-MAN

THE DARKEST HOURS OMNIBUS

by
Jim Butcher,
Keith R.A. DeCandido,
and Christopher L. Bennett

TITAN BOOKS

Spider-Man: The Darkest Hours Omnibus
Print edition ISBN: 9781789096040
E-book edition ISBN: 9781789096057

Published by Titan Books
A division of Titan Publishing Group Ltd
144 Southwark Street, London SE1 0UP

First edition: May 2021
10 9 8 7 6 5 4

FOR MARVEL PUBLISHING
Jeff Youngquist, VP Production Special Projects
Caitlin O'Connell, Associate Editor, Special Projects
Sven Larsen, VP, Licensed Publishing
David Gabriel, SVP Sales & Marketing, Publishing
C.B. Cebulski, Editor in Chief

Cover art by Justin Ponsor.

A CIP catalogue record for this title is available from the British Library.

Printed and bound in Great Britain by CPI Group (UK) Ltd, Croydon, CR0 4YY.

Book One

THE DARKEST HOURS

by Jim Butcher

ONE

MY name is Peter Parker and I'm the sort of person who occasionally gets in a little over his head.

"The most important thing," said the man in the dark hood, walking down the hall next to me, "is not to show them any fear. If you hesitate, or look like you don't know what you're doing, even for a second, they'll sense the weakness. They'll eat you alive."

"No fear," I said. "No getting eaten. Check."

"I'm serious. You're outnumbered. They're faster, most of them are stronger, they can run you into the ground, and if you're going to keep it under control, you're going to have to win the battle here." He touched a finger to his forehead. "You get me?"

"Mind war," I said. "Wax on. Wax off."

The man in the dark hood stopped, frowned at me, and said, "You aren't taking this seriously."

"People always think that about me," I said. "I'm not sure why."

"See, that's what I mean," Coach Kyle said. He tucked his hands into the pockets of his workout jacket and shook his head. "You go joking around with them like that, and that's it. You've lost control."

"It's a basketball practice," I said. "Not a prison riot."

Coach Kyle was about six feet tall, with a slender build. Dark skin, and dark hair which apparently hadn't started to go gray, though he had to have been in his late forties. He wore thick glasses with black plastic Marine-issue, birth-control rims. He'd been a Hoosier, starting guard, back in the day. He hadn't made the cut to the pros. "I see," he said with a snort. "You're upset because you were the one who got stuck with running the team."

"Well," I hedged, "I wasn't much for sports when I was in school."

"This was settled at last week's faculty meeting," he told me cheerfully. "If you hadn't been the last one to arrive at *this* meeting, you'd be halfway home by now."

"I know." I sighed.

"Guess you had something more important come up?"

I'd been crawling around about two hundred and fifty berjillion freight-train-sized shipping containers at the piers, looking for the one the mob was using to ship out illegal immigrants for sale on the slave market. Officially speaking, they weren't people, since they hadn't filled out the right paperwork and learned the secret American handshake from the INS. Unofficially speaking, scum who target people who can't defend themselves incite me to creative outrage. By the time I had the last of them webbed to the side of their slave container in the shape of the word "LOSERS" I'd been five minutes late to the faculty meeting already.

But that's not the kind of thing you can use as an excuse.

"The dog ate my homework," I said instead.

Coach Kyle shook his head, grinning, and we stopped outside the door to the gym. "Look. Your big worry is the tallest kid there. Samuel. Best strong center I ever had, and he could go all the way. Problem is he knows it, and he doesn't play well with others."

"The fiend," I said. "This is a job for Superman."

Coach Kyle sighed. "Peter. Samuel's mom works three jobs to make enough to feed him and his three little brothers and sisters. Their block isn't such a good one. He had an older brother who was a gangbanger— that is, until he got stabbed to death a few years back. That's when Samuel took over as man of the house. Looking out for the little ones."

I sighed, and dialed down my snark projector. "Go on."

"Boy's got a real chance of turning into a top-rate athlete, and if he can make it into a college, he can help out his whole family. Problem is that he's a good kid, at the core."

"That's a problem?"

"Yes. Because if he doesn't get himself under control and make it into a good school, he'll graduate and try to support his family."

I nodded my head, getting it. "And wind up in the same place as his brother."

Coach Kyle nodded. "He's big, tough, and can make good money in a gang. And it isn't as if he's going to have employers kicking down his door to get to him."

"I see." I glanced through the narrow window in the door to the gym. A lot of young people were running and screaming. Shoes squeaked on the floor. Many, many basketballs thudded onto the court in a rhythm that could only have been duplicated by a drunken, clog-dancing centipede. "What do you need me to do?"

"Right now, the kid is his own worst enemy. If he doesn't learn to work with his team, to lead on the court, no university will even look at him."

"But he hasn't realized that yet," I guessed.

Coach Kyle nodded. "I just want you to understand, Peter. Coaching the basketball team isn't just a chore that needs doing. It isn't only a game. The team might be this kid's only chance. Same goes for the others, to a lesser degree. The team keeps them off the streets, out of some of the trouble."

I watched the kids playing and nodded. "I hear you. I'll take it seriously." I met his eyes and said, "Promise."

"Thank you," Coach Kyle said, and offered me his hand. "To tell you the truth, I was hoping you'd be the one to keep an eye on them for me. I see you with some of the other kids. You do good work."

I traded grips with him and grinned. "Well, I'm so childish myself."

"Heh," he said. "Maybe I should come in with you for a minute. Just to help you get started."

"It's okay," I said. "I can handle it myself. Have fun getting lasered in the eyes."

He tapped his ugly glasses with one finger. "See you next week," he said. Then he headed out.

I sighed and opened the door to the gymnasium. After all, it wasn't like I'd never been outnumbered before. I'd gone up against the Sinister Six versions one through fifty or sixty, and the Sinister Syndicate, and those bozos in the Wrecking Crew, and . . . the X-Men? No, that couldn't be right. I hadn't ever taken on the X-Men and thrashed them, I was sure.

But those others, yes. And if I could handle them, surely I could handle a bunch of kids playing basketball.

Which only goes to show that just because I happen to be a fairly sharp scientist, the Amazing Spider-Man, and a snappy dancer, I don't know everything.

TWO

THERE'S something about gymnasiums. Maybe it's the fluorescent lighting. Maybe it's the acoustics, the way that squeaking shoes echo off the walls, the way thudding basketballs sound on the floor, or rattling against the rim, or the way "bricks" slam into the backboard and make the whole thing shudder. Maybe it's the smell—one part sweat and friction-warmed rubber to many parts disinfectant and floor polish. I'm not sure.

All I know is that every time I walk into a gymnasium, I get hit with a rush of memories from my own days of high school. Some people call that phenomenon "nostalgia." I call it "nausea."

Unless, of course, nostalgia is *supposed* to make you feel abruptly shunned, unpopular, and inadequate—in which case, I suppose that gymnasiums are nostalgic as all get-out for me.

The gym was full of young men in shorts, athletic socks and shoes, T-shirts and tank tops. The color schemes and fabrics employed were slightly different, but other than that they looked pretty much exactly like the b-ball players had when I'd gone to school here. That made me feel pretty nostalgic, too.

I hadn't had a very easy time of it in high school, particularly with the sports-oriented crowd who hung around in the gym. A radioactive spider bite had more than taken care of any physical inadequacies—but my memories of that time in my life weren't about fact. They were about old feelings that still had power.

Fine, so I had one or two lingering issues from high school. Who doesn't?

I also had Coach Kyle's whistle, his clipboard, and his practice schedule, complete with warm-ups, drills, and all the other activities which constituted a training session. Plus, I was an adult now. A teacher. I had the wisdom and experience of age—well, compared to a teenager, anyway. I was the one with the authority, the one who would command respect. I was not a big-brained high school nerd anymore. No one was going to give me a wedgie or a swirlie or stuff me into a locker.

Even if most of them *did* seem to be awfully tall.

I shook my head and grinned at my reaction to all those memories. These days, I'd have to work hard to be sure not to hurt any of them if they tried it, but the emotional reflexes were still there. You can take the nerd out of the school . . .

I stepped out onto the court and blew a short, loud blast on the whistle and rotated my hand in the air above my head. "Bring it in, guys, right here."

A couple of the kids immediately turned and shuffled over to me. Most of them never even slowed down, being involved in a game of seven-on-one against Samuel.

They probably just hadn't heard the whistle. Yeah, right. No fear, Peter. No fear.

I blew the whistle again, louder, and for as long as I could keep blowing, maybe twenty or thirty seconds of pure, warbling authority. Most of the stragglers came over after ten seconds or so.

Samuel, who was big enough and strong enough to dunk, slammed the ball in one more time after everyone else had come over, recovered it, and took a three-point shot for nothing but net. He finally turned to walk over about half a second before I ran out of wind.

"Afternoon, guys," I said. "I'm Mister Parker, and I'm a science teacher, in case you didn't know. I'm going to be standing in for Coach Kyle for a few days, until he's back on the job. The coach has left me a schedule of what he wants you to be doing so—"

"Shoot," said Samuel, with a disgusted exhale. He didn't say "shoot," exactly, but I wanted to give him the benefit of the doubt.

"You have a question, Mister . . ." I checked Kyle's clipboard. "Larkin?"

"Yeah," he said. "Where you played ball?" His expression was sullen and skeptical. The kid was ridiculously tall, and not just for his age. He would have been ridiculously tall at any age.

"I haven't lately," I told him.

"College?" he asked.

"No."

"High school?"

"No," I said.

"Shoot," he didn't say. "You don't know nothing about ball."

I didn't let it rattle me. "Those who can't do, teach," I told him. Then I held up the clipboard. "But I figure Coach Kyle knows what he's doing, so we're just going to stick to his plan, starting with a ten-minute warm-up run and stretching." I tucked the clipboard under my arm and tried to pretend I was a drill sergeant. I blew the whistle once, clapped my hands, and said, "Let's go!"

And they went. Slowly, reluctantly, and Samuel was still standing there glowering at me when the first of his teammates had finished the first lap, but then he shambled off to join them. Good-looking kid, very strong features, skin almost as dark as his eyes, and his voice held authority well. His teammates would look up to him, literally and figuratively.

Once the run was finished, I told Samuel to lead the team through stretching, which he did without batting an eye. He'd done it for Coach Kyle before, I supposed. I could see what the coach meant when he said the kid was a natural leader.

When the stretching was done, Kyle's plan called for passing drills, and that was when I saw what the coach meant about Samuel's bad attitude.

The team groaned when I said "Drill," and Samuel shook his head. "Screw that. That isn't what the team needs right now." He looked around. "Okay, we'll go half court twice. Starters against me on this end; Darnell, you take the rest to that end and split into four-on-four."

The kids went into motion at once.

Good thing I had that whistle. I blew another blast on it and called, "The coach wants you running passing drills. You are darn well going to run passing drills."

"Hey," Samuel said, "shredded wheat." He shot me a hard, swift pass that should have bounced the ball off the back of my head—but my spider sense, that inexplicable yet extremely cool sixth sense that warns me of danger, alerted me to the incoming basketball. I turned and caught it flat against my right hand, then gripped onto it with the old wall-crawling cling, so that it looked like I had caught it and perfectly palmed it to boot.

Samuel hadn't expected that—but it didn't faze him, either. "You're pretty fast for an old man."

"Thanks," I said, and flicked the ball back at him, making sure I didn't break his ribs with it out of annoyance. "Now line them up and run the drills."

"Screw you, Mister Science," Samuel said. "The team needs real practice."

I frowned at him. "The coach—"

"Ain't here," Samuel said, his tone harsh. "He's off on vacation, ain't he."

"Doesn't matter," I said. "We're running drills. We've got twenty minutes of full-court five-on-five at the end of the day."

The team groaned, and Samuel grinned at me. "Full-court five-on-five? Might as well send everyone else home and let me practice shots. 'Cause that's all that is gonna happen. My way, everybody gets to play."

"You aren't the coach," I said.

He shrugged. "Neither are you."

"I am today."

"Tell you what, Mister Science," Samuel said. "You come out here on the floor with me. We can go half-court one-on-one to five. You get even one past me before I hit five, or if I foul you even once, we'll do it your way. Otherwise you let someone who knows what he's doing run the practice."

I was tempted, but only for a second. Hammering my point through the kid's thick skull wasn't going to do him any good. "We're going to practice," I told him. "If you don't want to practice, that's cool. You can leave whenever you like."

Samuel just stared at me. Then he burst out into a rolling belly laugh, and most of the other kids followed along.

Clearly, the whistle's power was finite. The clipboard's additional failure was sadly disappointing. I was on the verge of trying my luck with pure alpha-male bellowing, when someone behind me cleared her throat, a prim little sound.

I turned to find my professional nemesis standing behind me.

Julie from Administration.

She was fortyish, fake blonde, slender as a reed, and wore a lavender business suit. She had a diamond the size of a baby elephant on her wedding ring, a thick pink clipboard in her hands, and was entirely innocent of original thought.

"Excuse me, Coach Kyle," Julie said without looking up. "I needed you to sign this report."

"I'm not Coach Kyle," I said. "Coach Kyle is a little taller than me. And he's black."

She looked up from the papers on her board and frowned severely. "Coach Kyle coaches the basketball team."

"Hence 'Coach.' Yes."

"Then what are you doing here?"

"He's on a medical leave."

Julie frowned. "I did not see the paperwork for it."

I sighed. "No paperwork? Clearly, Western civilization is on the brink of collapse."

She frowned at me. "What?"

Insulting Julie from Administration is like throwing rocks into the ocean. There's a little ripple, and the ocean never even notices it happened. "I'm standing in for him," I said. "Maybe I can help you."

Behind me, the kids had broken up into two half-court games as soon as my back was turned, just as I told them not to do. Gee, thanks, Julie.

"It's about Mister Larkin," she said. "His immunization record still hasn't been completed, and if he doesn't get his shots we'll have to suspend him until he does. I need you to sign here to show that you've been notified."

"That happens," I allowed, as she offered me the pink clipboard. I signed by the X. "How long does he have to get the shots?"

"Until Monday," she said. "If he doesn't have them Monday morning, he'll have to go into suspension."

I blinked at her. "It's Friday," I said.

"And I'm working late," Julie replied. "Because unlike *some* people who work at this school, I find it important to put in extra effort, instead of calling in sick every six-point-two-nine days. Like some people I could mention."

"Oh," I said, in a tone of sudden revelation. "You're talking about me." *Grrr.*

"Yes," she said. "I only hope your attitude doesn't affect Coach Kyle's job performance."

Grrr.

"You missed my point, though," I said as politely as I could. "There's no way to get him into a city clinic before Monday morning. They aren't open before then."

"Well," she said, exasperated, "his parents will just have to convince their family doctor to help."

"Parent," I said. "Single parent, working three jobs to support the family. I promise you, they use the clinic, not a private practitioner."

She sniffed. "Then they should have gotten him to the clinic sooner."

I gritted my teeth. "Have you notified him or his mother?"

"No," she said, as if I was a moron. "I required the signature of one of his teachers before I could run through all the forms, and you're the only one left in the building. You didn't sign for it until just now. Which makes it all your fault, really."

The ironic thing is that Julie is an enormous Spider-Man fangirl.

Deep breaths, Parker. Nice, deep breaths.

"But he didn't know he needed the shots." I blinked. "Still *doesn't* know, in fact."

"Letters were sent to all students' parents last July," she said firmly. "He should have had them before school even started."

"But you're only telling him *today*? When it's already too *late*?"

"It was a low organizational priority," she said. "More pressing matters have kept administration"—which was always Julie plus someone who was going to quit within two weeks—"far too busy to waste time doing Mister Larkin's parents' job."

I rubbed at my forehead. "Look, Julie. If this kid gets suspended, he'll be off the team—and it would make it more difficult for him to be accepted into a university."

Julie gave me a bewildered stare, as though I'd begun speaking in tongues. "University?"

I wondered if I'd get strange looks if I threw myself down and started chewing at the floorboards. "The point is that if he gets suspended over something like this, it's going to be all kinds of bad for him."

She waved a hand. "Well. Perhaps Mr. and Mrs. Larkin will be more careful about following immunization procedures next time," she said, and jerked her clipboard back. She tore off a pink copy of the form I'd signed and said, "This is for Mr. and Mrs. Larkin."

"Julie," I said. "Have a heart here. The kid needs some help."

She sniffed in contempt at the very idea. "I am only following the policy, rules, and law of the New York educational system."

"Right. Just following orders," I said.

"Precisely." She turned on a heel and goose-stepped out of the gymnasium.

My God, the woman was pure evil.

I glanced back at Samuel, who was currently playing four-on-one and winning handily. He wasn't talking smack to them, though. He was focused, intent, moving in his natural element. The kid was a stiff-necked loudmouth, insulting, arrogant, and he reminded me way too much of people who beat me up for lunch money when I'd been in school.

But no one deserved Julie from Administration.

And since Coach Kyle wasn't around to do it, this looked like a job for Spider-Man.

THREE

"TALK about disasters," I said, as Mary Jane came through the front door of our apartment. "It's like they could smell the high school nerd on my clothes. Mister Science. They called me Mister Science. And shredded wheat. Just did whatever they wanted. And the worst one, this Samuel kid, he challenged me to a round of one-on-one. Told me if I won, they would run the practice my way."

I might have sounded just a bit sulky. My wife got the look she gets when she's trying really hard to keep from laughing at me. "The basketball practice?" she asked.

"Yes." I scowled down at the stack of papers I was grading. "It was like herding manic-obsessive cats. I can't remember the last time I felt so stupid."

"Why didn't you play the kid?" MJ asked. "I mean, you could have beaten him, right?"

"Oh, sure. If I didn't mind the kids finding out that Mister Science has a two-hundred-and-eighty-inch vertical leap." I put my pen down and set the papers aside. "Besides. That isn't what the kid needs. I'm supposed to teach him to be a team player. If the first thing I do is go mano-a-mano with him to prove who's best, it might undermine that."

"Just a bit," Mary Jane conceded. "I thought you were going to go to the faculty meeting early so you wouldn't get saddled with coaching the team."

"I was," I glowered. "Something came up."

"Who could have foreseen *that*," she said tartly, and walked into our little kitchen and set down the brown grocery bag she was holding. If you'd asked my opinion when I was Samuel's age, I'd have said she looked like a million bucks. Since then, though, there's been inflation, and now I figure she looks like at least a billion.

But as we grew closer, I saw other things when I looked at her. I saw the woman who was willing to stand beside me through thick and thin, despite a mountain of reasons not to, despite the fact that just being a part of my life sometimes put her in danger. I saw the woman who was willing to spend many nights—far too many nights—alone while I ran around town doing everything a spider can, and leaving her to wonder when I'd be back.

Or even if I'd be back.

I might have been able to juggle compact cars, but I wasn't strong enough to do what she did, to be who she was. She was the one who had faith in me, the one who believed in me, the one who I knew, absolutely *knew*, would always listen, always help, always care. The longer I looked at her, the more beautiful she got, and the more thoroughly I understood how insanely lucky I was to have her beside me.

It was enough to disintegrate my frustration, at least for the moment. Honestly, if a man gets to come home to a woman like that at the end of the day, how bad can things be?

"Sorry, MJ." I sighed. "I ambushed you the second you walked in the door."

She arched a brow and teased, "I'll let it go. This time."

I started helping her with the bag. Not because she needed the help, but because it gave me a great excuse to stand behind her and reach both arms around her to handle the groceries. I liked the way her hair smelled.

She leaned back against me for a second, then gave me a playful nudge with one hip. "You really want to make it up to me? Cook."

I lifted both eyebrows. I cook almost as well as Ben Grimm embroiders, and MJ knew it. "Living dangerously tonight, are we?"

"Statistically speaking, you're bound to make something that tastes good eventually," she said. She took a frozen pizza out of the bag and passed it over her shoulder to me. "Back in a minute, master chef."

"Bork, bork, bork," I confirmed. She slipped off to the bedroom. I flipped the pizza box and went over the instructions. Looked simple enough. I followed the directions carefully while Mary Jane ran the shower.

She came back out in time to see me crouched on the ceiling, trying to get the stupid smoke alarm to shut up. She got that I'm-not-laughing face again and went to the oven to see what she could salvage.

I finally pulled the battery out of the smoke alarm and opened a window. "Hey," I said. "Are you all right?"

"Of course," she said. "Why would you ask that?"

"My husband sense is tingling." I frowned at her, then hit the side of my head with the heel of my hand. "The audition. It was this morning, right?"

She hesitated for a second, and then nodded.

Oh, right, I got it. She'd been bothered by something about it, but I'd been quicker on the draw in the gunfight at the co-dependent corral, and she didn't want to lay it on me when I'd been stressed myself.

Like I said. I'm a lucky guy.

"How'd it go?" I asked her. We got dinner (such as it was), a couple of drinks, and sat down on the couch together.

"That's the problem," she said quietly. "I got the part."

I lifted my eyebrows. "What? That's fantastic! Who'd they cast you as?"

"Lady Macbeth."

"Well of course they did!" I burbled at her. "You've got red hair. Redheads are naturally evil. Did I mention that this was fantastic?"

"It isn't, Pete."

"It isn't?"

"It isn't."

"But I thought you said it was a serious company. That working with them would give you some major street cred for acting."

"Yes."

"Oh," I said. I blew on my slice of pizza. "Why?"

"Because it's showing in Atlantic City."

"Ugh. Jersey."

She rolled her eyes. "The point being that I'm going to have to get over there several times every week."

"No problem," I said. "We can swing the train fare, I'm sure."

"That's just it," Mary Jane said. "I can't trust the train, Peter. Too many things could happen. If it's delayed, if I'm late, if it takes off a couple of minutes early, and I don't show up, that's it: I can kiss my career goodbye. I've got to have a car."

I scratched my head, frowning. "Does it have to be a nice car?"

"It just has to work," she said.

"Well," I said. "It's more expensive, but we might be able to—"

"I bought a car, too."

I looked down at the suddenly too-expensive pizza on my plate. MJ's career as a model had been high-profile, but not necessarily high-paying. I was a part-time science teacher, and the paycheck isn't nearly as glamorous and enormous as everyone thinks. We weren't exactly dirt poor, but it costs a lot of money to own and operate a car in New York City. "Oh."

"It didn't cost very much. It's old, but it goes when you push the pedal."

"That's good," I said. "Um. Maybe you should have talked to me first?"

"There wasn't time," she said apologetically. "I had to get it today because rehearsal starts Monday afternoon, and I still had to take my test and get my license and . . ." She broke off, swallowing, and I swear, she almost started crying. "And I failed the stupid *test*," she said. "I mean, I thought it would be simple, but I failed it. I've got a chance to finally show people that I can really act, that I'm not some stupid magazine bimbo who can't do anything but look good in a bikini in movies about Lobsterman, and I failed the stupid driver's test."

"Hey," I said quietly, setting dinner aside so that I could put my arms around her. "Come here."

She leaned against me and let out a miserable little sigh. "It was humiliating."

I tightened my arms around her. "But you can take the test again tomorrow, right?"

She nodded. "But Pete, I . . . I got nothing on the test. I mean, nothing. Zero. If there'd been a score lower than zero I would have gotten that, but they stop at zero. It isn't fair. I've lived my whole life in New York. I'm not *supposed* to know how to drive."

I wanted to laugh, but I didn't. "It isn't a big deal," I told her. "Look, I can help you out, you'll take the test tomorrow, get your license, and then we can plan your outfit for the Academy Awards."

"Really?" she said, looking up at me, those devastating green eyes wide and uncertain. "You can help?"

"Trust me," I told her. "I spent years as a full-time underclassman while spending my nights creeping around rooftops and alleys looking for trouble. If there's one thing I know, it's how to pass a test you haven't had much time to study for."

She laughed a little and laid her head against my chest. "Thank you." She shook her head. "I didn't mean to go all neurotic on you."

"See there? You're becoming more like the great actresses by the minute." I kissed her hair. "Anytime."

I heard a low, faint rumbling sound, and glanced out the window. I didn't see anything, but it took only sixty seconds for the sirens to start howling—police as well as fire department, a dozen of them at least.

"Trouble?" Mary Jane asked quietly.

I grabbed the remote and clicked on the TV. Not a minute later, my regular programming was interrupted by a news broadcast. The news crew camera was still jiggling as the cameraman stumbled out of a van, but I got enough to see what was going on: a panic, hundreds of people running, the bright light and hollow boom of an explosion and clouds of black smoke rising up in the background—Times Square.

"Trouble," Mary Jane said.

"Looks that way," I said. "Sorry."

"Don't be." She looked up and laid a swift kiss against my lips. "All right, tiger. Get a move on." She rose and gave me a wicked little smile. "I'll keep something warm for you."

FOUR

AH, New York on an autumn evening. Summer's heat had passed by, and let me tell you, there's nothing quite as miserable as webbing around the old town when it's so hot that my suit is soaked with sweat. It clings to and abrades things which ought not be clung to or abraded. My enhanced physique runs a little hotter than your average human being's, too—the price of having muscles that can bench-press more than any two X-Men, and reflexes that make Speedy González look like Aesop's Tortoise.

Autumn, though, is different. Once the sun starts setting and the air cools off, it feels just about perfect. There's usually a brisk wind that somehow smells of wood smoke, a golden scent, somewhere on the far side of eau de New York, that heralds the end of summer. Sometimes, I can stand on one of the many lofty rooftops around town, watching the moon track across the sky, listening to the passage of geese heading down to Florida, and letting the traffic-sounds, the ship-sounds, the plane-sounds of New York provide the musical score. Nights like that have their own kind of delicate beauty, where the whole city feels like one enormous, quietly aware entity, and though the sun was still providing a lingering autumn twilight, tonight was going to be one of those times.

Assuming, of course, that whatever had caused a third column of smoke to start rolling up through the evening air didn't spoil it for me.

I was making pretty good time through Manhattan when that twitchy little sensation of intuition I'd dubbed my "spider sense" (because I was fifteen at the time) let me know that I wasn't alone.

I managed to catch a blur in the corner of my vision, moving along a window ledge on a building parallel to my course, above and behind me, staying in the shadows cast by the buildings in the fading light, and rapidly catching up with me. If I continued in my current line of motion, my pursuer would be in a perfect position to ambush me as I crossed the next street—one of those midair impacts, when I was at the top of a ballistic arch and least able to get out of the way. The Vulture loved those, and so had the various Goblins. If I had a chiropractor, he'd love them too, on account of every one of them would make him money.

Me, I'm not so fond of them.

So at the very last second, just as I would have flung myself into the air, I turned around instead, hit the building my chaser was on with a webline, and hung on. The line stretched and recoiled, flinging me back toward the would-be attacker, and I added all of my own oomph to it and shot at my pursuer like a cannonball.

Whoever it was reacted swiftly. He immediately changed direction, leaping off a ledge and soaring through the air by swinging on some kind of matte black, nonreflective cable to a lower rooftop. He hit the roof rolling, and I had to flick out a strand of webbing to reverse direction again. He might have been fast, but not *that* fast. I hit him around the waist with a flying tackle and pinned him against the roof.

At which point I realized that I had pinned *her* to the roof.

"Well," drawled a languidly amused woman's voice. "This evening is turning out even better than I thought it would."

"Felicia?" I said.

She turned her head enough to let me see the smirk on her mouth and said, "This is hardly a dignified position for a married man. What if some nerdy freelance photographer for the *Bugle* came along and took our picture? Can you imagine the headlines? *Two Swingers Caught in Flagrante Delicto on Roof.*"

"I doubt that the Human Flattop would use that term," I replied. But she had a point. I read somewhere that full-body pins are not a proper greeting for an ex-girlfriend from a married man, so I got off of her in a hurry.

Felicia Hardy rolled over, leaned back on her elbows, and regarded me for a moment from her lounging position. She'd given her Black Cat costume a minor makeover, losing the white puffs at her calves and wrists.

Maybe they'd been harder to find since *Cats* closed. She still wore the catsuit, but this new suit was made out of some supple, odd-looking black material I'd never seen before, and it managed to give me the impression that it was some kind of body armor. Her hair was shorter than the last time I'd seen her, and she wore a black visor that covered her eyes, until she tipped it down enough to give me a wicked-eyed smile over the visor's rim, and extended her arm up to me. "Give me a hand?"

Part of me was happy to see Felicia again. There aren't a lot of people I'm comfortable fighting beside, but Felicia is one of them. Admittedly, we'd gotten off to a bad start, since she had been a professional burglar at the time, but eventually the bad first impressions became spilt milk under the bridge. She'd reformed—more or less. And she'd helped me out a couple of times when I really needed it.

We became involved during that time, and the romance had been . . . eventful. Tempestuous. On occasion, it had resembled pay-per-view professional wrestling. It had ended amicably, more or less, but I'd still been worried that she might go back to what she was doing before she met me. Apparently, however, her reform had been sincere, and she was, as far as I knew, on the straight and narrow these days.

I pulled her to her feet. "What are you doing here?"

"I needed to talk to you," she said, rising. She put her hands on the small of her back, winced a little, and stretched again. "Mmmm. I always did like it when you played rough, Spider."

"I could have killed you," I said. "What do you think you're doing, stalking me like that?"

"I was going to knock on your door," she said, "but I saw you leaving. I had to get your attention somehow."

"You know what gets my attention?" I said. "When someone shouts my name and says that they want to talk to me. One time, they even used this magical device called a telephone."

"You don't get it—" she began.

Another enormous crunching, crashing sound from Times Square, only a few hundred yards off, interrupted her.

"No, *you* don't get it," I said, and turned to go. "I don't have time for this right now, Cat. I'm on the clock."

"Wait," she said. "You can't!"

I ground my teeth under the mask and paused, webline in hand. "Five words or less, why not?"

Felicia put her hands on her hips, eyes narrowed, and said, holding up a finger with each word, "It is a trap." She considered and stuck out her thumb, too. "Dummy."

"A trap?" I said. "Whose?"

"That's just it," she said. "I'm not sure."

"You just know it's a trap."

"If you'll give me a second to explain—"

Down the street, a police car tumbled across the road, end over end, bouncing along like a child's toy, lights flashing. It knocked over a fire hydrant, sending a cascade of water into the air, then crashed through the front window of an adult bookstore.

"You've got to admit," she said. "It isn't hard for someone to get a rise out of you if they want to draw you out. That's what Morlun did."

I had been about to swing off, but her words stopped me cold.

Morlun.

Ugh.

Morlun had been . . . bad. A creature, some kind of entity that fed upon the life energy of vessels of totemistic power. That's mystic gobbledygook for superheroes who draw their powers from—or at least compare them to—some kind of animal. Say, for example, your friendly, neighborhood Spider-Man. He was an ultra-ancient being who only looked human, who devoured the life energy of his victims to sustain his own apparent immortality.

Morlun had asked me to dinner, and not as a guest. The invitation had come in the form of a rampage in the fine tradition begun by the Hulk. I sent him a two-fisted RSVP. As brawls go, it had been a long one. Days long. I can't remember anyone who's made me feel more physical pain, offhand. Morlun was strong. Really, really strong. And he took everything I could throw at him without blinking. Or talking. Which cheesed me off. How am I supposed to uphold snappy superhero banter when the other guy won't carry his end of the conversational load?

He almost killed me. God help me, I almost let him. I almost gave up. I'd just been that hurt, that tired—that alone. Morlun showed up in my nightmares for a good long while afterward, temporarily supplanting my subconscious's favorite bogeyman, Norman Osborne.

I came out on top in the end, but only by injecting myself with material from the core of a nuclear reactor, so that when he tried to eat me, Morlun got a big old mouthful of gamma-ray energy instead. After that, Morlun's day went down-hill pretty fast.

Here's the kicker, though.

I hadn't told anyone about Morlun.

Not Aunt May.

Not Mary Jane.

Nobody.

As far as I knew, the only one, other than me, who had known what was going on was a guy named Ezekiel. A man who had, somehow, acquired powers remarkably similar to my own, and who had tried to warn me about Morlun—and who had eventually helped me defeat him, nearly at the cost of his own life.

So how had Felicia found out about Morlun?

"Hey," I said. "How did you find out about Morlun?"

"I've turned over a new leaf, remember?" she said. "I'm a security consultant and investigator now. I investigate things, and some of what I turned up indicates that there's someone here to call you out." She slipped off the visor and met my eyes, her expression worried. "The details will take me a while to give you, but the short version is that you're in danger, Peter."

An ambulance siren added its wail to that of the police cars and fire trucks. I could see people running from the area, underneath one of the big flashing signs for the New Amsterdam Theater, where they were performing *The Lion King*.

"No," I said. "They're the ones who are in danger."

"But I already told you—"

"It's a trap, I know. But the longer I stay away from it, the more noise whoever is over there is going to make. I'm going."

"Don't," she said, touching my arm. "Don't be stupid. It's not as if there aren't a couple of other folks around New York who will show up to a disturbance this public."

"No," I said. "I can't let other people do my chores for me. If I wait for the FF to show up, or the Avengers, he'll scamper and do it all again another day." I felt myself getting a little angry, talking about it.

Like I said: I have issues with people who pick on those who can't protect themselves.

"I'm taking this guy down," I said. "Thank you for the warning. But I'm going."

Felicia didn't look happy with me as she jammed the visor back onto her face. "You stiff-necked . . ." She shook her head. "Go on. Go. Be careful."

I nodded once, dove off on my line, and flung myself from building to building down the street. I swung around the last corner, rapidly gathering momentum, and found a scene of pure chaos. Emergency units were trying to cordon off the square. Fires burned. Smoke rolled. Several police cars had been flattened—literally *flattened*—by blows of superhuman strength. Many of the lights were either out or flickering wildly, giving the place that crazed, techno dance club look. Broken glass lay everywhere. Car alarms and fire alarms beeped and wooped and ah-oohgahed. The air stank of burning plastic and motor oil. People shouted, screamed, and ran.

"It's like the mayor's office in an election year," I muttered.

At the center of it all, in the thick plume of black smoke, stood a single, hulking figure. I altered my course, spat a new line from my web shooters, and swung down to give whoever it was a big old double-heeled mule-kick greeting on behalf of the citizens of New York.

Did I mention that I have a tendency to get in over my head?

FIVE

I hollered, "Boot to the head!" as I swung through the black smoke and slammed into Newtonian physics.

Newton. Isaac Newton. You remember him. White wig, apple tree. Played poker with Einstein, Hawking, and Data in an episode of *Star Trek*. You can't really say he discovered the laws of physics, since they'd pretty much been there already, but he was one of the first to actually stop and look at them and get them written down. And while the next several centuries of scientific advancement proved that in certain circumstances he had dropped the ball—*bah-dump-bump-ching!*—he did a good enough job that it took the computer revolution to knock him off his pedestal a bit. Even then, pretty much anywhere on the planet (for example, Times Square), for pretty much everything you might bump into (for example, rampaging bad guys), Newton's material is a darned good rule of thumb.

One of them applied here: For every action, there is an equal and opposite reaction.

I came swooping down and delivered my double-heeled kick all right. Right into the Rhino's breadbasket.

Granted, I'm smarter than most, and I always have something pithy to say, and I can just be a gosh-darned wonderful person when I put my mind to it. But all of that fits into a pretty small package. I'm not big. I'm not heavily built. I weigh about one sixty-five, soaking wet.

The Rhino, now, he's built like a brick gulag. He's huge. Huge tall, huge across, huge through. Not only that, but whatever process was used to ramp up his strength, it mucked about with his cellular makeup somehow, because he weighs on the heavy side of eight hundred pounds. I'm sure some of that can be accounted for by the stupid Rhino hat he wears, but bottom line, he's an enormous gray block of muscle and bone, and even with my oh-so-stylish spider strength, I wasn't really set for this kick. Super strength is all well and good, but if you don't have yourself braced—like if you're swinging on a webline—you're at Sir Isaac's mercy.

But my Aunt May always taught me to make the best of things, so I let him have it.

The kick took the Rhino off guard, even with me shouting and all. Granted, he isn't exactly the shiniest nail in the box, and there were all kinds of bright colors and sounds around to distract him, but still. I think I might have caught him on the inhale, because the kick made his face turn green and threw him fifteen or twenty feet back and smashed him into a storefront.

Of course, the same amount of force came back at me. And since the Rhino weighs four or five or six times as much as me, I got flung a lot farther than fifteen or twenty feet. Then again, I'm the Amazing Spider-Man. Flying around in the air is what I do. So I hit a streetlamp with a webline as I flew by, hung on to be whipped around in a circle twice, arched up into a tumble, and came down in a crouch on top of an abandoned taxi about sixty feet away—where I could see the Rhino, enjoyed a clear field of view around me, and had plenty of room to move.

Felicia is no dummy. If she said that this was a trap, she probably had a good reason to think so.

"Well, well, well," I said. "The Rhino. Again. I thought maybe poachers might have shot you and ground you up to sell as medicine on the Chinese black market by now. They're doing that for all the other rhinos."

The Rhino lumbered back to his feet. Lots and lots of broken glass slid off of his suit and tinkled to the concrete. Rhino wore his usual—the thick gray bodysuit made out of some kind of advanced ballistic materials that I'd heard could blow off armor piercing rounds from antitank guns. I can understand the insecurity. I mean, when your own skin can only handle heavy explosive rounds, you want a little insurance in case some enterprising mugger comes along packing discarding sabot shells.

He had on the hat, too. It was made of the same heavy material, encasing his head in armor and leaving only a comparatively small, square area of his small, square face vulnerable. The horn on it was heavy, tough, and sharp enough that when he put his weight and muscle behind it, he could blow through brick walls like they were linen curtains. All of which is imposing.

But at the end of the day, the hat still looks like a Rhino's head. Good Lord, I keep hoping the NFL will approve a start-up team called "The Rhinos," because then he'll actually look like a comedic team mascot. I wondered if the Chicken could take him.

"Spider-Man," growled the Rhino, presumably after taking a few moments to collect his thought. His consonants were clipped, the vowels guttural, Slavic, though if he really was a Russian, he spoke English pretty well. "We meet again."

"Rhino." I sighed. "You have got to get some better writers for these high-profile events. How are people ever going to take you seriously if you go around spouting that kind of hackneyed dialogue? What you do reflects on me, too, you know. I've got an image to think about."

His face flushed and started turning purple. It's almost too easy to handle this guy. "It will be pleasure to squash you, little bug man," he growled. He seized a mailbox, ripped it up out of the concrete, and threw it at my head.

I moved my head, webbed the mailbox as it went by, and slung it around in a circle, using the elastic strength of the webline to send it back at him twice as hard. The impact made him stagger back a step. "Whoa there, big fella," I told him. "Throwing down with me is one thing. But you do *not* want to tick off the Post Office. They don't goof around."

"I will shut your mouth!" he bellowed. He rolled forward at me, and to give the guy some credit, he moves better than you'd expect from someone who weighs eight hundred pounds. He swung fists the size of plastic milk jugs at me, a quick boxer's combination, jab, jab, cross, but I was fighting my kind of fight and he never touched me. Instead, he pressed harder, throwing heavier blows as he did. I popped him in the kisser a few times, just to keep him honest, and he grew angrier by the second.

Finally, I wound up with my back against an abandoned SUV, and let the Rhino's next punch zoom past my noggin and right through the SUV's door. I hopped around to his rear, and he swung his other hand at me, sinking it into the engine block of another car, and briefly binding his hands.

I popped up in front of him, held up the first two fingers of my right hand in a V shape, poked him in the eyes, and said, "Doink. Nyuk, nyuk, nyuk."

That last bit was too much for him. Something in him snapped and he let out a roar that shook the street beneath me, his anger driving him wild. He flung the cars hard enough to free his hands, sending each of them flying with one arm, inflicting more collateral damage, and charged me with murder in his eyes.

Like I said: He almost makes it too easy.

When you get right down to it, that's how I beat the Rhino every single time. His anger gets the better of him, makes him charge ahead, makes him clumsy, makes him blind to anything but the need to engage in violence. He's stronger than me, grossly so, in fact, and he isn't a bad fighter. If he were to keep his head and play to his own strengths—overwhelming power and endurance—he could take me out pretty quick. That kind of thinking is hard to manage, though, once the rubble starts flying, and he's never learned to control his temper. If he could do it, if he could work out how to force me into close quarters where my agility would be less effective, he'd leave me in bits and pieces. He just can't keep his cool, though, and it's always just a matter of time before he blows his top.

Maybe it's the hat.

I evaded the Rhino's charge, and he kept coming at me. I let him, leading him into the street and as far away from the buildings and storefronts as I could—some of them would still be occupied, and I didn't want the fracas to set them on fire or knock them down. Once the Rhino goes . . . well, rhino, it's possible to turn his own strength against him, but it takes an awful lot of judo to put the man down.

He batted aside a car between us, just as I Frisbeed a manhole cover into his neck. He flung a motorcycle at me with one hand. I ducked, zapped a blob of sticky webbing into his eyes, and hit him twenty or thirty times while he ripped it off of his face. He clipped me with a wild haymaker, and I briefly experienced combat astronomy.

He chased me around like that while the police got everyone out of the immediate vicinity. Give it up for the NYPD. They might not always like it that they need guys like me to handle guys like the Rhino, but they have their priorities straight.

I led the Rhino in a circle until one of his thick legs plunged into the open manhole and he staggered.

Then I let him have it. Hard. Fast. Maybe I'm not in the Rhino's weight class, but I've torn apart buildings with my bare hands a time or two, and I didn't get the scars on my knuckles in a tragic cheese grating accident. I went to town on him, never stopping, never easing up, and the sound of my fists hitting him resembled something you'd hear played on a snare drum.

Once he was dazed, I picked up the manhole cover and finished him off with half a dozen more whacks to the top of his pointed head, and the Rhino fell over backward, the impact sending a fresh network of fractures running through the road's surface.

I bent the manhole cover more or less back into shape over one knee, nudged the unconscious Rhino's leg out of the manhole, and replaced the cover. My Aunt May taught me to clean up my messes. I checked the Rhino again, and then gave the nearest group of cops a thumbs-up.

That was when the trap sprang.

My spider sense is an early warning system hard-wired into my brain. It can somehow distinguish between all sorts of different dangers, warning me of them in time for me to get clear. A few times, my spider sense has become a liability, though. I was so used to its warnings that when I went up against something that didn't trigger it, for whatever reason, it made me feel crippled, almost blind.

When Morlun had come after me, my spider sense did something new—it went into overdrive. Terror, terror so pure and unadulterated that it completely wiped out my ability to reason, had come screaming into my thoughts. It almost felt like my spider sense was screaming "HIDE!" at me, burned in ten-foot letters upon my brain. It had been one of the more terrifying and weird things that had ever happened to me.

It happened again now.

Only worse.

The terror came, my instincts howling in utter dread, and the sudden shock of sensation made me clutch at my head and drop to one knee.

Hide.

Hide!

HIDEHIDEHIDEHIDEHIDE!

"Move, Spidey," I growled to myself. "It's fear. That's all it is. *Get up.*"

I managed to lift my head. I heard myself making small, pained, frightened sounds. Danger. It couldn't be Morlun. It couldn't be. I saw him die. I saw him turn to *dust.*

They came out of the New Amsterdam, where *The Lion King* was rolling onstage. Maybe they'd been watching the fight from the lobby. They came walking toward me, their postures, expressions, motions all totally calm amidst the chaos. Two men. One in a gray Armani suit, the other in Italian leather pants and a silk poet's shirt. Both men were tall and pale. Both had straight, fine black hair and wore expressions of perpetual ennui and disdain.

And both of them bore a strong resemblance to Morlun.

The third was a woman. She wore a designer suit of black silk and had on black riding boots set off by a bloodred cravat. She too was pale, her black-cobweb hair worn up in a Chinese-style bun.

She, too, looked a bit like Morlun—especially through the eyes. She had pale eyes, soulless eyes, eyes that neither knew nor cared what it was to be human.

She came over and stopped about five feet from me, her hands on her hips. She tilted her head and stared at me the way one might examine a messy roadkill in an effort to determine what it had been before it was squashed.

"You are he," she said in a low, emotionless voice. "The spider."

"Uh," I said.

I found myself at a loss for words.

She narrowed her eyes, and they flickered with cold, cold anger—and inhuman hate, something that could roll on through a thousand years without ever abating. "You are the one who killed our brother." Her eyes widened then, and a terrible hunger came into them as the two men stepped up to stand on either side of her.

She pointed a finger at me and said, "Kill him."

SIX

IT dimly occurred to me that at this point, if I was Han Solo, faced with a genuine threat to my life, I would officially have moral license to shoot first.

The thought flashed through my mind as swiftly and lightly as a wood chip passing over the surface of a rushing river, but it gave me *something* to grasp toward, and I was able to get my head above the surface of my instinctive terror long enough to grab on to another thought:

If one of them touched me, just *touched* me, I was as good as dead.

Right then. Don't let them touch me.

Tweedle-Loom and Tweedle-Doom stalked forward with a predator's economic grace, but I didn't want to give them time to shift gears when I scampered. I waited until the last second to pop them both in the face with bursts of webbing and jump back out of reach. A quick hop landed me twenty feet above the road on an enormous billboard, and I crawled up it, turning to study them. If they were anything like Morlun, they'd be walking tanks with nearly limitless endurance—but not a lot swifter, on foot, than anyone else.

As it turned out, the boys were apparently a lot like Morlun. They tore off the webbing with about as much distress as I would feel wiping off shaving cream, gave me dirty looks, and continued stalking toward me.

The woman had evidently stood in a different line when they were handing out superpowers. She hit the spot where I'd been standing with one foot and leapt—with grace and élan—up to the top of the sign I was scaling. She crouched there, her head still tilted at that odd angle. "You must know this is pointless," she said dispassionately. "You cannot stop us. You cannot save yourself."

My spider sense was still gibbering at me, but enough of my voice had come back for me to say, "Now let me think. Where have I heard someone like you say something like that before? Hmm."

A cold little smile touched her mouth. "Little Morlun was one. We are three."

Little Morlun? That wasn't encouraging. "I don't suppose it matters to you that I didn't kill him," I told her.

Her lips twitched a little. "He hunted you?"

"Yes."

"He died."

"Yes."

"You saw it. You allowed it."

"I . . ." I swallowed. When it came down to the wire, I'd had him at my mercy. I knew full well that if I'd let him live, he'd only come back another day. I hesitated. And before I could go through with it, Dex, Morlun's demented little attaché, had emptied a Glock into him from ten feet away and blew him to dust.

I'd like to think that if I'd been aware of Dex and his gun I would have stopped him. Part of me is sure I would have. But more honest parts of me aren't so sure.

"I did," I told her quietly.

"Then for his sake, you die."

"What if I'd tried to stop it?"

She smiled a cold little smile, showing me very white teeth. "Then you would die for mine. I am hungry, spider. I will devour you."

"Gosh, that's kinda intimate," I said. "We haven't even been introduced."

She lifted her chin a bit, and then inclined her head to me. "Mortia." She moved a hand in a simple gesture to indicate the other two. "Thanis in the suit. Malos in the silk."

"Spider-Man," I said. "I'm the one standing in the shoes which are going to kick all three of you back to wherever it is weirdos like you come from."

Mortia threw back her head and actually laughed a cold little laugh. "Such defiance." Her eyes widened, showing the whites all the way around. "And it makes you smell sweet."

"Well," I said, "they tell me my deodorant is *strong* enough for a man—"

She flung herself at me in mid-quip. She was fast, as fast as anyone I've ever seen. As fast as me—and my spider sense, already howling at maximum intensity about how much danger I already knew I was in, gave me no warning at all.

I moved, barely ahead of her—and if I hadn't been watching her, ready for it, I would have been too slow. I never thought I'd actually have a reason to be *glad* that that symbiotic maniac Venom had obsessed over me and done his best to make my life a living hell between bursts of attempted arachnocide. My spider sense never registered him, either, and it had forced me to learn how to bob and weave the old-fashioned way, using only five senses.

Her hand flashed out toward me as she passed by, and missed me by less than an inch. I hit the ground moving. Tweedle-Loom threw a television set at me, while Tweedle-Doom went with a classic and flung a rock with such power that the projectile actually went supersonic in a sudden clap of thunder, like a gunshot. I did not oblige either of them by behaving like a good target.

Besides, they were just distractions, and they knew it. For the time being, the woman was the real threat, and she was hot on my trail. She got better air than me, but she didn't have handy-dandy weblines to play with, and I was able to stay ahead of her—barely. I went bouncing around Times Square like a racquetball, playing a lunatic version of tag with the mystery lady while I struggled to come up with a plan. It was harder than usual. Normally, between my reflexes and my spider sense, things just sort of flow by, and it feels like I have all the time in the world to think. That's how I'm able to be all funny and insulting while duking it out with the bad guys. It feels like I've had hours to come up with the material.

This time, my spider sense had ceased to be an asset, and my speed was only just sufficient to stay ahead of the three of them. It took all of my attention to avoid her, plus dodging the occasional portion of landscape her homeys pitched after me—complicated by the fact that if I led them out of Times Square, which the Rhino's efforts had already cleared of most civilians, bystanders would get hurt. Morlun hadn't blinked an eye at the notion of murder, and I didn't think these three would be any more safety-conscious than he was.

It's hard to gauge passing time in circumstances like that, but I gradually got the impression that maybe the reason I couldn't think of a plan of action was that there *wasn't* one. I'd taken Morlun out with the aid of material from the core of a nuclear reactor, and I didn't see one of those around Times Square. The only Plan B I could come up with was for me to keep doing what I was doing until some of the other New York hero types turned on the TV, found out what was going on, and showed up to lend a hand.

Although "hope someone rescues me" was a pathetically flawed Plan B. I mean, I'm supposed to be a superhero. I'm the one *doing* the rescuing.

Thanis took the decision out of my hands. He threw something heavy that hit the car I'd landed on and knocked it cleanly out from under me. I dropped to the ground unsteadily and looked up to find that Mortia had anticipated her brother's action. She was already two-thirds of the way through the pounce that would pin me to the ground and kill me. Thanis's distraction hadn't cost me much, maybe half a second.

It was enough.

As fast as I was, I still wasn't going to be fast enough to get out of her way.

SEVEN

ONCE in a while, plan B actually works out.

As Mortia came down at me, there was a *phoont* sound of expanding compressed air, and a small, metallic grappling hook flew over my head and hit her right on the end of her upturned nose, trailing a line of fine, black cable. The instant it touched her, there was a flickering of blue-white light, and Mortia's body convulsed, hit by what I assumed was a hefty amount of electricity. She went into an uncontrolled tumble, and I got out of the way in a hurry.

"That's new," I said, hopping to my feet—which I happened to plant ten feet up a handy streetlight, so that I could be sure to keep an eye on Clan Goth.

"I went legitimate," Felicia replied tartly. She landed in a crouch on the streetlight's arm, above me, pushed a button on a small baton, and the cord and grapple reeled swiftly back in. "I never said anything about not finding new toys to play with."

Mortia came to her feet slowly, looking down at the concrete dust clinging to her suit with undisguised annoyance. She traded a look with Thanis and Malos, and then all three of them turned to stare at me.

Absolutely no one moved. The only motion in all of Times Square came from rising smoke and the whirling bulbs on the police cars. The only sound came from a few stubborn car alarms that had survived the fracas (evidently Thanis and Malos found them as annoying as I did), and the harsh clicks and buzzes of transmissions on distant police radios. Nothing happened for a long minute.

What the heck. Every tableau's got to be broken by something.

"What we need," I drawled to the Black Cat, "is a couple of tumbleweeds. Maybe a rattlesnake Foley effect."

"Grow up," she sneered, watching Mortia and her brothers as carefully as I did. "What we need is the Avengers."

"Only because we didn't bring them," I said. "If we had, we wouldn't need them."

"Well, better to have them and not need them than—"

"Do I criticize your equipment list?" I asked. "And, oh. Don't let one of them touch you."

"We aren't dating anymore," she said archly.

I grinned, underneath my mask. "Very funny. Just don't do it."

"Why not?"

"Because once they do, they can track you down. Follow you anywhere. Find you anywhere."

She pursed her lips, the expression made tough to read by the visor, and said, "Got it. We should leave now, then."

I hesitated.

It wasn't a macho thing. I had no idea what Mortia and company might try if I left the fight. In a bid to keep me close enough to kill, Morlun had promptly started brutalizing whoever was handy when I tried to break contact with him for more than a minute or two. That was why I was hesitant to leave.

It wasn't because I didn't want to tuck my webs between my legs and run in front of half of New York and my ex-girlfriend. It wasn't that. At all. Not even a little.

Of course, dying in front of half of New York and my ex-girlfriend didn't sound like much fun, either.

A news chopper came whipping down the street, lower than the level of the buildings; someone was going to get a royal chewing-out from the FAA and whoever else screams and rants about such things. It kicked up a lot of dust and debris in the Square.

Mortia saw it and made a disgusted little noise. "Mortals. So gauche." She glanced at her brothers, then turned to me and said, "We are introduced, Spider. And after all, a multicourse dinner calls for a more . . ."—she gave me an acknowledging nod of the head and another wintry smile—". . . intimate setting. Fear not. We shall be reunited."

"Won't that be ducky," I said.

She flicked her wrist, dismissive. "You and the aperitif may flee, Spider."

"What?" Felicia said, indignant. "*What* did she call me?"

"Come on, bonbon," I told her. "Let's git while the gittin' is good."

Mortia turned to walk away, then paused to consider the fallen Rhino. "Bring the brute," she told her brothers. "He may yet be of use to us."

The two men each took one of the unconscious Rhino's arms, lifted all of him without so much as a grunt of effort, and dragged him along like a giant, armored rag doll in a goofy hat toward the nearest subway entrance.

There was a stir at one of the police control points, and I spat out a breath as I saw the SWAT van roll up. "Come on. Something we have to do."

"What?" Felicia called after me as I swung over to the control point.

I landed on the street next to the police lines. A couple of beat cops stared at me. One of them laid his hand on the baton at his belt. That was actually a pretty good reaction, for me. Usually, the hands go right to the guns.

"Hey, guys," I said. "Who is in charge of this scene?"

"None of your business," one of the cops said. "You ain't the sheriff of this town. You ain't the one that makes the calls."

A spotter had his field glasses focused on the retreating shapes of Mortia and company and was speaking cool instructions into his headset's mike as the SWAT team locked and loaded.

"Guys, you've got to trust me on this one," I told them. "Leave those three alone."

"Look, buddy," the cop said, his face turning red. "You're lucky they aren't getting ready to come after *you*, you freakin' nutball."

"Gosh, officer. Don't be afraid to tell me what you really think."

"Jesus, Frank," the second cop said with a sigh, rolling his eyes. "There's no harm hearing him out."

Frank folded his arms. "He's probably in this with those four, somehow."

The older cop stared at him for a second, blinked his eyes, and, through what looked like a nearly miraculous effort of self-control, did not whack him upside the head. Then he looked at me and said, "Why?"

"Because these people are bad news," I told him.

"Big, bad news. They're willing to walk away without a fight, and they don't have any reason to hurt anyone but me, unless you force them to defend themselves. Your men can't stop them. If they try it, they'll die. For nothing."

"But you think you can handle them," he said.

"Not sure. But when I hit them again, I can at least do it someplace without all the civilian bystanders."

He squinted at me for a moment, then looked at the DMZ that had, until recently, been Times Square. He grunted. "You got anyone on the force will speak for you?"

"Lamont," I said promptly. "Fourteenth Precinct."

His thumb tapped thoughtfully on the handle of his baton. "Sourpuss? Cheap suit? Drinks a lot of coffee?"

"That's him."

The cop grunted. "Sit tight." He stepped a few feet away and spoke into his radio. Maybe five minutes went by, and the SWAT team broke into a measured jog, setting off to pursue the retreating weirdos.

"Ahem," I said. "Time is getting to be a factor, officer."

He glanced back at me, then at SWAT, then went on talking. A moment later, he said, "Check." Then he walked over to the spotter, who was evidently some kind of authority figure with a rear-echelon command style, and passed him the radio.

I couldn't hear the conversation, but it didn't take much more than a minute for the SWAT guy's face to go carefully, professionally blank. He tossed the radio back at the officer, spoke into his headset, and a minute later the SWAT team reappeared. I let out a slow breath in pure relief.

The officer ambled back over to his post, and I said, "Thanks."

He shrugged a shoulder. "I got an auntie I like. She told me you saved her from a mugger. Don't mean I like you."

"Good enough for me," I said. "Thanks anyway."

There might have been the ghost of a smile on his lips. "Stick around. Lamont wants to talk to you. He'll be here in five."

"Anything to help the fine men and women of law enforcement," I said.

It didn't take the whole five minutes for Lamont to get there. He looked like Lamont usually looked: rumpled, tired, grumpy, and tough as old boot leather. His hair was the color of iron. He was a career New

York cop who had been unlucky enough to retain his conscience and his concern for the citizens he protected. His hair had gone gray early. His eyes had perpetual bags beneath them, despite the large, steaming Styrofoam coffee cup in his hand. He wore a long black overcoat, his cheap suit and his hair were rumpled, he needed a shave, and his beady eyes glinted with intelligence.

He really didn't like me very much.

"Hey," Lamont said. "Let's walk."

We turned down the street and walked away from the police lines, passing in front of a long row of shops and stores, until we were far enough away to avoid being overheard.

He stopped and squinted at me. "You're doing that just to annoy me."

I shrugged. I was standing with the soles of my feet on a rail of the awning above us, looking at him upside down. "Come on, Lamont. Would I do something like that?"

He grunted and chose to ignore me. "So what happened here?"

I gave him the Cliff's Notes version of the evening's events and their players.

Lamont scratched at his head. "So these weirdos are here for you?"

"Yeah," I said.

"So that sort of makes it your fault, I guess." He sipped his coffee, eyes narrowed. It was as close as I'd ever seen him get to smiling. He nodded at the destruction surrounding us and said, "Where do we send the bill?"

"Call my accountant," I said. "You can reach him at 1–800-in-your-freaking-dreams."

He gave me a bland look, sipped some more coffee, and said, "Judging from the outfit, you wouldn't be good for it anyway."

"Look who's talking."

Lamont stared down at his cup, then up at the bright lights of Times Square. "You say these people are strong. Like the Frankenstein gangster?"

"I took him in a straight fight," I said. "He was from the farm team. These three are major league. Like Rhino, or the Hulk."

"The Hulk, huh."

"Pretty close," I said. "But they don't go in for mass destruction with the same kind of glee."

"So this isn't mass destruction," he said. He coughed as a stray breeze blew some black smoke our way. "That's good."

"Rhino did most of this," I growled. "Probably to get my attention."

"Draw you out in the open, huh."

"Yeah."

Lamont looked around some more, sipped some more coffee, and gave me a shrewd look. "You're in trouble."

I was quiet for a minute, then said, "Maybe. It could get really messy. These things don't care, Lamont. They could kill every man, woman, and child in New York and sip cappuccinos over the corpses."

"Christ." Lamont grunted. His face twisted up abruptly, as if he'd suddenly started sucking on a lemon spiked with jalapeño. "How can I help?"

"You having a stroke, Lamont? Your face is twitching."

"I might be," he said darkly. "Helping out one of the maniacs in tights. I might puke. Maybe on you."

I looked down at him from my upside-down position. "That would be difficult, considering."

"I'd manage. I'm crafty."

"Don't know if there's much you can do," I said. "Except for making sure you aren't putting pressure on the Addams Family. If you start a fight, they'll take you up on it."

"Good plan," Lamont said. "I solve most of my problems by standing around hoping they'll go away."

"If I could give you a better one, I would," I said. "Let me handle this one my way; give me some room to breathe. I'll take the fight to somewhere safe." I glanced at the square. "Well. Safer than *this,* anyway."

Lamont grunted again. "I'll see what I can do. No promises. And if something like this happens again, all bets are off."

"You try to take these guys down, cops are going to die."

He was stone-still for a moment. Then he murmured, "I know. So you damn well better take them out before it comes to that."

Trust is something precious and fragile. Once it begins to fracture, it isn't ever going to be strong again. Lamont didn't like me, I knew. But I hadn't realized that he trusted me. It was an enormous gesture, especially for him.

"I'll handle it," I told him, voice serious.

He finished the coffee, crushed the cup in a frustrated fist, and then pitched it down into the rest of the wreckage. "Right. Move along, then, citizen. Nothing to see here."

He was right, thank God. There wasn't.

Yet.

EIGHT

I found Felicia waiting on the same rooftop where I'd tackled her a little while before. Full night had come on, but in New York, that means little. Even up high where we were, there was enough ambient light to see by, easily. In spots, you could read by it. But when night's curtain is drawn over the azure face of the sky, the light takes on a sourceless, nebulous quality. It stretches shadows, gleams on metal and glass, and emphasizes the brooding shapes of gargoyles and statues and carvings on many of New York's architectural wonders. The sounds of the city come up, but lightly, as though they were little more than remembrances of their makers, no louder than the voice of the wind. It's a kind of fairyland, and it always makes me feel as if I am the only real, tangible object in the world. It's beautiful, in its own way, and peaceful.

I figured the next day or three might be real short on peace. So I sat down next to the Black Cat for a minute and soaked it up while I still could.

"Hey," she said after a moment of silence. "You're trembling."

"Am I?"

"Yes."

I shook my head.

She stared at me for a second. Then she took off the visor again. Her eyes were worried. "Peter?"

"I'm all right. It's what happens when I'm scared."

Her silver blonde eyebrows went up. "What?"

"Scared. Frightened. Afraid. Having the wiggins."

"That doesn't sound like you," she said.

I shrugged.

"How bad *are* these people?" she asked quietly.

"They aren't people," I said. "They look like us, but they aren't. I studied Morlun's blood. Their genetics are . . . almost an amalgam of hundreds of different species. Maybe thousands."

"What's so bad about them?"

"They feed on life energy," I said quietly. "The way I hear it, they're from the mystical end of the universe. They devour the life energy of totemic vessels."

"Totemic what?"

"People," I explained, "who have chosen to use an animal as a personal totem. Who, in some sense or fashion, draw power from that association." I pointed at the spider on my chest. "Like Spider-Man." I chewed over an unpleasant thought. "Or like the Black Cat."

She blinked. "Just because of my name? What if I were . . . I don't know. The Black Diamond or something."

I shrugged. "Don't ask me."

She frowned. "So, this Morlun. He tried to eat you?"

"Nearly did," I said. "He was . . . the Hulk's opening shot was kind of soft, compared to Morlun's. He was strong. Really strong. And he just kept coming. I fought him for about two days, almost nonstop." I glanced at her. "I hit him with everything I had, Felicia. He just kept coming." I shuddered. "Like the Terminator, only relentless. He could follow me everywhere. And every time I tried to bail, he'd start hurting people until I came back."

She grimaced. "How'd you beat him?" she asked quietly.

"I injected myself with radioactive material from a nuclear reactor. When he tried to feed on me, he got that instead. It dazed him, weakened him. I beat Morlun down. He had this little Renfield clone named Dex with him. When Morlun went down, Dex snapped and Wormtongued him."

"He what?"

"Doesn't anyone *read* anymore?" I asked. "Dex killed Morlun."

"Injected yourself with . . ." She shook her head. "That's insane."

"I was getting a little punchy when I came up with it," I said, agreeing.

"Still. They can't be all that tough. They turned tail and ran once enough people showed up." She frowned. "Right?"

I stared down at the city. "Morlun . . . he was just so old. He'd seen everything. He said he only fed once in a while. That I would have sated him for a century. But the hunt was something that was nearly a ritual with him, something that he had to get right. The only time I got him off me was when I blew up a building with him in it. He came out without a scratch, but his clothes had been incinerated. He called a time-out to go get dressed again, because he knew he had all the time in the world. He knew that I wasn't going to be able to stop him."

"And that's why Mortia stopped?"

"I think that she wants to be able to take her time, when she gets me. She wants to be able to do it right."

Felicia shuddered. "She's insane."

"No. Just inhuman. Though I suppose it amounts to the same thing." I glanced up at her. "Which reminds me. How in the world did you know about Morlun? And about these three?"

"I think that 'know' is probably too strong a word," she said. "Look, I told you I've been working in the private security sector, right?"

"Yeah."

"Well, I've been doing some private investigation on the side. A couple of years ago, I get hired by a man who wants me to find out the exact time of Spider-Man's first appearance in New York, and every time he has appeared in foreign cities."

I blinked. "What?"

She spread her hands. "Exactly. So I play this guy along, trying to find out more about him, why he's asking these questions like he did. I figure he was trying to figure out who Spider-Man really was. Who *you* were. Like, maybe he was looking for puzzle pieces, and he just wanted me to find one of them." She shook her head. "No clue why he'd do that. I tried to find out more about him, but the paper trails and money trails all ran into dead ends. Zip, nothing, like the guy didn't exist. All I got was his first name. Ezekiel."

I blew out a breath. "Wow. Ezekiel. He told me he had hired several investigators to find out pieces of my background. He kept them ignorant of each other so that none of *them* would realize who I was. He was protecting my identity."

Felicia looked even more surprised. "You know this character?"

"I did," I said quietly. "He's dead."

My tone did not convey the sense that further questions along this line were welcome.

Felicia, being Felicia, feared my wrath about as much as she would a bubble bath and a glass of chardonnay. "What did he want?"

I kept my temper and answered as calmly as I could. "To protect me from Morlun," I said. "To hide me in some big expensive life-support unit he built, so that Morlun wouldn't find me and kill me."

"That was nice of him," she said.

"Heh," I said. "He was only doing it so he could feed me to something *else,* later. Something that had been coming for *him.*" I clenched my teeth on my bitter tone and forced myself to lower my volume. "In the end, he didn't do it. Maybe he really did want to help. Maybe he didn't really know what he wanted. I don't know. Never had the chance to talk to him about it."

Felicia shook her head. "A few months later, I get another job. This time, someone wants to know about the recent appearances in New York of a missing family member named Morlun. Specifically, if he was ever seen in an altercation with the Amazing Spider-Man, and if so where. I dig, and find out that the description I've got matches this loser in a cravat who was seen trying to pound Spider-Man's face in."

"Made you suspicious, eh?"

"I'm always suspicious. You know that."

"True. What did you do?"

She ran her fingers back through her hair and let a cool wind play with the strands, her eyes distant in thought. "I fed them a little good information, a lot of false information, and played them along while I tried to find out everything I could about them." She shook her head. "I thought they belonged to some kind of secret society—like the Hellfire Club or something."

"Ah," I said fondly. "The Hellfire Club. What did you find out?"

"They're loaded," she said. "Seriously rich, managed through all kinds of law firms and accountants and hidden under enough red tape to choke a senator. They referred to themselves as 'The Ancients.' Like I said, it sounded like a club or something."

"The Ancients." I sighed. "You'd think they'd pick something a little less done to death."

"Maybe they had it first," she said. "I did some more digging and I managed to find several references to the Ancients—and eventually a picture of Mortia." She dipped a hand into the suit and drew out a slender PDA. It lit up, made a couple of beeps, and then she held up the visor. "Here. See for yourself."

I put the visor on, and was treated to an infrared display of New York. "Whoa," I said. "Predator-cam."

She touched a button on the side of the visor, and it cleared away to a light-enhanced image of the Big Apple, mostly black and white, the colors all oddly muted. I could see the bad toupee on a passing pedestrian thirty-five stories below. Then, an image appeared in front of me, as if on a projection screen—a newspaper clipping.

"It's from a microfiche archive I found at the University of Oklahoma," she said. "An article from the Dust Bowl era."

I read the article. It detailed the disappearance of a number of individuals from a traveling circus that had been passing through Tulsa, including a snake charmer, a lion tamer who was purported to actually wrestle the beasts, and the self-proclaimed world's greatest equestrian. They had last been seen in the company of a woman who generally matched Mortia's description. The article included an artist's rendering of the suspect as described by witnesses. It wasn't a perfect sketch, but it bore Mortia enough likeness to get the job done. "How did that connect you to the Ancients?"

"The owner of the circus attempted to bring a suit against the company that owned the hotel his people had been in when they disappeared. It was one of the properties owned by the Ancients." She was quiet for a moment. Then she said, "I also found this. A friend of mine got it out of the archives of the Texas Rangers, early fifties." Her PDA beeped again, and I saw another image—this time simply a photograph.

I took it for a photograph of a dry creek bed for a second. Then I made out the shapes in the picture. They were dried, desiccated human remains. Nothing was left except for the skin, stretched drum-tight over bones. Dead faces were locked in silent screams. Hair still clung to scalps, but other than their desiccated condition, there was not a mark on the bodies, as if even the animals and insects had refused to touch them.

"Two men, one woman," Felicia said quietly. "One of the men wore a gold wedding ring with an inscription that matched that of a ring owned by the lion tamer who disappeared from Tulsa."

I swallowed, staring hard at the wasted remains of what had once been human beings. This was what was waiting for me, if the Ancients had their way. This is what they had been doing to people for thousands, maybe tens of thousands of years.

I took the visor off, and the image of the wasted remains was replaced with Felicia's worried face. "Is this what they want to do to . . ."—she swallowed—"to us?"

"Looks that way," I said.

She shook her head. "I got this two days ago, and wanted to get a better look, so I tracked down the contact the Ancients had been using to speak with me, so that I could see him when I called him back with the information. It was an office building in Chicago. Mortia was there with him." She took a deep breath. "That's when the client starts asking me some of the same questions Ezekiel did."

I sat up straight. "What?"

She nodded. "I fed them some false information, and came to warn you, Pete. I told you, these folks were rich. And if Ezekiel can spend enough money to find out who Spider-Man is . . ."

"The Ancients can too," I breathed. "Mary Jane. If they find out about me, they find out about her."

"I'm sorry, Peter," Felicia said. "I didn't realize how serious it was or I'd have contacted you sooner."

"You did good," I said quietly. "Thank you."

She tried a smile. "You want to get home, I suppose? Make sure they aren't there?"

"They aren't," I said. I focused on my spider sense and peered around. "They're . . . on the other side of town somewhere."

She frowned. "How do you know that?"

"Mortia didn't manage to touch me," I said. "But I flicked one of my spider tracers into her pocket."

Felicia blinked at me. Then she said, "Gosh, and here I was going to feel all smug that I'd marked her with an isotope paste I put on the end of my grapple. I can track it from maybe three or four hundred yards out."

"Great minds," I said.

"We always did make a pretty good team."

I grinned at her, beneath the mask. Felicia couldn't see it, but she'd hear it in my voice. "Yeah. We work well together."

"What's the plan?" she asked.

I thought about it for a minute. Then I said, "I'm going to head back to the apartment. I'll know if the tracer gets within half a mile or so. I'll get on the net, see what I can find out about these things."

She nodded. "Let me get in touch with Oliver."

"Who's Oliver?"

"He works with me at the company," she said. "Mostly skip tracing, but he's a demon for research, too. He's good. If anyone can find out more about the Ancients, he can."

I mused. "See what he can get on the Rhino."

She gave me a skeptical look. "The Rhino?"

"He's a mercenary," I said. "Maybe we can find a way to make them default on their payment or something. I've got enough on my plate without fighting him, too."

"Are you kidding?" she teased. "You clean his clock every other week."

"Not that often," I said. "I've got his number, one-on-one, but that doesn't mean he isn't dangerous. If the Ancients had come after me before he went down, instead of after, I'd look like those poor circus folks right now."

Felicia slipped the visor back on, adjusted its controls, and said, "I'll see what I can do." She got out her baton and said, "We can handle this, Pete. Right?"

"Sure," I said cheerfully. "We're the good guys."

I'm fairly sure the Black Cat didn't believe me.

I'm fairly sure I didn't, either.

NINE

MARY JANE was in the living room when I came home. She was sitting there with the manual she'd gotten from the DMV, trying to look like she'd been studying. I had seen the lights of the television, though, when I came down the wall from the roof.

She got up from the couch when I came in. She was wearing one of my T-shirts and a pair of my socks. "I saw . . . I was watching it on the news. They said something about the Rhino, but the clips were all of these men throwing things. They were throwing *cars* at you."

I went to her and held her, very gently. "Did they get me from my good side?"

She hugged me back very hard. "The cameramen couldn't even find you. They just kept circling these blurs on slow-motion replay and saying it was you."

"My grade school pictures are like that too," I said. "I fidgeted. I was a fidgeter."

We stood there like that for a long time. Mary Jane shuddered once, then exhaled and leaned against me.

"I don't like this part," she said. "The part where I have to worry about people throwing *cars* at you. Cars, Peter. I must have seen twenty cars crushed up like beer cans." She let out a half-hysterical little laugh. "How much do you want to bet all three of those bullies have a driver's license?"

I just held her. "Well. They can throw whatever they want. They aren't going to hit me, so it doesn't much matter."

She finally looked up at me, and her eyes were clear and steady. "Tell me all of it."

I exhaled slowly, then nodded. I didn't want to scare her, but Mary Jane had earned the right to know what was happening—and bitter experience has taught me that keeping secrets from the ones close to you is just not a great idea, in the long term.

I got a glass of water, stripped out of my tights, and sat down with my wife on the couch. MJ settled herself under one of my arms and pressed against my side, which I liked enough to make it a little difficult to speak coherently, but I persevered. I'm brave like that. I gave her the whole story, starting with Morlun. She knew me well enough that I got the feeling she understood more than just the words I was saying.

"God, Peter," she said. "You never told me about that thing."

"Well. You weren't here at the time." We'd been in a rough patch, one we'd since left behind us. "And when you came back, we had enough on our plates already."

She let out a quiet laugh at the understatement. "I suppose we did." She spread the fingers of one hand out over my chest. "But Peter. I'm sorry I wasn't here for you." She frowned. "No. That's not exactly right. I needed the space. The time to think."

"We both did," I said, nodding.

She looked up at me. "I'm sorry you had to hurt alone."

"I'm over it," I said, quietly. "Started getting better when you came back."

Her eyes searched mine for a long time and then she said, "You aren't over it. You're afraid."

I nodded.

She watched me for a second more. Then she said, a faint smile on her mouth, "But you're not afraid of them. These Ancients."

"Oh, believe me. I'm afraid of them. They are not reasonable people."

She shook her head. "But you're not afraid of what they might do to you. You're afraid of what you might have to do to them."

People rarely expect a beautiful woman to have a brilliant mind. My wife is smarter than almost everyone gives her credit for. She'd just realized something I hadn't consciously admitted to myself yet.

"They play hardball," I said. "They'll kill people without losing a second's sleep. Even if I can beat them, if they walk away, they're going to find someone else to eat. Someone else will suffer instead of me."

She laid one hand over my heart, listening.

"I can't let that happen," I said quietly. "I don't know . . . what other choice I have. I know they can be killed. It might be the only way I can stop them." I looked up at her. "I'm just not a killer, MJ. And I don't want to be one."

"What can I do to help?" she asked quietly.

I shook my head. "Nothing I can think of."

She sat up and said quietly, her voice growing brittle, "But Felicia. She can help you."

I sighed. "MJ . . ."

"She's got all the kung fu and criminal training, after all. Maybe even some actual superpowers, unless she's just been lying about that all along. Plus she's got a costume." She walked away from me, over to the window I'd just come in. "But I'm only your wife. I'm not useful."

"Hey, hey, hey . . . ," I said, trying to keep my voice quiet and calm. "Where did this come from? Felicia and I are over. You know that."

Her shoulders stiffened, as did her voice. "Yes, Peter, I know that."

"Then what gives?" I asked her. "Why are you being like this?"

She turned around, green eyes hard and fierce and wet. "You are *my* husband. And I . . ." The tears fell from her eyes and she said, in a very quiet voice, "And I hate it that I can't be the one to help you."

She looked small and frail. Lost. Vulnerable. If I hadn't gone over to her and held her, I think something in my chest would have broken open. She leaned against me again. Her shoulders shook a little, but she didn't let me see her face when she cried.

"I want to help you," she said. "Instead, here I am crying on you. For the second time today. God, that ticks me off."

"What does?"

"Adding to your burden. Being extra weight."

I kissed her hair. Then I put my hand on her shoulder and lifted her chin with a finger, so that her eyes met mine. "MJ, there's more to it than costumes. You've got to understand that. Maybe you don't throw punches for me or blast people with cosmic rays, but you do more for me than you know. Having you in my life makes me stronger. Better. Don't think that you aren't helping me. Don't think that you're a burden. Not for a second."

She didn't look convinced. But I hugged her again, and she hugged back, a tacit, temporary agreement to disagree. "So," she said. "What's the plan?"

"Research online," I said. "And I'm going to call some people."

"For help?"

I hedged. "For information," I said after a moment. "These three are here because of me. I can't ask someone else to fight my battles for me. But maybe someone will know something about them. How to beat them some way other than . . ."

"Killing them," she said.

"Killing them." I looked at the clock and said, "Okay, tell you what. How about we spend a little while getting you ready for your test, huh?"

She looked up at me, blinking. "Are you kidding?"

"Not even a little," I said. "MJ, this is just another freak of the week. It isn't the first time someone's come gunning for me, and it won't be the last. If we start calling a halt to life every time some psycho with a bone to pick walks into town, we'll be spinning our wheels until we retire."

"I'm going to assume you meant that to sound encouraging," she told me, arching an eyebrow.

"I'm trying," I said, nodding. "Look at it like this. Next week, this is going to be over, and I'll be making wisecracks about it to you while you drop me off at school and tell me how your rehearsal is going. Unless we let the latest set of bozos scare us out of living our life and you don't get the license and don't get your part. So. Give me the manual and we'll get you set for the test. We can even go out to the car and I can coach you a little if you like. You can get to bed early, I'll stay up and research things for a while—it'll be fun."

"Fun," she said, her tone flat—but there was, at least, a flicker of life in her eyes again, something that might eventually grow into a smile.

"Studying is fun," I said.

"Once a nerd," she said, sighing, "always a nerd."

"You want to skip the written and go to the car instead?"

She folded her arms. "What if I do?"

"Give me a minute, and I'll go borrow a crash helmet and make sure my life insurance premium is paid up."

She gave me an arch look.

"Does the car have air bags?" I asked. "Because if it doesn't, I can web us in nice and safe."

Mary Jane rolled her eyes heavenward. "*Now* he gets creative with the webbing."

○———————○

"THIS is the car you bought?" I asked her. My voice echoed in the parking garage. The acoustics magnified my skepticism.

"I was kind of in a rush," she said. "And there wasn't much of a selection."

"And this is the car you bought?" I asked. "A lime green and rust red Gremlin?"

"Actually," she said, "it's just a lime-green Gremlin."

I leaned closer and flicked a finger at the car's fender. The rust red paint was, in fact, simply rust.

"I got a really good deal on it," she said.

"No air bags," I noted, walking around the car. "Too old for them."

"It's also all metal," she responded. "Being a really heavy car is really the next best thing."

I snorted. "Well," I said. "You can obviously drive. After a fashion, anyway. You took the car to the test, right?"

She raked some fingers through her hair. "Well. Yes. Though we stopped at the written. I was going to tell them my husband had driven me to the DMV, then went for coffee."

"Mistress of deception, huh?"

"Give me a break. I was working under pressure," she said. "And yes, I can drive. I mean, more or less. I didn't smash into anything on the way home, anyway. But everyone kept honking at me whenever I even came *close*. People in cars can be really rude."

I tried to imagine this scene, and had to keep myself from wincing. "Okay then. Let's get in and start with signals and right-of-way."

"Signals?" she asked. "Right-of-way?"

I couldn't help it. My lips twitched. "I'm not laughing at you," I said. "I'm laughing *with* you."

She gave me a very stern look.

I held up my hands. "All right, all right. I'll be nice. Get in the car, and we'll go one step at a time."

We got in, but she didn't put her key in the ignition. "You're a good man, Peter Parker," she said quietly. "I love you."

I leaned over and kissed her on the cheek.

"You know," she said. "We never made out in a car when we were teenagers."

"We didn't have a car," I pointed out. "Plus we weren't dating."

"All the same," she said. "I feel cheated."

She leaned over, pulled my mouth gently to hers, and gave me a kiss that rendered me unable to speak and gave me doubts about my ability to walk.

We got to the driving lesson.

Eventually.

TEN

I clicked the print button and my printer wheezed to life—though at this point, I doubted the dissertation on magical systems of power that it was currently reproducing would be helpful except maybe in an analytical retrospective, long after the fact. I muttered under my breath, and tried the next batch of Web sites, looking for more information, as I had been since Mary Jane went to bed.

There was a sudden, heavenly aroma, and I looked down to find a cup of hot coffee sitting next to my keyboard.

"Morning," Mary Jane said, leaning over to kiss my head. "I thought you weren't going to stay up all night."

"Marry me," I said, and picked up the coffee.

She was wearing my T-shirt, and I could not, offhand, think of anyone who made it look better. "We'll see," she said playfully. "I'm baking cookies for Mister Liebowitz down the hall for his birthday, so I might get a better offer."

"I always knew you'd leave me for an older man." I sipped the coffee and sighed. Then I glowered at the stack of useless information by the printer.

"How'd it go?" she asked.

I made a growling sound and sipped more coffee.

"Peter," she said, "I know that in your head, you just said something that conveyed actual information. But when it got to your mouth, it grew fur, beat its chest, and started howling at the moon."

"That's right," I said, as if reminded. "You're a girl."

That got me a rather sly look over the shoulder. Doubtless, it was the fresh, steaming coffee that made my face feel warm.

"I take it your research didn't go well?" she said, walking into the kitchen.

"It's this magical crap," I said, waving a hand at the computer. I got up from my chair, grabbed my coffee, and followed her. "It's such hogwash."

"Oh?"

"Yes. It's like we're reverting to the Dark Ages here. Which you're not actually supposed to say anymore, because it's not like it was a global dark age, and to talk about it like the whole world was in a dark age is Eurocentrically biased." I sat at the kitchen table. "And that's pretty much what I learned."

"You're kidding," she said.

"No. Eurocentrically biased. It's actually a phrase."

"You're funny." She opened the refrigerator door. "Seriously, nothing useful? Not even in the Wikipedia?"

"Zip. I mean, there's all kinds of magical creatures on the net, God knows. But how do you tell the difference between something that's pure make-believe, something that's been mistakenly identified as something magical, something that's part of somebody's religious mythos which may or may not have a basis in life, and something that's real?" I shook my head. "The only thing I found that was even close to these Ancients turned out to be an excerpt from a Dungeons and Dragons manual. Though I did run across a couple of things that led me to some interesting thoughts."

Mary Jane continued on, making breakfast and listening. I wasn't sure how she did that. Heck, I had to turn off the television or radio to be able to focus on a phone call. "Like what?" she asked.

"Well. These Ancients might have superpowers and such, but they still have the same demands as any other predator. They have to eat, right? And they're thousands and thousands of years old."

She nodded, then frowned. "But I thought that the super-powered types only started showing up kind of recently. I mean, fighting Nazis in World War Two, that kind of thing."

I shrugged. "Maybe. But maybe not, too. I mean, most of the super-powered folks who have shown up are mutants. I've heard some theories that it was nuclear weapons testing that triggered an explosion—"

"So to speak," Mary Jane injected.

"—in the mutant population, but that doesn't make much sense to me. I mean, the planet gets more solar radiation in a day than every nuke that's ever gone off. It doesn't make sense that a fractional increase due to nuclear weapons tests would trigger the emergence of superpowers."

"Worked for the Hulk," she pointed out.

"Special case," I said. "But I think that maybe what we're seeing—the rise in the mutant population—might be as much about the *total* population rising as it is about a sudden evolutionary change. We've got about six billion people on the planet right now. Two thousand years ago, the estimate is that there might have been three hundred million. If the occurrence of powered mutants is just a matter of genetic mathematics, maybe it just seems like there's a lot more mutants running around these days. I mean, they do tend to be kind of eye-catching."

She was making omelets. She assembled them as quickly and precisely as if her hands were being run by someone else's head while she carried on the conversation with me. "And you think that explains how these things ate before? By feeding on the occasional mutant with some kind of totemistic power?"

"Potentially," I said. "Even a reduced population might be able to sustain the Ancients. They only eat once in a while, sort of like a boa constrictor. Felicia thinks the last time Mortia ate was in the forties. Morlun told me that feeding on me would fill him up for a century or more."

"Tastes great," Mary Jane said. "More filling. I agree."

I coughed. "Thank you," I said. "But, ahem, getting our minds out of the gutter, think about it for a minute. How would people have described someone with, say, Wolverine's gifts, back when? He'd have been called a werewolf or a demon or something. Charles Xavier would have been considered a sorcerer or a wizard of some kind. Colossus would have been thought to be some kind of gargoyle or maybe a fairy tale earth-creature, like a troll."

She lifted her eyebrows. "So, you're saying that maybe a lot of folklore and mythology might be based on the emergence of mutants, back when. Like if . . . say, Paul Bunyan was actually a mutant who could turn into a giant."

See what I mean about brains? My girl ain't slow. "Exactly. Ezekiel told me that the African spider-god Anansi was originally a tribesman who had acquired spiderlike powers. Sort of the original Spider-Man. That he got himself involved with gods and was elevated to godhood."

"Actual gods?" Mary Jane asked, her tone skeptical.

"Hey," I said. "I ate hot dogs with Loki a few months ago. And I saw Thor flying down Wall Street last week."

She laughed. "Good point. You aiming for a promotion?"

"Not if I can help it," I said. "But think about it. Say, for example, something really odd happened and I joined up with the Avengers. All of a sudden, I'm running around with a new crowd, gone from home a lot, hanging around with Thor, all that kind of thing. If it was two thousand years ago, it sure would look like I'd been accepted by beings with incredible powers, whisked off to their world and welcomed into their ranks."

She nodded. Then asked me, "Would that be so odd? For you to join a team like that?"

"Captain America doesn't think I'd be a team player," I told her. "We've talked about it in the past. And there was that whole thing where I wanted to join the Fantastic Four, but when they found out I was looking for a salary they got all skeptical about me."

"You thought the FF *paid*?" Mary Jane asked.

"I was about sixteen," I said. "I thought a lot of stupid things."

She smiled, shook her head, and started dishing up the omelets. "Eat up, Mister Parker. Get some food in you."

I took the plate from her and set it on the table. "Anyway. I didn't make a sterling first impression on the superhero community. And I've had all that bad press, courtesy of the *Bugle*. So there's always been a little distance between me and Cap and most of the other team players."

"It just seems . . ." She paused, toying with her fork. "You know. If you were part of a team, it might be safer."

"It might," I said. "But on the other hand, the Avengers are pretty upscale when it comes to villainy. They take on alien empires, aggressive nations, super-dimensional evil entities, that kind of thing. I mostly do muggers. Guys robbing a grocery. Car thieves. You know—here, New York, with real people. There's no friendly neighborhood Thunder God."

"Did you call them up, at least?" she asked.

"Answering service," I said. "Who knows where they are this week. I left a message on their bulletin board system, but I don't know if they'll get in touch anytime soon since, you know. They mostly don't know who

I am." I paused. "The secret identity thing probably hasn't helped endear me to my fellow good guys, thinking about it."

"What about Reed Richards?" she asked.

"Called Mister Fantastic's lab at six A.M.," I said. "He'd been there for an hour already. He said he'd see what he could find out, but he didn't sound optimistic. And he has to take Franklin to the dentist later. He said he'd get word to me by this afternoon, but . . ."

"But he's a scientist," she said. "Like you. He doesn't like the whole magic thing, either."

"It isn't that he doesn't *like* it. It's that he likes things to make *sense*. Science makes sense. Some of it can be pretty complex, but it makes sense if you know what you're dealing with. It's solid, reliable."

"Predictable?"

"Well," I said. "Yes."

"You don't like things you can't predict," Mary Jane said. "Things you can't control. You don't know the magical stuff, and it doesn't seem to lend itself to being predicted or controlled—so you don't like it."

"So now I'm a control freak?" I asked.

She looked at me for a second. Then she said, "Peter. You've spent your entire adult life fighting crime, protecting people from bad guys of every description and otherwise putting yourself in danger for someone else's sake—while wearing brightly colored tights with a big black spider on the chest. I think it's safe to say you have issues."

"With great power . . . ," I began.

She held up a hand and said, "I agree, God knows. But an abstract principle isn't why you do it. You do it because of what a robber did to Uncle Ben. You could have controlled that if you were there, but you weren't and you didn't. So now you've got to control every bad guy you possibly can. Be there for everyone you possibly can. That's control freaky. Constructively so."

I frowned down at my eggs. "I haven't really thought of it that way before."

"That's right," she said, deadpan. "You're a man."

I glanced up at her and smiled. "I'm glad you remembered."

She blushed a little. She does it much more prettily than I do. MJ leaned across our little table and kissed my nose. "Eat your breakfast, tiger."

The door to our little apartment opened, and Felicia stepped in, dressed in a dark gray business suit-skirt that showed an intriguing amount of leg. She wore horn-rimmed glasses and had her silver blonde hair pulled back into a bun. "Pete, we're screwed. Hi, MJ."

I was still in my shorts, and MJ hadn't gotten dressed yet, either. I sat there with a bite of omelet halfway to my mouth. "Oh. Uh, Felicia, hey."

Mary Jane gave Felicia a glance and murmured to me, "Was the door unlocked?"

"No." I sighed.

Felicia closed the door behind her and peered out the peephole. "Sorry. I didn't want to stand around in your hallway and get spotted." She looked back at us and gave me an appreciative glance. "Well, hello there."

Mary Jane gave Felicia the very calm look that comes to people's faces only seconds before they load a deer rifle and go looking for a bell tower. She stood up, and I stood up with her, taking her arm firmly. "Uh, Felicia, give us a second to get dressed, okay?"

"You bet," Felicia said. She tilted her head, sniffing. "Mmmm. That omelet smells good. Are you guys going to eat that?"

"Why don't you have mine," Mary Jane said sweetly.

"Come on," I said, and walked Mary Jane out of the room. We got into the bedroom and shut the door.

"Are you *sure* she isn't evil anymore?" Mary Jane asked.

"Felicia wasn't ever really evil. Just . . . evil-tolerant. And really, really indifferent to property rights."

Mary Jane scowled. "But if she was evil," she said, "you could beat her up and leave her hanging upside down from a streetlight outside the police station. And I would like that."

I tried hard not to laugh and kissed her cheek, then put the uniform on under a gray sweat suit and stuffed my mask into a pocket. Mary Jane went with jeans and a T-shirt, in which she looked genuine and gorgeous.

"She's not that bad," I said as we dressed. "You know that."

"Maybe," she admitted.

"I think maybe you're having a bad day," I said. "I think that she's mostly a convenient target."

"Of course you'd say that," she snapped. Then she forced herself to stop, the harshness in her voice easing, barely. "Because you're insightful and sensitive. And because you're probably right."

"Yeah," I said. "That's hardly fair to you."

She lifted her hand in a gesture of appeasement. "Peter, I do my best to be rational and reasonable about everything I can. But I think maybe I'm running low on rationality where Felicia is concerned."

"Why?" I asked.

"Because she gets to help you when I can't," Mary Jane said. "Because you used to date her. Because she doesn't respect such banal conventions as marriage and probably wouldn't hesitate to rip off her clothes and make eyes at you, given half an excuse."

"MJ. She wouldn't do that."

"Oh? Then why is she dressed like some kind of corporate prostitute?"

I sat down next to my wife, put my hands on her shoulders, and said, "She wouldn't do that. And it wouldn't matter if she did. I'm with you, Red."

"I know," she said, frustrated. "I know. It's just . . ."

"It's a tough time, and between the two of us there isn't enough sanity to cover everything."

She sighed. "Exactly."

"No sweat. I've got it covered," I said. "I'll take care of business, release the pressure, Felicia will probably go back to her glamorous life in private security, and everything will be like it usually is—which is good."

She covered one of my hands with hers and said, "It is pretty good, isn't it."

"I always thought so."

She took a deep breath and nodded. "All right. I'll . . . somehow avoid clawing her eyes out. I can't promise you anything more than that."

"I'll take it," I said. I kissed her again, and we went back into the living room.

Felicia hadn't eaten anyone's omelet. She was, however, giving the fridge an enthusiastic rummaging, setting things haphazardly on the counter by the sink as she did.

Mary Jane paused, and her cheek twitched a couple of times. Then she took a deep breath, clenched her hands into fists, and sat down at the table without launching even a verbal assault. She began eating her omelet in small, precise bites while Felicia continued foraging in the refrigerator.

Felicia eventually decided on the leftover pizza and popped it in the microwave while I sat back down.

"All right," I said to Felicia. "What did you find out about Gothy McGoth and her brothers?"

"That we're in trouble."

"Gosh. Really."

She stuck out her tongue at me. "Mortia is connected, and in a major way. She controls at least half a dozen corporations, two of them Fortune 500 companies. She's visited the White House twice in the last five years and has more money than Oprah—*none* of which can be found in documented record or proved in a court of law."

I frowned. "How'd you find out, then?"

"Let's just say that I know some very intelligent and socially awkward men with a certain facility for the electronic transfer of information." She checked the pizza with her fingers, licked a blob of tomato sauce from them, and sent it for another spin cycle in the microwave. "The point is that these people have money, employees, and enormous resources. And bad things can happen to people who start sniffing around. Several investigators looking into their business turned up dead in really smooth professional hits. They looked like accidents."

"How do you know they were murders, then?"

"Because the Foreigner said so."

Mary Jane frowned at me. "The Foreigner?"

"Professional assassin," I said quietly. "He killed Ned Leeds. Hired a mutant named Sabretooth to kill Felicia."

Felicia smiled, and it made her eyes twinkle. "He can *cook*—oh my goodness! And his wine cellar is to die for."

Mary Jane blinked. "You dated him? Before or after he tried to kill you?"

"After, of course," Felicia said with a wicked little smile. "It made things . . . very interesting."

Mary Jane's fork clicked a bit loudly on her plate for a moment as she cut the omelet into smaller pieces with its edge.

"I'm out of the business," Felicia said, "but we keep in touch. I went skiing with him in South Africa last summer. Even the Foreigner's information on Mortia was very sketchy, but it gave me places to start looking." She took a bite of pizza. "And our best move is to blow town."

"What?" I asked.

"I picked up four plane tickets for London, and from there we can cover our tracks and get elsewhere. I can have new identities set up within the day."

Mary Jane blinked at Felicia and then at me.

I finished my omelet's last bite, swallowed, and set my fork down. "Four?"

"You, me, Aunt May, and MJ," Felicia said. "We have to get all of you out together."

"Why do you say that?"

"This is a no-win, Peter," Felicia said, her tone growing serious. "Without more knowledge, you can't take those three on. And if we start nosing around to get that knowledge, one of their managers is going to notice it and correct the problem."

"And hit men are supposed to be scarier to me than the Ancients?" I asked.

She finished the first piece of pizza with a grimace. "I guess you cooked, eh?"

"Stop trying to dodge the question," I said.

She looked down for a moment, her expression uncertain. Then she glanced at Mary Jane. "The Ancients are rich. One person has already found out about Peter's alter ego by spending a lot of money and using his brain. If they're willing to expend the money and manpower, it's only a matter of time before the Ancients know, too." Then she glanced at me. "And then you won't be the only one in danger."

My stomach felt cold and quivery, and my eyes went to Mary Jane.

Her eyes were wide with fear, too. "Aunt May," she said quietly.

Aunt May was out of town at the moment. Her friend Anna had won two tickets on an Alaskan cruise liner in a contest on the radio, and they were off doing cruise-liner things for the next few days. The brochure had said something about glaciers and whales.

It occurred to me that there really wouldn't be anywhere for Aunt May to run or anyplace to hide, trapped out on a ship like that.

"The people they send won't be obsessive, melodramatic maniacs like your usual crowd, Pete," Felicia continued, her voice calm and very serious.

"They'll use strangers, cold men, with years of skill, patience, and no interest whatsoever in anything but concluding their business and taking their money to the bank. They'll find you, stalk you, and kill you, and it won't mean any more to them than balancing their checkbook."

"All the more reason to take care of it right now," I said quietly.

"No," Felicia replied. "All the more reason to run right now. For the moment, the Ancients don't know any more about you than you do about them. If Peter Parker and his family vanish now, you'll be able to hide—to bide your time until we can figure out more about the Ancients or else get some help in taking them down."

"I'm not—," I began.

"Whereas if you wait," Felicia said, running right over me, "if you keep going the way you are, they'll find out who you are, probably within a few days. Then it's too late. Then they'll use their resources to keep track of you and everyone you care about, and you won't have the option of running anymore. You won't be able to get out of sight long enough to come up with a new identity."

Silence fell.

I've been afraid of bad guys before. That wasn't anything new. The people I care about have been put in danger before. That wasn't new, either. But this time was different. This time a choice I had to make would determine whether or not they'd be in danger. If I stood my ground, the Ancients would use them to get me out in the open, and the only way I could keep them absolutely safe was to hide them—or else to get eaten, in which case my loved ones would no longer be of value or interest to the Ancients.

But it would mean vanishing, maybe for a while. It would mean leaving behind a lifetime there, in our town, our home. New York can be dirty and ugly and rude and difficult and dangerous, but it is by thunder my home, and I would not allow anyone to just rip it away.

Bold words. But I wondered if I'd ever be able to look at myself in a mirror again if MJ or Aunt May got hurt because of my stubbornness.

I looked up at Mary Jane, searching for answers.

My wife met my gaze and lifted her chin with her eyes slightly narrowed, a peculiarly pugnacious look on her lovely face.

I felt my lips pull away from my teeth in a fierce grin.

Felicia looked back and forth between us and drew a small packet consisting of airline tickets held in a rubber band from her jacket pocket. She tossed it negligently in the trash can. "Yeah," she sighed. "I was afraid you'd see it like that."

ELEVEN

FELICIA accompanied me to the libraries, plural. The New York Public Library system is enormous, and it took most of the morning to get through the three different branches I wanted to visit. By the time I was finished hunting through the stacks of books, Felicia looked like she might simply explode from pure nerves.

"What's wrong?" I asked her. "Bibliophobic?"

"Never met a bibble I didn't like," she replied. "It's just that I haven't ever actually come to a library for the books before."

I blinked at her. "Why else would you be here?"

She gestured around us. We were down in the basement of this one, and it was nearly deserted, and quiet. "Look around, Peter. Lots and lots of long rows of books, lots of dim little crannies—not a lot of people." She tipped the rather frumpy horn-rimmed glasses down. "Imagine the possibilities."

"I'm imagining books getting damaged," I told her, half-amused. "And after that, I seem to remember that libraries occasionally carry rare books, and sometimes important documents or pieces of art."

"Why, Peter. I'm shocked that you would suggest such a thing." She sighed. "Besides, that isn't a terribly good market. It's difficult to move any of the take. It's all too identifiable. You've got to go to a foreign market to get decent money and it adds in several more middlemen who . . ." She gave me a brilliant smile. "Should I go on?"

"Please don't," I said.

"What are you looking for down here, anyway?"

"Stories," I said. "Folklore, specifically Native American folklore. There were powerful totemic images all through their society and their religious beliefs. Especially with regards to their shamans."

"What's a shaman?"

"It's like a wizard or a holy man," I said. "They were often the healers and advisers of a tribe. They communicated with the spirit world, negotiated with spirits for the benefit of the tribe. There was a lot of lore about them taking on the shape of various animals." I shrugged. "Maybe they really did. Or at least, maybe they could do some extraordinary things—like mutants."

Felicia nodded. "You think the Ancients did some feeding on them."

"I think it's worth investigating. It's possible that if anyone encountered them and survived it, it would make one heck of a good story. There's a chance that it passed into their folklore."

Felicia frowned. "Like . . . like if there was a real-live Pecos Bill who was a mutant who could control tornados? And he was used as the source of the myth? Something like that?"

Felicia isn't exactly a moron herself.

"Just like that," I said. Then I jabbed my finger down on the page. "Aha!"

"Do people really say that?" she asked. But she came around the table and sat down in the chair next to me. "What did you find?"

"This is the third mention I've found of a tribal shaman being pursued by a wendigo. It's a Native American manitou—a spirit creature. It's a kind of punishment that happens to people who resort to cannibalism to survive. They're possessed by the wendigo and transformed into a creature of endless hunger, doomed to haunt the earth forever, looking for victims to devour."

"Sounds like our Ancients all right," Felicia said. "Except that from what you've said, they eat energy, not flesh. And they aren't human. And they only eat once every several years. So it really sounds nothing like them."

I shook my head. "But the details of the story don't necessarily have to be accurate. Think about it. One of the Ancients gets hungry. It comes into a tribe, looking like one of them, to pursue its victim. Then, it and the victim go hunting, or gathering herbs or what have you. The Ancient attacks and leaves a dried husk behind. Later, concerned relatives and friends find the ruined corpse, which is nothing but bones and skin, as if the meat had been sucked out of it. And the new tribesman, the Ancient, has vanished." I shrugged. "Why not assume that the stranger had been a wendigo? Give me some time and I could probably make a case for the original Grendel of folklore being something similar."

"Ah," Felicia said, though she didn't look confident in my hypothesis. "So. Does it say how to kill a wendigo?"

"It's got a heart of ice," I replied. "The traditional way to kill it is to melt the ice."

"We could get Mortia a nice card," Felicia suggested. "Some roses, some chocolate, maybe a Yanni CD and a bottle of Chianti . . ."

"Very funny," I said. "Look, each of these stories is different. In the first two, the wendigo destroys the shaman it hunted. In the last one, though, the shaman had a twin brother, who was a great hunter. The two of them overcame the wendigo."

"I know one set of twin brothers," Felicia admitted. "Though admittedly, I'm not sure if they could take on an Ancient, even though they were definitely in great shape." She frowned. "Come to think of it, I'm not even sure I remember their names."

I snorted. "It wasn't that they were twins," I said. "It's that there were *two* of them fighting it."

"What makes you say that?"

"Comparative data," I said. "You notice how quick Mortia and her goons vanished after you showed up?"

Felicia blinked. "I . . . suppose they did."

"Mmmm. And there were police nearby, choppers coming in close. I think that it posed some kind of threat to them."

Felicia laughed. "Are you kidding? I'll be the first one to tell you how fantastic I am, but I'm not stupid, Pete. I couldn't last a round with any of them, let alone all three. I don't think I made them nervous. I don't think the cops made them nervous."

"Maybe," I said. "But *something* did."

"They didn't look nervous," she said.

"Maybe it was only a marginal threat," I said. "Maybe that was enough to make them cautious."

"Why would they do that?"

"It's the nature of predators," I said. "No matter how hungry one of them gets, there are some things they won't do. If the prey is too dangerous, a predator will look for an easier target if possible. They know that if they're wounded in the course of bringing down the prey, it will render them unable to continue hunting effectively. They don't take chances if they can help it."

Felicia frowned and nodded. "Throw the fact that they're immortal into the mix, too. If you had eternity to lose as the price of a mistake, you wouldn't take any chances, either."

"Right," I said. "So we know they've got a weakness. They don't want to face more than one target at a time."

"Good," Felicia said. "Now. How does that help us? Specifically."

"Working on it," I said. "Let me get back to you. What did you find out about the Rhino and his money? Any way we could nab it, get him to part company with the Ancients?"

"Not a prayer," she said. "The money trail looks like an Escher drawing. It could take months to sort it out."

"Mmmm," I said. "Anything more?"

"Quite a bit, actually. The Foreigner gave me a copy of his own file on the Rhino."

"And?"

"Aleksei Mikhailovich Sytsevich," she began.

"Gesundheit."

"Immigrated to the States from the Soviet Union, back when they had one. He'd come over to get a job that would pay enough for him to bring the rest of his family—the usual American dream. But since he didn't have much in the way of education, he couldn't get a job that would offer him enough money."

I grunted.

"He was big and tough, though. He wound up working as an enforcer for the mob. Someone—the Foreigner isn't sure who—offered him a chance to participate in an experiment. The one where they grafted the armored hide to his skin."

"Did they give him that hat, too?"

"Yes."

"The fiends."

"Stop interrupting," Felicia said. "Later, he went through another experiment that enhanced his strength as well, enabling him to go toe-to-toe with the Incredible Hulk. He lost, but he made the Hulk work for it."

"Engh," I said. "Well, it's too bad we couldn't subtract him, but he won't affect the equation too badly."

Felicia gave me a pointed look. "Equation? Peter. He's fought the *Hulk.*"

"So what?" I said. "*I've* fought the Hulk. The Hulk's personality being what it is, pretty much *everybody* has fought the Hulk."

Felicia leaned over and peered at my face.

"What you doing?" I asked her.

"Seeing if your eyes have turned green." She smiled at me. "The Rhino's had a lot of work with various villains, and has a reputation as an extremely tenacious mercenary. As long as no one sends him after the Hulk, apparently."

"Or me," I said.

She patted my hand. "Or you."

I scowled at her. "Why are you giving me a hard time about this?"

She shrugged. "Maybe it's my background. As mercenaries go, the Rhino isn't all that bad a guy."

"Not all that bad? He wrecks things left and right! Factories, buildings, vehicles—"

"And," Felicia said, "in the midst of all that destruction, he's never actually killed anyone. That says something about him, Pete."

"Even if he hasn't killed anyone, he's still breaking the law. He destroys property, steals money and valuables, and in general makes a profit off of his victims' losses."

Felicia removed her glasses and stared hard at me for a second. Then she said, her voice very quiet, "The way I used to do."

I frowned at that, and fell silent.

"I know you've got a lot of contempt for him," she said in that same quiet voice. "But I've been where he's standing—and I got into it purely for the profit, not to take care of my family, the way he did. He started off with better intentions than I ever had, and he's ended up in a much worse position. It's a bad place to be, Peter. I feel sorry for him."

"I don't," I said quietly.

"And what's the difference, Pete?" she asked. There was no malice in the question. "What's the difference between him and me? What's the difference between him and *you,* for that matter? I mean, I don't know if anyone ever explained this, but vigilantism isn't exactly smiled upon by the law in this town, and you do it every day."

Which was true, and really inconvenient to this debate. "So what? You think I should drop the mask, go to the police academy, and get a badge? Right. Like they'd ever let me do that."

She shook her head. "I just think you should think of him as a human being, not some kind of dangerous wild animal. Speaking of which," she said, "didn't it ever strike you as odd that the Ancients hired the bloody *Rhino*? A goon chock-full of totemic life energy?"

I blinked.

It hadn't.

"I'm not saying you should pull your punches," she continued. "I'm not saying we should give him a hug and sign him up for group therapy. I'm just saying that he's a human being with strengths and flaws, just like anyone else—and that he's in way over his head. He's in as much danger as you are and he probably doesn't even realize it."

I shut the book a little harder than was strictly necessary. "He hurts people for money."

"You hurt people for *free!*" she said tartly. "That just means he has better business sense than you."

"I fight criminals," I said. "Not bank guards and security personnel."

"One man's security guard is another man's hired thug," she said. "And when you get right down to it, men like the Rhino spend far more time pounding on other criminals than they do on law enforcement."

I stacked the books up to return to the shelves. Most people probably don't make enormous booming noises when stacking books. But I think they would if they had the proportionate strength of a spider and the proportionate patience of the crowd control guys on Jerry Springer. "So what are you saying? There's no difference between the good guy and the bad guy?"

Felicia arched an eyebrow at me. "They're both guys. Aren't they?"

"Yeah. One of them a violent criminal, and the other someone who *protects* people from violent criminals."

"My point, Peter," she said, "is that when you get down to it, there's very little difference between a wolf in the fold and the sheepdog who protects them."

"Like hell there isn't," I said. "The sheepdog doesn't eat *sheep*. Which is a really sorry metaphor to use for New Yorkers in the first place. Your average New Yorker is about as sheeplike as a Cape buffalo."

"Not everyone has a heart like yours, Parker," she snarled, her voice ringing out among the stacks. "Not everyone is as *good* as you. As noble. Not everyone *sees* the difference between right and wrong—and once upon a time you didn't, either, or you wouldn't be who you are." She folded her arms and brought her voice under control with some difficulty. "And I'd still be doing jobs on jewelers and vaults and . . ."—she gestured around us, wearily—"libraries."

True enough. Once upon a time, I hadn't seen the difference between right and wrong, and Uncle Ben died for it.

I sighed. "Look, there's nothing else to be gained here. You want to go?"

She nodded. "Yeah. Another library?"

"No," I said. "I have another stop to make."

TWELVE

COACH Kyle had been right. It wasn't a great neighborhood.

The Larkins' apartment building was well coated with graffiti and neglect. There wasn't a visible streetlight that hadn't been broken. The windows on the lower floors were all barred and covered in boards. There weren't a lot of cars around, and the ones that were looked far too expensive for anyone living there—except for one old Oldsmobile, which had been put on blocks and stripped to a skeleton of its former self.

Most tellingly, on a Saturday afternoon, there was almost no one in sight. I saw one gray-haired woman walking down the street with a hard expression and a purposeful stride. Several young men in gang colors sat on or around one of the expensive cars while a big radio boomed. Other than that, nothing. No pedestrians headed for a corner grocery store. No one taking out the trash or walking to the mailbox. No children out playing in the pleasant weather.

I'd filled Felicia in on Samuel, and she had listened to the whole thing without comment until we got where we were going. "You take me to the nicest places," she said. "Which building?"

"The one with those friendly-looking young men with the radio."

"I thought you'd say that," Felicia said.

We approached the building and got flat-eyed stares from the young men. They sat with the grips of handguns poking up out of their waistbands or outlined against their loose shirts. None of them were older than nineteen. One couldn't have been fifteen.

"Hey," said one of the larger young men, his tone belligerent. "White bread. Where you think you're going?"

I gestured with a hand without slowing down, as if it had been a polite inquiry instead of a challenge. "Visiting a friend."

The kid came to his feet with an aggressive little bounce and planted himself directly in my way. "I don't know you. Maybe you better just turn around." He looked past me to Felicia. "You're pretty stupid, coming down here with a piece like that. Where do you think you are, man?"

I stopped and looked around, then scratched my head. "Isn't this Sesame Street? I'm sure Mister Snuffalupagus is around here somewhere."

The kid in front of me got mad and got right in my face, eye to eye. The young men with him let out an ugly, growling sound as a whole. "You trying to start something, man? You gonna get a cap, you keep this up."

It was annoying. If I'd been wearing the mask, I could have taken these kids' guns away and scared them off. Peter Parker, part-time science teacher, however, couldn't beat up gangs single-handed. And if anything started, Felicia was sure to pitch in. She could handle herself as well as anyone I knew, but this wasn't the time or the place to look for a fight.

I lifted my hands and said, "Sorry, man, just joking with you. I'm here to see Samuel Larkin."

"What do you care?"

"I'm his basketball coach," I said.

That drew a round of quiet laughs. "Sure you are." He shook his head. "Time you're leaving."

"No," I said quietly. "I need to see Samuel Larkin."

The young man pulled up his shirt and put his hand on the grip of a semiautomatic stuck in his waistband. "I ain't gonna tell you again."

I met his gaze in silence, and didn't move. He expected me to, I could tell, and as the seconds ticked by he started to get nervous. He had his hand on a gun, all of his friends had guns, and I would have had to be insane not to be afraid. He had expected me to back off, or produce a gun of my own, or attack him—*anything*, really, but stand there calmly. The basic tactics of bullies hadn't changed since I was in school—cause fear and control people with it. Granted, they hadn't carried around the handguns quite so obviously. And if one of them had backed down back then, it probably would have meant a little bit of embarrassment. Depending on how hard-core this gang was, backing off could cost this kid his leadership—which could well mean his life, or at least everything he thought was of value in it.

I lowered my voice so that only he could hear it. "Don't," I said quietly. "Please."

He swallowed. Then his shoulder tensed to draw the gun.

"George," bellowed a deep voice from above us. "What you think you doing to my coach?"

I looked up and found Samuel's scowling face looking down from a window on the fourth floor.

George, presumably, looked away from me and put his hands on his hips to scowl up at Samuel. "I don't know no George."

Samuel rolled his eyes. "Oh, yeah. G. You just G now, huh. George got too many letters."

"You got a big mouth," George said, scowling.

Samuel barked out a laugh. "G, you always been a funny guy." Then he looked at me and said, "Hey, Coach Parker."

"Mr. Larkin," I replied, nodding. "Got a minute to talk?"

"Buzz you in," he said. "Don't be too hard on my man G. Nobody ever gave him a hug or a puppy or anything like that, so he grew up with a bad attitude."

I nodded to him and walked to the door.

Behind me, George stepped in front of Felicia and said, "Now you, girl. You're fine. Maybe you should stay here and hang with me. Me and my crew will keep you safe from the bad element."

Felicia took off the glasses and smiled at him. Not a pretty smile. It was a slightly unsettling kind of smile, very Lecter-like. "I *am* the bad element," she said, toothily. "The question you should be asking is, Who is going to keep you and your crew safe from *me*?"

George let out a laugh, but it sort of died a strangled death a second or two in.

Felicia kept smiling and took a step closer to him.

George took a wary step back from her.

"That's good, G," she told him. "That's smart. Smart men are sexy."

The door buzzed, and I opened it for Felicia. She sauntered through, giving George a dazzling smile on the way, and vanished into the building.

I nodded to George, pointed a finger at my temple, and spun it in a little circle.

"Yeah," George said, shaking his head as the door closed. "Crazy white people."

The elevator was out, so we took the stairs up to the fourth floor, then found the Larkins' apartment. I knocked. It took Samuel a minute to get to the door. He opened it, stepped out, and closed it behind him, so that we didn't get to see the apartment.

"Mister Science," he said. He looked from me to Felicia. "I really wasn't expecting to see this kind of thing until college recruiters started showing up."

Felicia asked me, sweetly, "How hard is it to play basketball without kneecaps?"

I put a hand on her arm and said to Samuel, "Thanks for stepping in with those guys down there."

He shrugged. "You get killed here, there's gonna be a lot of trouble for people I know. It ain't 'cause I like you, Mister Science."

"Yeah. I can tell what a public enemy you are," I said. "I came by to see if you'd had any luck with getting the shots set up."

"Oh sure," he said. "Soon as my driver gets back with the limo, he gonna take me to my private doctor. Doc's on vacation in Fiji, but I got my personal jet waiting to pick me up."

I gave him a flat look for a minute. Then I said, "I'm serious."

"Then you're stupid," he replied, his tone frank and not bitter. He stared at me for a second and then said, "Shoot." (Which he didn't say, again.) "You really think that I was gonna get to a doctor?"

"I think you really want to," I said. "I thought maybe there'd be something I could do to help you."

"And you came down *here*? And with your woman, too. And you face off with G." He shook his head. "You gotta be brave or stupid or crazy, Mister Science."

"I am not his woman," Felicia said, tartly.

"And my name is Parker," I said, putting a restraining hand on Felicia's arm again. "Look, Samuel, if there's something I can do to help you, I want to do it."

"Like what?" the big young man said. "You gonna get my father back to New York, back with my mom, maybe? So he can work a job, so my mom got time to get us taken care of? Maybe you can make her arthritis disappear." He shook his head. "That ain't gonna happen."

"I know that," I said.

"You even know any doctors?" he asked.

"Um. Not the medical doctor kind," I said. I didn't think Doctors Octavius, Conners, Osborne, or Banner would have the most recent inoculations sitting around ready to go. Reed Richards might, or might know someone, but I didn't like the idea of asking him for his help for something so . . . normal. Mister Fantastic's time is pretty well eaten up by cosmic devices and mad Latverian dictators and threats to the entire universe.

"What use are you then, huh? Part-time science teacher gonna save us urban kids. You're a bad joke, man."

Felicia's hands clenched, the way they did when she wore the gloves with the built-in claws.

"Easy," I said to her. "Samuel. Look. If you don't want my help, you can tell me that. You don't have to keep trying to insult Ms. Hardy and me so that I'll get mad and walk away."

Samuel fell quiet for a long minute, and the door to his apartment opened. A little girl, maybe four or five years old, came out. She was cuter than a whole jar of buttons, with little pink bows in her hair, blue overalls, and a pink T-shirt.

"Samm'l," she wheezed, rubbing at her eyes. "Chris'fer keeps kicking me."

Samuel glanced at us once, suddenly nervous, and turned to kneel down and speak to the little girl, picking her up as he did. "Did you tell him to stop that?"

"Yeah, but he's sleepin'."

"Oh," Samuel said, and his voice was warm and gentle. "Well, he doesn't mean to do that. You know that, right?"

"He won't stop."

"Uh-huh," he said. "How 'bout I put you in my bed for your nap." She frowned. "And Peter Rabbit?"

He snorted. "Okay. And Peter Rabbit. But only once."

The little girl smiled at him. "'Kay."

Samuel kissed her on the head and set her back down. "Go on. I'll be right there."

The little girl nodded, gave me and Felicia a shy little glance, then fled inside.

Samuel stood up slowly and shut the door after her. Then he turned to face us, clearly uncomfortable. "My little brother does a lot of running around in his sleep," he explained. "They share a bed. Hard on her sometimes."

"She's a beautiful child," I said.

Samuel glanced back at the door and smiled. "Yeah, she . . ." He was quiet for a moment, and the smile faded. "She's a sweetheart."

"Okay," I said. "You want to stop with the insults now?"

He rolled one shoulder in a shrug. "I guess you mean well, at least. You shouldn't have come down here, though. Dangerous." He looked up at Felicia and gave her a nod that somehow conveyed an apology. "Especially for you, Ms. Hardy. But there's nothing much you can do."

"Samuel," I said. "Maybe I can talk to someone. I might be able to—"

"I don't want you to," Samuel said, his tone hardening. "I don't want your help. Your charity. I'll do it on my own."

"Even if it means suspension," I said.

He shrugged. "Shoot. Good as I am, the college boys aren't even gonna look at that. Once they see me, that's that."

"They're going to have a hard time seeing you if you get suspended. I checked regulations. You aren't going to be eligible to play for the rest of this season."

He shrugged. "So I arrange something else. I don't need your help, Mister Science."

I exhaled heavily. "Everyone needs help sometime."

"Not me," he said. "Nice of you to come by, but it ain't helping me any. Best if you just go."

"You sure?" I asked him. "It could mean a lot, in the long run. Making sure you're on the team."

"My life. I'll handle it." He shrugged. "I can't do ball, I'll do something else. My mom can't do it alone no more."

"G and his buddies seem to like you," I noted.

"Grew up together here," Samuel said, nodding. "I don't like what they do, but . . . people gotta live."

I stood there for a moment, feeling stupid and awkward. Then I nodded to him and said, "Your call, then." I pulled a scrap of paper out of my notebook and wrote down my number. "But here's my number. In case you change your mind."

"I won't," he said, making no move to take the paper I offered.

"In case," I said. "Keep your options open."

He glowered for a moment and shook his head.

Then he took the paper and said, "Just to get rid of you."

○━━━━━━━━━○

WE headed for the nearest subway station, Felicia watching me steadily the whole time.

"Sometimes I don't know how you do that," she said.

"Do what?"

"Think about other people. You're up to your neck in trouble, but you're worried about some loudmouthed prima donna. Going out of your way to see him."

"I have to," I said.

"Why?"

"The same reason I won't leave town."

"Which is?"

"If I let my fear of the Ancients force me to abandon my life, if I run away from everything I think is important, they've already killed me. If I hadn't come here, then this time next week, I'd feel pretty bad about leaving Samuel in the lurch without even trying to help."

"If you're alive in a week," she pointed out.

"Right," I said. "I'm planning on its happening. That's one of the things that's helped me survive this long."

Felicia shook her head. "He seems like a pretty good kid, once you get past the attitude."

"Yeah," I said.

"You're going to do everything you can to help him, aren't you."

"Yes I am."

"Even though you're up to your tights in alligators already," she said, her voice amused.

"When am I *not*?"

She laughed, and we walked in companionable silence for a while. I stopped at the entrance to the subway.

She tilted her head at me. "What is it?"

"I hate this mystic stuff," I said, frustrated. "Way too nebulous. I've got nothing but speculation. Theories. Hot air. I've got the next best thing to nothing when it comes to empirical data. What I need is someone who's actually been around the Ancients, who knows them."

"Seems to me that they don't like to go public. I doubt anyone close enough to have seen them in action survived to talk about it."

"But without some kind of information, I'm at a dead end. There's no record, no evidence of—"

Suddenly an idea hit me, and I had to sit there frowning furiously until my brain ran the numbers.

"What is it?" she asked.

"There *is* evidence," I said. "Or there might be."

"What?"

"Renfield Dex," I said.

"Who?"

"He was Morlun's little buddy. Human. Took care of details for him. He was there when Morlun died." I shivered. "Morlun hadn't treated him well. When I beat Morlun down, Dex took a gun off an unconscious guard and emptied the whole thing into Morlun's chest."

Felicia's eyes widened. "There were two people there when Morlun died," she said. "Dex and you."

"Yeah."

"Then I guess we need to talk to Dex." She frowned. "What's the rest of his name? Where is he?"

"I don't know," I said. "But when the cops got to the reactor, they found the gun in the aftermath. I'm sure they lifted prints from it. If we can get the prints, maybe we can identify him. The police should have them on file, even if the weapon went back to its owner."

"Wouldn't they have done that already?"

"I doubt it," I said. "That kind of thing could take a lot of man-hours, and it isn't as though they'd found a murder weapon. What was left of Morlun when they got there couldn't have filled a thermos. The only crimes had been in trespassing and the assault on the guard."

She narrowed her eyes in thought. "That would put it a pretty good way down their priority list, wouldn't it. But they don't exactly leave the evidence room open to the public," she said.

"Felicia," I said. "I'm sure that if anyone can find a way to get them, it's you."

She beamed at me. "It's sweet of you to say that. Even if it makes the air smell just a little bit like hypocrisy, O great defender of the law."

I glowered at her. "Don't start with me."

She smiled, pleased to have needled me. "What are you going to do?"

"What I should have done last night," I said. "I was just hoping to avoid it, because every time I go there, I get the crap beat out of me by something, or shipped off to some funky dimension to get the crap beat out of me, or my astral self gets projected away from my body so that I'm getting the crap beaten out of me in two dimensions at once. It's bad. It's always bad. Every time it happens I swear to myself that I'm never going down Bleecker Street ever again."

"Ohhh," Felicia said. "Him."

"Time's a-wasting," I said.

She nodded, rising. "I'll call the office, and we'll see what we can do about finding Dex. Quick description, please?"

"White male, twenty-five to thirty-five, about five-eight, straight brown hair, one of those shaggy goatees, hazel eyes. Real thin face, long nose."

She nodded. "Got it."

I put a hand on her shoulder. "Watch your back," I said.

"Always," she said, smiling. She touched my hand lightly and then vanished into the subway.

I slipped into an empty alley, put on my mask, and set off to visit Doctor Stephen Strange, Sorcerer Supreme.

THIRTEEN

I headed over to Strange's place on Bleecker Street. It's easy to find from above. All I have to do is look for the funky round window with its oddly shaped panes. I didn't go in through the window, though. You don't just sidle into a sorcerer's place through the windows or the vents. Guys like Strange tend to protect themselves against that sort of thing. It's safest to go in through the front door.

I had my hand raised to knock when Wong opened the door and gave me a small bow. "Spider-Man."

Wong is tall for a native Tibetan and can look me right in the eye. He had a little piece of tissue paper stuck to a spot where he'd nicked himself shaving, on the top of his head. He wore trousers and a shirt of green silk with black embroidery, accented with threads the color of polished bronze. His expression was what it usually was—serene. To me at least. Wong's poker face was so good, it nearly qualified as a superpower.

"Wong," I said. "You busted up my groove."

"Did I?"

"Big time. I was going to do the Bugs Bunny routine on the Doc. I brought a carrot and everything."

Wong nodded, his expression serious. "My soul is impoverished by the sin of . . . busting up your groove? Additionally, I mourn my master's disappointment in being unable to properly experience your doubtlessly flawless impersonation of a cartoon rabbit."

I looked at him for a second. "Nobody likes a wiseass, Wong."

Wong's mouth twitched at one corner, though he came nowhere

close to actually smiling. "My master is expecting you. Please come in. May I take your . . . carrot?"

I'd picked it up from a vendor at a street market on the way. "No thanks," I said. I pulled up my mask enough to bunch over my nose. I swear, one of these days I'm going to get a mask that leaves my mouth free. I crunched into the carrot because it was good for me. And because I hadn't had lunch.

Wong watched me soberly, then nodded and led me to the doctor's office.

It was a big room, the size of a large study, packed full of books, scrolls, tablets, and oddities, all in neat order, all terribly well organized and clean, all set around an enormous mahogany desk. Though the ceilings were high and arched, the lighting there was always subdued, and lent it a cavelike mien. There was a fire crackling in a fireplace, and the air smelled of incense and cinnamon.

Stephen Strange sat behind the desk. He's a tall, slender man. He's got a neatly trimmed mustache and dark hair, with those perfect silver streaks at the temples that some men seem lucky enough to develop. He looks like an extremely fit man in his mid-thirties, though he's got to be older than that, judging from the sheepskin he keeps on the wall behind him. Neurology. He was wearing a very normal-looking outfit, especially for him: a pale blue golf shirt and khakis. I was much more used to the electric blue tunic and Shakespearean tights, plus the big red disco cloak.

"Spider-Man, master," Wong said in calm, formal tones.

"Thank you, Wong," Strange said. He had a resonant voice. "Our guest has not had lunch. Do you think you could find something appropriate?"

"Eminently so, master."

"Thank you," he said, and Wong departed. Strange leaned his elbows on his desk and made a steeple of his fingers. "Good day to you, Spider-Man. I thought you'd be by today."

"Saw me coming with the old mystical Eye of Agamotto, eh, Doc?"

He moved one finger, pointing at a flat-screen plasma TV on the wall beside his desk. "On the Channel Seven news." He moved his hand and picked up a copy of that day's *Bugle*. There was a picture of the wreckage in Times Square next to the headline

SPIDER-MAN RUNS WILD IN TIMES SQUARE

"You may not be the most subtle man in New York."

I pointed at the newspaper with my partly gnawed carrot. "That wasn't my fault."

"Of course it wasn't." Strange sighed. "Ignorance is part of the tragedy of the human condition. It is in the nature of man to fear what he does not know or cannot control. The average human being is no more comfortable in contemplation of his inner being than he is contemplating magic itself."

"You sound like Ezekiel," I said. "He was always trying to tell me my powers had come from some kind of mystic spider-god entity."

"Are you so sure they did not?"

"I was bitten by a radioactive spider. Period."

Strange smiled at me. "And who is to say that said spider was not the theoretical entity's choice as emissary? One does not necessarily preclude the other."

I looked at him. Then I sat down without being asked. "I was pretty sure I was done dealing with all this mystical muckety-muck."

Strange nodded. "Indeed, you are. The onus of that entire business has been appeased, the obligations completed, the balance restored, the necessities observed."

I tilted my head, like a dog who has suddenly heard a new sound.

"Your account ledger is cleared," he clarified. "That particular business is done."

"Well, it ain't, Doc. I take it you've heard of beings calling themselves the Ancients?"

Strange shrugged his shoulders. "Many claim such a sobriquet. Few deserve it."

"Morlun," I said. "Mortia. Thanis. Malos."

Strange hissed. "Ah. *Them.*"

"Them," I said. "Morlun tried to eat me. He wound up dead. Now his siblings are looking to return the compliment."

Strange lifted his eyebrows. "You defeated Morlun?"

"Yeah. With freaking radioactive material not unlike the radioactive freaking spider that gave me my freaking powers," I retorted. "No freaking mystical juju at all."

"Interesting," he mused. "Then their motive is not a factor of mystic balance, but one far older and more primal."

"Yeah," I said. "Payback. I need your help."

"Help?"

"Aid. Assistance. Advice."

Strange stared at me for a moment. Then he closed his eyes, settled back in his chair, and murmured, "Absolutely not."

Which made me blink. "What?"

"I cannot interfere in what passes between you and the Ancients."

"Why *not*?" I demanded.

He leaned back in his chair, frowning, his expression genuinely disturbed. "You understand, of course, that all forces in the universe act in balance. In a harmony of sorts."

"That's kind of Newtonian, but let's assume that you know what you're talking about," I said.

"Thank you," he said, his voice serious. "The powers at my command are part and parcel of that balance. I am not free to simply employ them on a whim without serious consequences resulting—and in fact, it would be dangerous to do so around one of the Ancients you face."

"Oh," I said. "I guess they deserve the name?"

"Indeed. They are older than mountains, older than the seas. Since life first graced this sphere, and since that life called out to the mystic realms, echoing in harmony and sympathy, these beings, these Ancients, have been there to feed upon it."

"Really, you could have said, 'Yes, they're old,' and it would have been enough."

"My apologies," Strange said. "I occasionally forget the limitations of your attention span."

"Thank you."

"Yes. They are old."

"And you can't do anything to them?"

Strange frowned. "It is a complex issue, and does not lend itself to monosyllabic explanation."

I cupped my hands to either side of my head. "Okay. These are my listening ears. I've got my listening ears on."

"Let me know if you experience any discomfort," Strange said, his voice dryly amused. Then he made a steeple of his fingers. "What you call 'magic' is a complex weaving of natural forces—life energy, elemental power, cosmic energies. And, like more familiar physical forces such as thermal energy, electricity, or gravity, they abide by a set of governing laws. They do not simply obey the whims of those who employ them. They have limitations and foibles. Do you understand that much?"

"Yes," I said brightly. "And I didn't get a nosebleed or anything."

"The nature of my access to these powers determines how I might employ them," he said. "I cannot simply randomly choose anything in my repertoire to counter any given situation, just as you could not expect to mix random chemicals and attain the desired results."

"So far, so good," I said.

He nodded. "The Ancients are predators, as you are doubtless aware. And while they are not a particularly pleasant part of the natural world, they are, nonetheless, a part of it. My powers are meant to defend and protect that world from those who would attempt to damage or destroy it. Were I to turn my powers against the Ancients it would be"—he actually turned a little green—"an abuse of that which is entrusted to me. A corruption of the energies in my charge. A most abominable blasphemy of the primal forces of our world."

"And what? The magic wand police would give you a ticket?"

"You speak lightly," Strange said. "But you are well aware of the evils that can be wrought with the abuse of power. Were I to turn the energies with which I work against the Ancients, the repercussions could be severe."

"Why?" I asked.

"Because of what and who the Ancients are. They are some of the eldest predators upon this sphere, creatures of enormous mystic strength—though they do not refine and utilize that energy in the way I do. It is, however, consciously focused by their force of will to give them enormous resilience, strength, and speed."

"Yeah. They're magically malicious. I figured that part out already."

"Their formidable physical attributes are minor compared to the enormous potential that dwells within them. Should I wield my powers directly against them, the results could be catastrophic."

"Uh-huh," I said, lowering my hands. "When you say 'severe,' and 'catastrophic,' you mean. . ."

"The end of all life upon this sphere."

"Right." I took a deep breath. "Couldn't you at least give me some more information about them? Anything would help."

"My personal knowledge of them is limited. And even were I to employ my arts to learn more, I would be constrained to tell you nothing."

"What? Why?"

"Knowledge is power—a fact with which I suspect you are intimately familiar. If I used my power to gain knowledge, and then shared that knowledge with you to affect the outcome of this situation, it would be as disruptive as if I had done so myself. It would upset certain critical natural balances and as a result, the eldritch portals would open in order to create a redressing of the forces so unbalanced."

"Which would be . . . ?" I asked.

"A series of confrontations like those you experienced a few months ago—beginning with Morlun and continuing through Morwen's incursion and confrontation with Loki, your battle with Shathra, all of which culminated in Dormmamu's attempted destruction of this reality on your birthday. You would again be a critical variable in the equation. It would expose both you and uncounted innocents to enormous peril. And so I must do nothing. Even having this conversation at all is potentially dangerous."

I shuddered. Then I slumped in my chair. My head suddenly felt really heavy on my neck. What was the point? For crying out loud, it had been nothing short of a miracle that I had survived Morlun, much less the rest of that mess. I wasn't asking Strange to make them go poof. I just wanted him to help me. Just a little.

Strange spoke quietly, and his voice was strained with regret and compassion. "I am sorry that I cannot aid you in this battle, as you have so often aided me in mine. It is unjust. Unfair."

"Since when has life been fair?" I asked.

Strange smiled. "In the long view, I think it might be worse if life *was* fair, and each of us received everything he deserved. My mistakes would have earned me torments to disturb the dreams of Dante himself."

"Amen," I said quietly, having pulled some epic blunders of my own.

"I wish you luck in your struggle," Strange said. He rose and offered me his hand. "But you should know that I believe you have the necessary potential to overcome this foe. Do not lose heart. There is more strength in you than even you know. I am truly sorry that I cannot do more."

I thought about just storming out, but Aunt May didn't raise me to be rude. Besides, if Strange said he couldn't help, he couldn't help, period. He might be weird, wordy, and unsettling, but he's not a coward or a liar. If he could have helped me, he would have. I believed that.

"S'okay, Doc." I shook his hand, and he walked me to the door of his office. "I never got the chance to thank you for that birthday present."

Strange inclined his head, a solemn gesture. "It was my pleasure and honor to be able to bestow it. Even so, it in no way lessens my gratitude and obligation to you for times gone by."

"Don't worry about me. I'm used to going it alone."

"Which is the problem," he said.

I stopped, blinked, and looked up at him. "Hey. Did you just—"

Strange smiled, very slightly, and quietly shut the door in my face.

Strange said he couldn't share information, but had he just tried to slip me something? If he was going to do that, why not just come out and say it? Why the heck does everything have to be so confusing when he's involved?

Freaking sorcerers. Freaking mystic muckety-mucks.

Wong entered the room on nearly soundless feet, carrying a paper lunch bag. I turned to face him.

"I have always found," Wong said, "that the master quite often is able to say something important without ever coming anywhere near it in conversation. I would humbly suggest that you consider his words singly, collectively and most carefully."

"Why does it always have to be twenty questions with him?"

"Because he is the master. Did your talk go well?"

I grunted. "Not really. I was hoping for a little good luck this time around."

Wong bowed his head, then offered me the lunch bag. "I regret that the outcome of your visit did not please you. I hope that ham on wheat will satisfy."

I accepted the bag as we walked to the door. "It's my favorite."

"Really? Then one might say that you found a little good luck after all."

I blinked at him. "Wait. Wong, did you just—"

Wong bowed politely and shut the door in my face.

I looked at the door.

I looked at the lunch bag.

"Their weakness is ham on wheat?" I asked the door.

The door was almost as informative as Strange and Wong.

"This is why I don't like messing around in this magic stuff!" I hollered at Strange's mansion.

People on the sidewalks stopped to stare at me.

I scowled. "I swear, one of these days I'm going to snap and throw a garbage truck through that stupid window." I shook my head, muttered some things I'd never say around Aunt May, and opened the lunch bag.

Ham-on-wheat sandwiches, two of them, in plastic bags.

An apple.

And a black-lacquered square box as wide as my hand, maybe half an inch thick.

Interesting.

It reminded me of a jewelry case. I opened it. Inside were three small, black stones, along with a folded piece of paper that looked like a page torn from a book.

I read over it.

Very interesting.

For the first time that day, I felt something almost like real hope.

I closed the lunch bag, tied it to my belt with a bit of webbing, and swung for home.

FOURTEEN

"LET me get this straight," Mary Jane said as she sat down across the kitchen table from me. "You went to ask for Doctor Strange's help, and he gave you magic beans?"

"Well. He didn't give them to me. Wong did."

"Wong did."

"And they aren't beans. They're rocks."

"Magic rocks. And he told you they would help?"

"No," I said.

"Wong did?"

"No," I said. "Wong gave me lunch. And rocks. And this. But he didn't tell me anything." I slid her the piece of paper Wong had packed in the lunch bag while I munched on the sandwiches.

The ham was that expensive honey-baked kind that Aunt May can only afford once a year, for Christmas, and it was delicious. The bread was wheat bread, sure enough, but homemade and fresh, and Wong had made it with a splash of Italian dressing and had somehow found a fresh-grown tomato, not one of those Styrofoam imitation tomatoes my grocery store sells. It was good.

Maybe I should think about asking Wong for cooking lessons. If only he wasn't such a wiseacre.

"Alhambran agates," Mary Jane read. "Long used to detain the most savage nonmortal corporeal beings. Touched to the flesh of a willing or insensible entity, they resonate with a static pocket dimension from which there is no simple means of egress." She frowned. "Static pocket dimension?"

"A tiny reality where not much happens, and where time doesn't progress at the same rate as everywhere else," I said. "It's like a combination prison cell and deep freeze."

"But magic," she said.

"Well. There are some quantum theories that indicate that something like this *could* be possible, but . . ."

She reached for one of the stones. "So you just touch the Ancient with the magic rock and poof?"

I caught her wrist gently before she could touch it. "I'm not sure exactly what they will and won't do," I said. "But they're evidently powerful and dangerous. I think it's best not to take any chances."

She blinked and drew her hand back. "Oh."

"Here's the thing," I said. "They have to want to go. Or else they've got to be unconscious. Otherwise, the rock doesn't work."

"Oh," Mary Jane said. "Well. That's doable, right? I mean, you can just punch their lights out and stick a rock in their ear. Can't you?"

I grunted. "I blew up a building with Morlun in it. Gas explosion. His clothes got flash-burned and he walked out of it naked as a jaybird and without so much as a bruise. It barely mussed his hair. And I put him through brick walls, smashed him with a telephone pole to the noggin, threw him off the roof of a thirty-story building—nothing."

Mary Jane folded her arms. "So, the magic rocks aren't going to help after all?"

"Not unless I can devise a way to knock out the Ancients," I said through a mouthful of sandwich. "Or else talk them into doing it willingly."

"I see," she said quietly.

One of those tense silences fell.

"How did the test go?" I asked her.

"Hmmm?" She shook her head a little and gave me a false laugh. "Don't worry about it. It's not really important."

"Sure it is," I said quietly.

She frowned at the table for a minute. "I passed the written," she said.

"Uh-oh."

She rolled her eyes and waved her hands in frustration. "It's so *stupid.* I got to the driving test and panicked. I couldn't remember anything I was supposed to remember. I mean, in the traffic and everything, and I was worried and it turned into one huge blur. I couldn't get my breath."

"Ah," I said. "What happened?"

"I just tried to figure out what to do by watching the professionals. I mean, I figured they knew what they were doing, right?"

"The professionals?" I asked.

She nodded. "Cabbies."

I choked. I couldn't help it. I bowed my head and tried to cough as if something had gone down the wrong way, to strangle my laughter before it could hurt her feelings. I looked up at her after a moment, with my face turning red from the effort of holding it in.

She sighed and shook her head with a small, rueful smile. "Go ahead."

I laughed.

"I just don't understand it," she said, when I recovered. "Locking up like that. It isn't as though it's particularly *difficult.*"

"The driving test, you mean?" I said.

"Yes."

I thought about it. "You say you were short of breath?"

"Yes."

"It sounds like a panic attack," I said. "They happen."

Mary Jane's mouth twisted in distaste. "Really? I used to make fun of the models who said they had them before a show. I never thought they might be real." She shook her head. "Maybe I should just check myself into a funny farm."

"Might be a little extreme this early in the game," I said. "I mean, we're talking about a reaction to psychological pressure—of which you have had plenty lately. You'd be crazy if you *didn't* have a twitch or two."

I didn't mention anything specific. No need to bring up the ugly details. Her abduction and imprisonment following her apparent death. Our split. Our happy reunion, but always with homicidal madmen, with or without costumes, prancing in and out of the wings. All the while, dashing around the world on planes, trains, and automobiles (admittedly, someone else did the driving) to appear in shows, to be photographed in exotic places, attending openings and soirees and all the other duties expected of a celebrity.

Mix in some pain, some trauma, some terror. Blend well. All of that would be more than enough to rattle anyone's cage.

"Then why do I feel like such a wimp?" she asked.

"I don't know," I said. "Sometimes I feel kinda wimpy myself. Look, MJ, this isn't a big deal. If we have to, I'll drive you down until you can pass the test."

She frowned and then shook her head. "No. I'll do it myself. I'll pass it Monday morning. If you can deal with immortal, unstoppable monsters, I can handle the DMV."

"Easy there, Superchick. If you're working up an archenemy, you don't want to start with the DMV. Go with someone a little easier to deal with. Doctor Doom, Magneto."

She smiled at me—more because I'd gone to the effort to make the joke than because it was funny. She glanced at the stones. "I'm not sure I like this Strange person," she said.

"The doc's okay," I said. "I get the feeling he's doing everything he can. He's got limits."

"I don't care about limits," Mary Jane said, her tone practical. "I care about you. He isn't doing well by you, and you're what matters to me."

I slipped my hand from her wrist, and twined her warm fingers in mine. "I think you might not be totally objective."

"Why would I want to be?" she asked. She leaned down and pressed a soft, warm kiss to my hand.

I pushed my food aside, and went around the table to kiss my wife. She returned the kiss with an ardent sigh, her arms sliding around my neck, holding on as tightly as she could.

She was afraid.

So was I.

So the kiss became our whole world. She became my whole world. I let her warmth, her desire, her love wash over me, and gave it back in kind. Words would have been a waste of sensation. So I picked her up and carried her toward our bedroom, where the fear, for a while, couldn't touch us.

○────────○

I hadn't really planned on falling asleep, but I'd pulled an all-nighter after a fairly strenuous round with the Rhino and a follow-up game of Dodge the

Ancient, so once I had relaxed body and mind, it was apparently inevitable. I woke to the sound of voices speaking quietly in the living room.

I got out of bed and suited up, put some jeans and a sweatshirt over my colors, and walked into the living room.

"There's nothing going on," Felicia was saying. "Even you must have that one figured out by now."

"Believe me, sweetie," MJ said in a poisonously friendly voice, "I do not regard you as a threat."

I thought about maybe putting on the mask and going out the window. Nothing I could possibly say or not say, do or not do, would let me avoid a fight. Although it didn't seem very heroic to go running and hiding like that. On the other hand, it didn't seem prudent to go rushing into the conversation, either. So I stayed put for the moment, listening.

"A threat? Now why would I be a threat to you?" Felicia asked. "Just because I can actually do something to help Peter—other than waving pom-poms and baking him cookies, that is."

If the barb scored on MJ, I couldn't tell it from her voice—which meant that it probably had. "Ah, yes, your job skills. I can't count how many times I've wished I knew how to steal cars or sneak around in an outfit from Strippers 'R' Us. It would be so helpful to Peter, in his day-to-day life, if only I could unzip my top a little farther down past my belly button."

Felicia let out a catty little laugh. "That's pretty bold, coming from the girlfriend of Lobsterman. Have I mentioned, by the way, how much I admired your acting in that fine film? I think the scene in the pink bikini was probably the most moving, though it must have been a cold day on the set. Did they get you an acting coach to tell you how to scream in terror, or did they just shove head shots of you on a bad hair day into your face?"

"It was traumatic," MJ said. "Thank goodness there was someone who wanted to share his life with me to help me recover. Does your husband comfort you after a hard day at work, Felicia?"

"If I ever find anyone I can put up with," Felicia said, "at least I'll make up my mind when I marry him, not bounce back and forth like an airy little Ping-Pong ball."

At which point, good sense departed, and I'd heard enough.

I pushed open the bedroom door, and said, in a very quiet, very even voice, "Felicia. That's my wife."

Felicia pressed her lips together before she could say whatever hasty response had come to her mouth.

She folded her arms and turned away from MJ and me, stalking stiff-spined to the window.

"MJ," I said in the same quiet voice. "That's my friend. And yours. You know that."

Mary Jane's face flickered with anger, but then she closed her eyes and shook her head once, and nodded to me. "I just . . ."

"We're all tense. This isn't the right way to handle it," I said quietly. "You're both better people than that. I need you to call a cease-fire. Please."

Felicia rolled her eyes at my reflection in the window. She was back in the Black Cat outfit again, though she'd slung a gauzy peasant skirt and a leather jacket, both dark blue, over it, and it would pass for a clubbing outfit to the casual eye. "Fine," she said. "MJ?"

"Yes," Mary Jane said in a measured tone. "There's no reason we can't be civil."

"Thank you," I said with exaggerated patience. Which was probably asking for trouble, but ye gods and little fishes, they were supposed to be adults.

"Are my leftovers in the fridge?" I asked my wife.

"Yes. Go ahead and eat," Mary Jane said.

I grunted and did, getting what remained of Wong's Shangri-la-level sandwiches out of the fridge. I took them to the table with a glass of milk and asked Felicia, "Did you get the prints?"

"Yes," Felicia said calmly.

"Do I want to know how?" I asked.

"Does it matter?"

I chewed on my sandwich. "It matters to me, I guess."

"Because I might have broken the law?"

"Yes."

"Ah," Felicia said. "You mean, the way the Rhino breaks the law. I mean, that's what you said made him a bad guy. How he broke the law all the time."

"What I said—"

"I mean, logically speaking, if you would have busted him for doing something illegal, I should expect you to treat me the same way. If I tell you that I broke all kinds of laws getting the prints, are you going to take me in, Peter?"

Mary Jane said nothing, but her lips compressed and her eyes narrowed.

"No," I said. "Don't be ridiculous."

"Ah," Felicia said. "Well. You'll be pleased to know that I broke no laws whatsoever."

That surprised me a bit. I guess it showed on my face, because Felicia laughed. "All I had to do was contact Lamont. I told him what it was about and that I was working with you and he was happy to let me get a copy."

I blinked. "He was? Why?"

Felicia fluttered her eyelashes. "I asked him in person."

I snorted and shook my head. "You're shameless."

"Why, thank you," Felicia said. "I'm told you had some success this afternoon? MJ said something about magic rocks."

"That remains to be seen. I don't see how they're going to be of any help to us—at least not yet." I explained the rocks and showed her the page describing them. "Were you able to turn anything up from the prints?"

"Too soon," she said. "Oliver's good, but it will take several hours, at least, to start comparing them to all the databases."

I nodded. "All right," I said. "Meanwhile, we need more information. I think we should head out and tail these creeps around a little, find out what they're up to, where they're staying."

She nodded firmly. "Way ahead of you. I think we should—"

My spider sense began to stir, a slow tingling that rippled lightly over my spine and scalp.

Mary Jane sat up straight, her eyes widening as she saw my face. "Peter?"

"My spider tracer," I said quietly. "It's close."

"What should—"

"Shhhhh," I said, trying to focus on the sensation. There. The electronic signal the tracer emitted resonated off of whatever it was that made my spider sense work. It was south of us, and coming closer, fast.

Just then, Felicia's jacket beeped. She reached in, grabbed her visors, and put them on for a moment. Then she let out a quiet curse. "My tracking paint," she said. "Closer than three hundred meters." She looked up with suddenly wide eyes. "Peter, we need to go *now*."

My spider sense quivered oddly, and I began to feel the first stirrings of the primal dread the Ancients caused in me.

"It's too late," I murmured. "They're here."

FIFTEEN

NO time. No time. Think fast, Spidey.

"Mary Jane," I said. "I want you to grab the credit cards, any cash we have, and a change of clothes. Now, move."

My wife nodded and hurried to the bedroom.

"Felicia," I said. "Get her out of here."

Felicia had never been much of a fan of tanning beds, but she looked especially pale about now. "Right. Where?"

"Aunt May's. Then we—"

Mary Jane emerged from the bedroom in a flowered dress and a fleece coat. She carried a nylon backpack in either hand. "That was fast," I told her.

"I thought it might be smart to have a traveling kit ready for emergencies," she said. "This one's mine. This one's yours. Cash, two credit cards we haven't used, medicine, a first aid kid, a blanket, some dried food, clothes."

I felt a surge of sudden pride. "That was pretty good thinking," I said.

"It never hurts to plan ahead."

I kissed her on the mouth. "All right. Felicia's going to get you to the car, and then you're both going to scoot to Aunt May's."

"What?" Mary Jane protested. "I'm not going to—"

"Be used against me," I interrupted. "You're going with her."

"Peter . . ."

"Don't worry about me, MJ. I'll just bounce around insulting them for a while and then run away." I pulled off my street clothes, put on the mask, and the whole time the sense of panic in me continued to rise. "This can't be a discussion right now. They're getting closer. Go."

She swallowed, nodded, then said to Felicia, "We should use the stairs."

Felicia detached the flimsy skirt, produced that grappling baton from a sleeve, and opened the window with a grin. "Stairs?"

"Oh my," Mary Jane said.

"Don't worry, MJ," Felicia said with a feline smile. "It won't be like with Peter, but I'll get you there." Her head tilted to one side as she presumably looked at something in the visor. "They're within a hundred meters already."

I checked in with my spider sense. "Yes. Mortia's almost directly below us. They're at the front of the building."

"They came in fast," Felicia said. "Come here, MJ." She produced a strap of nylon webbing, clipped one end to a ring at the waist of her bodysuit, and flipped it around Mary Jane. "I thought you said they had to touch you to track you down."

"They do," I said. "They must have found us some other way."

"Like what?"

"If I knew, I'd have been making sure it didn't work," I said. "Tick tock, Cat."

"Don't get your webs in a knot," she advised me. She ran the strap around Mary Jane and secured it to something on her own outfit with a muted click. "Okay, MJ. We go out the window on three. Hold on tight."

"Wait," Mary Jane said. "Do I have my car keys?" She fumbled a set of keys out of her pocket and clenched a plastic tag on the key chain in her teeth. Then she nodded, donned her backpack, and she and Felicia went out the window on the slender cable extending from the Black Cat's baton.

I went out behind them, part of my attention on Felicia and MJ as they descended at a controlled pace that Felicia couldn't possibly have managed on upper body strength alone. It was hard to tell in the near-dark, but I was betting that there was some kind of rock-climbing-type harness built into the suit. Felicia guided them down in long, smooth rappels, obviously being careful. That would be for my sake, I knew. Given a choice, Felicia generally likes to do things in the most insanely dangerous fashion she thinks she can survive.

I hit the building above us with a webline, let it stretch, and used the snap to get some more air and throw myself out into the autumn air, nailing the building's corner with another webline to swing around. I sailed clear across the street in front of our apartment, stopped on the building across the street, and froze in a shadow halfway up while my spider sense clubbed me with what had become an almost familiar amount of brainstem-level terror.

There was the usual foot traffic for that time of night, a cool autumn evening, and there were several people moving down the sidewalks while city traffic prowled by at a relaxed pace in the wake of rush hour. Couldn't the Ancients have waited until midnight? At least then, there wouldn't have been quite so many people around. Rude, these psychotic life-eating monsters. Very rude.

Mortia stood on the sidewalk outside my apartment building, wearing the same outfit as the day before, plus a long evening coat. She was staring thoughtfully at the building. The Rhino stood behind her in, I kid you not, a khaki trench coat you could have made a tent out of and a broad-brimmed fedora. He had a gym bag in one hand—it doubtless held the stupid hat.

My spider sense quivered, and I glanced down. Malos was on the sidewalk immediately below me, walking slowly down the length of the building like a pacing mountain lion, gazing thoughtfully up at lit windows. Down the block, Thanis was doing the same thing on the other side of the street from Mortia and the Rhino, neither of whom was headed into my building.

I sucked in a breath. So. They had a general idea where I was, but didn't know exactly where. That meant that they hadn't found out about Peter Parker, at least not yet, which in turn meant that they wouldn't know about Mary Jane—or Aunt May's place. Good. With that off my mind, I would be free to worry about myself—something which is really quite useful when one is in combat.

In fact, given that they were still searching, there was really nothing to be gained from a fight, except possibly getting tagged and tracked down. Not only that, but there were way too many people around who could get hurt. I decided to sidle out and run.

Which is when I got an object lesson in how important it is for prey to stay downwind of predators.

Hey, whaddya want from me? I lived my whole life in New York City. The only time I worried about the wind was during games at Yankee Stadium and in fights with real stinkers like Vermin and the Lizard.

Mortia suddenly tensed and then whirled, eyes intently scanning up and down the street—and then tracking up to me. I was hidden in deep shadow, invisible. *Invisible,* for crying out loud. There aren't many people on the whole planet who can sneak around better than me, and I know invisible when I do it.

I guess nobody told Mortia that, though. She bared her teeth in a very slow, very white smile, and as she did, both Thanis and Malos froze in their tracks and looked up at me as well.

The Rhino continued to look around, evidently bored. It took him a second to notice Mortia, and then he squinted upward and around, expression puzzled.

I dove off my perch just as Malos ripped a steel wastebasket off of the sidewalk and chucked it at me. I hit a flagpole sticking out from the building three stories up, flung myself up, flicked a web-strand at Mortia's feet in midair with one hand while sending out a zipline down the street and hurling myself forward with the other. Thanis leapt at me as I did, and I had to contort and twist in midair to alter my trajectory and avoid him.

I hit the sidewalk rolling, then hopped up over a mailbox and landed on its other side, with Thanis coming hard behind me. I reached out and seized the parking meters on either side of me and ripped them from the concrete, one in each hand as Thanis approached.

I caught him on the end of one of the four-foot lengths of metal, the broken concrete jabbing into his belly, and planted the actual meter on the ground beneath me. This had the effect of slamming him in the breadbasket pretty hard, as well as keeping him physically away from me, sending him flying over my head, his flailing fingers missing me by an inch or more.

It was harder without my spider sense working at full power, but I assumed the worst—that Malos was already closing in—and bounded to one side, then up onto the wall, then into a double backflip that carried me all the way to the roof of an old Chevy sedan parked on the street.

My fears had been well founded. Malos missed catching me in a simple tackle by a fraction of a second, but the flip carried me straight over his head and behind him. He whirled around to face me, expression furious. I played "Shave and a Haircut" on his noggin with alternating blows of the parking meters. I put a lot of extra oomph into the "six bits" part, and the meters exploded in mounds of silver coins when I did. Malos was driven back several steps by the impact, and his knees looked a little wobbly for a second.

But just for a second. Then he gave his head a shake, speared me with an annoyed glance, and started in again.

By that time, Mortia had torn her foot loose from where I'd webbed it to the sidewalk, and she was coming after me at a sprint. Wow, she was quick. And if she'd gotten out of my webbing that fast, she wasn't exactly as dainty as a schoolmarm in the muscle department, either.

Fighting all of them in the open was a losing proposition. Sooner or later Mortia and her brothers would be almost certain to inflict harm on the citizenry—and I had no illusions about outmaneuvering Mortia this time. If this went on too long or I got unlucky, she'd at least get to tag me. Once that happened, I could run, but not hide.

So, I needed somewhere to fight that would leave me with enough room to move around, while simultaneously being hostile to long lines of sight *and* relatively free of bystanders. New York being what it was— packed with people—unpopulated spaces tend to be the kinds of places no one wants to hang around in: places that are dangerous or unsettling to linger in, places where bad people do bad things.

So I headed for the nearest parking garage.

I leapt onto an awning, bounced on it to gain speed, and whirled around a traffic light to get airborne. I took a long, long swing and flipped myself into a helplessly ballistic arch with Mortia only a few leaps behind me. I was making an easy target of myself, and she went for the opening, coming after me.

Excellent. I flipped in midair, gave her some webbing in the face with one hand, stuck a line to a passing garbage truck with the other, then joined the two, and watched the truck jerk her off-course and begin dragging her down the street.

It looked painful. Also cool.

I landed in a backward roll, flipped up into the air, and used a webline to whirl in a couple of big circles around a streetlight before throwing myself up onto the garage's roof. A little ostentatious, maybe, but this way Malos and Thanis would be certain to spot me. They looked like the types who might not exercise their brain cells very often.

Malos showed up first, by climbing up the side of the parking garage. He wasn't sticking to the wall or anything amazing and stylish like that. Instead, he just made a claw shape with his fingers and sank their tips several inches into the concrete, like it was so much soft clay. He went up hand over hand very nearly as fast as I could have done it. He flipped himself up the last five or six feet and landed on his feet with credible grace. His silk shirt was torn in a couple of places where my follow-through with the meters had wreaked havoc, and both his shirt and his long black hair were covered with dust.

"You got dust all over that pretty shirt," I told him in a cheery tone. "And your hair, too. And look, there are security cameras. Everyone is going to see you all mussed and disheveled."

"Oh dear," he said in a very low, velvety-soft voice, and walked toward me in no great hurry. "However will I survive?"

Then he turned to a dark green Volvo and picked it up.

They might be the safest cars in the world, but when they're thrown from an eight-story parking garage, I really doubt that their Swedish engineering does very much to soften the blow. So I simply hopped off the roof, popped the garage with a webline, and swung back in on the sixth level, out of Malos's sight, and hoped that he wouldn't waste the effort to throw the car.

A distinct lack of crashing crunches told me I'd been right, and I breathed a little sigh of relief—right up until Thanis stepped out of the shadows of a stairway in his expensive Italian suit and threw a haymaker at me.

I didn't sense him coming until the very last second. I got a little lucky. If he'd just reached out to touch me with his near hand, it probably would have been fast enough to land. He'd gone for the whole enchilada, though, and I had time to get my head out of his way. I danced to one side with Thanis breathing down my neck and dodged another pair of quick blows. He was good at throwing them, but I was better at getting out of their way. I could keep this guy from laying a glove on me, if I was careful, and if he didn't get any help—and if he didn't realize that I had no intention of hitting him back.

But he figured that part out—and within a few seconds, to boot—and the shape of the fight altered. It's like that in hand-to-hand combat. If you can simply discard the notion of protecting yourself from counterattack, it's a whole heck of a lot easier to get through an opponent's defenses with a focused, concentrated offensive, and it was suddenly everything I could do to keep him off me—until I ducked under a sledgehammer blow aimed at my neck. Thanis's fist hit the wall behind me, and shook loose a fire extinguisher from its mount on the wall.

I caught it on the way down and hollered, "Batter up!"

I swung with both hands and hit him. I didn't hold *anything* back. I don't do that very often, but for Morlun and his kin, I cared enough to send the very best.

There was a sound halfway between the ringing of a gong and the thump of a watermelon hitting the sidewalk, and Thanis left the garage by way of having his head line-drived through a section of concrete wall.

Without pausing, I cleared the pin from the firing mechanism of the extinguisher and sent a cloud of white chemicals billowing out behind me—right into the face of Malos, who had emerged from the stairway in pursuit. He came through blind and aggressive. My second swing of the extinguisher lifted him from his feet and into the concrete roof above me, sending a web-work of cracks about twenty feet across it, and leaving the extinguisher bent into the shape of a boomerang.

"G'day, mate!" I shouted in a cheesy Australian accent, and whipped the extinguisher at him in a sidearm throw. The impact slammed his head back into the front grille of an old Impala, driving his skull into the body of the car up to his ears. "Spider-Man! That's Australian for 'Headache!'"

The ground started to shake in rhythm, and the Rhino came pounding up the car ramp at a modest pace of thirty or forty miles an hour. He'd ditched the coat, the broad-brimmed hat, and his bag, and he had the silly rhino-head hat on. The fashion slave. He doesn't corner well, and he had to windmill his arms to keep his balance as he bent his course around the ramp. Then he saw me, bellowed, and came my way, picking up speed fast.

Figures. Someone I can actually punch finally shows up and it's already time to leave.

I charged him right back.

He wasn't expecting that, but after a fraction of a second of surprise, he simply lowered his horn and came at me faster, letting out a bellow as he did.

I waited until the last second, then bounded straight up and over him, and clung to the ceiling. As he passed, I tagged his broad gray butt with a webline, then sent another web at Malos, who was just then regaining his feet. And since it had already worked once, I merely joined the lines together.

The Ancient looked down as the webbing plastered itself to his silk and the belt area of his leather pants. Then he tracked the line of the web-strand back to the thundering Rhino.

He closed his eyes in irritation and sighed. "Oh, bother."

I gave him a cheerful, upside-down wave from where I crouched on the ceiling.

The Rhino tried to brake, but he had too much momentum going. He went out through the wall.

The line stretched a little, so that there was a Looney Tune instant of motionlessness, and then it snapped back like a bungee cord and dragged Malos out of the garage after the plummeting Rhino.

"Sometimes I amaze even myself," I said in a cheerful voice. Then I hurried to the far side of the garage and beat a hasty retreat. I'd delayed the Ancients long enough for Felicia to get MJ out of there, so there was no point in staying. It was time to fade out and fight another day.

Except that in the middle of fading, I saw Mortia running down the street back toward me, running on *top* of the power lines as if they were as wide as a city sidewalk. She spotted me, bounced like a diver on a board, flipped through the air, and landed at a bounding run. I saw that she was wearing one of those tiny headsets some cell phones have, and she was speaking into it as she pursued me.

Maybe thirty seconds later, the Rhino caught up to us and joined her. He's a lot lighter on his feet than you'd think—he can top out at better than a hundred miles an hour, even if he can't change course much while he does so. Mortia looked like something out of Japanese anime, streaking along in a bounding run that would have run me down in about ten seconds flat on level ground.

I could use that speed against them, to keep them separated from Malos and Thanis.

So I poured it on, zipping down the street, using every trick I knew to move as fast as I possibly could. I didn't have an infinite amount of webbing, and I was burning through it fast, using its elasticity to maintain my momentum and add speed, while taking a lot of turns to prevent the Rhino from getting enough momentum to catch up.

Mortia came after me the way the Lizard always chased me—fast and nimble, bounding over cars and passersby, her feet hardly touching the ground. She leapt to sprint along window ledges occasionally, when traffic on the street was too high-volume.

The Rhino lumbered along the road in the middle of the right-hand lane, passing cars and at one point shouldering aside a cabby who had tried to change lanes and was crowding him. The cab flew into the side of a building.

I made sure to keep the pace down just enough that they seemed to be catching up with me, always gaining a little ground, and as a result they never slowed. We left the other two Ancients to trail along blocks behind us—because while they were super-strong, they just didn't have the raw speed necessary to keep up with Mortia and the Rhino. I started changing the pace as we pulled away, hopping over a block this way, then doubling back and heading three blocks the other way, until I was sure Malos and Thanis were nowhere in the immediate area.

I went by Shea Stadium on long, slingshot-style weblines, zoomed over a line of docks filled with small commercial fishing vessels and largish pleasure boats, and came down in the hangars on the eastern end of La Guardia. Ongoing renovations had several of the enormous buildings gutted and under repair, separated from the rest of the place by those orange construction fences, so there wouldn't be many people around. It was nice and dark there, plenty of three-dimensional space to play in, and not many people.

I swung over the fence and landed on a little open space between acres of yawning buildings, bounced up onto the side of one of the hangars, and made myself scarce and sneaky in the abundant shadows.

Mortia came down practically in the same spot my feet had landed in and froze, her stance a marvel of liquid tension, her eyes open wide. The Rhino wasn't far behind her. He had to jump over the fence to get to her, maybe a seventy-five-foot hop, and nothing his enhanced muscles couldn't handle. He landed on the concrete beside her. The impact sent several cracks running through it, and it took the Rhino a few steps to arrest his momentum.

Mortia gave him another contemptuous look.

Then she turned in a slow, slow circle, looking for me. But I'd kept downwind this time.

"You're quite clever," Mortia called out, turning in a slow circle. "But then, the spiders always are. Separating me from my brothers this way is an excellent tactic."

I wanted to make a comment about family therapy, but I kept my mouth shut.

"I should also like to thank you for your gifts," she said. She reached into a pocket and held up my spider tracer between two fingers. "My people tell me that this is some sort of tracking device. They say it was built quite cleverly, but out of unremarkable parts. Which told us that you were not a being of substantial material wealth. But then, spiders rarely are."

She held up the cravat next. "This potion upon my clothes, on the other hand, is quite expensive and quite rare. Even governmental military bodies do not use it; its availability and use is restricted to private security firms. And there can only be so many lovely young white-haired women with access to it."

True enough. Gulp.

"We *will* find you, spider. You will fall. It can be no other way. Once we learn your name, there will be no place for you to hide. There will be no way to protect those you love. But if you come forth and face me now, that need not happen. I do not know who your loved ones are, nor do I care. My business is with you. I have no interest in them, except in how I might use them to attain you. Come forth and we will depart, our business done. Deny me, and I will destroy them along with you."

For a minute I was tempted to deal with her. Anything I could do to keep the conflict between just myself and the bad guys was something that appealed to me. My fights had spilled over onto innocents far too many times. But I wasn't sure I could trust Mortia. If she really was here on a vengeance kick, she might well choose to take someone close from me, just as I had taken family from her.

Either way, the smart thing to do was to pull a swift fade, break contact, and let them flounder around looking for me. Definitely, that was the smart thing to do.

But no one threatens my family.

It took me maybe a second and a half to hit a scaffold on the opposite hangar, a heavy rig loaded with heavy steel structural support beams. I gave the scaffold a hard pull, and brought the entire stack of metal struts down onto Mortia and the Rhino, burying them in at least a ton of metal.

They weren't under it for long. The mess wasn't done settling before the Rhino started slapping struts away like they were so many drinking straws. Though Mortia did not seem to be the same kind of powerhouse as her brothers, she wasn't a wimp, either, and was able, with visible effort, to begin freeing herself from the tangled steel.

While she was doing that, I swung down at the Rhino and shouted, "Boot to the head!" as I kicked him there.

The Rhino flew into another stack of building materials—heavy-duty rebar and lumber. He came surging out of them with a bellow of anger and charged me, swinging. I let him do it like he always did it, barely dodging him—only this time I danced over toward Mortia, and just as she came to her feet, one of the Rhino's furious swings struck her squarely and slammed her back into the mound of twisted metal.

"Great hook! Thanks for the assist, big guy," I said in a cheery tone. Then I popped him in the face with a glob of webbing, goosed him, and ran.

But not far.

I doubled back to the far side of the hangars, nipped up to the roof, found a place where I'd be neither scented nor seen, and waited to see what happened.

The Rhino ripped the webbing off his face and bellowed in frustration. He spun around looking for me, and naturally did not spot me.

Mortia sat up, her hair mussed. She might be tough as nails, but when the Rhino tags you, you know it, and I don't care who you are. Where Mortia hit the thicket of support struts, they had been mashed into a definite indentation. It matched her outline exactly. Her cold eyes locked onto the Rhino. "Well?"

"He is gone," the Rhino replied. He let out a frustrated growl and then turned to Mortia to offer her a hand up. "My apologies, ma'am. It was not my intention to strike you."

The Rhino could be polite?

"I told you not to commit yourself against him until I signaled you," Mortia said, rising. "You disobeyed me."

"Da," he growled, frustration evident in his voice. "I lost my temper. He makes me angry."

"You allow him to do so," she said in that same cold tone. "You are a fool."

The Rhino looked like he couldn't decide whether to be angry or chagrined. "One day, he will not be lucky. One day, I will strike him, once, and it will all be over."

Mortia looked at him for a moment and then said, "No. I do not think that will happen."

The Rhino glanced at her, a question on his face.

"You have just become more liability than asset," she said, quite calmly. And then, in a motion so fast even I barely saw it, her hand shot out and clenched over the Rhino's face, her nails somehow digging into his superhumanly durable flesh. There was a flash of sickly greenish light beneath her fingers.

The Rhino screamed. Not a war bellow, not a cry of rage, not a shout of challenge. He screamed like a man in utter agony, screamed without dignity or any kind of self-control, and his superhumanly powerful lungs made it *loud,* loud enough to shake the ground and the shipping containers around him. His body bent into an agonized arch, and if Mortia hadn't been holding him up with one arm, he would not have remained standing.

Instead, she whirled with him, eyes burning with the cold light one might associate with a hungry python, and drove his skull into the same debris she had struck. "Pathetic little vessel. You are worthless, incapable of even simple destruction. Be grateful that your life will at last have *some* sort of purpose."

The Rhino screamed again. Weaker.

I watched it in pure horror.

She was killing him.

The Rhino was no friend. But he was a long-term enemy, and in some ways that's close to the same thing. I've butted heads with him, metaphorically speaking, since my earliest days in costume. And Felicia was right about one thing: The Rhino wasn't a killer. So much so, in fact, that one time, when the Sinister Somethingorother had me dead to rights, the Rhino had refused to participate in killing me with his fellow villains and had, in fact, argued against it. Sure, he hated my guts. Sure, he wanted to beat me down once and for all, prove that he was better than me, stronger than me.

But he wasn't a killer.

The Rhino was one of the bad guys, but there were worse bad guys out there.

Like the one murdering him in front of my eyes.

That unholy light poured up through her fingers, showing the outlines of oddly shaped bones that belonged to something else, something other, a creature who did not feel, did not fear, did not care. Who only hungered.

Aleksei was still a human being. There was no way I would leave a human being, *any* human being, no matter his sins, in the hands of a creature like that.

I couldn't make a fight of it; the wonder twins would be coming along any minute. So I took a cheap shot. I got to my feet, dove toward Mortia, and shot a webline at the wall of the hangar behind me. As the line stretched, it slowed me, and I stuck a second line to Mortia's rear. The first line snapped me back, and as the second line stretched, I gave it a sudden hard pull with all the power I could summon. The resulting combination of tension and strength ripped her away from the Rhino, sent her tumbling cravat-over-teakettle into the evening air, and flung her over the hangar and out of sight. She let out a wailing, alien howl of rage as she went, one that blended in with the roar of a jet lifting off.

I landed on the ground near the Rhino and said, "Right. Never say I've never done anything nice for you."

The Rhino didn't reply. Or move.

I hopped over and checked on him. He was alive, at least, and he let out a soft, agonized moan. There was blood on his face, trickles of it coming from the marks Mortia's nails had left there. The skin was horribly dry and cracked, flakes coming off as he moaned again, as if his face had been left out in the desert sun for several days.

He was barely conscious, even with his enhanced resilience. If I left him there, he was as good as dead.

"For crying out loud," I complained. "I haven't got enough to do?"

Mortia screamed again. It sounded like she was a lot farther away this time, maybe all the way to the edge of the inlet. A second later, I heard another brassy, weird-sounding call from the opposite direction. Thanis and Malos were closing in.

"No good deed goes unpunished," I muttered. Then I bent down and slung the Rhino over my shoulder. The extra eight hundred pounds was going to make web-slinging difficult, but I couldn't just leave the loser there to die.

So I got moving again, if more slowly, this time carrying an unconscious foe, avoiding the incoming Ancients, and making my way back to MJ and Felicia.

SIXTEEN

WHEN I tapped on the glass, Felicia opened the window of Aunt May's apartment. She looked at me. Then at the Rhino, wrapped in webbing from the shoulders down and strapped onto my back like a hyperthyroid papoose, the horn on his silly hat wobbling as his head bobbed in the relaxation of the senseless.

Then she looked at me again, blinked, and said, "You're kidding."

"Just open the window the rest of the way and stand back," I told her.

"I hope Aunt May is insured," she said, but she did it.

I climbed in with the Rhino on my back. I wasn't worried about hurting him if I banged him into something. I was more worried about the something. So I brought him in as carefully as I could and laid him out on the kitchen floor.

Aunt May's apartment is somewhat spartan, for an elderly lady. When she moved out of the house I grew up in, the one she had shared with Uncle Ben, she put many of her belongings in storage, rather than attempting to stuff them into her little apartment. She still has some of her furniture—a table, chairs for it, her rocker, her couch. She replaced their double bed with a single one; there's a small guest room where she put the double, for when Mary Jane and I visit. She keeps a couple of bookshelves filled with everything from *Popular Science* (which I'm still half-sure she only subscribes to so that I'll have something to read when I visit) to romance novels to history books. She has a few small shelves, a few knickknacks, and that's about it.

Mary Jane came in and hugged me tight, then stared at the man on the floor. "Oh, God. What happened to his face?"

The Rhino looked bad. No worse than he had when I had picked him up, but no better, either.

"Mortia did it to him," I said. "She decided he wasn't useful anymore and started feeding on him."

Felicia regarded the Rhino with a cool, distant expression. "He's dead, then?"

"Not yet," I said.

"Are you insane?" Felicia asked quietly.

Mary Jane gave her a sharp glance.

"If Mortia did this to him," Felicia explained, "she touched him. If she touched him, she can follow him, find him, as long as he is alive. Which means—"

"She can find us here," Mary Jane breathed. She looked at me. "Peter?"

"No names," I said quietly. "He's out, but he'll be coming to anytime now. He doesn't need to know any names."

"This is massively stupid," Felicia snapped. "You're going to get yourself killed. And me with you."

"She was going to kill him," I said. "What else could I have done?"

"You could have *let* her kill him," Felicia said.

I was glad that I had my mask on, because I wasn't sure I could have kept the anger I felt off of my face. "What happened to treating him like a human being? To his not being all that bad a person?"

"He might not be Charles Manson, but he chose which side to play for." She folded her arms. "It isn't a pleasant thought, not for anyone, but he knows there are risks in this kind of life. You should have let her have him. If nothing else, then she might not have been quite so hot and bothered about coming after *you*."

"So I guess he's not a person after all," I said, and I didn't keep the bitterness out of my words. "Is that it?"

"It isn't about that," she said. "It's about you putting your life at risk. If I had to choose between the two of you, it would be you. Without a second thought. All I was saying is that I wanted you to show a little respect for him. I never wanted you to throw your life away trying to save him."

"He isn't worth that?"

"Worth *you*?" Felicia asked, her voice tired. "No. You can't save everyone. This time around, you'll be lucky to save yourself. Don't throw your life away on some boy scout scruple you can't survive."

Mary Jane stood to one side of the kitchen, motionless, almost invisible, listening, her wide green eyes on me.

I forced myself to take a slow breath. Then I asked, "What do you think I should do?"

"Put him on a train. A plane. Throw him on a truck. Anything, but get him out of here until we can learn more about the Ancients. Once we get up close with these things, once they've touched us, we only have one chance to put them away. If you keep the Rhino here, they'll find us. Maybe in the next few minutes. Certainly soon. So you use him to lead them off and buy us more time."

"That would be the same thing as murdering him myself," I said quietly.

Felicia shook her head, frustration evident on her face. "You didn't ask him to come back to New York. You didn't force the Rhino to get involved with the Ancients. You didn't make them turn on him. He did that all on his own."

"Should that matter?" I asked.

"If your places were reversed," she said, "he'd do the same to you. In a heartbeat."

I looked down at the Rhino, maimed and helpless on Aunt May's kitchen floor.

What Felicia said was probably true. But . . . maybe not, too. The Rhino could have done nothing while Doc Ock and his buddies finished me. He'd opposed them. They hadn't worked up to a fight or anything, but he'd said something, at least.

If our positions were reversed, would he have stood by and done nothing? Would he have let me die to save his own life?

Probably.

But . . .

But in the end, that didn't matter. Regardless of what the Rhino might or might not have done, it did not change who I was. It did not change the choice I had to make. It did not change the responsibility I would bear in making that choice. It did not change what was right and what was wrong.

"Earlier," I said quietly, "you asked me the difference between people like the Rhino and people like me." I looked at the man, then slowly nodded. "Maybe it starts right here. I'm not letting them have him. I'm not letting them have *anyone*."

"Gosh, that's noble," Felicia said, her voice tart. "Maybe MJ can put it on your tombstone."

"Felicia," Mary Jane said, stepping up beside me, putting a hand on my shoulder. "You know he's right. If you could stop thinking about yourself for a minute, you'd realize that."

"Hey, Mrs. Cleaver. When I want your opinion, I'll read it in your entrails," Felicia snapped.

MJ's eyes narrowed. "Excuse me?"

"*Enough,*" I growled, loud and harsh enough that even MJ looked a little surprised. I turned to Felicia and said, "This is what I'm doing."

The Black Cat stared at me for a long moment, and then demanded, something almost like a plea in her voice, "For him? Why?"

"It doesn't matter who he is. I won't leave him to Mortia."

She got in my face, quietly furious, spitting each word. "This. Is. Suicide."

"Look, I get it that you're afraid—"

"Don't you patronize me," she hissed. "I'm not afraid of anything and you know it."

"I'm not saying you're a coward. There's no reason to feel ashamed of being afraid."

She jabbed a finger into my chest. "I am *not* afraid. I am also *not* going to commit suicide for some lowbrow thug too stupid to be careful who he works for."

I pulled the mask off, and met her eyes. "I'm not asking you to do it with me," I said quietly.

Her eyes narrowed, searching mine. Then they became hooded and unreadable, her voice calm. "Good," she said. "Then I don't need to tell you no." She spun on a heel and walked quietly to the door. "I'll call you if I find out anything else. Goodbye."

She slammed the door on the way out.

I flinched a little at the sound of it.

My head pounded in a dull, steady rhythm. My brush with the Ancients had left my spider sense screaming, and the headache was, I began to understand, some kind of natural aftereffect of having the gain on my extra sense turned up to eleven, some sort of psychic hangover. My mouth felt fuzzy. More than anything, I wanted to crawl into a dark hole for a while and rest.

I've noticed that you rarely get a chance to do any dark-hole-crawling when you seem to need it most.

Mary Jane's fingers touched my chin and gently turned my face toward hers.

"Why did you provoke her?" she asked, her manner very serious.

"Provoke her?" I said. "I don't know what—"

She rolled her eyes. "Oh, please. Don't try to deny it. I know you too well."

I felt my mouth turn up into a tired smile. "Well. Maybe a little."

She gave me a small, strained smile and slid her arms around me. "You're pushing her away. Trying to protect her."

I held MJ for a moment, closing my eyes. "Maybe."

"You're a good man," she whispered, her arms tightening. "Which makes me think that she must be right about how dangerous it will be to protect him."

"Maybe," I said.

"What's the real plan, then?"

"The Jolly Gray Giant here should wake up sometime soon. I hope. When he does, I'll tell him about the danger and send him on his way."

Mary Jane was quiet for a moment. Then she said, "How is that different from putting him on a train?"

"Because I'm not going to use him as a lure. I don't think Mortia will chase him down until she's concluded her business with me. He deserves to know what he's up against, and needs time to recover and prepare for it, in case I don't . . ."

I didn't finish the sentence. Mary Jane's arms tightened around me. We stood that way for a minute.

Then I said, "All right. The webs will hold him, but not for long. So I need to be here with him when he wakes up, so I can start talking right away. If he panics, he'll rip out of the webs in a few seconds, and God only knows what will get wrecked. So if he freaks, I'll pitch him out the window."

She nodded, biting her lip thoughtfully. Then she turned the kitchen lights out.

I frowned at her quizzically.

"I don't have a mask," she explained. "I'd rather not be someone he recognizes, generally speaking."

I gave her a small smile and put my mask back on, leaving my nose and mouth uncovered. It hit me that I was starving, so I opened Aunt May's fridge to rustle up something.

"How long will it take them to find us?" Mary Jane asked.

"Technically, they could have been right behind me. But you don't live for thousands of years by taking unnecessary risks. They'll come in carefully, quietly, checking out the area. With any luck, Sleeping Beauty here will wake up in the next few minutes. We'll let him go on his way, which ought to confuse them, at least. Then you and I will slip out and make them start looking for me all over again."

Mary Jane nodded slowly. "But you still don't know how to beat them."

"No."

"Do you know how to find out?"

"No."

"Then what good is running going to do?" she asked. "Ultimately, it's just a delaying tactic."

"So's exercise and controlling your cholesterol," I said, and it came out more frustrated than I meant it to. "I don't know how to deal with freaking magical, Spider-Man-eating monster people." I lost control of my voice completely and found myself shouting. "I'm scared, all right? I can't think! *I don't know!*"

"But you'd risk drawing them here, to both of us, for this man?"

I was quiet for a moment, staring at the inside of the fridge. Then I said, "I couldn't just leave him."

Mary Jane's voice turned warmer. "No. You couldn't."

"If it comes to a fight, I'm not going to stay around here. I don't want them to grab you."

She was silent. I assumed she nodded.

"I'll try to lead them off somewhere where it will minimize the damage. And . . ."

And what, Pete? Bounce around until you get tired, while they don't? Then miss a step. Then die.

"Here's a thought," Mary Jane said.

"Hmmm?"

"Maybe the doctor didn't mean those stones for the Ancients."

I frowned and blinked at her. "Huh?"

"Maybe he meant them for us." She shrugged. "I'm just saying. If it's some sort of timeless prison—maybe he meant us to use them to go there for shelter. Maybe he'd come and get us out."

"Maybe," I said quietly. "But . . . maybe he wouldn't. Or couldn't."

"Did he say that?"

I frowned. "He said that he believed I had what I needed to defeat this foe."

"Oh." She thought about it for a moment, and then said, "He's a difficult man to pin down."

I grunted. Aunt May's fridge was largely bare. Of course. She had been planning to leave for a week on Anna's prize cruise. She wouldn't have left anything in the fridge that would go bad. The freezer had TV dinners, but with any luck we'd be gone from here long before they could be done. So I made do with some microwave popcorn.

As the scent filled the room, the Rhino let out a groan.

I looked up sharply at Mary Jane and nodded toward the bedroom. She swallowed and went there in silence.

Popcorn rattled in the microwave. The Rhino muttered something I didn't understand, in what sounded like Russian. His head tossed left and right. Then he snorted and tried to lift his head.

"Take it easy there, big fella," I told him. The microwave beeped, and I took the popcorn out. "Yes, you're tied up. Yes, I'm Spider-Man. No, I'm not going to hurt you, or even turn you over to the cops. And to prove it, I'll split some popcorn with you if you give me two minutes to talk to you without you going berserkergang on me."

"Spider-Man," the Rhino spat. I could dimly see him bare his teeth in the shadowy kitchen. His basso voice rolled out the thick, half-swallowed consonants of his accent. "You think this is funny, I bet."

"No," I said. "Ow, hot popcorn. Augh, that steam, right when you open the bag? Anyway, I don't think it's funny. I think it's really scary. I think that both of us have bigger problems to worry about than one another."

The Rhino growled, a sound full of suspicion and not much in the way of intellect. "Then why am I bound?"

"What do you remember?" I asked.

"Mortia. She touched me and . . ." He shuddered. Eight hundred pounds of shuddering Rhino is a lot. The plates rattled in the cupboard.

"How are you feeling?" I asked.

"I . . . hurt." There was a note of almost childish surprise in his tone. The Rhino did not often get hurt. Heck, he wasn't even showing any bruises from the massive walloping I'd given him not twenty-four hours before. My knuckles, on the other hand, were still swollen. "Heat, on my face. Headache."

"Mortia and her brothers are extremely bad news," I said. "They feed on life energy like yours and mine."

"They eat super-powered people?" Rhino asked.

"Close enough," I said. "They had a brother who came to eat me several months ago. He got a case of the deads."

"So they came to even the score," said the Rhino. I had to give the big guy credit. Not much in the way of brains, but he understood the meaner things in life.

"Exactly. They hired you to draw me out. Then stood around doing nothing, by the way, when I beat the stuffing out of you."

The Rhino growled, and for some reason it was a much more threatening sound in Aunt May's kitchen than in Times Square.

"The point is," I said quickly, "they didn't exactly give you any backup. And when you inconvenienced Mortia, she decided to kill you."

The Rhino was silent for a second, and then he said, "You stopped her?"

"Yeah."

"Why?" he demanded.

"Despite what you may have read in the *Bugle,* I am one of the good guys. I don't let people get eaten on my watch."

"But I am your enemy," he said.

"Sorta, sure," I agreed. "But Mortia and her brothers are bad news in a big and scary way. You and I have had our disagreements. I imagine we'll keep on having them. But if they get the chance, those three will kill us.

Both of us. And they'll barely remember it a few days from now."

His mouth spread into a sneer. "And what do you want? For me to fight beside you?"

"No," I said. "I want you gone. Out of here, somewhere safe. This is going to be nasty, and no one sane is going to want any part of it. Get yourself clear until you have a chance to recover. I think they're coming after me first, but if they get past me, you'll be on your own."

"Da. Am always on my own," the Rhino said, a glower in his tone. "But what do you really want?"

"Nothing. I pulled your big gray butt out of the fire because you once did something similar for me. I just want you to get up and get away from me as fast as you can manage it. The way I see it, that'll balance the scales between us."

His voice became even more suspicious. "This is some trick."

"No trick," I said.

"Prove it," he said. "Untie me."

I haven't spent all this time as a human spider without learning to tie some outstandingly groovy knots. I leaned down, gave the webbing around him several sharp tugs, and the whole thing slithered away from him.

The Rhino sat up slowly, a little unsteadily, as if shocked that I had actually untied him. "Now, the blindfold."

"Uh?" I said. "There's no blindfold, big guy. I mean, it's a little dim in here, but . . ."

I saw him lift his fingers to his face. He drew his hands away after a single touch, and spat out something in Russian that probably should not be said in front of Russian children.

I turned and flicked on the kitchen lights.

The Rhino's ruined face looked awful, but not as bad as his eyes. They had gone entirely white, as if cataracts had entirely occluded them in the few seconds Mortia had touched him.

Holy Moley. This put a nice big old hole in the "get everyone away from Peter so he can fight the battle without them getting hurt or in the way" plan. There was no way I could send him out on his own like this— helpless, utterly unable to defend himself.

"*Bozhe moi,*" the Rhino said, staring sightlessly. "I am blind."

SEVENTEEN

THE Rhino sat on the kitchen floor munching microwave popcorn while I tried to figure out what would go wrong next. He went through the bag fast, though he didn't seem to hurry, and asked, "Is there perhaps water?"

The simple question startled me. I mean, of all the people I'd ever have thought I'd be talking to in Aunt May's kitchen, the Rhino was about third to last on the list. And the question was just so . . . normal. He ate popcorn. It made him thirsty. The Rhino was pretty much supposed to be all about bellowing and smashing—not being beaten, blind, and conversational.

I got him a glass of water and said, "Hold out your hand."

He did. I put the glass in it. He gave me a grave nod, making the silly rhino horn bob, and said, "Thank you."

The Rhino. Saying thank you. Excuse me while I boggle.

At this rate, I was going to have to reboot my brain before it locked up entirely and went into meltdown. A thought struck me. The Rhino was blind. There was no reason I had to keep wearing the mask.

I took it off and stared at it for a minute. It was just a piece of cloth, but it had done more to protect me—and the people I cared about—than any number of locks or security systems over the years. I'd thrown it away several times. I'd always picked it up again. Looking at it now, it just seemed a little worn.

I looked at the Rhino. I could count the number of times I'd seen him without looking through the mask on the fingers of one hand—and never from this close, this clearly. He finished the water and set the glass carefully to one side. I had half-assumed he would smash it in his fist when finished. Perhaps follow that by chewing up the pieces and swallowing. It was the sort of recreational activity I had expected from him: *I am the Rhino. My favorite movie is* Rocky IV *and my turn-ons include exotic haberdashery and rubble.*

"I assume," he said instead, "that we are in your secret headquarters."

"Secret headquarters," I said.

"Da," he said. "The armory and lab where you design your weaponry. The bulletproof, stealth-technology super costumes. All the equipment you have used over the years. The cloaking technology that hides all of it."

I nearly burst out into a laugh, but kept it from happening. "Ah. That headquarters."

"Mysterio once said it was the only way you could counter his illusion technology so completely. With access to advanced equipment for the design of countermeasures, like that of Mister Fantastic."

"Mysterio thinks a whole lot of himself," I said.

The Rhino snorted. "Da."

Wait.

I had just agreed with the Rhino on something.

I wondered if my brain would explode out of my ears or just sort of flow out of my nostrils in steaming gobs.

"I presume," the Rhino said, "your security measures are monitoring me."

Why not?

"Every single one," I said. "I'd prefer it if you didn't give me a reason to use them."

At that, he tensed a little, and his jaw clenched. "You think you can frighten me?"

"No," I replied. Normally I would have added something like: *You're obviously too stupid to be afraid of anything.* It would have been funny, but maybe not entirely accurate. Whatever else his faults, the Rhino was tough-minded, and no coward.

Besides. I didn't need to be a telepath to realize that he was scared. Who wouldn't be, in his position, blinded and captured by a bitter foe? But all I said was: "You've never had a problem with fear. There wouldn't be any point to trying to scare you now."

He grunted. We were both guys, so to me, the grunt sounded like, *Good, because I'm willing to fight you, blind and helpless and doomed, rather than let you think you frighten me.*

It was the kind of grunt I might have used myself, were things reversed.

"I am ready to go," he said.

"What?" I asked.

"Go," he said, tensing again. "You said you intended to set me free. Do you mean to go back on your word?"

"No," I said, tiredly. "But that was before I knew about your eyes."

The Rhino shifted his weight warily. More dishes rattled. "You did this to me?"

"No, bonehead," I replied, mildly annoyed. "But I'm not going to send you out there blind. God only knows what you might blunder into and smash." I shook my head, my voice trailing off. "Besides. When the Ancients came for you, you wouldn't have a prayer."

"Then I am your prisoner?" he asked.

"No. You're free to go." I paused for a second. If I just put my teeth together and kept them that way, the Rhino would be out of my hair. It would be simple, practical, and easy.

Who am I kidding? I've never really been all that good at simple, practical, easy things. Things like baking frozen pizzas and abandoning enemies to their gruesome fate.

"You don't have to leave," I said. "If you need some more time to get back on your feet, you can stay." I paused. "So long as you give me your word that you and I have a cease-fire until Mortia and company are dealt with."

The Rhino tilted his head, sharply, blank eyes staring at nothing. "My word? You would trust this?"

"Yeah," I said, and realized, as I did, that I meant it.

The Rhino was quiet for a long moment. Then he nodded and said, "Until they are dealt with and for twenty-four hours after."

Because he didn't want me pitching him into the pokey if we managed to survive. Understandable. "No rampaging while you're here, and you leave town peacefully after. Deal?"

He nodded. "Done."

I picked up his glass and got him some more water, and a glass of my own. Then I gave him his glass, clinked mine against it, and we drank in silence.

Suddenly, rap music with a lot of bass and someone chanting "Unh, unh, unhunh yeeeeaaaaah" blared through the room.

"What is that?" I asked.

The Rhino tossed off the rest of the water, set the glass aside, and said, "Is me." He fumbled a bit at the rhinoceros hat, then patted his legs and chest before saying, "Ah," and ripping open a panel in the gray-armored suit I had never seen before. The sound of Velcro tearing scratched through the room, and the music got louder as the Rhino produced a little cell phone from the hidden pocket. It looked grotesquely tiny for his enormous, blunt hands. He put it to his ear and said, "Da."

His jaw clenched.

He held the phone out in my general direction. "For you."

Well. That couldn't be good.

I took the phone and put it to my ear. "Da," I said in my best growling Russian accent. "Ivan's Pizza Shack. Ivan take your order."

There was a moment of puzzled silence, and then Mortia's cool, quiet voice asked, "Is this the spider?"

"If it isn't," I said, "he's going to be upset when he finds me running around in his tighty-whities."

"Your kind," she said, "are irritating in the extreme."

"Oh gosh," I said. "Now I'm going to blush, you sweet talker. We can go on like this, but I should warn you that your credit card will be billed at two ninety-nine per minute."

Mortia's voice got colder. "Spider. I grow weary of you. Listen well, for I will not repeat myself, nor make this offer again."

I let my tone get harder. "Speak."

"The Metro Used Auto Center in Flushing. Twenty minutes before dawn."

"Why?"

"Because it is more convenient to meet you there than to expend resources upon my optional initiative."

My stomach fluttered and felt cold. "Which is?"

"Look out the window to your left."

I froze for a second. Then I turned my head, just enough to see out the window.

Mortia crouched on a four-inch-wide window-pane across the street, on a level with Aunt May's place, balanced easily on her heels. She had a phone to her ear, and the wind blew her hair and coat around her in a fashion every bit as chilling and unsettling as Venom on a good day. She stared at me, at my partial profile, with the emotionless patience of a shark waiting for a bleeding seal to weaken.

It was scary.

I turned sharply away before she could see any more of my face.

"Meet me there," she said. "If you do not, I will kill you where you stand."

"You think you'd get away with—"

"Whether you escape or die," she continued, "my staff will detonate the explosive charges currently planted on the building in order to cover our tracks. There are, at present, nearly fourteen hundred people in your building. Including one hundred and twenty-six children."

At which point, the fear vanished, replaced by raw anger.

"And if I meet you?" I asked.

"Then I will withdraw my staff and the threat to the innocent."

"How do I know you won't blow up the building anyway?" I said.

"I have no interest in the residents. Only in you. You have five seconds to decide."

"I don't need *one*," I snarled. "I was planning on pounding you to scrap in any case. See you there." Then I hung up on her, turning enough to watch her indirectly.

Her eyes glittered, a weird and somehow insectoid sight, and then she leapt from the ledge in a flicker of black cloth and white teeth, and was gone.

I leaned down and put the phone back into the Rhino's hand. "What does she want?" he asked.

"A beating," I said.

Tough words.

But the bottom line was that in all probability, I'd be dead by the time the sun rose once more.

EIGHTEEN

I went into the bedroom and shut the door behind me. Mary Jane took one look at my face and went pale.

"Peter?" she whispered.

I sat down slowly on the bed while she hovered over me.

"The thing is," I heard myself say, "you've got to feel the traffic around you. You've got to have your eyes watching other people, making sure some idiot isn't about to turn in front of you. The laws, the lights, changing lanes, all of that really isn't hard at all. Most people can drive while they're half asleep and stand a reasonable chance of arriving safely anyway. You just have to keep an eye out for the idiots. It's the idiots that mess up an otherwise decent system of transportation. As long as you know you've got your eye on any potential morons, it's a lot easier to feel confident about the rest of it."

She shook her head, lips pressed tightly together.

"It's like listening to music. You know it when something starts going wrong. You know how it's supposed to sound, and when you hear that first difference, that's when you know you've got to look sharp. Or like science. You know what's supposed to be in a given environment, and when something changes, you can see it, see what caused it. It's the same on the road. You listen for the change in music. You watch for the active variable. That's really all there is to driving, MJ."

She sat down with me. "Peter. You're scaring me."

"I just . . . I just don't want you thinking that this driving test is something big or complicated. It's simple. Sometimes the simple things aren't easy. But it isn't anything that's going to stop you for long. You'll beat it."

She took my face in both hands and made me look at her. "What happened?"

I told her about the Rhino's blindness and Mortia's phone call.

"So. I guess we'll have this finished by dawn," I said.

We sat together in silence for a minute.

"I have to go," I said. "If I don't . . ."

Mary Jane gave me a quiet smile. Then murmured, "Yet do I fear thy nature; it is too full o' the milk of human kindness to catch the nearest way."

"What's that mean in English?" I asked her.

She kissed me. "That I love you."

We held hands for a while. Then she said, "Can you win?"

"Not that it matters," I said. "But I think so. If I could figure out how."

"You always do," she said.

"Yeah," I said, without really meaning it. "Maybe something will come to me."

"Well," she said quietly, "you'll need some dinner. And to get some sleep, if you can."

Sleep. Right.

"Come on," she said. "You'd better introduce me to our guest."

"MJ . . . ," I said.

"He's our guest, Peter. Didn't you invite him to stay? Offer your protection to him? Didn't he agree to a truce?"

"Yes," I said. "But . . ."

"Then he's probably hungry, too. I'll see what I can put together." She stood up to leave.

I touched her wrist and said, "Just, uh. Be careful of him. All right? Don't go within reach of him. I'll move him to the couch."

"Where is he now?" she asked.

"Um. The kitchen floor."

"Oh, *Peter*, for goodness' sake."

"I'll move him," I said. "As long as you promise to be careful."

"All right," she said.

"Oh," I said. "One more thing . . ."

"**I** am curious," said the Rhino as he sat on most of Aunt May's couch, with a cup of hot tea. The Rhino hat occupied the leftover space beside him. He held the cup between two fingers and stirred very carefully as Mary Jane sat the sugar bowl back on the coffee table. "What kind of salary does a high-profile superhero's majordomo require?"

"Never as much as I'd like," Mary Jane responded. "But the hours aren't bad and there are decent benefits." She walked back toward the kitchen and rolled her eyes at me. I gave her a thumbs-up, while she plundered the freezer. Aunt May had a bunch of frozen hamburgers left over from the big end-of-summer cookout we'd had, and some pasta, and some tomato paste, and Mary Jane set about making something out of it.

"Benefits," the Rhino said. "Never have gotten anything like that. That is a problem, working as an independent contractor."

I had a cup of tea, too, but I wasn't sipping. Still too weird seeing the freaking Rhino on Aunt May's couch. Sipping tea. "I like that phone," I said. "Great speaker."

"Da, is also MP3 player," the Rhino said, pleased. "When I first get into this business, tried to carry radio with me, but I had no pockets in the suit. I lose or break half a dozen radios, then cell phones, and one day think to myself, Rhino, what kind of idiot designs suit with no pockets?"

Mary Jane turned her head away and bit down on a wooden spoon to keep from laughing.

"Yeah," I said, glowering at her. "Idiot."

I was going to design pockets into my costume. Eventually. It wasn't like I didn't have better things to be doing with my time.

"Got to be practical in this business," I said.

"Exactly," the Rhino said. "Is business. Lot of people cannot accept this."

I was quiet for a minute. Then I asked, "Why'd you get into it?" The Cat had told me why he'd gotten his start already. I wanted to hear what he had to say.

The Rhino sipped his tea for a moment. Then he said, "The money. I had other ideas, back then. I was younger. Very naïve. Stupid." There was more than a little bitterness in his voice.

"When you're young it isn't necessarily stupidity," I said. "It only means that there's a lot you haven't learned."

He shook off what looked like bad memories and resumed speaking in a neutral, conversational voice. "No, this I admit: I was stupid. Made stupid, young-man mistakes. After getting the strength enhancement and that first job against the Hulk, I had to find work. If you believe this, I had planned to enter professional wrestling. To become a wrestling star and make money." He let out a rumbling chortle. "Of course, I am stupid, but not *this* stupid. I realize in time what a disaster it could be and ask myself, Rhino, what kind of moron gets superpowers and sets out to enter professional wrestling?"

"Hah hah," I chortled with him. "Hah hah, yeah. Heh."

Mary Jane's face turned bright red, and she had one hand firmly covering her mouth as she stood over the stove.

"Of course," the Rhino continued, "you know what happened next. The armored suit began to bond to my skin, and I could not take the costume off." He shook his head. "There I was, young man, big, strong, plenty of money, stuck in a gray suit I could not remove. Do you have any idea how difficult it is to pick up girls when you have been stuck in armored suit for six months?"

I thought about it and shuddered. In *that* suit? "Ugh."

"Da," he said with heartfelt agreement. "The smell alone . . . I had to go through car wash to get even a little clean. So I start taking more jobs, to get enough money to remove the suit." He shook his head. "Is like low-budget horror movie. I thought that suit was an incredible asset, but it turns into horrible curse. You have no idea." He shook his head, finished the tea, and carefully put the cup back on the table. "As I say, stupid. What kind of moron gets himself stuck into costume he cannot even remove?"

My face turned red and I glanced at Mary Jane.

Her whole upper body started jerking in little hiccuplike motions from the effort of holding in her laughter, and she had to leave the room.

"I've got to ask you something," I said. "Just something I've wondered." He nodded. "Da."

I did my best to keep my voice neutral and calm. "Why do you keep that look? The big gray rhino suit. And . . . the *hat.*"

"*Bozhe moi.*" He sighed. "The suit and hat. I hate the suit. I hate the hat."

I tilted my head and leaned forward. "Then why do you keep them?"

He waved both hands a little, a gesture of helpless frustration. "I have no choice," he said. "They have become business asset. Trademark."

I frowned. "What do you mean?"

"When I finally get the first suit off, I swear to myself never again. Hired a public image consultant. Bought myself business suit. Armani. Dark glasses. Big trench coat. Was good look, very hip, very professional." He sighed. "First contract was in Colombia and it falls apart."

"Why?"

"Because I reach employer for meeting, and he does not believe I am the real Rhino. He says I am fake. That real Rhino has hat with horn on it and big gray body armor suit. He says everyone knows that. So I must be fake, and I must prove I am real Rhino."

This conversation was like listening to a train wreck: fascinating, novel, and more than a little confusing. "What happened?"

"I get angry and prove it," he sighed.

"How?"

"I throw his yacht into his billiard room." He shook his head. "After that, no more questions, but contract falls through. Unprofessional. Is better for business to wear stupid costume. And stupid hat."

I shook my head. Good grief. Felicia was even more right than I thought. I had also been young and ignorant when I got my powers. There but for the grace of God, Spidey.

"You ever see yourself retiring?" I asked him.

His body language shifted, from politely conversational to totally closed. He shrugged a shoulder. "Do you?"

"Tried," I said. "Couldn't really stay out of it."

"Da," he said quietly, nodding. Then he relaxed a little and did a half-credible Pacino impersonation, complete with hand gestures. "They pull me back in."

I broke out into a sudden laugh, and he joined me.

Maybe three seconds later, both of us realized we were laughing with one another and not at, and there was an abrupt and awkward silence.

"Dinner," Mary Jane said with absolutely angelic timing. She'd returned to the kitchen unnoticed, but when she spoke I got a whiff of something delicious and my stomach threatened to go on strike if I didn't fill it immediately. She came out with spaghetti and meat sauce, flavored from Aunt May's own spice rack, and both me and the Rhino started wolfing it down.

In the afterglow, the Rhino sat back on the couch and covered a quiet belch with one hand. "Excuse, please."

"Why not," I said.

"You are not what I expected," the Rhino said.

I grunted. We were both guys, so the Rhino heard, *You aren't what I expected, either.*

"I do not like you," he said, his voice thick. "That is not something that changes."

"I hear you."

He nodded, evidently satisfied at the response, and settled onto the couch a little more comfortably. Even if his face hadn't been all messed up, he would have looked exhausted. Add in the damage of Mortia's touch and he looked like death. He was asleep and snoring within seconds.

Mary Jane frowned at the Rhino for a moment. Then she set her plate aside, took one of Aunt May's quilts from the little trunk next to the couch, and spread it over him. She turned to me and reached out a hand.

I took it and regarded the sleeping Rhino for a moment. Then we gathered up dishes and went back to the kitchen together. She sipped a cup of tea while I did the dishes.

"It was good to hear you laugh," she said after a while. "I like it when you laugh."

"It's weird," I said. "It's like he's a person."

Her eyes sparkled. "Amazing."

"Heh. Yeah." I kept at the task. The hot water on my hands was soothing. Cleaning the plates and the pan was comfortable, a job at which I could achieve tangible, immediate progress. I found myself moving more and more slowly, though. If I finished the dishes, I'd have nothing but time—and not much of that.

"You should try to rest," she said. "Even if you can't sleep. Get a shower, lay down, and close your eyes. It will be good for you, and you'll need your strength."

"Maybe," I said.

"Definitely. After you kick the Ancients back to wherever they came from, you're coming with me to the driving test Monday. You'll need all the nerve you can get."

I tried to smile at her, but her flippancy didn't change the facts any more than mine did. I was alone, and I had no idea how to survive the night.

"All right," I told her. "I just need to make a call first."

She'd figured me out a long time ago. She already had her cell phone in hand, and she passed it to me. "Aunt May left me several numbers in case we needed to reach her. They're in the phone book."

I took the phone and got a little misty-eyed. "What in the world did I do to deserve you?"

She kissed my cheek. "I have no idea. But I'm fairly sure it isn't the sort of thing to happen twice."

I took the phone into the bedroom with me and opened up its list of contact numbers. The time flashed sullenly on the little display screen, the seconds ticking down with relentless patience.

NINETEEN

THE silence wore on as I stared down at the little clock on the phone. I really, really didn't want to die.

It's going to happen eventually. I know that.

Death comes to all of us, sooner or later. That's just part of the deal of being born. All the same, though, I didn't want it to happen *today*.

I'd faced danger before, too, situations where I could have lost my life. Most of those situations, though, had been blazing seconds of fast-moving action, while I was high on adrenaline and the fury of a fight.

The fear I felt now was a different flavor. It was patient. It had hours and hours in which to keep me company and it was comfortable doing so with each inevitable second that went by. To make things worse, I was relatively rested, alert, and not in any particular pain, which meant that all my attention was free to feel the fear. To watch death coming.

There was some part of me, the part that had made me try to walk away from the mask, that was simply furious at my stupidity. I didn't have to be doing this. I could run, and to hell with all the people who would suffer for it. What had they ever done for me? I'd spent my life trying to protect them, and despite that I still got scorn and derision and hostility as many times as I received any gratitude. Even if a thousand people died because I ran, I figured I had saved the lives of three or four times as many as that—and that was directly, face-to-face, not counting the times where I'd shut down some maniac who would have killed tens of thousands with various gases, bombs and death rays. If I bugged out (ha, get it?) now, I'd still be ahead by the numbers.

Maybe I was just getting set in my ways, because I knew I wouldn't do it. But part of me really, really wanted to. It made me feel ashamed.

Weak. Tired. Simultaneously, though, there was a sort of peace that came along with it. That's the one good thing about inevitable death. It clears the mind wonderfully. Once it's done, it's done. There would be no more agonizing questions, no more of others suffering for my mistakes, no more madmen, no more victims. I had done all that I could, and I would be able to rest with a clean conscience, more or less.

The worst part was that death would mean saying painful good-byes.

I wasn't sure how much time passed before I turned my attention to the phone, but the lighted panel had gone out, and seemed far too bright to my eyes when I turned it on.

When I finally got through the cruise ship's phone system to Aunt May, there was a lot of talking in the background and a slight lag in speech from the satellite transmission times. "Peter!" she said, her voice pleased and warm. "Hello, dear."

"Hi, Aunt May," I said. "How's the cruise?"

"Scandalous," she said happily. "You wouldn't believe how many self-styled Casanovas and Mata Haris are on this ship. It would not shock me to find a complimentary Viagra dispenser in every bar."

That made me smile. "Sounds noisy there. What's going on?"

"We're at a glacier," she told me. "Everyone's quite impressed that the water is blue and that one can see through it. They're off cutting ice from the glacier now, so that we can have hundred-thousand-year-old ice cubes in our drinks. Despite the fact that up until now we've been given perfectly good fresh ice. And there are whales."

"Whales?"

"Yes, some sort of whale, at any rate. They look like half-sunken barges to me, but everyone's at the rail taking pictures. Then there's going to be some kind of drinking game, as I understand it. Most disgraceful."

I laughed. "Just don't drive afterward."

"Oh, I won't be drinking, naturally. It's far more amusing to watch a fool drink than to be the drunken fool. The sun is still up, can you imagine? It must be, what? Nearly midnight there."

I checked the clock. "Pretty close."

"Apparently, night is only a few hours long this far north. I think it may have contributed to how juvenile everyone is acting."

"You're loving it, aren't you," I said.

"I can't remember the last time I laughed so hard," she confirmed with undisguised glee. "We're having a ball. How are you?"

"Oh, great," I said. "They put me in charge of basketball practice at the school Friday afternoon. I'm supposed to coach the team until next Thursday."

"Well, you always did have such a fondness for sports," she said, her voice dry. "How is it going?"

"I'm supposed to be teaching their star athlete to play nice with the team," I said. "He's not having anything from me, though. And everyone else is following his example. I figure by Tuesday they'll try to give me a wedgie and shut me into a locker. Gosh it's nice to be back in high school."

Aunt May laughed. "I take it your star player is talented?"

"Too much so for his own good, apparently."

"That can be difficult," she said. "Sooner or later he'll run into something he can't do alone. It's important that one learns to work with others before that happens."

"That's why the coach wanted me to teach him different." I sighed. "But I've got no idea how to get through to him."

"Think about it for a while," she suggested. "I'm sure it will come to you. And I suspect it might be good practice for when you have children of your own."

I blinked. "What?"

"Oh, I'm not lobbying for an instant baby, mind you," Aunt May said. "But I do know you, dear. You'll be a wonderful father." She paused for a moment and said, "Is that enough small talk now, Peter, or shall we make a little more before you tell me what's wrong?"

"Oh, nothing's wrong, Aunt May."

"This is a cruise ship, Peter dear. Not a turnip truck."

I didn't have another laugh in me, but I smiled. Aunt May would hear it in my voice. "There's nothing unusually wrong, then," I said.

"Ah," she said. "A business problem, then. Have I mentioned, Peter, how glad I am that you are willing to discuss your business with me now?"

"About a hundred times," I said. "I was so glad that we could . . . talk again."

"It is a very good thing," she said in warm agreement. "How is MJ?"

"Worried about me," I said.

"I can't imagine what that must be like," Aunt May said, her tone wry. "But I'm glad she's with you. She loves you to no end, you know."

"I know," I said quietly.

"And so do I," she said.

I closed my eyes, still smiling despite the quiet ache in my throat and the wetness on my cheeks. "I know. I love you too, Aunt May."

She was silent for a moment before she said, "If I could do more, I would, but in case no one has told you, remember this: You have a good heart, Peter. You've grown into a man to be admired. I am more proud of you than I can possibly describe—as Ben would be. You have always faced the true test—the times when you are alone, and when it seems that everything is as bad as it possibly could be. That's the moment of truth, Peter. There, in the darkest hours, not in whatever comes after. Because it is there that you choose between music and silence. Between hope and despair."

I sat with my head bowed, listening to her voice. I could smell her perfume in the room around me—the scent of safety and of love and of home. I hoped the phone was waterproof.

"You have only to remember this, Peter: No matter how dark the night, you are not alone. There are those who see your heart and love you. That love is a power more potent than any number of radioactive spiders."

I couldn't say anything for a minute. Then I whispered, "I'll remember, Aunt May."

"Listen to your heart," she said, her tone firm and quiet, "and never surrender. Even if you are not victorious, Peter Parker, no force in creation can defeat a heart like yours."

What can you say, faced with a love, a faith like that, warm as sunshine, solid as bedrock?

"Thank you," I whispered.

"Of course," she said, and I heard her smiling.

A bell rang somewhere in her background. "Well. It is time for me to go to supper and wait for the floor show. I'll leave you to your work."

"I love you, Aunt May."

"I love you."

We hung up together.

Neither of us said goodbye.

My peace was gone, shattered by the conversation. Hope can be painful that way, and part of me longed for the return of peace and quiet. That peace, though, is not for the living—and I was alive.

And I intended to stay that way.

So long as there was a breath left in my body, the fight was not over and the darkness was not complete. I had faced and overcome things as deadly and dangerous as Mortia and her kin, and I'd be a monkey's uncle before I accepted defeat. I was rested. I was smart. I had the kind of home and life and happiness a lot of people can only dream about.

I refused to let Mortia take that from me. I refused to allow my fear to make me lie down and die.

I rose from where I sat on the bed and felt suddenly clear, focused, and strong. Nothing had changed. I still had no idea how I was going to get myself out of this one. But I would. I would find a way. I suddenly felt as certain of that as I was that the sun would rise in the morning. I always felt that my powers came to me for a reason, and while I did not know what that reason might be, with God as my witness, it had *not* been to feed some psychotic monster-wench and her kin.

I would beat these things. I would find a way.

The phone in my hands suddenly let out a series of chiming notes, the theme from *Close Encounters of the Third Kind*. I don't know why Mary Jane used them as her ring tone. She said it just made her happy.

I flipped the phone open and said, "Hello?"

"It's me," Felicia said, her voice cool and professional. "We found Dex."

TWENTY

MARY Jane appeared at the door, eyebrows lifted in inquiry.

"Felicia," I reported, handing back the phone. "Oliver, her guy at the company, found Dex."

MJ nodded, frowning. "What are you going to do?"

"They're bringing him here," I said quietly. "I'm going to go talk to him."

Her mouth quirked at one corner. "Aren't you getting a little old to be throwing parties when Aunt May is out of town?"

"We'll party tonight and clean it up tomorrow," I responded. "What could possibly go wrong?"

She put her hand over my mouth and said, "If you don't shut up, you're going to bring on a montage."

"Is that some kind of seizure?"

"Actually," Mary Jane said after a moment of thought, "that's not a bad description." The whimsy faded out of her face. "Seriously. Up here?"

"They're bringing a car. I'm going to go talk to him."

"I see," Mary Jane said. She glanced from me to the recumbent Rhino. "And I stay here?"

"I think you'll be all right. I'll be on the street right outside the building," I said. "I put Felicia's cell number on your speed dial. If you even *think* there *might* be a problem, you hit that, and I'll be up here inside of fifteen seconds."

Mary Jane considered that for a moment, and then nodded. "I suppose I'll make some coffee, then. Stay alert."

"Keep the lights dim," I said, "and stay away from the windows."

Mary Jane's eyes glittered. "I'll keep an eye on our guest. If he gives me any trouble, I'll subvert him with cheesecake."

"There's cheesecake?" I said. "I didn't see any cheesecake. Why didn't I get cheesecake?"

"Because I haven't made it yet."

I considered that for a moment. "I suppose I'll accept that explanation."

"You're a reasonable man," MJ said. Then she stepped close to me and pressed herself against me. I held her quietly, eyes closed, until her phone beep-beep-beep-BOOP-booped. She flipped it open and checked the screen. "Felicia." Rather pointedly, she did not answer the phone.

I released her reluctantly, walked to the window, and looked down. A white van that looked like an unmarked bakery truck pulled up on the street outside. A pair of professionally unremarkable cars pulled out from spaces they'd somehow secured, making room for the van, which slid up to the curb and came to a halt.

I gave MJ a quick kiss, hit the fire escape, flipped myself across the street so that I wouldn't be approaching the van from the direction of Aunt May's place, and moseyed on down, landing on the van's roof. Then I stuck my head down in front of the driver's face and said, "I hope you guys take credit cards, 'cause I can't find my checkbook and the only cash I have is a bucket of pennies."

Felicia looked back at me without any amusement whatsoever in her expression. She shook her head, then turned and vanished into the back of the van. The side door whispered open, and I crawled on in.

The inside of the van looked like a cramped office. There were several low seats and an abbreviated desk, complete with a clamped-down computer and monitor. There were several people in there. Felicia, dressed in her bodysuit and leather jacket, sat behind the desk, her legs crossed, her eyes cool.

A small man hovered next to the desk, and he was the only one there short enough to stand up. He was a dapper little guy in a casual suit of excellent cut. He had sparse, grizzled hair, spectacles, an opaque expression, and unreadable blue eyes.

"Spidey," Felicia said. "This is Oliver."

I folded my legs, Indian style, only I sat on the ceiling. It's a rare man who can honestly say that his butt has a superpower. "'Sup, Oliver?"

His eyebrows lifted. He didn't say anything. He looked like the kind of man who was used to patiently suffering while other, more intellectually limited people tried to catch up with him.

Sitting across from the desk were three men. Two of them were bruisers—though older and more solid than most of the thugs I've tussled with. They also had suits and wedding rings. Law-abiding bruisers, then, I supposed. Security personnel.

"Mister Walowski," Felicia supplied. "Mister Gruber."

"Howdy," I said to them. Then I tilted my head toward the last man, who sat between them, his shoulders hunched defensively. He was as skinny as I remembered, almost famished-looking. His hair was a mess, his eyes sunken and lined with what almost looked like bruises rather than bags. He hadn't shaved in a few days. He was dressed plainly, in jeans, a T-shirt, and a blue apron bearing the words, "Sooper-Mart!"

His eyes, though, were dark, intent, calculating.

He reminded me of a trapped rat, spiteful and stubborn, holding still in hopes that the predator might simply leave, but ready to fight with berserk desperation if pushed too far.

"Is this the guy?" Felicia asked.

"Yeah, that's him. Where'd you find him?"

"Hartford," Oliver said. He had a very calm, quiet voice. "The convenience store where he works was robbed, and another clerk was stabbed. They took prints from all the store's employees so that they could sort out which belonged to the suspect. The prints were put on file and the company found them."

"You found them, Oliver," Felicia corrected.

He favored her with a small smile.

I nodded at the bruisers. "You been sweating him?"

"Just doing a lot of looming," Felicia said. "Apparently, he doesn't scare easy."

I snorted. "No. He wouldn't. Hi, Dex."

Now that I'd spoken to him by name, Dex let out his breath in a hiss. "I did what you told me to. I stayed away from New York."

"That's good," I said.

"Then what do you want?" he asked.

"I want you to talk to me about Morlun."

"He's dead," Dex said in a monotone, and closed his eyes. "What else is there to say?"

"I'm sure there must be something," I told him. "His sister and his two brothers seem to be really upset about the whole situation."

Dex looked up at me sharply, and for a second his expression became frightened, before congealing into that ratlike calculation again. He said nothing.

"Dex? Did you hear me?"

"Yes." He took a deep breath. "What makes you think I know anything?"

"You were with Morlun for a while. You ran his errands. Handled his books. Went out for coffee. You were his Renfield."

"No," Dex said, in that same flat monotone. "Renfield got to die; Dracula killed him. Morlun kept promising, but he never would do it."

I wasn't sure which was creepier—the words Dex had said, or the way my instincts told me that the faint shades of longing in his eyes were entirely genuine.

"Dex," I said. "I know he was a monster. But I'm looking at three more just like him up here, and I need to know whatever you can tell me."

"Or what happens?" A faint sneer colored his voice. "You tell them about me?"

"No," I said. "They're blaming me for his death. I doubt they know or care who you are. You aren't in any danger."

"I wouldn't say that," Felicia said sweetly. "Dex, Spidey is a longtime associate of mine. I'd be very upset if something happened to him."

"Oh," Dex said. He paused for a moment, then asked, "What are you going to do to them?"

"Whatever I have to," I said.

And then something in the man's demeanor changed. In that instant, his weakness and fear abruptly vanished, and his eyes widened, gleaming.

"Kill them," he said, his voice suddenly hard-edged, hot, eager. "You beat him. You *beat* him. You can do it again; you can beat them again. You can kill them. Kill them. *All* of them. Promise me you will kill them, and I'll tell you everything you want to know."

He stared at me, panting as if he'd run up a long hill, fever-bright eyes locked on my face. I'm not a therapist, but I've been around it enough to know what crazy looks like, and Dex was it. Something told me that if I pushed him or put him under any pressure or strain, he might crack.

Violently.

After all, I'd seen him do it once before.

I had to give him what he wanted. Or at least a reasonable facsimile thereof.

"Talk to me," I said, gently, "and I promise you that I will send them to the next world."

Dex choked out a breath and his eyes sagged halfway shut. He let out a low, shuddering sigh, a disquietingly intimate sound, and closed his eyes. Then he said, "What do you want to know?"

"Tell me about Morlun's feeding habits," I said.

He paused for a moment, frowning in concentration, gathering his thoughts. "Morlun was never alone when he fed. Sometimes he would dismiss me for days. But always, when he fed or hunted, I was there. Always."

"I thought they only fed every few years," I said.

"From the source, yes," Dex said. "The pure, primal life energy. Like yours. But others have the same energy, though in lesser quantity, very diluted. It wasn't very satisfying to him, but it pleased him to snack on such folk from time to time."

"Like popcorn," I said.

Dex smiled at me. His teeth had been stained by cigarettes. Too much of the whites of his eyes showed. "Like popcorn. Normal humans with some kind of personal association with a totemic source. Something about their personality brushed on the source, gave them a minuscule amount of the same energy."

"Someone like a lion tamer," I said quietly. "Or someone who worked with and rode and loved horses. Maybe Grizzly Adams."

"Yes," Dex said. "Those, he'd take every few months. And always he made sure I was there."

"Why?"

"To watch for intrusion," Dex said. "To notify him if anyone approached. He was very specific about it. Paranoid, really, even for him. He would repeat the instructions every single time, in full, every time."

"Do you remember them?" I asked.

Dex shuddered and licked his lips. "I remember everything." He folded his arms and shook his head several times. I gave him a minute to work himself up to it. Felicia leaned forward and began to speak, but I made a small, discouraging gesture with one hand. She saw it, and for a second I thought she'd go ahead anyway—but then she settled back into her seat and waited.

Dex looked up and spoke. His voice, when it came out, hardly sounded like his own—it had gained richness and depth and had taken on a faint, vaguely British accent. It sounded a lot like Morlun. "Pay attention, Dex."

Then Dex answered in his own voice, toneless and quiet. "Yes, Morlun."

His voice changed back to that echo of the Ancient's. "The usual arrangements are in place? A private suite?"

"Yes, Morlun."

"Security has been notified that I wish privacy?"

"Yes, Morlun."

"You are armed?"

"Yes, Morlun."

"You have checked the locks?"

"Yes, Morlun."

"The windows?"

"Yes, Morlun."

"The outer cameras are in place?"

"Yes, Morlun."

"The new locks to my chamber door are installed?"

"Yes, Morlun."

"Give me the keys."

Dex held out his hand, his eyes focused on nothing, as if dropping something. "Yes, Morlun."

"You will remain on guard outside my door."

"Yes, Morlun."

"If the security measures are disturbed, by anything whatsoever, however small, you are to make me aware of it at once. If any unauthorized persons appear, you are to slay them."

"Yes, Morlun."

Silence fell. Oliver looked more than a little uncomfortable. The bruisers were creeped out. Heck, even Felicia had that narrow-eyed, casual stare she got when she put her poker face on.

Dex hadn't simply been sharing a memory. He'd been all but reliving it. For him, it had been almost as real in replay as in real life. God, what torture, to remember every twisted detail experienced under the thumb of a thing like Morlun.

"Eidetic memory," I said quietly. "And then some."

Dex opened his flat, lifeless eyes and shrugged a shoulder. "It's why he chose me. It made me more useful to him."

"I take it he would bring victims back to a prepared location," I said.

"Yes. It wasn't difficult for him. He was charming, when he needed to be."

"Must have been the cravat," I said. "Did he always use additional security forces?"

"Yes. Sometimes hired bodyguards. Sometimes hotel or resort security. Sometimes he would use underworld muscle."

I nodded. "Sounds like he shut even you away."

"Yes. Morlun never wanted to be disturbed while he fed."

While he fed . . . Blast it, the answer was there. It was in there somewhere, so close I could taste it. I had what I needed, but for the life of me, I couldn't piece it together. Literally. It was like working out a badly tangled cord—if I could just find one end and get it out of the first stubborn knot, I was sure the rest would be workable.

"Dex," I said quietly. "Thank you."

"Will that help?" he asked, his voice again surging with smoldering rage. The sudden shift in tone made the bruisers tense up. "Will it help you kill them?"

"It might."

"Don't hesitate," he snarled. "Don't think twice. Kill them."

"Dex," I said. "You need to calm down, man. You don't want to—"

"You have no idea!" he shouted. There was spittle collecting at the corners of his mouth as his breathing became labored again. "You don't *know* the things I saw. You must kill them. Kill them. *Kill them all.*"

He snapped on the last phrase, screaming and thrashing. The bruisers piled onto him, telling him to relax. Dex fought with more strength than I would have given him credit for, howling up a storm as he did. I felt a little bit sick. Dex had been hanging on by a thread, and all my questions hadn't done anything to make his situation less precarious.

"He's getting a little worked up," Oliver noted quietly. "Do you have any further need of him?"

"Spidey?" Felicia asked.

"I'm good," I said.

She nodded while the bruisers subdued Dex. They were careful about it, not using any more force than they had to while holding him down to prevent him from harming himself or others.

"Perhaps we should step outside," Oliver suggested.

"Good idea. Spider?"

I went out first, crouching on the roof of the van as Felicia and Oliver exited and closed the door. The noise from the van cut out at once, but I knew that inside Dex was still struggling, because the van was rocking back and forth.

I bit my lip beneath the mask, looked at Felicia, and asked, "He going to be okay?"

"Relax. They won't hurt him," Felicia said quietly.

"Unless he forces them to," Oliver contradicted her. "That young man is clearly disturbed and dangerous."

"They won't hurt him," Felicia said again, louder.

Oliver glanced at her, sighed, and then drew a cell phone from a pocket and stepped a few feet away to make a call.

"I'll see to it," Felicia said quietly.

"Dex suffered," I said quietly. "Maybe a lot more than I thought he had. He needs help. Not getting dragged off to be interrogated in the middle of the night." He probably hadn't needed to be banned from New York on pain of torment and death, either. Granted, I hadn't exactly been in a state of perfect clarity after my marathon beating from Morlun, but all the same. I hadn't seen Dex as another of Morlun's victims. Maybe I should have. It made me feel bad, that I'd added to his suffering by dragging him here.

Except that I hadn't.

I frowned. "Why didn't you just make a phone call, instead of bringing him here?"

"They were fairly close," Felicia said. "We thought it would be best for you to see him in person. He wasn't exactly the soul of cooperation."

I nodded, feeling my lips purse thoughtfully. "I need to make a call," I said. Then I turned to Oliver, as he lowered the phone and turned back to us. "Can I borrow your phone?"

Most people wouldn't have seen it, but Felicia froze in place for a tiny moment, her head tilting a fraction to one side in interest.

"Hmm?" Oliver said. "Oh, certainly. How often does one get to lend a phone to a superhero?" He offered it up to me.

"Thanks," I said. I reached down from the van's roof and took the phone from him.

"I'm impressed, Oliver," Felicia was saying behind me. "This was quick work, even for you."

"I was well motivated," Oliver replied. "Whatever I can do to help one of New York's most colorful heroes."

Felicia smiled widely. "Two of them."

"Yes, two. Of course."

My, but Oliver had a neat phone. It had all kinds of things in it, a full PDA among them. People seem to take security much more lightly when it comes to PDAs, for some reason. Maybe it's because they're always kept safely tucked in a pocket. I opened Oliver's e-mail. Then I looked at his call logs.

The PDA beeped a whole lot while I did, and Oliver noticed it. "Hey," he said. "Hey, what do you think you're doing?" He came over and reached up as if to take the PDA out of my hands. Like that was going to happen. I held it maybe six inches out of his reach and kept going. "Give me that!"

The incoming calls all had neat identifying tags on them—except for one, which was quite conspicuously blank. I checked the outgoing calls. Ditto. Oliver kept everything neatly labeled—except for a single phone number. I dialed that one, and told Oliver, "You got an e-mail, by the way. Your offshore bank confirms a money transfer with a bunch of zeros, Oliver."

The phone rang once, and then Mortia's voice spoke. "Do you have the cat? The spider?"

"Tick tock, Mortia," I told her in a cheerful voice. "Don't be late for our appointment."

I hung up the phone and tilted my head at Oliver. "Thanks, bud. All done. Hey, Felicia, where'd you get your phone?"

"From the company . . . ," she said, after a moment. Then she corrected herself. "From Oliver."

"His has a GPS built into it," I said. "Betcha yours does, too. And on a completely unrelated note, do you remember how we were wondering how Mortia and company found us back at the apartment? Any thoughts on how that happened?"

Oliver stood frozen for a moment. Then the traitor bolted.

TWENTY ONE

OLIVER was awfully quick for a man his age.

Felicia let out a snarl like a furious mountain lion, startling and savage enough to make me wonder—again—about the source of her grace and agility, and she flung herself after Oliver.

His suit was an expensive one—it hid the gun Oliver was carrying to perfection. He drew the weapon and pegged a pair of shots at Felicia, slowing down enough to make sure they went more or less in her direction. She flipped into a lateral tumble—though with uncontrolled shots like that, you run almost as much risk of dodging *into* a badly aimed bullet as you do of dodging an accurate shot.

I gave them enough of a lead to make sure I wasn't going to be crowding Felicia, and then went after them.

Oliver darted down an alley between two apartment buildings, and I shook my head. The runners are always doing things like that. Maybe it's some kind of burrowing instinct left over from our ancestors, little mammals hiding from dinosaurs, right before a big rock fell on them. Whatever the reason, Oliver went down the alley, throwing glances over his shoulder.

One thing about the narrow alley, I supposed. Had Felicia simply sprinted after him, he'd have had a really hard time missing her when he opened fire again. Oliver might have been smart enough to have thought that through. Most of the time, though, it's just a side effect the thugs aren't really bright enough to appreciate. There are several means of ending a chase in a place like that, and Felicia employed my personal favorite. She outthought Oliver and got ahead of him.

He was a few feet from the other end of the alley when a patch of shadow erupted into movement, and the Black Cat fetched Oliver a kick to the belly that took him from a full sprint to a full stop as he folded around her boot. He went down, the wind knocked all the way out of him. Felicia, furious, stomped down on his gun hand until he dropped the weapon. She kicked it away. Then she picked him up by the front of his coat and slammed him against one wall of the alley.

"You greedy little *toad*," she snarled, slamming his shoulder blades against the wall for emphasis. "What did you *do*?"

"Ms. Hardy," he gasped, hardly able to speak. "Contain yourself. This is not a professional means of—"

She threw him against the other wall of the alley, then popped him in the back of one thigh with a simple snap kick. He cried out as his leg buckled, and fell onto his side. Felicia's boot flashed out again, this time striking Oliver's head in a firm push, trapping it between her foot and the brick wall.

"Oliver," she purred. "I am not prepared to be a sensitive, reasonable, professional individual right now. I'm not feeling my normal, elegant, stylish, and ladylike self." She leaned toward him a little, making him writhe at the additional pressure, and her voice sweetened. "So I want you to believe me when I tell you this: You get one chance. If I even *think* you're trying to lie to me in any way whatsoever, I'm going to crush your skull and wipe your brains off my boots with your expensive jacket. Have I expressed myself clearly?"

He let out a pained sound and gave her as much of a nod as he could manage.

Felicia leaned back slightly, folding her arms and supporting herself against the alley's other wall as casually as if she'd been resting one foot on a crate instead of on a man's temple. "What did you do?"

"She's a big-money client, Felicia," he said. "She's hired the company before. There's an established relationship. She came to me complaining that you were stalling and feeding her false information."

"Yes. Because I suspected she was plotting murder. Doing the fieldwork for murderers is not good business, Oliver, and it never will be." She paused and then said, "How much did she offer you?"

"Enough," he said, grimacing.

"What did she want?"

"To keep tabs on you," he said. "And when she heard about this Dex person, she wanted him as well."

"The going rate on this kind of thing is, I believe, thirty pieces of silver. I hope she offered you that much, at least."

Oliver lifted one hand in a gesture of surrender. "It wasn't personal, Hardy."

Felicia went completely still and silent for a second. Then she whispered, "Not personal?"

"No."

"This creature you worked for has attempted to kill my friend twice. If it gets the chance, it will kill me, too—not to mention all the bystanders who might get hurt when the music starts. And you pointed them *right* at him." She twisted her heel, grinding it slowly into the side of Oliver's head. "In what way is that 'not personal'?"

"Wait," Oliver choked out. "Look, it doesn't have to go down like this. We can negotiate, cut you out of the deal. That was what I was trying to do from the start. Trying to look out for one of the company's assets."

"And to pick up some money on the side while you did it?"

"Don't do this," Oliver said. "You don't know these people, Hardy. They're rich, richer than rich. They've got connections, power. You *can't* survive being their enemy. But if you let me help you, I think I can work something out. Protect you."

Felicia snarled, bent down, lifted Oliver against the wall again, and suddenly flicked out the fingers of her right hand.

I tensed. She had the gloves on. The deadly, razor-sharp talons built into it deployed with a wicked little rasping sound. Very deliberately, Felicia reached out and ran her clawed fingertips lightly down the bricks beside Oliver's head. Sparks flew up. There was an awful, steely sound.

Oliver turned white. He glanced aside at the five long furrows Felicia had dug into the wall. Sweat beaded his skin.

Felicia picked up his tie with the same hand, her fingers idly toying with it—and soundlessly slicing it to slivers as they did. "Oliver," she said. "I am disinclined to let you betray me and simply walk away. So there's something I want you to think about."

His eyes were all on the claws. A cut across one cheek was bleeding a little. "I'm listening."

"First, you're going to go back to the van. You're going to get Dex somewhere safe, without telling anyone anything about him. You will never speak to Mortia or her flunkies again. Resign. The money you took to betray me is forfeit. You will find a place for it to go. A good place, where it might help someone."

"I have done nothing wrong," he said. "I have broken no laws."

"Which might matter to courts and lawyers," Felicia said pleasantly. And then her eyes blazed and she struck suddenly and savagely at the wall again, this time gouging out a six-inch-long section of brick as deep as the second joint of her fingers. "But you hurt my *friends*," she snarled. "Do it, Oliver. Or I'll destroy you."

"You aren't a killer," he said, eyes narrowing.

"Who said anything about killing? By the time I'm finished with you, you won't have a penny. You won't have a home. You won't have a job. What you will have is nothing. And everyone you've ever crossed is going to know exactly where to look you up."

Oliver licked his lips, and his voice trembled. "You wouldn't do that."

She released him, springing the claws on the other hand, and simply leaned the tips of her fingers against the bricks on either side of his head, creating a steady trickle of sparks, a grinding, growling chorus of scrapes and tiny shrieks of protesting brick.

Her eyes turned wide and cold and angry, and leaned in close enough that he had to have felt her breath on his face. "Try me," she purred.

Oliver shivered and looked away.

"Get out," she said, her voice quiet and full of contempt. "Get out of my sight."

She stepped back from him, and Oliver tried for a dignified retreat.

She kicked him hard in the seat of the pants as he left, sending him out onto the sidewalk in an undignified sprawl. Oliver hurried away, limping.

Felicia watched him go for a minute. Then she recovered his gun, disassembled it in a single smooth motion, and dropped the pieces into several different trash cans. She put the lids back on the cans, shook her head, sighed, and looked up to where I sat thirty feet up the building's wall in a patch of heavy shadow. "I thought you'd have come down there, at the end."

I dropped to the alley to stand with her. "You had him under control. Why would I do that?"

She did not look at me, and shrugged. "The bit with the claws. I figured you'd grab my wrist any second, all worried that I was about to kill him in cold blood."

"What?"

"If the positions had been reversed, you'd have stopped Oliver."

"Well, yes, but—"

"If it had been the Rhino, you'd have stepped in."

"Felicia," I said, a little frustrated. "Where are you going with this?"

Her eyes grew cold, and she said, "Nowhere. Never mind. You'd probably want to help Oliver if he was in trouble. Just like you're helping the Rhino. No one is too black-hearted to be worthy of the Amazing Spider-Man's protection."

Then she began walking back down the alley toward the van.

I stared after her, and in a sudden flash of insight I finally understood her recent attitude—at least a little bit.

Felicia wasn't defending the Rhino.

She was defending *herself.*

I knew that she'd tried, she'd really tried to be one of the active good guys, but . . . well, she hadn't been all that *good* at it. Her past sins had weighed against her, and she'd had a rough path to follow.

She'd given up, largely, on the whole freelance-hero gig. Now she worked in private security. Like the Rhino, like Oliver, she was a mercenary—one on the side of the law and civilization, true, but a mercenary nonetheless.

Maybe my initial contempt and antipathy toward the Rhino bothered her, because she saw too many similarities in herself. Maybe it made her wonder if I harbored some degree of the same contempt for *her.* Maybe she wondered if she had just been another sad charity case on whom I'd taken pity. Maybe that was why we hadn't worked out. Maybe my opinion, which had been important enough to her to help motivate her to abandon a life of crime, was *still* important to her.

If so, then by causing her to question the nature of our relationship, maybe I was eroding the foundation of the new life she was building.

I sighed.

Maybe if I rented a crane, I could pull my foot out of my mouth.

I caught up to her, prowling along the wall at head height while I tried to talk to her. "Felicia, wait."

She never slowed her pace or glanced aside at me. "Look. I found your toady for you. And you made it clear that you don't want me involved in your problems. So has MJ. So I'm leaving."

"Don't do this," I said. "Come on, would you hold up a minute?"

She didn't slow down or answer me, and I stopped as she stepped out of the far end of the alley.

"You were right," I said quietly. "You were right about the Rhino. And I was being a pigheaded idiot about it."

She stopped in her tracks. She turned her head enough that I could see the curve of her cheek.

"Only a real friend would have tried to point out a blind spot like that," I said. "And I didn't even try to listen to you. It was stupid and arrogant of me, to disrespect you like that. You deserve better from me, and I apologize."

The lines of her body shifted almost imperceptibly. Her shoulders sagged a little. Her neck bowed her head forward a couple of degrees.

"Yes," she said after a minute. "A pigheaded idiot."

I dropped to the ground and walked over to her, crossing my arms and leaning my shoulders against the wall. "I haven't ever said this," I said. "But I admire you, Felicia. When you went legit, you picked a hard road for yourself. You knew it would be hard, but you did it anyway. That took a lot of courage."

She turned to look at me. Her eyes were misty.

I put my hands on both her shoulders. "You're beautiful and strong, and you don't let anyone tell you how to live your life. You're a good friend, and you have a good heart. When the going gets rough, you always have my back, and I trust you there."

She blinked her eyes rapidly. Her voice came out quiet and a little shaky. "Then why don't you want me to help you with this?"

"Um," I said.

Felicia suddenly tilted her head to one side and her eyes widened in understanding, then narrowed in anger. Her hands came up and slapped mine from her shoulders. "You were trying to *protect* me! Like I'm some kind of china doll!"

"No," I said. "Wait."

"You *pig*," she said, pushing her fingers stiffly at my chest. "You arrogant, reactionary, egotistical . . . My God, I ought to pop you in the mouth right now!"

"I'd really rather you—"

"I don't need your protection," she snapped. "I'm not a child. How *dare* you make that kind of decision for me! How dare you take that choice away from me!"

I rubbed at the back of my neck. "Listen. If I just hit myself in the mouth a few hundred times, would it make this rant go away any faster?"

"You're going to be hearing about this for years, Parker."

I sighed and lifted my hands in surrender. "All right, all right."

"So no more noble-defender crap. From here out, I've got your back. Right?"

I nodded. "Right."

Her cheeks grew a little rounder as she kept a smile off of her face. Then she nodded back and said, "Apology accepted."

"Sheesh," I said.

"So," she said. "Did it help? You figured out the silver bullet?"

"I think so," I said. "But it's right on the tip of my brain and I can't get it to come out."

She fought off another smile. "The tip of your brain?"

"You know what I mean," I said. "I've got all these facts, and once I put them together the right way it should be possible."

"Which facts?"

"Paranoid solitude during feeding," I said. "Feeding upon smaller victims for between-meal snacks. My fight with Morlun. The folklore accounts. The information you discovered. The way the Ancients shy away from crowds. The fact that Mortia was, apparently, interested in finding you, even *after* I agreed to meet her."

The Black Cat frowned. "Mmm. Maybe we should get everything written down. Brainstorm. Two heads will be better than one, right?"

And suddenly it all fell into place, like the wheels on a slot machine coming up all cherries. Suddenly I saw what had been right there in front of me the whole time. I had picked out the false note, made a positive identification of the active variable.

I could beat them.

"That's it," I heard myself whisper. "I can *beat* them."

Felicia's eyes widened. "You've got it?"

"Eu-freaking-reka," I confirmed. I ran over the solution in my head a few times. It seemed sound. "But I can't do it alone."

She arched a brow and then smiled sweetly. "So what you're saying is that you need my help."

"Um. Yes," I said.

"How *interesting*." She folded her arms, expression amused. "Say 'Please.'"

"Please," I said.

"'Pretty please,'" she prompted.

"Pretty please. I need your help."

She sniffed. "It wasn't nice of you to provoke me into a fight so I'd walk away, you know."

"Then why'd you fall for it?"

She rolled her eyes. "I'll think about it. But I'll walk you home first. You'd just get lost on your own."

"Very generous," I said.

She gave me a pious smile. "What are friends for?"

TWENTY TWO

I led Felicia back to Aunt May's apartment, filling her in about the Rhino and Mortia's phone call on the way. We went in through the same bedroom window by which I'd left earlier. I shut it behind us, and we headed into the living room.

Mary Jane had turned out the lights, presumably to let the Rhino sleep. The only illumination came from several candles on the kitchen counter, where Mary Jane was sitting with a copy of the Scottish Play, a notebook, and a pencil.

She glanced up at Felicia and me as we appeared from the bedroom, and arched an eyebrow. "You know," she said, "a lot of wives would not react to this particular situation with patience and understanding."

I sighed.

MJ smiled, mostly with her eyes, and said, carefully polite, "Felicia."

Felicia nodded to her. "MJ."

"I thought you had left," my wife said.

Felicia shrugged. "I got bored. I decided not to let your husband hog all the excitement for himself."

Mary Jane considered her for a moment, and then nodded. Her voice warmed considerably. "It's good to see you again. Tea?"

"Please." Felicia smiled and then looked down, settling on a chair at the kitchen table.

"The Rhino?" I asked.

"Out like a light," she said. "He snored for about five minutes. Some plaster fell out of the ceiling. How did the interview go?"

I stripped off my mask, leaned against the kitchen counter, and smiled at her.

MJ took one look at my face, and there was a sudden fire in her eyes. "You figured it out," she said.

"I think so," I said. "It was right there in front of us, too."

MJ gave me a mock scowl and asked Felicia, "Isn't that annoying? The way he makes you ask him to explain things?"

"It's his great big brain," Felicia said, nodding.

"He likes to remind everyone about it, to make up for all his other shortcomings."

"Look," I said. "The real problem with fighting the Ancients is their sheer durability. They can fight for days without slowing down, and it's all but impossible to fight them head-on. They don't get hurt and they're strong. So every little ding and bruise they inflict on you makes you tired faster, while they just shrug off whatever you do back to them. They grind you away."

Mary Jane shivered. "Go on."

"I was looking for a weakness, but I had already found it—partially, anyway. Morlun got hurt twice. The first time was when he had me down and was starting to do to me what Mortia did to the Rhino. Ezekiel jumped him and bloodied his nose for him, literally. It was the first time in maybe eighteen hours of fighting I saw him injured.

"The second time was at the reactor, when he started taking a bite of me and got a mouthful of uranium instead. See?"

Felicia tilted her head, frowning. "From what Dex said . . . that's when they're vulnerable. When they feed. Right?"

"Right," I said. "Strange told me that the Ancients' powers were a result of their will focusing all the latent energy they've devoured. Morlun wasn't super-strong and nearly invulnerable all the time. He had to be concentrating on it, *willing* himself to be that way. When he started to feed, he couldn't keep his focus, or at least it seriously reduced his defenses—and when he panicked, at the end, he couldn't use them at all."

"It explains why they get nervous at taking on more than one opponent, too," Felicia said. "More distractions."

"And why Mortia didn't stay on your trail after you saved the Rhino," Mary Jane added. "You hit her at the only moment when she was vulnerable. For all she knew, you knew exactly what you were doing when you did so. You probably scared the wits out of her."

I nodded. "Exactly. So we use that against them."

Mary Jane sat a cup of tea down in front of Felicia. "How?"

"I don't think I like where this is going," Felicia said.

"We decoy them," I said. "We tempt them into feeding."

The Black Cat sipped her tea. "I was right. This plan has a major flaw in it."

"Flaw?" Mary Jane asked. "Which part is flawed?"

"The part where they have to be feeding when we attack," she said. "To feed, you have to have, well, *food*. I don't want to be food. That's really the point of the whole exercise, isn't it."

"It's a risk," I admitted. "But if I'm right, it could work. We wait until they start, blindside them, knock them out, and use the magic rocks to get rid of them."

Felicia's eyebrows went up. "Oh, sure. And if you're wrong?"

"I didn't say it was a perfect plan," I said quietly. "That's why you're carrying the rocks and I'm going to be the decoy."

Felicia shook her head, rising with the teacup to pace restlessly. "That isn't a good idea."

"Sure it is."

"No it isn't. I'm good, but you're better, and a lot stronger. Of the two of us, you're the one most likely to be able to KO one of the Ancients, even if they are in a weakened state." She smiled, showing teeth, and took a few hip-swaying steps across the room. "And let's face it, Parker. I've forgotten more about distraction than you'll ever know."

"I hate to point this out," Mary Jane said quietly. "But once they start feeding, whoever they're attacking is essentially paralyzed. Right?"

I chewed on my lip and nodded. "Yes. Morlun barely got started on me before Ezekiel decked him, but the pain was . . ." I shivered. "Yes. You can't put up much of a fight after one of them starts on you."

"There are three of them," Mary Jane said. "No matter which of you is the decoy, there are still going to be two of them who *aren't* feeding. Do you think they'll just stand around and let you knock the third one out?"

I shook my head. "We'll have to separate them."

"Like you did last night?" Felicia asked.

"Exactly."

"Last night, when you scared Mortia to death?" Mary Jane asked. "Do you think she'll be as careless and confident this time? Do you think she'll be dumb enough to get separated from the others again?"

It was a big worry of mine, too, but I tried not to show it. "Maybe. Maybe not. Either way, this is pretty much the best plan we've got."

Felicia laughed. "That's because it's the *only* plan we've got."

"You say tomato . . . ," I said.

We stood there, looking at one another for a silent moment.

"That's the plan, then," I said quietly, taking MJ's hand.

"Right," Felicia said. She checked her watch, and her mouth twisted with distaste. "Now comes the fun part. Five hours of waiting."

I nodded. "I know what you mean. I hate waiting, too. I think Aunt May has some cards. We could play a round or two, or—"

Felicia lifted both hands. "No offense, Pete, but you could really use a shower first. Really."

"Thank you," Mary Jane told her. Thinking back later, there was a little bit of emphasis on the phrase I didn't notice at the time. "I didn't want to be the first one to say something."

Felicia grinned at MJ. "No problem. Go on, Pete. I'll keep an eye on Snoozy here." She took a sip of tea and regarded the Rhino. "Awww. He's kind of cute when he's sleeping."

"Fine, fine." I sighed, and trooped off to the bathroom for a shower.

TWENTY THREE

I actually slept. Not for long, but every minute of it was precious. I woke up in the quietest part of the night, hours after the bars had closed, hours before the heavy Sunday morning traffic would be under way.

I lay in bed for a moment, my arm around Mary Jane, and she sighed in her sleep. The night showed me only a ghostly image of her, absent of makeup or artifice of any kind. Nor was her face touched with worry or fear—only the relaxation of peaceful sleep.

My God, she was beautiful.

I'm a lucky man.

After a few minutes, I rose and went to the window, staring out at the quiet city. It was a quiet moment. A good moment. I faced the city I have always fought to protect, focused on what was before me. There was a chance I would prevail, a good chance. Victory was by no means likely, but I had that fighting chance.

That's all I've ever had, really.

And it's all I need.

After a little while, I felt Mary Jane's presence behind me. Her reflection in the window wore only the loosely wrapped sheet from the bed. She stepped up to press against my back, and wrapped her arms and the bedsheet around me. She rested her cheek upon my shoulder and stared out at the city with me, sharing my silence, her warmth and love pouring into me through her touch.

We stayed that way until the eastern sky began to lighten.

I turned to her, and nodded. She smiled a little, then brought me my colors. I started to put them on, but she gently pushed my hands back down to my sides, and dressed me herself. She stood up with the mask last, and pulled it slowly over my head—leaving my mouth uncovered. Then she leaned into me and gave me one more kiss on the lips, slow and sweet. I returned it the same way, as gently as I knew how.

She broke off the kiss after a time, and murmured, "For luck."

I smiled a little and said, "You want to go out for some dinner later?"

"Not Thai. Never again."

"Not Thai," I agreed.

"I'll think about it," she said.

"You are quite a tease, Mrs. Parker."

She lifted her hands to cup my face, green eyes bright. "I'll make it up to you."

I smiled again, and turned to the door. I opened it as quietly as I could, and when it began to open, I heard voices. MJ touched my hand, silently telling me to wait and let her listen.

"Is not so much that I am stupid," the Rhino was rumbling. "But I do not think well on my feet. I try to plan ahead, da? To be careful. But he always makes all plans fall apart."

"Believe you me," Felicia answered, "I know exactly what you mean."

"Is maddening. Someday I will beat him, my way."

"Yeah?" Felicia asked. "Even after tonight?"

The Rhino paused before saying, "He is man of honor. Maybe I have more respect for him. But I must beat him. I *will* beat him."

"You're more alike than you realize," she told him. "I've read the files on you. I know why you volunteered for the procedures for the armor, the enhanced strength."

The Rhino grunted.

"I'm just saying, I understand your motivations. He would, too."

"Maybe you are right. It changes nothing."

"Why not?" Felicia asked.

"Because of what I am," he said. "A mercenary. A criminal. An enemy to him and those like him."

"So far," Felicia argued. "What's to say that the future can't be different?"

There was a silence so long that I thought maybe the Rhino had fallen asleep. But then he said, "Is too late for me."

"Why?"

"Because of what I have done. The alliances I have made, the mistakes I have made. There is no going back."

Felicia exhaled slowly and said, "What about your family? Do they think that?"

The Rhino's voice gained a faint edge of bitterness. "When they hear I am criminal, they disown me. My brothers and sisters hang up phones when I call. My mother sends back all my mail unopened."

"It's never too late, Aleksei," Felicia said. "My past isn't exactly white as the driven snow. But I turned things around."

"Your past had less blood in it. I have made enemies, and I owe too much to some of my allies," the Rhino replied. "Money. Favors. I try to leave now, I will not survive it." The couch creaked. Maybe he had shrugged. "I am a man who pays his debts. Besides. I have nothing else to do. Nowhere else to go."

Mary Jane pushed the door silently shut, frowning.

"What?" I asked her.

"I'm not sure," she said. "There's something about his attitude . . . I feel like I should be understanding something about him, but it's eluding me."

"Ah," I said. "Yes. Nothing is so subtle as the elusive Rhino."

She stuck her tongue out at me. "I'll think of it sooner or later." She frowned. "The poor man. He made himself into a criminal to try to provide for his family and bring them to the States—and he lost them because of it."

"Yeah. Breathe in the irony." I frowned and said, "Must have been tough to live through."

"Ready?" my wife asked me.

"Yeah," I said. "Let's do it." Then I opened the door and walked out into the living room. "Morning," I said to Felicia. "Rhino."

"Spider-Man," he replied with a nod. His ravaged face was no longer swollen, though there were still heavy welts and marks, and the way the skin was flaking off was none too pretty. Still, he was visibly less damaged than only a few hours before, and it was possible that the cataracts on his eyes were not as densely white as they had been. He also looked more relaxed. He must have been in a lot of pain earlier that night; he'd endured it long enough to allow him to sleep. He took a sip from a small silver flask, and then passed it back to Felicia, who sat in Aunt May's armchair.

"Tell me you're sober," I said to Felicia.

"Sober enough to know how crazy this is," she replied, taking another hit off the flask. "Mellow enough not to mind."

"As long as you don't throw up on me. You ready?"

"Yes," Felicia said, standing.

"Da," Aleksei said, rising.

"Whoa," I said. "Who said anything about you going, Rhino?"

"I did," he said. "Just now."

I sighed. "Ladies. Could you excuse us for a minute, please?"

The Black Cat narrowed her eyes for a moment—but then glanced at MJ, waiting for her response.

Mary Jane nodded at her and said, "Sure." The two of them withdrew down the little hall to the bedroom.

"There is something you wish to say?" the Rhino rumbled.

I picked up a cork coaster, and flicked it at him. It bounced off his face. The Rhino scowled and rubbed a finger on his nose.

"You're blind," I said, my tone frank. "And even if you weren't, there's a big difference between calling a cease-fire and believing you've got my back."

"The Black Cat told me what you have learned about the Ancients, and your plan," the Rhino said. "I wish to help."

"I'll say it again: You're blind. You'd do more harm than good."

"Perhaps not," he said.

"Oh?"

"I cannot see," he rumbled. "But I do not need to see to serve as your decoy."

I lifted my eyebrows, surprised into a brief silence.

The Rhino's ugly mug slid into a grim smile.

"You'd be willing to do that?" I asked him quietly.

"Da."

"Why?"

"If the Ancients kill you," he said, "I will be their next meal. There is better chance for survival in cooperation."

"That's not what I meant, exactly," I said. "You'd be running a huge risk. If an Ancient starts in on you, there's no guarantee we'll be able to get to you in time. Even if we do, if my hypothesis is flawed you could die anyway." I snorted. "For that matter, how do you know that I won't just let you get eaten?"

"Because you already didn't," the Rhino pointed out.

I folded my arms, frowning. "You're willing to trust me to save your life?"

"You are Spider-Man," he said, as if the phrase embodied some kind of answer.

"What's that supposed to mean?"

He let out a caustic little laugh. "Of course. You cannot see it. Or you would not be who you are."

"Um. What?" I asked.

"Give me your word," he said. "That if I do this thing for you, you will do your best to save my life. Not that you will. Just that you will try."

"I will," I told him.

"That is enough," he said. *Tempus fugit.*

"It is," I said, thoughtful. "Be right back."

I went down the hallway to the bedroom and opened the door. Felicia and Mary Jane were sitting on the edge of the bed together, hugging. Felicia looked . . . absolutely awkward. She wasn't the sort who'd had a lot of girly friends.

"You know," I drawled. "It's not just every husband who would walk in on this and be patient and understanding instead of leaping to conclusions." I leaned on the door frame. "Carry on."

They broke the hug, gave each other a glance, then in practically a single voice said, "Men are pigs."

I beamed. "I figured putting the two of you in one room might get you to talk. Or start a fight. I'm not sure which one I was rooting for."

My spider sense warned me about the incoming pillow as Mary Jane threw it, but I let it bounce off my face.

Felicia folded her arms, too dignified to fling objects at me. "Well?"

"Well what?"

She arched a brow and then glanced pointedly past me.

"Oh. Cat . . . I've worked with you before," I said quietly. "But him . . ."

"Come on, Spidey," the Black Cat teased. "Who *haven't* you teamed up with at one time or another?"

"That doesn't mean I enjoy it."

"Why wouldn't you?" she asked.

I grunted and muttered under my breath.

"I'm sorry. What was that?" Felicia asked.

"I said, there's a reason it's 'the Amazing Spider-Man,' and not 'Spider-Man and His Amazing Friends.'" I shook my head. "You know that if I had a choice, I'd be doing this alone."

"But you don't have a choice," Mary Jane said quietly. "Thank God."

I sighed. "MJ . . ."

"I know." She sighed. "You're a great big he-man and you don't need anyone. Been working on your own for years. But I worry about you being alone out there, because I'm your wife and that's what I do. I'm glad Felicia is going to be there. And if our guest can help, too, more power to him. You should take all the help you can get."

Felicia's expression sobered. "Believe me, I know what you're feeling. I don't play well with others, either. But Aleksei's got a point. If we can use him as our stalking horse, it will leave the two of us to handle the two Ancients who are still focused. I can try to distract those two while you finish off whichever one is taking a bite."

"Simple, eh?"

Felicia nodded. "That's the idea. Take one down, rinse, and repeat."

I took a deep breath, and released it slowly, thinking it over. Sure, the plan sounded swell—well, sweller than doing it with just me and the Cat, anyway—but I wasn't entirely convinced that the Rhino wouldn't be nearly as dangerous to Felicia and me as he would be to the Ancients. On the other hand, I didn't think I could manage to get myself into all that much more danger even if I tried. I still would have preferred to be the only one at risk.

And I suddenly felt like an arrogant high school basketball prodigy, too young and foolish to realize that no one can do everything alone.

That realization sparked another idea—a way to minimize the risk the Rhino's undisciplined strength presented, and to further use the Ancients' own natures, their confidence and their arrogance, against them.

"Okay," I said, feeling newly confident, and raised my voice. "You're on the team, Aleksei."

His expression grew pained. "Please," he called back. "Rhino. From you, Rhino."

I grinned, heading for the living room, beckoning MJ and Felicia to follow me. "Okay, Rhino. We're short on time, so huddle up. Here's the plan."

TWENTY FOUR

THE murky light of predawn fell on the auto yard. Colors were washed out to various shades of blue, darkening to perfect black. The streetlights nearby were mostly broken, but where they were on, they added the occasional shaft of yellowish light. The low light softened edges and deepened shadows. It made the stacks of crushed cars and mounds of discarded parts look positively alien, and the mounds and mounds of deceased vehicles created an oxidized labyrinth. The place smelled like rust and rot and old motor oil. Pools of liquid rippled under a ghostly wind, and the light reflecting from them danced through too many colors for them to be puddles of water.

The whole place was on a long lot, behind a high fence. It was maybe a hundred yards in length, maybe half as wide. About the size of a football field, in fact. Maybe that was just a coincidence. But then again, maybe Mortia picked it for that exact reason—to tell me that I was simply a game to her.

If so, that was all right. I can play games, too.

Two features in the yard stood out: first, an enormous industrial machine, one of those dinosaur-sized hydraulic car-crushing gadgets. The other, not far from the entry gate, was a small and run-down building with the word "Office" painted on the door. A small and dilapidated mechanics' garage was attached to the building.

My spider sense started twitching when I was a block away from the junkyard. By the time I actually swung over the fence to land high atop the car crusher, it was screaming at maximum volume. The Ancients were there ahead of me.

I remained in place for another two minutes, just to be punctual, and then called out, "Mortia! Thanis! Malos! It's on!"

The three of them appeared from the interior of the run-down garage, their pale faces visible first, so that they gave the appearance of three skulls drifting toward me. Eventually, they came out enough for me to see that once again, they had all come in pseudo-formal attire. It made sense, I supposed. MJ and I dress up a little when we plan on a nice dinner, too.

Mortia stopped a step ahead of her brothers, smiling up at me. "Ah. I am glad that you saw reason."

"I'm a reasonable guy," I said. "Which is why I have a proposal for you."

She tilted her head to one side. "Oh?"

"A trade," I said. "I looked it up and it turns out that Spider-Men my size only make a decent meal for two, not three, and that I'm full of carbs and bad cholesterol. I thought I might be able to arrange something healthier and more profitable."

And with that, I pulled the Rhino, once again bound limply into a cocoon of webbing, off of the papoose-style carry on my back, and began lowering him to the ground. "I figure this ought to stick to your ribs better than me. I'm all string and gristle."

Mortia touched a forefinger to her chin, a pensive gesture. "And why would you offer such a thing?" she asked.

"Because I'm not an idiot," I said. "What happened with Morlun was a fluke. I'm never going to be able to survive the three of you."

Mortia gestured at the Rhino. "Yet it is a poor gift you offer. We can take him at will."

"Think of him as a down payment," I said. "I can set you up with all kinds of totemistic super folk. I can point you to a Lizard, an Octopus, a Vulture, a Scorpion, a Sabretooth—oh, and Serpents. There's so many of them that they formed their own society."

"You would doom others of your ilk to preserve your own life? It seems uncharacteristic of your behavior."

"They're all enemies," I said. "Criminals, thugs, and good riddance to them. I can't beat you, but I *do* want to survive. It's an acceptable compromise from which both of us profit."

Mortia turned and looked at each of her brothers in silence. They returned an equally placid, inhuman gaze. Then she turned back to me and said, "Lower the brute."

My mouth felt a little bit dry. "Here we go," I whispered. "All set?"

"*Da,*" the Rhino whispered.

I lowered him slowly, steadily to the ground. Mortia and her brothers walked over and stood there in their little formation as the Rhino sank to the ground at Mortia's feet.

She regarded the Rhino with hooded eyes, then looked up at me.

"Do we have a deal?" I called.

Mortia's sharklike smile returned, and she murmured, "Arrogant worm. Kill them both."

Let the games begin.

"You're going to wish you hadn't said that," I predicted.

She regarded me with scorn. "Why?"

"Because even a blind man can find you when you yammer on like that."

The Rhino ripped out of the cocoon as if it had been made of tissue paper—and parts of it were—and seized Mortia by the ankle. Then he grunted, rolled, and threw her.

Here's a business secret not everyone knows: Super strength, after you get to a certain point, suffers from a case of diminishing returns, especially in combat. That's just physics, old Sir Isaac rearing his oversized melon. When you lift something heavy, you're pushing up at it, but it's pushing *down* at you, and through you to the earth. That downward force eventually gets to the point where it starts forcing your feet into the ground.

Sure, the Hulk can free-lift better than a hundred tons, but when that much weight is pushing down on a relatively small area—like his feet—it tends to drive them down like tent stakes. (Not to mention that there just aren't all that many hundred-ton objects that won't fall apart under the stress of their own weight when lifted.) Similarly, the Thing can throw a big punch at a brick wall, but if he uses too much of his strength, the impact of the blow will shove against him, pushing his feet across the floor or even throwing him backward. He has to brace himself if he's really going all-out.

(Which is one reason I've done pretty well in slugfests against guys a lot bigger and stronger than me, by the way—my feet *always* hold on to the ground, or wall, or whatever, allowing my punches to be delivered far more efficiently than those of most of the powerhouses.)

Anyway, once you get into the heavyweight division of super strength, the differences are kind of academic, and they only really stand out in a couple of different areas.

Ripping an object apart between your hands is one of them. It's isometric. Throwing things is another.

The Rhino can trade punches with the Hulk. He can flip an Abrams main battle tank with one hand. And, apparently, he can throw gothed-out brunettes halfway to Jersey.

Mortia shrieked and flew out of the junkyard like a cruise missile in a red cravat. She clipped the edge of a ten-story building a block away, sending up a cloud of dust and a spray of shattered bits of masonry. The impact didn't even slow her flight down. She just kept on going, tumbling end over end, over the nearest buildings and out of sight, screaming in feral rage all the way. The scream faded into the distance.

For a second, the remaining Ancients were stone-still in surprise, and it was time enough for the Rhino to come to his feet in a fighting crouch, arms spread. He might have looked intimidating if he hadn't been facing approximately ninety degrees to the left of his foes.

Malos moved, quick and certain, his body darting for the Rhino, dropping, spinning, so that he kicked the big man's legs out from under him. The Rhino had far too much of a mass advantage on the Ancient. Malos's kick was viciously strong, but he wasn't properly braced to transfer enough of that strength into upsetting the Rhino's balance, and all he was able to do was kick the Rhino in the ankle hard enough to annoy the big guy.

The Rhino kicked him back. It was a blind kick, and didn't land with full force, but it was still strong enough to send Malos flying into a half-stripped old pickup truck, slamming him through the safety glass to a painful impact with the steering wheel and dashboard.

We had to work fast. The Rhino had taken Mortia out of the equation, at least for a little while. I had no idea how far he'd actually thrown her, but if she didn't hit something solid, wind resistance would slow her down eventually—say, within half a mile. Then she'd land and head back. Given how fast I'd seen her move, we had maybe a minute to take out at least one of the other Ancients; ninety seconds, tops.

That made me eager to mix it up as soon as I possibly could—but that wasn't the plan. We had to see if my theory was correct, and to do that I had to let them start on the Rhino. So I clenched my hands into fists and waited.

Thanis closed on the Rhino in perfect silence, and as a result slammed his first couple of hits in without opposition. Hits like that probably would have broken my neck. The Rhino just grunted at the first, and was a savvy enough brawler to roll with the second. He swiped one huge hand in an arch and got lucky, more or less. The blow landed, and Thanis staggered back a pair of steps.

Great. Of all the times to have a great opening round, the Rhino picks *now,* when he's supposed to be *losing.* At this rate, he'd probably rough them up just long enough for Mortia to return. I debated tripping him or something. It wouldn't be like I was trying to get him killed. I would just be sticking to the plan, which was everyone's best chance of survival.

As it turned out, I didn't need to do it. Malos came back into the fight with a vengeance, literally seizing the Rhino by the horn and sweeping him up and over to slam the big guy's back onto the ground with earth-shaking force. The impact stunned the Rhino. Malos stepped forward and, with brutal efficiency, stomped a heel down on the Rhino's head, a motion similar to that of a man crushing an empty can of beer. The Rhino's thick skull withstood the impact (of course) but the sheer power of it drove his skull six inches down into the gravel and mud of the junkyard's ground, and it seemed to daze him even more thoroughly.

"Take him," Malos snarled, and lifted his eyes to me.

Thanis bared his teeth in a nasty smile, lifted a hand, fingers spread, and then drove it flat against the Rhino's chest, where another burst of sickly light flared out between his fingers. The Rhino screamed again, and the sound sent a surge of adrenaline and rage through me.

I went into a swan dive, aiming for the Ancient kneeling over the Rhino. As I expected, Malos threw himself in the way, leaping up to meet me in the air. I folded into a roll and, as the Ancient met me, brought both heels into a lashing kick that tagged him squarely on the forehead and killed both his momentum and mine. We dropped the last fifteen feet or so to the ground and landed ten feet apart, facing one another over one of the chemical-spill puddles of various auto fluids.

On the way down, I hit the top tire of a stack behind me with a short webline, and used the elasticity of the line and my own strength to fastball it into Malos's chest. The blow knocked him back—because super strength doesn't mean you suddenly have more mass. Malos might have checked in at around two hundred and fifty pounds, and the tire hit him hard enough to take him off his feet and dump him onto his butt. Best of all, the old tire had been half-full of stagnant water, and it splashed all over his fancy clothes. He looked up and directed a snarl of hatred in my direction.

"Welcome to New York, chump," I said. Then I bounded up onto the tire stack, and from there went over a twelve-foot-high wall made of crushed cars.

Malos let out an angry snarl and chased me. He came sprinting around the corner, focused entirely on my red and blue costume, intent on catching up to me and neutralizing me before I could take a swing at his brother.

Of course, if I had been *in* the costume he was chasing, it probably would have worked better.

Instead, I hopped up to a shadowy section of the wall of cars and froze, while Felicia bounded through the predawn dimness in my backup costume. In better light, or if she'd been still, there would have been no way anyone with eyes would have mistaken her for me—but wouldn't the Ancients have thought of that kind of thing before they set up the time and place for the showdown?

Malos ripped free a heavy mirror that had somehow survived its parent truck's crushing, and flung it after Felicia. The Black Cat dodged it with contemptuous grace, cleared the wall of cars, and hit the car crusher with her grappling line, then retracted it, hurtling through the air as it pulled her, just ahead of the enraged Ancient, leading him away from the Rhino.

I went back over the wall and flung myself at Thanis. Once upon a time, I probably would have said something cute to make him turn around before I hit him, but wasting time on such a thing in this kind of fight could get me killed.

That said, though, I'm freaking Spider-Man.

"Warning!" I shouted. Thanis blinked and half-turned his head, just in time for me to lay a haymaker directly across his jaw. He flew back from the Rhino and slammed into the side of a junked school bus, and I followed right on his heels. "The surgeon general has determined that attempting to eat the Rhino may result in unanticipated side effects." He bounced off the bus and ran into my fist. I heard teeth break, and felt a rush of furious satisfaction. "Including but not limited to dental problems." I gave him a double-handed sledgehammer blow to the guts. "Nausea." I sent a flurry of jabs at his head, pretending it was a speed bag, and bounced his skull off the bus maybe fifty times in seven or eight seconds. "Headache."

Thanis wobbled forward, his eyes gone glassy, his face broken, bleeding, swelling. He could barely keep his feet. "And," I said, drawing back. "Drowsiness."

It's rare for me to go all-out, but I hit the jerk with every fiber of my body and sent him clear *through* the bus's metal siding.

The bus rocked a time or two, but the Ancient did not arise. He lay sprawled and motionless inside.

Not bad. Maybe it wasn't as impressive as a Rhino-strong blow, but for a guy who weighs in at one sixty-five, it was a pretty good hit. Even better, my hypothesis had been proven. Thanis had indeed been vulnerable as he fed.

"Don't let me down, Doc," I muttered, and flicked one of the three Alhambran agates at the downed Ancient.

There was a whisper of sound, no louder or stranger than that of a door sliding closed, and Thanis—and the agate—vanished. Gone. Poof. Just like . . . well. Magic.

Hot diggity dang, it worked!

I threw myself over to the Rhino's side. He lay on the ground, his breathing labored. "Aleksei," I said. "You all right?"

"I," he wheezed, "think I do not like these Ancients. Did it work?"

"Yeah. One down. Can you move?"

He shuddered, and after a second I realized that he was trying to get in a sitting position. He gave up with a groan. "It would seem not."

"Okay," I said. "I'll get you out of here."

"No!" he wheezed. "You must finish them before they realize the danger. You may never get a second chance like this one."

"I can't just leave you here. Mortia won't be gone long, and she'll be angry."

The Rhino growled, and swiped an arm weakly at me. It was an improvement, of sorts. "Will be fine in a moment," he said, glaring in my direction. "Now, you must fight. You are using your wits. Speed. They have only strength. And they do not know the danger they are in. This is your kind of battle, Bug Boy. Take it to them."

"Bug Boy?" I said, and felt myself grinning.

"Spidey!" called Felicia's voice from the other end of the junkyard. "I lost him! He's heading back to you!"

A vise-clamp settled on the back of my neck, and bounced my head off the nearest car. Which was twenty feet away. It hurt.

An undetermined amount of time later, I managed to sit up, only to find Malos standing over me. He leaned down and grabbed the front of my costume, hauling me to his level. "You forget that you touched me," he said in a quiet voice. "It struck me that while I seemed to be pursuing you, my sense of your presence told me that you were, in fact, behind me. A clever enough ruse, little spider. But your bag of tricks is now empty."

My spider sense's terror-reaction was nothing to that of my mind, as I scrambled to gather up my wits and try to defend myself.

I was too slow, the blow to my head too severe. Malos held me high off the ground with one hand, made a talon of the other, and his fingers suddenly dug into my abdomen.

Pain.

Pain.

Pain.

White hot. Ice cold. Nauseating. Terrifying. My senses were overloaded, the pain something that somehow gained sound and taste, color and texture and scent. The pain was as fundamental, solid, and real as I was—in fact, more so. I tried to scream, but the pain had priority on reality, and no sound came out. This was worse than what Morlun had tried to do. He'd barely touched me for a second. This went on for an eternity, and mixed itself with a horrible sensation of something being *ripped* out of me, like someone had shoved a blender into my belly and turned it to puree.

Somewhere behind the pain I could dimly sense the real world, but it was disconnected and unimportant, a shadow play being performed far away. I saw it all through a hallucinogenic haze. Saw myself running atop a wall of crushed steel. Saw myself take off my mask and become Felicia. Saw her look up at the power lines passing by on the street, saw her raise her baton, saw a thin black line extrude from it as the hook arched up and up, sailed over the power lines, and then fell—onto Malos.

The Ancient's expression was quite calm—except for the maddened frenzy of hunger dancing in his eyes—and he paid the shadow-play world no mind. But his expression turned to shock and sudden agony as the Black Cat's line touched him and electricity from the power cables surged through to him.

I felt it, too. It hurt, but not necessarily in a bad way. The burning tingle was an honest pain, a real-world pain, not the nightmare agony of the feeding Ancient. I felt my body contort along with Malos's—and then the agony was gone and I was in my body again, burned and breathless and utterly exhausted.

I lifted my head enough to see Malos stirring, attempting to rise. I had to get on him right away, knock him out before he gathered his wits and focused his power into his defenses. I managed to wobble upright. Then I staggered over to him and kicked him in the chops. The blow was weak, and it knocked me down, but it got the job done. He fell to the ground in a pile of loose limbs beside me.

I fumbled out the second agate and flicked it at his nose. It missed and struck his cheek, but once more, without a flicker of showy lights, with barely more than a whisper of sound, the Ancient simply vanished.

I heard Felicia come running toward me. "Spidey?"

"Mmm, fine," I slurred. "Jusht ducky." I started to stand up and staggered again.

Felicia had to catch me. "Is that all of them?"

"Two," I managed to say. "We got two."

"What about Mortia?" Felicia hissed, looking around.

She turned her face directly into a blindingly swift blow. The Black Cat went straight down, body gone instantly and entirely limp—unconscious or dead.

Mortia, her dark clothes and hair soaked from her landing in the river, looked coldly down at Felicia for a moment. "Don't worry, darling," she purred. "I'm sure she'll turn up."

TWENTY FIVE

I managed to keep my feet and throw a punch. It wasn't a fast punch or a strong punch, but it was the best I could do.

It wasn't good enough. Mortia slapped it aside, seized me, slammed me into the same car her brother had not two minutes before, and then threw me through the air to land near the Rhino.

"Quite the interesting morsel you are," she murmured, regarding me with amused eyes.

I counted birdies and stars. At least she'd hit the *other* side of my head. That way, my brain could be equally bruised on both sides. The agony of the Ancient's devouring touch was fading as my heart kept on beating, and I felt some of my balance returning.

Mortia flicked a bit of debris from her sleeve. "But all things in their due course, trickster. First, the tart little aperitif."

With that, she turned and walked deliberately toward Felicia.

At which point I found myself suddenly angry enough to chew barbed wire and spit nails. I'll say this for the bad guys: Just when they pound me the worst, they have this ongoing tendency to provide me with oodles of motivation.

So I motivated Mortia right through a mound of scrap metal by way of saying thanks.

She came out on the other side furious, her jacket and pants in tatters. The steel had torn the expensive clothing to rags, though it hadn't broken her pale flesh. "Do you have any idea," she snarled, "how difficult it will be to replace this outfit?"

"You're one to talk!" I shot back. "At least you can get someone *else* to make yours!"

She came at me hard and fast, leaping from the ground to propel herself off the fence around the yard and straight at me.

This time there was no dodging, no webs, no tricks. I stepped forward to meet her and swatted her out of the air with a punch that killed her momentum cold. She bounced back from it with a spinning kick imported straight from Hong Kong that nearly took my head off. I managed to get away from it with nothing worse than a chipped tooth, but was reminded that I couldn't fight stupid against Mortia. She was too fast.

I ducked a second whirling kick, knocked her ankle out from underneath her with one leg, and got in a good stomp on her stomach, but then she drove her knuckles against the side of one of my knees, forcing me to hop away before I got knocked to the ground. After that, she came in close and brought a lot of hard, vicious, swift punches with her, throwing everything from less than a foot away, and all of it aimed at my eyes and nose and neck—Wing Chun, I think it's called. She'd had formal training somewhere.

I'd done all my learning in the school of hard knocks, and even if I don't have a pretty martial arts sheepskin, I can get the job done. I did a lot of bobbing and weaving, more boxing technique than anything else, spoiling the occasional blow with a quick slap of one hand. We closed and struck and counter-struck and parted a couple of times, each exchange several seconds long.

Whether it was the formal technique or just her sheer weight of experience and untiring speed, I missed a beat and took a chop to the side of the neck, followed by a stiff blow from the heel of her hand to the tip of my jaw that snapped my head back in a sudden whiplash.

I barely blocked a haymaker of an uppercut, and in a single motion splashed a blob of webbing into Mortia's face and followed up with a hard, driving strike with the same hand. I caught her on the forehead and knocked her tail-over-teakettle into one of the toxic-looking pools of the junkyard's liquid refuse.

She rose from the pool, her pale eyes cold and angry.

"There's something on your face," I told her.

She only stared at me with that intense, alien stare, and replied, "You're getting tired. You're slowing down." She prowled around the little pool toward me. The top of her head never changed height as she walked; you could have balanced marbles on it. Her eyes, similarly, never varied in height above the ground, just floating along, wide and intent. It was extremely graceful in an insectlike way, and highly creepy.

Especially because she was right. This wasn't going to be like my fight with Morlun. With him, even after I'd gotten tired, I had still been a lot faster than he was. With Mortia, I'd barely had an advantage when I was fresh, if I'd had one at all. As fast as she moved, it would not take much fatigue to slow me down enough to be overwhelmed by her sheer speed.

"Tired, mortal," Mortia murmured. "It's almost over. You can't avoid me for very much longer."

"Maybe not," I said. "But at least *my* outfit's still clean."

I guess she expected more whimpering and pleading, because my reply clearly enraged her. She came at me like she intended to tear my head off, and it was suddenly all I could do to stay alive.

The fight got blurry after that. I had no frame of reference for time. Every move she made came at me too quickly to see, and at the same time it seemed to take forever, if not longer. I remember landing a couple of good ones, and shrugging off a lot of lighter blows—a whole lot of them. She wasn't trying to KO me. All she wanted was to continue to inflict pain through smaller, repeated blows, to grind down my endurance.

It must have worked. I saw bloody knuckles rush at my face—her knuckles, my blood—and then a flash of white light.

After that, I stared up at the slowly brightening sky, which looked like it was getting ready to turn into a pretty day, and wondered why I wasn't back home in bed with MJ.

"My brothers are gone," she said. Her voice echoed and rang oddly, as if coming to me down a long tunnel. "Which I admit is mildly disturbing, but probably inevitable." She picked me up and threw me into a heavy beam supporting the structure of the car crusher. I struck sideways across the small of my back, and heard things crackle when I hit.

"They were always incautious, you see. Impatient. Once they saw the prey, they could only pursue it, devour it." She paused over the weakly stirring Rhino and crushed her heel down upon his head in several vicious kicks as she spoke in a conversational tone. "Ultimately, of course, I would have had to kill them. The world will not bear the strain of feeding even the few of our kind who remain, in the next several thousand years. As the source drains from this world, fewer and fewer of your kind appear, spider. And subsisting on lesser beings"—here, she paused to step over the unmoving Felicia—"is simply no way to live."

I got up and hit the car crusher with a webline near the top, using my left hand, intending to jump and swing and get some distance from Mortia. I was moving too slowly, though, too weakly.

"All in all," she said, "I suppose I should be thanking you, in some ways." She seized my left arm, and with a squeeze and a twist she snapped the webline—and broke my wrist. I felt and heard my bones cracking under her viselike fingers.

Fiery pain took away whatever strength was left to me, and I fell to my knees.

"Yet," she continued in the same conversational tone, "they were family. Companions over the empty years. They would have amused me, somewhat, until I had to kill them." She threw me with both hands— she wasn't as strong as Malos had been, but was at least as strong as I. I slammed into the mechanics' garage and left a deep dent in the rusty corrugated sheet metal that passed for its walls.

It hurt. A lot.

"Your struggle has been useless, of course," she said. She kicked my ribs several times, and all I could do about it was to try to exhale when her foot impacted me. It hurt even more. I'd have been screaming about it if I'd been able to get a breath. I'd have been running away if I could have managed to stand. "That's the way of the world, spider. Predators and prey. Your fall was inevitable. But the tricksters are always the most interesting hunts. Certainly more so than the brutes."

I tried crawling away, around the office building and garage. I dimly remembered that the chain-link gates had been there.

She picked me up with one arm and slammed me into the office building. I could see the gates, see the street outside through the chain links. It wasn't thirty feet away—but I'd never reach it.

"Truth be told," Mortia purred, her voice growing deeper, huskier, "the brute will make a more than acceptable meal. But you will taste simply divine. A spirit such as yours will be most rich; most delightful."

She idly ripped off the front of my costume, and pressed a kiss against my chest. Flickering sparkles appeared in my vision, and the nauseating pain of the Ancient's hunger brushed against me for a minute.

Mortia looked up, licked her lips, and shivered. "But your passing need not be agony. I can take you gently. Peacefully. It will be like falling asleep in my arms." Her eyes brightened. "All you need do is ask me to be merciful." She pinned me to the wall with one hand, looking up at me with the same horrible hunger I'd seen in the eyes of Morlun and Malos, just before they fed. "Beg, spider."

So this was it.

Huh. I hadn't really figured today would be the day.

But then, who does? Am I right? You never really wake up and think that it's your last day on this rock.

She leaned closer, almost close enough to kiss me. "Beg, spider."

I swallowed and faced her, no longer attempting to struggle or escape. I was through. No one was left to attack her when she fed. I was alone. I was going to die alone. But I'd taken down three out of four, and I hadn't abandoned anyone doing it. Not bad. Not bad.

"I have seen gods and demons at war," I told her, my voice hoarse. "I have seen worlds created and destroyed. I have fought battles on planets so far from Earth that the light from their stars has never reached us. I have seen good men die. I have seen evil men prosper, and I have seen scales balanced against all odds. I have seen the strong oppress the weak, the law protect criminals instead of citizens. I have fought with others and alone against every kind of enemy you can imagine, against every kind of injustice you can imagine." I met her eyes and said, quietly and unafraid, "And because of what you are, Mortia, you will never understand why."

She tilted my head, staring at me as though puzzled, the way someone might regard a talking lobster being held above the pot.

"In all that time," I said, my voice growing weaker, "I have never surrendered." And all the defiance I had left in me rose—too weak to stir my limbs, but giving my voice a hard, hot, edge of anger. "I will never beg you for anything. So you'd better stop flapping your stupid mouth and kill me. Or so help me God, I will destroy you just like I did your brothers."

Those cold, alien eyes grew colder. "Very well," she said, her voice low, throbbing with excitement. "Then you will feel every second. May you live long enough for the pain to drive you mad."

Her hand slammed flat to my bared chest.

My world *drowned* in pain. This time, as she began ripping at me, I wasn't even strong enough to writhe.

The shadow play of the world went on in the background.

I saw a bright white light, from far away, begin to rush closer. And closer. And closer.

A roaring sound began, and I thought to myself that heaven needed to get itself a new muffler.

The shadow play rolled on, and what I saw there sent hope pouring through me again, one last surge of defiance that I had never imagined could have survived what the Ancients had done to me. It gave me one last tired wave of awareness, one last weak and weary burst of motion. I managed to twist my body enough to get my feet onto the wall of the junkyard office, then walked them sideways and up, until they were level with my head.

Mortia let out a flushed, ecstatic laugh at this last, tiny defiance, as she ripped into me.

And then Mary Jane's rusty, lime-green Gremlin blew through the junkyard's chain-link gates at seventy or eighty miles an hour and smashed into Mortia and the office building, ripping her hands away from me as the car's hood went entirely through the wall beneath me, taking Mortia with it.

The Gremlin's engine surged. Smoke and steam were coming from under the hood, but it backed out of the hole it had pounded in the office wall, and then crunched to a stop. Mary Jane got out, wearing her jeans, a sweater, and leather driving gloves. She opened the trunk, her expression focused and smooth, though her hands were visibly trembling, and emerged with a tire iron.

Mortia staggered out of the wreckage, bloodied, one of her arms smashed beyond recognition, one of her legs obviously broken. Dust clung to her damp clothing and hair, and her expression was dazed, almost childishly confused.

Mary Jane walked to face the battered Ancient, eyes narrowed, and tapped the tire iron against her palm.

Mortia stared at her, dumbfounded. "Who . . . who are you?"

"That which hath made them drunk hath made me bold," Mary Jane quoted. And delivered a two-handed blow with the tire iron. Mortia staggered. My wife's voice, full of fury, rang out in the predawn air as she swung again. "What hath quench'd them hath given me fire."

She struck the Ancient on the head, and Mortia fell senseless to the ground.

Mary Jane snarled at the fallen Ancient and spat, "What's done is done."

"MJ," I croaked. I fumbled at my left hand with my right, where I'd stuck the last agate to my glove with a bit of webbing, and passed it to her.

She took it with a nod, knelt down, and after a second of consideration, shoved the stone hard into Mortia's ear.

The last Ancient vanished, and Mary Jane stood up. She stared at her tire iron for a moment, then at the car, and then she came to me. I more or less dropped off the wall, and she crouched down to wrap her arms around me. Compared to the last hellish minutes, her touch was pure heaven.

"Thanks," I told her, and meant it.

She shivered and cried a little. Then she pressed a fierce kiss against my head and whispered, "I love you."

I smiled at her. "You," I croaked, "are going to make one heck of a Lady Macbeth."

TWENTY SIX

I don't know how we would have gotten Aleksei home if Wong hadn't driven up in a heavy-duty pickup.

He just pulled up without a word, lowered the tailgate, and wheeled out a hand truck. I wasn't in terribly good shape, but I was able to web up the Rhino—again—and attach him to the hand truck. Getting him into the back of the pickup was another issue with one arm out of commission, but with Wong's help I managed it. Wong isn't big, but he's wiry. Not wiry like me, but stronger than he looks. I was still kind of unsteady on my feet, though, and Wong and MJ moved Felicia themselves.

Wong drove us to Strange's place, and MJ followed in her now-wheezing car. No one seemed to take any notice of us. Granted, it was sunrise on a Sunday, but even so no one seemed to actually make eye contact with the vehicles or any of their occupants. Maybe Strange had done some of that voodoo that he do so well. Or maybe it was just because we were in New York. It would take something a lot weirder than a cocooned bruiser in a Rhino hat, a shirtless Spidey, and a bald Tibetan martial arts expert in a pickup being tailed by a stunning redhead in a crumpled, wheezing lime-green Gremlin to attract attention.

Wong had a pallet ready on the floor of the reception hall, and he put Aleksei on it. He glanced at me, and I pulled the webbing off of him. Felicia rated a cot, and Wong and MJ put her there. Wong examined the large swelling on the side of her head for a few moments, then drew out an old leather valise and opened it, filling the room with the pungent, pleasant fragrance of herbal medicine. He applied a fragrant salve of some kind to her head, another to her neck, and bound a bracelet of some kind of braided plant around her left wrist.

Within minutes, Felicia blinked her eyes open, peered around groggily, and said, "We win?"

"We won," I said.

"Go, us," Felicia mumbled. "You owe me big time, Spider." She then stripped out of my spare costume, staying only more or less covered by the blankets as she did. She sighed in contentment, dumped the clothing on the floor, rolled over, snuggled naked under the blankets, and promptly went to sleep.

Wong looked somewhat startled and uncomfortable at the sight.

I was next to get the herbal treatments. I don't know what Wong has growing in his garden, but his stuff makes Tiger Balm look positively anemic. I had so many bruises that he had to open a second jar, and MJ helped him slather it on me. Then he got to Aleksei, applying medicines to his much-abused face and head.

The pain began to fade, and it was a delicious sensation. I sat there hurting less and breathing deeply despite the twinge in my back and my broken wrist, and loved every minute of it.

Wong got to my wrist, frowned, and left.

He returned with the doc, who settled down next to the chair I was slumped in to examine my wrist.

"A clean break," he said. "I can set this for you, if you like."

"Can't you just fix it, O Sorcerer Supreme?" I said in a whimsical voice. "For you, this is just a bippity-boppity-boo-boo, isn't it?"

Strange arched an eyebrow. "Healing magic is quite complex, and its employ must take into account several and various factors which—"

I winced, though he really couldn't see it through the mask, and interrupted him. "Doc. My head."

His eyes wrinkled at the corners. "No," he said.

"Now was that so hard?" I asked him.

"You've no idea," he said.

"Wong," he said to his servant, "I was looking for my Alhambran agates, and I couldn't find them anywhere. Do you have any idea where they are?"

Wong bowed at the waist. "Abject apologies, my master. I seem to have misplaced them."

"Ah," Strange said. He glanced at me. "It's always the little things you wonder about." He bowed his head to me and said, "Congratulations on your victory. It was well done and well won."

"Thank you for your help," I said.

Strange put a hand over his sternum. "'Help'? I can't imagine what you mean. One ought not confuse my natural concern for your current state of health as partisanship in your recent struggle with the Ancients, which would be against my obligation to maintain a strict balance of mystic forces."

"Oh, right," I said. "Sorry. Thank you for the not-help."

"It was my pleasure not to provide it," he said, his voice warmer. "Let me check on your allies." He circled to Felicia and Aleksei. He lingered longer over the Rhino, murmuring something to Wong, and then returned to me, his expression grave.

"Bad news, Doc?" I asked.

He spread his hands in a noncommittal gesture. "He has taken a terrible beating, and in more than a merely physical sense, but he should recover within the next few days."

"His eyes?" I asked.

"Those too. He seems to be most resilient."

"Yeah," I said. "Annoyingly so."

"You sound as if you do not care for him," Strange said.

"I don't," I said. "Well. I do. I mean, I didn't want him to get killed or anything, but . . ." I shook my head. "I guess it might have been simpler if he had. He's dangerous."

"Dangerous?" Strange asked.

"You've seen him," I said. "What he's capable of."

"True," Strange said. "And I have seen what you are capable of, as well, I might add. You yourself can be most dangerous, Spider-Man. As can I. And Wong. And, apparently, even Mary Jane."

"You aren't going to rampage anyone into the ground, though," I said. "Neither is Wong or Mary Jane. But the Rhino, I'm not so sure about. He's habitual."

"Ah," Strange said.

"I'm the one who saved his life," I said quietly. "Whatever he does with that life in the future, I'm going to share some of the responsibility for it. If he hurts someone. Or kills someone . . ." I shook my head. "How would I live with that? I feel . . . really stupid."

"Do not think the less of yourself for your ignorance. It is a weighty question," Strange said. "Many wise men have struggled to answer it. I am aware of none who have done so."

"Maybe I should do something, then," I said. "Maybe I have a responsibility to try to limit the harm he could do."

"Or the good," Strange said.

I grimaced. "Do you really think he's going to do anything good, Doc?"

"It seems to me that he aided you and the Black Cat only this morning."

I sighed. "Yeah, he did. It's making it hard to figure out what to do."

Strange nodded. "If you like, I shall summon the authorities."

I thought about it for a minute more. Then I shook my head. "No. We had a deal, and he more than lived up to his end. In fact, without him, we would never have been able to pull it off. He's got twenty-four hours before I make any moves."

Strange got an odd little smile and nodded once. "I am glad to see that you are still a man of your word—as he is. Good never came of treachery. It wounds betrayer and betrayed alike."

The conversation—and his offer—had been a test, then. A lesson. Freaking wizards. Strange really needed to get out among the nonmystical crowd more often. Maybe go bowling. Put back a cold one or two. Watch a movie. But he's the Doc. He's pretty much all about the weird wizardly wise man shtick. And he was probably right.

"We just do what seems right," I said.

He nodded. "We're only human."

"Maybe you could do me a favor," I said. "Besides the wrist, I mean. The Rhino, ah . . . maybe it would be better if he woke up here, and you could call him a cab."

"Certainly," Strange said. "I am pleased to be able to offer you more conventional help."

I frowned at the unconscious Rhino for a moment. "How are you at fortune-telling, Doc?"

Strange followed the direction of my stare. "The future of beings like the Ancients is easily seen. They have no true sense of self-determination, you see. They are driven by their needs. Ruled by their impulses and fears." He shook his head. "The future of mortal beings, though, is generally imponderable."

"Stop dancing," I said. "Do you think he can straighten out?"

"He *can,* certainly. Though I sense there would be a very heavy price to be paid—perhaps one which would be too high." Strange shook his head. "The question is will he choose to do so. In the end, his future will depend upon his choices. Just as yours does."

I frowned and nodded. "I suppose I shouldn't expect much."

Strange smiled faintly. "Even should he dare to change his path to run along near your own, I think it would little change his attitude toward you."

"Gee. Why doesn't that shock me," I said.

Strange actually chuckled. "Let's get that wrist straightened out, hmmm?"

Mary Jane leaned into me and murmured, "He *is* a real doctor, right? Not like a doctor of magicology or philosophy or something? He's qualified to do"—Mary Jane glanced at Strange and gave him a very mild, elegantly reproachful look—"something? This time around, anyway?"

Strange blinked at her, then at me, and let out a very brief, very quiet sigh. I savored the moment.

"There," he said, a few uncomfortable minutes later. He had my wrist set, held stiff by layers of wrapped tape. "It's a simple fracture. Leave it for a day or so, and you should be fine, given your own exceptional recuperative capacity."

I sighed. "Thanks, Doc."

He put a hand on my shoulder and squeezed. "Of course. Is there anything else I can do?"

I blinked at him. "You know," I said, "there is. There are two things, actually."

His eyebrows went up.

"Doc," I said. "I assume your doctoring credentials are still good. You know, like, legal?"

"As far as I know," Strange said, his tone cautious. "Why?"

"And do you know if Wong plays basketball?"

"Excuse me?"

"Simple question," I said. "I mean, it's not brain surgery, is it? Does he shoot hoops?"

"I'm . . . actually, I'm not sure," Strange mused.

Somewhere in the background, Wong started whistling "Sweet Georgia Brown."

"Peter," Mary Jane said, smiling at Strange. "I'm sure you shouldn't press the good doctor. After all, he's done so *much* to help you already."

Strange looked helplessly at her and then lifted both hands. "Mercy, lady, I beg you. By all means, Spider-Man, just tell me what I may do."

TWENTY SEVEN

THE gang wasn't loitering around outside of Samuel's apartment at eight o'clock on Monday morning. I guess it isn't exactly gang-hanging prime time. The doc and I took the subway and walked the last couple of blocks. He was wearing fairly normal clothes again, and had added an old bomber jacket to his ensemble, as well as an archetypal doctor's bag. Even in the "civvies," though, he didn't exactly fit in on the street. Strange . . . is. It goes deeper than just mystical mumbo jumbo and Shakespearean wardrobe. It's no one thing I can put my finger on, but Strange never seems to fit in much of anywhere, unless maybe it's in the middle of serious trouble.

It's probably one reason we get along so well.

I cruised up to the Larkins' apartment and knocked. Sounds murmured through the gap beneath the door—children running, talking, laughing, the tinny sound of a television playing one of those seizure-inducing cartoons, and the occasional sound of a strident, confident woman's voice. I heard rushing footsteps and then Samuel's little sister, the one I'd seen wheezing on my first visit, opened the door. She stared up at us for a minute, then slammed it shut. Her footsteps retreated.

A minute or two later, Samuel opened the door.

The big young man glanced from Strange to me, then frowned like a thundercloud. "What."

I made a show of checking my watch. I didn't have one, since my wrist was still all bandaged up, but I didn't let that stand in the way of good drama. "You're late for school, Mister Larkin."

"That's real funny," Samuel said, his glower deepening. "You know the score. Office lady already got me suspended. I ain't there no more."

"Samuel," said the woman's voice. "Who are you being rude to?"

"Nobody good, Mama," Samuel said.

"Look, if you're more than two hours tardy, you aren't going to be eligible to practice tonight. We'd better get a move on."

"You deaf?" Samuel growled.

"Samuel Dewayne!" snapped the woman, and she came to the doorway. She was nearly as tall as her son, her hair was threaded with gray, and she wore a waitress's apron over a gray dress and comfortable shoes. She regarded me and Strange with a wary eye, then asked, "Something I can help you gentlemen with?"

"Hi, Ms. Larkin," I said. "My name is Peter Parker. I teach science at Samuel's school, and I'm temporary coach of the basketball team."

"What do you want with Samuel?"

"Just to get him to school, ma'am," I said. "We're already several minutes late."

She shook her head. "I thought he got suspended."

"Only if he doesn't get his vaccinations up to date," I said. "This is Doctor Stephen Strange. He's agreed to help with that."

Ms. Larkin pressed her lips together. "I don't have the money to pay you for this. You might as well go on."

"There's no charge," I said.

Samuel scowled and lifted his chin—maybe in unconscious mimicry of his mother, who did the same thing. "We don't need charity," she said.

"This isn't charity," I told her. "The doc here is part of a new neighborhood health program some of the action groups have kicked off. He'd have been here in a few more days, anyway, to get your kids looked after—he just started here, as a favor to me."

Strange arched an eyebrow at me, but nodded. "Indeed."

"Mmm-hmm," Ms. Larkin said. She was clearly skeptical, but she didn't push it. Instead, she just glanced at Samuel, as if waiting for him to speak.

Samuel looked from his mother to me and back, biting one lip and clearly uncertain. It made him look like the boy he still was.

"Well?" I told him in my exasperated-coach voice. "What are you waiting for, Larkin? Me to carry you on my back? Let the doc look at you and then let's get to school."

Samuel looked as if he didn't know whether to sneer at me or hug me, but he finally sighed and said, "Yeah, all right."

"If there's time," Strange said, "I can take a look at any of your other children, ma'am, and make sure they're all caught up on their shots."

Ms. Larkin almost smiled. "Well," she said, "if you hurry. I have to drive the rest to school in ten minutes."

"Don't worry," I assured her. "He's the fastest mouse in all Mexico."

"Come in, then," she said. "Come in."

Strange was good to his word, if not precisely popular with the little ones. He diagnosed a burgeoning ear infection and left a bottle of children's antibiotics for it, as well as providing the wheezy little sister with an inhaler after she described what sounded like a fairly heavy asthma attack.

"Samuel," Ms. Larkin said. "Help me get them all in the car, and then you can walk to school with Coach Parker."

"Yes, ma'am," Samuel murmured, and set about doing just that while Strange and I exchanged farewells with Ms. Larkin and left to wait outside.

"A new neighborhood help program?" Strange asked me, once we were alone.

"Brand-new," I said. "You up for it? It isn't glamorous or exciting, and there aren't any demons or super magical powers involved—but you know how hard it is to get good health care these days. Especially for folks like the Larkins. People in this area can use the help you could give them. It's not brain surgery, but it's a *good* cause, Doc."

Strange looked from me, to his medical bag, and then up toward the Larkins' apartment. He let out a long and rather satisfied sigh, the kind of sound I make after I hear a favorite song that hasn't been on the radio in a while, and his eyes wrinkled at the corners. "Why not."

"Yeah," I said, folding my arms in satisfaction. "Why not."

○━━━━━━━━━━○

WONG met me outside the gymnasium after school.

He wore simple gray shorts, a loose gray top, and a gray sweatband around his shaved head. He had worn, simple high-topped basketball shoes on his feet, and held under one arm a standard Wilson basketball so well used that barely any of the pebbling remained on it.

"You any good?" I asked him.

Wong gave me his Wong face and a little bow. "I saw the Globetrotters once when I was young."

"You shouldn't brag so much, Wong," I said.

When we walked in, it was the same as Friday. The team was all over the place, shooting and jawing and goofing off to no end, with Samuel driving himself hard, working out against several teammates.

I blew the whistle. No one even looked at me.

I blew the whistle again, louder. A couple of the kids drifted a few grudging steps toward me.

I sighed. Then I stripped out of my button-down shirt and my pants. I wore a tank top and shorts underneath. I walked over to Samuel and took the ball away.

Maybe I cheated and used my super-duper spider reflexes, just for the hand speed. But it was for the boy's good. I slapped the ball aside when he was in mid-dribble, and bounced it over to Wong.

That got his attention. The gym got quiet, fast.

Samuel turned to loom over me. "Ain't like I don't appreciate your help," he said. "That don't make you Coach Kyle. Give me the ball and get out of the way."

"I decided to take you up on your offer, kid," I said.

His mouth twisted into a white-toothed smile. "Shoot. Half court. We go to ten. You playing with one hand, so I'll spot you six. Then when you lose you can go sit down."

"No," I said. "We play two-on-two. No points spotted."

"What?" he asked.

"Two-on-two," I said, and jerked my head at Wong. "Me and him. You and whoever you like. And when you lose, I run practice the way I'm supposed to, and you go along."

"Don't need whoever I like. Take you both by myself. Don't need anyone else."

"Sure, if you say so," I said. "But I don't want you saying it wasn't fair when you lose."

"Whatever, man," Samuel said after a moment's hesitation. "A-Dog, you up for this?"

"Sure," said the second-tallest kid on the team.

I bounce-passed the ball to Samuel. "You want it first?"

He bounced it back. "Age before beauty, Mister Science."

I nodded to Wong, who came over and nodded pleasantly to the two boys. Everyone else went to the sidelines to watch. I went to the top of the key, passed the ball to Wong, and the game started.

Let me tell you something.

Wong got game.

He blew past A-Dog while he was still flat-footed, faked to one side on Samuel, then rolled around him for an easy basket.

Samuel frowned at Wong and narrowed his eyes.

After that, he got serious. He nearly blocked my next pass to Wong, and was all over him on defense. Wong had more quickness, but not much more, and Samuel's long arms and prodigious talent made up for it. Wong missed his next shot, and Samuel recovered it, took it out, and then drove back in for his own point.

Wong gave Samuel a smile and a little bow and then said, "School's in, Grasshopper."

Wong and I had talked it out earlier. Samuel pressed him again, but Wong passed off to me and I mimed a shot, forcing Samuel to turn to me. Instead, I shot it back to Wong, who went through A-Dog and scored again.

The game went like that, with Samuel getting more and more frustrated, trying harder and harder, his efforts growing almost violent. Every time he pressed one of us, the other was there for an outlet. Neither A-Dog nor Samuel seemed to have a real solid grip on the idea of coordinated effort, and their defense was never quite quick enough to make up the difference. I took a few shots, and made one. Wong did the rest, and I was happy to set him up. I played the harder defense for us. Samuel was too much for Wong to handle, but he rarely passed, and the kid was nowhere near fast enough to get by me. I tried to keep my effort down to just footwork and hand speed, taking the ball from his control whenever he came by.

And somewhere between Wong's seventh basket and his ninth, Samuel got what was happening. He started looking for his partner, passing more, actually working with A-Dog, or at least trying to. It was too little, too late. Final score: Team Spidey 10, Samuel and A-Dog 6.

Samuel was angry about it for maybe a minute. Then he shook his head and snorted, regarding me thoughtfully. "You ain't never played before, huh."

"Not really," I said.

"Where'd you find Little China?"

"Little Tibet," Wong corrected with a small bow.

"Friend of mine," I said.

Samuel grunted. "Guess I lost the bet."

"Guess you did," I said.

He passed me the ball, jerked his head at A-Dog, and then started off, running laps around the gym. The rest of the team followed him. I watched them for a moment. My wrist ached a bit, but I didn't mind. Wong started whistling "Sweet Georgia Brown" again.

"Thanks, Curly," I said quietly.

"You are welcome," Wong replied.

o————————o

I went back home, grabbed a shower, and took the wrapping off my wrist. My hand opened and closed without the same sharp pain I'd felt yesterday, though it was still tender. I didn't want to do any web-swinging or wall-crawling for another day or two, but it could have been a lot worse.

The injuries I'd received weren't life-threatening, but recovering from them always left me hungry. My stomach started growling loudly enough that I half-expected a neighbor to pound on the ceiling or a wall, and I stuffed my face on anything I could find in the kitchen that didn't take too much effort to prepare. Then I crashed on the living room couch.

I woke up when a square of light fabric landed on my chest. I opened my eyes to see Felicia, in jeans and a T-shirt, her hair held back in a ponytail, standing over me. She smelled like strawberry shampoo and a delicate floral perfume. The red and blue outfit she'd borrowed now lay on my chest, laundered and folded.

I gave her a smile. "Hey."

"Hey," she replied. "I brought your suit back."

"Thanks."

"Don't mention it. Red and blue aren't a good combination on me anyway."

I shook my head and met her eyes. "No, Felicia. *Thanks.* For coming here. For staying by me."

She frowned and shook her head. "I was stupid, Pete. I led the bad guys right to your home. To MJ."

"Not your fault," I told her. "You didn't think Oliver would stick a knife in your back."

"But I should have thought of it," she said.

"Maybe next time. Did you find out how he was tracking you?"

She rolled her eyes. "How *wasn't* he? GPS in the phone, the visor, the power unit on the suit—and tracking chips woven into the fabric of the suit itself. I had to ditch it."

"Back to the old outfit?"

"It's not old," she said. "It's classic. Or at the worst, retro."

I snorted out a little laugh. "As long as it isn't the one with the shoulder pads and the headband. How's our buddy Oliver?"

She gave me a smile filled with very white teeth. "He's out of the company already. He's probably out there trying to plot a way to keep his money without me ruining his life."

"Seems to me if he could subtract you from the equation, he could do that."

Felicia shrugged. "He wouldn't be the first to try it."

"Just so long as he's not the last."

She gave me a coy little look and shifted her hips. "I'm a big girl, Petey. I can take care of myself."

"Just be careful," I said.

"Maybe I'll get a bodyguard," she said. "If I could find one who would guard my body instead of ogling it."

"You and MJ worked things out, I guess?"

"'Worked out' is a rather strong term. We called a cease-fire," she replied. "News flash, honey: It's a rare thing for wives and ex-girlfriends to get along. I don't think she's ever really gotten past that portrait I had taken for you." She smiled. "Watson's got guts, though. I'll give her that."

I remembered said portrait of Felicia, and hoped my blush didn't show. "And how," I said. "Thank you for helping me protect her."

Her expression grew serious for a moment. "I know you think the world of her. Maybe we aren't together anymore, but I care about you. A lot. So even if she tried to claw my eyes out every time I came in the room, I'd do the same thing next time. It'd kill you if something happened to her. I don't want that. And she loves you, too, Pete. She makes you happy."

"Yeah. She does." I smiled for a moment and reached up to take her hand for a moment, squeezing. She squeezed back, then leaned down and kissed me on the forehead. "Don't be a stranger," I said.

"Of course not," she replied. "And don't wait for it to get as bad as this before you call me for help, either. No one does it all alone."

"I'll remember," I said.

"Tell MJ I said goodbye?"

"Will do."

She winked at me on her way out. "Take care of yourself, Pete."

"Don't do anything I wouldn't do," I replied.

"You're no fun at all," she said, and closed the door behind her.

○———————○

MARY Jane got in late—after eleven o'clock. But she came through the door smiling and humming to herself. I was dozing in front of the TV. My metabolism gets me back on my feet faster than the average bear, but mending broken bones really takes it out of me.

"Hey there," I mumbled, and smiled at her. She came to the couch and kissed me thoroughly and then just sort of draped herself over me. "Someone had a good day," I observed. "The car ran? The driver's test went okay?"

"The car," she said, smiling, "is fixed. You'd never know I crashed it into anything at all."

I blinked. "How . . ."

She wriggled pleasantly, and drew an old business card from her pocket. The front said, "Stephen Strange, MD." She flipped it over. The back read, in Strange's scrawling script, "Bippity-Boppity-Body Shop."

I laughed and hugged her. "And the test?"

"Somehow, it seemed a whole lot less dramatic on Monday than it had been on Saturday," she replied, her tone smug.

"There's a shocker," I said. "How was your first rehearsal?"

"Wonderful," she said, and kissed me again. "The lead was all surprised that I had a mind. He thought he was just getting to hang around with a bit of mobile scenery."

"So long as he looks with his eyes and not with his hands," I drawled. "You need me to beat anybody up, you let me know."

"I think I'll manage that on my own, should it become necessary. Which it won't, of course." She kissed me again, then drew back, eyes bright. "How was practice?"

"Wong got game," I said. "Apparently he saw the Globetrotters when he was a kid. I guess when he wasn't learning mystic kung fu and herbal remedies, he was teaching himself whatever he could about basketball."

"The plan worked?"

"And how," I said.

"Broken wrist and all?"

"Yep," I said. I grinned. "I cheated. Just a little. Not enough to look weird."

Mary Jane grinned back. "I thought you said cheating would defeat the purpose."

"One-on-one, sure," I said. "But the kid needed to learn that sometimes you run into something you can't handle on your own. So I made sure he couldn't." I put on a pious face. "It was for his own good."

She laughed again. "Did Felicia get out of town all right?"

"Yes," I said. "She said to tell you good-bye."

"Good."

"Good that she said that, or good that she's gone?"

"Yes," Mary Jane said in a cheerful tone. "You're never going to believe who came by the rehearsal."

The phone rang. I sighed and fumbled around for it. Mary Jane sort of wormed her way up my stomach so that she could reach the phone. Which was quite nice, really.

She picked up the phone and held it up to my ear for me.

"Hello?" I said.

Wong's voice came over the phone. "The Rhino asked to speak to you before he left. I took the liberty of contacting you so that he would not know the number I called."

"Right," I said. "Put him on."

"Spider-Man?" the Rhino asked, the strong Russian accent thick and rolling.

"Da?" I said.

He snorted. "You kept your word to me."

"Yes," I said. "It's been more than twenty-four hours."

"I know. Called to tell you am keeping to our deal in any case. Am on the way out of town in a moment. No trouble for you or anyone."

"Good," I said. "Don't suppose I could talk you into extending the deal."

The Rhino grunted. "You going to pay my debts? Give me job?"

"No."

"Then is no deal." His voice turned thoughtful. "Maybe one day, things are different. But for now, is no help for it."

"Too bad," I said. "Someone like you could do a lot of good. It wasn't bad working *with* you for once."

"Maybe. But things between us do not change," he said. "One day, I will beat you. My way. One day, I will show you."

"Well," I said. "We'll just see about that."

I swear, I could hear the big guy's smile. "Da. We will."

And we both hung up.

"You know," she said thoughtfully, "I think I've worked out what was bothering me about him. Our friend Aleksei is not stupid."

I frowned. "He's not Gump or anything, maybe, but I promise you he's not the crispiest chip in the bag."

"I'm not so sure," she said, voice intent. "You think that because you've always thought it, and so now you expect him to be a big dope. But stop and think for a minute. *Everyone* in your circle expects it, don't they?"

"Well. Yes. I mean, everyone knows that the Rhino isn't all that bright."

"What if he's bright enough to be hiding it from everyone?" Mary Jane asked. "When people expect you to be an idiot, assume you haven't got a brain in your head, letting them continue to think so can be very advantageous." She gave me a wry smile. "Believe me. When it comes to people's assuming abject stupidity based on expectation and appearance, I know what I'm talking about."

I blinked and thought about that one for a minute. "Then how come when he fights me, he keeps falling for the same routine, over and over?"

"Exactly," Mary Jane said. "Even a moron would have changed their tactics by now. I think it's become a matter of principle for him. He wants to beat you his way, and he won't be satisfied until he does." She mused. "You know, I'll bet you anything that he wasn't unconscious as long as you thought he was, when you brought him in here. If he was as stupid as everyone thinks, do you really think he would have been so calm and rational when he woke up blinded and bound?"

"Admittedly," I said, "I was sort of surprised that he let me talk to him. I knew the webbing would hold him long enough to let me throw him out a window if he got rowdy, but all the same, he did take it awfully calmly."

"Right. I think that was because he'd been listening and he already knew you had no intention of hurting him."

The Rhino with a brain. That notion was at least as disturbing as the occasions when the Hulk had managed to hold on to Banner's intellect. "I don't know . . ."

"I'm not saying he's going to be a *Jeopardy* champion or anything. But think about how many mad geniuses he works with. The Goblins, Doc Ock, Mysterio. I think he knows that they're a lot smarter than he is. So he hides the brains he does have, so that if it ever comes to a fight, he'll have a card up his sleeve."

I hated to admit it, but I knew MJ might have a point. "If that's true," I said, "then he might have heard my name. Or yours."

She nodded. "If he did?"

"If he did . . ." I shook my head. "He's just got first names. And I don't think he'd do anything with them, anyway."

"Why not?"

"Because you're right about one thing: He wants to beat me his way. Man to man."

Mary Jane smiled. "Then you've got nothing to worry about. You're more of a man than anyone I know, Mr. Parker. Russian Rhinos included."

"You sound awfully certain about that, Mrs. Parker," I murmured, and kissed her.

"I am," she said, gorgeous eyes half-lidded. "Let me show you why."

And she did.

ACKNOWLEDGMENTS

A big thank you to Cam "It's Australian for Death" Banks, for giving me the issue that inspired this book. Another big thank you to April, for the most professionally well-timed Christmas present EVER.

And one more for Jen Heddle, for the opportunity to play in the Marvel universe.

ABOUT THE AUTHOR

JIM BUTCHER picked up his first Marvel comic during the Mutant Massacre story line in *Uncanny X-Men,* went back and bought everything from the Secret Wars on, and spent the next four or five years buried in every original Marvel comic printed, with a particular focus on every issue of *Amazing Spider-Man* he could get his hands on. The vision and skill of Stan Lee and dozens of talented writers and artists fed a young man's imagination all too well, and when he grew up he wound up writing stories of his own, albeit wholly in print.

For him, when *Spider-Man* hit the big screen it was like seeing a geeky old high school friend made good, and when offered an opportunity to actually write Spidey, he jumped at the chance with the proportionate strength of a long-term fan. The author of the best-selling *Dresden Files* series and the critically-acclaimed *Codex Alera,* he lives in Independence, Missouri, with his wife, son, and a vicious guard dog.

Book Two

DOWN THESE MEAN STREETS

by Keith R. A. DeCandido

To Kyoshi Paul,

for everything he's taught me

HISTORIAN'S NOTE

DOWN *These Mean Streets* is consistent with the continuity of the Spider-Man comics published by Marvel, though one does not need to be intimately familiar with those comics in order to follow the action. However, for those who are concerned with such matters, this story takes place sometime after Mary Jane Watson decided to take up theatre work in *Amazing Spider-Man* #509 (published in August 2004).

CONTENT WARNING

CONTENT contains depictions of drugs and smoking. Discretion is advised.

"DOWN these mean streets a man must go who is not himself mean, who is neither tarnished nor afraid. . . . He is the hero, he is everything. He must be a complete man and a common man and yet an unusual man. He must be, to use a rather weathered phrase, a man of honor, by instinct, by inevitability, without thought of it, and certainly without saying it. He must be the best man in his world and a good enough man for any world."—RAYMOND CHANDLER

ONE

PETER Parker looked at the clock on the wall, smiled, and said, "We've got a few minutes, so let's go to the next chapter: 'The Periodic Table of Elements.'"

A roomful of teenagers moaned and whined.

Peter smiled, remembering hearing similar moans in science class when he was a student here at Midtown High School and the teacher jumped ahead. Of course, Peter never indulged in those complaints himself—he was always three steps ahead of the rest of his classmates, especially in the science classes, whether it was in physics, chemistry, biology, or the general sciences that he now, years later, was himself teaching.

"Now, now," he said chidingly, "the periodic table was part of the reading you were supposed to have done by *yesterday's* class. So you all *should* have it down pat by now." He walked over to the side of the classroom, to the bulletin board situated between the room's two doors on the right-hand side from where the kids sat. "Besides, it's been up on the board all year."

"Dude, I thought it was a movie poster," Tommy Ciolfi muttered. Several of the kids around him tried, and mostly failed, to swallow a laugh.

"Well, it has been coming soon to a *classroom* near you." Peter winced even as he made the bad joke. *Why is it I'm hilarious when I'm beating up bad guys, but all the jokes I make as a teacher are lame?* "All right, who can tell me why the isotopes are in the order they're in?"

He looked around the room; only two hands, those of Marissa Blaustein and Suzyn Baptiste, went up. *Hardly surprising,* Peter thought. *They're two of the brightest kids in the class.* Marissa was pretty, popular, had perfect diction, and was on the junior-varsity cheerleading squad; Suzyn was overweight, unpopular, spoke with a Haitian accent, and was in the chess club. Both were brilliant, and they seemed to be in competition with each other academically. Marissa couldn't stand the idea of the social misfit being better than her, and Suzyn despised Marissa and everything she stood for. Peter had to admit, it made for good theatre.

However, this was a ridiculously easy question, and one that anyone who had actually *done* the homework would know. So he looked out over the class to see who besides these two really did the work.

Actually, only a few were looking at him. Most of the thirty kids were studying either their notebooks, or the window, or the floor, or the clock in the hopes that it would move faster. Peter's freshman general sciences class was scheduled for last period, and it was always difficult to hold kids' attention during the final class of the day, particularly in a required class that most of them didn't give a damn about.

Still, he was there to teach, and they were there to learn. He fixed his gaze on Javier Velasquez, the class's biggest troublemaker. Javier wasn't the only kid in the class with a rap sheet, but he was the one who took the most pride in it. "Javier?"

"What?"

Peter exhaled. "Answer the question, please." Knowing full well the kid hadn't heard it—since he hadn't paid attention to anything Peter had said all year—he threw Javier a bone and re-asked it: "What order are the isotopes on the Periodic Table in?"

He shrugged. "Alphabetical?"

One kid almost laughed, but stopped at a glare from Javier.

"L doesn't usually come before B," Peter said. "At least not in any language I'm familiar with."

"You 'familiar' with the language of kiss my ass?"

Peter grinned. "Yup. It's the language you'll be talking if you don't do your homework—or if I decide to tell the principal about the switchblade you've got stashed in your locker."

The look on Javier's face was priceless. Normally, a kid talking to a teacher like that—or, for that matter, carrying a weapon into the school—would get detention or a suspension, but Peter didn't much see the point in punishing Javier. He knew that Javier lived with the threat of getting shot or stabbed every day. Detention was going to neither scare him nor dissuade him from future infractions; suspension would just put him back on the streets for a few days, and he might decide to make it permanent, in which case, nobody won.

Peter looked around the room. "Anyone else?"

Slowly, Gregory Horowitz raised a meek hand. Gregory had the highest grades of anyone in the class, but he rarely raised his hand, despite Peter's encouragement. Seeing this as a good sign, Peter called on him.

"A—atomic mass?"

"That's right."

Indignantly, Marissa said, "No it's *not*! The book says it's atomic *weight*."

In a barely audible voice, Gregory said, "Sci—scientists prefer the term atomic mass now."

In a stage whisper, Tommy said, "Oooooh, Geekory's hangin' out with *scientists* now."

"Actually, you're both right," Peter said, overlaying Tommy. "Unfortunately, the textbook we're using is about five years old—or, to put it in simple terms, the same age that Tommy's acting—" That got a quick laugh from several kids, with the notable exceptions of Tommy and Javier. "—and since then, as Gregory said, scientists have come to prefer the more precise term 'atomic mass' to 'atomic weight.'" *Let's hear it for budget cuts,* Peter thought with a sigh. The text they were using wasn't much farther along than the one *he* had used as a fourteen-year-old.

He pointed at the upper-left-hand portion of the chart. "H is for hydrogen, which has an atomic mass of 1.00797—or just 1, for our purposes. How do you figure out the atomic mass, Marissa?"

Since Marissa had obviously done the reading, Peter figured she'd give the right answer. Without hesitating, she confidently said, "By adding the number of neutrons and electrons."

"Close. Suzyn?"

With a triumphant look at her classmate, Suzyn said, "The number of neutrons and *protons*." Marissa stared daggers at Suzyn.

"Right. It's the particles in the nucleus that make up the atomic mass. The electrons orbit the nucleus and don't figure into it."

Tommy rolled his eyes.

"Something bothering you, Tommy?"

Shifting uncomfortably in his seat at the sudden attention, Tommy said, "Uh, no, Mr. Parker, it's just—well. I mean, c'mon, who gives a damn about this crap? Atomic weight, atomic mass—it don't mean nothin'!"

Peter sighed. When he took this job, he knew it was going to be an uphill struggle. Most of these kids would rather be playing with their Xboxes or chatting with their friends online or text-messaging each other from across the room, or whatever it was that kids did these days. Peter didn't even know what kids did when *he* was that age. He had been as much an outcast as Gregory and Suzyn were: the geek, the dexter, the nerd, the one who went to a science exhibit instead of the football game or the homecoming dance.

And imagine what life would've been like if I hadn't gone to that science exhibit . . .

Looking out over the mostly apathetic faces of kids desperate to get out of school as fast as possible, he let out a long breath and walked back to the front of the class, away from the chart, and sat on the edge of his desk. "Look, I know this all seems meaningless—but look at what we're talking about here." He pointed at the chart. "This is *what everything's made of.* You, me, the desks, your books, the pavement outside, the lockers, the trees, the SUVs, the buildings, your clothes, your cell phones, your video games—this is what it's all made out of. These are the building blocks of the world. How can you not be excited by that?" Quickly holding up a hand, he said, "Don't answer that." Several chuckles followed. "I know, you don't think this is a big deal, but it really is."

He glanced at the clock. The bell would be ringing momentarily. "Any other questions?"

Ronnie Hammond raised his hand. "Yes, Ronnie?"

"Kr stands for Krypton, right?"

Peter nodded.

"I thought that was a planet."

Before Peter could give that the answer it deserved, the bell rang. "We'll pick this up tomorrow." His words could barely be heard over the din of books and notebooks closing, desks sliding on the linoleum floor, and classmates talking to each other. Peter noted that Suzyn and Gregory weren't talking to anyone. *There but for the grace of a radioactive spider go I,* he thought wistfully. "And don't forget," he said louder, "there's a test on chapters four, five, and six on Friday!"

That was met with predictable moans and whines.

Javier was one of the last to get up. He stared at Peter the whole time, then got up and walked out, never taking his eyes off Peter.

For his part, Peter met the stare. By the time he reached the door, Javier looked royally pissed off that Peter didn't blink.

Poor kid. If only he knew . . . Peter looked like a wussy white guy from Queens, and Javier usually ate teachers like that for breakfast. But Peter had spent all of his life since he was only a little older than Javier dealing with people who would eat Javier for breakfast.

Gregory made his way out of the class slowly, not wanting to get in anyone's way for fear that someone might notice him. Peter recognized that walk oh so well. That was how he had walked all over Midtown High. It was also how he had walked into that science exhibit on that fateful day, sponsored by a company in the Pacific Northwest that was doing demonstrations at high schools across the country. He had entered slowly, shuffling his feet, not wanting to bother anybody, and therefore had been stuck at the back of the room, barely able to see the demo. When a spider had gotten into the workings and became irradiated, Peter had been the one it bit in its death throes, the radiation changing the spider bite from something potentially fatal to something wondrous. Standing at the back as he was, nobody had noticed Peter stumbling out of the exhibit hall, wandering aimlessly down the streets of the Forest Hills section of Queens, wondering why he felt so strange.

Now, Peter walked more confidently through the school's halls, preparing himself to head home to his wife. *No, head home to an empty apartment,* he amended. Mary Jane had rehearsal tonight. His lovely wife had a supporting part and was understudy to the female lead in a way-the-heck-off-Broadway play called *The Z-Axis.*

"Hey, Mr. Parker!"

Peter turned to see Tommy standing at his locker, wearing the same smart-aleck grin that Flash Thompson used to wear when he was about to torment young Peter Parker. Some of Tommy's friends were nearby, cleaning out their lockers and grabbing their jackets and books. "Yeah, Tommy?"

To Peter's surprise, the grin fell, and Tommy sounded serious. "That speech you gave today—I gotta say it really really really sucked." By the time he reached the last two words, the grin was back.

Putting a hand on Tommy's shoulder, Peter said, "Well, Tommy, under *normal* circumstances I'd say that you just have to tough it out until June, at which point you'll never have to take general science again."

Tommy looked confused. "Whaddaya mean 'normal circumstances'?"

Peter smiled. "Well, if you keep going the way you're going, you're gonna have to take it *all* over again in summer school after you flunk." Removing the hand, and taking pleasure in the guffaws from Tommy's friends, Peter continued walking toward the faculty lounge.

He entered the tiny room that served as the teachers' refuge from the students. The furniture was brand-new when it was purchased shortly after World War II, the refrigerator sounded like a motorcycle with a muffler problem and only intermittently kept its contents below room temperature, and the grout in the tilework around the sink could, at this point, qualify as an alien life-form.

Just remember, Parker, you chose this job. If nothing else, it provided a more steady income than freelance photography ever had.

"How do you do it?"

Peter turned to see one of the math teachers, Elizabeth Doyle, sitting on the green sofa with the red cushions, clutching a can of diet soda for dear life.

"Do what, Liz?"

"Keep that smile on your face." She shook her head. "Damn newbies, always thinking this job's a *calling* and that it's *noble*. It's a *job*. And like every job, it sucks."

Walking over to the coffeemaker on the counter, Peter said, "Oh believe me, Liz, I've been at jobs that suck." He saw that there was about one cup left in the pot, and reached for the handle with one hand while opening the cabinet to retrieve his mug with the other. "But here at least I feel like I'm accomplishing something."

Liz looked at him like he'd grown another head. "If you say so. Don't you have Velasquez in your class?"

Peter nodded as he poured the coffee into the mug, steam twirling up from it.

She shook her head. "That's an expulsion waiting to happen. I'm telling you, the only way he's not expelled by the end of the year is if he gets himself killed."

Whatever Peter was going to say in response was lost when he made the mistake of actually drinking the coffee. Closing his eyes and trying not to think too hard about what he was doing, he swallowed it. "I see they're still using yesterday's dishwater for the coffee."

Holding up her can, Liz said, "That's why I stick with the soda machines. Safer."

"Yah." Peter poured the rest of the coffee into the sink. *I can always grab a cup at home before going on patrol.* "Anyhow, I think it's important—"

Liz held up a hand. "I swear, Pete, you tell me you took this job to give something back to the school that taught you so much, I *will* throw up right here on this sofa."

Peering at the cushions, Peter smiled and said, "Might improve the color."

Shaking her head, Liz hauled herself up from the couch and drank down the rest of her soda. "You're a crazy man, Pete."

"I think that was part of the job description when they hired me. 'Must have been crazy since the age of eighteen.'"

Liz chuckled. "Sad, but true. You need a lift home?"

"Nah, I'll walk. Thanks, though." Peter had accepted lifts home from Liz a few times, but with MJ not being home, he wasn't in any particular rush. The walk back to the apartment would help him decompress.

"Smart man, no car in this town. Wouldn't have one myself, but *you* try gettin' to Bayside by mass transit from here."

Having spent most of his youth navigating the Queens bus lines, Peter felt Liz's pain. The only subway that came close to Bayside, the 7, didn't come through Forest Hills. She was definitely better off with a car, even the '86 Chevy junker that she drove.

After saying his good-byes to Liz, Peter went by the science office to drop off his books and check his mail. Peter had spent most of his time since high school learning to travel with what he could put in his pockets. His school-related stuff remained in the science office—he didn't have anything to grade tonight, and he'd prepare for tomorrow's lessons in the morning—and everything else he needed fit in either his pants or jacket. It was a bit nippy out on this spring day, but Peter was wearing a skintight outfit underneath his button-down shirt, jacket, and slacks, so he figured he'd be warm enough.

Bidding farewell to his fellow science teachers—several of whom made their usual disparaging remarks about Peter's leaving all his work at the office—he headed toward the exit, allowing the teenagers dashing through the halls to get to their parents' cars or the bus stop or just *out* to zip past him. Among the many gifts the dying spider had conferred upon him was a sixth sense that he referred to as his "spider-sense," which allowed him to avoid danger. In practical terms it meant that, in a hallway full of high school kids desperate to be outside, not one of them crashed or bumped into Peter.

The biggest buzz from that extra sense came just as Peter was approaching the metal door at the end of the hall and was about to push the horizontal bar in to release it. Stopping his forward motion and moving to the side gracefully—and so quickly that he doubted anyone would even notice—Peter avoided being rear-ended by Javier. For his part, Javier stumbled forward unsteadily, not even acknowledging Peter's presence.

I was expecting another dirty look from him at the very least.

Resolving to live with the disappointment, Peter followed Javier to the sidewalk. During the one hour after school let out, this side street was closed to vehicular traffic except for the city buses that Midtown High commissioned to serve as shuttles to various neighborhoods. They were lined up one in front of the other on the curb, kids milling toward the front doors, faculty proctors making a valiant (and futile) attempt to keep the students in some semblance of single file. Peter shuddered, knowing that he would catch this duty in two weeks and dreading it.

Then he whirled back toward Javier—mainly because the spider-sense buzz Peter got off the kid hadn't died down.

In fact, it was intensifying.

"Yo, Javier, 'sup with you, man?" asked one of his friends. Peter didn't know the kid's given name, but had seen him before hanging out with Javier, who called him Nariz. Given the enormous schnozz on the kid, the nickname—the Spanish word for "nose"—fit.

Nariz held up his hand, expecting Javier to clasp it in return, but Javier was just standing unsteadily in the middle of the sidewalk. "You gonna leave me hangin', yo?"

With each passing second, Peter's spider-sense buzz increased in intensity. Javier was wobbly on his feet, but he didn't move or speak.

Just as Peter was about to find a place to change into his other outfit, Nariz lightly tapped Javier on the shoulder with the back of his hand. "'Sup, yo, you dissin' me now? What up with *that?*"

"Get *offa* me!"

Even as Javier said the words, he backhanded Nariz in the face. In and of itself, that would have been unremarkable, except that the blow sent Nariz twenty feet down the sidewalk, knocking over a group of seniors who were congregating.

Fourteen-year-old kids don't usually have that kind of strength, Peter thought as he realized that he wasn't going to have *time* to change clothes.

Especially when he saw that Javier's complexion had changed from its usual dark skin tone to an emerald green.

There is absolutely no way this can be good. Super strength and green skin was a combination that generally meant enhancement by gamma radiation—the most spectacular example being the Hulk. *How does a street kid from Queens get gamma-irradiated?* Peter asked himself, but saved it for later. *Maybe he got bitten by a radioactive wombat—worry about that when he isn't about to tear up the street and the students.*

One of the security guards at this door was a retired cop named Pat "Lefty" Lefkowitz, who'd been keeping an eye on things at Midtown High since before Peter's student days. Upon seeing Javier clock someone, he waddled over toward the kid, hand on the butt of his .38 revolver. Peter, hoping to keep this civil and knowing full well he probably couldn't, also moved toward Javier. *If nothing else, maybe I can keep Lefty's gun in its holster.*

"'Ey, Velasquez, wha'd I tell you about—"

Javier turned around and snarled. His face was getting greener by the second, and Peter noticed that he was also growing, his new physique straining against his clothes.

"Sweet Jesus!" Lefty cried, and unholstered his revolver.

Before he could fire a shot, Javier was on the retired cop, punching him in his huge belly, sending Lefty sprawling against the metal door, wheezing. Peter swore he heard the sound of bones cracking.

Kids and faculty alike started screaming, but Peter tried not to pay attention to any of it. Grabbing Javier's arm, he whirled the kid around into one of the metal doors, hoping that his own super strength would give the push enough force to render the kid at least insensate for a few minutes until one of the other guards showed up with a pair of handcuffs.

Unfortunately, being smashed into a metal door served only to make Javier angry. "Kill you!" he cried as he jumped at Peter, who could only let Javier knock him to the ground, using his abilities to roll with the attack enough so that it only hurt a little when they collided with the pavement.

"Get offa him, Velasquez!"

Peter recognized the voice of the other security guard assigned to this door, an ex-jock with delusions of competence named Brian Klein, but Brian's words concerned Peter a lot less than Javier's face. He was as green as the Hulk now, and based on the way he'd slammed into Peter's rib cage, he was starting to get near the Hulk's strength class, too.

Before Peter could kick Javier off him—and later come up with a feeble explanation for how a skinny white science teacher could toss a superstrong kid around—Javier suddenly screamed as if he was in pain, rearing his head back and shouting at the clear sky.

Then the kid collapsed right on top of Peter.

Deciding discretion was the better part of keeping his secrets safe, Peter played the helpless teacher and whimpered, "Uh, help?"

Javier, now a dead weight on Peter's chest, started twitching. A moment later, the weight was gone, as Brian had rolled him off. Clambering to his feet, Peter looked down to see the green hue fading from Javier's epidermis, even as the kid was convulsing.

From the ground, Lefty said, "I called 911." Peter turned to see Lefty still on the ground, but holding a cell phone. He clambered to his feet, wincing in a manner Peter recognized as that of a man with cracked ribs.

"Good call, old-timer," Brian said.

Lefty snapped, "Don't call me old-timer, you little punk." Lefty, Peter knew, had never had much use for Brian. "You okay, Pete?"

Peter nodded. "Just a little winded."

Brian stared at Peter. "That was a brave thing you did, Parker—throwing him into the door like that."

"Brave, hell, that was just stupid." Lefty was now clambering slowly to his feet. "Leave the security to the guards next time, Pete."

"Yeah, like you flat on your ass?" Brian asked with a sneer.

Javier's convulsing started getting worse. Peter also noticed he was sweating.

"Ambulance should be here in a minute," Lefty said, ignoring Brian. "Figures that Velasquez is usin' as well as dealin'. We—"

"I *kick* his ass!"

Peter whirled around to see that Nariz was back on his feet.

"Where the hell is he, I gonna kick—"

Even as he spoke, Peter had moved to intercept him faster than Brian or Lefty could have. "Easy, Javier's already down."

"Get out the *way*, teacher-man, I gonna—"

Peter forcibly stopped Nariz, putting his right hand on the boy's left shoulder and his left hand on the kid's right biceps.

Giving Peter a menacing look that probably would've scared most science teachers, Nariz—who was bleeding from his outsized hooter— said, "You *best* be lettin' go'a me, teacher-man."

"Javier's not going anywhere, Nariz. Take a look." He gestured with his head to the ground, where Javier was still twitching, without actually taking his eye off Nariz. Nariz looked down at Javier. "*Damn*." He looked at Lefty. "Wha'd you do to him?"

"He didn't do anything," Peter said quickly before Lefty or Brian responded in kind. "He just collapsed. Is he on anything that would do that?"

Nariz just stared at Peter. "You got two seconds to be lettin' go'a me 'fore I get up in yo' *face*."

Peter let go just as he heard sirens growing closer.

Turning his back on Peter, Nariz walked away. "This ain't over."

The ambulance pulled in behind one of the buses. Only then did Peter notice the crowd that had gathered, barely being held in check by a couple of faculty members and the other security guards, who'd come to check out the ruckus.

One of the English teachers, a small woman named Constance Dobson, looked at Peter and shook her head. "The guard was right about what you did, y'know."

Not sure which guard she meant, Peter asked, "About being brave or about being stupid?"

"Both."

Unable to help it, Peter laughed. "Yeah, maybe. Still, if I hadn't done anything—"

"Lefty or Brian woulda taken care of it. Leave that to the pros, Parker."

"I'll remember that," Peter lied. He'd stood by and done nothing when he had the power to help once. It was a mistake he would never make again.

The EMTs started working on Javier, and based on their chatter, they were assuming he was coming down off a shot of ecstasy. Peter frowned. *That doesn't track—he was straight in class. He had to have taken it after the bell rang. But you don't burn through an X high that quick.*

But then, an X high didn't turn you green and give you superstrength.

Nariz was right, Peter thought as he brushed off the paramedic who approached, assuring her that he was fine. *This isn't over.*

TWO

AN old saying had it that familiarity bred contempt, which explained why Eileen Velasquez hated Parkway Hospital so much. She'd certainly spent enough time here, and she'd come to despise the place.

It all started when she was pregnant with her first child, Orlando. The pregnancy was deemed high-risk by the doctors, and she spent the four months leading up to his birth checked into the OB/GYN ward on twenty-four-hour bed rest. She hadn't wanted another child after that, and she had talked her husband, Carlos, into letting her get one of those fancy birth control implants. Unfortunately, something about the implant didn't work right, and she became pregnant with Javier. That pregnancy went fine, though the labor took twenty-three hours, and she spent all twenty-three back here again. Somehow, Carlos talked her into a third child, which became four when her doctor told her she had twins: Jorge and Manuel.

Then Orlando got into that accident with his bike, necessitating an emergency-room trip. Then Javier got into a fight at school, the first of many. Then they found out that Manuel had a bone disease, one not shared by Jorge. That meant lots more trips to and from not only Parkway Hospital, but also Mount Sinai in Manhattan, to visit the specialist.

And then there was the accident.

Eileen worked at Dilmore, Ward, and Greenberger, Attorneys-at-Law, as a receptionist. It was there that she got the phone call from Mr. Harrington, the principal of Midtown High, saying there was an "incident." Usually that was code for "Javier got into a fight," which it turned out was true again as far as it went—but that Javier had been high on something was a new twist.

She knew Javier had been dealing. She didn't know he was also taking.

Mr. Ward, the managing partner, was completely okay with letting her go early, so she hopped on the V train and made the oh-so-familiar walk from the 71st Street station to the Parkway Hospital emergency room. The whiff of antiseptic mixed with sweat that characterized the hospital's E.R. filled her with an overwhelming feeling of disgust.

She had hoped never to come back here again.

Walking past the waiting area, with its cracked and dirty plastic chairs, she proceeded to the long, high desk, behind which sat a harried-looking white man in his twenties wearing light blue scrubs, though he didn't seem to be a doctor or nurse. He didn't have the casual arrogance that every doctor Eileen had ever met carried, nor the seen-it-all look that most nurses had. The desk was at Eileen's neck level, and the receptionist was seated, so she had to peer down at him.

The young man was on the phone. "Excuse me," Eileen said.

Holding up a finger, the receptionist said, "No, Fred, we need them down here *now*. Yeah, I know they're backed up, but we got a serious situation here. It's sixty degrees out, Fred, we really don't need the AC on full blast. Look, I—"

"Excuse me," Eileen said a bit more forcefully. "I need to see my son."

Again, the receptionist held up a finger, this time mouthing the words *just a second*.

"Fred, I've got Doc Shannon crawling up my butt, and he ain't gonna leave there until this gets fixed. Can you *please* just send somebody. I don't even care if they fix it, just have someone *show up*, okay? Thank you." He hung up the phone and looked up at Eileen. "Sorry 'bout that, it's crazy here. Now who—"

"My son—Javier Velasquez."

Even as the receptionist started typing something onto his keyboard, the phone next to him rang again. He picked it up. "E.R. Yeah. Yeah. Yeah. No. No, she's not on right now. No, she's not due back until tomorrow. Yeah. Yeah. Yeah. I really don't know that, you'll have to ask her. *Really*, ma'am, you have to ask her. Yeah. Sorry. Bye." The receptionist let out a long breath. "Sorry 'bout that. What's your husband's name again?"

Through clenched teeth, Eileen said, "It's my son, Javier Velasquez."

"Could you spell that, please?" Before she could, the phone rang again. He picked it up. "Hang on. E.R."

Eileen was two steps shy of reaching down and yanking the phone out of the floor jack it was plugged into when a voice from behind her said, "Excuse me, are you Javier's mother?"

She turned to see another white man in his twenties, but this one had darker hair and a kinder face than the harried receptionist. He was dressed in a sports jacket, button-down shirt, and slacks. Nothing fancy—nothing like her coworkers at Dilmore Ward—and obviously not a doctor or a detective. *A teacher, maybe?*

"Yes, I'm Eileen Velasquez."

"Hi, I'm Peter Parker—I'm Javier's science teacher."

I was right. "Were you the one—?" She hesitated.

"I, uh—I was the one who subdued your son. Kind of." He smiled. "Actually, he pretty much subdued himself and I happened to be standing closest. It was right after school was over, so I figured I'd come down, make sure he was okay."

"I—I just got here, I—" She shook her head. "That was really nice of you, Mr. Parker, thank you."

"Call me Peter, and, uh, don't thank me yet—there's a detective from the 112th Precinct here, and he's probably gonna want to talk to you. Not to mention the doctor. I've already spoken with both of them."

"Did they tell you anything about Javier?" To her own ears, Eileen sounded like a woman desperate for news—which she supposed she was, even though a big part of her didn't want to know the answer.

"Nothing I didn't already know. Looks like he took a hit of ecstasy, apparently, and then just went nuts—he hit one of the other kids and one of the guards, then jumped me before he collapsed into a pile of goo. Not literally," he added quickly, though Eileen had assumed he was speaking figuratively.

Though with the way the world is today, it wouldn't be the craziest thing I ever heard of.

Parker then said, "Ms. Velasquez—I know Javier's had some problems, but I've never known him to take drugs before. Deal, yes, but—"

"I don't know, Mr. Parker. Truth is—I don't know my son anymore.

Javier's my second oldest—his older brother went off to college, and he's got two younger brothers, but—" She took a deep breath. "One of them, Manuel, died a couple years ago, along with my husband."

"I'm sorry." Parker sounded like he meant it, which Eileen appreciated. "And as I said, it's Peter."

Eileen didn't think it appropriate to refer to one of her son's teachers by his first name. "I wasn't really there for Javier much, especially after Manuel and Carlos died. I've got my hands full raising him and Jorge, and with the lawsuit—" She cut herself off. Parker didn't need to know about that.

"'Scuse me, Parker?"

Parker turned around, and Eileen followed his gaze. The speaker was a heavyset black man in a dark suit, a shoulder holster bulging from under his pinstriped jacket, a gold-colored badge attached to his belt. *This must be the detective Mr. Parker was talking about.*

"Hi, Detective—uh, Detective Pierce, this is Eileen Velasquez, Javier's mother."

Pierce's eyes widened. "Oh yeah? Good, I need to talk to you, ma'am." The detective removed a pad of paper from his inner jacket pocket and started flipping through it to a blank page, the paper making crinkling noises.

"I need to know what happened to my son."

"The doctors are taking care of him, ma'am, but he'll be okay. Now I need to ask you—"

"I have to see my son," Eileen snapped.

Parker said quickly, "Would it hurt to let her see Javier, Detective?"

Pierce looked all put-upon, but Eileen didn't care. Finally, he said, "Yeah, okay. Follow me."

The detective led them down one of the corridors to a room with four beds in it. Back here, the antiseptic smell was still strong, but the sweat was gone. She supposed out of the way of the craziness of the reception area, that was to be expected.

Eileen didn't pay attention to the other three beds, focusing solely on the one closest to the door, where Javier lay sleeping.

That's the most peaceful I've ever seen him.

"What's wrong with his skin? I've never seen him look so pale," she said after a second.

"Actually," Parker said, "that's an improvement. At his highest, he was green."

"Green?" This was the first Eileen was hearing about this. "Why was he green?"

"Excuse me." At the new voice, Eileen turned to see a young Asian woman standing in the doorway alongside a tall black man in a nurse's uniform. "You people aren't supposed to be—" Then she noticed Pierce. "Oh, it's you. The kid's not waking up for a while yet, Detective, there's no need—"

"Dr. Lee, this is Javier's mother."

"Oh. I'm sorry, Ms. Velasquez, nobody told me you were here."

"That's okay. Can you tell me what happened to my son? Mr. Parker here said it was ecstasy."

"Not quite," Lee said. "It's a new variant that's been hitting the streets—laced with gamma radiation, which is why they turn green when they get high. It's called 'Triple X' on the street. He's lucky, though."

Eileen couldn't imagine how that could be. "What do you mean?"

"Your son's the fourth case I've seen in the last week. He's not showing any signs of radiation poisoning—which puts him one up on the other three. That means he's probably only taken it once or twice."

Pierce put a hand on Eileen's shoulder. It took all of her willpower not to shove it off violently. "Thanks, Doctor—let me know when he wakes up, okay? Ms. Velasquez, if you'll come with me, I've got to ask you those questions now." The detective led her out of the room. As they went, she heard the doctor say something quietly to the nurse. The nurse responded in a loud, deep voice: "Will do, Doctor."

Once in the hallway, Eileen did shake off the detective's hand. "I don't need you to push me, Detective, I can walk on my own."

"I'm sorry, ma'am, but I need—"

"I know what you need. So ask your questions, so I can be with my son."

She provided him with some basic information—address, full name, her job, phone numbers where she could be reached, and so on—and then he asked about their family situation.

"It's just me, Javier, and Jorge now. My oldest, Orlando, is at college in Florida. He doesn't come home anymore. Jorge's nine."

"Anybody else? Husband?"

"My husband and Jorge's brother, Manuel—they died two years ago."

"Were their deaths drug-related?"

Eileen snapped again. "What, you see Latino family, you figure drugs right off?"

"Take it easy, Ms. Velasquez." That was Parker—Eileen hadn't even heard him come out of Javier's room. "And Detective, go light on her, willya?"

"This ain't your business, Parker."

"Javier's my student—that makes him my responsibility."

Pierce rolled his eyes. "What a load of crap. Look, unless you can tell me something new about Javier that you didn't tell me before—"

"I told you everything I know."

"Fine, then shut the hell up. Ms. Velasquez, I'm trying to find out what happened to your son. Yeah, okay, maybe I jumped the gun with what I asked, but when you do what I do—"

Eileen didn't care to hear the man's rationalization. "My husband and son died in a car accident. Manuel had a bone disease, and we had to see a specialist in Manhattan. Carlos was driving him home after visiting that doctor, and a piece of concrete hit the car. It came from one of those super hero battles."

Eileen had spent a long time in the emergency room after the car was totaled, hoping that Carlos and Manuel would awaken from their comas, knowing that they'd both probably be crippled for life even if they did survive. Three days after the accident, Manuel died; Carlos's older, stronger body gave out another four days after that. Life had been a succession of nightmares since then.

Jorge became sullen and uncommunicative without his twin brother. Javier's descent into criminality got worse, to the point of his being arrested more than once, though nothing that resulted in any kind of jail time. Orlando had gone off to college in Florida and refused to ever come home.

Her subsequent wrongful-death lawsuit against the Avengers, who had been fighting a group that called themselves the Wrecking Crew at the time Carlos and Manuel happened along, had been going on for some years now. Despite the lengthy interval, Eileen kept at it.

Maybe if I hadn't kept at it so hard . . .

She shook her head. "So it didn't have anything to do with Javier—

unless you think the Avengers gave him this Triple X stuff."

"Yeah, well, it wouldn't surprise me," Pierce muttered.

"What does that mean?" Parker asked.

"Nothin'. Look, I'm sorry, Ms. Velasquez, but I just need—"

"You got everything you need," Eileen said, turning her back on the detective and heading toward the waiting area.

To her relief, Pierce didn't follow. However, Parker did. Walking alongside her back to the front of the emergency room, he said, "The guy was just trying to do his job."

"What'll he do, Mr. Parker? Find out who did this to my son? He doesn't need to do that, I know who—it was me. I haven't been there for my son, and this is what happens."

"It's not your fault," Parker said in a gentle voice. "With what happened—"

She shook her head. "You don't understand."

And he wasn't about to—the fact was, Eileen had never wanted Javier, and she had treated him that way ever since he was born. She resented him: the baby that wasn't supposed to happen. Sure, it was easy now to blame it on the accident, to say that Carlos and Manuel's deaths made her neglect her son. *But what was my excuse the ten years before that?*

Instead of telling this to Parker, she just asked him, "Javier'll be expelled for this, right?"

The teacher hesitated. "That *is* the school policy," he finally said. "But let me talk to the principal. Maybe I can . . ."

He didn't say what he would do. In truth, Eileen knew that there wasn't anything he *could* do. But at least he was trying. "Thank you, Mr. Parker. Really. I know Javier isn't the best student in the school."

"Actually, he's not that bad."

She gave him a look. "I know what he's like. I know he's a problem in class, and I *do* see his report card."

Parker smiled ruefully. "Yeah. But still, he deserves a chance. They all do."

Eileen let out a breath. "I don't know if I can believe that anymore, I really don't."

"I have to." He grinned. "Part of the job description." He reached into his pocket and pulled out his wallet, retrieving his business card. "This has my number at the school." He removed a pen from his jacket pocket and wrote a number with a 917 area code, which meant it was probably a cell phone. Sure enough: "I'm writing my cell number on it, too. If you or Javier need anything, just call."

She took the card, stared at it a second, then looked at this young man who was doing all this for her and her son. "You teach science, you said?"

Parker nodded. "Javier's last-period general science class, yeah."

Looking down, she saw a wedding band on the teacher's left ring finger. "You got a wife to go home to, and you're taking time out of your day to talk to me and make sure my son's okay. My son, who I know got a D in your class last term, and who'll probably be expelled."

"Yeah," Parker said with a shrug.

"Why are you doing this?"

Another shrug. "Like I said before, he's my student, so he's my responsibility."

She snorted. "What's the *real* reason?"

A pause. "I lost my parents when I was really young, so I was raised by my aunt and uncle. I learned a lot from both of them, and one thing that Uncle Ben always taught me was that I should always take my responsibilities seriously."

Smiling, Eileen said, "Sounds like your uncle's a good man."

"He was. He, uh, he died a while back. Got shot by a burglar."

Eileen shook her head. "Makes you wonder why anybody lives in this city."

"I guess."

She looked at the kind young man. "Thank you again, Mr. Parker. I'm going to go sit and wait for my son to wake up. You get back home to that wife of yours. She's probably worried sick about you."

Grinning, Parker said, "Actually, my wife's an actor, and she's got rehearsal tonight, so right now she's mostly worried about hitting her marks. So I can stick around if you want."

"No, I—I think I'd like to be alone for a bit, if that's okay."

Parker nodded. "Okay. Call if you change your mind."

"I will," she said, though she had no intention of bothering him anymore. He'd already done far more than his fair share for her son.

"Dr. Lee! The patient's crashing!"

Eileen looked up sharply. *I know that voice.* It was the deep voice of the male nurse who was with Dr. Lee, checking on Javier.

Oh God, no.

She ran down the hall, Parker following behind. As soon as she got to the door, the nurse—who was fairly large—blocked her way. "Ms. Velasquez, you can't come in here."

"My son's in there, you have to let me in!"

Behind the nurse, the doctor said, "CI—get me epi, *stat!*" Eileen had no idea what that meant.

Perhaps noticing her confusion, the nurse softened and said, "CI is a cardiac infarction, ma'am—your son's having a heart attack. The doctor's gonna help him, but you have to wait outside."

Parker put a hand on her shoulder, one she found far more comforting than the detective's. "Ms. Velasquez, the nurse is right. Let them do their jobs," he said in a quiet voice.

Nodding, she let Parker lead her back toward the waiting room. The teacher was talking as they walked. "I read somewhere that Henry Pym of the Avengers, when he was Giant-Man, had heart problems relating to changing size all the time. The same thing might've happened to Javier because he changed size."

Eileen nodded absently. *My son is dying, and there's nothing I can do.*

She swore that if Javier lived through this, she would make their lives different—make them better. She'd lost Carlos and Manuel and Orlando already, and she was damned if she'd lose any more.

THREE

"ALL right, but I think you're crazy."

Mary Jane Watson stared at Valerie McManus. Mary Jane's line was a cue for the blond-haired woman standing across from her on the cramped stage. Between them was Lou Colvin, the third actor in this scene.

For her part, Valerie just stared blankly back at her. In the silence that followed, Mary Jane could hear the whispers of the tech crew and the costuming people as they dashed about doing their appointed tasks to get *The Z-Axis* ready for its forthcoming opening.

Then Valerie blinked. "Oh God, my line's next, isn't it? I'm sorry, I just totally blanked. I'm *so* sorry. I'll get it right this time, honest."

Somehow, Mary Jane managed not to scream—which was more than could be said for Dmitri Voyskunsky, the play's director and writer. "Valerie, my darling girl—you are aware, are you not, that we are opening in *one week*?"

"I'm sorry, Dmitri," Valerie said. "I'll try to—"

"No! No no no *no*!" The Russian got up from his seat at front-row center in the tiny fifty-seat theatre and started pacing in front of the stage. "We are off book now. My play, it opens in one week, and I do not wish to hear about not knowing the lines. The time for 'try' is past. The time is now for not 'try.' Time is now for 'succeed.' Okay?"

Lou whispered, "Thank you, Yoda." Valerie giggled.

Dmitri stopped pacing and stared at Valerie—an effect diluted by the sunglasses that the playwright always wore, along with a battered old Brooklyn Dodgers cap. With all that, and his full beard, only the presence of his nose made it possible to be sure he actually had a face. "Oh, this is funny, you think? My play is going to open with leading lady who stares at the back of the wall with mouth hanging open, and you are laughing?"

"Sorry, Dmitri," Valerie said, "I was—I was thinking of something else, honest. I wasn't laughing at you. Really, I wasn't, okay? Can we take it again?"

"Okay." Dmitri retook his seat and adjusted his cap. "From Jane Mary's line."

Having long since abandoned any hope of getting Dmitri to stop mangling her name—she was half-convinced that he did it on purpose to annoy her anyhow—Mary Jane simply turned to Valerie and said once again, "All right, but I think you're crazy."

"You *want* me to think that, don't you?"

Valerie must have noticed the look Mary Jane was now giving her, because she then said, "Oh no, that's not the line, is it?"

"No!" Dmitri said. "That is line from *next act*. Okay?" Mary Jane was about to say something, when Valerie started waving her arms back and forth. "I got it this time, really, I got it. Honest. I got the line down pat this time, you watch. Let me try again."

"Hang on a sec," said Heidi. She was congregated around the soundboard with several other members of the tech crew. "These levels are wrong. Give me two seconds."

"I will give you five seconds, but no more!" Dmitri said.

Mary Jane knew *that* was a lost cause. Heidi had been complaining about the wonky sound system from the get-go.

They were standing on the second floor of Village Playhouse Central, a small theatre on MacDougal Street in the heart of Manhattan's famous Greenwich Village neighborhood. Downstairs was the lobby and box office, as well as the VPC offices. Within an hour or two, people would start milling about on the first floor to see tonight's performance of *Up the Creek Without a Fiddle,* a show by a different playwright. It would be running for one more week, at which point *The Z-Axis* would debut. *Up the Creek* had a minimal set—just a leather couch and a wooden rocking chair—which had been moved upstage and out of the way so Dmitri could run *The Z-Axis* without his actors tripping over the other play's set.

Although the place seated only fifty, most of the shows didn't sell out. Mary Jane was playing the supporting role of Irina, and she was also Valerie's understudy for the lead female role of Olga.

If she keeps up like this, I'll get that lead. In truth, Mary Jane was starting to truly worry about Valerie. She'd blown lines before, but she usually just cursed and got it right. She didn't babble a mile a minute the way she had been doing today.

Ever since she and Peter Parker had ended their thankfully brief separation and she moved back to New York, Mary Jane had been doing more theatre work, mainly in the hopes of improving her acting chops. As good as she was at modeling, she found acting to be much more fulfilling—and to offer more long-term possibilities once she got too old to represent products targeted to women or to stand next to products targeted to men. However, her acting experience to date consisted of a wretched soap opera and low-rent action movies, so she had recently decided to take advantage of the city's tremendous theatrical opportunities.

Despite the playwright's abrasive manner, she had found *The Z-Axis* to be a challenging piece—her smaller part of Irina was actually a stronger one than Valerie's lead. Olga was too reactive for Mary Jane's tastes; she just let things happen to her and didn't really appear to grow. Irina was more proactive, and actually went through changes as the play went on. It was a role that, despite the comparative paucity of dialogue, required nuance.

She looked closely at her costar, and noticed beads of sweat forming on Valerie's face. The lights weren't all that bright, and it wasn't all that hot in the room.

"Okay," Heidi said half a minute after Dmitri gave her five seconds, "we're ready to go."

Before Mary Jane could say anything, Valerie looked up and said, "All right, but I think you're crazy."

Dmitri uttered a stream of words in Russian, none of which Mary Jane knew, though she suspected that their equivalents in English were mostly spelled with four letters. Then Linnea, the costuming director, walked over to him, holding three swatches in her hand. Mary Jane figured that they were about to get into yet another fight over the color of the dress that Olga was supposed to wear in the opening scene. *That'll distract Dmitri for a few seconds at least.*

"You okay, Val?" she asked.

"Yeah, yeah, I'm fine. Really, I'm fine. Honest, let's do this and do it right."

Dmitri waved his hand in front of Linnea's face and yelled at Valerie. "Do it *right*? Oh, this is your brilliant plan now, to do it *right*?"

"I got it, Dmitri, really, I just . . ." Valerie put her head down and trailed off. "I'm fine, really, I—oh, shit."

Mary Jane moved closer, and saw that Valerie was starting to look a little green. "Dmitri, I think she's sick."

"*She* is sick?" Dmitri got up and started pacing again, ignoring the daggers that Linnea was staring at him. "No, it is *I* who am sick! We are opening in a *week*, and . . ."

Ignoring Dmitri's rant, Mary Jane put her hand on Valerie's shoulder. The other woman's head was down, her blond hair covering her face. "Val, you okay? Val?"

Lou had also moved closer. "Yo, Valerie, c'mon, get with the—"

Then Valerie raised her head.

The face Mary Jane saw was mostly recognizable as belonging to Valerie McManus. It had her hazel eyes, her prominent cheekbones, her button nose. There were, however, two major differences. One, her mouth was twisted into a snarl, revealing sharp, pointed teeth.

And two, her skin was now emerald green.

"Val?" Mary Jane said in a small voice.

Then Valerie let loose with a scream that Mary Jane felt in her spine. As she screamed, she struck out at Mary Jane and Lou. Crying out in pain as Valerie's fist collided with her stomach, Mary Jane stumbled backward, falling off the stage—which, thankfully, was less than a foot higher than the floor—and landing awkwardly on her shoulder, wrenching it.

She looked up at the stage to see that Lou had been knocked back to the wings at stage right, where he'd stumbled into two of the tech crew who'd been adjusting one of the lights.

As for Valerie, she was now green all over. What appeared to be bat wings had ripped through the back of her costume.

Several people behind Mary Jane screamed, including Linnea, who dropped her swatches on the floor next to Mary Jane.

Valerie started flapping her new wings and slowly rose toward the rafters. Then, with a burst of speed, she went through the rafters and to the ceiling beyond it. With a resounding crunch of shattered concrete, she then flew *through* the ceiling.

Several chunks of debris and insulation and plaster fell down onto the stage, which was now occupied only by the couch and rocker from the other play and Lou, who shouted several expletives when a piece of concrete landed on his leg.

"Lou!" Mary Jane awkwardly got to her feet and, holding her wrenched shoulder, hopped onto the stage. Right behind her was the stage manager, Anne Grace, who joined her and the tech guys as they crowded around the injured actor.

"Oh my God!" That was from the audience: Michael—the high-strung guy playing Sasha—whose eyes had gone wide. Next to him, his boyfriend, Joseph, was just staring with his mouth open, drool hanging off his lip-ring.

As for Lou, he was bleeding profusely from the leg. Mary Jane shook her head. "Looks like you broke a bone there, Lou."

One of the lighting guys looked at her with surprise. "You can tell *that* just by looking?"

Mary Jane had spent a significant chunk of her adult life being very close to a full-time super hero, including a fair amount of time recently being married to him. The sad reality was that she knew a broken leg when she saw one. However, she couldn't very well say that out loud. "OhmyGodohmyGodohmyGodohmyGodohmy*GodohmyGodohmyGod*!"

Mary Jane looked over to see Heidi screaming and waving her arms. Some of the other tech crew were trying to hold her still. One of the tech guys was hiding under the soundboard asking if it was safe to come out.

Jumping down off the stage, still holding her shoulder, Mary Jane went to her purse, took out her cell phone, and turned it on.

"Who you call, Jane Mary?" Dmitri was staring at Mary Jane. He had removed his glasses and was cleaning plaster dust off them with his shirt.

"An ambulance—Lou's hurt, and everybody's freaking out."

"No, there is no need. We can bring him to St. Vincent's, okay? Do not need to bring ambulance. Ambulance bring police, police close theatre, no show tonight, then Alfredo angry. Alfredo angry, maybe he decide *The Z-Axis* no good."

Before Mary Jane could say anything, Anne stepped down from the stage. "Dmitri, shut up. There's a big hole in the ceiling, Heidi's having a nutty, Lou's leg is broken, and I'm about two steps away from a heart attack. The theatre is gonna be *closed.*"

Dmitri was too smart a director to argue with his stage manager, and so he said nothing. As soon as she got a signal, Mary Jane dialed 911.

Waiting for an answer, she wondered what happened to Valerie to cause that kind of transformation. Unfortunately, being married to a super hero meant she had some pretty reliable theories on *that* score as well.

○————————○

THE ambulance and the police arrived almost simultaneously, the former from the very same St. Vincent's Hospital that Dmitri wanted to take Lou to—*And what were we supposed to do,* Mary Jane wondered, *call him a cab?*—and the latter from the 6th Precinct. The EMT who checked her over was a fan, as it turned out, with fond memories of Mary Jane's brief role on the soap opera *Secret Hospital,* and not only pronounced Mary Jane fine, but even gave her a small packet of painkillers. They had also managed to calm Heidi down, get both Linnea and Joseph to come out of their stupors, and help Anne when she started hyperventilating.

As for the cops, what surprised Mary Jane was that once they learned what happened to Valerie, one of them immediately contacted their dispatcher and asked for someone whose name she didn't get from "the Two-Four." She also heard the word "task force." Mary Jane's knowledge of police procedure was limited to secondhand information from Peter and watching *Law & Order,* but she knew that that meant the 24th Precinct, which, if she remembered correctly, was uptown. Certainly nowhere near here. *Which means that Valerie isn't the first person to turn all green and super powered, and the NYPD already have a task force dealing with it. Wonderful.*

After the EMT finished with Mary Jane—the ambulance had long since taken Lou to St. Vincent's—a uniformed cop walked up to her. He was about Mary Jane's age, with short black hair that had been moussed within an inch of its life, sideburns that were tailored to the height of fashion, and no discernible neck. His nameplate read SPINELLI.

She gave him her best smile, and asked, "What can I do for you, Officer Spinelli?"

He returned the smile and said, "Just gotta ask a few questions, Ms.—?"

"Mary Jane Watson." She provided her personal information first, and then described what happened to Valerie in as much detail as she could.

When she was done, and had answered a few follow-up questions, Spinelli said, "If you don't mind my sayin', Ms. Watson, you're takin' this a lot better'n—well, anybody else."

She shrugged. "It's New York."

"Yeah."

After asking one or two more questions, Spinelli said, "It's gonna be a little while more. But if you want, we can take you home when we're done. Or, uh, anywhere else you, uh, you wanna go." He smiled widely at that.

Oh God. "I'm sure my husband'll be very glad to know that I'm getting a police escort all the way back to Forest Hills."

The smile fell. "Well, just let me or Officer Pérez know. 'Scuse me." He beat a hasty retreat.

Just as he did, two people walked into the theatre area from the door at the rear: a tall, pale, lanky man in a beige trench coat over a brown suit, and a short, stocky, freckled redhead wearing a green pantsuit. Both had badges on their belts. *I'm betting these are our task force detectives.*

Spinelli and the other officer—Pérez, presumably—talked with them for a few moments, then Spinelli pointed at Mary Jane.

"Ex*cuse* me! I wasn't done *talk*ing to you two!" A short, skinny man with jet-black hair cut close to his scalp, a small goatee, and wearing an NYU sweatshirt came in behind the two detectives. This was Alfredo Garber, the owner and operator of VPC, and one of the more excitable people Mary Jane had ever met. "I simply *can*not have this! It's out*rage*ous!"

The male detective spoke in too low a volume for Mary Jane to hear, but whatever he said didn't placate Alfredo in the least.

"I have a *show* tonight! Do you know *noth*ing of the theatre? The show *must* go on!"

After a moment, the male detective left it to his partner, who didn't seem pleased at being left to deal with Alfredo by herself. She continued to talk to the theatre owner, leading him back out the door and downstairs to the lobby, where Alfredo could continue to shout.

The detective made a beeline for Mary Jane. "Hello, Ms. Watkins, I'm Detective Shapiro."

"It's Watson, actually."

"Of course," Shapiro said, sounding wholly uninterested in the subject. "Officer Spinelli tells me you saw the whole thing."

Mary Jane nodded. "Valerie was having trouble holding on to her lines, and then she turned green and grew wings, and flew through the ceiling." *Just another day in the big city.*

Shapiro remained expressionless. "I take it that Ms. McManus has never shown any indication of having super powers before?"

She shook her head.

"Does Ms. McManus take drugs?"

That question threw Mary Jane for a loop. From what she knew, both from the news and from Peter, super powers usually came about because of industrial accidents or exposure to radiation or genetic mutation.

"It's a simple yes-or-no question, Ms. Watson," Shapiro said after Mary Jane didn't answer for a moment.

"She's an actor, Detective. She—" Mary Jane hesitated.

"Do you do drugs, Ms. Watson?"

"I don't see that that's any of your business." He shrugged.

"You're an actor, Ms. Watson."

She sighed. "We've been to a couple of parties together. She wasn't always one hundred percent straight. Beyond that, I'm not really prepared to say without an attorney present."

Shapiro rolled his eyes. "Cool down, Ms. Watson, I'm just trying to paint a picture here."

"I'd rather my friend wasn't framed, if that's okay." She sighed again. "Look, there were drugs at the parties. There was coke, there was X, there was booze, there were cigarettes." She hit Shapiro with the same smile she used on Spinelli.

Shapiro did not return the smile. He just made notes and then said, "So she took ecstasy?"

"Probably. I wasn't really keeping track."

"Did she look like she was on something this afternoon?"

Mary Jane chose her words carefully. "She was having trouble with her lines. She was a little sweaty. It's possible she was high. It's also possible she had a fever or half a dozen other things." She pursed her lips. "Detective, is anyone out *looking* for Valerie?"

Shapiro nodded. "We've got an APB out, Code: Blue's looking for them, and we've alerted the Avengers and the Fantastic Four, since they tend to pick up on this kinda thing." Code: Blue, Mary Jane knew, was a special NYPD unit that dealt with paranormal activity.

The detective then asked, "Do you know if Ms. McManus associated with any known super heroes? Spider-Man, Daredevil, anybody like that?"

Shaking her head, Mary Jane said, "Not that I know of. And she would've mentioned it. She met Hugh Jackman at a party once and has yet to stop talking about it, so if she knew a super hero, she'd have said. You should probably talk to her boyfriend."

For the first time, Shapiro looked something other than bored. "She has a boyfriend?"

Mary Jane nodded. "Greg Halprin. They live in an apartment on Avenue C around 10th. I'm not sure of the exact address—Anne, the stage manager, she probably has it. She's the one breathing into a bag over there."

After writing that down, Shapiro closed his notebook and got up. "Thank you, Ms. Watson. You're free to go." He reached into the pocket of his trench coat and fished out a business card. "If you have any other information about Ms. McManus you'd like to share, please call me. And I may be calling you again as well."

Mary Jane reached up and took the proffered card. Sure enough, Detective Jeroen Shapiro worked at the 24th Precinct, located on West 100th Street.

Alfredo came back in, the redhead behind him. "Ex*cuse* me, but this *wo*man is telling me that we can't have our *show* tonight!"

"This room's a crime scene, Mr. Garber. Until I release it, it stays as is."

"But the *show*—"

"Your show is canceled, Mr. Garber. Live with it." Shapiro then went to talk to one of the uniforms.

Alfredo stormed over to Dmitri. "Can you be*lieve* this?"

"The police, they are the same everywhere," Dmitri said in a more subdued voice than Mary Jane had ever heard him use.

"Oh, people are going to hear about *this,* let me tell *you!* I *know* people, and they will most *def*initely hear of *this.* That Detective Shapiro is walking a *beat* by Friday! You *watch!*"

Mary Jane got up and joined the two men, as did another actor, Regina Wright, a willowy blonde who had a lead role in the play currently running at VPC and who was serving as Mary Jane's understudy for *The Z-Axis.* "Uh, Alfredo?" Regina said. "There's, like, a *hole* in the ceiling? We're supposed to perform here tonight, *how,* exactly?"

Alfredo rolled his eyes. "You've *nev*er heard of open-air theatre?"

Regina sighed. "Whatever."

"Dmitri," Mary Jane said, "if it's okay, I'd like to go home."

"Your shoulder, it is okay?" Dmitri asked.

Nodding, Mary Jane said, "Yeah, the paramedic gave me some pills. I'll be fine."

"Okay. You need to be your best—Olga."

Mary Jane sighed. She had been expecting this. "Dmitri, I—"

"You are understudy." He looked at the blonde. "Regina, you will play Irina and Jane Mary, you will play Olga."

"But Valerie—"

Dmitri adjusted the bill of his Dodgers cap. "I cannot have Olga with wings and green skin. The green skin, that perhaps Svetlana could work with in makeup, but wings? No good."

Mary Jane sighed. *The show must go on.* However, unlike Alfredo, she couldn't bring herself to actually utter the cliché aloud.

Regina snorted. "As *if* we're gonna even get to rehearse with Detective Sipowicz over there on the case."

Sounding confused, Dmitri said, "His name I thought is Shapiro."

"*NYPD Blue?*" Regina said with an incredulous look. "Hello, television?"

It was Dmitri's turn to snort. "I do not watch television. It is for fools."

"Whatever."

"I'm gonna get going," Mary Jane said.

"Night-night, MJ," Regina said. "You sure you're okay?"

Mary Jane nodded. "Yeah, I'm fine." She'd been terrorized by super villains in her time. By comparison, this was a walk in the park, wrenched shoulder notwithstanding. Right now, what she wanted more than anything was to be home with her husband.

However, she couldn't bear the notion of taking up Officer Spinelli's offer of going home in a blue-and-white police car. She passed by the uniformed cop as she headed to the exit. She also heard the redhead talking to Shapiro. "Look, I'm willing to finish up the interviews, but I don't think Garcia's gonna sign off on more OT without more of a case than we got. The shift ended at four, so—"

"Fine," Shapiro said, "then we'll go home after this. But let's finish the interviews."

Whatever the redhead said in response was lost to Mary Jane as she went downstairs. She grabbed her denim jacket and awkwardly put it on, trying to take it easy on her bad shoulder, then headed out the door to MacDougal Street.

The sun was starting to set, and was behind most of the buildings, leaving MacDougal pretty well shaded. A slight breeze tousled Mary Jane's red hair, and was blowing a plastic bag in circles on the street, causing a rattling sound. A man yelling profanities into a cell phone crossed in front of Mary Jane as she stepped down the stoop that led to VPC's front door.

She decided to take a cab home. It would be a bit pricey to go out to Queens from here, but after the day she'd had it was worth it to not have to deal with the subway.

Predictably, the first three cabs she saw were occupied, but the fourth pulled right in front of VPC and disgorged a passenger who was, Mary Jane suspected, about to be disappointed with regards to tonight's performance.

As she clambered into the cab and gave the driver her address, she thought, *Can't wait to tell Peter about my day. For once, mine is likely to be more exciting than his. . . .*

○———————○

SPIDER-MAN stood on the roof of an apartment building, staring out at his city.

His current perch was right on the Long Island Expressway, not far from

Parkway Hospital, where Peter Parker had changed into his red-and-blue uniform, complete with full face mask and gloves, and made his way here. He needed a few minutes to himself, and one of the advantages his super powers gave him was a wide range of options for places to go and quietly think.

It wasn't completely quiet, of course. It was now well into rush hour, so cars heading out to Long Island were backed up on the LIE, horns beeping, engines revving up and slowing down in the bumper-to-bumper traffic. Someone in one of the top-floor apartments had the window open and was watching the local news at a loud volume while frying something on the stove, the anchor's words competing with the sizzle of the pan. *Smells like chicken . . .*

But for now, Spider-Man was focused less on sounds and smells than he was on sights. He was perched on the cornice of the west-facing wall of the thirty-five-story building, staring down the ribbon of the LIE to the Midtown Tunnel, and beyond it to the Manhattan skyline, the slowly setting sun bathing the skyscrapers in a lovely yellow-and-orange glow.

When he was a kid growing up in Forest Hills, Manhattan was the mecca, the holy grail, the light at the end of the Midtown Tunnel. Young Peter Parker loved taking trips to Times Square and Rockefeller Center and Chinatown and Central Park and especially the American Museum of Natural History (his science geek cred was established early in life).

Now, though, he looked out on the skyline and mostly was reminded of conflicts. Each landmark prompted a memory of a fight against one of the dozens—maybe hundreds at this point—of costumed loonies he'd faced over the years. Even the campus of his alma mater, Empire State University, had as many super villain clashes associated with it as it did academic memories.

And now I've got students Hulking out.

"What're you, nuts?"

Spider-Man turned around to see a large black woman exiting the rooftop access door. She was waving her arms back and forth as she walked toward him, the metal door slamming shut behind her.

"Get the hell down from there, you crazy?"

"I'm, uh—I'm not crazy, ma'am, I'm just—"

"Shyeah, right, not crazy. Standin' there in some whacked-out costume on the edge of the roof. You jump, we get cops all up in here, and I ain't havin' that. Hell, that ain't even a decent Spider-Man costume. Don't look *nothin'* like the real thing."

Smiling under his mask, Spider-Man said, "Really?"

"Yeah, really. I seen Spider-Man up-close-like, and his costume looks *much* nicer than that thing you wearin'. Now get yourself *down* from there, 'fore you hurt yourself."

"Nah." Spider-Man turned his back on the woman. "Think I'll just jump."

With that, he leapt off the roof. With a double tap of his palm, a line of webbing shot out from the web-shooters in his wrists and snagged another building across the way.

As he swung around in the general direction of home, his only regret was that he couldn't see the look on the woman's face. *I love this town. . . .*

The wind whipped against Spider-Man's mask as his body sliced through the air in an arc. When that arc reached its apogee, he shot out another web, letting go of the first one. The new web struck a billboard advertising an upcoming movie, and Spider-Man hit a new arc.

This is the only way to travel.

He wouldn't admit it out loud—not even always to himself—but this was the part of being Spider-Man that Peter Parker loved most. When he first started, web-swinging had been difficult—constantly having to figure out angles of trajectory, where to leap, which parts of buildings to have the webbing adhere to, etc.—but soon enough, all of that became second nature. He didn't even think about that sort of thing anymore. Mary Jane once called it "Zen and the Art of Web-Swinging."

Now, he just enjoyed himself. The freedom of movement; the magnificent view of the city from that high up, with the people and cars looking like toys; the sound of the wind shifting (one of the first tricks he learned was to discern wind changes by listening); and so much more.

When he swung among the buildings of his hometown, he could lose himself in the joy of it all.

As he approached the apartment he and Mary Jane shared, though, those troubles came back to the fore. Dr. Lee said that Javier wasn't her first case with this so-called Triple X drug.

He planned to stop only for a moment and check in with his wife, who he knew should be coming home from rehearsal soon, but then he saw the yellow cab on the street below discharging a familiar red-haired figure. *What's she doing taking a cab home?* Peter was making a steady, if small, salary at Midtown High, and Mary Jane was still doing modeling work in addition to the acting, plus they both got occasional checks from past work—residuals from old acting parts of hers, royalties from reprints of his photographs—so they weren't in danger of starving anytime soon. But they generally weren't shelling out for cab rides from Manhattan without a good reason, either.

Coming in through the window as soon as his spider-sense died down enough to assure him that no one would see Spider-Man going into Peter Parker and Mary Jane Watson's apartment, he removed his mask and went to greet his wife.

As she opened the front door, Peter put his hands on his hips and said, "I spend all day working my *fingers* to the bone beating up bad guys, and is dinner waiting for me? No-o-o-o-o-o-o."

Mary Jane looked up in surprise, apparently not expecting Peter to be home, then gave him a wry smile. "Tiger, if that's what you were expecting, you *definitely* married the wrong woman."

"Well, I know *that's* not true, 'cause I have it on good authority that I married very much the *right* woman."

Peter looked at his wife and, for about the eight thousandth time, marveled at his luck that this woman had chosen to spend the rest of her life with him. Mary Jane was tall, with a huge mane of red hair framing her gorgeous face, knowing smile, and magnificent green eyes. She had been pretty much destined for a modeling career from high school, and she had excelled at it.

The day he met her was still seared on his consciousness. His aunt and Mary Jane's aunt, who had been best friends and neighbors for years, had been trying to set them up for months, but they kept missing each other. Peter had been convinced that Anna Watson's niece was some dull, uninteresting, unattractive woman. So when Peter—who at that point had had at least a few possibilities of relationships with other girls, among them fellow ESU student Gwen Stacy—finally met the gorgeous Mary Jane, he was totally floored.

"Face it, Tiger," she had said then, "you just hit the jackpot."

It wasn't until years later that they finally settled down to get married. For one thing, there was Gwen, and the rough period he went through after she was killed, and then Mary Jane had disappeared from his life for a while. In retrospect, however, their being together was inevitable. Mary Jane had known that Peter was Spider-Man long before he ever thought to tell her, and she had come to love him even more because of it. Though their marriage had had some rocky roads—from a pregnancy gone wrong to a miserable separation—they had come out of it stronger than ever. Having the woman he loved to come home to had made his life mission as Spider-Man in many ways more important—it gave him something concrete to fight for.

Now, he walked up to her and was about to give her a hug, when he noticed the way she was favoring her right arm. "What'd you do to your shoulder?"

"Oh, thereby hangs a tale. Brew me some coffee, and I'll tell you all about it."

Soon, they were sitting on the couch, each holding a steaming mug of coffee. Peter had handed his wife the mug with the dictionary definition of the word coffee written on it; for himself, he'd taken the one with the tiger engraved on it that Mary Jane had given him for his birthday last year, in honor of her longtime pet name for him. Peter waited to sip, for the moment enjoying the warmth and the smell of the drink. He neither smoked nor drank, nor purposely took any illicit drugs—super powers and impaired mental function were a dangerous mix—but Peter would never have been able to survive all these years without coffee.

Mary Jane then told Peter a story that floored him—not so much for the actual events, which, sadly, were pretty ordinary happenings in New York City these days, but for their similarity to those of Peter's day. By the time she was done, he'd set the mug down unsipped from.

After she finished talking about Valerie, Peter told her about Javier.

"That can't be a coincidence," she said.

"I'm thinking not, no." Peter finally drank some of his now-lukewarm coffee.

Mary Jane shook her head. "I have to admit I fibbed a bit to the detective. The fact is, every time I've seen Valerie at a party, she's been high on *something*—her and her boyfriend both. Thing is—it's only been at parties. When she's on the job, she's *never* stoned."

"Yeah, well, I didn't know Javier ever sampled the product he was dealing, either." Peter sighed. "I'm thinking this Triple X is some *seriously* good stuff."

"Well, if it turns you into a—what's the buzzword?" Mary Jane asked with a smile. "Paranormal? That's a pretty good incentive to take it right there."

Putting his mug back down on the coffee table, Peter said, "Just what this town needs: a drug that doesn't just get you high, but puts you in a position to damage more property than the Hulk and the Avengers combined—*and* will probably kill you."

"People don't usually die from X, Tiger."

Grimly, Peter said, "This stuff is laced with gamma radiation. Yeah, it gives you powers, but Dr. Lee at the hospital said that she's seen cases where the user has radiation poisoning. And Javier suffered a heart attack, probably because of the size changes. Who knows what other problems might crop up?"

"Oy."

Peter nodded. "'Oy' is right." He stood up. "The cops already seem to have a bead on this. I should head over there, see if they'll share info."

Mary Jane fixed her husband with a dubious expression. "You think that's likely?"

Letting out a breath, Peter said, "I dunno, MJ, but it's worth asking." In his career Spider-Man had been both hunted and helped by the police. It was always a crapshoot as to how any given member of the NYPD would respond to his presence.

"Well, I wouldn't bother tonight. When I left they were talking about how they were going off-shift and their supervisor wouldn't sign off on overtime for them. So they're probably not there until tomorrow."

Peter shook his head. "Figures. Well, I should still do my nightly patrol. Don't want the criminals thinking Spidey's taken a night off."

Mary Jane stood up and put her good arm on Peter's shoulder. "Go get 'em, Tiger. Me, I'm gonna take a hot bath."

"Good plan." His wife was far less accustomed to the bumps and bruises that were part and parcel of Spider-Man's daily existence. The hot bath would do her good. He gave her a deep, heartfelt kiss, then put his mask back on and, once his spider-sense gave the all-clear, leapt back out into the evening air.

FOUR

HECTOR Diaz threw his books into his locker with a little more force than was probably necessary. He got the usual from Mom this morning—like it was any of *her* business what he was doin' with his life. Not like she gave a damn before; he didn't know why she was up in his face now. It was like as soon as he hit high school, suddenly it was time for her to start bein' a mom after not giving a damn for fourteen years. Hell with that.

Biggie came up to him when he closed the locker. Hector didn't even know what Biggie's real name was—didn't matter none, since he was bigger than any other damn person in the school, even the seniors and the teachers, and he was a sophomore. Any other name wouldn't'a meant nothin'.

"Yo, Hector, what up." Biggie offered his massive hand. Hector took it, his own full hand smaller than Biggie's palm. "Listen, I got the good stuff, yo."

Hector winced. "Naw, man, I can't be doin' that. My Moms is all up in my face."

"The hell's that got to do with nothin'? I'm talkin' quality product here, you feel me?"

"Yeah, man, but I can't be doin' that. Not right now."

Biggie shook his head, which looked pretty crazy since Biggie didn't have much by way of a neck. "That's messed up, yo. Look, this be the high you been waitin' all your *life* for. You can't be passin' this up."

Hector thought this sounded like a big pile of crap. "This the same stuff Javier be takin'?"

"Man, why you want to be bringin' that up?" Biggie let out a big breath. "Look, Javier ain't right in the head."

"All's I know is, Javier went crazy, then went to the hospital."

Biggie shook his head again. "Look, this ain't stepped-on, a'ight? Now Javier be buggin', but you ain't Javier, yo. He think he all that, but he ain't. You can take this."

Hector closed his locker. "Nah, man, I can't. My Moms, she's all up in my face right now. I get high, she'll be tossin' my ass to the *street*, yo."

"A'ight, I get what you sayin'. But you change your mind, you know where I be?"

Biggie was part of Ray-Ray's crew, and that meant the Robinsfield Houses in Long Island City. "Same bat-time, same bat-channel?"

"Most def."

Hector nodded. *Still at them Houses, then.* Biggie held up his hand. Again, Hector returned the handshake.

Not that Hector planned to take Biggie up on that offer. He might go down there to score some blow or some weed, if he couldn't figure out a way to get it on his own, but Triple X? No way. No matter what Biggie said, Javier wasn't no fool, he was hardcore, and if that was sending his narrow ass down to the hospital, Hector was stayin' the hell away from it. He got high 'cause it was nice and 'cause it beat the hell out of sitting at home watching his mom drink herself to death the way she been doing since Dad walked out on them.

But when high started to mean hospital, Hector wasn't playing.

Martha Diaz came up to her locker, which was right next to Hector's, since the lockers were assigned alphabetically. Martha and Hector weren't related, of course—there were a total of ten Diazes at Midtown, and the only ones who were family were Martha and her older sister Wilma—but they'd been tight since grammar school.

"Hey, girl, you hear from Javier?" Hector knew that Martha's best friend was Javier's cousin, Rosanna.

Martha opened her locker door. "He still in the hospital. Last I heard, he ain't even waked up yet."

"Damn. That's messed up." Hector shook his head. "You figure they gonna expel his ass?"

Shrugging, Martha gathered up her books for the day. "School policy."

"Yeah. He been arrested?"

Frowning, Martha said, "I don't think so. Rosanna didn't say nothin' 'bout that."

"That don't make no sense. He hit Nariz and that fat guard, and Mr. Parker."

"Yeah, but I'm feeling a *lot* better now."

Hector turned around to see Mr. Parker. Both he and Martha immediately straightened up. Teachers hated when kids had bad posture, Hector learned that much in the first grade.

Mr. Parker shook his head. "Why do kids always do that?" He smiled. "Look, as long as you do your homework, I don't care if you look like the Hunchback of Notre Dame. Just stand the way you always do."

"The whoback of what?" Hector asked. Like most teachers, Mr. Parker didn't make no sense most of the time.

"Never mind. Look, I'm sorry, but I heard you two talking, and I think I know why Javier hasn't been arrested."

"Oh yeah?" Hector didn't see how a science teacher would know about that.

"I was talking to the doctor at the hospital."

That confused Hector at first, but if Mr. Parker was one of the ones who got hit when Javier went all crazy, then he woulda been at the hospital, too.

Mr. Parker went on: "She said there's a concern that Javier might get radiation poisoning from the Triple X."

"Triple X? What's that?" Hector asked, hoping he sounded cool.

"Calm down, Hector, I'm not wearing a wire. Right now, the main thing I'm worried about is this drug. If Javier *does* get radiation poisoning, then he's gonna be in the hospital for a long time—which is probably why they didn't arrest him."

Hector exchanged a quick look with Martha, who looked as confused as he felt. "What's that got to do with it?"

"If Javier's arrested while he's checked into Parkway, the NYPD then becomes responsible for his hospital bills. They're not gonna pay for that, and besides, it's not like he's going anywhere. If he's released, they'll probably read him his rights on the way out the door."

"That's messed up." Hector slammed his locker door shut. "Them cops are *totally* messed up." Then he looked again at Mr. Parker. "How you be knowin' all this about policin'?"

Mr. Parker grinned. "I wasn't always a teacher, Hector." Then he got all serious again. "Look, I need to ask you if either of you know where Javier got the Triple X."

Hector gave the teacher a nasty look. "Thought you said you weren't wearin' a wire, yo."

"I'm not. I'm just worried. Nariz and Mr. Lefkowitz and I were lucky that we weren't hurt too badly. The next person who gets in the way of a Triple X junkie may not be so lucky."

"Javier ain't no junkie," Martha said.

"Sorry, I didn't mean to say he was," Mr. Parker said. Hector was surprised to realize that it sounded like the teacher actually meant it.

Still, Hector wasn't buying Mr. Parker's act. He figured that the cops set him on the kids 'cause maybe the kids would talk to him. And for a teacher, Mr. Parker was okay. He made stupid jokes a lot, but he also talked to the students like they was people instead of pets like most teachers did.

But what got Hector going was what Mr. Parker said about why Javier wasn't arrested.

"What'll happen if Javier got radiating poison?"

"*Radiation* poison—and if he does have it, his cells will break down, his hair will fall out, he may get cancer. No matter what, he's pretty likely to die."

"I thought radiation give you super powers or whatever."

"It can. It can also kill you. Sometimes it does both. And who knows, Javier may be fine. But what about the next kid?"

Hector thought about what would happen if his hair all fell out and he got all sick. Then he looked up at Mr. Parker. "Look, I ain't sayin' nothin' here, a'ight, but—well, if you wasn't so white, I'd say you might want to check out Long Island City."

"I won't blend in, huh?"

"*Hell,* no." He turned around. "Look, I gotta be gettin' to class."

"Me too," Martha muttered.

Both Diazes packed up their books and went to their homeroom, leaving Mr. Parker behind.

As soon as they were out of earshot, Martha got all up in Hector's face. "What you be *tellin'* him that for?"

"Look, it's one thing gettin' high, but hair fallin' out? Dyin' of cancer? No way. Old folks die of cancer. I ain't seein' nobody goin' like that."

"He a *teacher*, Hector. He just tell the cops, you watch. 'Sides, what the hell *you* care about all this? You ain't takin' it, right?"

"Hell no!" Hector wondered why he *did* tell the teacher. If Javier got all dead, it wasn't nothing to him.

He thought about it all the rest of the day.

○━━━━━━━━━━━○

THE cacophony of the *Daily Bugle* City Room assaulted Peter Parker's senses: the sight of interns dashing back and forth, running errands for the reporters; the sound of reporters talking on their phones and typing on keyboards with rapid-fire clacks; and, of course, the lingering smell of publisher J. Jonah Jameson's cigars.

There are times when I've really missed this place.

Peter came here straight from school, the route from Forest Hills to the East Side's *Daily Bugle* Building so ingrained in his mind he barely even had to pay attention. This was the first of two Manhattan stops he needed to make this afternoon, especially after what he'd heard from Hector, and after Mary Jane's voicemail informing him that no one had seen Valerie since she flew through VPC's roof.

He navigated unerringly among the desks that were all butted against each other, his spider-sense allowing him to avoid collisions with interns rushing to run errands and reporters rushing to chase stories and editors rushing to berate reporters. He caught sight of several former colleagues and gave them each a polite wave.

Walking over to Betty Brant's desk, he saw her talking on the phone and typing on the keyboard of a small laptop that sat amidst the papers and Post-it notes on her desk.

Betty had dropped out of high school to work as Jameson's assistant at the *Bugle* when her mother became too sick to continue in that job. She was also Peter Parker's first crush—mostly by virtue of being the first woman who ever gave Peter a second look, or even a first one. Sadly, their relationship never really went anywhere romantically.

She had also been through more than any six people should. Her brother had been killed by Dr. Octopus; her husband, Ned Leeds, was brainwashed by the Hobgoblin and then killed by an assassin known as the Foreigner; and she herself was taken in briefly by a cult.

Somehow, though, she'd come out the other side of all those traumas stronger than ever. No longer a glorified secretary, she was now an investigative reporter, and a good one. She brought down both the Hobgoblin and the Foreigner with her mightier-than-a-sword pen, had reported stories from as far away as Latveria, and had won a couple of awards to show for it.

Every time he looked at her, he remembered something she'd said to him shortly after Peter started taking photos for the *Bugle*. Jonah had been engaged in one of his usual rants, with Peter as the subject. Betty— who, up to that point, was just the person Peter got his pay vouchers from, but not much else—sidled up to him and whispered the words that became imprinted on his brain: "Don't feel too bad, Peter. I may only be JJ's secretary, but *I* think you're *wonderful*."

Nobody had ever called him *wonderful* in quite that tone of voice before, and certainly not while wearing lilac perfume. Peter long suspected that the only reason why he had the courage to even talk to the likes of Gwen and Mary Jane was because Betty had expressed interest in him back then.

She smiled at Peter as he approached and mouthed the words *hang on* while she listened and typed. "Yeah, Marty. Yeah. Yeah. Okay. Great, thanks for the tip. Yes, you'll get credit. *Yes,* that means your name in the paper. I'll even spell it right. Okay, thanks, Marty. Bye."

Hanging up the phone, she immediately stood and wrapped her arms around Peter. "Long time no see, Petey!"

Returning the hug, Peter said, "Too long, Betts. How goes the reporter's life?"

"Busy as always. I'm actually working on a pretty big story right now. How's that corruption of the youth of America coming?"

Laughing, Peter said, "Slowly but surely. Actually, the youth that I'm corrupting is why I'm here. I had one of my kids Hulk out after school, and the E.R. doc said he was on a new drug called Triple X. It's a gamma-hyped ecstasy. One of MJ's fellow thespians is taking it, too—she knocked a hole in the ceiling of the theatre last night. I was wondering if anybody was covering this for the *Bugle* or not."

Betty grinned. "Trying to bring us a scoop?"

Returning the grin, Peter said, "Nah, my days in the fourth estate are behind me."

"Really?" Betty gave him a dubious look.

"Yes, really."

Shaking her head, Betty said, "I don't buy it. You'll be back to taking pictures eventually. It's in your blood. You forget, I knew you when you *started* as a shooter."

Peter shrugged. "Maybe someday, but today isn't that day. Right now, I'm just looking to find out more about this. I get the feeling this kid isn't the only one at Midtown High trying it out, and I'm worried."

Sitting back down at her desk and offering her guest chair to Peter, Betty picked up a pen off her desk and started tapping her cheek with it. After Peter sat in the guest chair, she said, "Actually—*that's* the story I'm working on." She pointed at the phone. "Marty there is a nurse at St. Luke's uptown. They've gotten a few cases up there—in fact, the first one was in a housing project up on Amsterdam in the 90s."

That explains a lot, Peter thought. The 24th Precinct was located on West 100th Street, so if they'd caught the first case of Triple X, it made sense that the task force would have been formed there.

"Do you know who's dumping this crap on the street?"

Betty snorted. "I wish. If I had the supplier, I'd have the story of a lifetime—and a way to get at the creep. Whoever it is, they're making a mint. From what I've been able to find out, the dealers slinging this stuff are raking in three times their usual take. They can probably carry some heavy weight if they keep this up. Unfortunately, all I know is that it's been showing up more and more and people really like it. And who can blame them, really? I mean, it not only gives you the same high you get from X, you've got the high *and* the super powers. Every day, you hear about the latest super hero fight. They're all over the place, especially in this town, and—our publisher's preferences notwithstanding—they're mostly glamorized." She chuckled.

"You know that, since he was revived, Captain America's been on the cover of *Time* and *Newsweek* more than the sitting president?"

"Doesn't surprise me." Peter tried not to sound bitter, but he himself rarely got that kind of publicity. The Avengers and the Fantastic Four were major celebrities, true, and other heroes tended to get lavish news coverage right alongside the actors and the sports stars. Spider-Man, though, had never had that kind of luck.

"So if you're the type of person who fits the profile for taking drugs—down on your luck, crappy home life, not much hope of improvement—" Betty hesitated.

Peter felt a pang of sympathy—Betty could very well be describing her own life before she got it together.

She shook it off. "You're that type of person, and you see the super heroes getting all the ink and news coverage, and you think, *I wanna be that*. Triple X gives you that chance. Not surprising that it's the hottest new drug."

"Yeah, right up until it kills you from radiation poisoning."

Betty nodded. "But that doesn't really make it any different from any other drug. They all kill you in the end, it's just a question of how." She leaned forward. "Anyhow, that's all I've really got so far. I don't know how it'll help your student or Mary Jane's friend, though."

Grinning, Peter said, "Well, like I keep telling my kids, knowledge is power. Thanks, Betts."

"Parker! What the hell're *you* doing here?"

Peter looked up to see the ever-scowling face of J. Jonah Jameson, framed by his flattop haircut and highlighted by his trademark Charlie Chaplin mustache. Wearing his usual white shirt and suit pants—rumpled from a day of ranting and raving—with his omnipresent cigar between the first two fingers of his right hand, the lanky Jonah stood over Betty's desk.

"Just dropping by for a visit, Jonah."

"This is the City Room, Parker, not a Starbucks. Last time I checked, you didn't work here anymore, and that makes you a trespasser in my newspaper office."

"Actually," Betty said before Peter could respond, "Peter's a source on my Triple X story. He was just telling me about two more cases."

"Really?" Jonah's eyes lit up. He popped the cigar in his mouth, puffed, and blew out a cloud of acrid smoke. "Don't suppose you have pictures?"

"'Fraid not, Jonah. I'm just an ordinary citizen talking to a reporter."

"Bah! You were never 'ordinary,' Parker, that much I'll swear to. Well, all right, Brant, keep this ingrate around—let him sit there and pretend that I never brought him up from nothing and made a celebrity of him, only to have him turn his back on me. But when he's done, he's gone, got it?"

"Absolutely, Jonah."

"Hmph." Jonah took another puff. "You used to call me 'Mr. Jameson.'"

Betty smiled sweetly. "I used to be your secretary. All the other reporters call you Jonah."

"Yeah, that was my first mistake." Something caught his eye. "Snow! What the hell are you doing here? Why aren't you out covering that damn press conference?"

Jonah stalked off to yell at Charley Snow. Once he was out of earshot, both Betty and Peter burst out laughing.

"Sorry about that, Peter."

Waving her off, Peter said, "Don't worry about it. Honestly, it was kind of refreshing."

Looking at him like he was crazy, Betty said, "You're kidding."

"No. It's kinda nice. It brings stability to my world to know that, no matter what else might happen, Jonah's still a cantankerous old coot."

Again, Betty laughed. "That's for sure. Look, I'd better type up these notes I got from Marty—hey, since I already told Jonah you were a source, can you give me specifics on your kid? Or Mary Jane's friend?"

Peter hesitated. He didn't want to make Eileen Velasquez's life any more difficult. "I'd rather not give a name."

"I'll be vague—a high school student in Queens and a theatrical actress in Manhattan?"

"That's fine," Peter said with a nod. "The kid turned into a mini-Hulk, and the actress turned into a green harpy."

Betty typed all that into her computer. "Great. I may call you later, run the text by you?"

"Thanks, Betts, I appreciate that."

"And if I learn anything that can help your student or Mary Jane's friend, I'll try to pass it on."

Putting a hand on Betty's hand, he said in a quiet voice, "Thanks again."

"Hey—always willing to help out a friend, Petey. And you've always been one of the best."

FIVE

"AND then she asks me why the DNA tests ain't done yet."

Jack Larsen, the desk sergeant at the 24th Precinct, was only half-listening to Detective Christopher Carter. Most of his energy was focused on filing the day's run-sheets. Inspector Garcia was on a paperwork kick ever since he got reamed at the last ComStat meeting for the Two-Four's crappy paperwork, so of course the inspector was taking it out on Larsen.

But the desk sergeant was always willing to let Carter go off on one of his rants, mainly because Larsen knew that the short, bald, pudgy detective had worn down the patience of the other occupants of the precinct house. It didn't bother Larsen any, and it kept Carter out of the other detectives' hair. Usually, Larsen was able to use this service as currency to actually get the damn run-sheets in on time. It mostly worked—he'd gotten everyone's but O'Leary's today, and O'Leary was working on hers right now.

"So I tell her, I says, 'Look, lady, we only got the soda can yesterday. It'll be *weeks* before we get the results.' And she just looks at me, and she says, 'But on *CSI* they do DNA tests in a couple of hours!' Can you believe that crap?"

Having caught the interrogative, Larsen quickly said, "Yeah, it's nuts." Then he went back to searching for Detective Wheeler's run-sheet. *It was here a minute ago.*

"I dunno what's worse, TV or the damn costumes." Carter shook his head. "Nah, it's the TV. Costumes at least sometimes help out, y'know? But TV don't do nothin' but spread misinformation to an already sad and pathetic general populace."

Larsen took Carter's brief pause for breath as an opportunity to make an incoherent grunt, thus creating the illusion of paying attention. Right now, he was running his hands through what was left of his red hair and getting seriously concerned about Wheeler's run-sheet. The detective had brought it by, talked for a few minutes about his latest conquest—a student at the Fashion Institute of Technology with what Wheeler called the hottest lips he'd ever kissed on a woman—and then gone to check on something for the Triple X Task Force.

"*CSI*'s the worst. Like anybody'd let some crime scene geek near a suspect. Or give 'em a weapon. Hey, can you imagine *Gardner* with a nine in his pants?"

"No, I can't." In that, Larsen was honest. Steve Gardner, the head of the Crime Scene Unit, wouldn't know what to do with a nine-millimeter pistol that he wasn't bagging for evidence.

"'Course it ain't all bad. Wish the job was like *NYPD Blue,* where you can yell at suspects for half an hour without them lawyering up. I swear, I never saw nobody ask for a lawyer on that damn show. You know what the only show that got it right was? *Barney Miller.*"

"Oh yeah?" Larsen asked as he riffled through the existing run-sheets for the fifth time, on the ever-less-likely theory that Wheeler's got mixed in with someone else's. If that didn't work, he was going to bang his head against the ugly white-and-bright-green walls that made the whole precinct house feel like a 1950s public school.

"Yeah. On *Barney Miller,* they spent all their time fillin' out paperwork and dealing with whack-jobs in the squad rooms. Sounds like my day-to-day, lemme tell ya. We won't even talk about—"

"Carter, would you mind explaining what in the seven levels of *hell* your posterior—not to mention the rest of your rather sad-looking self—is doing out here?"

Larsen turned to see the sergeant in charge of the dayshift detectives, Bill Green, in the entryway to the squad room, his tiny hands resting on his ample hips. The sergeant was affectionately known to his detectives as "The Jolly Green Giant," generally simplified to "Joll." He weighed about three hundred and fifty pounds, which he proudly proclaimed was "all fat—especially what's between my ears." Joll was shaped like one of those clowns that you punched that bounced back up, complete with thick middle and ovoid head—covered with a thick patch of brown hair that the balding Larsen was jealous of, especially since Joll was older than Larsen by five years.

Carter rolled his eyes. "Just givin' the sarge here my run-sheets, Joll. I—"

"What you were doing, *Detective,* was wasting the good sergeant's time with your tiresome diatribes on the televisual medium's portrayal of our noble calling. This is in direct opposition to what you should be doing, which is being by the phones, seeing as how you're up."

Carter straightened. "We got a call?"

Green nodded and removed a Post-it from his shirt pocket. "Break-in at 98th and CPW. You're taking Barron with you."

Wincing as he took the proffered Post-it, Carter asked, "Does it have to be Barron?"

Putting his hand over his heart, Green asked, "What's this? Can it be that you have a problem with the good Detective Barron? Is it possible that there is strife in the heretofore calm and friendly ranks of the Two-Four's detective squad?"

"It's just—" Carter sighed. "She insists on driving."

"So?"

"You ever been a passenger with her?"

Green shrugged. "It's rush hour—how fast can she go?"

"She'll find a way," Carter said gravely. "I gotta go to my desk, get my Dramamine."

Kelly Barron then came bursting out from behind Green, holding up a set of car keys and heading to the front door. "C'mon, Carter, let's go. I got us a car."

Rolling his eyes, Carter followed her. "I'm driving."

"I got the car."

"Like hell you do, I ain't taken my Dramamine."

"Don't be such a wuss."

Larsen watched them leave, unable to hold back a chuckle. Green turned to him, grinned, and said, "It's always so touching whenever the kids leave home for the first time, isn't it?" Growing serious, he asked, "How're we with the run-sheets?"

"Almost perfect."

Green looked pensive. "I like the word 'perfect.' It has a certain ring to it. Flows off the tongue almost effortlessly. That is, when it's by itself." Fixing Larsen with a hard look, he added, "It's when it has that modifier that it loses some of its innate charm. The word 'almost' ruins the effect—to the point where it is likely to make our wise and beneficent precinct commander unhappy. And when Inspector Garcia is unhappy, he tends to kick downward—at his sergeants. Meaning thee and me, my good friend. So what is this 'almost' crap?"

Sighing, Larsen said, "I can't find Wheeler's run-sheet. He dropped it off, talked for half an hour about that FIT student he bagged—"

"The one with the lips?"

"That's the one," Larsen said with a nod. "Now I can't find it. I looked everywhere."

"Well, it's not up here."

The voice scared Larsen out of about ten years of life, mainly because it came from above him. He jumped back, his hand automatically going to his weapon.

Looking up, he saw a strangely contorted figure with no face hanging from the cheap tile-work that passed for a ceiling.

After a second, he realized that the figure was human, and wearing a blue-and-red bodysuit, down to the mask. After another second, he realized that it was Spider-Man. He was hanging by one of his web-lines, upside down, knees bent and feet together, both over his head, which was now looking down at Larsen.

"How the hell'd you get in here?" Larsen asked.

"Ah, c'mon, Sergeant, you can't expect me to give away all my trade secrets. They'll make me turn in my hero union card." If he squinted, Larsen could see a jaw moving under the mask, but it was still creepy. The eyes in the mask were opaque and didn't blink, and Larsen could only make out the shape of a nose—and no mouth. That was the creepiest part.

"You guys have a union?" Larsen managed to ask.

"I wish. It'd save me a bundle on dry cleaning."

Green asked, "Would you mind explaining your presence in our precinct house, kind sir?"

"'Kind sir'? I like that. I'm trying to find some information about Triple X. Word on the street is that the task force is here, so I figured I'd just drop in."

Larsen wondered if the pun was deliberate. Probably, he thought.

"Most of the task force is out with their ears to the proverbial ground right now. However, you're in luck—one Detective Una O'Leary is still present and accounted for. She's finishing up her run-sheet." Green said that last with a look at Larsen. Larsen swallowed. Then Green smiled up at Spider-Man. "She's a bit late with it."

"That's the nice thing about my end of this business—no paperwork."

Green gazed at Spider-Man for a couple of seconds. "Maybe, but I don't think I'd be able to pull off wearing the spandex." For emphasis, he patted his ample belly with his hands, then he pointed to the door to the squad room. "Go through there, and then head upstairs. O'Leary's the redhead."

"Much obliged, uh—?"

"Sergeant Bill Green, at your service. And what do I call you?"

"Spider-Man's fine—or Spidey. I also answer to 'Hey you.'"

"Fine, Mr. Hey You, just head through there."

Larsen heard a chuckle from Spider-Man. "Everyone's a comedian. Thanks, Sergeant!"

With that, he swung around and leapt over to the squad room door in a manner that just was not natural. Somehow he jumped without having anything to push off, and twisted his body around to land hands and feet first over the door. Then he skittered through the doorway. It made Larsen nauseous just to watch it.

He turned to Green. "You're just gonna let that creep run loose in the squad room? In the precinct?"

Green fixed Larsen with a gaze. "You remember Jean DeWolff?"

"Oh yeah. She was good police," Larsen said. DeWolff was a captain downtown, till she got herself shot by a fellow cop who had gone nuts and begun to call himself by one of those crazy costume names, Sin-Swallower or something like that. Larsen had liked DeWolff; her father was a cop, too, and she was carrying on the tradition, like a real police. "What about her?"

Pointing at the door through which Spider-Man had just gone, Green said, "That's the gentleman that caught the bastard who killed her. And he was right there from the very beginning of the investigation, trying to avenge her, working with us. Far as I'm concerned, that man's welcome in my house."

Larsen wasn't entirely sure he agreed—but that was mainly because he was still feeling the burrito he had for lunch crawling back up his throat from watching Spider-Man twist and turn and jump. "Yeah, okay, whatever. But if Garcia asks what he's doing here, I was in the bathroom when he came in."

"Why don't you go to the restroom now, Jack—see if Wheeler's run-sheet's in the urinal?"

Letting out a long breath, Larsen said, "I'll find it, Joll, I'll find it."

"See that you do, Sergeant, because if the inspector does get in a kicking mood, I'm gonna make sure that, despite my own gluteus maximus providing a much more inviting target, the only behind his foot finds is yours. Am I perfectly clear in my meaning?"

Nodding, Larsen said, "Yeah, like a glass, Joll."

UNA O'Leary hated doing run-sheets.

No, it was more fundamental than that. She hated doing paperwork of any kind. For some reason, when she became a cop she thought that she'd spend all her time chasing bad guys and grilling suspects, and doing all the fun stuff you saw on television. She'd be like the Invisible Woman or the She-Hulk or the Wasp—her role models, really, women who made a difference in the world. Yeah, they had super powers, but O'Leary figured she could make up for it with her training at the police academy.

However, as Carter was happy to carry on about at a loud volume, life wasn't like it was on television, especially if you were a cop. Instead, you had lots and lots of paperwork.

And it got worse when she made detective. She was only a third-grade, and she had tons of the stuff, three times what she had as a uniform, and it would only get worse as she moved up to second- and first-grade.

Assuming I live that long. Assuming Joll doesn't string me up by my short hairs for not getting the run-sheets done. One advantage she had was that she had learned how to touch-type at a young age. Her mother had insisted, as it meant she'd have "a skill you can *use*" when she got older, never imagining for a minute that her little girl would become a police officer. O'Leary had been on the job seven years, and her mother was still trying to wrap her mind around the idea.

In any case, she was up to a hundred-and-fifty words a minute—which also meant that she was the one who usually got stuck typing up reports and such. But it was worth it not to have to suffer the agony of watching Wheeler hunt and peck with his right index finger. He wouldn't even use his left; drove her crazy.

Right now, the clacking of her keyboard was the only sound in the detectives' squad room. Carter and Barron were out on a call, Johannsen and Ursitti both were on vacation, McAvennie had called in sick, and the rest of this shift's detectives were, like O'Leary, on the Triple X Task Force, and were all following up leads. That left O'Leary alone with her run-sheet.

The squad room took up most of the tiny second floor of the Two-Four. The upper story was really the attic, but a few years ago it was converted to offices for the detectives during a rare instance when the city provided *more* money for the cops instead of less. However, with the pipes running along the already-low ceiling, that left them without much head clearance—really only a problem for Fry, who was six-eight.

"Wow, that's some fast typing."

O'Leary looked up, but didn't see anyone standing by her desk, and she hadn't heard anyone come in.

"Up here."

"Ohmigod. You're Spider-Man," she said as she looked up, but before her conscious mind entirely registered that the hero in question was hanging from one of the pipes.

"Your friendly neighborhood," the hero said jauntily. "I bumped into Sergeant Green outside—he said you were the person to talk to about Triple X."

I don't believe this. Spider-Man's coming to me *for advice. This is so cool!*

Then she came to her senses. *This has to be a joke.* "Wheeler put you up to this, right? He's still pissed at me 'cause of what happened at the pizzeria. C'mon, who's that under the mask?"

"Uh, Detective, I'm hanging upside down from a pipe." Then, suddenly, the costumed figure did a triple forward flip, landing squarely on his feet in front of her desk. Then he did a backflip, landing perfectly on O'Leary's guest chair.

Okay, so maybe this really is him.

"So," she said without missing a beat, "you want to know about Triple X."

"Yup. I've been coming across it lately, and—well, it's not good. People getting super powers while in a drug-induced haze isn't exactly a recipe for keeping the peace."

"That would be a big no." She opened one of the drawers in her desk and pulled out one of the dozens of files they had on this case. "This is one we pulled yesterday—woman rehearsing a play in the Village, turns into a harpy and flies through the ceiling."

"Boy, even these off-Broadway plays are getting special effects budgets these days."

O'Leary couldn't help but chuckle. "Yeah. From what we can tell, the woman's already a druggie—an actor taking drugs; what're the odds, right?—and she graduated to Triple X."

"'Graduated'?"

Nodding, O'Leary said, "This isn't a beginner's drug. This is the stuff they go to when they're tired of their regular high. Every case we got so far has a history."

"And it started around here?"

Again, O'Leary nodded. "Down on Amsterdam in the 90s. Some kid turned all green and got a big head. Started throwing things with his mind."

It was Spider-Man's turn to nod. "Telekinesis."

"Whatever. All I know is that the kid wrecked the lobby of his apartment building and one of the parking lots across the street from it before he came back down. Docs found weird stuff in his blood—like X, but not really. We only know the name Triple X from some of our CIs."

Spider-Man paused. She wondered if his face changed under the mask, but she couldn't really see it. *God, I love that disguise.* Finally, he said, "Cardiac infarctions?"

"Confidential informants. It's all any of them are talking about." She leaned back in her chair. "The biggest problem is that we don't have a sample of the drug itself. Every victim we've found has swallowed all of what they got." She looked at Spider-Man, who was impossible to read, just sitting there in his full face mask and being enigmatic. "This help you?"

"A little."

"Good. Can you give me anything back?"

Spider-Man seemed to consider it for a second. "I know that this stuff might be coming out of Long Island City."

That surprised O'Leary—she really hadn't expected a positive answer to her question. "Why didn't you say that before?" She riffled through the papers on her desk trying to find a pen, then remembered she'd stuck one in her hair to hold it up. She removed the pen, causing her red tresses to fall sloppily onto her shoulders. "LIC, huh? That means it might be one of the crews in the Bridgeview Houses or the boys at the Robinsfield Houses." She wrote down both names on a Post-it. "Or somebody we don't know."

"I'd lean toward that, honestly," Spider-Man said. "This stuff has some serious science behind it. Irradiating a drug—especially with just the right amount of gamma radiation to do what this stuff is doing—is not something that just anybody can do."

O'Leary nodded. "Again, no sample, no luck."

"Tell you what—if I find myself facing off against a crazed horde of green druggies, I'll try to get at their stash and send it to you guys."

That surprised O'Leary. "Really?"

"You sound surprised."

And he sounded amused. "Well, you guys aren't known for being all cooperative." She leaned forward, having wanted to have this conversation for *years*. "And you really *should*. God, if we could share information with you guys more often, we could do the job so much better. You guys have access to stuff we can't get near. And people will talk to a super hero who won't come near a cop. Besides, you guys have anonymity, which I think is great, really. Yours is the best—the way that mask covers everything, and the way you stand all hunched over like someone folded your spine in half. How's anyone supposed to ID you? You white, black, Hispanic, Asian, what? Can't tell height, can't tell facial hair, can't tell hair or eye color. Best we can do is weight, and your build looks slightly above average, but that's about it. And I'm babbling again, I'm really sorry—it's just that I've always wanted to meet one of you guys and talk about this stuff."

"That's—that's all right," Spider-Man said slowly. "Look, we'll get a chance to talk again, I promise. Right now, I want to head out and see what else I can find. And I'd definitely check out those places in Queens."

O'Leary snorted. "Yeah, like I can use the word of a guy in a mask as PC for a search." Inspector Garcia would have her head if he knew she was even talking to a "costume," as he, and several others in the department, called them. If he found out Spider-Man was her probable cause, he'd go ballistic. "Still, I can talk to the One-Oh-Eight, tell them to keep an eye out."

"Great. I'll do likewise." Spider-Man jumped to the floor from his squatting position on the chair.

He didn't move from that position the entire time, and now he doesn't even look like he cramped up. How does he do that?

She threw some papers and Post-it notes around, finally finding her card-holder. "Here's my card—stay in touch, okay? I think if we work together, we got a much better chance of beating this thing."

"I hope you're right, Detective. Thanks!"

After putting the card in a compartment in his belt, he jumped up to the ceiling pipe, crawled along it to the window, opened it, and then leapt out. O'Leary heard the *thwip* of his web-shooters.

She got up, walked past Wheeler, Ursitti, and Petrocelli's desks, and closed the window behind him—it was too chilly to let the late-afternoon air in. Besides, O'Leary liked it warm in here, even if the pipes overdid it sometimes, and since she had the place to herself . . .

I just talked with Spider-Man. And I'll probably talk to him again! This is so cool!

Sighing, she sat back down at her desk, wiggled her mouse to reactivate the screen—which had gone into standby mode while she talked to Spider-Man—and stared dolefully at the run-sheet file. After a moment, she started typing again, determined to get the thing to the sarge and out of her hair ASAP.

Can't wait to tell Shapiro about this . . .

○——————○

AS he swung amidst the buildings of the condominium complex that took up the space between 97th and 100th Streets on Central Park West, Spider-Man couldn't help but grin under his mask. *A cop who's a super hero groupie. I've now officially seen everything.*

Still, he knew more than he did before he made the trip to the Two-Four, and he'd also given the cops a tip on the source of the Triple X. *Assuming, of course, that Hector's reliable. Only one way to find out.* Mary Jane would be busy all through the evening—VPC was having its roof repaired, but the director had apparently rented a space on Bleecker Street for the night, so they'd be rehearsing late—freeing Spider-Man to investigate the possibilities in the early evening. One of the reasons he'd gone to talk to the cops first was to narrow Hector's intelligence down a bit. Long Island City was, after all, a decent-sized neighborhood, so Spider-Man appreciated Detective O'Leary's giving him a couple of starting points.

Just as he swung out over Central Park West and prepared to shoot a line onto one of the trees in the park itself, his spider-sense tingled a warning. So ingrained had his spider-sense become to the way he functioned that his right arm swung around behind him and his fingers tapped on his web-shooters before he'd even consciously acknowledged that his spider-sense was buzzing. The web-line hit one of the tall apartment buildings that faced the park on the southwest corner of 97th, and acted as a fulcrum to bring Spider-Man around and back over the street instead of into the park.

Landing on another building on Central Park West, closer to 96th, Spider-Man had no trouble identifying the source of the warning.

Four people knocked over one of the ubiquitous hot dog stands that had been selling their wares on Manhattan street corners for longer than Peter Parker had been alive. These four all shared one feature: each of them had skin that was an emerald green.

Triple X strikes again, Spider-Man thought as he shot a web-line to one of the trees that was both across and down the street a bit, then slid down it, taking him toward the quartet.

As he slid, he noted that one of them, a female, was bigger than the others, and currently smashing the hot dog stand to little pieces. A second—also female—was jumping up and down and yelling. A third was male, and had an outsized head, and was yelling something at the fourth one, also male. That last one fired a green ray-beam out of his mouth (which struck Spider-Man as more than a little gross) at the hot dog vendor, who collapsed to the ground even as Spider-Man let go of his web-line to land on the cobblestone-like surface of the Central Park West sidewalk.

"Now, now, boys and girls, just because he put too much sauerkraut on your dog, is that any reason to get crotchety?"

"Spider-Man?" the big-headed one asked.

"See, I just *knew* that hiring a publicist would do me good."

"Your feeble wit indeed identifies you as the wall-crawler," Big-Head said in a mocking tone. "I had hoped to pit my considerable intellect against a worthier foe, but you shall have to suffice. Attack, my minions!"

His spider-sense warning him of danger even as it was being loudly announced by Big-Head, Spider-Man leapt straight up toward a bus stop enclosure, doing a front flip and landing square on top. Meanwhile, the bruiser jumped for the spot where Spider-Man had been standing, just as Ray-Beam Mouth spit out a blast at the same location. Sadly, this meant that the beam hit the bruiser, who grunted her great annoyance.

"I'm sorry," Ray-Beam Mouth said, but that just caused another beam to hit the woman. She stumbled backward, but, unlike the vendor, did not fall.

"Buffoons!" Big-Head cried. "I am beset by buffoons! How many times must I remind you never to speak, Adrian?"

"You know," Spider-Man said, "when you talk like that, you sound just like Stewie from *Family Guy.*"

"I'm tired'a this," the other woman said, and she also jumped into the air, and then stayed aloft parallel to Spider-Man's position on top of the kiosk. "I'm takin' you *down,* Spidey-Man." She then thrust out her arms, and green needles shot from her fingers.

Leaping easily out of the way and landing back on the sidewalk behind Ray-Beam Mouth, Spider-Man said in a mock-exasperated tone, "Please, it's *Spider*-Man, or just *Spidey.* Really, don't you people read the papers? Kids today, I swear."

Spider-Man then grabbed Ray-Beam Mouth—or, rather, Adrian—and tossed him gently upward into one of the trees that overhung the park. As Adrian landed in the tangle of branches, Spider-Man shot a web from each wrist-shooter, sealing his mouth shut but leaving his nose free to breathe.

"That's some case of halitosis you got there, pal. This oughta do until you can find some mouthwash."

Then he leapt once again into the air, warned by his spider-sense even as the bruiser came running at him.

"Now, now, stop rushing, you'll all get your turn to be embarrassed by me."

Deprived again of her target, she kept going, crashing into the other woman, who was just coming in for a landing.

"On the other hand," Spider-Man muttered as he held on to a lower branch from the same tree Adrian was now in, "looks like you guys really don't need my help for that." The one who could fly was now on the ground, dazed. The bruiser—who had yet to utter anything more coherent than a grunt—let out a moan of anguish.

Big-Head looked up at Spider-Man, one of the veins in his massive forehead throbbing. "You find yourself amusing, Spider-Man?"

"Well, I generally don't fly in the face of public opinion."

"You'll be laughing out of the other side of your—"

The rest of Big-Head's sentence was cut off by the webbing on his mouth. Spider-Man found that that was an even better use of webbing than the similar shot on Adrian in the tree.

Another spider-sense buzz prompted Spider-Man to jump off the tree just before the bruiser slammed a fist into it.

Oh no. As he landed on the sidewalk, Spider-Man looked up to see that Adrian had also been knocked loose by the bruiser's blow. Whirling around, Spider-Man spun his web-shooters frantically to form a web cushion for Adrian to fall on. It barely formed in time for him to land on it.

Unfortunately, the time he spent doing that gave the bruiser plenty of time to leap at him, and this time they collided, as the only way Spider-Man could have dodged was to stop making Adrian's web cushion. *I hate this job sometimes,* he thought as he found himself knocked to the ground by a gamma-enhanced crazy person for the second time in two days.

Now, though, he could cut loose. He kicked upward, sending the woman flying into the air and grunting in shock. Spider-Man then leapt to his feet and—hoping like hell that she had a concomitant invulnerability to go with her superstrength—stood under her, preparing to catch her and toss her into the wall that separated the sidewalk from Central Park.

As he did so, he noticed a dimming in his spider-sense. *The danger's passing,* he thought even as he noticed the woman's skin tone becoming less green.

This is gonna hurt. If the woman was reverting to normal, no way he could toss her into a stone wall with his strength—there was a very real chance he'd kill her. So instead he simply caught her and then buckled his knees to help cushion her weight.

Pain sliced through his shoulder as he caught the woman, then wound up dropping her to the sidewalk rather than have her collapse on top of him. True, he didn't want to kill her, but he wasn't going to go out of his way not to hurt her, either.

Not that much hurting would be going on at this point. Just as with Javier, all four of Spider-Man's foes started experiencing convulsions—Adrian's restricted by being tangled in the hastily spun web cushion—and turning back to their natural complexions.

My God, Spider-Man realized, *they're only kids.* These four couldn't have been much over eighteen. Then again, Javier was only fourteen, but Spider-Man knew his history from being his teacher.

Spider-Man focused his concern on the victim. The vendor was lying on the ground, drooling out of the corner of his mouth, and starting to mutter something. The kids could wait—they knew damn well what they were doing when they took the Triple X, and from the sounds of it, Big-Head had made plans relating to it.

People started gathering around. Their murmurs were just audible over the sirens approaching from the north.

"Hey, you see that? Spidey beat up those kids!"

"Nah, man, he be takin' them kids down—they was bustin' up Igor!"

"Spider-Man's the one who beat up Igor. Let's get 'im!"

"*You* get 'im!"

"Them children was whalin' on Igor somethin' fierce. Spider-Man saved us."

I love a mob. The only thing you can count on is that you can't count on them, Spider-Man thought, not for the first time.

Remembering his conversation with Detective O'Leary, Spider-Man went over to the one with the enormous cranium—now normal-sized and -colored—and riffled through the kid's pockets as best he could while the kid was shaking and muttering something that was muffled by the webbing covering his mouth. "Don't worry, kiddo, it'll dissolve in an hour.

Hope you're still not doing the shtick when it does—it's bad enough when guys like Dr. Octopus use it, but at least he's *earned* the right to talk like an old movie serial. You, though? Nuh-uh."

Then he hit paydirt: in the kid's front right jeans pocket was a ziplock bag full of some small tabs. They looked like ecstasy tabs, except they were colored green. Spider-Man suspected that was less a by-product of their being irradiated and more a case of food coloring used for marketing purposes.

Two blue-and-white NYPD cars pulled up to the curb, each disgorging two uniformed police officers. All four cops unholstered their weapons. "Hold still, webhead," one of them, a young white man with a nameplate that read CARCETTI, said. Spider-Man also noted the number 24 in gold on both of his collars, as well as those of his four fellows—and, after a glance, on the two vehicles as well.

Holding up his hands, he said, "Easy, Officer, I'm on your side. And you'll want to call in your precinct's Triple X Task Force on this one. Groucho, Chico, Harpo, and Zeppo here just beat up this guy—" He pointed at the vendor, Igor. "—while all green and ferocious. And this—" He held up the ziplock bag. "—is, unless I miss my guess, some actual Triple X." He set the bag down on the sidewalk.

"I said hold still!" Carcetti yelled, but his partner, a Hispanic woman with RODRIGUEZ on her nametag, put her hand on his shoulder.

"Ease off, Mike, he's one of the good guys."

"Like hell—I don't know what happened here, and this guy's a witness."

Spider-Man, not really wanting to stick around, leapt back up into the tree.

"Hey! I'll shoot—"

"What, pigeons?" Rodriguez said. "Let him go."

Calling down from the tree as he shot a web out to another tree, Spider-Man said, "Talk to Detective O'Leary, she'll vouch for me—and tell her I'll call her tomorrow!"

Whatever Carcetti, Rodriguez, or their two comrades might have had to say in response, Spider-Man did not hear. Sticking around would not have been a good idea, especially with the fickle crowd and Carcetti's itchy trigger finger.

As he swung through the trees like a latter-day Tarzan, Spider-Man mused on his tempestuous history with the NYPD. He'd had good relationships with several cops over the years—among them, Captains George Stacy and Jean DeWolff, both deceased, and more recently a lieutenant named William Lamont—but also plenty of bad ones. Cops, Spider-Man had noted over the years, didn't take kindly to people getting in their way or trying to do their jobs for them or making their job more complicated, and Spider-Man had at various times done all three. By the same token, he also could deal with threats that the cops were simply ill-equipped to handle. Once or twice, representatives of the NYPD even recognized that and he'd cooperated with them. But that was rare—it was far more common for him to be met with Carcetti-style disdain.

Still, he thought as he swung over to the Metropolitan Museum of Art, ran across its roof, and then leapt out over Fifth Avenue, snagging one of the snazzy apartment buildings across the street from the Met, *I'll probably get some good brownie points with O'Leary by giving her those tabs. With luck, their lab can identify it properly, maybe get a clue as to who did this.*

Not that there were a lot of candidates. Top of the list was probably Dr. Bruce Banner—the identity of the Hulk when he wasn't big and green, and the foremost authority on gamma radiation—but Spider-Man couldn't imagine a circumstance under which he would manufacture a designer drug.

Of course, just because I can't imagine it doesn't mean it's untrue. And it wouldn't even make the top fifty list of Crazy Stuff I've Seen Since That Spider Bit Me. So he reluctantly put Banner at the top of the short list of people who had this capability.

Working his way south-southeast through the East Side of Manhattan toward the Queensboro Bridge, a second name came immediately to mind: Otto Octavius, better known as Dr. Octopus. He was a more likely choice than Banner, truly, given not only his credentials in the field of radiation, but also his criminal bent. *Still, drug trafficking isn't Doc Ock's usual MO. And if he was trying to set himself up as a new drug kingpin, he'd be proclaiming it to the world—his ego wouldn't allow anything less. Subtlety ain't his strong suit.* Nonetheless, he was a likely candidate.

Some other names—including some of the faculty at Empire State University under whom Peter Parker had studied as an undergraduate and a grad student—came to mind, and he made a mental note to investigate them. Or, possibly, pass their names on to O'Leary as well. *The cops have better resources for this sort of tracking than I do, and since O'Leary likes me, I might as well take advantage.*

The detective hadn't been wrong when she'd suggested that closer cooperation between him and them wouldn't be a bad thing, for all the reasons she gave. But so many people distrusted Spider-Man both on and off the force that he wasn't sure if that was really practical.

Attaching a web-line to the cable-car station that took passengers to Roosevelt Island, Spider-Man swung around in an arc that took him to the top spire on the Manhattan side of the Queensboro Bridge, which would take him right into the Long Island City section of Queens.

It was still light out, and Spider-Man suspected that, in his bright red-and-blue bodysuit, he'd have an easier time spying around the two housing projects O'Leary suggested at night, but he didn't want to waste any more time. The rampage on Central Park West highlighted how widespread this drug was becoming, and the consequences for it would be dire—not just for the users, who risked radiation poisoning, but for the poor schlubs who got in their way while they were using their super powers in a drug-induced haze.

The Bridgeview Houses were just north of the Queens end of the bridge, so Spider-Man went there first. The red brick buildings extended into the sky, all close to each other, linked on the ground by courtyards that had patches of greenery—bushes and trees—fenced off. Perching on the roof of one building, he saw one gray-uniformed person dolefully picking up litter off the ground with a stick and putting it in a bag slung on his shoulder. Groups of kids and smaller groups of adults wandered around, most of them heading to a particular doorway of a particular building. Nobody looked up at Spider-Man—his spider-sense was quiet—which wasn't a shock.

So how am I supposed to find the dealers in here?

He took a moment to restock his web-shooters with fresh cartridges from his belt, which he hadn't done in a couple of days. He'd gone through a lot of webbing against the four kids, and he wasn't sure how much he'd need once he found the Triple X market.

As he restocked, he paid closer attention to the walking patterns of the people below. He soon realized that several kids were standing alone. Some talked to people as they passed by. *I'm guessing those are the barkers.* Of the ones who stopped to listen to what the barkers had to say, some then went around to a spot Spider-Man couldn't see. He saw a few people playing that barker role, and after about twenty minutes, he noticed that all of them were sending people to an area behind the easternmost of the buildings that made up the Houses.

Staying low on the rooftops, Spider-Man made his way over to that building, leaping across when necessary. Peering over the edge of the south wall, he saw the ones sent by the barkers handing money to a person leaning up against a Dumpster. They were then directed to a staircase that probably led down to the laundry room—or storage, or whatever it was that the Bridgeview Houses kept in their building basements. People were going in there, but Spider-Man didn't see them leave.

There's gotta be another way out of there. He ran over to the other side of the building. The east wall was alongside 21st Street, and Spider-Man doubted that so careful a setup as what they had here would have any business being done on an open street. Obviously the crews dealing the junk were trying their best to avoid surveillance by the police. The offer of drugs, the payment, and the providing of the merchandise took place in three different locations. Each was handled by three different people, the last in a place out of plain sight in the windowless basement of a building. *Very efficient,* Spider-Man thought dolefully.

The west wall was up against another one of the buildings, which left just the north wall.

Sure enough, when he got there, Spider-Man found another staircase just like the one on the south wall, and people were climbing the stairs. He even recognized one of the buyers.

Okay, enough recon. Let's get some confirmation. Spider-Man followed an unsteady-looking man with light brown skin who could have been either black or Hispanic, and who looked like he had neither bathed nor changed his clothes since the Carter administration, as he made his way through the courtyards and then out onto the street. After a few minutes of following him down 21st, Spider-Man realized they were heading toward Queensboro

Plaza. He figured that the tangle of overpasses, elevated subway trains, and streets leading to the bridge was an ideal place to lose oneself and have a snort or smoke or whatever in peace.

Spider-Man stayed on the rooftops of the tall industrial buildings that made up most of the area near the bridge, keeping a close eye on his junkie.

His guess had been correct. The junkie found a spot wedged in behind a support beam for the subway tracks. Spider-Man leapt down from one of the buildings to the underside of the inbound tracks, even as an outbound W train was going by on the other side, shaking the support beam a bit and rattling his teeth.

Jumping over to the support beam on the other side, he saw the junkie lean against the beam and slide down into a sitting position. He pulled something out of his pocket and studied it.

Deciding to pull the same trick on the junkie that he pulled on the two sergeants at the 24th Precinct, Spider-Man webbed the underside of the subway track above him and let the line hang down to just over the junkie's head. Spider-Man then slid down to the end of the line, hanging upside down.

"That stuff 'll kill you, you know."

The junkie looked up. This close, he looked even worse than he had from the rooftops. He had thatches of hair on his cheek and neck, sores on his nose that hadn't been cared for, and a bleary look in his eyes that Spider-Man was sure was the result of too many days spent doing what he was about to do.

"You ain't got no face, boy."

Spider-Man almost laughed. "Nah, I got one, I just hide it."

"You must be pretty goddamn ugly then, 'cause I ain't never seen no one who covered up his face like that, 'less it was winter." He frowned. "We didn't hit winter and nobody told me, did we?"

Shaking his head, Spider-Man said, "Nah, it's still spring."

Relieved, the junkie said, "That's good. You got a name, boy?"

"I'm called Spider-Man."

"What kinda name that be?"

Again holding back a laugh, Spider-Man said, "It's what folks call me."

"Well, folks be doin' some right foolishness, you ask me. Now as for me, I got me a proper name. It's Albert."

"Pleasure to meet you, Albert. That Triple X you got there?" Even as Spider-Man asked, he knew it wasn't—this close he could see that it was white, not the trademark green.

"You know, I'm thinkin' you really ain't got no face, 'cause you can't see worth a good goddamn. This look like Triple X to you? If this be Triple X, it be green."

"So it's heroin?"

"When you gonna start making sense? It's blow, son. ."

"Okay, then, Albert, say I wanted to get some Triple X."

Albert frowned. "Don't see what good that be doin' you with no mouth or nothin'."

"All right, say *you* wanted some Triple X. Would you get it in the same place?"

Shaking his head, Albert said, "Naw, they don't be havin' that at Bridgeview. If ol' Albert want him some Triple X, he got to be sendin' one of them young'uns over to get it for him. See, they don't like Albert in Robinsfield."

The Robinsfield Houses. "Persona non grata, huh?"

"If that means I can't go there no mo', then yeah, persona no greater. Ray-Ray's boys be throwin' me out on account'a my bein' short two bills last month. Them boys got *no* sense'a respect for a junkie tryin' to make a livin'." Suddenly Albert shot Spider-Man a hopeful look. "You got five bucks?"

That surprised Spider-Man. "Why?"

"When them narcos be askin' Albert for tips, they usually give me five, ten dollars. Uniformed police, too. Now you, you ain't got no face, so I settle for five. And if you *ain't* payin', then I gotta ask you to move along and leave me be."

Spider-Man couldn't bring himself to actually pay Albert. In fact, he was seriously tempted to take Albert's drugs away, and the only thing restraining him was the same thing that kept him from giving Javier detention for mouthing off at him: it would do no good. All he'd be doing was denying an addict his fix, without giving him any viable alternative. That wasn't being a good guy, that was just making a bad problem worse.

Instead, he asked the question that had preyed on his mind since he first started observing the movements inside the Bridgeview Houses. "Albert—why are you doing this?"

"Askin' you for money? Don't you know what kinda world we live in? Don't nothin' cost nothin', you know what I'm sayin'?"

"No, no," Spider-Man said quickly, "I mean why do you do *this*? Why take the—the blow while sitting against a subway support beam?"

Albert snorted. "You got a better idea, you let me know. I ain't got no skills, I ain't got no looks, and I ain't got nothin' else. Oh, I had it once, but that was a long time ago. *Long* time ago. Ain't nothin' left for ol' Albert. I expect to be dyin' sometime soon. Least this way it don't hurt all the damn time. So if you don't mind, 'less you got Mr. Lincoln hidin' in that no-face body of yours, you best be movin' along and leavin' me be."

Spider-Man found he had nothing to say to that. Instead he reached out his left hand and shot out a web-line, heading eastward toward the Robinsfield Houses.

SIX

"RED caps! Red caps! We got red caps, yo!"

"WMD! WMD!"

"Triple X here, Triple X, Triple X."

Hector Diaz walked through the big courtyard at the center of the Robinsfield Houses. The tall buildings formed a square donut around this courtyard, with an archway on the 34th Avenue side to let folks in and out on foot.

The courtyard made it easier for all the slingers to do their business. Hector didn't pay attention to none of the crazy-ass names the slingers came up with. All the names were bullshit—just like commercials on TV, lying so people will buy it. "WMD" tried to make folks think of a weapon of mass destruction like what they heard about on the news, and "red caps" made it sound like it was the good stuff from the old-school times. That was back when Hector's cousin was slingin' for "Bell" Ring, before Bell got caught by them narcos. He was doing his twenty in Ryker's, unless he got him some parole. Meanwhile some fool was trying to make like he had Bell's package by using his old name: "red caps." Only thing the fool's dope had was the same as Bell's product was that it was covered in red.

Hector didn't care. Dope was dope, and that was what he wanted. Regular dope, not no WMD, not no fake red caps, and sure as hell no Triple X.

Walking up to the guy barking for Triple X—some skinny kid in a white hat whose name Hector didn't remember—he asked, "He around?"

Without saying anything, the kid took a cell phone out of the pocket of his baggy pants, flipped it open, and held down one button. "It's me.

Hector's here, wants to talk to the man. A'ight." Closing the phone, he nodded to Hector. "He in B39 today."

Hector nodded back and went over to Tower B. Ray-Ray always moved around where he'd keep the stash—always belonged to someone in his crew who lived in the Houses. It was never Ray-Ray's own place. In fact, thinking on it, Hector didn't even know where Ray-Ray lived. The elevators in Tower B were busted—again—with three white folks from the city trying to fix it. Hector didn't know why they bothered—just be broken again tomorrow. *Good thing Ray-Ray ain't in 154 like he was last week,* Hector thought. Walkin' fifteen flights of stairs *hurt.* But three flights were cool.

Each floor had nine apartments, and 39 was way the hell on the far side of the hallway. He knocked twice when he got there, pretending not to notice the rat that scurried along the floor. Hector remembered when this place was built—was supposed to be better than the old housing projects, better kept up, and whatever. That's why they called them "Houses." That lasted for about the first year, then it was just back to being the projects, except they don't call it that no more. It was just like the names for the drugs—fancy new name for the same old shit.

Cap opened the door. Taller than the doorway, and all thin, Cap kept his short dreads hidden under a backwards Yankee hat. Hector heard that he wasn't called Cap because he wore no cap, but because he busted a cap in Big Junior back in the day.

Holding out his hand, Cap said with a big grin, "Hector Diaz in the house! What up, yo?"

Hector grabbed his hand. "Doin' a'ight. He in?"

"Yeah, come on back."

Three guys Hector didn't know were counting money in the living room. Hector knew the dope was in the bedroom, and that door was closed. Ray-Ray was sitting at the kitchen table, talking to some young'un.

"I ain't tellin' you again, boy, if you come up short one more time, Cap's gonna take you *out,* you feel me?"

The boy nodded.

"Get your ass outta here."

Before Ray-Ray had finished talking, the boy was practically out the door. Hector wasn't sure his little feet touched the floor.

Raymond Johnson had been called Ray-Ray for as long as Hector knew him, and that went back to when Hector was in nursery school and Ray-Ray was a third grader. Where Cap was tall and thin, Ray-Ray was short and round, but it was all muscle. Ray-Ray didn't have no neck, and had a goatee that made him look even fiercer. Ray-Ray always wore big-ass sunglasses. Hector knew it scared the young'uns, but still thought it was stupid. Since Hector saw him last, he'd shaved his head.

Ray-Ray had dropped out of high school and taken over Bell Ring's package when Bell got busted last year. Hector figured that the Triple X came from one of Bell's old connections, since Ray-Ray didn't have that kind of weight on his own yet.

"What up, Hector?"

"You heard about Javier?"

"I heard. So?"

"He in the *hospital*, yo."

Speaking more slowly and menacingly, Ray-Ray repeated, "I *heard*. So?"

"We can't be puttin' this stuff out there. I heard he got radiating poison and he might die."

"Yeah, or the fool might catch a bullet tomorrow when he pisses off the wrong person like he *always* do." Ray-Ray stood up from the kitchen table and looked down on Hector. "What you askin' me, Hector?"

Hector shook his head. "I don't know, it's just—this Triple X, it's *bad*, yo."

Ray-Ray grinned. "Bad? You crazy? I got the only package anybody *wants*. That little knucklehead with his 'red caps' that he done stole from Bell, he gonna be *history*, you feel me? Robinsfield'll be *mine*, yo, and I'll be movin' to Bridgeview next, and I'm takin' blocks all over the city. This my *ticket*. And you come runnin' up in here tellin' me it's *bad*? What, that people be droppin' *dead*? Hell, they be droppin' dead anyhow. Gonna happen no matter what, but in the meantime, I'm gonna make me some cash *money*. And look, yo, you wanna be part of it, just say the word." Ray-Ray sat back down. "You smart, Hector—you always been smart, even when you was a young'un, and I could use smart. Blowback, he good at the details, but he ain't got the brainpower, you feel me?"

Hector shook his head. Bernabe Martinez—"Blowback"—was Ray-Ray's second-in-command, but that was mainly because he did everything

Ray-Ray told him to, was as tough as anyone, and remembered stuff better than anyone. But he wasn't smart.

It was precisely because Hector had brains that he said, "Nah, man, I can't be doin' that. I start spendin' all my time here, my Moms'll be all up in my face. I shouldn't even be here now, yo, but after what happened with Javier—"

"Don't be worryin' 'bout Javier. Look, I 'preciate you carin' an' all that, but *don't* be, a'ight? It's all cool."

"A'ight," Hector said, even though he didn't really believe it.

"Yo, Cap!" Ray-Ray called out into the living room.

Cap was watching ESPN on the TV. "Yeah?"

"Call De, tell 'im that Hector here get half off whatever he want."

Nodding, Cap pulled out his cell phone.

That surprised Hector. Ray-Ray didn't give discounts. "Thanks."

"Nothin' to it, little man. Like I said, you smart. An' the offer still stands, yo, if you change your mind or your Moms gets off your ass."

"A'ight."

Ray-Ray held out his hand, and Hector clasped it.

But even as Cap opened the door to let him out, he didn't feel no better.

When he got outside, he headed back to the barker who'd called up before—*De, that's his name,* Hector thought, remembering that his first name was DeCurtis. "Cap says you get half off, yo," De said as soon as Hector walked up. "You want blow, you gotta wait for the re-up. H, we got right on—"

"*Cape!*"

Hector looked up. The voice had come from somewhere above him—probably one of the small terraces where they kept the lookouts. "Five-oh" meant the cops. "Cape" meant a super hero.

Given a choice, Hector preferred the capes. They actually played nice more than the cops, maybe because they didn't have to. Hector knew that lots of folks—himself included—broke the rules 'cause the rules sucked and were a pain all up the ass. But capes didn't have to play by the rules in the first place, they did this 'cause they *wanted* to—so that meant they followed them pretty close. Meant folks didn't get beat as much.

As soon as the word "Cape!" rang out across the courtyard, the barkers all stopped. Two people started running off. Hector saw that they were from one of the new crews. *Fools.* Most slingers knew better than to keep the stash out here like that.

Then Hector saw the red-and-blue figure of Spider-Man swinging down on some kind of rope into the courtyard.

Hector didn't know much about Spider-Man except for his name. Didn't care much, neither.

The cape landed right on the bench next to where De was standing and started crouching. Hector had never seen a cape up this close before. It startled Hector when he started talking, since his face was covered by his mask.

"I hear this is the place to get Triple X," the cape said, his voice muffled by the mask. It was hard to tell, but Hector felt like he was looking right at him. "We just hangin', yo," De said.

"Right. And that guy on the terrace over there yelled 'Cape!' when I showed up because he was expressing his appreciation, not so you guys could hide the drugs."

"Ain't no drugs, hero-man. We just two citizens havin' us a conversation, which you intrudin' on."

Now Hector knew that Spider-Man was looking at him. "That true, Hector?"

Oh, man. "My name ain't Hector, yo."

"Yeah, sure. I know everything, Hector. I know about Javier Velasquez. I know about Valerie McManus. I know about those kids on the Upper West Side. I know about the radiation poisoning. And I know about Ray-Ray and that he's dealing Triple X."

Hector didn't have no idea who this Valerie lady was. But Spider-Man knew who he was and who Ray-Ray was and that Ray-Ray was dealing in Manhattan now. That scared him. The reason he didn't care nothing about capes was because they didn't care nothing about him. He saw them in the sky a lot, but that wasn't anything either.

"Now, you gonna tell me what I want to know?"

"Sound like you know everything." Hector cursed to himself; he sounded all scared.

De lifted the bottom of his windbreaker, showing the Sig Sauer he had in the band of his pants. "You best be movin' along, hero-man."

"Or what? Kid, I eat punks twice your size for breakfast every morning."

"Yeah?" De didn't look impressed, though Hector'd heard that Spider-Man could take out twenty guys without trying too hard.

"Yeah."

"Well, bring it, bitch. But ain't no drugs here, and ain't no Ray-Ray here, and ain't no Triple X here. You got a problem, then step to me. Otherwise, get yo' red ass outta here 'fore I call the cops an' tell them you trespassin' on city property."

Spider-Man just stared for a second.

"Fine." Then he thrust out one arm. Some kind of gooey rope shot out from his wrist and hit De's gun.

Before De could do anything, the cape yanked his arm back, pulling De's gun out of his pants.

Spider-Man then held the weapon in his right hand and brought his left hand down on the barrel, smashing it.

He threw it to the ground at De's feet. "It's for your own good—you could put an eye out with that thing. Toodle-oo!" Then he jumped straight up toward the wall of Tower D and started running *up* the side of the building. After he got to the roof, Hector lost sight.

"Hey, he done busted my gun, yo!" De sounded like someone'd killed his pet cat or something. "That was my *gun!*"

"So tell Ray-Ray to get you another one," Hector said.

"What, I'm supposed to tell Ray-Ray that some dude in *tights* broke my gun? Are you flippin'?"

"Whatever." Hector turned to walk away. "I'm gone, yo." He wasn't in the mood anymore, even at half off.

First Javier, then Mr. Parker, then Spider-Man. This Triple X is bad. *I don't care what Ray-Ray says, I'm staying the hell away from this.*

○———————○

UNDER any other circumstances, Mary Jane Watson would have simply gone straight from rehearsal to the West 4th Street station to hop a subway home. Or perhaps she would have taken Anne up on her offer to join the rest of the tech crew at the Back Fence to decompress. Dmitri had put them through a brutal rehearsal, made worse by the fact that there were three understudies coming in—not just Mary Jane for Valerie, but Regina for Mary Jane, and the male understudy, Mike Rabinowitz, substituting for Lou, whose broken leg was keeping him off the stage as well.

But circumstances *weren't* different. Mary Jane was worried about Valerie. Nobody had heard from her—she hadn't called anyone, and calls to her cell phone were greeted with a message saying her voice-mail box was full. Valerie worked at a Starbucks on 14th Street, but she had taken this week off in order to gear up for *The Z-Axis* opening, so while nobody there had seen her, that wasn't really indicative of anything. From what Peter had told her, the powers Triple X gave its users were temporary, so Valerie couldn't have stayed a green harpy for long.

Mary Jane had tried calling Valerie's live-in boyfriend, Greg, but he wasn't answering his cell or returning messages, either. He and Valerie never bothered getting a landline installed, since they both had cell phones and could get Internet access via cable modem. Unfortunately, that meant that if Greg left his cell off, he couldn't be reached. Greg was famous for forgetting to turn his phone on, and for not checking his messages on those rare occasions when he did.

So Mary Jane took a brisk walk across Manhattan to Alphabet City, so named for the names of the avenues east of First Avenue that made up the neighborhood: Avenue A, Avenue B, and so forth. Apartments were small and cheap in this area, and many actors had taken up residence here due to both that factor, and its proximity to many of the small theatres where they plied their trade.

I just hope that Valerie's okay and she's just all weirded out because of what happened, Mary Jane thought as she walked up the steps of the crumbling stoop that led into the small apartment building. None of the names on the buzzers matched the names of the tenants, of course, but Mary Jane remembered that they were 4W, and she pushed that button.

A burst of static followed, with the vague hint of a voice under it.

"It's Mary Jane Watson," she said slowly, hoping the other end had better speakers.

The dirty glass door to the building emitted a low buzz, and Mary Jane pushed the door open. As she entered the dark, narrow hallway, she had the usual New Yorker's concern that she misremembered the apartment number and some stranger just let her into the building. Still, it was a common enough occurrence that it didn't really elevate above a concern to a worry.

Local zoning laws stated that any building six stories or higher had to have an elevator. For that reason, there were a lot of five-story apartment buildings in New York, and many were like this one: a corridor no wider than the doorways, a winding staircase wedged into the back of the building to allow access to the higher floors. Mary Jane trudged up the four levels—trying to maintain her footing on stairs that hadn't been swept in months, and trying not to think about the odd smells from the second floor—then went to the door on the west side of the building and knocked.

A muffled voice from behind the steel-and-wood door said, "S'open!"

Mary Jane turned the knob—sure enough, the door was unlocked. She'd been here only a few times before, but the door had always been locked; Valerie had always been paranoid about someone robbing her place. Then she recalled that Greg had been more blasé about it. *Which means that Greg's probably home alone, which doesn't really bode well.*

The door opened to a small living room. A battered old couch was against one wall, opposite a television that was currently tuned to the Discovery Channel. Wearing only a T-shirt and boxer shorts, Greg Halprin sat on that couch amidst several remotes, empty food wrappers and bags, and unopened pieces of mail. His short brown hair was spiked upward in a manner that suggested he hadn't combed it since he'd slept awkwardly on his pillow, and he hadn't shaved anytime recently. Greg was supposed to be an actor, too, but it didn't look like he was in any physical shape to audition. He was also "between jobs," as Valerie had put it.

"'Ey, MJ, how's it hangin'?" Greg's words were so slurred, Mary Jane could barely distinguish the consonants. "What brings your babelicious face to the humble abode?"

"I was looking for Valerie. She—well, disappeared from rehearsal yesterday."

"Ain't seen her." Greg sounded wholly unconcerned as he looked back at the television. "Dude, can you *believe* all this stuff about dinosaurs? I mean, it's so totally out there, y'know?"

"You haven't seen her in over a day?"

Greg shrugged. "Figured she was out partyin' or somethin'. Wouldn't be the first time."

Mary Jane walked over to Greg and sat down on the vinyl ottoman with the splits along the side that sat randomly placed in the middle of the living room floor. Greg's eyes looked awfully vacant. "Greg, have you guys been doing Triple X?"

Now those vacant eyes lit up. "Is that what that's called? Valerie was talkin' 'bout scorin' some kinda special X. Our guy, he said it'd make her brain work better an' stuff. She thought it'd make her 'member her lines better. But I ain't seen her since then, so I don't know if she did score it." He frowned. "Bitch is probably hoardin' again. She always does that with the good stuff."

"Who's your guy?" Mary Jane asked.

"I dunno, the *guy*. Valerie knows 'im from back when they was in college. He had some weird lady with him. What're you, the cops or somethin'?" He grinned. "Or you tryin' to score, too?" Laughing, he added, "Knew that Ms. Perfect thing was just a thing, right? You're startin' to 'preciate the fine qualities of a good—"

Getting up quickly, Mary Jane said, "I gotta go."

"Naw, c'mon, MJ, stick aroun'. I got some weed 'round here somewhere." He looked on the floor in front of the couch and on the couch itself, rooting around the detritus, but not actually getting up. "Get some MJ for MJ— hey, get it?" He tittered at his own stupid pun.

"Hilarious." Mary Jane had never been all that thrilled with Greg, and now she actively wanted to run screaming for the nearest shower. "Look, if you see Valerie, tell her to call me right away, okay?"

"Fine, whatever." Greg sounded disappointed that Mary Jane didn't stay to get high—with him. "Dude, those dinosaurs really *rocked*."

Mary Jane exited the apartment, closing the door behind her, and walked as fast down the filthy stairs as her legs would carry her.

SEVEN

"I'M sorry, Peter, I can't help you. And I must say, I'm disappointed that you're even asking."

Peter Parker squirmed in the guest chair in the Midtown High School principal's office. The chairs were designed to be uncomfortable, something Peter had always ascribed to the principal's wanting to keep any students in here ill at ease. He was learning now that it applied to the employees under the principal's supervision as well. "Mr. Harrington, I wouldn't ask, but I met his mother at the hospital, and—"

"Peter, Peter, Peter." Harrington shook his white-haired head in a manner that made him look for all the world like a grandfather reproving a grandson who didn't know better. "I realize that you're comparatively new to teaching—although you did put in a certain amount of time as a TA at ESU, so I would think you wouldn't fall for these kinds of things."

"I'm not falling for anything," Peter said defensively, "I—"

"They *all* have mothers, Peter. And the ones that don't, have fathers. Some are even lucky enough to have both. And they've *all* got a story, they *all* have extenuating circumstances, but none of it matters."

"It does matter. We're talking about *people,* Mr. Harrington, and—"

"And I'm talking about abstract concepts, is that it?" Again he shook his head. "Peter, this *is* about people—specifically about the people who attend this school. I cannot keep a student enrolled in this school who takes drugs and then inflicts harm upon his fellow students and the employees of this school—including, I might add, you. Now I appreciate that young Mr. Velasquez has a mother. But so do Pablo DeLaVega, Lourdes Escobar, Peter Bain, Ian Chantal, and David King."

Peter frowned. "Who're they?"

"Mr. DeLaVega is the one Mr. Velasquez punched. The other four are the ones Mr. DeLaVega landed on. You say that it's not fair to Mr. Velasquez's mother to saddle her with a son who has been expelled from this school just because of some arbitrary rule in a book somewhere. I counter by pointing out that while people are affected, people also wrote that rulebook, and they were not imbeciles—and also that it's not fair to the parents of Mr. DeLaVega, Ms. Escobar, Mr. Bain, Mr. Chantal, and Mr. King to allow their children to remain in a school that has a shape-changing, rampaging drug addict among their fellow students." Harrington let out a long breath. "I'm not unsympathetic, Peter, but I'm also not going to fall for a sob story I've heard several thousand times before. And I certainly can't change the rules because one woman loves her child and one brand-new science teacher vouches for her. Am I making myself clear?"

In fact, he had made himself clear several sentences earlier, but Peter didn't think it was appropriate to mention that to his boss.

Especially when he's right. Harrington had been very kind to Peter, and he had hoped to prevail upon that kindness. But Peter found himself unable to argue with anything the principal said. *Not that that'll make talking to Eileen Velasquez any easier.*

He got up from the guest chair. "Thanks, Mr. Harrington. I, ah—I had to give it a shot. I promised Ms. Velasquez, and—"

"I understand," Harrington said, leaving Peter to wonder how often people ever got to finish their sentences when in this office. "And I'm glad to see you taking such an interest in your students—though I would recommend your time be given over to the students who've actually earned it."

"The ones who've earned it aren't always the ones who need it—or the ones who get it," Peter said without thinking. *Ouch.* He would have given anything to take the words back. *Why can't my spider-sense warn me when I'm about to say something stupid?*

To Peter's relief, Harrington took the rebuke sportingly and laughed. "A fair point, Peter. I'll see you tomorrow."

Peter nodded and turned and left the principal's office. His shoulders slumped, he meandered through the empty halls toward the exit. Most of the students had left for the day, with only those involved in extracurricular activities still around, and most of those were in whatever room they performed those activities in.

He had sleepwalked through most of his classes today. After his trip to the drug markets of Long Island City, he had gone on his usual nightly patrol, which involved a dustup with a would-be jewel thief on West 4th Street. It was almost 4 A.M. by the time Peter stumbled in through the apartment window, at which point Mary Jane woke up and told him about her failed attempts to track Valerie down. As a result, he'd taught today on precious little sleep.

He walked down the streets of Forest Hills, the late-afternoon spring sun shining pleasantly on his face, looking for a pay phone. He had a few phone calls to make, and at least one of them needed to be made from a public pay phone, as opposed to a cell phone that was easily traceable to Peter Parker.

Reaching into his sport jacket pocket, he retrieved his cell phone and turned it on. As soon as it acquired a signal, the phone played the theme music from *The Simpsons,* which indicated that Peter had voice mail.

Opening the phone as he continued walking down the street, he called the voice mail to find two messages. The first was an I-love-you from Mary Jane. The second was from Eileen Velasquez, informing him that Javier had recovered from the heart attack, but had lapsed into a coma and Dr. Lee was concerned about whether or not he'd survive. Apparently Peter's theory—that the strain of changing size had put a strain on Javier's heart—was correct.

Peter returned that call but, to his disappointment, got only Eileen's voice mail. "Hi, Ms. Velasquez, it's Peter Parker. Thanks for your message, and I'm really sorry—and, uh, I'm afraid I don't have any better news for you. I talked with Principal Harrington, but he's pretty adamant about there being no exceptions. I'm afraid Javier's no longer a student at Midtown High. I'm, ah, really really sorry. Call me back when you get a chance. Uh, bye."

He hit the END button, then let out a long sigh. *Wish I could've talked to her in person—that's lousy news to have to give in a voice mail message.*

Turning a corner, he saw a bodega that had a pay phone outside it. Better yet, the phone was at least twenty feet from the entrance, which cut down on the likelihood of eavesdroppers. He pulled Detective O'Leary's card out of the belt he wore with his Spider-Man suit under his clothes and the change that had originally been earmarked for laundry. After depositing the coins, he dialed the number. Using his calling card number would have had the same security risks as the cell phone—better to play it safe.

"O'Leary."

"Hi, this is, uh, this is Spider-Man," Peter said, realizing too late how ridiculous it would sound.

"Yeah, sure."

"It really is me—you did say to call when we met yesterday. I told you about Triple X coming from Long Island City, and you told me it started on Amsterdam in the 90s with a telekinetic, and you didn't know what that word meant."

"I did *too* know what it meant!" O'Leary said indignantly. "Whatever—it *is* you, I guess."

"I did say we'd talk further," Peter said. "Wanted to know about that package I left for you guys yesterday afternoon."

"We just got the prelim on that from the lab. Oh, and before I forget, stay away from Officer Carcetti for a while."

"Yeah, I got the feeling he wasn't about to join my fan club," Peter said with a smile.

"Not hardly. Anyhow, we rushed the test, and they knew what they were looking for, so the prelim says it's probably a variant on ecstasy, with a heavy presence of gamma radiation. So much so that the lab techs are all wearing lead aprons when they work with the stuff."

That surprised Peter. "The rad levels are high enough to be toxic?"

"How the hell should I know? Christ, I'm not even sure what you just *said;* that's what we keep the geek squad around for. Unfortunately, we ain't keepin' a lid on this. The *Bugle* had a piece on it today."

That must be Betty's story, Peter thought. "Well, you shouldn't believe everything you read in the papers."

"I don't—it's what the great unwashed out there believe. I swear, this is gonna cause a panic. People are used to the guys like you and the FF—the people who've been around a while. But bring something new in, and everyone gets skittish. And this hits all the press hot buttons: paranormals *and* drugs." She sighed. "There's good news for us, though—they signed off on OT, finally. I guess when it's kids disrupting schools and articles in the *Bugle*, then it's worth paying overtime money for. I hate the bosses sometimes. Oh, and our first gamma-head, the telescoping kid?"

Grinning, Peter said, "That's telekinetic."

"Whatever—he's got radiation poisoning. Docs give him a week at best. And another one—a kid in Queens—just fell into a coma." Peter winced, assuming that to be Javier. O'Leary continued: "Hell, with that news, I'd be wearing a lead apron if I was in the lab, too."

"Yeah. Oh, listen—I think I know where the Triple X is coming from. The Robinsfield Houses."

Somewhat snidely, O'Leary asked, "You willing to come in and sign a sworn statement to that effect?"

Peter didn't answer.

"I'll take your sudden silence for a 'Hell, no.' Which leaves us right where we were yesterday, with Narcotics keeping an eye on Robinsfield like they always do. Problem is, the crews there are good. We can't get up on them without months of surveillance and wiretaps and things, and right now, that's not a priority in the department."

"Not a priority?"

"*Don't* get me started," O'Leary said in a long-suffering voice. "Besides, it doesn't matter. Even if you could sign that statement, it'd be weeks before we'd get anything off it. Unless those boys mess up—and these crews are too good to mess up that bad—there isn't much we can do except bang doors down. And we may do that, but we need better PC than a phone call from you."

Peter was suddenly reminded why he didn't work with the cops more often. He understood their need to follow procedure, but sometimes it really got in the way. Before he could say anything else, an automated voice asked him to deposit more money for the next three minutes.

"You're on a pay phone?" O'Leary said incredulously after he'd deposited more quarters. "I'd think with the way you move around, you'd have a cell."

"Who says I don't? Cell phones are wonderful things—flexible, mobile, and they tell you the identity of who's calling."

"Ah, okay. Fair enough."

Another question occurred to Peter. "What about those four kids on Central Park West?"

"College kids," O'Leary said dismissively. "Thought it'd be cool to get super powers."

"They should try having them," Peter muttered.

"What's that supposed to mean?"

Regretting the words, Peter quickly said, "Nothing." *I need more sleep—I keep putting my foot in my mouth.*

But the detective wouldn't let it out of her teeth. "Like hell it's 'nothing.' C'mon, spill. Listen, I know Joll signed off on you talking to me, but Shapiro's in charge of this task force, and he'd go nuts if he knew I was talking to you on the phone—and worse, telling you lab results."

Smiling, Peter said, "Shapiro not fond of me, huh?"

"Don't take it personally—he hates all you costumes. Says you're all prima donna glory-hounds with delusions of relevance."

Peter rolled his eyes. It wasn't the first time he'd encountered that particular slur. "Well, as long as it's not personal."

"He's full of it, but he's good police. Anyhow, you got me offtrack—what do you mean 'they should try having them'?"

"Remind me never to be interrogated by you."

O'Leary chuckled. "Hey, I do this for a living."

"Yeah." Peter hesitated. A breeze kicked up, blowing some garbage out of the overfull public trash can at the curb toward him. "Let's just say Shapiro's dead wrong—I *don't* do this for the glory. A casual perusal of the *Daily Bugle* would show just how little glory I get in this business anyhow. No, it's not that."

"Money?"

"I should show you my Visa bill."

"Hey, for all I know you patented that webbing. No, actually, you couldn't have, 'cause then I'd see it all over the place. Come to think on it, why the hell *didn't* you patent it?"

"Long story," Peter said quickly. "The point is—I don't do this 'cause I want to. I do it 'cause I have to."

"Someone put a gun to your head?"

"No—to someone else's. And pulled the trigger, and I didn't do anything to stop it." Peter's right fist clenched. After all these years, thinking about Uncle Ben—more to the point, thinking about the man who shot

Uncle Ben, whom Spider-Man could have stopped if he wasn't being so self-absorbed—still made him feel wretched. And angry.

O'Leary said, "Okay, fine. So you've got an overdeveloped sense of guilt. Jewish or Catholic?" Before Peter could even attempt to answer that, O'Leary said, "What's that?" Her voice was more distant—talking to someone else. "Oh, okay." Her voice went back to normal. "I gotta go—keep in touch, okay?"

"Yeah, sure," Peter said even as a click on the other end indicated that O'Leary had hung up.

Why did I open up that much? Peter thought back over the conversation and realized he'd told the detective more than he'd told a lot of people who knew him only as Spider-Man about his life and his motivations. *I guess that's why they pay her the detective money.*

Peter walked over to the bodega entrance. Right by the door was a blue wire-frame stand that held copies of the *New York Times,* the *Daily Globe,* and the *Daily Bugle.* He grabbed a copy of the latter. While he doubted that Betty had put anything in her article that she didn't tell him yesterday, it didn't hurt to take another look.

○────────────○

AS Mary Jane descended the staircase into the VPC lobby, the strains of the Beatles' "Norwegian Wood" hit her ears. She looked down the stairs to see that tonight's musical act had already started. Two men stood on the raised platform near the front door, both with long hair and beards. One (whose hair was red and beard was gray) played a guitar and sang Lennon and McCartney's song, the other (whose hair and beard were both a dark brown) sat and lay down a beat on a pair of bongos wedged between his knees. The crowd for this evening's performance of *Up the Creek Without a Fiddle* was milling about, most not paying attention to the music, which Mary Jane thought was a shame—these two guys weren't bad.

As they ended the song and then segued into "Under the Boardwalk," Mary Jane's cell phone started to ring to the tune of "Cool" from *West Side Story.* Removing her phone from her purse, she saw that the caller ID couldn't identify the caller.

With an apologetic look at the musicians for her disruptive ring tone, she dashed out the front door to the short stoop in front of the building that housed VPC. Opening the phone, she said, "Hello?"

A familiar voice said, "Oh, thank *God* you answered, MJ." It was Valerie. "Greg isn't answering his *goddamn* phone, and my sister's still in Michigan, and I didn't know *who* else to call, and—"

"Valerie, where are you?"

"What?" Valerie seemed confused by the question. "Oh, I'm at that homeless shelter on 39th and 10th—they *finally* let me use the pay phone, since I lost my cell. A shelter, can you believe that? The people here just smell *awful.*"

"How'd you get there?" Mary Jane asked, immediately heading down the stairs to the street and looking for a cab.

"I have *no* idea. I didn't even realize it was Friday until one of the volunteers told me. Look, I hate to ask you this, but I need you to come down here—and could you bring me some clothes?"

Mary Jane lowered her hand at that, waving off the free cab that was coming down MacDougal Street. "Clothes?"

"I don't know what happened, but I'm still in costume, and it's all ripped—Linnea's gonna have a cow. It's weird, it's like I was attacked or something, but I'm not bruised or cut or *anything.* MJ, I don't know what the hell *happened.*"

Mary Jane walked down MacDougal toward a clothing emporium of a type common in the Village. She'd pick up something cheap and simple for Valerie to change into. "We'll talk when I get there, okay?"

"Is Dmitri pissed?"

Trying to sound jovial, Mary Jane said, "He's awake, so of *course* he is. Look, don't worry about it right now, okay? We'll talk when I get there."

"Thanks, MJ, you're a *goddess.*"

Feeling several kinds of awful, Mary Jane closed her phone and put it back in her purse. She couldn't bring herself to tell Valerie the whole story over the phone—that she had turned into a green harpy, or that she had been replaced in *The Z-Axis.* Or, for that matter, that she was wanted for "questioning" by the police.

She picked up a cheap blouse, a pair of jeans that she was pretty sure would fit Valerie's slim legs and all-but-nonexistent hips, and a pair of crappy-looking moccasins, in case her shoes were trashed. Mary Jane had forgotten to ask, but the footwear was cheap and she couldn't call her back.

Once the purchases were made and placed in a bright red shopping bag with the store logo on both sides, Mary Jane hailed a cab and told it to take her to 39th and 10th. Then she flipped open her phone and called Peter.

"Good timing," he said when he answered. "I was just about to head out to do a little patrolling."

Mary Jane smiled, imagining him standing by the window in his Spider-Man suit, except without the mask on, allowing her to see his sweet face. There had been many times over the years when she hated that Peter was also Spider-Man, but ultimately she always came back to one simple fact: the qualities that made him Spider-Man were the same qualities she loved most about him. He'd tried to stop being Spider-Man on several occasions, both before and after they got married, and it never took. She knew now that it never would—and, more to the point, never *should*. If he were to stop being Spider-Man, he would stop being the man she fell in love with.

"You'll never guess who I heard from, Tiger."

"Ed McMahon, telling you you've won a major sweepstakes?"

Chuckling, she said, "No."

"The Avengers, accepting your application to become their spokesmodel?"

"Uh, no."

"Then I'm stumped."

"Valerie called—from a homeless shelter." She filled Peter in quickly. "My guess is that she came down off the high and someone from the shelter found her lying on the ground, convulsing, with her clothes ripped to pieces."

"Or a cop found her," Peter said. "Either way, she sounds like she's in better shape than some of the other gamma-heads."

"Gamma-whats?"

Letting out a bark of laughter, Peter said, "That's what Detective O'Leary was calling them. Guess it stuck." Peter then told her about his conversation with the detective.

"I don't know," she said when he was done. "Sharing confidences with another woman—should I be worried?"

"She's a redhead, too."

"I know, I met her back at VPC when Valerie went harpy." Mary Jane chuckled again. God, it felt so good to talk to him. "It's a good thing I trust you, Tiger."

"Believe me, MJ, you have absolutely *nothing* to worry about."

"I love it when you're sincere. You're so *good* at it."

Peter's smile was almost audible as he said, "Years of practice."

Growing serious, Mary Jane said, "Look, Peter—don't tell O'Leary about Valerie, okay? I'll try to get her to talk to them on her own, but if not, I don't want Shapiro and his goons hassling her."

There was a long pause. "Okay, but if she doesn't go on her own, all bets are off."

"Fair enough."

"Look, I gotta go beat up some bad guys—and try to stop any more rampages by green-skinned addicts."

Mary Jane smiled encouragingly, even though the expression was lost over the phone. "Go get the gamma-heads, Tiger. I'll keep you posted about Valerie."

"Great. Love you."

"Love you, too."

As she closed the phone and put it away, Mary Jane wondered why she was being so protective of Valerie. *Maybe because I'd probably be her right now if it weren't for Peter.* She had been the original party girl when Peter first met her in college, but she had also stayed pretty clean, on the theory that modeling and acting required her body to be in pristine shape. On top of that, she and Peter had both lived through their mutual friend Harry Osborn's travails with substance abuse, which was enough to cure any sensible person of wanting to get hooked.

But she also lived the life, and she saw what everyone around her was doing. There were times when it was sorely tempting to join in the drinking, the snorting, the ingesting that everyone around her was enjoying.

Still, Peter was right—Valerie did need to talk to Shapiro and O'Leary and the others.

The cab pulled up in front of the shelter. Mary Jane paid the fare plus what she hoped was about a fifteen percent tip—she was never all that great at doing that kind of math on the fly—and then went in through the glass doors to the tall white building.

Her nose wrinkled as soon as she entered the waiting room. *There must be a dozen air fresheners in here,* she thought. The cloying artificial scents permeated the air; Mary Jane could almost taste them. *Then again, given the clientele, this smell is probably better than the alternative.*

A large Hispanic woman dressed in a sweatshirt and jeans was walking a short man wearing a winter coat and no shoes toward one door. The door buzzed and the woman pushed it open. Once they were gone, Mary Jane was alone in the reception area. A black woman was sitting behind a glass window—probably bulletproof—with a speaker's hole in the center and a tray in the bottom, reminiscent of teller windows at banks.

"Excuse me," Mary Jane said as she approached the window and placed the shopping bag on the floor next to her, "I'm here to collect Valerie McManus—blond, skinny, about five-four, five-five, wearing ripped clothes that look like Russian peasant wear."

The woman looked suspiciously at Mary Jane. "Just a second." She picked up the phone and dialed a four-digit number. "We got someone to see that skinny blond girl who came in yesterday. Yeah, she's a redhead. Bag'a clothes, too. Yeah, okay." She hung up. "Go on back."

Mary Jane nodded, picked up the bag, said "Thank you," and went to the door the other woman had gone through. It buzzed as she got near, and she pushed through it.

A small brunette waited for her on the other side. Mary Jane didn't think she looked old enough to be let out on her own.

"Hi, I'm Aimee. You must be Mary Jane?"

"Yes, I'm Valerie's friend."

"It's really good to see you, Mary Jane. I was kinda worried that, well, like, that you weren't, y'know, *real*."

Mary Jane couldn't help but laugh. "You thought Valerie was crazy?"

"Not really, but you never know. So many people come in here with all kinds of notions. When people lose their homes—"

"Well, Valerie didn't. She lives on Avenue C. She just had—well, something happened."

Aimee led Mary Jane back to the place where they kept the beds. There were more fresheners in the air, but now they didn't even put a dent in the problem. Mary Jane saw dozens of people of all races and both genders, with clothes in various forms of disarray.

The one thing they had in common was a lack of hygiene that was inevitable, given their circumstances.

"Oh, thank *God*."

Mary Jane looked over to see Valerie getting up off one of the pallets.

"Now do you believe me, you little *bitch*?" Valerie snarled at Aimee. "I *told* you I didn't belong here!"

Completely unperturbed by the abuse—Mary Jane supposed it was a regular thing around here—Aimee looked at Mary Jane and said, "Thanks very much for your help, Mary Jane. If you need anything, Carmen up front can find me."

"Thanks, Aimee."

As soon as Aimee turned to leave, Valerie muttered, "*God*, what a ditz. I so *hate* earnest little—" She shook her head. "Never *mind*, I just need to get out of these *clothes*. Can you believe this place?"

Mary Jane didn't say anything.

"C'mon, there's a bathroom back here."

If anything, the large bathroom smelled worse than the room they'd just left. Mary Jane immediately gagged, reflexively covering her nostrils with the sleeve of her denim jacket. She could feel her eyes watering. Seemingly unaffected by the stench—or so desperate to change clothes that she didn't care—Valerie eagerly took the red shopping bag and went into one of the stalls.

"So, MJ, can you *please* tell me what the hell happened?"

Mary Jane paused, and then said through her sleeve, "Look, Val—I know you're doing drugs."

"*Duh*, MJ, you were at Philo's party with me. I was the one trying to get you to—"

"I know you're doing Triple X, Val."

Silence. Then: "What're you talking about?"

"Val—"

"I don't even know what that *is*. Okay, look, Tuesday night, Zeke and some lady came over with some X that was all green, and he said it'd make me know my lines better, but—"

Remembering what Peter had told her about the tabs he found on the kids on the Upper West Side, Mary Jane said, "Val, that's a new drug. It's called Triple X and it doesn't just get you high, it changes you temporarily. Wednesday night, as God, Lou, Dmitri, and the rest of the cast and crew are my witness, your skin turned green, wings grew out of your back—which is why your costume got ripped—and you flew out *through the ceiling* of the playhouse."

Valerie opened the stall door, now wearing the clothes Mary Jane had purchased. For a moment, Mary Jane allowed herself to feel pride at having guessed Valerie's blouse, pants, and shoe sizes properly.

"MJ, that's the stupidest goddamn thing I ever heard!"

"Val—"

Shaking her head and holding up a hand, Valerie said, "No, no, *screw* you, MJ. You just want the lead, right?"

Mary Jane felt her mind boggle. "What?"

"You made up some stupid-ass story so you could be Olga. Well, fine, I'm sure it worked." She thrust the red bag, which now had her old clothes in it, at Mary Jane and said with no sincerity whatsoever, "Thanks for the clothes. I'm going home."

As soon as Mary Jane's hand wrapped around the shopping bag handles, Valerie stormed out of the bathroom. "Val!" Gritting her teeth, Mary Jane went after her.

Valerie ignored Mary Jane's imploring her to stop as she made a beeline for the door that led to the lobby. It did not require someone to buzz it to let someone else out, only to come in, a design flaw that Mary Jane was not especially thrilled with.

"Val, will you wait a second, please?" Mary Jane yelled across the lobby as she followed Valerie to the glass door that led to the street.

Her husband had always joked about the "Parker luck," and how it was all bad, and it seemed that today being married to a Parker was enough for Mary Jane to have it as well—as soon as Valerie stepped outside, a free cab pulled up. She got into it without another word.

Probably going home to Greg, Mary Jane thought with a sigh, *and to a nice buzz to take the edge off losing the part.* Naturally, all the other cabs in sight were occupied.

Had Valerie given her the chance, Mary Jane would've explained that she had never *wanted* the part of Olga, and that she certainly wouldn't make up a story like that. But Valerie wasn't being particularly rational on the subject—not that Mary Jane could blame her.

I didn't even get to tell her that the police want to talk to her.

She sighed and went back in. Aimee was in the lobby, a concerned expression on her face. "Is everything okay?"

"Yeah," Mary Jane said quickly, not wanting to drag her into this particular nightmare. She handed over the red shopping bag. "It's not much, but maybe it'll help someone here."

Aimee went back to her smile. "I'm sure it will do somebody some good. Thanks *very* much, Mary Jane. Have you ever considered volunteering?"

"I'm afraid I don't have the time right now." The words came out almost by rote. It was impossible to do everything kind and noble that she wanted to, and like so many others who didn't have enough hours in the day for what they *had* to do, much less wanted to, she had the stock answer perpetually on the tip of her tongue for when she was asked such questions.

Aimee didn't seem even a little put out. "That's fine. Thanks again!"

Mary Jane went back outside, opened her cell phone, and redialed Peter's number while heading eastward on 39th toward Times Square and the subway home.

Unsurprisingly, she got Peter's voice mail without a ring. He generally turned off the phone while patrolling. Shortly after first obtaining the cell phone, he'd had it on while in the midst of a fight with the Shocker. The ringing that emanated from his belt distracted him for just half a second, which was enough to keep him from ducking one of the Shocker's trademark electrical blasts.

"Hi, this is Peter Parker's cell phone. You've gotten this message because I've either turned the phone off, am on another line, or recognized your number on caller ID and don't want to talk to you right now, so there, nyah nyah. Leave a message after the beep and I'll get back to you as soon as I feel like it."

After the beep, Mary Jane said, "Bad news, Peter—Valerie not only denies that she turned into a harpy, she denies that she took Triple X. She thought it was regular X that was just colored green. She stormed out and went home, I guess, so, uh—I'd keep an eye out for harpies menacing Alphabet City in the next few days." She let out a breath. "I feel like I came all this way for nothing. I'll see you at home, Tiger. Love you!"

She closed the phone and continued down 39th, hoping that Valerie would be okay.

EIGHT

IT only took a couple days to get them Russian boys off the stretch of Amsterdam.

Bernabe "Blowback" Martinez, Ray-Ray's second-in-command, had taken charge of the operation. Ray-Ray told his people to check out the major corners and projects and see who was hurting 'cause they didn't have no Triple X, then start moving their asses in.

Technically, them boys on Amsterdam weren't Russian, they was as black as Ray-Ray or as Hispanic as Blowback, but that's 'cause, on this part of Amsterdam, white boys didn't really blend. Only white folks you saw here were either buyers comin' farther uptown to score the good stuff, or cops.

Nobody wanted blow or crack or X or weed now. They just wanted Triple X, and Ray-Ray had the package. You got the package, you got the real estate, and now a block that was all Russians a week back was now all Ray-Ray all the goddamn time. *Supply and demand, baby,* Blowback thought with a smile that flicked the toothpick he always kept in his mouth upward, *supply and goddamn demand. Yeah.*

It was the slow part of Saturday—late morning, when the early risers, or them that ain't gone to bed yet, were done buying and the afternoon crowd ain't woke yet—so two of Blowback's slingers were on one of the stoops, waiting for the clientele. Sweet, who was tall and skinny and wearing a do-rag on his dome and a Yankees shirt with Derek Jeter's name and number on the back, was trying to get Lemonhead, a short round kid with a head that he kept shaved, to come up with somebody who could beat the Hulk.

Running his hands over his dome the way he always did when he thought—which meant, far as Blowback was concerned, he didn't do it near regular enough—Lemonhead finally said, "Iron Man."

"No *way*," Sweet said, looking at Lemonhead like he was all nuts. "He just some guy in a suit. Hulk'll take that armor and crack it open, *pow!* Then Iron Man ain't shit."

"All right then, the Thing."

"Nah."

"What you mean 'nah,' you ever *see* the Thing? He big as shit, and all rocky, yo!"

"Nah, man, ain't gonna happen."

Lemonhead stood up all pissed off. "What you talkin' about? The Thing can kick his ass."

"Yeah, but the Thing ain't got that mean streak, yo. That's the edge. Maybe an even match, no problem, but Hulk's got that bad-ass temper." Sweet shook his head. "Try someone else."

Lemonhead climbed up onto the stoop's arm and sat up there so he could look down at Sweet. "You just gonna make shit up so you win."

"Am not, but you ain't comin' up with nobody that could do the job."

Blowback was about to chime in when he saw something.

Coming down Amsterdam was a big car that was slowing down as it got closer to them, even though it was still most of a block away from a traffic light that was still green. At first Blowback figured it was a customer.

Then he saw the gun muzzle.

"Get yo' ass *down*!" he shouted even as he ducked behind the stoop.

He saw one of the guns fire before he got out of sight, then he heard at least ten shots get thrown. A second later, the car was driving *mad* fast down Amsterdam, turning at the light with its tires screeching and heading off with serious speed. Only thing Blowback saw was that all three dudes in the car was white folks.

Goddamn Russians. Gotta be. Blowback hadn't even had time to get his Sig Sauer out. He stood up and looked over to see that Sweet and Lemonhead both had caught at least three bullets each. Sweet got one in the leg and two in the chest, both of them right on the interlocking NY of the Yankees logo on his shirt, which meant a heart shot; two of Lem's bullets were in the face, with the other one in his arm. Neither of them'd be slingin' no more. *And I gotta be tellin' Cutty that his little brother caught a bullet. Damn.*

Across the street, Blowback saw some citizen on a cell phone lookin' like he'd peed in his goddamn pants. *Probably callin' 911, which means I gotta get my narrow ass outta here.* He ran around to the other side of the stoop and removed the big brick that was hiding the stash—no sense in letting the cops take their product.

Blowback's ride was four blocks down the street—nearest goddamn parking space—so he ran that way after shoving the bags in his jacket and pants pockets. He had to tell Ray-Ray *now,* which meant heading back to Robinsfield. Ray-Ray didn't talk on the phone—cops got wiretaps all the time, and Ray-Ray wasn't taking no chances—and Blowback wasn't about to do this through one of those knuckleheads he had in the Houses. Nah, he had to tell him in person that Sweet and Lem was dead and them Russians was starting a goddamn war.

○————————○

JANNA didn't even know what club they were *in.*

Laura and Terri had dragged her out of the dorm practically kicking and screaming. "It's Saturday night," they said. "You need to get out," they said. "Have some fun once in a while," they said.

Okay, it was true she hadn't been going out much since she broke up with Steve, and yeah, she was mopey because Steve started dating that skank Katie Turner within, like, five *minutes* of her breaking up with him.

But she really didn't want to be here. Sure, Terri and Laura loved coming to these places because they were ohmygod *so* hip, but as far as Janna was concerned, they were just *incredibly* loud, *way* overcrowded, *much* too dark, and were playing music that Janna thought sucked. They called it "dance music," which Janna just didn't get, since she never wanted to dance to it. *Play some Red Hot Chili Peppers or Queen or Led Zeppelin if you want me to dance, not this techno crap.*

She had every intention of telling Laura and Terri this, but it was so *loud* in here that she couldn't make herself be heard without shouting at the top of her lungs, and she just didn't *feel* like it.

So she sat on the curved couch that the three of them had taken over in one corner of the club. And she drank. The drinks weren't even any good.

The only tequila they had was José Cuervo, which was the tequila equivalent of drinking Budweiser. Decent enough if that was all that was available, but not something anybody who appreciated the drink would go near.

More than anything, Janna wanted to go back to the dorm, open her own private stash of Patrón Añejo tequila, and come up with ways of murdering Steve with a fork.

She had gotten up to dance a few times, which involved barely moving while being pressed on all sides by sweaty, icky people. If Janna wanted to do *that,* she'd ride the 4 train at rush hour. She couldn't believe that she had to stand on line and pay a cover charge for the same experience here. When Terri or Laura got up to dance—they never all went up together for fear of losing their couch—they had each made sexy dancing gestures in the vicinity of two guys, but nothing came of it. *Thank God.*

Laura came back from her latest dance and then went to the bathroom. Terri leaned over and said, "Isn't this *great?*" Janna only knew she said that because she read her lips.

"No," Janna said honestly.

Terri scootched over right next to her so she could be heard more clearly. "You're not having fun?"

"Hel-*lo?* I've been, like, totally miserable since we *got* here!"

Looking crestfallen, Terri said, "But we were doing this so you'd have *fun!*"

Before Janna could answer that, Laura came back, holding a bag. She said something, but Janna couldn't make it out.

"What?" Janna prompted.

Laura sat down on the other side of Janna from Terri and held out the clear plastic bag. Inside were three ecstasy tabs, only green. "I said I scored this from a girl in the ladies' room. Triple X, baby!"

Janna wondered how, after the cover charge and the drinks, Laura had any money to pay for this stuff.

Laura said, "The girl said it was twice as fast and twice as good as regular X."

At this point, Janna was willing to do *anything* that might at least have a chance of making this night not suck, so she eagerly took the tab.

I think Laura got robbed, was Janna's first thought after taking it and waiting several seconds. She found that it just increased her bad mood because she had grabbed onto the concept of a buzz like a drowning person grabbing a life preserver and it just wasn't coming and it was driving her nuts and why couldn't anything go right and wow the lights in here are so incredibly bright and shiny and loud and pretty and her fingers started to tingle a little bit and suddenly she wasn't so much sitting in the chair as she was floating in the air above everyone and God she felt so incredibly good and this was the greatest thing she'd ever experienced in her whole entire life and nothing mattered whether it was stupid Steve or skanky Katie or anybody else because everything was just wonderful and the floor was so far away it was like she was flying through the air and maybe she really was since she was really really close to the strobe lights and her fingers were even tinglier and look at that something came out of her fingers like a laser beam only green and now everyone was screaming and why was Terri all big and muscular and green all out of nowhere and Laura was nowhere to be seen though there was a green blur in the room and why was everyone screaming and running all over the place all of a sudden weren't they all having a great time like Janna was?

Janna decided to ignore the shouting, ignore the screaming, ignore Terri ripping the bar up off the ground, ignore the green blur that looked a lot like Laura knocking things and people over, ignore *all that,* and just *fly.* Because she could fly, like that cute guy in the Fantastic Four who got on fire, he was a hottie in *every* sense of the word and maybe now that Janna could fly they could go out on a date or something together, he had to be better than Steve, but *anybody* would be better than Steve.

She had to get out of this place. There wasn't room to *fly* in here! So she thrust her tingling fingers out and then there was more green and then a big hole in the wall and Janna was free to fly wherever she wanted . . .

○———————○

FOR Spider-Man, the best part of web-swinging was the apogee—that moment at the end of the swing on one web-line before the double-tap on his web-shooters to send out a new line, when he hung in the air unfettered. He'd never gone skydiving, but he wondered if that moment was what it was like for divers in freefall before they opened their chutes: the total freedom from physical attachment to anything, just *being* in midair.

Just at the moment, though, he was in no position to appreciate it as he swung out through the cool evening air over Union Square, his web-line attached to the big bookstore on the north boundary, coming around and landing on a large apartment building on the southeast corner.

Over the course of a Saturday afternoon that he should have been spending doing a lesson plan, or maybe finally grading the pop quiz he'd given a week and a half earlier, not to mention the previous day's test, Spider-Man had been on the lookout for gamma-heads—and finding them. He'd stopped three of them who were harassing families and scaring animals in the Central Park Zoo, another who had gained telepathy with his X high and was using it to force everyone in Madison Square Park to walk out onto Broadway into oncoming traffic, and yet another who came very close to breaking the Bronx-Queens leg of the Triborough Bridge in half. Somewhere in there, he'd taken the time to check out the Robinsfield Houses again, but found nothing useful. *At least I didn't see Hector around, either.*

Each time he'd found something, he'd left a message with Detective O'Leary from a pay phone. This strategy was proving less efficacious than he'd hoped, as he was running out of quarters. *Maybe I should just head up to the Two-Four and hope for the best.*

Before he could do that, though, he had to fulfill a promise to Mary Jane to swing around Alphabet City and make sure that Valerie hadn't gone harpy again. Jumping off the apartment building, he shot out a web-line to the Con Edison building to the east and leapt out over the 14th Street traffic.

The one thing he hadn't been able to devote much thought to, focused as he was on stopping the gamma-heads' assorted rampages, was the party responsible. He had left his theories on one of his messages to O'Leary, but to the best of his knowledge, there was no forward movement beyond that. *Of course, O'Leary hasn't actually returned my messages—mostly by virtue of my not leaving a number—so that's not indicative of much of anything.*

He hadn't had time to check out his old ESU professors, though he assumed that to be a dead end in any case. *Still, probably a good idea to eliminate them, if nothing else.* The two most likely candidates remained: Banner and Octavius.

By the time he worked his way over to Tompkins Square Park, though, such thoughts were banished by the buzz of his spider-sense, which enabled him to barely get out of the way of the green-skinned woman with batwings flying down toward the park's tree line.

Yup, she's gone harpy again.

Doing a quick forward flip, Spider-Man landed on the park's fence and saw that Valerie—assuming it was her, and not some *other* gamma-head who got turned into a harpy—was heading toward a group of kids, plus one adult, who were kicking a soccer ball around. She was also terrorizing the pigeons, a large group of which flew out of the park in a huff, with the exception of one that Valerie had nabbed in her hands. Spider-Man also noticed that those hands were more like talons now. *Mary Jane didn't mention that. Could be a further mutation from repeated exposure.*

While biochemist Peter Parker was fascinated by the process, the super hero Spider-Man had to deal with more immediate concerns—like those kids, some of whom were now panicking at the sight of a green winged lady with a pigeon in her clutches. Leaping down at Valerie, he said, "Hey, c'mon, you don't want to eat that, you don't know where it's been."

He tackled Valerie head-on, and they both went down and over into a nearby tree—an oak with a crowded tangle of branches that ripped at Spider-Man, making him rethink the efficacy of his plan. On the bright side, she let go of the pigeon, which took off at great speed toward one of the apartment buildings across the street.

Valerie screamed and slashed at Spider-Man's chest. He tried to jump back, but his progress was impeded by the branches of the oak, so the talons sliced through his shirt and scratched his chest.

"Ow! Hey, that hurts! You may want to see your manicurist." He kicked outward as he said that, trying to make it more of a push than a kick. He didn't want to hurt Valerie, just stall her and keep her from hurting anyone, or anything, until she came down off the high.

Unfortunately, all the kick did was clear her of the tree, allowing her to fly off.

Great, there she goes again. At least she's decided not to bother with those kids.

As he extricated himself from the oak and shot out a web-line to a building in order to give chase after Valerie, who was now flying northeast toward the river, a thought occurred to him. *She has wings, idiot. Web the wings.* He'd been going for several days straight, both teaching and heroing, without enough sleep, and it was obviously affecting his ability to think things through.

By the time he caught up to her, she was over 14th Street, heading toward the East River and the FDR Drive. Leaping onto a streetlight, he shot webs upward out of both shooters, waving his wrists in a long-practiced motion that would cause the webbing to wrap around what he hit.

As planned, the webbing snared Valerie's torso and the wings on her back. Screaming, she flailed her arms about even as she started to plummet toward the pavement. Spider-Man then launched himself off the streetlight with sufficient force that the metal rod vibrated with a clang as he pushed off, on a path roughly parallel to the height of the streetlight. If he got his angles right—and after all these years of web-shooting, he rarely screwed up such geometric calculations—he would catch her as she fell. This would have worked perfectly had Valerie not spoiled the plan by ripping through the webbing with her talons, thus freeing her wings.

The Parker luck is running true to form, I see. Spider-Man shot out a web-line to snag a fire escape on a nearby building, and swung up and around to land on Valerie's back. *Sometimes, you just gotta do it the old-fashioned way.*

What Valerie had in strength she lacked in hard experience—and possibly brains, given that her vocabulary in this state consisted entirely of snarls and grunts. An experienced flier like, say, the Vulture could knock Spider-Man off his back like a bronco disposing of an inexperienced rodeo hand—and in fact had done so several dozen times. But Valerie had never had someone riding on her back, much less one with super strength and the ability to adhere to whatever he held on to, and so she found him impossible to shake.

Not for lack of trying, mostly in terms of bucking and weaving in a manner that would've made someone who didn't spend most of his time on a roller-coaster ride through the rooftops and canyons of Manhattan throw up. He sometimes wondered what would've happened if that spider had bitten an agoraphobe or someone with a weaker stomach than Peter Parker's. For now, though, it meant that no matter what Valerie did—and she did plenty—Spider-Man did not let go.

Then, all of a sudden, they started to descend slowly—heading right toward the FDR Drive's 34th Street entrance ramp. Looking down at Valerie's back, he saw that the wings were shrinking and her neck was growing pale. *She's coming down—in more ways than one.*

Reaching out, Spider-Man shot as much webbing as he could, simultaneously kicking his legs into Valerie's stomach in the hopes that it would force her to lift up a little so they'd overshoot the entrance ramp and land in the gas station beyond it.

Sure enough, it worked, if only for a second, before the wings shrunk away completely and he and Valerie became two dead weights falling through the air carried forward by momentum alone.

By that time, however, Spider-Man had made a handy-dandy web pillow that they both landed on—not softly, but at least it was a superior alternative to the hard pavement.

A customer was pumping gas into her car, and cried, "Jesus!" when they landed.

Spider-Man extricated himself from the web pillow. Valerie—and it was definitely her, for she had reverted to normal—was in no shape to do likewise. Just like Javier and the kids on Central Park West and the other ones he'd dealt with, she was barely conscious and twitchy inside her torn clothing.

He glanced around the gas station for a pay phone, but the only one he saw was dangling loosely off the hook, the earpiece having been broken off. *No luck there.*

Looking over at the woman pumping gas, he asked, "You have a cell phone?"

"Uh yeah—why?"

"Call 911."

"I can't do that!" The woman sounded aghast.

Spider-Man frowned under his mask. "Why not?"

"You crazy? I use a cell phone in the gas station, it'll blow up!"

"That's an urban legend," Spider-Man said with a sigh. "Don't you watch *MythBusters*? Trust me, it'll be fine."

He then leapt up to the top of the gas station's kiosk, shot out a web-line to one of the tall buildings on the other side of the FDR, and swung westward in search of a working pay phone. Even if the woman didn't call

911, he could still let O'Leary know. But he was down to the last of his change, so he wouldn't be able to do this for much longer.

To his amazement, O'Leary answered her own phone this time. "This is Detective O'Leary."

"Detective, it's Spider-Man, and *please* don't make me go through the same rigamarole again, just trust that it's me, and that we've got another gamma-head at the gas station by the northbound 34th Street entrance to the FDR. There'll probably be a 911 call about it soon."

"Nice job," she said. "I hear you've been all over everywhere today."

"Just doing my bit. I can do one bit better on this one, though—her name's Valerie McManus."

"Valerie McManus?" O'Leary sounded surprised. "Greenwich Village Valerie McManus? Turned into a flying green thing or whatever?"

Spider-Man nodded, though the gesture was lost over the phone. "That's the one." He was about to tell her that she was stronger this time, but the only way he could explain how he knew that was to say that he was married to one of the witnesses to Valerie's first transformation.

"Good. We've had a hell of a time getting ahold of her, and her actor chums were all stonewalling."

That caused a wince, since Spider-Man knew that Mary Jane was one of the stonewallers.

"Listen, can you come up here?"

"I thought Detective Shapiro didn't like 'costumes.'"

"He doesn't—but there are other detectives in this house who feel different. Especially after what's been going on the last couple of days." She let out a long breath. "Look, just get your webbed ass up here, okay?"

"All right, all right." Spider-Man was a bit taken aback by O'Leary's insistence, and wondered what it was she wasn't telling him. "I can be there in about twenty minutes or so—assuming I don't run into any more gamma-heads."

"Or shoot-outs," she muttered.

That took Spider-Man even further aback. "Shootouts?"

"Yup. We got us a bona fide drug war on our hands."

○———————○

UNA O'Leary nursed what she figured had to be her thousandth cup of coffee in the past hour as she sat in the coffee room of the 24th Precinct. When Jerry Shapiro had called a meeting of the whole task force, he'd put it in here, since the second shift was now on and using the squad room. Shapiro was standing on one side of the refrigerator, with Fry towering over the other side of the appliance. *It isn't bad enough he has to be taller than everyone else, but he never sits down,* O'Leary thought uncharitably, not in the least because she was the shortest person in the Two-Four's detective squad. Fry's presence at least kept her from being the youngest, as the immense black man was six months younger than she, though his appearance tended to mute any cracks about his age.

Shanahan, by contrast, was always sitting down, complaining about his knees the whole time. The old, fat, bald detective was just six months from being on the job for thirty years, and he was counting the microseconds until that day came so he could "get the hell away from this job and live a real life" with a veteran's pension to live off of. He sat opposite O'Leary at the large table. Between them, and perpendicular to both, was Petrocelli, who was chewing and popping his omnipresent bubble gum.

They were waiting on two people. One was Wheeler, who finally came in holding a ream of paper. Wheeler was tall, young, well-built, and good-looking, which would've been fine if he himself hadn't been so overwhelmingly aware of all four qualities. If she saw Wheeler in a bar, she'd think about talking to him, but five minutes after meeting him, she probably would've been inclined to throw a drink in his face. At least he was good police . . .

The other, known only to O'Leary and Fry, was Spider-Man.

O'Leary had confided in Fry, because she figured he'd be reasonable. Petrocelli had his head too far up Shapiro's ass to do anything Shapiro wouldn't like, and O'Leary neither trusted nor liked Shanahan or Wheeler.

Meanwhile, Wheeler held up his ream. "Just got the faxes in from the One-Oh about that club mess. Two people were killed when they got trampled and a whole lot more were hurt, a few more were injured when one of the girls ripped the bar out of the floor, a few more by the super-fast one who knocked people over, and the last one bruised a bunch with her ray-beams. The girls were ID'd as Laura Silverstein, Terri Bowles, and Janna Gilman, all students at ESU. Silverstein's the one who bought the

Triple X, but she didn't know the girl she scored it from—just someone else in the club." Wheeler shrugged.

Shanahan shook his head. "This is outta hand."

"That's why we have a task force, Pat," Petrocelli said.

"You wanna contribute somethin' useful, do it, or shut the hell up."

Pointing an accusatory finger at Petrocelli, Shanahan said, "Shut your yap, you little—"

Petrocelli just laughed. "'Shut your yap'? You're Damon Runyon all of a sudden?"

"*Both* of you, shut *up!*" Shapiro didn't raise his voice often, but when he did, the windows shook. The coffee room went silent.

After a moment, Shapiro looked at Fry. "We got anything from any of the other gamma-heads?"

Shaking his head, Fry said, "Nah, most of 'em are unconscious or ain't talkin'."

"We got somethin' else," Petrocelli said. "I talked with Narcotics, and they ID'd the two vics up on Amsterdam from this morning as well as the one who got shot at over on 110th—all three are part of a crew run by a dealer named Ray-Ray, and the one on 110th had a whole lotta bags of Triple X on him, so we're talkin' dealers here, since street yo's like that don't buy in bulk, usually."

O'Leary perked up. "This Ray-Ray work out of Long Island City?"

Petrocelli nodded. "In the Robinsfield Houses."

Looking at Shapiro, O'Leary said, "That matches—"

Before she could finish, Shapiro held up his hands. "*Don't* start that again, Una."

"Spider-Man told me this stuff was coming out of LIC."

"I don't really care, Una, we're not dealin' with no costumes."

O'Leary looked over at Fry. He was about to say something when Shapiro looked back at Petrocelli. "Anything else off that shooting we can use?"

Again, Petrocelli nodded. "Yeah—the guy I talked to at Narcotics nearly blew a gasket when he realized they were all Ray-Ray's crew. Both blocks that got hit belonged to a buncha Ukrainians for the last year or two. Now we got new crews in both locales and matching shoot-outs. And the witness up on Amsterdam says he saw white guys in the car that threw the shots."

"Yeah, that's probably the Ukrainians," O'Leary said. "Ray-Ray's taking their territory, now they're hitting back."

"Makes sense." Shapiro sighed. "Christ, this is only gonna get worse."

There was a pause. O'Leary gave Fry a significant look, since she knew that if she said anything, it would be dismissed out of hand. Picking it up, Fry turned to Shapiro. "Jerry, I think Una's right—we need to bring the web-head in on this."

Shapiro shot Fry a look—diluted by having to look up so far at the tall detective's face. "What're you, high?"

"Jerry's right," Shanahan said. "We don't need no costumes screwin' us up."

To O'Leary's surprise, it was Wheeler who said, "How's he screwin' us up? Right now, he's the only one containing this. We've got seven incidents involving gamma-heads in the last two days. A bunch of them had people injured and about half a dozen fatalities. You know how many of them ended with *nobody* hurt? Three—the three that Spider-Man's been involved in. He saved those people down at Madison Square Park and in the zoo, and one that just got called in to the One-Seven with some lady in a gas station."

O'Leary smiled. *Looks like I didn't give Wheeler enough credit.* "He called me after that one—Spider-Man did," she amended quickly. "Said that's Valerie McManus, from that theatre downtown."

Shapiro almost snarled. "And that means I'm supposed to let some costume into my house? No way."

"Aw, but I promise I'm housebroken."

O'Leary turned around to see Spider-Man sitting on the wall by the door to the coffee room, his back and feet flat against the wall, his knees bent. Standing in the doorway was the corpulent form of Sergeant Green.

Shapiro stepped forward and looked accusingly at O'Leary. "What the hell's he doing here?"

Before O'Leary could try to defend her decision to invite him, Green spoke up. "*I* let him in, *Detective*. You have a problem with that, *Detective*?"

Transferring his look to the sergeant, Shapiro started to say something, then thought better of it, knowing what Green's reaction would be if he said the wrong thing. "I'm just peachy with it, Joll."

A broad grin spread on Green's round face. "Good. I like 'peachy.'

'Peachy' is good. 'Peachy' means harmony and happiness and, best of all, a task force that can bring a case in, necessitating a nice press conference in which the commissioner sings the praises of the fine detectives of the Two-Four and makes us all look good to the bosses. It is my considered opinion that the presence of this costumed gentleman"—he pointed a pudgy finger at Spider-Man—"will make that happy outcome considerably more likely. It is also the opinion of Detectives O'Leary, Fry, and Wheeler, three detectives that you specifically requested for this detail, leading me to think that maybe you trust their judgment. Am I making myself entirely clear here, *Detective* Shapiro?"

"Yeah." Shapiro looked over at Spider-Man on the wall. "You got something useful to tell us?"

"A couple things. I—"

"Before you do that," Shapiro said, "I just want to say one thing for the record. I don't like you. I don't want you involved in police work." He looked over at Green. "My sergeant says otherwise, so I'm letting you help us out, but I just want you to know up front that I think you're an asshole who hides his face and doesn't deserve to be in the same room with real police."

Spider-Man sounded nonplussed in his reply. "Sorry you feel that way, Detective. But I'm here to help however I can. You don't want me, I'll go back out there and keep those gamma-heads from tearing up the city."

Petrocelli said, "We got Code: Blue for that."

Rolling her eyes, O'Leary said, "The same Code: Blue who had their budget slashed last year? The same Code: Blue whose equipment is breaking down?"

"Detective Shapiro," Green said, "you seem to be having some difficulties focusing your task force."

Shapiro smiled insincerely at the sergeant. "Just a free exchange of ideas, Joll. Keeps the police work fresh."

"Good rationalization," Green said. "Spider-Man, welcome to the Triple X Task Force. That's the task force commander, Detective Jeroen Shapiro. We all call him Jerry, mainly 'cause Jeroen's a sissy name."

Normally that got a smile out of Shapiro, but he was too busy staring daggers at the new arrival.

Green continued. "The landmass to Detective Shapiro's right is Detective Jimmy Fry, who looks down on all of us." Moving over to the sink: "Over there is Detective Ty 'Pretty Boy' Wheeler—I believe the nickname's etymology should be self-evident. Seated at the table are Detectives Lou Petrocelli and Pat Shanahan. And, of course, you know Detective Una O'Leary."

O'Leary smiled at him.

"Pleased to meet you all," Spider-Man said with a nod and sounding much more polite than O'Leary expected. *I guess his momma raised him right.*

"It ain't mutual," Shanahan muttered. "What the hell you gonna tell us we don't already know?"

Spider-Man actually seemed to consider Shanahan's mouthy words. "Well, for starters, I can tell you that this Ray-Ray kid who's dealing the drugs isn't the supplier. I've checked out his HQ, and he's got mostly teenagers working for him. To make ecstasy do what this stuff is doing requires a level of smarts that very few people have."

"We're already looking into that," Shapiro said. O'Leary snorted.

"Something wrong, Una?" Shapiro asked snidely.

"Not at all, Jerry," O'Leary said quickly. She had suggested looking into it two days ago, but Shapiro kept taking her off it every time she started. To be fair, that was in part because so many gamma-heads were turning up, combined with the sudden drug war, so there were more immediate things for her, and the rest of the task force, to be involved in.

"Most of the users seem to be students," Spider-Man said.

"That don't mean nothin'," Shanahan said. "X is a kids' drug. If you really belonged in this room, you'd know that."

Looking at O'Leary, Spider-Man asked, "He always this cheery?"

"We keep him around for morale," O'Leary deadpanned.

"Good work." Spider-Man gave Shanahan a thumbs-up.

Shanahan gave Spider-Man the finger.

Shapiro looked at his watch. "Christ, it's after midnight. All right, we all need some sleep. Una, keep checking those possibilities on the supplier. Ty, Jimmy," he said to Wheeler and Fry, "keep on the hospitals where the gamma-heads've been taken. Maybe one of 'em'll decide to talk. Lou, Pat," he said to Petrocelli and Shanahan, "do the same for the families of the three shooting vics."

Petrocelli looked at him like he was nuts. "You really think they'll talk?"

"They sure as hell won't if you don't talk to them," Shapiro snapped. He then looked up at Spider-Man. "As for you—do whatever it is you do. You find out anything useful, tell us."

"Unfortunately, I'm running out of change to call you guys—and if you have something for me—"

"Like *that's* gonna happen," Shanahan muttered.

Ignoring him, Spider-Man continued: "—it'd be nice if you could call. Like if you hear about a gamma-head rampage that your guys can't handle."

"You think we can't handle this?" Shanahan asked.

Spider-Man stared at him with his featureless mask. "You ever take on someone who was high on X and could bench-press the Empire State Building, Detective? I have, several times over the past few days."

To O'Leary's amazement, that shut Shanahan up.

Then she rose from her chair. "I got an idea. We can give him Ursitti's phone."

Shapiro frowned at her. "Ain't Ursitti too busy usin' it?"

O'Leary shook her head. "He left it in his desk when he went on vacation so nobody could reach him."

"Figures," Petrocelli muttered. "Fine, that'll work," Shapiro said.

"Thanks," Spider-Man said to O'Leary.

"No problem."

"All right," Shapiro said, "let's get moving." He looked over at Green. Green just nodded and turned and left the coffee room.

Aside from Shanahan, just Spider-Man and O'Leary were left in the coffee room after a moment, and she was only staying to finish off her coffee before going to Ursitti's desk to retrieve his phone. O'Leary assumed that Shanahan wanted to take his time getting up from the chair.

However, he apparently wanted to fire a few more verbal shots at Spider-Man. "No way I'm callin' this guy on no police phone."

"You have a problem with me, Detective Shanahan?"

"I got lotsa problems with you, but the biggie is that thing on your face."

"What, my mask?"

Shanahan nodded. "Yeah. I don't like somebody who claims to be on this side of the fence who can't stand behind what he does."

"Look, Detective—I really kinda *have* to hide my face. Occupational hazard."

"Bullshit."

"Excuse me?" Spider-Man said.

"Look," O'Leary said, "we're—"

Shanahan ignored her, like usual, instead turning around to look at Spider-Man. "I said 'bullshit.' You *have* to hide your face? That's the biggest load'a crap I ever heard in my life, and I been alive a lot longer than you."

O'Leary found herself jumping to Spider-Man's defense. "If people knew who he was, there would be all kinds of consequences to his family and—"

"Was I talkin' to you, girlie?" Shanahan snapped.

"Hey, watch it," Spider-Man said, a defense that O'Leary appreciated, but didn't really need. That Shanahan was a sexist jerk was hardly a news flash.

Shanahan turned back to Spider-Man. "You think, 'cause you deal with scumbags all the time, that you gotta hide who you are? You wanna know somethin'? I deal with scumbags all the time, too. An' when I arrest one of 'em, I'm wearin' a badge with a number on it that belongs to *me*. An' when I bring 'em back here, I type up a report that has *my* name on it. An' when that scumbag goes into the system, *my* name gets attached to his sheet. An' when it goes to trial, if it goes to trial, then I get on a goddamn witness stand in front of a judge an' a jury an' lawyers an' whoever the hell else is in the courtroom, and I give my name an' address an' testimony that's entered in the public record." He stood up slowly. O'Leary could hear his knees crack. "Ow! Goddammit!" He put one hand to his left knee, then turned back to Spider-Man. "You don't stand behind what you do, then what you do ain't worth shit."

With that, he hobbled out of the coffee room.

O'Leary was almost afraid to look at Spider-Man. "You didn't deserve that."

In a low, bitter tone, Spider-Man said, "'Deserve' got nothin' to do with it." He shook his head. "Guess that's part of his job as morale officer. C'mon," he said snidely, "let's get that phone so I can go back out and keep people safe."

"Point taken," O'Leary said, and led him into the squad room.

NINE

PETER Parker awoke to the smell of bacon.

It was his second-favorite aroma in the world to wake up to. The top spot was, naturally, taken by the smell of his aunt May's wheatcakes, which were about as close to heaven as Peter ever figured himself likely to get in this world.

But bacon did the trick in a pinch.

He climbed out of bed, only then noticing that he was still in the pants of his Spider-Man outfit. He had removed the shirt, mask, gloves, and footwear before collapsing on the bed at whatever ludicrous hour he had come in. After the oh-so-charming meeting at the Two-Four, he'd done another run around Manhattan and Long Island City—and not finding anything, which was something of a surprise for a Saturday night—before coming home to collapse beside his slumbering wife. She woke up long enough to kiss him, then fell back asleep. Mary Jane had long ago grown accustomed to his hours, and she knew that he'd wake her if something really terrible had happened. Since he didn't, she assumed it was a normal night.

Of course, for us, "normal" is a night of me beating up bad guys and risking life and limb. . . .

Padding into the kitchen, he saw a spread of waffles, bacon, sausage, toast, home fries, coffee, and orange juice, with Mary Jane moving from the stove to the serving plate, holding a pan full of scrambled eggs.

"Wow—you did all this?"

Mary Jane grinned. "Nice try, Tiger. I did the scrambled eggs and the toast. The rest is way beyond my culinary capacity, as you well know, and came from the diner."

"That'll do. I can eat a whole henhouse right now." Peter sat down at the small kitchen table and started wolfing down the eggs. "Mmm, nice and fluffy, the way I like 'em."

"I figured a nice Sunday brunch was the right way to go for both of us after the week we had."

"I didn't get a chance to ask you," Peter said as he chewed. "How'd rehearsal go?"

"Don't talk with your mouth full, Tiger—I *know* May raised you better than that," she said with another grin. "Oh, that reminds me, May called. She said we're welcome to come over for dinner tonight unless, and I quote, 'Peter's trying to stop that awful drug I heard about on the news.'" She sat down and dug into her waffles. "Anyhow, I told her you probably would be, and she said that was fine, and to feel free to stop by for leftovers since she knows you forget to eat."

"That's my aunt." Peter smiled warmly as he popped a slice of bacon into his mouth. *Best thing I ever did was confide in her.* May Parker had only recently found out that her nephew was also Spider-Man, and from Peter's perspective it was like a giant weight had been lifted from his shoulders. Rather than proving too big a shock for the elderly woman to handle—which had been Peter's rationalization for not telling her for so many years—it was instead a huge relief, since she had thought there was something terribly wrong with Peter, the way he kept sneaking around. In retrospect, keeping the secret from her all these years had been horribly selfish and unfair of him, especially since it meant he had to constantly lie to the woman who raised him. Such behavior was unbecoming of someone who tried to live up to the ideal of being a hero. While Peter had good reason to keep his identity secret from the world at large, he had come to understand that deceiving his loved ones was not always such a hot idea.

That train of thought led him to Detective Shanahan's diatribe. "MJ—I went to the 24th Precinct last night."

"Really?" Mary Jane sounded surprised.

"Detective O'Leary asked, and her sergeant signed off on it, even though Shapiro, the head of the task force, didn't like the idea."

"Shapiro's the one I talked to at the theatre," Mary Jane said through a mouthful of waffle. "He's a jerk."

Grinning, Peter said, "Don't talk with your mouth full. Anyhow, one of the detectives, a cranky old jerk named Shanahan, started ripping into me after the meeting broke." He summed up the gist of Shanahan's comments to Mary Jane.

Mary Jane chewed thoughtfully on some sausage when he finished, swallowed it, then finally spoke. "Like you said, he's a jerk."

"Yeah, but let me tell you, he definitely struck a nerve. I can't help but wonder if he's right. I mean, I originally only wore the mask as a way of creating a new identity for myself as a showbiz performer separate from Puny Peter Parker, the Geek Supreme of Midtown High. After that, it just kinda got to be a habit. Maybe I'd've been better off—"

"Stop right there, Peter." Mary Jane was pointing her fork at him. "I know you've been feeling a little weird about the whole secret identity thing since May found out—hell, since *I* told you that I knew about it all along. But I only have three words to say to you: Green, Goblin, Venom."

Peter shuddered, the home fries turning to ashes in his mouth. Venom was, in many ways, Spider-Man's deadliest foe, in part because he was immune to his spider-sense, in part because he knew Spider-Man and Peter Parker were one and the same. His first encounter with Venom was when the latter showed up at the apartment he and Mary Jane shared shortly after they got married, where he proceeded to terrorize her.

And then there's Osborn . . . The first person to don the costume of the Green Goblin was a lunatic industrialist named Norman Osborn. He learned that Peter was Spider-Man, and his knowledge of that fact led to more hardship and strife than Peter could have imagined. Osborn killed Gwen Stacy, as well as a man who was very much like a brother to Peter. For a time, he made Peter believe Aunt May was dead. Plus there was the abuse he heaped on his own son, and Peter's best friend, Harry, which led to his losing his mind and also taking on the mantle of the Goblin until he died as well.

Spider-Man had made many enemies in his career, but those two were arguably the worst.

"Point very much taken," he said, dolefully scooping some eggs into his mouth. "Still, Shanahan wasn't entirely wrong, either. It's not like these guys don't take risks, too. And they don't have the proportional strength and speed of a spider to protect them."

"That's their choice. And they do actually get *paid* for this."

"Second point taken." Peter sipped his coffee. "I guess he just got me thinking is all."

Before the conversation could continue, the strains of the theme to *Rocky* could suddenly be heard from the bedroom.

"What is *that*?" Mary Jane asked. "You change your ring tone again?"

That jogged Peter's memory. *Ursitti must be a Stallone fan.* "That's my temporary phone." He dashed into the bedroom, saw the name O'LEARY on the display, and flipped it open. "Yo."

"Look, Shapiro doesn't know I'm calling you, so don't tell him, okay?"

"What is it, Detec—"

"We got word from the Two-Eight that some slingers are gathering on 113th Street on one of Ray-Ray's blocks. Nobody's doing anything right now, 'cause it's Sunday morning, but—"

"Sunday morning? What's that got to do with anything?"

Sounding like she was talking to a five-year-old, O'Leary said, "It's *Sunday.* There's always a truce on Sunday morning—*nobody* messes with that."

"Are you serious?"

"No, I risked my task force commander reaming me out *again* for talking to you without cause just to make a joke. Will you just shut the hell up for a minute? It's already a quarter to twelve, and as soon as it hits noon, the truce is off, since most people are back from church by then. You gotta get over there. I don't trust those boys at the Two-Eight to do much of anything, frankly."

The detective put a lot of disdain into that last sentence, making Peter wonder what exactly the officers of the 28th Precinct did to deserve such treatment. *Then again,* he thought, *there's always a level of interdepartmental rivalry and disdain in any profession. No reason for cops to be any different.*

O'Leary continued: "That's why I'm telling *you*. You're there, maybe no bodies."

Peter swallowed. *But no pressure.* "Yeah, okay, I'll get right over."

"Good." She hung up without another word.

Turning around, he saw Mary Jane standing in the doorway. "Your cop phone has a loud volume—I heard the whole thing."

"Yeah, so I better get going." He placed the phone back in his belt and put it on, followed by the shirt.

Mary Jane walked into the bedroom. "You know, I think she has a crush on you."

"MJ, c'mon."

"Seriously, she's definitely hot for you. I think I may have to get a restraining order." She was grinning ear to ear. "At the very least, you may want to read one of those tell-alls that groupies have written—get some idea what you're dealing with."

"She's not a groupie, she's a detective who's putting up with enough garbage from her fellow officers, and who's trying to make my job easier, and that's sounding *way* more defensive than it should, isn't it?"

The grin had fallen a bit, though not entirely. "A little bit, yeah."

"Sorry." He sighed as he put his boots and gloves on. "It's just that she really thinks I can contribute, which is a nice change from the usual. I mean the best I generally get, even from the cops who *like* me, is a yeah-okay-we'll-deal-with-you-'cause-we-gotta attitude. And then there's folks like Shanahan and Shapiro."

Mary Jane kissed him before he could put his mask on. "Don't sweat it, Tiger, I was just teasing. And I think it's good that you've got someone on your side for once. Now get your cute little butt over to 113th before the truce ends." She hesitated. "They really have a Sunday truce?"

"Apparently." Spider-Man pulled the mask over his face. "I love you, MJ."

She dazzled him with her best smile, the one that never once failed to melt his heart. "Love you too, Tiger."

As he leapt out into the sunny Sunday morning air, he realized that he never did find out how Mary Jane's rehearsal went. . . .

o————————o

JESUS "Save" Martinez couldn't believe that them damn Ukrainians hadn't heard about Sunday morning.

Boris—he had a real name, but Save just called him Boris 'cause he didn't like having to remember no three-syllable name that was all Ds and Vs—was all shocked when Save told him that he had to wait to take out Ray-Ray's boys on 113th until noon.

"You don't be violatin' Sunday mornin'," he'd told Boris down at his crib in that crappy diner in Brooklyn. Save hated going there 'cause it was full of white folks who didn't speak English, but that was the only place Boris would meet, and as long as the Ukrainian dude was payin', Save'd go wherever.

"Why do you care?" Boris had asked with that accent of his that made him sound just like the guy in the *Bullwinkle* cartoon that Save had decided to name him after. Then Save had finally figured out how to put it so Boris would understand it. "How come you don't order no killin's on no Friday nights?"

"It is the Sabba—Ah!" he had suddenly said, looking like someone shined a damn light on his face. "This is your Christian observance, yes?"

"Damn right. So we ain't shootin' nobody till noon. You violate Sunday mornin', then all hell breaks loose, know what I'm sayin'?"

"Not particularly, but I do not care that much," Boris had said while sipping that weak tea he always drank. "As long as it is done."

Now Save was sitting in the crappy Toyota he used for work—he only used the Lexus when he was taking out one of his ladies—and waiting for it to be noon so he could go around the corner to take out Ray-Ray's slingers and show them boys who they was messing with.

Next to Save, Bee was listening to his iPod. Checking his watch, Save saw that it was 11:58. "Yo," he said to Bee.

Bee was lost in the rhythm of his music.

Save reached across the front seat and ripped the earpiece from his left ear. "I'm *talkin'* to you!"

"What up with you, dog? I'm listenin' to—"

Save didn't want to hear it. "It almost twelve. You know what that mean?"

Bee's eyes went wide, as he looked at something behind Save. "Holy—!"

Whirling around, Save saw a dude carrying a nine-mill pointed right at the back of Save's head, saying, "Truce's over—*ow!*"

That last part was on account of he got kicked in the head by a red blur.

"Start the car, yo, start the *car*!" That was Bee, screaming his fool head off.

Instead, Save took out his own hardware, a Beretta he took off a security guard from a job he did a few years back. He'd been saving it for the right occasion, and he figured this'd be it, since he'd have to dump it when he was done.

Suddenly the blur turned into a man who said, "Hey, didn't your mother tell you it's not polite to point?" Then he did some kind of flip and landed on the hood of the car.

Damn. It was Spider-Man. *Hell with this, Boris don't pay me to deal with no capes.* Now he did turn the car on, but just as he was turning the key, glass came flying all *over* the place, and Save felt like a hundred knives done nicked his face. Then a fist grabbed his Jets jersey and yanked him forward onto the hood.

"Now now," Spider-Man said, "leaving so soon? The party just started. Word to the wise, by the way—if you're casing a joint, do it from a *little* farther away. *I* figured out you were planning to ice Ray-Ray's crew from way the heck up on the rooftops, and our friend who's sleeping on the floor over there"—he pointed to the pavement, but Save couldn't stop staring at Spider-Man's face, which was just *scary*— "figured it out, and I don't think he's much of a candidate for Mensa. And where're *you* going?"

With the hand that wasn't holding Save, Spider-Man shot out a web-line to his left. Save still couldn't look, but he heard the distinctive shouting of Bee, which meant Spider-Man probably got him with his webbing.

"Where was I? Oh yeah, Ray-Ray's people will probably be wondering why they haven't heard any shots yet, soooo . . ."

Save started feeling dizzy, and then he heard shots being thrown. Spider-Man was leaping in the air, still holding on to Save.

Then a hot pain sliced through his shoulder, and he cursed loudly and repeatedly, realizing that he'd caught a bullet.

"Hey, c'mon, guys, the whole object of the exercise was to *stop* the shooting!" That was Spider-Man again. Save closed his eyes, unable to look, and in a lot of pain from the bullet hit. He heard more shots and the thwipping sound of Spider-Man's webbing, and then sirens.

Now the cops. Should've kept my damn mouth shut about the damn truce.

More pain pounded into his shoulder as he hit the pavement: Spider-Man must've dropped him. He decided to open his eyes.

He saw Spider-Man's feet, the feet of some cops, and voices yelling, "Get *down* on the ground, *now*! Move it, scumbags!"

Save tried to reach for Spider-Man's ankle with his good arm, figuring maybe to trip him up and get away—but *damn* if Spider-Man didn't dance out of the way. "Hey, none of that to the guy who kept you from getting shot in the head."

Save tried to speak, but he couldn't make his mouth move. And his vision was getting all blurry. *And, after all that, they got me anyhow.*

"Yo, web-head," another voice—sounded like a cop—said, "our sergeant says you're on our side for this one."

"I'm on your side for *all* of them, Officer—and this kid's been shot. I'm gonna get him to St. Luke's before he bleeds out."

"Fine, whatever. We got plenty to talk about, don't we, scumbag?"

That was the last thing Save heard before he blacked out.

o——————————o

IT had only taken Spider-Man a few minutes to convince the emergency room doctors at St. Luke's to take the guy in the Jets jersey to one of their trauma rooms—he suspected it was more the way the kid was bleeding all over the floor than anything Spider-Man said. *Good thing the costume's mostly red,* he thought dolefully as he stared down at the bloodstains. He was about to turn around and head out—and maybe catch a nap, as whatever energy he'd gotten from MJ's brunch was wearing right off— when a familiar voice spoke.

"Good Lord, they'll let anybody in here."

Whirling around and leaping to the ceiling just in case, Spider-Man saw the tall form of Detective Fry, walking alongside the shorter Detective Wheeler. Fry was wearing the same suit he had worn the night before and hadn't shaved in the interim, whereas Wheeler was cleanshaven and wearing a rather snappy suit.

"Well well well," he said, "if it isn't Big Man and Pretty Boy."

Rolling his eyes, Wheeler said, "I'm gonna kill Joll, I swear."

"Yeah, yeah," Fry said. "What brings you here?"

"There was an attempted shoot-out on 113th. One of the shooters got himself shot, so I brought him here."

Fry asked, "He gonna live?"

Spider-Man shrugged as best he could while crouched on the ceiling. "Probably. He bled a lot, but the bullet only got him in the shoulder."

Looking down triumphantly at Wheeler, Fry said, "You owe me twenty bucks."

Grumpily, Wheeler said, "The kid could die yet."

Confused, Spider-Man asked, "What're you—"

"After Una called you," Fry said, "I bet Ty here that you'd keep anybody from getting killed if you got there before the bullets flew."

Looking at the shorter detective, Spider-Man said, "Your confidence in me is touching."

"Bite me."

"Don't tempt me," Spider-Man muttered.

"Actually," Fry said, "you should probably come with us."

"Oh?"

Fry started walking down the hall. Spider-Man followed by coming out of the crouch and walking upside down along the ceiling, avoiding fluorescent light fixtures as he went. Wheeler trailed a few steps behind, muttering something about how costumes were weird.

"Got a call from the attending. They got another gamma-head—he busted up a fancy restaurant on Columbus—only this is a middle-aged white guy in a suit."

Fry had said that like it should mean something. "So?"

"Like Shanahan said, X is a kids' drug, mostly. Anybody over the age of thirty who takes it is probably a junkie or homeless or something. This guy don't fit the profile. That makes him worth talking to, assuming he's out of his coma."

"Does our middle-aged white guy have a name?"

Before Fry could say anything, Spider-Man experienced a mild buzz of his spider-sense. He resumed the crouching position on the ceiling, which got him out of the path of the gurney that was coming down the corridor behind them at top speed, even as a nurse yelled, "Coming through!"

Fry and Wheeler dashed to the side of the corridor as the gurney went past, navigated by emergency medical technicians, nurses, and doctors toward one of the trauma rooms. One of the EMTs was saying, "GSW to the chest, BP eighty over thirty, pulse—"

The victim's pulse was lost as they went around the corner.

"Never a dull moment," Spider-Man said.

Fry nodded in agreement.

"I don't get that," Wheeler said, shaking his head. "Why do they say 'GSW'?"

"Same reason they say 'BP,'" Fry said. "It's an abbreviation."

"No it ain't. 'GSW' is five syllables; 'gunshot wound' is three. The whole point of the abbreviation's so they can convey the information faster and maybe save the guy's life. Those extra two syllables could make the difference between life and death."

Spider-Man smiled under his mask even as Fry said, "I doubt it."

"How the hell do *you* know? You catch a bullet—sorry, a 'GSW'—right in the heart, your life's down to nanoseconds. I don't want to die 'cause some EMT was too busy pronouncing all three syllables of the letter W."

Looking up at Spider-Man, Fry said, "I begged Jerry—*begged* him—to pair me up with Una. But he stuck her on phones talking to scientists all day, so I got stuck with *him*."

"*You* can bite me too, Jimmy."

"I ain't bendin' over that far. Here it is," Fry said quickly before Wheeler could reply to that. "This is the room where they're keeping the gamma-heads."

"You never told me the guy's name," Spider-Man said as he skittered over the top of the door frame to enter the room. There were eight beds inside, all occupied. Spider-Man wondered how many other hospitals in the city had devoted entire rooms to victims of this drug.

"Right." Fry reached into his jacket pocket and pulled out his notebook. "It's, a doctor, named—hang on."

Spider-Man, however, no longer needed the detective's assistance in identifying the latest addition to the ranks of the gamma-heads. He recognized the pale man with the brown hair and matching mustache lying in the bed nearest the door, having first encountered him very shortly after he became Spider-Man. "Kevin Hunt."

Both Fry and Wheeler looked at Spider-Man with surprise. "You know this guy?" the latter asked.

"Yup. Brain specialist, right?"

Fry nodded. "He's working at the ESU Medical Center."

Nodding, Spider-Man said, "Yeah, I'd heard that. When I first met him, he was working at Bliss Private Hospital in Westchester. He was the physician of record when a man was checked in after being caught in an explosion at the U.S. Atomic Research Center." Spider-Man turned to the two detectives. "That patient was Dr. Otto Octavius."

"Oh, great," Fry muttered.

Wheeler asked, "Who the hell is Dr. Otto Octavius?"

"You probably know him better as Dr. Octopus," Spider-Man said. "I know I do."

Hunt was still in a coma, from the looks of it. Spider-Man probably wouldn't have even remembered him if he hadn't appeared on television a while back to discuss Octavius. Specifically, he'd been recanting his initial diagnosis of brain damage—a diagnosis that had always been used as the explanation for Octavius's insanity. However, Hunt was saying, what he'd assumed to be damage might have been the synapses of his brain reordering themselves to accommodate the four new limbs that were now a part of Octavius's body, and ones that didn't follow the muscle-over-joint pattern of virtually every other human limb. Octavius had mental control of his metal arms, even after they were separated from his body, and that would probably have meant changes to his brain chemistry.

Spider-Man remembered that interview mostly because it drove home the very real possibility that Octavius *wasn't* insane—that he was that much of a creep normally.

Fry walked over to the bed. "I ran this guy before coming down here. No priors, no history of drug use—hell, according to what the woman at ESU told me, he doesn't even smoke or drink."

Spider-Man remembered what O'Leary had told him when they first started talking. "This isn't a beginner's drug."

"Right. Like I said, this guy doesn't fit the profile."

Hunt's eyes suddenly fluttered. Spider-Man leapt over the bed to the other side and grabbed the doctor's right hand, since the left one had various tubes and leads in it. "Doc, it's Spider-Man, can you hear me?"

In a very muddled voice, Hunt said, "Spi-Man?"

"Close enough."

"Dunno—wha' happen. Was jus' eatin' brunch like always an' somethin' happen." Then he drifted back to sleep.

Looking up at Fry, Spider-Man asked, "What was the restaurant?"

Checking his notebook, Fry said, "Place called Mark's on Columbus and 83rd."

Turning around, he saw that there was a window in the room—along with seven other patients, most of whom were asleep or staring openly at Spider-Man. He leapt toward it, causing one of those staring patients to bark out an astonished scream. "I'll meet you guys there."

"We already had units canvass the restaurant," Wheeler said. "Nothin' weird there."

Before Spider-Man could respond to that, a weak voice said, "Spider-Man? That you?"

Looking over at the bed closest to the window, Spider-Man saw a face that he hadn't seen in years. A pale, flat face, a nose that had been broken at least once, curly black hair—now receded a bit—and matching thick mustache, this was the face of a man who, among other things, was partly responsible for the death of Betty Brant's brother Bennett, as he'd been working with Dr. Octopus at the time.

"Blackie Gaxton, as I live and breathe."

"You know this guy?" Wheeler asked.

"Yup. Haven't seen him in years, though."

"That's 'cause I'm *clean*," Gaxton said.

"Sure you are," Wheeler said as he and Fry walked over to Gaxton's bed. "That's why your sheet in Philly's as long as my arm."

"In Philly, yeah," Gaxton said. "After I went up against *this* guy, I went straight, moved to New York. I been workin' as a store manager since then."

Spider-Man had to admit to a certain pride, and a desire that more lowlifes would decide, after facing Spider-Man, to go straight the way Blackie had. *At least that explains why I haven't heard boo from him since Bennett's murder.*

Fry asked, "So how'd you wind up in the Triple X ward?"

"The what?" Gaxton sounded confused. "Look, all's I know is I got sick, felt something weird on my legs, and then I woke up here."

Spider-Man checked his chart. "You took Triple X, Blackie—it's a new drug that's like X, only with super powers."

"What the hell's X? Oh, wait, ecstasy, that garbage the kids're doing? Jesus, I don't *do* that stuff. Talk to my parole officer, I been *clean*."

Looking up at the detectives, Spider-Man said, "I believe him."

Wheeler looked at him like he was nuts. "Mind tellin' me why?"

"Why would he lie?"

Fry said, "Using illegal narcotics would qualify as a parole violation."

"Jesus Christ, I'm *clean*," Gaxton said.

"What if he has been?" Spider-Man asked. "What if somebody fed him—and Hunt—the Triple X?"

Wheeler rolled his eyes. "Gimme a break. Maybe you costumes are big on conspiracies, but in the real world, things ain't that complicated. This hump's a gangster with a sheet who ain't exactly outta the profile."

"I told you, I'm *clean*!"

Ignoring Gaxton, Wheeler pointed back at Hunt's bed. "*That* one's a doctor who sees drugs all the time, and works in a medical research center. For all we know, he *made* the stuff. It ain't any more complicated than that."

"What if it is?" Spider-Man asked.

Before Wheeler could say anything else, Fry asked, "What're you saying?"

"If Blackie here has been clean—"

"I am!"

Looking over at Gaxton, Spider-Man said, "Shut *up*, Blackie, willya?" Turning back to the detectives, he said, "These two guys have one thing in common: Doc Ock. And he's one of the top suspects for creating this drug in the first place. He's got the smarts to create it."

Fry nodded. "And he's enough of a sociopath not to care about distributing it."

Wheeler looked up at his fellow detective in shock. "You're buyin' this, Jimmy?"

"No, but I'm not dismissing it, either. You were the one who said he'd be useful."

"For keeping the gamma-heads in line, not for police work. He's a thug, we're detectives—*we* should be doin' the detecting!"

Fry looked away from his partner. "Say it is Octavius. What's the next step?"

Spider-Man shrugged. "Find him."

"He's got half a dozen warrants out on him already," Wheeler said. "We're already lookin' for him." He shook his head. "This is nuts. Why's it always gotta be costumes with you people?"

"Occupational hazard. Look," Spider-Man said, turning to Wheeler, "I'm gonna head out and do my thug thing by keeping the gamma-heads in line. I'll also press some of my contacts, find out if anybody knows what ol' Ockie's up to these days. Who knows? Maybe I'm wrong. But it's worth checking out."

"We'll keep in touch," Fry said.

"Speak for yourself," Wheeler muttered.

As Spider-Man opened the window and leapt out it, he heard Gaxton say one last time, "Goddammit, I told you guys, I'm *clean!*"

TEN

THE last person Hector Diaz expected to see in the lobby of his building on Monday morning was Biggie, but there he was, standing in the corner by the mailboxes. As soon as Hector came out of the elevator, Biggie looked up and said, "Yo, Hector, time to be suitin' up."

"Suitin' up for what?" Hector asked as he and Biggie shook hands. *I swear, one of these times, I ain't gonna get my hand back,* he thought as Biggie's massive palm enveloped his.

"You been livin' in a cave, dog? There's a *war* on, yo, and we got to be retaliatin' on them Russians."

Hector was now completely confused. "Biggie, what you talkin' 'bout?" He headed to the dirt-streaked glass door that led to the lobby. Briefly, he wondered how Biggie got in without a key, but he probably just waited until someone came out and then walked in. Happened all the time.

"Ray-Ray been expandin' into the city, hornin' in on some real estate that used to belong to some Russians—till Ray-Ray came in with the product. So them Russians done gone and shot up Sweet and Lemonhead and Jay."

That drew Hector up short. "Sweet's dead?"

"All *three* of 'em, dog. And it's time for some righteous retributatin', know what I'm sayin'?"

Given their relative sizes, Hector figured it was best not to let Biggie know that "retributating" wasn't a real word. He walked down the street toward the bus stop that would take him to school. "So what's the drill?"

"The drill be, get yourself to them Houses soon as you're done with classes."

"Why we waitin' that long?"

"'Cause them Russians ain't stupid, dog. They got boys workin' for 'em that might be noticin' if everyone in Ray-Ray's crew ain't in school today, you feel me?"

Hector nodded. "A'ight, I be there."

"Good." Biggie offered his hand, and Hector's got swallowed up in it again. "Later, dog."

Biggie stomped off in the other direction. Hector got to the corner just when the bus showed up. He dropped his MetroCard in, pulled it back out, and went to the seat in the back corner. He didn't know nobody on this bus, which was weird, but happened sometimes. Just luck and all.

Sweet's dead. Hector couldn't believe it. Elwood Candelario got the nickname "Sweet" when he was in grammar school with Hector, mostly on account of hating his first name. He was always going on about capes and their different powers, when he wasn't talking about baseball. Hector used to joke that if Sweet ever met Derek Jeter and Captain America on the same day, he'd just die right there 'cause he wouldn't have nothing else to live for.

And now he's dead.

Drugs was one thing. Hector didn't think he'd be able to get through life without drugs, and it didn't make no sense to him that people could buy all the booze and cigarettes they wanted, but couldn't get blow. Hector had seen people drunk and had seen people high. Drunks killed people and shot people and beat people, but when you was high, you was mellow.

But dropping bodies? *That ain't right. People shouldn't be dying.*

And there'd be more if Ray-Ray was talking war. He was starting to think that maybe he wasn't gonna be heading down to no Robinsfield Houses after class. *I ain't ending up like Sweet. No way.*

He arrived at school, said yo to folks he knew, and went to his locker. Martha was just closing her locker when he got there. "'Sup, Martha. How's Javier doin'?"

Martha just shook her head. "Still in a coma." Then she went off to homeroom.

Hector headed to the bathroom before following her to homeroom. He pushed the big painted metal door open and sauntered in. Nobody else was inside, which suited Hector fine. He didn't want to deal with nobody right now.

Instead of going to a stall or a urinal, though, he walked over to one of the tiny white sinks, dropped his bookbag on the tile floor, and stared at his reflection in the dirty, cracked mirror.

This ain't right.

"Hey, Hector, got a sec?"

Hector turned to see that Mr. Parker had followed him into the bathroom. "What, this gonna be a thing with you now, Mr. Parker?" Then he looked at the teacher more closely. He had bags under his eyes and he was walking slowly, like his legs hurt. "The hell happened to you?"

"Rough weekend," he said quickly. "Listen—I need your help."

"*You* need *my* help?"

"I know you're involved in this, Hector. It's bad enough that people are winding up in the hospital by the dozens—"

"Dozens? What you talkin' 'bout?"

His voice getting harder, Mr. Parker said, "Every hospital in this city has at least three or four people who are sick and dying because of Triple X. Or they've got people who've been beaten, bashed, zapped, or mind-controlled *by* someone on Triple X. And on top of that, you see the papers this morning? There's a drug war on—Spider-Man stopped a major shoot-out on 113th Street yesterday, right before he kept five other gamma-heads from tearing up the town. This is getting out of control, and it has to stop."

Hector had been thinking the same thing, but hearing it come out of some white teacher's mouth made him realize how stupid he'd been. "What, *you* gonna stop it? You makin' me laugh, Mr. Parker."

Mr. Parker shook his head. "Hector, you owe it to—"

"To what? What you askin' me to *do*? Roll over on my people? Ain't happenin', yo. They my *friends*. They *family*. I ain't flippin' them."

"Hector, you don't understand—"

"Oh, and *you're* gonna explain it to me? You makin' me laugh again, Mr. Parker, livin' the good life and trying to tell *me* how it is."

Then Mr. Parker laughed. "Now *you* think it's funny?"

"I do actually, yeah—you really think *I'm* living 'the good life'?"

"You expect me to believe you ain't? Grew up in your house in the suburbs an' shit." Hector turned his back on the teacher and twisted the handle on the sink. Cold water dribbled from the faucet; Hector shoved his hands under it.

Mr. Parker laughed again. "I grew up right here in Forest Hills, Hector—and the house was barely big enough to fit me, my Aunt May, and my Uncle Ben."

That surprised Hector. "No parents?" he asked as he walked over to the paper towel dispenser.

"They died when I was a kid. My aunt and uncle were pretty old, but they raised me anyhow. And then Uncle Ben died when I was only a little older than you, so it was just me and Aunt May. I had to take on work as a photographer when I was still in high school just to pay the bills. To give you an idea how incredibly lucrative *that* profession is, I took on teaching instead, and I think you have a good idea how little *we* make. So don't think you've got the monopoly on a crappy life, Hector. And even if you did, that doesn't mean you or your friends should just throw your lives away for a drug that's *killing people*—whether it's the users, the people they're hurting, or the pushers who're shooting each other over it."

Hector didn't say anything as he finished drying his hands and balled the cheap paper towel up into a ball.

"Fine," Mr. Parker said. "Stand by and watch people die, knowing you could've done something about it."

After tossing the towel into the trash bin, Hector whirled around and pointed a finger. "Yo, don't be *puttin'* that on me, Mr. Parker!"

"Who else am I supposed to put it on?"

With that, Mr. Parker turned around and left the bathroom.

Hector stared after him for a few seconds, then picked up his bag, slung it over his shoulder, and went back into the hallway.

He spent the rest of the day in a kind of daze, wandering from class to class without paying much attention, except in Mr. Parker's class. For some crazy reason, he wanted to act natural in his class. Not draw attention or nothing.

As soon as school let out, he practically ran out the door, not even bothering to stop at his locker. He hopped the bus that would take him to them Houses to talk to Ray-Ray. He went to the back, and saw somebody left a copy of the *Daily Bugle* on the seat. Picking it up, he started flipping through it. On page ten, he saw a story about Triple X.

It was written by a reporter named Betty Brant, and it talked about the task force the NYPD formed, and people who'd been put in the hospital 'cause of Triple X. It also talked about how Spider-Man was keeping the folks high on it—"gamma-heads" is what Mr. Parker called 'em, and now Hector knew why, since that's what the article called 'em, too—from going too crazy or hurting people. He couldn't be everywhere, but he was doing his best.

And he was up in them Houses last week trying to find out.

It took almost half an hour 'cause of the damn traffic, but Hector finally made it to Robinsfield, walking through the graffiti-covered archway on 34th Avenue that led to the courtyard.

Nobody was barking today. No other crews were slinging. Hector looked for De, so he'd tell him where Ray-Ray was holed up, but when he saw De over at Tower A, he also saw Ray-Ray, along with Blowback, Biggie, Cap, and some other folks he didn't know by name, though one of 'em was the kid Ray-Ray was chewing out last time Hector was up in here.

When Hector walked up, Ray-Ray said, "My *man!* Glad you could join the party, dog!" He held up his hand, which Hector clasped. "We be takin' down some Russians, yo."

Hector winced. "Takin' down?"

Ray-Ray stared at him through his big sunglasses. "They got Sweet, they got Lemonhead, they got Jay, and they *almost* got Blowback. Time for some *pay*back!"

Everyone around Ray-Ray made all kinds of "Yeah" and "Damn right" noises.

"This is *wrong,* yo," Hector said. "Where is it gonna end?"

Holding up a hand, Ray-Ray said, "Back up off me, Hector. Ain't nothin' to be doin' but unto them what they doin' unto us, you feel me?"

"This ain't right. Look, you give people dope, that's cool, nobody gives a damn 'cause everybody be dopin', but now you killin' folks! With the Triple X and now this." Hector shook his head. "Forget that, what about the cops? You start droppin' bodies, them cops gonna be out here, yo. In force. They already got a task force."

"Say what?" Ray-Ray was looking at him like he was buggin'.

Hector shoved the *Bugle* in his face. "Was in the paper, yo, they formed a *task force* just for Triple X. You know what that means?"

Knocking the paper to the ground, Ray-Ray said, "Don't mean *shit*, a'ight?"

Cap said, "We wastin' time, Ray-Ray. We gots to be *goin'*."

Shoving his hand at Hector's face, Ray-Ray turned around and said, "Let's be movin'."

They all started to walk away from Hector into the courtyard toward the exit. Hector could see that they all had bulges in their pants or jackets—they all was carrying. He only had one thing left to say. "What about Spider-Man?"

That stopped all of them about twenty feet from the archway. Ray-Ray turned around and said, "Spiderwhat?"

"He came by here the other day—broke De's gun."

Ray-Ray whirled on De, who started backing up. "Yo, you told me you *lost* that gun."

De didn't say nothing.

Hector kept talking. "He all over this, and he ain't gonna be lettin' up. What happens when—"

Whatever Hector was going to say next was cut off by the squealing of tires. He looked over and saw that two cars had pulled up onto the sidewalk and were in the archway, blocking it.

Four white guys got out and started shooting.

Hector thought he heard shouting, but he wasn't sure 'cause Ray-Ray and his crew opened up, too, and the guns was so *loud*. He fell down to the ground, but he wasn't sure why except that everything was so *loud* and his stomach hurt and then he couldn't breathe and *what the hell's going on, is that blood, oh. . . .*

Then everything went black.

o————————o

SPIDER-MAN swung across the North Lawn of Central Park en route to the 24th Precinct, having spent the day trying desperately to keep his eyes open while teaching. After leaving the hospital yesterday, he'd stopped five different gamma-heads, as he'd told Hector, as well as stopping some kid from breaking into a synagogue. Apparently, the kid had the mistaken impression that there'd be valuables inside. Spider-Man took a certain bitter amusement out of educating him to the fact that the only thing he'd find in there worth anything was the Torah scroll, but that had more spiritual than monetary value. Besides, he probably wouldn't find a fence for it. *Though in this town, you never know.*

He'd also been digging through his contacts, but nobody he found knew anything, and he hadn't seen any of his usual Octopus-related stoolies. *Then again, Sunday night's not usually the best time for seeking out lowlifes.*

All this meant yet another late night. He'd gotten a message on Ursitti's phone from O'Leary to come by the Two-Four for a meeting in the afternoon, which he'd barely be able to make if he came straight from Midtown High. He had been hoping for an opportunity to tail Hector after class—since direct questioning and a guilt trip weren't doing the trick, and right now Hector was all he had—but he didn't want to squander what little goodwill he had with the NYPD. *If nothing else, it might come in handy later.*

He leapt out over the 100th Street exit to the park and swung around the face of the tenement-style buildings on the north side of the street, then the buildings of the condo complex on the south side, then took a big swing off the Health and Human Services building across the street from the precinct house before landing on the roof. This time he came in through the same window by which he departed on his last two trips here: the one that led to the detectives' squad room. Sure enough, all six members of the Triple X Task Force were present, as was Sergeant Green and a Hispanic man wearing a pink shirt and yellow tie. O'Leary, Shanahan, Wheeler, and Petrocelli were all seated at their desks, with Green sitting in the guest chair at O'Leary's desk; Shapiro was standing, as were Fry and the other man.

"Sorry I'm late," he said as he came in and climbed across the big pipe on the ceiling. "Couldn't catch a cab."

"Inspector," Green said, indicating the man in pink, "this is our civilian assistance."

"Cute way'a puttin' it." The man looked up at Spider-Man. "Esteban Garcia. I command this precinct. I appreciate the help you're giving us."

Both surprised and pleased, Spider-Man said, "Thanks—glad to do it. I just wish I could do more than knock around the gamma-heads." He said that last with a look at Wheeler.

"Actually, you have." Shapiro sounded like he would've liked anything in the world more than to have to say those words. "Una?"

Sounding much more excited, O'Leary said, "We've got two more gamma-heads that don't fit the profile. One was on Ryker's, a kid named Jeff Haight."

Spider-Man frowned. Ryker's Island was the largest prison in New York City, located on the East River between the Bronx and Queens. The name sounded familiar, but it took him a few seconds to finally place it. "Oh, jeez, Haight? He was an idiot, but I never pegged him for a druggie."

"He isn't," O'Leary said. "Somebody offered him a hit of Triple X in the cafeteria and when he didn't take it, he got the shit kicked out of him."

"Figures. Haight can't even do something intelligent right." Haight was a photographer who wanted to become Dr. Octopus's personal shooter. All it got him was busted for conspiracy and harboring a fugitive, a term he was still serving.

O'Leary continued: "The other one's a man named Nat Fredrickson. Also no history of drug use, though he has a couple of DUIs. The kicker here is, he's the ex-husband of Carolyn Trainer."

Spider-Man winced. "This just gets better and better." Trainer was a devotee—one might say a groupie—of Otto Octavius, having followed his career even before the accident. When Ock was killed, Trainer took on the mantle of Dr. Octopus for a time, before figuring out a way to resurrect Octavius through means Spider-Man still had to admit to not entirely understanding. Then again, Ock was hardly the only bad guy in his rogues' gallery who'd cheated the Grim Reaper.

Fry said, "Looks like you were right—Octavius may be involved in this."

"And like I said before," Wheeler said, "so the hell what? We still can't find the sonofabitch."

"We can look harder," Spider-Man said. "I've already put a few feelers out."

"To who?" Shapiro asked.

Chuckling, Spider-Man said, "Gee, Detective, you gonna give me a list of your CIs?"

O'Leary laughed, but broke it off at a stern look from Shapiro. "We have contracts with our CIs."

"And I have understandings with mine."

Shanahan said, "'Understanding' my ass. You bust their heads, right? Hell, we should arrest him for brutality."

"That's enough," Garcia barked. "Detective Shanahan, you're out of line."

In a wholly unapologetic tone, Shanahan said, "Sorry, sir."

"Something I don't get," O'Leary said.

Shanahan muttered, "There's a surprise."

Somehow, Spider-Man resisted the urge to punch Shanahan in the face—or, at the very least, web up his mouth.

"Octopus has never had any kind of underworld contacts." O'Leary turned to Spider-Man. "Right?"

"Just the usual rent-a-thugs. He was never a player in the same way that other guys have been. He wouldn't lower himself, to be honest— the only times he's worked with other people, it's been a marriage of convenience in order for him to achieve his own ends." He was thinking in particular of the times Octopus hooked up with some of Spider-Man's other regular sparring partners to form the so-called "Sinister Six," mostly in an attempt to do together what none of them had managed alone: kill Spider-Man. There'd been several incarnations, sometimes with more or fewer than the usual six, and they'd mostly been done in by their mistrust of each other—and, in Ock's case, by his own massive ego.

Petrocelli asked, "If that's the case, how does he hook up with a Long Island City slinger?"

"He doesn't," Spider-Man said, "but he doesn't have to. Look, we know that Ock's involved because there are people being hit here who don't have a history of drug use, but who *do* have a history of getting in Ock's way. Hunt's the doctor who worked on him after the accident— Ock thought Hunt was trying to imprison him in the hospital. His deal with Gaxton went south when I stopped them. Haight was an annoyance. There may be others, for all we know."

"What about Fredrickson?" Fry asked.

"That's the key," Spider-Man said. "Carolyn Trainer doesn't have Octavius's book smarts, but she's got plenty of street smarts, and I know she *did* develop the kinds of contacts that Octavius would consider beneath him. I can't see him being able to facilitate a deal with Ray-Ray, but I can see Trainer."

"We still gotta find Octavius," Petrocelli said.

"Yeah," Wheeler said. "Question is, how?"

"Let me work my angle."

Shapiro pointed at Spider-Man. "If you do find him, you *call us,* you understand? I'm not having my case trashed because some costume can't follow procedure again."

Frowning, Spider-Man said, "'Again'?"

"You know how many times we find a guy webbed to a lamppost for no reason? You put your cute little *'courtesy your friendly neighborhood Spider-Man'* card on it, but there's no stolen merch, no witnesses, no victims, just a couple of knuckleheads webbed to a lamppost—and *they* ain't talkin'."

"Detective—" Spider-Man started. He'd heard this complaint before.

However, Garcia interrupted. "All right, Detective, you've made your point."

Glowering at Spider-Man, Shapiro said, "Yeah."

"As for you," Garcia said to Spider-Man, "if you're gonna keep cooperating, you will cooperate. That means following the rules, understand? I don't want a glory hound screwing our case."

"Inspector, the next time I seek glory will be the first. Like I've already told your detectives, that's not why I do this."

"Fine." Garcia walked to the door. "I want this drug war ended and this case *closed,* people. Do a job."

As soon as the door to the squad room closed behind Garcia, Shanahan said, "'Do a job,' Jesus. Knute Rockne, he ain't."

"All right," Shapiro said, "enough. Let's get to the hospitals, keep trying to get *something* out of the vics. Maybe one of 'em knows their dealer." To Petrocelli, he said, "Narcotics is keeping an eye on Ray-Ray, right?"

Petrocelli nodded. "It's been quiet, though. That in itself is scary."

Oh man, Hector, why couldn't you talk to me? Spider-Man shook his head. Hector was a good kid, but Spider-Man couldn't entirely blame him for not rolling on his buddies. How many secrets had *he* kept to protect his friends and family over the years, after all?

"Keep in touch with them. I wanna know—"

The desk sergeant Spider-Man had met on his first trip here burst in all of a sudden. "Jerry, we just got a call from the One-Oh-Eight—shots fired in the Robinsfield Houses. There're some narcos there, and they told the One-Oh-Eight to call you."

Without hesitating, Spider-Man leapt for the window. "I'll meet you guys there." He was out the window before anybody could object, swinging across the street and through the condo complex to the park, making time as fast as he could to Long Island City.

Now, Spider-Man wished he had tailed Hector. True, it would've meant not getting the confirmation on the Ock connection right off, but if that kid wound up dead . . .

With great power comes great responsibility. That was something Uncle Ben had told him, something that had become his lifelong credo. *But sometimes the responsibility really sucks. And I just can't be in two places at once.*

It took about fifteen minutes to wend his way to LIC, and by then it was all over. Ambulances and blue-and-whites were surrounding the Houses, lights flashing, casting a red glow on the entire area. Spider-Man could smell the gunshot residue as he approached, which meant a *lot* of gunfire.

"Yo, web-head!"

Spider-Man saw a short black woman waving at him. She was dressed casually, but had a badge on her belt. He twisted in midair to do a backflip onto the top of an ambulance, then leapt over to the roof of the car next to where the cop was standing. "Can I help you?"

"Joan Barnes, Narcotics. Una O'Leary called and said I should talk to you when you got here."

Making a mental note to buy O'Leary flowers when this was all over, he asked, "What happened?"

"Drug hit. We got one of the shooters, but the rest rabbited. Two of our guys got hit—the one shooter we got laid down cover fire for his buddies."

"They okay?"

Barnes nodded. "We're stakin' out a drug market, you *bet* we're all wearin' Kevlars."

Looking closely, Spider-Man noticed the impressions of the Velcro flaps of a bulletproof vest under Barnes's sweatshirt. "Who's the shooter you got?"

"White guy—talks with an Eastern European accent. I figure it's a Ukrainian crew working out of Brighton Beach. They're the ones getting pushed out by Ray-Ray."

"Anybody else hit?"

At that, Barnes actually smiled. "That's the fun part. Ray-Ray took one in the chest—and he wasn't wearing a Kevlar."

"Anybody else?"

Opening her notebook, Barnes started flipping pages. "Lessee—two of Ray-Ray's crew. Ambo took 'em to Parkway." She got to the right spot. "Robert Billinghurst, street name 'Cap,' and a new kid, Hector Diaz."

A fist of ice clenched Spider-Man's heart. "They took 'em to Parkway?"

"Yeah, why, you—"

But Spider-Man didn't hear the rest of the sentence, as he leapt off the roof and made his way to the hospital. *I should've tailed Hector. I knew I should've tailed Hector!*

ELEVEN

AS opening night fast approached, the minds of the cast and crew of *The Z-Axis* were turning to thoughts of homicide.

Mary Jane was working out just fine in the role of Olga, if she did say so herself. The part was, after all, less challenging than that of Irina, so plugging into it wasn't too difficult. Dmitri had been effusive in his praise—which, for Dmitri, meant that he only told her that she was awful and was ruining his show once or twice, as opposed to constantly.

The problem was with Regina in the role of Irina. Regina was also, after all, playing Fiona, the lead female part in *Up the Creek Without a Fiddle,* the about-to-close show currently running at VPC. Fiona was a not-too-bright prostitute with a drug problem who was the victim of the men around her; Irina was a smart, prim young woman who believed in the best of people. Thus they were two radically different parts of the type that most actors would be thrilled to have on their resumé in order to show off their range.

The problem was, Regina was having a hard time getting out of Fiona mode and into Irina mode, as it were.

This had a domino effect on everyone else. Dmitri was so frustrated that at Sunday's rehearsal, he actually succeeded in ripping his prized Dodgers cap in two (it had since been replaced with a Mets cap). Regina was annoyed at herself for not getting Irina down pat, and was taking it out mostly on the crew, who proceeded to take it out on the entire cast by screwing up cues and set changes. This in turn got the cast members annoyed and upset, which they took out on each other and Dmitri, who was aggravated at all of them. *Thank God we have Monday off,* Mary Jane had thought after Sunday's disaster.

That union-mandated off-day on Monday was a huge help, as Tuesday afternoon's rehearsal—the last one before previews began Wednesday night—went swimmingly. They were going through the climactic scene in Act 2 when Irina chews Olga out for being an idiot. Regina put her all into the chewing-out, and Olga's response—during which she emerges from her shell for the first time in the entire play—was as intense as Mary Jane could make it.

When they were done with the scene, and the lights went out, Mary Jane was stunned to hear clapping from the audience.

The houselights came up, as they did after every scene so Dmitri could nitpick them to death before going on to the next scene, and she saw that it was Dmitri who was clapping.

"Now *that*, my good friends, *that* is acting. Jane Mary, Regina, for the first time in a week I believe that you quite possibly might not be ruining my play."

"Gee, thanks, Dmitri," Mary Jane said dryly.

Regina touched Mary Jane's shoulder. "God, MJ, I'm so sorry I've been such a bitch."

"Don't worry about it," Mary Jane said quickly, even though Regina had, in fact, been one. "It's the usual preopening jitters."

"Yeah, but I don't *get* those. It's just—I don't know, what happened with Valerie is *so* totally weird. It's got me so *totally* freaked out."

"I know." Mary Jane tried to sound understanding, though her own tolerance for weirdness was higher than that of most folks who didn't actually wear super hero suits.

"Excuse me?"

Mary Jane looked to the rear entrance to see a good-looking man in a suit, holding a small pad of paper.

Dmitri turned around and threw up his hands. "This is closed dress rehearsal. You cannot be here!"

Regina whispered to Mary Jane, "I don't mind if he stays a while." Mary Jane tried to hide a smile at Regina's sudden switch to flirt mode.

The man opened his jacket far enough to show a badge on his belt, as well as a shoulder holster. "'Fraid I can. I'm Detective Ty Wheeler. I need to talk to, uh"—he checked the pad—"Ms. Regina Wright."

"Lucky me." Regina sounded like a cat about to pounce on a mouse. But then, Regina tended to go through men the way buzz saws go through trees. Remembering Peter's description of Wheeler's lousy behavior at the hospital, she decided not to say anything and just let Regina loose on him.

Regina jumped down off the stage, but Dmitri moved to stand between her and Wheeler. "What is this about?"

"You're Mr. Voyskunsky, right? This is follow-up on Ms. Valerie McManus."

"Ms. McManus is not in this play anymore, so you have no business here."

"No, but Ms. McManus's boyfriend said that Ms. Wright might be able to help us with our inquiries. I'm afraid I have to insist, Mr. Voyskunsky."

Regina put her hand on Dmitri's back. "It's okay, Dmitri. I want to help Valerie." She then walked past Dmitri, and Wheeler led her over to the back corner seats to talk.

"Okay," Dmitri said. "We will take five."

Fat chance it'll only be five minutes, Mary Jane thought with a smile. "I need something to drink. Anybody want anything?"

Mike Rabinowitz, who had taken over for Lou Colvin, said, "I would just *kill* for an apple juice."

"I think we can avoid murder, especially with a cop in the room," Mary Jane said with a smile as she grabbed her purse from the front-row seat where she'd left it.

She walked downstairs to the small counter behind the box office where nonalcoholic drinks were served, and asked the volunteer whose name she couldn't remember for an apple juice and a diet soda.

Then her cell phone rang. Cursing herself for forgetting to turn it off during rehearsal, she reached into her purse, pulling out both wallet and phone.

To her surprise, it was Valerie's number showing on the display. Flipping open the phone, she said, "Val, you okay?"

"It's Greg." Valerie's boyfriend sounded absolutely awful. "I'm calling from Cabrini, I—oh, *God.*"

Cradling the phone in her shoulder, she paid for her drinks while saying, "Greg, what is it, what's wrong?"

"It's Val—the doctors—they say she's *dying*, MJ! I don't know what—"
Then he stopped.

"What is it?" she asked after a second.

"Sorry, the nurse just said I can't use the cell in here. Look, MJ, I gotta talk to you, okay? Can you come by here tonight?"

Peter would probably be spending most of the night trying to keep a lid on the Triple X problem, so Mary Jane didn't hesitate to say, "I'll be there as soon as rehearsal's done, okay?"

"Great. We're in Room 310 at Cabrini."

"Got it," she said as she walked back upstairs, juice and soda in hand.

God, she thought as she ended the call and turned the phone off before putting it back in her purse. *She's dying. This is insane. Please, Peter, find out who's doing this, and stop them. . . .*

○———————————○

EILEEN Velasquez had just finished leaving her tenth message on Orlando's cell phone voice mail when the doctor walked up to her in the waiting area.

Dr. Lee wasn't, in Eileen's opinion, a very nice woman. If she'd met her under any other circumstances, Eileen probably would've walked across the room to avoid the doctor. But she had been very straightforward and honest with Eileen about what Javier was going through, and Eileen appreciated that right now. The doctors who had treated Manuel always danced around with fancy words and false hopes and fake promises. Dr. Lee didn't do any of that.

"I'm afraid the news isn't good, Ms. Velasquez. Javier has a brother with bone marrow edema, yes?"

Eileen winced. "Had a brother—Manuel died in a car accident a few years ago."

Lee shoved her hands into the pockets of her white lab coat. "Has Javier been tested for it?"

Nodding, Eileen said, "Every year, I always make sure Javier and Jorge are tested. They've been clean." Eileen did not like where this conversation was going.

"Javier isn't showing any signs of radiation poisoning," Lee said, "but it looks like the radiation in the drugs he took is having an effect on him. He's tested positive for the edema. By itself, it's probably treatable, but his heart is still weak—the treatments for the edema would probably trigger another heart attack. In fact, it's pretty likely that he'll suffer another one in due course anyhow. He's not coming out of his coma, and I'm not sure he's going to."

The doctor said some more things, but Eileen didn't hear them. At some point, Lee walked away but Eileen didn't notice that, either. All she could think about was that she was soon going to lose another member of her family.

She was startled out of her nightmare by the chirp of her cell phone. To her amazement, the display indicated that it was Orlando.

"Orlando, baby, thank you for calling m—"

"What do you *want*, Ma?"

The hostility in Orlando's voice was like a slap. "Didn't you get my messages?"

"Yeah, I got 'em. I know what's goin' on, so—"

"Javier's *dying*, Orlando."

"And I'm supposed to give a damn *why*, exactly?"

Eileen tried to gather up outrage, but found she couldn't. The fact of the matter was, Orlando's behavior was completely consistent with how he'd been for years. Why should he act any different now?

Still, she gave it a shot. "He's your *brother*."

"He never gave a damn about me—don't see why I gotta be returning the favor. Look, I got homework, okay? I gotta go. I got your messages, so stop calling me."

Orlando cut off the connection.

Eileen held the phone to her ear for several seconds. She felt a tear roll down her cheek.

"Hey, you okay, Ms. Velasquez?"

Closing the phone, Eileen looked up to see Peter Parker standing over her, looking concerned.

"I'm fine, Mr. Parker. Just trying to keep my family together—and like usual, screwing it up."

He sat down next to her. "What happened?"

She told him what Dr. Lee had said about Javier. "And I've been trying to reach my oldest boy, Orlando, but he wants nothing to do with me or Javier."

Putting a hand on hers, Parker said, "I'm sorry. I wish there were something I could do."

Somehow managing to get her face to form a smile, she placed her other hand on top of Parker's. "Unless you're willing to fly down to Florida and kick Orlando's butt, there isn't much you can do." She and Parker both got a quick laugh out of that, then she added, "You did enough just by caring, Mr. Parker. Thank you."

"No problem. And like I keep saying, it's Peter." He extricated his hand and stood up. "I gotta go—another of my students wound up here in a drive-by yesterday."

"You're not careful, you'll be spending all your time in here." Eileen found the words to be bitter ones, given how much time she herself was spending in this messed-up place.

"Yeah, I know. See you later."

What kind of world is this where a teacher Javier can't even stand cares more about him than his own brother?

———○————————○———

WHEN Hector woke up, he panicked, because he couldn't feel anything below his neck.

He tried moving, and then got pins and needles all up in his chest and legs. And everything smelled funny. . . .

Looking down at his body, he realized he was in a hospital gown—in a hospital bed. He could feel bandages on his chest.

Then he remembered everything. *They shot me!*

"About time you woke up."

Hector saw Mr. Parker standing in the doorway. He turned over so his back was facing the teacher. "What do *you* want?"

"Heard you got shot."

"Yeah. You gonna be puttin' *that* on me, too?"

"No, I put that on the guys who shot you. Ukrainians, from what I heard."

Wondering how a science teacher knew so much, then deciding that he really didn't care that much, he said, "Yeah, you know everything, don't you?"

"What's your problem, Hector?"

Hector turned back over and shot Mr. Parker a look. "What's my *problem*? My problem is that I *listened* to you, and I got *shot*! The hell you *think* my problem is, yo?"

"I'm sorry about that, but—"

"Only reason I *went* down there was 'cause I listened to you. I was just gonna go home an' stay low, but naw, I gotta listen to Mr. Teacher Man who knows all about how baaaaad my life is when he really don't know *shit*!"

Mr. Parker just stared right back at Hector. "So now what, Hector? You're just gonna lie here and feel sorry for yourself?"

"*Hell*, no. They done *shot* me, and I'm gettin' back at them!"

"Oh, *good* idea!" Mr. Parker walked up to the bed.

"'Cause as much fun as getting shot at is, dead is so much better."

"And you got all the answers, right?"

Putting his hands on the metal railing, Mr. Parker said, "I know that if you'd told me—or the police, Spider-Man, *anyone*—about where the Triple X was coming from, it wouldn't have come to this."

Hector turned back over again, not wanting to look at Mr. Parker's stupid white face. "I don't roll on family, yo."

"Family? The people who got you shot are family now?"

Turning his head around, he said, "*You* the one who got me shot!" Then he looked back at the wall. "Ray-Ray'll take care'a me, then there'll be—"

"Ray-Ray's dead."

Hector turned around again. "What?"

"Took one in the heart."

"Fine, then Blowback take over. So what?" Even as Hector said that, though, he wondered what it would mean. Blowback didn't have Ray-Ray's head.

"And Javier's dying, too. Doctors figure he won't live out the week. And then there's all the other Triple X cases, and—"

"I told you, that ain't on me!"

Mr. Parker kept talking all calm. "Maybe not, but you *can* do something about it. And if you don't do something to stop this when you have the means, then you become just as bad as whoever it is who's making this drug. Then you *are* responsible." The teacher turned his back on Hector and walked to the door. "You live with that, Hector."

And then Mr. Parker left.

Good goddamn riddance, Hector thought. His chest started to ache.

○――――――――○

GREG Halprin didn't look much better today in Room 310 of the Cabrini Medical Center than he had when Mary Jane visited him last week, although he was better dressed. Now wearing a Columbia University sweatshirt and faded jeans, he still had slept-in hair, and even more beard stubble.

When he looked up, Mary Jane saw one other change—his bloodshot eyes indicated someone who was most definitely not high on anything, but who also hadn't slept in a few days.

Valerie McManus was lying in the bed next to the chair Greg was sitting in, which was the one of the three beds in the room closest to the door. The other two were occupied by elderly men who slept and had no company.

"Hey, MJ." Greg's voice was much weaker than it had been last week. "Can you believe this? She's *dying*. The docs say it's some kinda radiation poisoning."

Mary Jane stood behind Greg and put a hand on his shoulder. "I'm sorry."

"It's crazy. I mean, we been doin' everything, you know? Weed, coke, blow, X, you name it, and all we got was high. But this—" His voice broke. "The guy said it'd make her smarter. He didn't say it'd make her dead."

Remembering what both Greg and Valerie had told her, Mary Jane said, "Greg, you told me that Zeke—the guy—he had a woman with him."

Greg nodded. "Yeah, some purple-haired lady."

Jackpot, Mary Jane thought, clearly remembering a purple-haired woman with mechanical arms who had taken on the mantle of Dr. Octopus after the first one died, and who later went on to resurrect her predecessor. Peter had filled Mary Jane in on the working theory that the source of the Triple X was Otto Octavius and Carolyn Trainer, and if Greg and Valerie's supplier had a purple-haired lady with him, that went a long way toward proving the theory right.

She walked around to face Greg. "Listen to me, Greg—you need to go to the police and tell them about your suppliers."

Looking at her like she was nuts, Greg said, "Are you out of your *mind*, MJ? I ain't talkin' to no cops about no suppliers. I ain't rattin' the guy out, okay?"

"Fine, then, don't rat the guy, just the purple-haired lady. *She's* gotta be the one who came up with the Triple X, right? Zeke didn't have the stuff until she showed up?"

"Yeah," Greg said, "that's true."

"So just give her up. Keep Zeke in the clear." Mary Jane knew she was encouraging at the very least that Greg commit a misdemeanor, but the important thing was to get *someone* to corroborate that Trainer was the one pushing the Triple X.

Shaking his head, Greg said, "No way. Nuh-uh. She'll kill me."

Oh, God, Trainer threatened them. "Look, the cops can protect you from the purple-haired lady, you just—"

"I don't mean her, I mean Val! If I talk to the cops—" Again, his voice broke. He looked over at Valerie on the bed.

Mary Jane followed his gaze. Right now, Valerie looked peaceful, as if she was sleeping, even with the IV in her arm and the oxygen tube in her nose and wrapped around her ears. *God, she may never wake up from that.* There were no outward signs of radiation poisoning yet, but Mary Jane knew that was only a matter of time.

"Jesus, she looks so peaceful," Greg muttered, his words echoing Mary Jane's thought. "She ain't gonna make it, is she?"

"I can't answer that," Mary Jane said honestly. "But if she isn't—do you really want the person responsible for killing her to stay free?"

Greg closed his eyes. "Dammit, I don't know. It's usually Val who decides this stuff, I'm just—" He hit the arm of the chair weakly with his fist. "I'm just a guy, y'know? Just doin' my thing, I don't know nothin' 'bout—" He slumped.

Reaching into her purse, Mary Jane pulled out the card that Detective Shapiro had given her at VPC. "Listen, after Val changed the first time, I talked to this detective. He's up at the 24th Precinct on 100th Street, and he's in charge of the whole Triple X thing. You can talk to him."

It took a few seconds for Greg to take the card. "Yeah, okay. I'll go tomorrow."

Mary Jane didn't like the sound of that. "Greg, go tonight. I'll stay with her."

"Okay, but—let me sit with her a few more minutes, all right?"

Looking around the room, Mary Jane found another chair and brought it over next to Greg. She sat down and said, "Okay. I'll sit with you."

"Yeah, thanks." Greg kept staring at Valerie. "Jesus." They sat alone in silence after that.

TWELVE

SPIDER-MAN was very grateful for the fact that wearing a mask meant nobody in the Triple X Task Force could see that he could barely keep his eyes open.

He'd slept in today, having called in sick to work Monday night right before collapsing in a heap on the bed and sleeping until two on Tuesday, then heading to Parkway Hospital to visit Hector. Then Mary Jane called him from Cabrini saying that she had stuck Greg in a cab that would take him uptown to the 24th Precinct, and he should get his red-and-blue butt over there.

Monday he had made a wholly futile attempt to find Dr. Octopus. Unfortunately, Sunday's run through his usual stoolies proved prophetic for Monday's: nobody knew anything, and those that might have were nowhere to be found. Spider-Man was starting to get a complex.

The closest he got to good news was hearing that Elias Kitsios would be at Amsterdam Billiards for a tournament Tuesday night. Kitsios was one of the go-to guys if you wanted to buy equipment, usually stolen, of the type needed by guys like Dr. Octopus. When Ock needed anything, from lab equipment to an air conditioner, there was a good chance that Kitsios would be the one to get it for him.

The good news was, at least Spider-Man was able to stop a few more gamma-head rampages, though several straight days of keeping super-powered druggies from doing too much harm, while trying not to do too much harm to them, was taking its toll on even his enhanced stamina. The extra sleep this morning and afternoon had helped, but not nearly enough. As he sat on the wall of the Two-Four's detective squad room once again, he felt the bones of his arms and legs turning to liquid. He hadn't had a decent meal in days, though he had promised Aunt May, in a hasty phone call right before he webbed over to the precinct house, that he and Mary Jane would come over for a late dinner tonight. Thrilled at the prospect, Aunt May said she was heading out to the Associated Supermarket on Queens Boulevard to get all the fixings.

Shapiro, Shanahan, and O'Leary were present. Petrocelli was out chasing a lead. Shapiro and Shanahan studiously ignored the wall-crawler, leaving O'Leary to do all the speaking. Given their hostile attitudes, compared with O'Leary's friendliness, this suited Spider-Man fine.

Fry and Wheeler came walking in, the latter with two mugs of coffee in his hand. To Spider-Man's surprise, he handed one of those mugs to Spider-Man.

"Heard you been goin' full tilt. Figured you might need this," Wheeler said with a small smile.

"Thanks, Detective." Spider-Man took the steaming mug, figuring this to be a peace offering from Wheeler.

Lifting his mask up to his nose, he took a sip, and then had to gather up all his willpower not to spit it out. This was even worse than Midtown High's faculty lounge coffee, and that stuff was often mistaken for sewage. *Maybe it's not so much a peace offering as revenge.*

Wheeler looked at Shapiro. "So who's this guy comin' in?"

"Greg Halprin," Spider-Man said. "He's the boyfriend of Valerie McManus, and he's giving up his supplier."

Shapiro shot Spider-Man a look. "How'd *you* know that?" He looked at O'Leary. "Did you—?"

Quickly, O'Leary said, "I just told him we had a possible witness."

Sitting down at his desk, Wheeler said, "Hang on—Halprin? I talked to that guy today. He sent me back to the theatre, said one'a the other actresses had somethin' to say." He grinned. "She didn't, turns out, but, *man,* what a babe."

Fry shook his head. "You hitting on witnesses again, Ty?"

"Didn't need to—this one was coming on to me."

O'Leary laughed. "Well then, she couldn'ta been much use as a witness, 'cause if she was hitting on you, then she's gotta be blind."

Wheeler good-naturedly tossed a paper clip at O'Leary, who batted it aside.

"If you kids are finished . . . ," Shapiro said. Everyone else settled down. "Petrocelli's following up on someone in Inwood who matches Octavius's description. Meanwhile—"

One of the uniforms walked in, along with Greg Halprin, looking pathetic.

O'Leary leapt to her feet, leading Greg over to her desk. Mary Jane had said in her phone message that Greg was not handling Valerie's decline very well, and seeing him now, Spider-Man could see that clear as day. As Peter Parker, he had met Greg only once, when they were both in the audience during the callbacks for *The Z-Axis,* each of them, as Greg had put it, "lending our womenfolk some moral support." He'd seemed a nice enough guy—a little slow on the uptake, perhaps, but harmless. Based on what Mary Jane had told him, however, he'd been at his best at that callback.

He certainly wasn't now. When O'Leary asked him his name, he struggled with the concept, and his address took several seconds.

But once he got to the meat of the statement, the words started to flow better. "Look, we took stuff, okay? You try getting through an audition or a callback straight—or try sittin' around hopin' that they'll call you, even though you know they're gonna go for someone else. You're too tall, too pale, not blond enough, too wide in the shoulders, not skinny enough, what-the-hell-ever. Can't expect a dude to face that straight, you just *can't.*"

Spider-Man found himself drinking the awful coffee just to cover the bark of derisive laughter he had on standby. He was married to someone in the same business—who'd also spent plenty of time as a model—and she faced it just fine straight. Apart from a bout with cigarettes, Mary Jane had stayed clean.

Then again, not everyone has MJ's strength.

"So we met this lady. Dude, she was *intense.* Never got a name, but she had a hawk nose, and purple hair, I remember that much. Wasn't even stylin' or nothin', just regular hair 'cept it was purple."

O'Leary, who had been typing Greg's words into the keyboard on her desk, stopped, nodded, then looked at Fry. The tall cop brought over a booklet and dropped it on O'Leary's desk. She flipped it open to the middle. Peering over, Spider-Man saw that the page O'Leary opened to had five mug shots of women, all in color, each woman with purple hair. *Why does it not surprise me that there are four purple-haired women in this town besides Trainer with rap sheets?*

Greg didn't even hesitate. "That's her." His index finger landed right on the picture of Carolyn Trainer.

"All right," Shapiro said, "Detective O'Leary's gonna print out your statement. I want you to read it and sign and initial it everywhere the detective tells you, okay?"

Nodding, Greg said, "I just wanna get the people that did this to Val, y'know?"

"I know, son." Shapiro put a hand on Greg's shoulder, and spoke in as kind a voice as Spider-Man had heard him use.

O'Leary stood and led Greg over to the printer on the far side of the squad room.

Looking over at Shanahan, Shapiro asked, "We got an address on Trainer?"

"Yeah, but I dunno if it's current."

Spider-Man pulled the mask down over his face. "Where?"

"Hang off a second," Shapiro said, holding up a hand toward Spider-Man. "We take Trainer, I don't want you within a thousand feet of us."

"I beg your pardon? Detective, this lady *was* Doc Ock for a while, and she was actually pretty good at it."

Shapiro shook his head. "I don't care, this is the first real lead we've had since they formed this damn unit, and I ain't lettin' it get screwed up by some technicality 'cause we brought a civilian in a costume on the bust."

"What difference does it make?" Spider-Man asked. "Can't you just arrest her on old charges?"

Shapiro said, "There *are* no old charges."

Spider-Man blinked under his mask. "What're you talking about? She was wearing the tentacles, she—"

"Wearing metal arms isn't a crime," Shapiro said. "But she was arrested, and—"

Fry spoke up, then. "And she was brought to trial, and a jury of her peers found her not guilty of any of the charges, mostly because the DA couldn't put a decent case together and her lawyer ripped the prosecution case to shreds. Not surprising, really, since their only witness was her father, who—"

Wincing, Spider-Man said, "Who was killed by the Green Goblin."

"Yup," Fry said. "No witness, no case, no conviction."

"Well," Shapiro said, "there was one other witness."

He stared right at Spider-Man. "But he wears a big red mask and doesn't testify at trials."

"How do you like *them* apples?" Shanahan asked with a nasty smile.

Before Spider-Man could respond in kind—or web Shanahan's mouth shut, an option that was looking more pleasurable by the second—Shapiro went on. "So I can't take the chance of having you there on Trainer's bust. Hell, we don't even know if the address we got for her is current. But if it is, we'll take her in and get her to flip Octavius."

Spider-Man couldn't help it. He laughed. "What's so goddamn funny?" Shanahan asked.

"You're not gonna get Trainer to give up Octavius. Not on a drug charge, not on an assault charge, not on the charge of being the second coming of Lucrezia Borgia."

Shanahan gave him a dirty look. "You think we can't flip some broad?"

"I know for a fact you can't flip this one. She's so devoted to Octavius *she had him resurrected from the dead*. You really think she'll give him up?"

"Even if she doesn't," Shapiro said before Shanahan could say something else stupid, "she's still in on this. Right now, we need an arrest. We need to show the inspector and the commissioner and the mayor and the newspapers that we're *doing* something. An arrest will go a long way toward keeping people calm."

"Maybe," Spider-Man said, "but I'm not about to just sit on my hands and let you guys—"

The desk sergeant—Larsen—burst into the squad room. "We just got a call from the One-Twelve. Some old lady in a supermarket's turned green and is firing ray-beams outta her eyes."

For the second time in two days, a fist of ice clenched Spider-Man's heart, but this one was bigger and colder. "What supermarket?" he asked.

Looking down at the Post-it he was holding, Larsen said, "An Associated on Queens Boulevard over by—"

The word "boulevard" had barely escaped Larsen's mouth when Spider-Man was out the window.

Of all the people Ock would go after, Spider-Man had hoped, had prayed, that May Parker would have been left off the list. After all, she hadn't actually done anything to him. *Then again, neither did Gaxton, really, and that didn't stop Ock from hitting him with the drug. . . .*

Years ago, Dr. Octopus had learned that May was in line to inherit an island containing a nuclear power plant. When Spider-Man later learned the whole story, he had thought it an odd thing to bequeath, but May would only say that it was from the "side of the Reillys we try not to talk about." In order to get his hands on the plant, Ock had courted May, and got her to agree to marry him. Spider-Man hadn't actually stopped them himself, being beaten to it by a mob boss who went by the sobriquet of "Hammerhead." Between them, Ock and Hammerhead blew up the power plant and destroyed the island, though both somehow managed to escape with their lives. With the island gone, so too was Ock's interest in marrying Peter's aunt.

I guess, Spider-Man thought as he webbed across Manhattan in record time, *it was too much to hope that Ock would've forgotten about her.* May had been at death's door more than once since Peter Parker became Spider-Man, and he even thought her to be dead for a brief time, and he wasn't about to let her be taken from him by Ock's sick revenge scheme.

Queens Boulevard, one of the major thoroughfares of the borough for which it was named, had both a main road and a service road. Traffic on the eastbound side was snarled, as the cars couldn't get past the giant crater on the divider between the eastbound service road and main road, as well as the tree that had been knocked across the road, both right in front of a giant Associated Supermarket.

A green beam of light shot across and hit one of the street lamps. People were shouting and running away from the supermarket as Spider-Man swung into the parking lot, which seemed to be the source of the beam.

Several blue-and-whites were surrounding a single female figure, with over a dozen uniformed officers standing in a position that kept their cars between them and her.

Said figure was skinny, green, and shooting beams from her head. Even from this distance, and with the new skin tone, Spider-Man instantly recognized May Parker.

As he swung into the parking lot he saw another beam fired and heard a familiar voice yelling, "I'm sorry! So sorry!"

Spider-Man landed on a car behind one of the blue-and-whites. "Not your usual gamma-head, is she?" he said to the one cop not in a uniform.

Whirling around, the cop—a heavyset Latino man with a bald head and a thick mustache—said, "About time you showed up. Shapiro said you'd be here."

Nice to be wanted. "I think I can convince her to come quietly."

"Yeah, we tried that." The detective pointed at one of the blue-and-whites, which was missing its entire trunk. "But I ain't about to tell these guys to open fire on an old lady, even if she *is* green. Christ, she must be, like, ninety years old or somethin'."

"As it happens, she's a fan of mine. Wrote some nice letters to the *Daily Bugle* and everything. So I think I've got a shot here."

"Good—'cause if you don't, I do."

Nodding his understanding and silently swearing he wouldn't let any harm come to his aunt, Spider-Man leapt over to a car next to her. "Mrs. Parker, this is Spider-Man. Just take it easy."

"Spi—Spider-Man?" Another beam shot out and demolished a Dumpster.

"Easy, Mrs. Parker—listen, just close your eyes."

"But then I can't see."

His spider-sense buzzing, Spider-Man leapt just as another beam shot out of his aunt's eyes, totaling the car he was on. *Hope the owner's insured.*

Landing in front of her as she said, "I'm so sorry!" Spider-Man grabbed her arms.

"It's okay, Mrs. Parker, really."

"I don't feel very well," she said. "Ever since that nice woman with the purple hair gave me those free ice cream samples, I . . ."

Then she collapsed in his arms.

"Move in!" the detective cried, just as an ambulance pulled up.

Waving off the uniformed cops who ran toward him, Spider-Man said, "She's fine, I got her."

"Sir," one of the uniforms said, "we got to—"

"I said, I *got* her! Back off!"

Refusing to let any cop near her, Spider-Man waited until the EMTs rolled up with their gurney, at which point he gently placed his aunt on it, then let the pros take over.

He then tore into the supermarket itself, making a beeline for the frozen foods section. Sure enough, there was a table with some small spoons and empty cups on it, with a sign reading FREE SAMPLES.

The supermarket had been evacuated, of course, and somehow Spider-Man doubted that Trainer would hang around once her objective of poisoning Aunt May was accomplished. *I wonder if she just pushed it on everyone here, or had a special batch ready for when Aunt May came by.* Probably the latter, since Queens Boulevard wasn't being overrun with gamma-heads.

Spider-Man ran out the front door and leapt up to a nearby high-rise, being careful to avoid any of the cops or EMTs—or members of the press, for that matter, several of whom filmed his departure.

When he alighted on the roof, he took out Ursitti's cell phone and called O'Leary.

"Everything okay?" she asked.

"I want Trainer's address, and I want it *now.* I'm going to beat that woman until she bleeds."

"I can't do that, and you know why. Shapiro's getting the warrant on the address right now. It's gotta be a clean bust."

"I don't care! What she and Ock are doing—" Spider-Man cut himself off. He couldn't very well tell O'Leary that the latest target was the woman who raised him.

"You think we don't know what they're doing? But if we don't do this right, Trainer will *walk,* especially since our only witness is a drugged-out actor whose girlfriend is dying. We gotta be real careful with her." She paused. "But only with her."

"What do you mean?"

"Well, Trainer's clean, but Octavius isn't. Got about a dozen outstanding warrants, at least. Doesn't matter *how* he's brought in."

Spider-Man started to say something, then stopped. "What time is it?"

"About six-thirty. Why?"

Forcing himself to calm down, Spider-Man said, "I've got a pool game to catch." He closed the phone without another word.

Shooting a web-line off to one of the trees on the Queens Boulevard service road, Spider-Man thought, *The tournament isn't starting until nine, but if Kitsios is playing pool for real tonight, chances are he's at that place on 8th that has the cheap booze he likes, so he can liquor up. . . .*

○—————————————○

ELIAS Kitsios leaned over the crappy pool table and lined up a shot. He'd knock the seven in the corner and bank it off the side to sink the two. After that, the eight-ball would be all set up and he'd take this idiot's money.

This was all just a warm-up for Kitsios. Tonight was the tournament, playing on a *real* regulation table, not the dinky thing they put in bars like this dump on 8th Street. Usually, he just came here for the drinks—this was the only place in Manhattan that had *ouzo* at what Kitsios considered a reasonable price—but when some black kid started trash-talking about how he was a pool god, Kitsios decided to make a little extra money. It'd be good prep for tonight.

And the extra cash didn't hurt. Not that he needed it. He had plenty of clients, including one who was rolling in it and spending like there was no tomorrow.

Now just gotta sink the last two and take this idiot for everything he—

"The important thing," a voice from above him said suddenly, forcing Kitsios to scratch his shot, "when you're playing pool is to focus, to *never* lose your concentration."

Slamming the stick down on the table, Kitsios whirled around. "Who—?"

But there wasn't anybody in the bar who hadn't been there before. The ones who were, though, were all looking up.

Kitsios followed their gazes to see Spider-Man hanging upside down from the ceiling.

"What do you want, *arachne*?"

"Dr. Octopus."

Letting out a breath, Kitsios asked point-blank, "I tell you where to find him, you let me get back to my game?"

"That's the idea. C'mon, I know Ock's hatching a scheme, and with him, schemes usually mean fancy-shmancy equipment, and fancy-shmancy equipment usually means yo—"

"He's at 91st Street—the abandoned subway station under Broadway. I got him the generators and lights and some lab stuff."

Spider-Man didn't say anything for a second. "That's it? I don't have to beat you up or anything?"

Kitsios sighed. "I got a game to finish and a tournament to play uptown. I don't have time for you. Besides, what can Otto do to me?"

"You really don't want to know the answer to that one, Kitsios."

Waving off Spider-Man, Kitsios picked up his cue stick. "Nobody can get what I can get. That makes me too useful to beat up, except by people like you. So the best way to keep you from doing that is to tell you what you want."

He walked toward the table, but his opponent used his own stick to block Kitsios's path. "Nah, man, it's *my* shot. You scratched."

Pointing at the ceiling with his thumb, Kitsios said, "That was because of—"

"I don't care if yo' Moms came in to tell me how much fun she had with me last night, you don't hit nothin', you scratch, *my* shot, got it?"

Kitsios looked up, only to see that Spider-Man was gone. *Good riddance. Those super heroes just get in the way of things.* Then he looked down at the table, seeing that his opponent had several good shots and might be able to take the table before Kitsios had another chance.

"Yes," he said slowly, "I 'got' it. Take your shot." He stepped off to the side and took his cell phone out of his pocket.

THIRTEEN

FOR Otto Octavius, it had begun three months ago when he visited his mother's grave.

Technically, one could argue that it had started longer ago than that. The notion of infusing gamma radiation into one of the many drugs of which the doltish members of the human race partook, thus increasing its potency and also imbuing the user with one of the common paranormal side effects, had first occurred to him several years ago. But he had never bothered to marry that thought to an action.

But Octavius had goals, ones that required resources he didn't have, and could only acquire with money that he also didn't have. Petty thievery of the type in which he had once indulged was no longer practical—too many banks and depositories were equipped with security designed to stop people like Octavius. Circumventing that, while possible, wasn't cost-effective given the actual monetary gain he'd realize from the theft.

On a winter evening three months ago, the anniversary of Mary Lavinia Octavius's death, he visited her grave. He wasn't entirely sure why he had chosen to visit on this particular anniversary. Several such had come and gone without his marking it, but this year, on the eve of his most recent plan's commencement, he had done so.

For the longest time, he had been devoted to his mother, particularly after his father, Torbert Octavius, died. Father was a thug, a construction worker who labored with his hands and had very little patience with people who used their intelligence. He was also good enough to die in a construction accident, thus freeing Otto from his endless tirades about how Otto should defend himself against the school bullies "like a man"—as if any but a simian would respond in such a manner.

Father was dead, so he no longer mattered. Liberated from his verbal and physical abuse, both Otto and Mother had flourished. Encouraged by Mother to excel, Otto had graduated at the top of his class both as an undergraduate and a graduate student, attaining his doctorate in the minimum time.

Though he'd taken many jobs, and developed a reputation as one of the premier atomic scientists in the country, it was as a project manager at the United States Atomic Research Center that he had come into his own. His cousin on his mother's side, Thomas Hargrove, worked there—one of only two competent people employed at the center. The other was Mary Alice.

Ah, Mary Alice.

Unlike the other dolts at USARC, Mary Alice understood his work. More to the point, she understood *him* in a way no one else but Mother ever did.

Sadly, their relationship was not to be. Mother was furious at the notion of Otto's abandoning her. Foolishly, Otto agreed, not wanting to disappoint the woman who raised him, who encouraged him.

To this day, Otto wondered what he had been thinking listening to Mother. With Mary Alice, he would have been happy. Instead, he shunned her, got Hargrove to fire her from USARC, and devoted himself fully to his work.

It had been all he had left.

Mary Alice went on to marry some other man. Eventually she died of complications resulting from a blood transfusion that was tainted with HIV.

Perhaps it was all for the best. The work was what mattered.

Certainly Mother didn't, even before her death. Otto came home early one night—a rare occasion when he *didn't* work a twenty-hour day— to find Mother dressed up, preparing for a date.

Otto, naturally, was livid. He had sacrificed his own happiness with Mary Alice for Mother's sake, yet she felt free to gallivant around with some imbecile behind his back.

They argued. Never a skinny woman, Mother couldn't handle the strain of her prodigious bulk and the stress of their contretemps. A cardiac infarction ended her life.

She no longer mattered, either.

Liberated from her simpering, he was able to accomplish great things. Already the world's leading authority on radiation, he had, months earlier, designed a set of four mechanical arms that allowed him to manipulate volatile materials from a safe distance. Then came the explosion that fused the arms to his body, granting him full mental control over the dextrous limbs.

On that day Otto Octavius—wretch, outcast, the prototypical "mama's boy"—died, and "Dr. Octopus" was reborn from his ashes. The nickname had been given to him as a sneer by those inferior minds at USARC, and Octavius took great pleasure in throwing it back in their faces as the name he took as a recognized genius.

True, the press insisted on labeling him a "super villain," but Octavius was far more than that. He'd been belittled, betrayed, and bothered by so many for so long. Lesser minds had kept him from achieving his goals.

And it had all started with dear old Mother.

What would my life have been like if she had died with Father? he had thought that night at her grave months ago. *Or if so many others who got in my way had not been present to ruin my plans? When people die, they stop mattering. So it's time some of them died. Especially that irritating arachnid . . .*

Spider-Man had been the one to stymie Octavius's plans the first time, and most of the times after that. Octavius's first jail sentence was light— Mother's final gift to him, as her recent death was cited by his lawyer as the main reason why the bench should take it easy on him, and the judge agreed—and what few prison stays he'd had since were short-lived.

No jail could hold a man of his superior intellect for long. Mother may have appreciated his genius, but she never understood it.

No one did.

Certainly not Spider-Man, despite his continued meddlesome presence, which was sufficiently routine that Octavius had, on this occasion, taken steps to prepare for it.

The phone call a few moments ago from Kitsios confirmed that those preparations were about to bear fruit, as did the sound of rending metal that signaled the door to the dome's caving in.

The dome had been constructed in the 91st Street station mostly by Octavius's arms at his direction, using material supplied by Kitsios. As a youth, Octavius had made a study of the various abandoned underground caverns located throughout the New York metropolitan area—abandoned military bases, unused land, power stations, and the like—which he had used in adulthood as bases of operation. Abandoned subway locales were also beneficial, whether the caverns constructed for the abortive attempt at a subway in the late nineteenth century, or places like the 91st Street station, originally built for the still-running subway constructed in the early twentieth.

Made of reinforced steel, the dome served to protect Octavius's ears from the din of the 1, 2, 3, and 9 trains that rattled by at high speeds on their way to and from the 96th Street station, and his sensibilities from the muck-encrusted, graffiti-covered, rat-infested walls and floors of the long-abandoned platform. Only someone with Octavius's strength could get through the dome's walls and single door.

Whatever the arachnid's failings, he was a creature of considerable strength. He stood now in the gap in the dome created by his rending of the door, his costume covered in a layer of soot and grime from traversing the subway tunnels in order to arrive here.

"It's over, Ock."

Smiling, Octavius said, "I doubt that very much."

Octavius had expected the arachnid to arrive much sooner. Kitsios had informed him that Spider-Man had spent the last several days in search of Octavius. Since Octavius's only outside contacts on this endeavor were Carolyn Trainer and Elias Kitsios, he instructed the latter to make his movements known and, when his and the arachnid's paths inevitably crossed, to provide Spider-Man with the 91st Street locale.

Now that he had been good enough to show up, Octavius attacked Spider-Man with two of his arms. Predictably, the arachnid jumped out of the way—and just as predictably, Octavius attacked with a third arm.

To his surprise, Spider-Man succumbed to the attack, the end of the arm colliding with his masked head.

However, Spider-Man recovered quickly, and ducked out of the way of the fourth arm, leaping onto the curved wall of the dome and projecting one of his tiresome webs toward Octavius's face. Octavius deflected it easily with two of his arms, the webbing sliding off the specially treated metal surface of his arms. Long gone were the days when Octavius would succumb to so minor an inconvenience as the arachnid's artificial web.

The remaining two arms had Spider-Man cornered near the floor of the dome, but he was able to grab each with one hand to stave them off. "It wasn't enough for you, was it, Ock?" Spider-Man asked through what sounded like clenched teeth. "You couldn't just poison the streets with your radioactive garbage, you had to target innocent people?" There was a tone in the voice that surprised Octavius: an anger, a resentment that was almost personal.

Octavius laughed. "Your definition of 'innocence' differs from mine. All those who were targeted offended me in some manner—a guilty charge in my own court." His other two arms went for Spider-Man's legs. Octavius planned to grab one extremity with each arm and toss him aside like so much garbage. He hadn't defeated Spider-Man this quickly since their first meeting. *It can't be this easy,* he thought.

And, indeed, it wasn't. Still holding on to two metal arms, the arachnid leapt forward in a flip that took his feet around two hundred and seventy degrees to land with his feet on the wall of the dome. It was, Octavius had to grudgingly admit, an impressive move, one a normal human simply could never have made.

"Guilty, huh? What about May Parker?"

At that, Octavius snarled. In truth Mrs. Parker had done nothing bad to him—it was because of that foolish, deformed gangster that Octavius lost his chance at that power plant. Mrs. Parker had been kind and generous to him.

Just like Mother was . . .

No, she too had to die. Just like Gaxton, Haight, Hunt, and the others, including Carolyn's former husband.

They had to die so they would no longer matter.

"Cat got your tongue, Ockie?" Spider-Man asked as he pulled on the metal arms in his grasp, hoping to yank Octavius off his feet. However, the arms were not at their full extension, and all the arachnid's foolish pulling did was extend them.

Octavius commanded them to retract once again, in the hopes of doing what Spider-Man intended to do to him: pull him off the dome wall. However, Spider-Man simply let go of the arms.

"I have no need to justify my actions to anyone, arachnid, *least* of all the likes of you."

Leaping up to the top of the dome, Spider-Man spoke in the same angry tone. "It's over, Ock. The cops've got your groupie, and I've got you."

As Spider-Man dropped down, apparently hoping an aerial assault would prove more fruitful than a frontal one, Octavius raised all four arms and had them attack Spider-Man at different points in his descent. Even he would not be fast enough to evade all four.

I wonder if he speaks the truth about Carolyn, or is simply trying to bluff me. No matter—she has served her purpose. The funds from peddling the gamma-irradiated drugs to the unwitting fools of this city had amounted to more than he needed to bankroll his latest endeavor.

Two of Octavius's arms collided with the arachnid's form, sending him flying across the dome. Spider-Man managed to recover enough to land feetfirst on the dome wall, using his ability to stick to surfaces to land safely. Octavius then tried to club him with two of his arms, but his foe managed to dodge them—and leave himself open for a blow to his ribs with a third arm. Spider-Man grabbed that arm, but Octavius simply yanked it out of his foe's grasp.

The dance continued for several more minutes, and Octavius had to admit to a certain disappointment: Spider-Man was barely holding his own. Octavius was not sure whether he was still reeling from the initial blow to the head, or not thinking straight due to the anger Octavius detected in his voice, or both. His enemy was also forgoing his usual attempts at wit—for which Octavius was frankly grateful—which alone bespoke an unusual state of affairs.

Perhaps I will be able to kill him as well. That was almost too much to hope for. Despite all his attempts over the years, he had never been able to deal the arachnid a fatal blow, and Octavius wasn't naïve enough to believe that today would change that—but that didn't mean he wouldn't try his best.

Spider-Man leapt about the dome like a dervish, but as fast as he was, Octavius's arms were faster, moving as they did with the speed of thought. The confined space of the dome did not permit the wall-crawler his usual freedom of movement, and Octavius was able to deliver several blows to the head, ribs, and stomach. For the arachnid's part, he was able to get anywhere near Octavius only twice, and both times, Octavius was able to use his arms to remove Spider-Man from proximity to his person.

Then, Spider-Man leapt to the ceiling once again and looked at the lab table at the far end of the dome from the entrance.

"Nice little setup you've got here, Ockie." Spider-Man's voice sounded slurred, as if he were too tired to go on, and he seemed unsteady. "What is it with you and underground holes, anyhow? It's no wonder you're so pale."

"My motives are not for such as you to divine, arachnid."

"Y'know, Ock, that's what I love about tussling with you—I mean, let's face it, most of the guys I throw down with have the cranial capacity of a fried egg. But you, you're the only one who uses 'divine' in a sentence—as a verb, no less."

Truly I was hoping to avoid the inane banter. Octavius snarled and thrust an arm toward the ceiling, but Spider-Man leapt behind the lab table. He kicked it hard enough to send it flying through the air at Octavius, who had to use all four arms to deflect it.

When he had done so, the arachnid was nowhere to be seen.

Turning and looking out through the opening left by the shattered door, Octavius saw a web-line swinging limply from the ceiling, obviously abandoned within the last few seconds. Spider-Man had used the desk as a distraction to make his escape. *No doubt he realized his defeat was imminent.*

Octavius at once considered and rejected the notion of giving chase. It would be foolish to expose himself at this stage. *Let him make his futile attempts to stem the tide of the drug, or to find me again. He will fail at both.* This particular hideaway was simply a front for the inevitable confrontation with Spider-Man. The arachnid had no idea where Octavius's true base of operations was, nor would he ever find it.

Then Octavius smiled, remembering one of the arachnid's tired tricks. He quickly found one of those ridiculous "spider-tracers" on his back. Shaped like a small red spider, the device served as a homing beacon. Too many times in the past, Spider-Man had found Octavius by attaching one of the infernal devices to his person.

Smashing the small tracer to pieces with one of his arms, he thought, *Not this time, fool.*

The dome shook as an uptown train went careening down the tracks, headed toward 96th Street. With the door smashed, the dome had lost much of its usefulness, and Spider-Man's awareness of it—and subsequent thrashing—disposed of the rest of it. Grabbing his hat and camel-hair coat, he contracted his arms and headed toward the tracks.

All is going precisely according to plan.

JEROEN Shapiro stared at the purple-haired woman on the video monitor.

He was standing with Fry and Wheeler in the cramped video room, which had the monitors that got the feed from the video cameras in the two interrogation rooms. Anybody who watched television knew that interrogations weren't conducted in secret, and nobody was fooled by the old two-way glass anymore, so many precinct houses had just installed video cameras and had done with it. Besides, having a video record of interrogations was useful at times.

Carolyn Trainer had just been coming home when Shapiro and his task force, along with some uniforms, burst into her home, warrant in hand. They had found a stash of Triple X in her closet behind a false wall—Fry had been the one to notice that the depth of the closet didn't match the layout of the house—and had brought her to the Two-Four. Shanahan was continuing to supervise the search of Trainer's house, while Petrocelli was heading to Parkway Hospital in Queens to interview May Parker, the latest unwitting Triple X junkie. She was in recovery and, according to a rather peevish-sounding doctor, was eager to talk to the police even though the doctor said she should rest. Shapiro just wished all witnesses were so willing to help out.

O'Leary was walking in, putting her cell phone on a clip on her belt. "Just left a message for Spider-Man. No word from him on Octopus."

"We don't need to," Shapiro said, "we got her."

"What if Spider-Man was right?" O'Leary asked.

Shapiro whirled sharply on her. "He wasn't. Jimmy and I will get her to flip."

Shaking her head, O'Leary said, "I don't think you will, Jerry. She's devoted to him."

"And you're a little too devoted yourself."

Defensively, O'Leary asked, "What the hell's *that* supposed to mean?"

"You've had your nose in spider-butt this entire case."

Fry interposed his massive form between Shapiro and O'Leary. "That's outta line, Jerry—and you know it. Una's right—Spider-Man *has* been helpful, and he hasn't been wrong yet."

Shapiro looked up at Fry, then walked toward the door, pushing past O'Leary. "Let's go do our interview."

The fact was, Fry was correct, both about his being out of line and about Spider-Man and O'Leary's being right. As irritating as O'Leary's hero worship was, it hadn't interfered with the police work. What chafed Shapiro most was having that damn costume shoved down his throat by Green and the inspector. This was *his* unit; that should've been *his* call.

He shook his head. *Right, like the bosses have ever given a crap about that kind of protocol before.*

Speaking of which, he bumped into Green in the hallway between the video room and the interrogation room where they'd placed Trainer. "So, at last we have an arrest."

"Yeah, Joll. I'm on my wa—"

"Inspector Garcia is practically wetting his pants, he's so tickled by these joyous tidings. He's calling a press conference and everything, talking about the mass quantities of Triple X that the good Detective Fry here found in the suspect's closet. Of course, if he was also able to say that the aforementioned suspect had given up her partner in this endeavor, said partner being one of the most wanted fugitives in the country, I suspect that the inspector would be positively orgasmic."

"We're gonna go try that now," Shapiro said.

A huge grin bisected Green's round face. "Excellent news! I'll go inform the inspector now."

Shapiro watched the sergeant continue on his way down the hall, a noticeable spring in his step.

Fry asked, "Did he just skip?"

"Don't even go there, Jimmy." Shapiro shuddered. "I hate this."

"Hate what? Joll's happy."

"This kinda happy means he'll be *seriously* pissed off if we screw this up." He looked at Fry. "So let's not screw this up."

They entered Interrogation Room 2 to find Carolyn Trainer, still wearing the apron and all-maroon outfit she used to give free ice cream samples to the customers at the Associated at Queens Boulevard, including one laced with Triple X to feed to May Parker. She even wore a metal nametag that said HEYER, which belonged to an employee of the ice cream company who had called in sick that day, and who also had a substantial deposit recently put in her savings account. Uniforms were already on the way to Heyer's apartment to pick her up.

The interrogation room was painted an unfortunate shade of green, and no one had applied a new coat since Shapiro transferred to the precinct. There were no windows, and the only features besides the two rickety metal chairs and Formica table were the video camera in a far corner and the air vents. During some interviews, the detectives would alter the temperature to help put the suspect ill at ease.

"I gotta tell you," Shapiro said to Fry as they walked through the door, "I don't know why we're bothering with talking to her. We got the drugs, we got her, we got two witnesses that say she's dealing this crap. Why don't we just toss her into the cage and be done with it?" He closed the door behind him.

Fry, picking up the cue smoothly, said, "Well, y'know, Jerry, I was looking at this woman's background. I mean yeah, she's got a Ph.D., but that's in computer science. She doesn't have any kind of chemical skills."

Shapiro just stared dumbly at Fry. "C'mon, Jimmy, what's she need chemical skills for? All she's gotta do is get this stuff in the hands of some slingers, and she's set."

"I don't know, Jerry." Fry shook his head and folded his arms, leaning his tall frame against the wall. "You heard what the lab geeks said—somebody with some serious test-tube smarts made this stuff. That ain't this lady."

Sitting down in one of the two chairs opposite Trainer—who was held fast via a single handcuff that was bolted to the table—Shapiro said, "Yeah, that's a good point."

For the first time, Trainer spoke. She was smiling. "Cute act, boys, but you're wasting your time. I want my lawyer."

Shapiro winced. "Now, see, you really shouldn't do that. If you ask for a lawyer, this conversation ends."

"That was the idea. I know my rights. You were kind enough to read them to me earlier, after all."

"This is true, you do have that right. But if this conversation ends, we write this up like what it looks like."

Fry added, "And it looks pretty shitty for you."

Counting his points off on his fingers, Shapiro said, "We've got the Triple X drugs in your house. We've got a witness who admits you sold him Triple X. We've also got the crew you sold the drugs to—they got shot up by some Ukrainians who didn't appreciate the competition. Most of these guys are brain-dead, and their head guy got himself shot, so I can pretty much guarantee that one of them will be more than happy to shave off a few years so he can put in the one who sold them their stuff. We got the lady from the ice cream company that you bought off to borrow her uniform. We got all that on you—plus, I'm pretty sure the old lady you gave the ice cream to will be able to ID you, too."

"You know, if you're gonna do this stuff seriously," Fry said thoughtfully, "I'd lose the purple hair. It makes it real easy to pick you out of a lineup, y'know? Even if you're a half-blind old lady like May Parker. And what's the big deal with her, anyhow? I mean, in order to have been there when she was, you would've had to stake out the supermarket, and maybe her house, too, for, like, *weeks.*"

Trainer shook her head and looked away. "I really wish I'd killed that old hag when I gave her that stuff."

Shapiro looked up at Fry. "What's this? Detective Fry, I do believe that I heard Ms. Trainer say something that can and will be held against her in a court of law."

"I believe you're right, Detective Shapiro."

Looking wholly unintimidated, Trainer said, "Nice try, boys, but the only way to prove that I said what I just said is to show the videotape that camera up there's feeding to, which will show that my statement came after the part where I asked for my lawyer. Which I'm asking for again. Until he shows up, you can't use a damn thing I say to you—which is why I'm going to tell you this." She leaned forward in the chair. "I will never say anything that will lead to Otto's being imprisoned. I don't care how much time I'm likely to get, either from the DA in a deal or from a jury. If it helps Otto, then I'll do it, and that's all there is to say."

Then she leaned back, a triumphant look on her face.

Shapiro stared at her for several seconds. She didn't have her mechanical arms—they hadn't been found yet in her house—and without them, she was just a normal woman. A very small part of Shapiro wanted to turn off the video camera and beat the living crap out of her.

And that would accomplish what, exactly? She's not gonna give Octavius up.

So without another word, he got up and left the room, Fry right behind him.

As soon as he shut the door behind him, Fry said, "Spider-Man was right, sh—"

Whirling on Fry and pointing a finger up at his face, Shapiro said, "Don't *ever* say those words in my presence again, Jimmy! You understand me? I put up with that costume 'cause Garcia said to, but I will *not* listen to that. Bad enough I'm getting it in both ears from Una."

Before Fry could reply, O'Leary came out of the video room. "I told you she wouldn't flip."

"So did I," Fry said, "and so did Spider-Man."

"Since when do we start consulting costumes about police work?"

O'Leary said, "It's the same as when we talk to any expert about a particular case. Spider-Man knows Dr. Octopus better than anyone."

"And, more to the point," Fry said, "he's better equipped to deal with the gamma-heads *and* Octavius than we are."

Shapiro had had more than enough of this. "So what? A bodybuilder's better equipped to subdue a brain-dead hopped up on meth, but we ain't about to start using one. He ain't trained, he ain't accountable—he doesn't have a badge."

"Maybe," O'Leary said, "but he ain't going anywhere, either. And I'd rather have him working with us, given a choice."

Although Shapiro had several responses to that, Green's arrival forced him to squelch them. "That was a remarkably speedy interrogation, Detective. I have to confess, your prowess in encouraging suspects to trade up continues to improve."

"No it hasn't," Shapiro said. "She lawyered up the minute we walked in. And even if she hadn't"—he gritted his teeth—"the costume was right, she ain't givin' Octavius up. We need to get him some other way."

Green stared at Shapiro for a few seconds.

Here it comes, Shapiro thought, dreading the thermonuclear explosion that was about to issue forth.

"Then we'll get him some other way. Meantime, we've got the redoubtable Ms. Trainer, and she'll make a dandy top story on the five o'clock news, and an even dandier headline. Nice work."

Green slapped Shapiro gently on the arm, and continued down the hall.

Silence reigned for several seconds before O'Leary asked Fry, "Did he just *not* kill Jerry?"

"Apparently not," Fry said dryly.

Shapiro let out the breath he hadn't realized he was holding. "Guess Trainer's good enough for Garcia's goddamn press conference. So let him have her. Like Joll said, we'll find Octavius some other way."

FOURTEEN

PAIN sliced through Spider-Man's chest as he gingerly swung his way toward Central Park. *That's at least a couple of cracked ribs. Probably a concussion, too. I love my life.*

When he got to the park, he leapt from tree to tree, which was also painful, but not as much as raising his arms to swing on a web-line was. He'd have to do enough of that once he got out of the park, but he wanted to do as little of it as possible. To that end, he worked his way down to 59th Street, then leapt across to one of the trees hanging over the fountain in front of the Plaza Hotel.

"Mommy, look! It's Captain America!"

Spider-Man looked down to see a little girl pointing up from the sidewalk. The mother in question said, "That's nice, dear," in a distracted voice.

I've got too much of a headache to correct her, he thought with a smile, so he gave her a jaunty wave, then shot out a web-line and attached it to the FAO Schwartz building across the street, took a mighty leap, and swung around to alight on the side of Trump Tower.

Okay, that was a mistake. The action of swinging sent white-hot agony coursing through his entire torso. Leaping over to the Schwartz building, he climbed gingerly up to the roof and decided to simply run across rooftops until he got to the Queensboro Bridge, then run across that. *Anything else hurts too much.*

When he reached the bridge, he pulled out Ursitti's cell phone and turned it on. There was one message, from O'Leary: "We got Trainer—she was just coming home when we came to deliver the warrant. Was wearing some kinda weird apron or something."

Spider-Man sighed as he started running up the frame of the bridge. Trainer had obviously gone straight home from the supermarket after poisoning Aunt May. *Her bad luck,* he thought with a certain malice.

O'Leary continued. "She's already made it clear she won't give Octavius up. You're right, she's really devoted to that nut job. I'll let you know if anything changes—hope you're having better luck with Octavius."

As he reached the top of the first tower, Spider-Man put the phone away. There wasn't much point in letting the cops know about Ock's little hidey-hole—it wasn't his real base anyhow. It took him a while to really take a look at the equipment Ock had in his 91st Street abode, but once he did, it was obvious. All he had was a couple of test tubes and a Bunsen burner. It wasn't anywhere near enough equipment to do what Ock had been doing. Heck, it wasn't enough for one of Peter Parker's "Intro to Chemistry" students to work with, much less a scientist of Ock's caliber. *It was just a place to lure me and kick my butt. That's why Kitsios gave the location up so easily.*

Working his way to the second tower, he sighed and chastised himself. *Ock's one of your three or four deadliest foes, web-head—you should know better than to take him on when you're not thinking straight.* If he hadn't been so focused on his anger over Aunt May's being poisoned with the Triple X, he might have questioned Kitsios's easy acquiescence, or recognized the inadequacy of Ock's setup at 91st Street right away instead of after Ock used him as a punching bag for half an hour. *Which means the next time I face him, I won't be as aggravated, but I'll still be exhausted, and badly injured to boot.*

Gritting his teeth against the pain—the buildings were too far apart in Queens for his rooftop-running gag to do the trick—Spider-Man swung his way home.

To his surprise, Mary Jane was waiting for him. He thought she'd be at rehearsal. She got up and walked toward him as he came in the bedroom window—she had been lying on the bed reading a magazine.

"Tiger, you"—her nose wrinkled—"smell *really* bad." He laughed, then clutched his side. She noticed that, walked more quickly to him, guided him to the bed, then went straight for the first-aid kit.

Gingerly removing his costume shirt, mask, and gloves while seated on the edge of the bed, he asked, "What happened to rehearsal?"

"They're running the scenes I'm not in—Dmitri's focusing all his energy on Regina—so I got to come home early."

"Lucky me."

Mary Jane came back with the kit and started taping his ribs. "So what happened to you *this* time?"

"Good news and bad news. The good news is, Greg gave his statement, and it was enough for Shapiro and his band of loonies to serve a warrant on Carolyn Trainer."

Emphatically, Mary Jane said, "That's *great* news."

Peter smiled wryly. Mary Jane didn't exactly have good memories of Trainer's brief tenure wearing the tentacles. He continued: "The other good news is that I tracked down Ock."

"And the bad news is he kicked your butt all over Manhattan?"

"No, just all over the little dome he built in the old 91st Street station. Thing is, he was waiting for me so he could beat the daylights out of me." He shook his head, an unwise move with the concussion, and he had to steady himself on the bed. "I can't believe I let him walk all over me like that."

As she finished taping his chest, Mary Jane said, "As I recall, the first time you and the good doctor met, he cleaned your clock, too."

"Yeah." Peter remembered the day clearly. It was the first time he'd ever been defeated in his nascent super heroic career, and he had been convinced that he'd have to hang up his webs forever. Only when he attended a lecture by the Human Torch of the Fantastic Four—who revealed that the FF had been defeated themselves a few times, but always got up off the mat, as it were—did he regain his confidence and go back after Octopus. He said to Mary Jane, "I don't think I'll be able to fuse his arms together again like I did then, though."

"No, he'll expect that." Mary Jane put her hands on his shoulders and stared at him with those beautiful green eyes of hers. "So you'll have to do something he won't expect."

"God, MJ, the two of us have gone 'round and 'round so many times, I don't think either one of us can really surprise the other, unless—"

Suddenly his face brightened. He had the perfect solution. It would take a bit of work, and he'd need to track Ock down via the spider-tracer. *But it's so crazy, it just might work.*

He stood up. Mary Jane stared up at him. "I know that look, Tiger. It's the I've-got-an-idea-that's-so-crazy-it-just-might-work look."

Grinning, he said, "You know me entirely too well. I'm gonna need to swallow an entire bottle of aspirin, and then I need to make a call."

○────────────○

OTTO Octavius had always been happiest in the laboratory. It was the only place on this wretched planet where he was able to exert total control. He was the master of it all: the chemicals, the isotopes, the equipment, the elements themselves.

And the plan had worked beautifully. Creating a designer drug was the work of only a few days, and most of that was finding the right proportion of radiation to infuse the drug with so that it would have the proper effect. The fools of the city would jump at the chance to give themselves paranormal abilities in addition to a high. Even better, the drug killed them that much faster, thus reducing the population, which was always a plus for Octavius. His eventual goal was to control everything outside the lab as well as inside it, and control was easier when the overall numbers were smaller. Carolyn's criminal contacts were more extensive than Octavius's— he never bothered with such minutiae, simply employing extra sets of arms when he needed them—and so he let her do the legwork. She was now rotting in a holding cell in the 24th Precinct for her troubles, but Octavius had decided to reward her when the time was right.

Targeting the others—Hunt, who had tried to imprison him after the explosion; Gaxton, who so ineptly mishandled the job in Philadelphia; Haight, who presumed too much; dear Mrs. Parker, the simpering old fool; and the others, such as Carolyn's ex-husband—was a two-edged bonus. For one thing, he was able to rid the world of those who had annoyed him—so they would no longer matter. For another, they were, to some degree or other, innocents, and therefore would push all the right buttons with the arachnid. Spider-Man was always at his sloppiest when bystanders' lives were in danger. Octavius had scored one of his greatest victories when he killed a retired police captain whose name Octavius could no longer remember. Spider-Man had been blamed by the fourth estate for the murder, and, though he won in the short term, the death of that old man had long-term consequences for Spider-Man, both personally and perceptually. Their recent tussle at the dome under 91st Street had also served that purpose adequately. *The only flaw was that I was unable to finish him off. But that will come in time. The arachnid is reactive, much like the creature he emulates—he waits until his prey comes into his web before dealing with it. I am proactive, and unlike him, I can afford to lose. He can lose only once—and that will be a good day indeed. . . .*

His current plan made use of the facility that once headquartered the United States Atomic Research Center in lower Westchester. Before it was shut down by the Department of Defense and left abandoned, the facility had had an isolation that appealed to Octavius when he started working there. Since the shutdown, an industrial park had been constructed nearby. Still, the location itself was ideal for Octavius's researches.

Selling the drug had given him the necessary capital, as well as a distraction for the police and Spider-Man. Now, with the materiel and equipment he'd purchased from Kitsios, he could start the next phase.

"Now this—*this* is a laboratory! Not like that kids' chem set you had at 91st Street."

No. It cannot be! But when Octavius whirled around and looked up at the ceiling, he saw the hated arachnid hanging from it. "How did you find me? I destroyed your infernal spider-tracer!"

"Correction, Ockie—you destroyed *one* of my infernal spider-tracers. I left two on you, in case you found one." Octavius sometimes forgot that the arachnid, while limited in so many ways, was still cleverer than most. "No matter. I will defeat you as easily as I did before."

And with that he came at Spider-Man with all four arms.

o———o

OKAY, Spider-Man thought as he leapt off the ceiling to avoid Ock's attack, *this really has to work now.*

This time around, he didn't bother with any kind of offensive maneuvering, for two reasons. One was that the plan called for him to lure Ock out to the industrial park. And the other was that he was in enough pain just dodging Ock's blows. One day later, his ribs felt better, especially taped up, but every move still gave him at best a poke of pain, and at worst searing agony throughout his entire thoracic region.

He just moved on instinct, letting his spider-sense warn him when the blows were coming and dodging out of the way, making sure to keep his distance, forcing Ock to stretch his arms to the limit.

"Cah-*mon,* Doc, is that the best you can do? The Scorpion can tag me with one tail more often than you're getting me with all four of those goofy arms of yours."

Even as he taunted Ock, he moved toward the staircase that led to the aboveground portions of the former USARC. Ock had holed up in the basement, which was where all the good labs were. Spider-Man had noted that the section which held the room where the explosion that created Dr. Octopus took place was still sealed off by lead blast doors. *Probably won't be safe for human life for a bunch of years yet.*

As Spider-Man ran up the stairs, his spider-sense buzzed a warning. One of Ock's arms was heading not for his head, but for the metal staircase in front of him. Leaping into the air even as the arm came down on the stairs, rending them into smaller pieces of scrap with the spine-vibrating squeal of metal on metal, Spider-Man flipped around over the smashed stairs and reached down to grab an arm.

That was a mistake, as Dr. Octopus retracted the arm with a jerk. Spider-Man didn't let go for a second, which was long enough for the motion to aggravate his ribs.

Stick with the plan, doofus, he thought, continuing upstairs and clutching his ribs with one arm.

"You will not escape me again, arachnid! You will die in this place, just as I was born here!"

"As usual, Ock, you're the master of cheap symbolism." Spider-Man leapt up to the top of the stairs, then ran across the wall of the giant hallway that served as the entryway to the USARC.

"You imagine yourself to have an advantage in the open spaces, do you?"

"Well, I've always had a healthy imagination," Spider-Man said as he kicked his way through the large doors and out into the open air beyond the facility.

He had gone about fifty feet toward the industrial park when his spider-sense buzzed, just after hearing the sound of rending metal. Unfortunately, he was in midleap, and was able only to curl himself into a ball to try to avoid the door, which Dr. Octopus had ripped from its hinges and tossed at Spider-Man.

His attempt was only partially successful—the door clipped his left arm, knocking his momentum off and sending him careening toward the ground.

Reaching out with his right arm, he shot out a web-line at a tree that was at least fifty feet off. He snagged it and used it to swing up in the air, shooting out another line to snag a different tree, which he pulled himself toward. All the while, his chest and arm were throbbing a conga-drum line in his head. He'd been going full tilt for days, with not enough sleep, plus his teaching duties (even with taking Tuesday off), he had cracked ribs, and now a bruised arm, and he was trying to avoid being killed by a powerful super-villain.

Just a typical Wednesday evening in the Parker life, he thought with a sigh as he shot a web-line from the tree out to the parking lot at the center of the industrial park. There were only a few cars in the lot, but there shouldn't have been any, since the park was supposed to be evacuated.

Alighting for a landing in the northwest corner of the lot, as far from the few cars as possible, Spider-Man turned and waited for Ock to show up.

He didn't have to wait long. Using his arms to stride forward, Dr. Octopus entered the parking lot, the pincers on the ends of his arms smashing into the asphalt.

"This ends now, arachnid!" he said, his arms holding him still about thirty feet in front of Spider-Man.

Smiling under his mask, Spider-Man said, "You don't know the half of it. Look down."

"What are you playing at?" Dr. Octopus couldn't help but lower his head—only to notice two dozen red dots suddenly appearing on his chest.

Stealing a glance upward, Spider-Man saw that every roof of every building that adjoined the parking lot was filled with black-clad NYPD sharpshooters.

"It's over, Ock."

"Do you truly believe that this will dissuade me from killing you?"

"Get real, Ock—there are twenty-four guys up there. Yeah, you can deflect *a* bullet. But even you can't stop two dozen MP5s fired by experts."

A snarl formed on the doctor's face.

Nobody moved.

There was a very small part of Spider-Man's brain that wanted Doc

Ock to make a move, to force the cops to take him down. It was no less than he deserved for all the deaths he'd caused, from Bennett Brant and Captain Stacy on down the line.

But that would mean placing myself above the law. And no matter what Shapiro and Shanahan and the rest of them might think, I'm not gonna do that.

Then, after several seconds passed, the snarl became a smile. He retracted his arms, bringing him down to the ground. "Well played, arachnid. I surrender."

Shapiro, O'Leary, and a few troopers from the state police came out from inside one of the buildings. O'Leary was holding some kind of bulky device that looked like a jet-pack from an old B-movie.

"Otto Octavius," Shapiro said, "you are under arrest for about half a dozen crimes I really don't feel like listing right now. You have the right to remain silent."

As Shapiro read Dr. Octopus his rights, O'Leary, with the aid of the troopers, placed the device on his back. As soon as they did, Ock's metal arms went limp. Spider-Man knew that the neutralizer was a standard piece of NYPD equipment for taking in paranormal fugitives. In fact, the villain slipped into it with the ease of long practice—after all, this wasn't his first arrest.

"Do you understand these rights as I've read them to you?" Shapiro asked.

"I daresay better than you, Detective." Octavius was still smiling. "I also understand that this changes nothing in the long term."

A large NYPD truck had pulled up while he was being fitted for his new accessory. The troopers led him into it.

O'Leary grinned at Spider-Man. "Nice plan."

"Thanks." He had tracked Ock to the old USARC building the previous night, then called O'Leary and tried to sell the police on his crazy idea. Spider-Man had to be the one to lure Dr. Octopus out and into an open space where the sharpshooters could do their work. For one thing, the facility was a maze, one Octopus knew intimately, and if they tried to storm it, Doc Ock could fend them off for hours, with a virtual guarantee of casualties among the cops. For another, the facility was technically federal property. Getting a warrant for it would probably mean going through the FBI, which not only added to the paperwork, but also meant they'd have to share the bust with the feds, something Inspector Garcia was loath to do. It was hard enough for Shapiro to convince him to cooperate with the state police.

The parking lot was the ideal spot for the takedown, as it was an open space that gave everyone a clear shot.

Shapiro shook his head. "I still can't believe he just surrendered."

"I'm not at all surprised," Spider-Man said. "In fact, I was counting on it. Look, if he surrenders, he just goes to jail. Five'll get you ten he breaks out—God knows, he's done it enough times before. If he doesn't surrender, he gets shot. Maybe he lives, but he probably doesn't, and he's already been dead once. Would *you* want to repeat the experience?"

Snorting, Shapiro said, "Hell, I don't want to do it the once, thanks. You realize we don't have him on Triple X. I mean, he's got a dozen outstanding warrants, so it's no problem sticking him in Ryker's."

Spider-Man shrugged. "Arresting Trainer got the Triple X off the streets. Arresting Ock guarantees there won't be any more to replace it. No more gamma-heads, and probably no more gang war, since Ray-Ray's crew doesn't have it to deal anymore. Isn't that the important part?"

O'Leary sighed. "There'll probably still be some territorial crap, since the Ukrainians might wanna take their blocks back. But that's business as usual."

"Yeah," Spider-Man said, "and you get the credit for arresting Dr. Octopus."

Finally, Shapiro smiled. "That doesn't suck."

Offering his hand, Spider-Man said, "It was a pleasure working with you, Detective."

For a moment, Shapiro just looked at Spider-Man's proffered hand like it was diseased. Then, tentatively, he clasped it in a handshake. "Thanks for the assist."

Looking at O'Leary, Spider-Man said, "You too, Detective."

Grinning, she said, "The pleasure was all mine. And remember what I told you."

Spider-Man nodded, figuring that O'Leary's notions about hero/cop cooperation wouldn't go over well with Shapiro, which was why she was vague. "See you around," he said as he shot a web-line out to one of the buildings and swung away toward home.

I'm going to sleep for a week. . . .

EPILOGUE

HECTOR Diaz stared at the ceiling, waiting for the doctor to show up with his personal stuff and tell him he could finally go the hell home. His mom had crappy insurance, so he couldn't do any of the physical therapy that the doc said he was supposed to do without paying extra for it, and they didn't have extra to pay.

So he was just going home. *About damn time.*

Someone knocked on the door. He looked over to see some white lady wearing a suit. She wasn't wearing a lab coat or nothing, so she probably wasn't a doctor.

"Are you Hector Diaz? My name's Betty Brant; I work for the *Daily Bugle*."

Hector blinked in surprise. He knew that name from somewhere—that was it, that article he read on the bus. *What the hell's a reporter doin' talkin' to me?*

Then he figured it out. "I ain't talkin' to you, lady."

"You sure?" She smiled. "Lots of people like to see their name in the paper."

"Bitch, you stupid or somethin'? My name go in the paper, I catch another bullet, and this won't just be my shoulder, you feel me?"

The Brant lady sat down on the guest chair. "It's just—well, we have a mutual friend. Peter Parker."

Figures. "Mr. Parker ain't no friend. He a teacher."

"He sees it differently, I guess. Anyhow, he said I might be able to get you to comment on something."

Hector rolled over so his back was to the reporter. *Where's that damn doctor?* "I ain't sayin' nothin'."

"You sure? See, I have some information here. In the last two days, thirteen people died from radiation poisoning because they took Triple X. Fifty more have been diagnosed, and some of them may die of it, too. Ten more people have died from other complications—including a schoolmate of yours named Javier Velasquez, who suffered a fatal heart attack last night. At least seven people have died of gunshot wounds because of the turf war between Ray-Ray and the Ukrainians, plus people like you who were wounded. And I guess I wanted to know what you had to say about that."

Hector rolled back over. "Ray-Ray's dead. We got us a new crew chief now, bitch. And we'll be payin' those Ukrainians *back*. Now get your ass out my room!"

She stood up, and she wasn't smiling no more. "You know, Peter said you were a good kid—and that you were a smart kid. Too smart to get caught up in all this. But if Ray-Ray's old crew is 'we' to you now, then obviously Peter was wrong. You're just another slinger who's too stupid to realize that he's gonna die before he's old enough to vote."

Turning around, she left the room.

Hector rolled back over. Blowback had already done told him that they'd be getting back at them Russians—and that Hector had a place in the crew if he wanted it. "Ray-Ray was always talkin' you up, yo," Blowback had said. "And we needs us some good soldiers."

But, even though he told the reporter bitch that he was hooked up with them, the truth was, Hector hadn't said yes.

Yet.

He stared out the window. *Where that damn doctor at?*

○———————○

EILEEN Velasquez hated the fact that she had to break her word.

At Carlos and Manuel's funeral on a long-ago cloudy Saturday morning, she swore that she would never again bury one of her children. Now, thanks to that terrible drug, she was doing it again. She heard on the news that Dr. Octopus created the drug, which meant that yet another one of those super-powered people were destroying Eileen's family.

"And so we commend this poor young soul to heaven, where he now resides with our Lord Jesus Christ after being taken from us too young."

No, she thought as the priest told all his lies about where Javier was now, *it's not because of the drug. The drug just gave him a road to take to hell, but if it wasn't that, Javier would've found something else. And that's my fault.*

"We take solace in knowing that Javier is in a better place now."

She looked through her veil at the faces of those who sat in the chairs or stood around the grave that already had two members of her family and awaited the third in the closed coffin hovering over the big hole in the ground. (Although the heart attack that killed Javier left his body in perfectly fine shape, Eileen insisted on a closed coffin for the wake so she wouldn't have to look at her son's face in death.) Her sister came, along with her daughter Rosanna, as did Carlos's brother and mother, the latter bawling her eyes out at the death of her grandson. Somehow, she found tears that Eileen couldn't, so disgusted was she with herself.

A few of Javier's friends were there, and Eileen was ashamed to realize that she didn't know any of their names. She had never paid close enough attention to what Javier was doing to even be aware of them.

Also present were the dean of students from Midtown High School— earlier, before the burial started, she conveyed the alleged regrets of Principal Harrington, who supposedly had another engagement—as well as Peter Parker and his wife. The science teacher's presence did not surprise Eileen. He was a good man, and she hoped that his other students appreciated him more than Javier did.

Then she looked down to her right at Jorge. The boy looked sullen and angry and fidgety, like he wanted to go home.

"In the name of the Father, and of the Son, and of the Holy Spirit, amen."

Eileen crossed herself as the priest spoke, and said, "Amen."

"Please rise."

As she and the others stood up, she finally let go of the vain hope that Orlando would come. She had left messages on his cell phone saying when the funeral was, and when she'd called his dorm hall phone, his roommate said he had gone off-campus for a few days.

But he didn't turn up. *And why should he? He didn't care any more about Javier than—*

She didn't let herself finish the thought.

After they lowered Javier's body into the ground and the proceeding broke up, Eileen stood about twenty feet from the grave, holding Jorge's hand. Several people came over to offer their condolences. Well, the adults did—the kids went off on their own, and the dean from Midtown High did likewise.

When Parker and his wife came over, he clasped her free hand in both of his and said sincerely, "I'm really sorry I couldn't have done more for Javier, Ms. Velasquez."

"You have nothing to be sorry for, Mr. Parker. You did everything you could. More than most. And I'll always be grateful to you for that." She even managed to give him a small smile through the veil.

Indicating the tall redhead next to him, Parker said, "This is my wife, Mary Jane Watson."

Parker's wife's smile could have lit up a Christmas tree. "Peter's said a lot of nice things about you, Ms. Velasquez—I wish we could've met under better circumstances. I'm sorry for your loss."

Bending over to look at Jorge, Parker said, "You must be Jorge."

Jorge nodded.

"I'm Mr. Parker—I was one of Javier's teachers. Maybe when you go to high school, I'll be your teacher too."

"I'd like that," Eileen said.

"'M not."

Looking down sharply at her son, Eileen said, "What are you saying, Jorge?"

"'M gonna die too, right?"

Eileen felt her chest tighten. "Oh God, no, baby, that's not gonna happen." She got down on one knee and let go of Jorge's hand so she could put both her hands on his shoulders. Looking him straight in the eye, she said, "I'm not gonna lose you too, Jorge. I won't let it happen. We're both gonna make it, you hear me?"

Jorge didn't say anything. Eileen supposed that was better than his denying it.

Soon enough, they walked out of the cemetery. Carlos's mother was still crying, and was being comforted by her remaining son. Eileen's sister was driving them all back to her house in Flushing so the family could gather, for which Eileen was grateful. She even invited the Parkers, but they politely declined, saying they'd promised to take Parker's aunt out for lunch.

After getting into the passenger seat of her sister's car, Eileen removed her cell phone from her purse and turned it on. As soon as she got a signal, the phone beeped to indicate voice mail. As her sister started the slow drive through the winding roads of the cemetery, she listened to the voice mail message.

"Hey, Ma, it's Orlando. Look, I'm—I'm sorry about Javier. He wasn't that bad of a kid—and even if he was, y'know, he deserved better than that. I tried to get some time off to come up, but my boss said he'd fire me if I didn't make my hours, and I can't really lose this job, y'know? So, uh, look—I'm sorry, okay? I'll try to call you later, Ma. Bye."

Eileen found herself playing the message a second time, simply refusing to believe that this was really Orlando.

But it was. Maybe he didn't make it up here, but he did make the effort—and he was considerate enough to call and say he'd call again later.

It wasn't much, but Eileen clung to the sound of her oldest son's voice like it was a life preserver.

Maybe there's a chance for this family after all. . . .

IT was a solemn Peter Parker who entered his aunt's house, his wife at his side. Both were dressed formally, and in black, having just returned from Javier Velasquez's funeral.

It was only their first funeral of the weekend. Tomorrow was Valerie McManus's. She'd died of radiation poisoning. Tonight was opening night of *The Z-Axis,* after two good preview performances, and Mary Jane told Peter that Dmitri had agreed—after much bitching and moaning—to dedicate the show to Valerie's memory.

For now, though, they were visiting Aunt May, who had been discharged from the hospital the previous night . . . and who was very lucky to be alive.

As soon as Peter walked in, a spring entered his step almost involuntarily as a familiar—and beloved—aroma caressed his nostrils.

She made wheat cakes. God, I love this woman.

By the time he reached the kitchen doorway, rational thought took over. He saw his aunt standing over the stove, wearing the KISS THE COOK apron he and Mary Jane had gotten her for her birthday, and fixed her with a stern gaze. "Aunt May, *what* are you doing? We were gonna take you *out* to eat."

"Don't be ridiculous. Now take a seat, both of you. These will be ready any second."

In a more gentle tone than Peter had used, Mary Jane said, "May, you really shouldn't be straining yourself like this—you just got out of the hospital."

As she turned her head, Peter saw a familiar twinkle in his aunt's eye. It was the one she got whenever she was about to lecture Peter or Uncle Ben. "When you get to be my age, getting up in the morning is straining yourself. Either you let it ruin what's left of your life, or you get used to it and do what you want."

Chuckling, Mary Jane said to Peter, "And people wonder where you get your stubborn streak."

"Oh, I don't wonder it at all." Peter loosened his tie and entered the kitchen. "Guess we should give in to the inevitable."

"Looks like, yeah."

Aunt May flipped over the wheat cakes, and then turned all the way around. "Now let me get a look at both of you." She shook her head. "My, but you look snappy. What a pity it took such an awful occasion to get you to look so nice."

"Yeah." Peter sat down at the kitchen table. "I'm glad we went. Javier wasn't a bad kid—well, okay, he *was* a bad kid, but still. I just wish I could've done more for him. Maybe if I'd had a chance . . ."

Mary Jane put her hand on his. "Tiger, don't start this *again*. You can't help everyone."

Aunt May slid the wheat cakes off the skillet and onto a serving plate. "But it's good that you try. Such a pity that Otto did what he did."

Shaking his head, Peter said, "I never did get what you saw in him."

"The same thing you saw in that boy," Aunt May said, the twinkle back in her eye. "Who knows? If Otto had had a teacher in high school who cared as much about him as you did about that boy, he might have become a productive member of society instead of the horrible man he turned into."

Peter thought back on what he knew about Ock before the accident. *What would he have been like if he had started out as a good person? Would having the power the arms gave him still have turned him bad?*

Then Peter thought about Hector. He had steered Betty to him, in the hopes that maybe he'd listen to her, since he'd shut Peter out ever since getting shot. However, based on the message Betty had left, she wasn't holding out any hope for him.

He speared his wheat cakes with a fork. "Maybe you're right, Aunt May. And maybe I *can't* help everyone, but I'm gonna try to help as many as I can." He popped the wheat cake into his mouth, and it proceeded to deliciously melt and explode all at the same time. For a brief moment, Peter was a teenager again, being fussed over by Aunt May and Uncle Ben.

"That's my boy. Oh, and did you get to see that press conference the other day?"

Nodding as he swallowed, Peter then said, "Yup. Shapiro didn't tell me he'd invited a camera crew along to Ock's capture—they were probably hiding behind one of the parked cars."

Predictably, a press conference had been held at the 24th Precinct announcing the arrests of both Trainer and Ock, which included Inspector Garcia's showing off the huge stash of Triple X they took from Trainer's house, while the commissioner sang the praises of Shapiro and the task force. New York 1, a local cable news station, also had footage of Ock's capture at the industrial park. Peter wasn't sure why a dinky cable station got that exclusive, nor was he entirely happy that the fourth estate had been invited to the takedown, but he wasn't about to argue with the good press, especially when the commissioner also thanked Spider-Man for his assistance—while a nearly apoplectic Shapiro looked on.

"I bet Jonah swallowed his cigar over that one," Peter added.

"Good," Aunt May said. "He's been riding you for far too long, and it's long past time you got proper credit for what you've done."

Laughing, Peter said, "Thanks, Aunt May."

The twinkle came back. "And what's so funny, young man?"

"It wasn't all that long ago that you were talking about 'that awful Spider-Man.'"

"It also wasn't all that long ago that I thought Otto was worth marrying.

But we all learn as we grow older, even when we're already old."

Turning to Mary Jane, Peter said, "Hey, speaking of proper credit, I never gave you yours."

"Me? What'd I do?" Mary Jane asked through a mouthful of wheat cakes.

"You were the one who talked Greg into talking to Shapiro. That's what got them the warrant for Trainer. That was a pretty big part of the whole thing."

Mary Jane patted her husband on the shoulder. "You can take all the credit, Tiger. I'll stick with acting."

Aunt May smiled. "I don't suppose there's the possibility of a seat at tonight's opening performance?"

Reaching behind her, Mary Jane unslung her purse from the back of the kitchen chair and removed an envelope from it. "Ask and ye shall receive. Two tickets, one for you and one for Aunt Anna."

Looking disappointed as she took the envelope, Aunt May asked, "Won't you be joining us, Peter?"

Peter shook his head. "Saturday nights are always bad out there, and there's still a turf war going on. And even though the Triple X is out of circulation, there's still plenty of it on the streets, which means more gamma-heads. I want to do what I can to keep the body count to a minimum. Besides," he added with a grin, "MJ could only get two freebies, and it's much better for two good-looking young single ladies to have a night on the town."

"Oh, Peter." Aunt May chuckled as she set the envelope aside. "Eat your wheat cakes."

"Yes, ma'am."

○————————○

THE sun shone brightly on West 100th Street, casting its warm glow on Una O'Leary's pale face. Wheeler and Fry had joined her for a quick pizza lunch, and they were on their way back from Sal & Carmine's on Broadway. All that was left for the Triple X Task Force was paperwork, which they'd been doing for two days straight—hence the need for a pizza break.

"Dr. Octopus. *Damn.*" Wheeler was shaking his head.

O'Leary looked up at Fry. "Has he said *anything* else for the last two days?"

Fry shook his head.

"You realize what this *means*?" Wheeler asked. "Press conferences, big drug busts, and Dr. Goddamn Octopus. And you were definitely right about the web-head, Una. I don't care what Shapiro and Shanahan say, he was definitely in the right."

"Wait a minute," Fry said, "you're admitting that you were wrong about something? I gotta write this down, mark this day on my calendar."

"Hey, I can admit when I screw up," Wheeler said defensively.

"You can't prove that with any evidence that'll stand up in court, Detective," O'Leary said with a cheeky grin.

"Fine, bust my chops all you want. Doesn't matter, 'cause I'm in too good a mood. You *know* we're all gonna get promoted for this."

"Except Shanahan," Fry said. "This close to his thirty, they ain't gonna waste the pension."

O'Leary nodded. "And don't be so sure about the rest of us. I bet Garcia takes all the credit—and maybe Shapiro, especially after he got the bust on TV." She smiled at that, remembering that Shapiro owed a favor from almost a year back to Rosita Sanchez, a New York 1 News TV reporter, which he repaid by giving her exclusive footage of the Octopus bust, footage that would be shown—with the NY1 logo in the corner—on every other news outlet in the world for at least a week or two, and which now meant the station owed the precinct a favor, which was always useful.

Wheeler was still grinning. "Best of all, we got lots of OT, which means I can put more to the fund."

Rolling her eyes, O'Leary said, "You're never gonna get that bike, Ty. You're gonna get distracted by some pretty little thing and spend all your motorcycle fund on her. I guarantee it."

As they arrived at the front door of the Two-Four, Wheeler said, "I'm telling you, that Harley will be *mine*."

"Yeah, yeah."

Sergeant Larsen intercepted them as soon as they entered. "I'm still waitin' for twenty-four-hour reports from all three of you."

"We *know*, Sarge," O'Leary said. "We'll do it right after the arrest paperwork, the CSU paperwork, the paperwork from the state cops, and the paperwork requesting permission to burn all paperwork."

"Very funny." Larsen turned around and headed to the men's room. "Oh yeah, you got some flowers from your boyfriend. It's on your desk."

O'Leary blinked. "I don't have a boyfriend."

"Coulda fooled me," he said as he went through the door.

Fry looked down at her. "Didn't you and Mike break up?"

"Twice." O'Leary went through the door that led up to the detective squad room.

"There's only one person it could be from," Wheeler said. "I mean, c'mon, she's been mooning over him the whole case."

"What are you *talking* about, Ty?" O'Leary asked with a murderous look at Wheeler as they started up the stairs.

"C'mon, Una, don't be so coy. Man of mystery, superstrong, agile— he's probably *great* in bed. You gonna get all kinky and make him keep the mask on?"

"You're gonna have a hard time riding that Harley after I break both your legs," she said as she entered the room.

Whoops and whistles sounded throughout the squad room as they came in. At the sight of her desk, O'Leary saw why: two dozen roses sat in a vase right next to her keyboard.

"So," Carter asked, a big grin on his face, "you two set a date yet?"

Petrocelli said, "Or is this a forbidden affair?"

"The love that dare not speak its name—or spin its web," Wheeler said, his grin matching Carter's.

Barron, the only other woman in the detective squad, walked up to her, put a friendly hand on her shoulder, and said, "Ignore them, Una. They're pigs. In fact, they'd have to improve to be as good as pigs."

"Which raises the question," Wheeler said, "of what's better, pigs or spiders?"

Deciding to take Barron's advice and ignore them, O'Leary instead walked over to her desk. The flowers were beautiful, and smelled fantastic, making the squad room—which always felt to O'Leary like it was one step removed from a locker room—a much more pleasant environment.

There was a note attached. THANKS FOR STICKING UP FOR ME. ALL THE BEST, FROM YOUR FRIENDLY NEIGHBORHOOD SPIDER-MAN. Also attached was a cell phone, which O'Leary realized was Ursitti's.

"So, is it gonna be a big church ceremony, or you gonna elope in the spider-cave?"

That was Shapiro, standing behind her. He did not look especially amused.

"Look, Jerry, he sent me flowers. It was probably because I actually treated him like a person instead of—"

"A vigilante? A masked scumbag who works outside the law?"

"How 'bout a person who helped you get Triple X off the streets, got you on TV as the guy who nailed Dr. Octopus, gave you a way to repay Sanchez in spades, and made the task force and the precinct look good to the bosses? Not to mention everything he did with the gamma-heads."

"We didn't need him."

"For all of it? Maybe not. But we wouldn't have gotten Octavius without him, and we'd have a lot more bodies without him."

Shapiro just stared at her for a second or two, then walked off without a word.

Guess I won't be inviting him to the wedding, she thought with a chuckle.

The jokes wouldn't be stopping for at least a week, but she didn't care. For years, she had been insisting that the NYPD would be better off working *with* the costumes instead of independently of them. This case had proved her right, finally.

Maybe some good will come out of it. . . .

○————————○

OTTO Octavius waited for his lawyer to arrive.

He sat alone in the huge visitors' room at Ryker's Island Penitentiary. Normally, up to two dozen prisoners could speak to visitors here, separated by special glass designed by Reed Richards of the Fantastic Four—proof not only against bullets, but most forms of direct energy. Today, however, Octavius had the place to himself, with all other visitations postponed until his was completed.

Surveillance cameras recorded every activity—though no sound, as the conversations that went on here were constitutionally protected. Three guards wearing specially designed armor stood at both the visitors' door and the door Octavius used to enter, supplementing the facility's guards. Those guards, as well as the ones in his cell block, which he had to himself, would remain for the duration of Octavius's stay. As far as the justice system was concerned, that span would be determined at Octavius's arraignment the following morning.

As far as Octavius was concerned, the span would be considerably shorter than that.

The door opened, and a tall, thin man with dark hair and small wire frame glasses held up by a large nose entered. This was Alan Schechter, Octavius's attorney. The Armani suit he wore had been purchased with the exorbitant fees that he had extracted from Octavius over the years.

Setting his briefcase down, Schechter took a seat opposite Octavius and picked up the phone that would allow him to converse with one hand. With the other, he opened the briefcase and removed a PDA.

"The guards out there are ridiculous," Schechter said. "And I understand they've got you isolated?"

Octavius, who had picked up his own phone, nodded. "I have the entire cell block to myself, yes."

"Tomorrow, I'll file a motion—this is cruel and unusual punishment. Without your arms—"

"Where are they?" Octavius asked a bit too eagerly. But he was always concerned when lesser minds had access to his arms.

"Right now they're in a federal facility." Using the wand for his PDA, he called up some information. "A warehouse in Elizabeth, New Jersey. I got a court order to keep them locked away there until your trial."

Octavius nodded. That could not have been an easy thing to accomplish—scientists were always eager to poke and prod at Octavius's work—and he found himself reminded as to how Schechter could justify taking so much of Octavius's money.

"In any case, I'll go to Judge Hernandez tomorrow and get them to move you—"

"Do not concern yourself. It is only fitting that they take such extraordinary precautions. I consider it a sign of respect that I so rarely get from law enforcement. Besides, the prattling of the other inmates annoys me."

Schechter nodded, and again used the wand on his PDA. "Fine. Anything else you need?"

"I find arraignments to be tedious. Anything you might do to delay this one until next week would be appreciated."

"Hm." Schechter tapped his cheek with the wand, then smiled and made a note on his PDA. "I've got a friend in the U.S. Attorney's Office. You were on government property when Spider-Man attacked you, and a lot of your outstanding warrants are federal. I should be able to get her to file a motion to have the case moved to Washington. It'll take at least a week to straighten it out."

Octavius smiled. "Excellent. By then, it will no longer matter. I will be gone from this place."

Schechter winced. "Will you *please* not tell me things like that? Lawyer-client privilege is one thing, but I'd just as soon you *didn't* make incriminating statements in my presence."

Scowling, Octavius said, "You work for me, Schechter, a job for which you are very well compensated. Do not presume to lecture me on what I can and cannot say."

"Fine, fine." Schechter made a few more notes, and then carried on about other legal minutiae that Octavius found tedious to deal with—which was another reason he paid Schechter so well.

The secondary aspects of his plan had gone imperfectly. In retrospect, he should not have entrusted that to Carolyn. Though she had great enthusiasm, she lacked subtlety. And by targeting Hunt, Haight, May Parker, and the others, he'd provided a signpost to allow the police and the arachnid to suspect him.

But his capture and incarceration were of little consequence. The designer drug had already served its true purpose: of providing him with sufficient income to at last bring his latest plan to fruition.

Soon enough, the world would tremble at his feet. . . .

o———o

SPIDER-MAN swung out over the Bridgeview Houses, heading homeward after a long night. He had stopped a group of Ray-Ray's old crew, now run by a guy called "Blowback," before they were about to go shoot things, and the cops apparently got a tip on one of the Ukrainians' stash houses, so there was no turf war tonight. He'd encountered a few more gamma-heads, including a couple who were menacing some theatregoers on 45th Street and a bunch of college kids stomping through the Cloisters.

Just one more thing to take care of.

Swinging around the Houses for a few minutes, he finally found what he was looking for. Lowering himself on a web-line, he hung over a tree above the bench on which his quarry sat.

"Hi there, Albert."

The junkie looked up in surprise. "No-face! The hell *you* want, boy?"

Reaching into a compartment of his belt, Spider-Man pulled out a crisp five-dollar bill. "Just wanted to pay up my debt. You said five bucks was the going rate for the intel you gave me, right?"

"Uh—yeah, I guess. Don't remember—just remember that you ain't got no face."

Spider-Man hesitated. Albert would probably just spend this money on more drugs. *Although, based on how slurred his voice is, he's probably already high. Maybe I'll get lucky and he'll get some food. And if not—at least I can't say I didn't try.*

He handed Albert the bill. Albert stared at it for a second. "You should keep it. Buy y'self a face."

"I'll be fine. But you look like you could use a bowl of soup."

"Guess I *am* a little hungry." Albert snatched the bill. "Thanks, No-Face Man."

"You're welcome."

With that, Spider-Man climbed up his web-line to the tree, shot out another line, and swung toward home and his wife and his bed for a good—and, he thought, well-earned—night's sleep.

ACKNOWLEDGMENTS

PRIMARY thanks go to my enthusiastic, encouraging, and excitable editor, Ed Schlesinger, who has been an absolute joy to work with; my effervescent agent, Lucienne Diver; and the ever-encouraging publisher Scott Shannon.

Secondary thanks to Stan Lee and Steve Ditko, without whom we wouldn't have Spider-Man, and to the dear departed *Electric Company* children's show, which introduced me as a kid in the 1970s to Spidey.

Tertiary thanks to various Spidey scribes who've written the character in both comics and prose form in the years since Stan and Steve's day, and to whom I also owe a huge debt: Pierce Askegren, Samm Barnes, Brian Michael Bendis, Kurt Busiek, John Byrne, Adam-Troy Castro, Chris Claremont, Gerry Conway, Peter David, Tom DeFalco, J.M. DeMatteis, Todd Dezago, Diane Duane, Eric Fein, Danny Fingeroth, Craig Shaw Gardner, Glenn Greenberg, Paul Grist, Paul Jenkins, Terry Kavanagh, Howard Mackie, Bill Mantlo, David Michelinie, Mark Millar, Fabian Nicieza, Denny O'Neil, Jim Owsley (aka Christopher Priest), Dean Wesley Smith, Roger Stern, J. Michael Straczynski, Brian K. Vaughan, John Vornholt, Zeb Wells, and dozens of others that I know I neglected to mention by name. I would also be remiss if I didn't thank my collaborators on two previous pieces of Spidey prose: John Gregory Betancourt (my cohort on "An Evening in the Bronx with Venom") and José R. Nieto (my partner in crime on *Venom's Wrath*).

Village Playhouse Central is very loosely based on the Manhattan Theatre Source in Greenwich Village. Like VPC, MTS has musicians playing in the lobby before showtime—I know, because I've been one of those musicians several times. Thanks to all the good people there who've treated me well. Trust me, any negative aspects of VPC were for dramatic purposes and in no way reflect on the fine folks at MTS.

Thanks also to Ian Wakefield, Bruno Maglione, Ruwan Jayatilleke, and all the other fine folks at Marvel; the New York Police Department's most excellent and informative website (http://www.nyc.gov/html/nypd/home.html); SpiderFan.org, the best online resource of info about this novel's hero; the Elitist Bastards, just on general principles; Magnum Comics in the Bronx, which had back issues when I rather desperately needed them; and Tom Brevoort and Kurt Busiek, for some timely research assistance.

The usual gangs of idiots: the Geek Patrol, the Malibu folks, the Forebearance, CITH, CGAG, all the people at Riverdale Kenshikai, and the folks on various online bulletin boards, e-mail lists, and LiveJournal, who all keep me going to some degree or other. Also them that live with me, both human and feline, who do likewise.

Finally, a big thank you to some folks I worked with in the past, who deserve a moment of due respect in print: Keith Aiken, Jeff Albrecht, Nathan Archer, Pierce Askegren, Michael Asprion, Terry Austin, Dick Ayers, Mark Bagley, Robin Wayne Bailey, Steve Behling, Julie Bell, eluki bes shahar, John Gregory Betancourt, Dennis Brabham, Ginjer Buchanan, Mark Buckingham, Jim Burns, John Buscema, Kurt Busiek, Steven Butler, Richard Lee Byers, Dennis Calero, Adam-Troy Castro, Joey Cavalieri, Joe Chiodo, Manny Clark, Dave Cockrum, Nancy A. Collins, Richard Corben, Greg Cox, Roger Cruz, Peter David, James Dawson, Tom DeFalco, Tom De Haven, Thomas Deja, Dave DeVries, Sharman DiVono, Colleen Doran, Max Douglas, John S. Drew, Diane Duane, Jo Duffy, Tammy Lynne Dunn, Emily Epstein, Vince Evans, Steve Fastner, Eric Fein, Danny Fingeroth, Sholly Fisch, Ron Frenz, Michael Jan Friedman, James W. Fry III, Alex Gadd, John Garcia, Craig Shaw Gardner, Gabriel Gecko, Christopher Golden, Glenn Greenberg, Ken Grobe, Tom Grummett, Bob Hall, Ed Hannigan, Tony Harris, Glenn Hauman, Doug Hazlewood, Jennifer Heddle, C.J. Henderson, Jason Henderson, Greg and Tim Hildebrandt, Nancy Holder, Bob Ingersoll, Tony Isabella, Bruce Jensen, Joe Jusko, K.A. Kindya, Scott Koblish, Dori Koogler, Ray Lago, Michelle LaMarca, Andy Lane, Bob Larkin, Katherine Lawrence, Stan Lee, Steve Leialoha, John Paul Leon, Rick Leonardi, Rebecca Levene, Clarice Levin, Steve Lightle,

Ron Lim, Scott Lobdell, Steve Lyons, Elliot S! Maggin, Alexander Maleev, Leonardo Manco, Ashley McConnell, Bob McLeod, David Michelinie, Grant Miehm, Al Milgrom, Tom Morgan, Will Murray, Duane O. Myers, José R. Nieto, Ann Nocenti, Patrick Olliffe, John J. Ordover, Carol Page, George Pérez, Dan Persons, Byron Preiss, Ayesha Randolph, Bill Reinhold, Darick Robertson, Madeleine E. Robins, Steven A. Roman, John Romita Sr., Luis Royo, Paul Ryan, Jenn Saint-John, Joe St. Pierre, Robert Sheckley, Evan Skolnick, Louis Small Jr., Dave Smeds, Dean Wesley Smith, Steranko, Michael Stewart, Steve Rasnic Tem, Mike Thomas, Stan Timmons, Juda Tverski, Deborah Valcourt, Brian K. Vaughan, John Vornholt, Matt Wagner, Robert L. Washington III, Lawrence Watt-Evans, Len Wein, Richard C. White, Casey Winters, Chuck Wojtkiewicz, James A. Wolf, J. Steven York, Mike Zeck, Ann Tonsor Zeddies, Phil Zimelman, Dwight Jon Zimmerman, and Howard Zimmerman.

ABOUT THE AUTHOR

KEITH R.A. DECANDIDO'S writing career has spanned twenty-five years. In addition to his original novels he's produced licensed fiction that includes TV shows (*Star Trek*, *Supernatural*), games (*Summoner's War*, *World of Warcraft*), movies (*Cars*, *Serenity*), and comics (Spider-Man, Thor). In 2009 the International Association of Media Tie-in Writers gave him a Lifetime Achievement Award. Keith is a third-degree black belt in karate, and avidly follows the NY Yankees.

Book Three

DROWNED IN THUNDER

by Christopher L. Bennett

For Angela,

who's MJ and Gwen rolled into one.

THE whole problem with the world is that fools and fanatics are always so certain of themselves, but wiser people so full of doubts.
—Bertrand Russell

HISTORIAN'S NOTE

DROWNED in *Thunder* does not require the reader to be familiar with the specifics of *Spider-Man* comics continuity. For the benefit of continuity buffs, however, this novel takes place after Mary Jane begins her theatrical career but before Spider-Man joins the Avengers. It also takes place before the transformation Spider-Man underwent in *Spectacular Spider-Man* 15–20 ("Disassembled," August–December 2004).

ONE

IN THE CHILL

IT was a bright and stormy night.

It never got particularly dark in midtown Manhattan, except when acts of nature or supervillainy resulted in blackouts. It was at night, Peter Parker thought as he gazed down at the city from rooftop level, that New York City most clearly displayed the abundance of life and energy that made it the most exciting city in the world, as millions of multicolored lights from windows, signs, streetlights, spotlights, and cars shone out in defiance of darkness, declaring to the universe that New Yorkers were about their business and would not let anything as mundane as the rotation of the Earth tell them when to sleep.

Which was good for Peter Parker, since at the moment he was attired from head to toe in red-and-blue spandex and free-falling from a twenty-odd-story building, relying on a thin strand of webbing fired from his wrist to adhere to the next skyscraper and swing him safely forward down Eighth Avenue. This was just part of the routine nightly patrol of a friendly neighborhood Spider-Man, and the bright lights were an invaluable aid to him in seeing where he was going, as well as keeping an eye peeled for crimes and crises in the streets below.

But stormy? That was another matter. Even on a normal day, Spider-Man had to be alert to the vagaries of the high-altitude winds that gusted between the towers, amplified by the wind-tunnel effect of Manhattan's canyonesque streets. A strand of spiderweb, even the scaled-up synthetic-polymer stuff that sprayed from Spidey's webshooters, was a gossamer thing, easily blown off course by a sudden gust. Web-slinging was a thrilling, liberating way to travel, fifty times better than any roller-coaster ride—

totally unconfined, soaring and swooping at exhilarating speed, free from the miasma of car exhaust and cigarette smoke and the perpetual game of chicken played by hypercompetitive drivers, pedestrians, and cyclists. But it would have been a suicidal undertaking if not for Peter's "spider-sense"—the preternaturally heightened awareness of his surroundings that a fateful bite from an irradiated spider had given him years ago, along with the proportional strength and agility of that selfsame arachnid. The spider-sense tingle in his head alerted him to imminent attack by his many foes, let him dodge bullets before they left the barrel, and so on, but it also helped him at more mundane tasks—like sensing that the web strand he was about to fire would be blown off course by a sudden shift in the wind, giving him the chance to adjust his aim to compensate.

Well, most of the time! Spidey thought, as an extra-strong gust kicked in just after he'd depressed his palm-mounted trigger and let the web fluid spray out into a long, quick-drying strand aimed at the New Yorker Hotel. The wind yanked it back over his shoulder, and he promptly released the trigger, letting the strand fly free as the pinch valve cut it off. Long experience had taught him not to release one webline until the next had found an anchor, so he allowed himself to continue his upswing as he sighted and fired again. The webline struck the Art Deco hotel higher on its ziggurat-like upper half than he'd intended, meaning that as he swung forward, his webline would get hung up on the corner of the lowest terrace. He readied himself for it, letting it swing him around sideways to alight on the Eighth Avenue face of the building, clinging to the wall with his hands and feet.

And slipping. Normally, his digits could adhere to just about any surface. But the wind was accompanied by a steadily worsening rainfall, making the hotel's brown brick surface slippery. It wasn't too bad yet—all it took was a little more pressure to secure himself. "But if this rain keeps getting worse," he muttered to his masked reflection in a darkened window, "maybe I'd better take the F train home instead." A flash of lightning and the subsequent clap of thunder, too close for comfort, drove home the point. Like the real thing, his synthetic webbing was nonconductive when dry, but could carry a charge when wet. And lightning tended to strike at the tops of buildings, making them less-than-ideal places to hang around (or from) in weather like this.

Unfortunately, he didn't have a change of clothes handy to let him ride the subway as Peter Parker. He'd gone directly out on patrol from his LoHo apartment, but hadn't realized he'd forgotten to check the weather report until he was halfway to Greenwich Village. And he couldn't call Mary Jane to do it for him, since—as usual these days—his lovely wife was out rehearsing for her latest off-Broadway play. He'd tried sticking his head in a couple of windows and asking if anyone would be so kind as to switch on the Weather Channel for him, but it was just his luck that both apartments' occupants had belonged to that sizable segment of the New York populace who considered him a menace rather than a hero. The first had come at him with a baseball bat, and the second had roused the entire neighborhood with her screams and accusations of attempted ravishment. Both times, he'd found a hasty retreat preferable to sticking around to offer explanations to neighbors and police. And since then he'd been kept busy proving his naysayers wrong (not that they'd notice) with various acts of derring-do against the forces of crime and chaos, so that even though he'd sensed the oncoming storm, he'd been unable to wend his way homeward in time to avoid the rain.

"Why couldn't spider-sense come with a long-range forecast?" he asked the universe at large as he shot out another strand of webbing, making sure it anchored securely on Five Penn Plaza before he swung into action again. "Scattered showers this evening, with a 30 percent chance of Scorpion. Tomorrow, hail of .38-caliber bullets is expected. And now, here's Joey with sports." Okay, so he was talking to himself. It was a habit he indulged in when he got nervous. He talked to himself quite a bit.

Now the rain was starting to fall harder, the lightning coming more often, and he tried to pick up the pace toward home, veering east to soar over Madison Square Garden and continue diagonally across the next few blocks toward Broadway, planning to follow it and the Bowery toward home. But halfway between Seventh and Eighth, he felt a faint, familiar tingle of danger raising his hackles. The rainfall interfered with his arachnid senses as well as his normal ones, but not yet enough to obscure a twinge this strong. He tasted it like a connoisseur: sharp, angry, but removed, an act of human violence a couple of blocks away, not aimed directly at him—not yet, anyway. A fraction of a second later, the sounds of a gunshot and screaming reached his ears, then again as they echoed off the Two Penn Plaza building behind him. From the way the tingle intensified as he swung, he could home in on the incident better than he could from the sounds alone. It led him back north, toward Herald Square.

Even as he homed in, the physical horripilation of the spider-sense was accompanied by a familiar anxiety. Not the kind of anxiety a normal, sane person (the kind of person who wouldn't go out in public in red-and-blue spandex) would feel upon rushing headlong into a gun battle; he'd been in so many of those, and faced so much worse, that they held no terror for him anymore. What did fill him with terror was the question: *Am I too late? If I hadn't let myself get slipped up by the wind and rain, could I have swung by here in time to sense the danger before the shot was fired? Did a human being just die because I failed to do enough—again?*

Spider-Man knew he couldn't be everywhere, couldn't save everyone. He'd long since grown accustomed to that bitter truth. But he could not forgive himself for the lives he could have saved and failed to.

Time for that later, Pete. Right now, if there were other lives in the balance, he wouldn't let them down.

As he reached Broadway and swung into his descent, he spotted his quarry. A gang of thieves was running out of Macy's, heading for a getaway van, while a wobbly security guard tried to get a bead on them with his pistol. The guard's other hand was clutching his upper right arm, its sleeve stained red—a minor injury, little more than a graze if he could still hold his gun. A surge of relief went through Spidey. No one had died—yet. But this was a crowded intersection, and the guard's aim was shaky. New York's Finest were trained not to fire their weapons in a crowd, but would this rent-a-cop have as much sense?

Spidey couldn't risk it. He needed to catch both the thieves and the guard off, well, their guards. Landing on the green metal awning over the front doors, he raised the hem of his tunic to expose his utility belt and triggered the spider-signal (his admittedly pretentious name for what was essentially a cheap belt-buckle flashlight with a spider-mask transparency over its lens), aiming it at the thieves. But nothing happened. *Confound it! The batteries are dead!*

He couldn't waste any more time. Leaping to perch above a window in front of the guard, he pressed his two middle fingers down on the web trigger with firm, continuous pressure, causing the fluid to come out as a thick gluey stream that clogged the guard's gun barrel. "Hold it!" he called. "Too many people around! Let me handle them!"

"Screw that!" the guard cried. "You're probably with 'em!"

"Let me guess—another satisfied subscriber to the *Daily Bugle.*" The guard was pulling at the web-glob on his gun, trying to get it free. Just to keep him from accidentally pulling the trigger and blowing his hand off with the backfire, Spidey shot out a thin strand to snag the gun and yanked it away, letting it fall atop the flat surface of the front-door awning, safely out of reach. Then he fired another glob of webbing to coat the guard's wounded arm as a makeshift bandage. "That should hold you until the ambulance arrives. Put that in your next letter to the editor."

Now the bad guys' van was screeching out into Broadway traffic, so Spidey set off in pursuit. But during his little heart-to-heart with the guard, the sky had opened up. He tried firing a strand of webbing to snag the getaway van. His original webbing formula wouldn't have solidified in heavy rainfall, but he'd long ago licked that problem. However, solidified or not, the light strand was pummeled to the ground by the torrent before it could reach the van. Spidey was forced to pursue the thieves on foot. Fortunately, superstrength meant superspeed as well—not in Quicksilver's league, but more than enough to catch up with a van in Manhattan traffic during a downpour. Especially since he could leap from roof to roof across the cars. A stream of honks and curses from disgruntled drivers followed him. *Ah, the lullaby of Broadway.*

Finally, he landed atop the getaway van as it tore through Korea Town. Pulling open the rear doors, he ducked his head down to see what he was facing. After years of experience, the fact that he was seeing it upside down was no impediment—but the raindrops drenching his mask lenses were another matter. Everything was a marbled blur of movement. Luckily, there were no raindrops between him and the occupants of the van, so his spider-sense was able to warn him of the imminent gunfire and let him pull his head up out of the way before the shots rang out. "It's the bug!" someone in the van cried.

The bug? What was the world coming to? In the old days, whenever he swung down on a gang of hoods, he could always count on one of them to cry out "Spider-Man!" like an emcee giving an introduction. These days, it seemed, they just took him for granted. *Where's the respect?*

He didn't even need spider-senses to know what would happen next; he'd seen enough action movies for it to be obvious. Bad guys in vehicle plus hero on roof equals perforated roof. These guys must have seen the same movies, since the rain of lead from below came right on cue, counterpointing the rain from above. But Spidey was already leaping out of the way, starting to flip around the rear edge of the van's roof like a gymnast on a bar. With the thieves firing upward, he could come right in through the back doors and take them down with a double kick.

Except that wasn't the way it happened. He'd grown used to relying on the adhesion of his fingertips rather than a good firm grip, and in the heat of the moment he forgot to override that reflex on account of rain. All his fingers adhered to was a bunch of water molecules, so instead of doing a graceful two-axis flip and landing inside the van, Spider-Man tumbled hard onto the rain-slicked pavement. Only the sound of a horn and screeching tires warned him of the oncoming car, and only his heightened reflexes let him roll out of the way in time. *But the bruises to my pride may be terminal. Brilliant move, web-for-brains. And on top of everything else, now I've got "Lullaby of Broadway" stuck in my head.* "That's it," he said, leaping to his feet and over car roofs in pursuit of the van once more. *The rumble of the subway train . . . a-jing-a-jing . . . the rattle of the ta-a-xis . . . stop that!*

But it was getting harder to see; not only were his lenses covered in rain, but in these cold, wet conditions they were starting to fog up on the inside as his breathing grew harder. He landed too far forward on a yellow cab and went sliding on his can over the hood. "Hah!" the cabbie cried. "Good move, web-ass!"

"Yeah, well—use less Turtle Wax next time! And get outta here, they've got guns!"

"Hey, don't tell me where to drive, creep! And get off my cab before I start the meter!"

Gritting his teeth in frustration, Spidey wiped off his right lens with his glove, got a good grip on it with his fingertips, and tore it clear out of the mask so he could see where he was going. He stuffed it in his utility belt for safekeeping as he set out after the van once again. But it wasn't much of an improvement, since there was now nothing to keep the fat raindrops from battering his right eye and making it sting. He had to hold his hand over his exposed eye as he ran. *Note to self: invent umbrella that can fit in utility belt. Naah—on a night like this, it'd get blown away in two seconds.*

The gunmen were taking potshots from the back of the van again. *I've got to stop them fast, before they kill someone!* But how? The rain was pummeling him so hard it gave him flashbacks to his last battle with Hydro-Man. His webs were useless, his sticky fingers were useless, his spider-sense was useless—*and I'm getting chilled to the bone in these sopping-wet tights.* He could do what he usually did when he had to let the bad guys go and fire a spider-tracer at the van—but the hammering downpour would interfere with that as surely as with his webs. What did he have left?

Only the proportional strength of a spider, you idiot! he realized. He needed to throw something big at the shooters, and fast. But what? He looked down for a manhole cover, but the gun battle had brought traffic to a standstill, and every manhole in range had a car tire planted solidly atop it.

Just then, a horn blared from behind him, and a familiar voice followed. "Hey, web-ass, I got fares to get to! Outta the freakin' way!"

For the first time this night, Spider-Man grinned. It was just too perfect.

The cabbie's reaction when Spidey ripped the hood off his cab was not one that Peter Parker's former newspaper colleagues would have deemed printable. Neither was the reaction of the thieves in the van as they saw it flying toward them almost faster than their eyes could track. But their curses were cut off abruptly when the hood slammed into them, knocking them against the back of the van and felling them for the count. Unfortunately, the cabbie was not so easily silenced. But at least he still had breath to draw.

The van swerved, its driver startled by the impact from behind, and slammed into the back of a parked car. Spidey ran to confront the driver, ripping off the door, but found him dazed as his airbag deflated before him. Spidey's webshooters were still waterlogged, so he gave the guy enough of a tap on the jaw to send him to dreamland until the cops came—which, judging from the sirens he could now hear over the rain and thunder, would be any moment.

He took a moment to check the two thieves in the back, since he'd hit them pretty hard with that cab hood. One of them had broken ribs, the other a broken arm from trying to block the collision, but both their vitals were strong. That was a relief. He didn't like getting this rough when he could avoid it, not against mere mortals, and was glad he had as potent a nonlethal weapon as his webs to fall back on most of the time. But circumstances had left him no choice but to employ greater force to protect innocent bystanders. He was lucky the damage hadn't been worse.

Still, he knew the cops wouldn't be inclined to see it that way, so he made his retreat in haste, ducking into the nearest alley. The walls would still be too rain-slicked to climb, so he jumped up to the nearest fire escape (a short hop for someone who could clear three stories in a single bound) and clambered to the roof. Leaping from rooftop to rooftop, he made his way clear of the area, knowing the police would be searching for him, wanting as always to bring him in for "questioning" about the incident. Really, he couldn't blame them; all too often, the villains he caught were out on the streets again before long since they couldn't be convicted without his testimony. But falling into police hands would mean the exposure of his identity. The first time it had happened, years ago, a sympathetic police captain named George Stacy had forbidden the removal of his mask pending a legal consultation over his civil liberties. Spidey had subsequently escaped before the matter could be resolved. But Captain Stacy was long dead, and few in the police today would be as concerned with protecting his identity. And civil liberties weren't exactly fashionable in recent times, especially for the superpowered. Despite the risk of letting the bad guys walk, he just couldn't reveal his identity and operate openly. There were too many people he cared about, people who would no doubt become targets if his enemies knew who he was. It had happened too many times already.

Am I doing the right thing? he asked himself for the millionth time as he huddled under a rooftop water tower and waited for the rain to let up. *Swinging around in a mask, beating up the bad guys as a rogue element? I could work for the government, get my loved ones in witness protection. I could try to join the Avengers and work as part of the system. I could sell my web formula to the police, let them use it to catch crooks while I stay home and focus on my family.*

But every time Peter Parker's thoughts went in that direction, they came back to the one argument he could never escape. Once, he had been willing to leave the fight to someone else. Once, after he'd first gotten his powers and begun using them for profit as a TV showman, he had stood by and let a burglar escape even though he'd had the power to stop him. And that burglar had gone on to murder Peter's Uncle Ben.

As long as I have this great power, I have to shoulder the great responsibility that goes with it. I can't risk letting anyone else die because I failed to act. He knew that implicitly. It was why he had begun using his Spider-Man identity and powers to fight crime, why he continued doing so to this day despite the constant hardships and dangers. And though he often wondered if his methods really were the most responsible way of wielding his powers, every alternative he'd ever tried had been too limiting, too much of a compromise. There were things he could only do as an independent operator, skirting the letter of the law in the name of a more fundamental justice.

But is it worth the trade-off? Is there a better way I'm overlooking?

As always, the only answer to that question was a roaring silence. Followed by a roaring sneeze that he just barely had time to lift his mask for. "Just what I need—to come down with a cold." All he wanted now was to get home, to get out of his wet Spidey suit and into a nice hot tub. Hopefully with the magnificent Mrs. Mary Jane Watson-Parker as his companion. She was the one who made it all worthwhile, who kept him strong and hopeful in spite of everything. She was the one person he would give up being Spider-Man for, and yet her support and understanding of his double life were what enabled him to carry on as Spider-Man. The anticipation of going home to her at the end of the night was what gave him the strength to keep fighting through all odds and never give in to defeat. Just the thought of it warmed him, and inspired him to push off toward home again. It was only twenty or so blocks now.

But then the alarms started sounding from the other direction, then the screams started, and Spidey sighed heavily, reversing course. MJ would just have to wait a little longer.

TWO

SPINS A WEB, ANY SIZE

IT wasn't until morning that Spider-Man was finally able to make his way back to the building where he resided as Peter Parker. Hoping his waterlogged spider-sense had cleared up enough to alert him if anyone was watching, he slipped down to his apartment via the fire escape. Luckily, the only spectator was Barker, the very strange and ugly Rottweiler living in the apartment across the way, whose chief activity seemed to be staring menacingly at Peter's window—when he wasn't having dress parties thrown for him by his doting owner Caryn or making strange noises inside her apartment. Despite the lack of spider-sense tingle, Peter sometimes suspected Barker of being a closet supervillain.

Even if that were true, though, he was too tired to bother with it now, so he just climbed in through his apartment window and pulled off his mildew-scented mask. "Hi, honey, I'm home," he called out feebly.

He was hoping for a warm embrace from his gorgeous wife, a caring lecture on making her stay up all night worrying about him, and then that nice hot morning bath together. Instead, Mary Jane just stuck her copper-tressed head briefly into the bedroom, and said, "Hey, honey. Rough night?" in a distracted tone.

"I've had better," he said, peeling off his gloves and shirt. "I tried climbing up a waterspout, but down came the rain and washed me out. You'll never guess what happened next. Come here, and I'll tell you all about it."

"Ohh, I can't. I'm running late for rehearsal as it is." She rushed in and gave him a quick peck on the lips, but hurried away before he could respond.

"Hey, that's all I get?"

"Sorry—can't go to rehearsal smelling like wet superhero. We'll talk tonight, okay, tiger? Love ya, 'bye!" And like that, she was gone.

After a few moments, Peter snapped his mouth shut, lowered his outstretched hand, and sighed. It wasn't what he'd been hoping for, but he couldn't just think of himself. MJ may have been his loving helpmate and all, but she had her own life to lead. After years as a successful supermodel and struggling actress, she'd found it difficult to get casting directors to take her seriously as more than a pretty face (make that ravishing face, and long, shimmering red hair, and legs that went on forever, and . . . ahem). Aside from a brief soap-opera gig a few years back, she'd found it difficult to get cast as anything other than skimpily attired love interests in B-grade action movies. And she was growing keenly aware, as she edged closer to thirty, that the shelf life of a supermodel-cum-Hollywood-starlet was severely limited and that she would need to branch out eventually for the sake of sheer survival. So she'd recently taken up a theatrical career to improve her chops as an actress and broaden her long-term career options. Combined with the occasional modeling work she still did to pay the bills, it kept her busier than ever.

Indeed, MJ had become consumed by it lately. The critics had panned her turn as Lady Macbeth, dismissing it as stunt casting while dismissing her as a gorgeous face with little beneath it. (The wisecracks had been predictable, at least for those who knew their Bard: "All flower and no serpent." "Unsexpot me here!") Since then, she had striven to work harder on her acting and was throwing herself fully into her new play, trying to make the most of her supporting role. She seemed to be devoting every available minute of her life to the rehearsal process, either with the cast at the theater or at home running over her lines.

There were moments—okay, maybe more than moments—when Peter resented the competition for her time. He'd been without her for far too long. Last year a man had abducted her and faked her death, holding her prisoner for months before Spider-Man had finally rescued her. He had been profoundly relieved to have her back, but it hadn't lasted. She'd needed time to recover from the trauma and find herself, to compensate for the feelings of helplessness she'd endured for so long. And so she had left him for a time, moving to Los Angeles and working to build a life for herself as something other than Mrs. Spider-Man.

She'd succeeded in that goal; the work she'd gotten might not have been as classy as she'd hoped, but she'd regained her belief that she was strong and resourceful enough to get by on her own and stand up to hardship. And Peter had finally won her back when he'd convinced her, not long ago, that he depended on her strength and love to keep him going. Every day, he was thankful that she had been willing to come back to him. But it was frustrating that her new career left her so little time for him, especially when he still felt as though he'd only just found her again. He knew, though, that MJ felt the same way about his web-slinging career, and yet she accepted and supported it in spite of everything. Peter owed her no less.

Besides, she had a point. He held up his tunic, studied it, caught a whiff of it, and turned away. "She's right, Petey. Being Spider-Man stinks sometimes." He sneezed violently. "And if I can smell it through this congestion—bro-ther!"

On top of which, he realized, he had less than an hour to get to Midtown High (his oddly misnamed alma mater over in Queens), or his Honors Bio students would be without a teacher—again. He was already having enough trouble keeping his part-time teaching gig despite his frequent absences and his limited ability to come up with good excuses for them. The only reason Midtown High kept him around was because there was a shortage of decent science teachers in the public school system, at least ones brave enough to take on the rough-edged inner-city students placed in his charge. Years of battling the Green Goblin, Dr. Octopus, Kraven the Hunter, and Venom had prepared him for the challenge of facing a class of surly, suspicious, possibly armed teenagers and trying to convince them to open their minds to new ideas. Well, it had almost prepared him. Battling supervillains was actually easier since he could just hit them when they didn't cooperate.

Plus, at least he had adrenaline to keep him going in a fight. Today, after a sleepless night in the pounding rain and only a quick shower, coffee, breakfast, and more coffee to get him past it, he had to stand in front of a roomful of canny, recalcitrant teenagers and convince them he knew what he was talking about—or at least that he was awake. He'd worked hard to penetrate their skepticism over the past few months, but he knew that if he showed any sign of weakness, he risked losing them. Though with the head cold he had coming on, it was a struggle even to speak coherently. *Thank heaven I have years of experience learning to enunciate clearly through a full-face mask.*

His lecture on genetically modified organisms didn't go so well, however. Susan Labyorteaux, a slightly chubby, blonde-haired senior from a strongly religious background, didn't react well to the subject, any more than she had to his talks on evolution in earlier classes. "We shouldn't be tampering with God's design for nature," she insisted. "We don't have the right."

"Yeah," put in Bobby Ribeiro, a slim boy from an Afro-Cuban family. "And who knows what kinda monsters we could make? Damn scientists shouldn't mess with things they don't understand." Some of the students nodded and made noises of agreement.

"Well, you're not the first people to raise objections," Peter said. "A lot of stores won't sell foods with GMOs in them, and there are even laws restricting their use. And you're right, Bobby, that there are things that can go wrong if we're not careful.

"But the fact is, we've all been eating genetically altered foods all our lives." At the students' startled reactions, he explained. "That's right— virtually every food item we eat has been altered from its native form through centuries of domestication and selective breeding. Take bananas. They're handy, convenient, uniform. They have nice protective skins that can easily be peeled off and even come with built-in handles. You think nature made them that way?"

"God did," Susan said.

"Yeah, I saw it in a George Burns movie," interposed Joan Rubinoff, the class clown. Susan didn't join in the chuckling, but didn't get angry at Joan either, being an easygoing sort despite her impassioned beliefs.

"Actually, God didn't," Peter said, "not directly, anyway. Wild bananas are small, tough, green, practically inedible things. Bananas as we know them today are the product of centuries of artificial breeding. Heck, they can't even reproduce naturally anymore, since they're seedless. They're all literal clones—in the original sense of a plant grown from a cutting, not the Dolly-the-sheep sense—that came from a single original plant. In fact, that's cause for concern, because if a disease comes along that can infect them, it could kill every banana plant in the world because none of them would be genetically different enough to survive. And that could ruin the economies of whole countries—not to mention breakfasts the world over."

'Well, that just shows how wrong it is to try to play God," Susan said. "We can't do it well enough."

Peter had always found that argument a little strange. Humans were God's children, right? And didn't most parents *want* their kids to follow in their footsteps? But he supposed Susan's point was that humanity was still too childish for the responsibility. "Maybe," Peter acknowledged. "But can you suggest a way to fix the problem without using genetic engineering to add more variety to bananas?"

"No," she admitted. "But that doesn't mean there isn't one."

"Fair enough. Still, bananas are just one case." He went on to give them more examples of how humans had been "tampering with nature" for centuries. He told them about how natural carrots were purple and had been specifically bred to be orange to pay tribute to the royal house of Orange. Though in his condition it came out sounding more like "Ordge."

"But that's not the same," Bobby stressed. "That's just breeding things naturally, not reaching in with tools and screwing around with their genes."

As usual, Bobby was quick to find a good counter-argument. Peter admired his deft, independent thinking, his insistence on asking questions rather than just passively writing down what his teachers said without bothering to consider it as anything more than a rote answer for the next test. But it made him a tough sell, particularly today, when Peter had to struggle to make his own brain work. "Well, um . . ." It took him a moment to remember the response he'd prepared for such a question. "Reaching in with tools, you say. Well, the thing is, the main tools that are actually used in genetic engineering are viruses. And for them, sticking new sequences into other organisms' genes *is* natural. Scientists estimate that as much as . . . umm . . . as much as 8 percent of the normal human genome already consists of genes that retroviruses have been splicing into it for countless millions of years. You could say that modern genetic techniques are just a way of harnessing that natural process to serve human objectives rather than viral ones." In the back of his mind, he pondered a new question that might be worth exploring if he ever willed his body to science. Did that irradiated spider have a retrovirus in its system? Was it really the virus, rather than the spider, that had been altered by the radiation? Had it spread throughout his body as an infection and inserted genes taken from the spider into his own genes?

He realized that he'd let his mind wander, and the class was staring at him expectantly. 'Anyway, um, for our purposes, the main difference between selective breeding and gene-splicing is that gene-splicing is much more precise. Instead of slamming two whole genomes together and hoping you get good results with few side effects, you can go in and change exactly what you want and leave the rest alone. It's like the difference between microsurgery and a bone saw."

"Okay, okay," Bobby said. "But with that much control, what if somebody wants to use it to screw around with people's genes on purpose? Say, change their babies to make 'em white?" A lot of the students expressed displeasure with that possibility.

"Well, sure, you have a point," Peter acknowledged. "That precision makes it a much more powerful technique, and that means it can certainly do a lot more harm in the wrong hands. But it can also do much more good in the right ones."

A new hook occurred to him, and his tentativeness faded. "As my Uncle Ben used to say, 'With great power there must come great responsibility.' Power isn't evil—it's just powerful. Whether it does good or harm depends on how responsibly you use it."

"Are any of you diabetic?" he asked. A couple of hands were raised, including Susan's. "The insulin shots that save your lives every day are the result of genetic engineering. They're made by *E. coli* bacteria that have been engineered to produce human insulin. Until a couple of decades ago, you would've had to use insulin extracted from the pancreas of a cow, a pig, or a fish. And you might've suffered a dangerous allergic reaction to it."

He told them about how genetic therapy could potentially provide cures for cancer, cystic fibrosis, Parkinson's, and other diseases. He talked about the research into engineering fruits with genes that let them produce oral vaccines naturally, letting people in impoverished countries get vaccinations cheaply and conveniently through the crops they grew themselves, rather than having to rely on a medical infrastructure that they couldn't afford if it even existed in their countries. That was a point that struck home with these kids, most of whose living conditions weren't much better than one would find in a Third World country. (Bobby Ribeiro lived with six other family members in a tiny tenement room that was little better than a cardboard box under an overpass. Jenny Hardesty didn't even have that, living with a group of homeless, parentless kids who sheltered in condemned buildings and tried to stay clear of the cops until they turned eighteen and could legally fend for themselves.) The prospect of getting vaccinated through a fresh banana or apple rather than a sharp needle had its appeal as well.

"But what about mutants?" Bobby objected. "Or freaks like the Hulk and Spider-Man? They prove that messing around with genes is dangerous."

"Yes, it can be." Peter certainly understood his concerns, having faced a number of dangerous results of genetic science gone awry, not to mention having been personally mutated into one or two of them (sometimes his sides still itched in recollection of the four extra arms he'd briefly owned). "But a lot of mutants and other genetically altered beings use their powers for good. Or at least try to. Genetically modified organisms are as likely to save the world as threaten it. Like I said, it's not the power that makes the difference, it's the responsibility." Of course, he couldn't exactly let on that he was himself a genetically modified organism—particularly since Spider-Man was widely considered more a menace than a hero, thanks to years of bad press from the *Daily Bugle*.

The bell rang too soon, as always, and he could only hope he'd given them enough information to make wise decisions about the issue. After all, they might grow up to be the ones whose decisions about genetic research could determine whether it was allowed to save lives or suppressed out of fear of the unknown. Even in a world of superhumans and wannabe gods, knowledge was still the greatest power.

Which reminded him: "Don't forget," he yelled at the outrushing students, "field trip to the New York Public Library tomorrow! Make sure your persimmon slips are in order!" *Did I just say "persimmon" instead of "permission?" Ohhh, I need my sleep!*

Unfortunately, he still had his freshman general science class to teach, and that wasn't until last period, so he couldn't go home just yet. Instead, he headed for the faculty lounge, hoping it would be quiet enough to let him catch a nap on its dilapidated couch. Of course, "quiet" was a relative thing, given the constant motorcycle growl of its antique refrigerator. But Peter had spent most of his twenties in tiny apartments with paper-thin walls, and had learned out of necessity how to sleep through the worst traffic noise—particularly since his nocturnal web-slinging meant he often caught up on sleep during morning rush hour. In an odd way, his spider-sense had helped with that skill as well; he'd grown so used to relying on it to alert him to danger that he didn't startle as easily in response to other stimuli such as loud noises. As long as there was nobody in the lounge interested in engaging him in conversation, he could count on a little shut-eye.

When he arrived, he found the lounge empty except for Dawn Lukens, a fortyish but still-pixieish English teacher who had an inexplicable knack for keeping her students in line despite her tiny build and little-girl voice. She was a friendly enough colleague, but right now Peter hoped she'd be content to ignore him in favor of the Web surfing she was doing on her laptop, courtesy of the Wi-Fi hookup she'd been instrumental in persuading the school board to install at Midtown High—as much to sate her own Web addiction as to serve the students' educational needs. *Web addiction. Hah. I'm one to talk.* As always, he was tempted to ask something like how many Spider-Man Web sites there were, but his desire to downplay his connection to the infamous wall-crawler overrode his love of bad puns. Just barely.

So instead he gave Dawn the briefest of polite greetings followed by a studied yawn, hoping she'd take the hint and leave him to sack out on the couch. Instead, she said, "Hey, Pete, come and look at this. You used to work for this guy, didn't you?"

"Huh?" Silently lamenting his long-lost sleep, he came around to peer over her shoulder—and recoiled as an unwelcome face glared back at him from the screen. Haircut like a shaving brush, a moustache that went out of style with Eva Braun's boy toy, a cigar as foul as his expression—it was J. Jonah Jameson, all right. *Thank heavens he didn't try smiling for the camera—that's the only thing scarier than his scowl.*

Peter's relationship with the irascible publisher of New York's *Daily Bugle* was as long and schizophrenic as his crimefighting career. From the beginning, for reasons that continued to befuddle Peter, Jameson had latched on to Spider-Man as Public Enemy Numbers One through Ten inclusive and asserted it at every opportunity. The number of words of anti-Spider-Man rhetoric he'd written in editorials, spoken on specially purchased TV spots, and delivered in private tirades to his newsroom staff could rival the collection of the New York Public Library for verbosity. His rabble-rousing and the controversy it had manufactured had scuttled Peter's early attempts to turn Spider-Man into a TV sensation and had subsequently made him the most hated crimefighter in the city. And yet, even as he'd destroyed one career for Peter, Jameson had provided him with another, since he could always be counted on to pay for photos of Spider-Man to accompany his biased coverage of the wall-crawling menace. Peter Parker had been in a unique position to take such pictures, once he'd purchased a miniature camera he could carry on his belt, set on automatic, and web in place to overlook his superbattles. Peter hadn't been crazy about helping Jonah assassinate his own character, but it had paid the bills through many lean, difficult years. (And at least Jameson always spelled his name correctly, with the hyphen and capital M. *As* the saying went, that was the most important thing. Too many people rendered it "Spiderman," which in Peter's mind looked like a Jewish surname. "Hey, honey, it's the Spidermans from across the street!")

"Yeah, JJJ and I go way back," was all he said to Dawn. "You never forget working for that man—even after years of therapy. What's he gotten into now?"

"The blogosphere. He's finally given in to the twenty-first century and started his own daily journal. '*The Wake-Up Call.*'"

"Really?" Peter asked. "I'm surprised Jonah's willing to have anything to do with something called 'the Web.'" Dawn chuckled. "Then again," Peter mused, "how could he ever pass up a new way to tell people what he thinks?"

Drawn to it like a rubbernecker at a freeway pileup, he leaned in, unable to resist reading what Jolly Jonah had to say. In a screwed-up way, he almost missed Old Pickle-Puss's diatribes. Inevitably, the subject of the column was Spider-Man—specifically his actions in foiling the previous night's robbery at Macy's:

> . . . Like I've always said, that wall-crawling miscreant doesn't have the sense to come in out of the rain. Fine by me—I'm praying for a terminal case of pneumonia. But that

glory hog isn't content to put himself out of our misery, he has to make others suffer along with him! First, he dares to attack a wounded security guard named <u>Eddie Barnes</u>, a brave man struck down in the line of duty yet driven to push forward in the pursuit of justice even as his very life's blood poured from a near-fatal wound. This is a real hero, ladies and gentlemen, not like those flamboyant freaks who hide themselves behind fright masks and terrorize the good people of New York with their endless self-absorbed brawls! Perhaps Spider-Man recognized that and attacked brave Eddie Barnes out of jealous spite! More likely, though, he was in cahoots with the criminals, acting as their lookout and using his disgusting webs to throw off pursuit.

But there's no honor among thieves, so minutes later, the rancid arachnid turned on his own accomplices, no doubt wanting to take all the loot for himself and make it look like he'd captured the criminals. <u>As always</u>, he persists in his attempts to fool the good people of New York into believing he's on the side of law and order. Hah! Lawlessness and chaos is more like it, as Spider-Man's actions on that busy Manhattan street went on to prove! Randomly vandalizing the vehicles of innocent motorists as he went, he got into a running gun battle with his former felonious fellows, putting countless civilian lives in danger! When a brave cabbie, <u>Nicholas Kaproff</u>, dared to speak out in protest, Spider-Man started to tear apart his cab, and might have done the same to Nick himself if New York's Finest hadn't arrived on the scene. Thankfully, they scared off the sniveling Spider-Man before he could abscond with the loot.

But how are honest citizens like Eddie Barnes or Nick Kaproff to seek compensation for the damages inflicted on them? How can they press charges or file suit against a coward who hides behind a stocking mask and always flees the scene of the crime? How . . .

It went on in that vein for some time. Peter didn't need to read any more, though; he'd long since memorized JJJ's act. Although the new forum that he of the triple palatal approximants had found for his views seemed to have inspired new creativity in him. "'Rancid arachnid'? I don't think I've heard that one before."

"Still," Dawn said, "through all the bluster, he kind of has a point. Even if Spider-Man wasn't working with the thieves, he did his share of damage. A lot of the stolen goods were trashed in the fight. And what makes superheroes think they have the right to tear up other people's property and use it as weapons whenever they feel like it? It's like they care more about showing off how powerful they are than about stopping crimes. Spider-Man may think he was doing good last night, but his methods leave a lot to be desired."

Peter kept his mouth shut, not trusting himself to think of a reply. He'd been trying to take Jameson's new forum for arachnophobic attacks with good humor, but the criticisms from a fellow teacher whom he liked stuck in his craw. He'd done everything he could to keep people safe, and had needed to strike as hard and fast as he did to prevent fatalities from stray bullets. He'd been left with no other choices. Hadn't he?

He lay down on the couch for a while, but his eyes stayed wide open.

THREE

HEY, YOU GUYS!

THE next day's field trip did much to raise Peter's spirits. The New York Public Library's main building on Fifth Avenue was an inspiring place, its massive Beaux-Arts facade and interior "noble spaces" bestowing the place with a sense of grandeur and awe that befitted the purpose and power of a library. Ben and May Parker had brought their nephew, Peter, here many times in his childhood, and the majesty and beauty of the place had done much to inspire his love of learning. He, Dawn Lukens, and the other teachers who'd organized this trip hoped it might do the same for some of their students, which was why they'd made the trip from Forest Hills.

"As you know," Dawn called out to the students as they clambered from the buses and neared the front steps, "Queens has its own separate library system, as does Brooklyn."

"While the New York system," Peter interposed, "takes Manhattan, the Bronx, and Staten Island, too." He waited for a laugh but got nothing. Typically, the kids didn't realize there had ever been any culture or music before their own lifetimes. But then, Dawn didn't seem to get the joke either. *I guess it comes from being raised by older relatives,* Peter realized. *Uncle Ben and Aunt May got me interested in a lot of old-time movies, music, radio shows, you name it.* His favorites were the old-time radio comedies; he could swipe their best material as Spidey, and people would think he'd made it up. Although most of his comedy was wasted on unappreciative audiences who were busy trying to shoot him, dismember him, or pummel him to death. *Hecklers. They'll kill ya.*

"But the New York Public Library is something special," Dawn went on. "It's one of the leading libraries in the entire country, even the world.

Its collection is immense and includes an original Gutenberg Bible. Now, this building isn't really a circulating branch, but holds the Humanities and Social Sciences collections of the Research Library. The circulating branch is right over there on the opposite corner," she said, pointing to the unassuming storefront-style establishment on the southeast corner of Fortieth and Fifth, "and we'll be dropping by there later today. For now, let's come this way . . ." As Dawn went on with the lecture, leading the class up the stairs, Peter shook off his reverie, turned, and abruptly found himself looking up at one of the mighty lion statues that flanked the entrance. He almost jumped back in alarm, remembering the time he'd had to fight these statues when they'd briefly come to life during that Inferno mess a few years back. Besides, with his archenemies on his mind, he couldn't look at a lion without thinking of Kraven the Hunter, one of the most relentless foes of his career. *Great. Now I'm a Kraven coward.* He hurried ahead to catch up with Dawn at the front of the group, humming "If I Only Had the Nerve" to himself.

The sweeping interior spaces of the building brought some oohs and ahhs from many of the students, and even some of the ones determined to maintain a tough, unaffected facade had impressed looks in their eyes. For his own part, Peter gazed lovingly at the building's elegantly crafted walls, ceilings, and columns, and found himself wanting to sneak in after hours and just crawl all over this lovely architecture. *Parker, you're a very strange person.*

Before the students could get into the main body of the library, they had to get their bags searched by the guard at the door—the trade-off that every great New York landmark had to make in this day and age, when subtle infiltrations in the name of terror had proven as effective at mass destruction as the worst supervillain flamboyance. It was slow going, particularly since some of the searches turned up contraband that the teachers would have to deal with. Peter fidgeted, impatient to get on with the field trip. He couldn't wait to see how the students would react to the Rose Reading Room, a single vast chamber that was nearly as long and wide as the whole of Midtown High. Its walls were lined with two stories' worth of reference books comprising over twenty-five thousand volumes, and its many crystal chandeliers hung from an ornate fifty-two-foot-high ceiling containing murals of billowing salmon-hued clouds—

appropriately, since the room was practically big enough to have its own internal weather system. He dared even the most jaded student to enter that room and not be struck by the sheer weight of learning it contained.

But before the students had cleared the security sweep, Peter heard the familiar wail of sirens racing along Forty-second Street. *Lots* of sirens. Moreover, he was getting a faint twinge from his spider-sense: something several blocks away, not immediately threatening to him, but big enough to raise his hackles. *Oh, no.* Not only did he have to miss the reading room, but he had to think up an excuse for abandoning his class. Now that he was a teacher rather than a photographer, he could no longer claim to be heading off to cover the story. And the sirens outside scuttled the old standby of "Wait here, I'm going to call the cops."

Dawn had come up to him. "What do you think is going on?" she whispered.

"I wish I knew."

"If it's serious, we may have to cancel. I'd hate that, but I don't want to risk these kids." In any other city, her concern might be exaggerated. But the superbeings who tended to congregate around New York had a way of inflicting serious property damage in their frequent combats, so the citizenry had learned to be ready for the worst.

He was grateful for the opening. "Tell you what—I'll just pop outside and see if I can find something out. You watch the kids."

"Good idea. But be careful."

Why start now? Peter answered silently as he headed for the exit and squeezed past the remaining students. Once outside, he hurried over to the north side of the entranceway and ducked around it. All the pedestrians' eyes were to the north, so nobody saw him as he climbed up the wall and onto the roof of the library. By now, he could hear crashing noises and alarms from several blocks to the north. *Sounds like my kind of dance, all right.*

Superhuman speed and years of practice let him complete the change in under fifteen seconds: First he kicked off his shoes and socks, pulled off his jacket and T-shirt (no buttons for quick removal, dark color and high thread count so the red and blue wouldn't show through), and dropped his pants. He retrieved the compact webshooters that hooked to his utility belt, slid them over his wrists like flexible watchbands, then flipped forward the palm electrodes and locked them into place. Then on with his uniform stockings and gloves, making sure the web nozzles poked through the small slits in the gauntlets. And finally the mask (a spare, since he hadn't gotten around to fixing the lens in the other), whose long neck he tucked into the tunic. He bundled his street clothes and—as much to test the webshooters as to protect his property—sprayed a loose cocoon around them.

The web nozzles were complex pieces of micro-engineering he'd labored long and hard to perfect. The hemispherical nozzle caps had several tiny holes through which the web fluid sprayed, forcing its long chain polymers to extrude and air-harden into long, wispy strands. With a quick series of brief, repeated taps on the palm electrodes, Peter produced a loose spray of short fibers that clung together in midair to form a fine, almost fabriclike mesh. By moving the shooters around, he could "weave" the diaphanous mesh into a variety of shapes, such as the cocoon around his clothes. Since the mesh partly dried in midair and had a low surface area, it didn't stick to them badly, and it would biodegrade in an hour anyway.

Of course, whatever the problem was, Spidey hoped to be done with it in much less than an hour, since the students were waiting. Taking a running start across the library roof, he leaped skyward and gave his right palm electrode a quick double tap, holding it down on the second. This caused the web fluid to fire in continuous strands, the nozzle cap rotating like a lawn sprinkler from the fluid pressure and twisting the strands into a strong ropelike bundle. A thicker glob of fluid discharged at the beginning provided an effective anchor as the webline connected about halfway up the 500 Fifth Avenue building across the street. The elastic webbing contracted as it dried, pulling him up like a bungee cord and giving him added velocity. He let the swinging line carry him forward and upward through the air shaft between skyscrapers, and at the top of his arc, as he fired off another strand, he began to see signs of the crisis over the lower rooftops beyond. A cloud of dust and smoke was rising from Forty-seventh Street between Fifth and Sixth Avenues. *Well, whaddaya know? The Diamond District. Somebody's going ice-fishing.*

If you were looking for diamonds, the stretch of Forty-seventh known as Diamond and Jewelry Way was the ideal place. Nearly 90 percent of all the diamonds sold in the United States passed through this single block.

But of course security was ferociously tight. Your run-of-the-mill jewel thief would be crazy to try to rob any of its shops or exchanges. But from the mess up ahead, it was already clear that whoever Spidey was about to face was no ordinary criminal. *And most supervillains are crazy anyway. At least the ones I slum around with. Well, birds of a feather.*

As he swung toward the pounding and crashing noises—now joined by the sound of gunshots, heralding the arrival of the police on the scene— Spidey cast an eye north to the roof of the Baxter Building, hoping to glimpse the Fantastic Four racing down from their headquarters to tackle the crisis. That would save him the trouble, and he could get back to his students. But of course he had no such luck. Even if they weren't off saving some distant planet from being eaten by a mutant space goat or something, the FF tended to concentrate on fate-of-the-world stuff and left street crime to street-level heroes like him. *Face it, Captain Kirk, you're the only ship in the quadrant again.*

Spidey came in for a landing atop a building on the south side of the street and peered down over the edge. His eyes widened beneath his mask as he saw the source of the danger. "Aw, nuts! Not robots! I *hate* robots!" But robots they were, over a half dozen of them. They were six-legged and heavily built, nearly the size of horses, and they were methodically making the rounds of the street from east to west, smashing in the fronts of the diamond exchanges and using elaborate manipulator arms to steal the diamonds and dump them into hoppers in their backs. Or so Spidey extrapolated from his quick glimpse of multiple robots in various stages of their operations, and from the shattered storefronts in their wake. Another couple of robots were now emerging from buildings, and Spidey wondered how many more might still be inside. The police were firing at the armored beasts with no effect. *If these things suddenly sprout wings and propellers, I'll know I'm in an old Fleischer cartoon!*

Normally he'd prefer to swoop in and clobber the bad guys unannounced, taking them off guard. But he wasn't sure these robots had a guard to be taken off of—or whatever—and he didn't want to catch any stray bullets. So he hopped along the rooftops toward Sixth, snagged a webline on one of the fancy-schmancy steel-sculpture streetlights at the end of the block (with diamond-shaped light fixtures on top, oh, how precious), and swung down to perch atop the subway kiosk alongside the police. "I'd heard those new robot toys were a smash, but this is ridiculous!" he called by way of introduction.

The cops turned to register his arrival. "Stay out of this, wall-crawler," said one of them, a burly young brown-skinned man.

"Hey, wait a minute," said his partner, an older man with a salt-and-pepper moustache and big square glasses. "We aren't having much luck with these things. I've been around this town a long time, and I've seen Spider-Man tackle worse menaces than this."

"We're supposed to protect civilians, not let them fight for us."

Spidey waved. "Hello, crouching right here! For the record, I prefer the term 'talented amateur.' And for the record, I'm going in there whether you ask me to or not. I'd just appreciate it if you avoided firing bullets at the area I'm about to be in. Okay?"

The older cop smiled. "You got it. Now face front!" Spidey did as the cop advised and saw that one of the robots was trundling his way. He flipped forward, pushed off the subway rail with his hands, did a mid-air somersault, and shot out a web to snag one of the light fixtures extending from the Jewelry 55 Exchange building, up above the sign that boasted "WORLD'S LARGEST JEWELRY EXCHANGE" in big red letters. Luckily, the cops seemed to be holding their fire. He clutched the webline two-handed and swung down to kick the approaching robot in what looked like its forward sensor cluster.

But its manipulator arms moved with striking speed, clutching his ankles before they hit. The force of his impact pushed it back a few feet, but its legs moved deftly to keep it in balance. It tossed Spidey back over its body and continued on its way. He caught himself on a lamppost and swung around it to hurtle back at the robot. Landing on its back, he coated its manipulators with a thick layer of webbing, using a firm, continuous pressure on the electrodes to push the nozzle cap forward, allowing the web fluid to goosh out around its edges in a thick, gooey stream, its stickiest form. "You shouldn't go out without your mittens. You'll catch your death of cold!"

The manipulators strained against their web cocoons without success, so Spidey began clambering over the robot to look for a control panel or something. "Ro, ro, ro your bot," he sang. But then his spider-sense twinged, alerting him that the robot had deployed a pretty potent laser and was using it to cut the webs free. He clambered under the robot's body as its arms reached back for him, but found that to be a mistake as its middle pair of legs tried to squash his head between them. "Whoa! Not so gently down the stream!" He pulled back and webbed them together securely, hoping the laser couldn't reach underneath.

Now that I have a moment, let's try the obvious. Twisting over to get his legs under him against the pavement, Spidey thrust upward and flipped the robot onto its back. *That was easy.* But the robot's back was rounded enough that it was able to rock itself and regain its footing even with one pair of legs hobbled. It then continued its course for the 55 Exchange building. *These things are tough! At least for once the deadly robots aren't after me personally. They don't attack me unless I attack them.*

But his spider-sense was still twinging, and his eyes told him there were still people inside the exchange. He sighed. *So here I go attacking them again.*

He decided to play it smart this time. He leaped back up to one of the light fixtures, hit the robot's rear with another webline, and jumped down, using the fixture's support pole as a pulley to lift the robot into the air. "Oh boy, a piñata!" He kicked it with all his might as it rose past him, hoping to damage something inside it. The force of the kick was sufficient to send it up and over the light fixture, more or less. A collision with a window air conditioner halted its trajectory, and as it fell, it smashed the light fixture itself and a security camera before crashing against the corner of the exchange building's metal awning and toppling from there to the sidewalk. One of its legs snapped off, and Spidey grinned. *Now we're getting somewhere!*

But his spirits sank as another robot trundled out of the adjacent smashed-up storefront and used its laser to cut the first robot's middle legs free of Spidey's webbing. The damaged robot clambered up onto its five remaining legs and came forward once more, awkwardly but effectively. "Who built these things?" Spidey demanded. "Timex?"

The damaged robot was still heading for the exchange, with its rescuer close behind. Spidey had to delay them long enough for the people to get out. Luckily, the guards inside had seen the robots closing in and were directing the occupants to the exits. Spidey leaped up to perch on the "EXCHANGE" sign and sprayed a wide-angle mesh between the corner of the building and the lamppost out front, and then another between that and the adjacent lamppost, forming a barricade between the robots and the fleeing occupants. If he'd gauged their behavior correctly—reactive rather than anticipative—they'd try to push through the webbing first, and it took Hulk-level strength to do that. But then they'd no doubt deploy their lasers to cut through it. That was something he'd have to stop.

But his webshooter LEDs began blinking under his gloves while he was still spraying the second barrier, alerting him that they were running dry. He plugged in new cartridges from his belt as quickly as he could, but one of the robots was already starting to push through the incomplete web. Spidey had no more time to replace all the web cartridges, so he had to settle for just a couple of fresh ones in each shooter. *Let's kill two birds with one stone,* he thought, and used the fresh web supply to trap the robot within the barrier and pin it to the ground. It strained with no success, and though its laser began cutting its front clear, Spidey doubted the beam could reach to the back. But its fellows could help it get free, and they were drawing closer.

Hoping to hurry the evacuation along, Spidey ducked down into the exchange building, climbing in over the heads of the evacuees, and called, "Hurry, everybody, out while you can!" But that was easier said than done, since that big red sign out front wasn't lying. The place had been packed with vendors and buyers before the attack; since a diamond merchant didn't need more than a small booth to do business from, there was room for hundreds of them. Many of the dealers were still busy trying to secure or pack up their stocks, and Spidey's eye caught a number of civilians hanging around despite the risk, perhaps hoping to swipe some diamonds in the chaos. But Spidey couldn't be bothered with that now. He cried, "Move, move, move!" at the top of his lungs, hoping that people would either respond to whatever authority he carried as a superhero or, more likely, be afraid to face the wrath of the creepy bug guy. He hustled people out of the building as fast as he could with help from building security, hoping they and the cops would search everyone for contraband once they were safe and clear. "Come on, people! Diamonds are forever, you aren't! Hurry up!"

The tingle in his skull intensified, and he rushed back out to see that the robots had nearly cut through his webbing. He clambered up to his former perch, readying himself to launch into a renewed attack. But his hairs suddenly stood on end, as much from a sudden charge in the air as from his spider-sense, and he reflexively jumped clear just as a lightning bolt struck his position, blowing several letters off the sign and shattering a couple of windows directly above it. Pulling himself up on the flagpole again, Spidey focused in on the source of the attack—a green-and-yellow-garbed figure who stood atop a redbrick building across the way. "Oh, no. Don't tell me!"

"That's right, Spider-Man!" came a familiar gravelly voice in reply. "Electro's back, and he's got company!"

Electric company? Why does that sound so familiar? "And Spider-Man is sick of villains who introduce themselves in the third person!" Electro was an old-school supervillain, one of Spidey's earliest foes though not one of his most active. A former electrical lineman named Max Dillon, he'd gained the power to control and channel electricity in some freak accident and had used it to turn to larceny. The accident had also apparently crippled his fashion sense; his green-and-yellow outfit was one of the most garish ones Spidey had encountered, with lightning-bolt patterns in a sort of weird suspenders shape running from waistband to shoulders, and a black cowl with a big yellow lightning/starburst sort of *thing* on the front, its jagged points sticking out stiffly from the sides of his face with a big one sticking up on top. *Honestly, it looks like a cardboard mask from a school play. I'm a happy little starfish, except I'm not so good with scissors.* But Dillon was tough and dangerous, so Spidey supposed he could get away with looking like a complete doofus.

"Besides," he went on, gesturing at the damaged sign, "why would you want to rob the World's Largest Jewelry Hange?" Spidey shot a webline, but the veteran thug saw it coming and dodged. Spidey hurtled across the street at him, but Electro jumped up to the wall of the taller building next door and began scaling it, clinging to the building electrostatically, not unlike how Spidey did it, albeit by amplifying his body's charge rather than relying on molecular Van der Waals forces. He climbed around to the front of the building as Spidey followed. "Come on, Max, you can't beat me at my own game!"

"Oh yeah? Remember this trick?" Electro extended a hand toward Spidey, who suddenly found himself slipping. He fell several stories before he caught himself on a building ledge.

I'd almost forgotten he could do that. I thought he had, too. Once, when

Spidey had been foolish enough to taunt him with some crack about "static," Electro had had the idea to draw all the static electricity in the area toward him, canceling out Spidey's clinging ability. It was a trick Electro had rarely tried again; he wasn't the brightest bulb on the marquee, and in the heat of battle, he generally didn't bother to reason it out. But he seemed to be in top form today.

"Neat trick, Sparky! Now let me remind you of some of mine!" He leaped up after Electro, grabbing windowsills to pull himself up. But Electro let himself slide down the side of the building, firing off a lightning bolt at Spidey as he slid past. Spidey jumped clear and fired a web across the street, swinging down to the sidewalk to meet Electro at ground level. *Electro. Ground level. There's a pun in there somewhere, but it's not worth it.* Spidey was in the mood to talk with his fists for a while.

But there was a crackle in the air, and a robot trundled forward to stand between Spider-Man and his prey. "I got a few new tricks this time, wall-crawler!" Spidey looked around to see several other robots closing in on him. "Computer commands, mechanical movements . . . it's all done with electric signals. I could fry you myself, but I think I'd rather let my friends do it while I sit back and enjoy the show."

Spidey was glad his mask hid the expression of dismay on his face. If Electro had figured out how to manipulate electronic devices, he could be virtually unstoppable. He could rip off ATMs, bring traffic to a standstill, crash planes, and worse. Spidey only hoped that Dillon's limited imagination hadn't reached that realization yet. Outwardly, he kept up his usual mocking front. "Great, so you've turned yourself into Remote Control Man!" he called, leaping up to perch on another wall. "Do me a favor and hit rewind, will ya?"

"How about eject?" Electro gestured, and a robot took aim at Spidey with a laser beam. Luckily they were slow-moving, and Spidey had no trouble leaping clear.

But the equation had changed now. Before, their target had been the diamonds, and he had simply been a distraction. Now these titanium Tinkertoys were targeting him. And any laser that could cut through his webbing could easily cut through flesh and bone.

I've got speed on my side, though. So let's make the most of it! Instead of waiting for the robots to strike, he took the fight to them, diving into the fray and relying on his speed, agility, and spider-sense to stay one hop ahead of the lasers. While the robots were still trying to get a bead on him, he was able to grab or web their laser arms and rip them free, ducking or leaping clear of their manipulator arms before they could catch him. He smashed at robot joints with hands and feet, looking for weak spots. He was able to cripple a few limbs, but not enough on any one robot to put it permanently out of action.

Then one of them got in a lucky blow. His danger sense warned him, but he was hemmed in and couldn't fully twist away before a cutter arm slashed across the back of his neck. *Yikes! An inch closer and I'd have been the Amazing Quadriplegic Man—or worse!* As it was, it was just a bad pain in the neck and some blood trickling down his back. Before it could get any worse, he reached back, grabbed the cutter arm, and ripped it free. He used it as a club to smash some robot limbs aside and jump clear to regroup, although he sustained another slash across the thigh before he could. He took a second to check his wounds, confirming that they were nothing more than moderate cuts. Thinking, *Hey, it worked for the night watchman,* he sprayed a bit of webbing on the wounds to staunch the bleeding.

"Hah!" Electro crowed. "First blood's mine! Keep at him, boys, you're wearing him down!"

Spidey leaped to the side of a building, figuring he'd taken care of most of the lasers and would be safe up there. But the robots' legs dug into the brick wall and began climbing after him. *Oy vey,* he thought, as Electro cackled.

Hey, wait a minute! Electro could be pocketing a fortune in diamonds while his pets take care of me. So why's he standing there playing armchair quarterback? He's not the type whose sole purpose is revenge against li'l old me. He had no way of knowing I'd even show up for this! True, there had been that one time after Spidey had saved his life, which Dillon had seen as a humiliation. He'd used his temporarily souped-up powers to defeat Spidey and make him beg for mercy, a loss that still stuck in his craw even though he'd come back and taken Electro down again. But that had been the end of Dillon's revenge kick, and though they'd clashed a couple of times since, it had been when Electro was working for someone else or pursuing a different agenda. *So why is he focusing on this battle instead of the diamond heist? Maybe because he* has *to! He has to be consciously directing the robots.* That was a relief, actually; if he was just puppeteering their bodies, controlling the electrical impulses in their servos, rather than actually affecting their programming, that meant this new ability was not as dangerous as it could have been. *Shut him down, and I bet the robots shut down, too.*

Maybe the police were thinking the same thing, since they were now calling, "Electro! Stand down or we open fire!" With a contemptuous sneer, Electro turned his gaze on the fancy diamond-themed streetlights flanking the cops. Both fixtures exploded with sparks, and blue-white electric arcs began leaping between them and licking out at all surrounding metal, including the police cars and guns. The cops scattered. The older, mustachioed officer from before had the presence of mind to leap into his cruiser, its metal body serving to insulate him from the lightning, and pull the car away out of range. The other car in the blockade was abandoned, erupting into flames after taking several hits of lightning. Luckily, a fire truck was already on the scene.

But Spidey was already taking advantage of Electro's distraction. He leaped across the street and ricocheted off a building to come at Electro from an unexpected direction, firing a glob of webbing to cover the felon's mask and blind him. Electro reflexively grabbed at the obstruction, getting his hand caught in the still-drying web, but a second later he began burning the web away with an electric discharge from his fingers, using the other hand to fire a lightning bolt that Spidey dodged. Hoping Dillon would need time to recharge after that, Spidey stuck out a leg as he landed in a crouch and swept around to take his enemy's feet out from under him. But just that brief contact was like kicking a live cable. The current running through his muscles forced them to contract, folding up his leg and canceling much of the force of the kick. Electro only staggered and regained his balance, while Spidey gasped in pain and rolled away to gain some distance.

Electro laughed. "Too bad you left your rubber costume at home, hero! You can't touch this!"

"I never liked that song," Spidey countered, registering that the street around him was strewn with pieces torn off of the robots, including a heavy leg not far from him. "How about '*Domo arigato,* Mr. Roboto?'" he called as he snagged the leg with a webline and slung it at Electro.

Dillon knew better than to try to zap it with lightning. He might heat it up, even partially melt it, but he wouldn't cancel its momentum, so he'd just end up getting hit with molten titanium instead of the solid kind. So he deferred superpowered gimmicks and just plain ducked, covering his head. Which gave Spidey enough time to leap forward and spray him with a web-mesh to pin him in his crouch. Dillon fired finger-bolts to snap the threads and struggled back upright, then fired lightning again as the web-spinner came closer. Leaping around him, dodging lightning bolts, Spidey kept coming, binding Electro's hands and pinning his feet with webbing. Then he picked up the robot leg again and hefted it as a club. *Luckily titanium isn't very conductive,* he thought as he prepared to knock Dillon out with it.

But Electro was laughing. "Might want to look behind you."

Spider-sense told him that was no ruse. He spun to check on the robots, and his heart sank. The robots were now stomping along at random, spreading out in all directions, smashing aside cars and knocking over streetlamps. A few were already out of the Diamond District and on their way out of his sight, shrugging off police fire. *Oh, no. No! With Electro distracted by the fight, the robots didn't shut down, they went out of control! They're running wild!*

He turned back to Electro. "Shut them down! *Now!*" he cried, brandishing the robot leg menacingly.

The villain laughed. "I don't think so. Knock me out, and they just keep going and going and going. Let me go, and I just might stop them for you."

"Stop them now, and I'll consider it."

"No deal. How do I know you'll keep your end of the bargain?"

Spidey cocked his head. "Hello? Me champion of justice, you career scumbag. Which of us is more trustworthy?"

Electro shrugged. "All I know's what I read in the *Bugle.* According to Jameson, you're as crooked as I am. So I'd like some insurance."

"How about we say 'Mazel and Broche' and shake hands?" he said, referring to the traditional words of accord still considered binding by the mostly Jewish dealers on this street.

"How about you do what I tell you? Walk away, let me do the same, and I'll stop 'em." More crashing sounds came from over Spidey's shoulder. "Better decide fast, wall-crawler."

Spidey knew he had no choice. Even he didn't have the strength to snap his own webbing, but he was able to dig his fingers in between the strands where it met Electro's sleeve and tear one of his hands free. Then he leaped clear while Electro zapped the rest of the webs away. "Now stop the robots!"

"Why? They make such a great distraction!" He laughed over the sounds of spreading mayhem. "Better get moving, champion!"

Damn it! Dillon had him but good. Grinding his teeth beneath his mask, Spider-Man backed away from Electro, heading toward the nearest robot. Laughing, Dillon turned and moseyed—yes, actually moseyed—away. Hoping to salvage something, Spidey reset his webshooter to activate its spring-loaded launcher, firing a spider-tracer to connect with one of Electro's calves in hopes of tracking him later. But the tiny, arachnid-shaped microelectronic tracker shorted out on impact with Dillon's charged body.

Roaring in frustration, Spider-Man pounced onto the robot, unleashing his anger by smashing at its joints and vital spots. It fought back, but he tore off the front half of its remaining arm, then did the same with enough of its legs that once he flipped it on its back, it was unable to regain its footing. But in the time it had taken to do that, the remaining eight or nine robots had made more headway out into the city, and he could hear more screams and sirens coming from all directions. *Which way? How can I stop them all?* There were so many places within just a few blocks that could be endangered—Rockefeller Center, Saks, St. Patrick's Cathedral, Radio City, Times Square—the *Library!*

But if he went after his kids, thousands of other people might be endangered. *I can't take them all out before they do some real damage. How do I choose?* He considered going back and recapturing Electro, finding some way to coerce him into stopping the robots. But he'd tried that already with no success. Even if he could somehow intimidate Electro into backing down, it would take too long.

As he pondered his options, Spidey shot a webline and climbed to the top of the block's tallest building to get the lay of the land. The robots were spreading out, following the streets. A couple were heading up toward Rock Plaza and St. Pat's, at least one was nearing Broadway, and one was heading in the general direction of Grand Central. But two were on their way down Fifth, already halfway to the Library. *Do I have the right to place the people*

I personally care about above everyone else? he asked himself. But he realized there was more to the equation than that. Spider-Man was responsible for the whole city—but Peter Parker was responsible for those students in particular.

Besides, he added as he swung back to the southeast, *I've failed to save too many people close to me over the years. Uncle Ben, Gwen and George Stacy, Harry Osborn, Flash Thompson. If anyone's entitled to choose to save the people he cares about, I am.* He rationalized it by telling himself he'd go right back to stop the other robots the moment he was sure the kids were safe.

One of the robots on Fifth seemed to be veering east, away from the Library, so Spidey took a chance and tackled the other one. Unfortunately, this one still had two intact manipulator arms that grabbed at him when he landed on its back, clamping around his head and shoulder and tossing him forward into the street. *Ow! I wasn't counting on that. I thought they were out of control.* Apparently they still had autonomous self-defense programming even without a guiding will to give them direction. He shot webs at the manipulator arms, but they flailed away, and he missed their business ends. *Was that a lucky accident, or are they learning from experience?*

With a sense of déjà vu, Spidey dived under the robot, dodging its arms, and began striking at its joints and ripping away legs. He got carried away and dismembered it enough that the body fell squarely on top of him, knocking the wind out of him for a moment. Angry at himself for letting that happen, he flung it off him and watched as it arced through the air and crashed down hard. It convulsed a few times and fell still. Spidey looked around for the next one, the one that had been heading east.

Except it wasn't heading east anymore. Its drunken walk had taken it back in the other direction, straight for the Library. It was already scuttling across Forty-second, climbing over a pair of cars that had collided with each other in the chaos, and Spidey was a block away. But Spidey could cover a north-south Manhattan block in a single swing. He fired a webline at the nearest corner of the 500 building . . .

And it fell short. He was empty again! He'd been too distracted to note the blinking LED on the right shooter. He used the left one to fire the strand and made the swing. But one of the people in the wreck was stuck in the car and bleeding, so Spidey took a moment to drop down and tear off the door. Then he jumped up into the treetops to see—

My God, no! The students were right there, part of the crowd being evacuated by the police. All three pairs of large, ornate front doors were open, being used as emergency exits. The students and Dawn were just coming out the nearest one—and the robot was heading right toward them, smashing aside tables and chairs in the courtyard and clambering over the fountain. Spidey leaped to the side of the building and fired his left webshooter—

And it sputtered! It was empty, too! Its LED must have been damaged in the fight. "No!" Spidey cried, just as the robot collided with the massive marble urn sculpture next to the steps, cracking its narrow base and sending it down onto the screaming students beside it. The wild automaton then barged forward into the crowd of students, half of whom were trying to rush back inside and colliding with those still trying to push out. It was a recipe for disaster.

Spider-Man jumped down, grabbed the heavy marble sculpture, and heaved it off to the side, where it shattered against the fountain. Desperate, having no time to reload his webshooters, he jumped onto the robot's back and grabbed its flailing manipulator arm, the one it had left. He realized the arm was slick with blood, and his heart choked his throat. There was no safe place to redirect the robot, except *up.* He jumped onto the column abutting the entrance arch and began to climb, pulling the robot up after him. It was a gamble; there were injured students on the steps below, and if the blood-slicked arm slipped through his fingers, the robot could tumble over them. On top of which, it was flailing wildly and sending chunks of marble flying from the column. So he had to act fast. He hauled on the robot with all his might and tossed it into the courtyard, where it crushed a marble shrubbery pot beneath it. He jumped down after it and pounded and ripped it apart until well after it was dead.

But then he pulled himself together. *The kids!* He bounded over to see if they were all right. Paramedics were already on the scene, getting stretchers ready. "Are they all right?" Spidey asked.

"Do they look all right?!" It was Dawn Lukens, standing shakily with blood on her clothes and hair. But then she caught herself. "No . . . I know you mean well. But you can't always arrive just in time. And there's nothing more you can do now."

Her cool forgiveness was more damning than fifty Jameson editorials.

Especially when he took in the faces of the students being loaded into ambulances. All of them were faces he knew Bobby Ribeiro . . . Susan Labyorteaux . . . Joan Rubinoff . . . Koji Furuya . . . Angela Campanella. *My students. My responsibility. I've failed them.*

"Peter?" Dawn was calling now. "Peter, where are you?" She got out her phone and speed-dialed him. Up on the roof, Spidey knew, a cell phone inside a web cocoon was vibrating silently. Normally, he would rush to the roof, answer the phone, and concoct some excuse. But he had no time to worry about secret identities now. There were still other robots running rampant.

As he reloaded his webshooters, he called out to the nearest cop, who was just getting off her walkie-talkie. "Hey, where are the rest of the robots headed?"

"Don't worry yourself, Spider-Man," the stocky, curly-haired brunette told him. "Your pals have it under control."

"What?"

"Yeah, the Avengers just showed up in Times Square, a few of 'em, anyway. They're mopping up now. And the Thing and the Torch just saved St. Pat's. Oh," she added proudly, "and the boys in blue just took out the one heading for Grand Central. We get our licks in sometimes, too." She shook her head. "It's a real mess, though. Lots of damage, dozens heading for the hospital. I'd hate to be the one who gets sued for this."

Spidey's head was reeling, and not from the fights. "Electro," he remembered. "Max Dillon, Electro. He started this. I have to find him—"

The cop smiled. "Don't worry. I hear She-Hulk caught him just north of Times Square. Knocked him out with one finger. Talk about the night the lights went out on Broadway, huh?" She stared. "Hey, what's the matter? I thought you were a guy who appreciated a good joke."

Spider-Man gazed at the blood covering the library steps. "This is no joke, Officer."

FOUR

WHEREVER THERE'S A HANG-UP

JEWEL-THIEF ROBOTS
BUILT FOR VENUS
by Ben Urich

NEW YORK—Visitors and patrons in the Forty-seventh Street Diamond District could not be blamed for wondering if they were being invaded from outer space when a horde of six-legged metallic monsters rampaged through the block late this morning. The *Daily Bugle* has learned that the ten robotic devices unleashed upon the block by Maxwell Dillon, a costumed metahuman known by the nom de guerre Electro, were actually designed as interplanetary travelers.

The robotic probes were stolen from Cyberstellar Technologies, a private aerospace firm commissioned by NASA to construct the devices for an extensive survey of the planet Venus. The second planet from the Sun, Venus is much hotter than Earth and possesses a dense atmosphere bearing thick clouds of sulfuric, hydrofluoric, and other potent acids, with a surface pressure close to a hundred times that of Earth's atmosphere. To date, of the landers that have reached the surface of Venus, none has lasted longer than 127 minutes.

The Cyberstellar probes were designed for a more ambitious survey, one that involved traveling across Venus's rocky surface and taking mineral samples for return to Earth. They were thus equipped with versatile legs for maintaining balance on unpredictable terrain, powerful grippers and cutting lasers for the taking of samples, and extremely strong durable shells to withstand the crushing and intensely corrosive atmosphere. All these features combined to make them extremely effective adversaries for the police and other crimefighters who took them on. Spider-Man, the first costumed adventurer to arrive on the scene, was unable to contain them on his own. Some witnesses claim that his confrontation with Mr. Dillon caused Mr. Dillon to lose control of the probes, precipitating their subsequent rampage through Midtown and requiring the intervention of members of the Avengers and Fantastic Four. However, sources within the police department have stated that the means by which Mr. Dillon controlled the probes has not yet been determined, so that the role Spider-Man's actions may have played in the rampage remains unclear. Mr. Dillon is a former electrical lineman, able to manipulate electric fields and currents directly through paranormal means, but is not known to have any training in computer programming or robotics.

The theft of the probes from Cyberstellar's Westchester facility occurred early last Thursday. This afternoon, District Attorney Blake Tower announced his intention to file indictments against Mr. Dillon for the Cyberstellar theft as well as the attack on the Diamond District. A source in the District Attorney's Office indicates that Mr. Dillon is also being investigated in connection with last Saturday's burglary of industrial equipment from an Oscorp facility in Nassau County, since damage inflicted on the facility in that theft appears to match the damage in the Diamond District. Upon being reminded that Mr. Dillon's conventional modus operandi tends toward simple larceny and large-scale vandalism, often as an employee of more powerful underworld figures, Mr. Tower declined to speculate on the reason for Mr. Dillon's change of tactics . . .

"It's not your fault."

Peter had been hearing those words from Mary Jane all afternoon, even as the news channels continued to broadcast the footage of his failure. Or so it seemed to him. True, there was some footage of Spider-Man battling Electro while the robots rampaged outward from the Diamond District, but most of the news coverage was dominated by action footage of the Avengers defeating the robots and Electro, shot from a hundred different angles.

There was never a shortage of cameras in Times Square, and it had been quite a spectacle. After all, there was probably nowhere else in the city where so much electricity was in use all at once—at least not so visibly. Electro had been in his element, siphoning up power from the clutter of garish, flashing signs and video screens that made Times Square into a cross between a *Blade Runner* cityscape and a giant pinball game. He had briefly rivaled those displays for intensity, firing gouts of lightning at his pursuers, while three of his robots had been causing serious property damage and sending shoppers and tourists screaming for cover. It had been a dramatic and exciting battle, but Spider-Man had been conspicuous only by his absence. Overall, the media were treating him as a sidebar to the story.

But J. Jonah Jameson, in his *Bugle* editorial column (and no doubt his new blog as well), was being as loud-mouthed as usual about Spider-Man's role in triggering the disaster. Of course, JJJ would blame Spider-Man for the *Hindenburg* and the fall of Pompeii if he could find a way. But this time, Peter thought, he had a far more legitimate basis for his accusations. "I'm the one who started it," he told MJ. "I distracted Electro, made him lose control of them."

"You can't think that way," she insisted. MJ was taking time out of her busy rehearsal schedule to help him through this, but it made him guilty to feel good about it; he didn't want to be a distraction from her career at a time when it was so critical to her. "Electro was the one who stole the robots and used them. He was the one who decided to send them rampaging around the city."

"But only after I caused him to lose control. He took advantage of my blunder."

"How do you know he didn't plan to send them on a rampage anyway to cover his escape?"

"Then how would he have gotten away with the diamonds?"

MJ studied him. "All that staring at the news, and you're not really listening, are you? The Torch found sample canisters full of diamonds ejected from the robots, sitting on top of a nearby building. Electro must've planned to collect them later."

"Oh yeah." Peter vaguely remembered hearing that. The canisters must have been intended for returning the samples to Earth. Electro would have had to reduce the thrust of their rockets significantly to keep the swag from blasting into space. "But that was a backup plan at most. He wouldn't have gone to the trouble if I hadn't forced the issue."

"And if you hadn't, he would've gotten away with gazillions' worth of diamonds, and a lot more people could've been hurt or killed. You did what you had to do, Peter."

"Not well enough."

Before MJ could argue further, the phone rang. When Peter answered, Aunt May's kindly voice replied. *"Peter, dear, I just got back from shopping, and I heard what happened. I wanted to make sure you were all right."*

He smiled. "Don't worry, Aunt May, I'm fine. Well, physically, anyway." The smile gave way to a sigh.

"I understand, dear," May said after a pause. *"But don't you go punishing yourself for this. I know it's hard not to, you're such a sensitive young man, but I know you, and there's not a doubt in my mind that you did everything you possibly could for—well, for everybody involved,"* she finished, trying to remain cryptic about the details while on an open phone line.

In spite of himself, Peter smiled at her awkward attempt to cope with the reality of his life. Aunt May's recent discovery that he was Spider-Man had turned out to be one of the best things that had ever happened to him. For years, he had assumed the shock would be too much for her weak heart to bear, though in retrospect he realized he should've known better. May had been strong enough to bear the loss of his parents and later her beloved Ben, to nurture and inspire him through a lonely childhood, and to weather the ongoing madness that seemed to affect everyone in Peter's life in the wake of that spider bite, whether through deliberate manipulation by foes who knew his identity or simply through the lunatic fortune that seemed to be his lot. Her discovery had been a grave shock to her—she had learned it in the worst possible way, letting herself into his apartment and coming upon a battered and bloody Peter asleep in half of his uniform after a particularly rough battle—but the effects had been more emotional than physical, and she had wisely taken time to think it over before confronting him and working it through. Until then, she had feared and loathed Spider-Man, but now she was striving to accept what he did, still disturbed by his vigilantism but believing unswervingly in her nephew's basic goodness.

Still, although it was usually refreshing to be able to talk to May about his problems as Spider-Man after years of hiding them from her, today her reassurances stung more than they healed. *"You did the right thing looking out for your students,"* she told him. *"You should be glad that you have so many— er—like-minded friends who were able to take care of the other . . . aspects of the problem. You really should consider teaming up with them more often."*

"You know I've never been much of a team player, Aunt May," he replied. It was odd—somehow, over the course of his career as Spidey, he seemed to have teamed up with virtually every other superhero on the planet (and some from beyond), yet despite that he was still a habitual loner, rarely following through on those opportunities to forge closer bonds with the hero community. He'd tried to join the Fantastic Four at the start of his career, but had handled it badly and alienated them, leading to an ongoing rivalry with the Human Torch. He'd later been able to turn to the FF for help when he'd really needed it, but had still kept his distance behind the mask. He'd actually been a reserve Avenger for a little while, but that status had been lost in one of their periodic disbandings, and he'd never tried to regain it.

Is May right? he wondered. If he'd been part of a team from the start, would they have taken care of the robots before they'd gotten out of hand? Before they'd sent his students to the hospital?

The truth was, when he looked at the news footage of She-Hulk taking Electro down and her fellow Avengers trashing the robots, he didn't feel gratitude for their assistance. He felt embarrassed at his failure to defeat one of "his" villains on his own, at needing other super heroes to clean up a mess he'd caused—particularly in such a public way. But he was too embarrassed by that embarrassment to admit it to May or MJ. He didn't want to sound like he cared more about his wounded pride than the safety of the citizenry.

If anything, he felt oppressed by their efforts to talk him out of feeling guilty. Because Peter knew that it was hollow comfort, that ultimately they knew as well as he did that he *had* failed in his responsibility to protect the innocent. To protect his students. So after a while he said his goodbyes to May and made an excuse to get out of the apartment.

Unfortunately, the excuse he made on the spur of the moment was: "I promised I'd go downstairs and check on Flash." Once he was out the door, he belatedly realized that was the last thing that could distract him from his guilt.

Eugene "Flash" Thompson had been Peter's greatest rival in high school and college, the football jock and BMOC who'd relentlessly picked on "Puny Parker," but in later years they'd mended their differences and become fast friends. More recently they'd drifted apart, but that hadn't kept Norman Osborn from targeting him. Osborn had been Spider-Man's greatest foe for years, both as the masked berserker called the Green Goblin and as a devious manipulator working behind the scenes—in large part because he knew Spider-Man's true identity. He had kept that secret to himself due to the rules of whatever mad game he thought he was playing, but had not been above striking at Peter's friends to hurt him. Flash Thompson had been the latest victim, framed in a drunk-driving accident that had left him in a vegetative state. Aunt May had arranged for him and a full-time nurse to be moved to the vacant apartment below Peter's, and Peter's friends and fellow tenants had taken it upon themselves to look in on Flash regularly, trying to engage his dormant mind in the faint hope of stimulating it back to some level of activity.

That's the thing about being Peter Parker, he thought as he knocked on the door to Flash's apartment. *I never have to travel very far for a guilt trip.*

The door opened, but instead of Flash's nurse, Peter found Jill Stacy standing there. "Hi, Pete!" the pretty young brunette said, smiling. "Come on in! Hey, Liz, Pete's here!"

"Hey, Pete!"

Oh, great, Peter thought. *Two more reminders.* Jill was the younger cousin of Gwen Stacy, the first great love of Peter's life, whom the Green Goblin had murdered years ago. Liz Allan, meanwhile, was the widow of Osborn's son Harry, who had fallen victim to his father's legacy of madness and ultimately left Liz a widow and single mother. Despite her own problems and responsibilities, Liz had shown unfailing loyalty to her old high-school flame Flash Thompson since his injury, coming to visit him almost every day.

Everyone in this room has suffered terribly from Osborn's feud with me, Peter thought as he came in. *Everyone in my life seems to get hurt sooner or later, even if they have nothing to do with Spider-Man. Why do I keep letting this happen?*

Outwardly, he tried to keep his expression cheerful, but with limited success. Liz and Jill saw his melancholy but didn't divine the full reason for it. "Aww, Peter, we heard about what happened to your students," Liz said, drawing him into a hug that Jill joined in on. "Thank God you're all right."

"Well, I'm certainly feeling better now," he replied, keeping his tone breezy.

"Hey, don't forget you're a married man there, Mr. Watson-Parker," she teased as she pulled away.

"Trust me, MJ would never let me forget that. Nor would I wish to."

"On pain of a horrible death, I'm sure," Jill added, then cleared her throat when the joke fell flat. "Sorry. Bad taste."

"That's okay," Peter told her. "The doctors think all the kids will pull through."

"I hope so," Liz said, suddenly turning toward Flash. "And I hope they all get . . . back to normal." She gave a nervous, breathy laugh, wiped a bit of drool from Flash's chin, and took his hand. "Like you'll be anytime now, right, Flash? It just takes time to heal, is all." Peter winced.

Just as he was trying to think of a way to change the subject, Peter's phone buzzed in his pocket, startling him. He grinned sheepishly as he pulled it out. "Don't be alarmed, ladies. I have my phone set on 'vibrate my bottom.'" After an embarrassing and life-threatening incident or two, he'd gotten into the habit of keeping his phone in silent mode when he was out as Spidey, and sometimes he carried that over into civilian life.

Reading the caller ID, he answered the phone. "Dawn? Hi, what's up?"

His fellow teacher sounded angry. *"Peter, have you seen Jameson's blog today?"*

"Uhh, no, why?"

"That son of a—he—I don't even know if I can talk about it. Just . . . I think you need to see this."

"Okay, hold on." He lowered the phone, noticing Liz's laptop sitting on Flash's coffee table. "Liz, can I borrow your laptop?"

"Sure."

The laptop was in standby mode, coming on automatically when he opened it. Checking with Dawn for the address, he browsed to Jameson's *Wake-Up Call* blog and started skimming the latest entry. It started out with the expected Jameson boilerplate: Spider-Man is a menace, started the rampage, glory hound, no respect for public safety, yada yada yada . . .

Then he scrolled down and saw the pictures. "No," he breathed. But looking closer, there was no doubt. The first image was an embedded YouTube clip, home video footage of the attack on the library. Reluctant to watch but having to know, Peter clicked on the image. It was shaky low-resolution footage, but it showed the robot attacking, the urn toppling, the students falling under the debris as Spider-Man arrived seconds too late. That was horrifying enough, but below it were a number of still photos apparently taken at the hospital afterward: photos of his students, battered and bloodied as they were rushed to the emergency room. Susan, Bobby, Angela, all of them. Their faces were visible. Their names were named. Below them, Jameson had written:

> Some may question the taste of showing these images
> in public, but they are already out there, thanks to the
> anonymous hospital employee who took these photos
> and posted them online. The ethics of it are a debate for
> another time, but if this kind of total exposure is the nature
> of our culture today, then maybe in this case that can serve
> a positive purpose. The public needs to be shown the true
> horrors that Spider-Man and his ilk inflict on the innocents of
> the world in their never-ending testosterone contests. People
> need to see that despite their flashy, flamboyant personalities
> and wisecracking antics, at the end of the day theirs is a
> legacy of blood. These are the faces of Spider-Man's victims.
> Angela Campanella, Koji Furuya, Susan Labyorteaux, Roberto
> Ribeiro, Joan Rubinoff. Say if you like that the hospital worker
> violated their rights by taking these photos, or that I violated
> good taste by posting them. But never forget that it was
> Spider-Man who violated them most of all. Look well on what
> his reckless vigilantism did to these fragile innocents and
> remember. Yes, it is shocking to show you these images.
> But sometimes we must be shocked, must be angered and
> offended, before we can be inspired to take action.

But Peter barely saw those last sentences through the red haze filling his vision. "Jameson! How dare he!"

"Peter!" Liz cried in alarm. Peter turned his head to where both women were reading over his shoulder, regaining enough presence of mind through his fury to follow Liz's gaze and realize he'd crushed the phone in his hand.

But right now he couldn't be bothered to worry about protecting his identity. He only regretted that it hadn't been Jameson's throat. "I'm okay," he said through clenched teeth. "Sorry, I have to go."

"We understand," Jill said. "That jerk, how dare he?"

"Take care of that hand, okay?" Liz called after him as he stormed from the apartment. But his hand was fine. The injury ran much deeper.

No, he realized as he climbed the stairs. What he felt was not an injury, not another pang of the guilt that already weighed so heavily on his heart. Something had snapped inside him, yes, but it had brought him a new clarity, a new strength. He had been pushed too far, and now something inside him was pushing back.

By the time he reentered his apartment, he was still angry, but it was a focused, controlled anger rather than the ferocious rage that had threatened to overtake him before. He sat on the couch with MJ and told her what had happened in a tight but level voice. "I can't believe it!" she said when he was done. "Jonah's pushed the limits of good taste before, but putting up photos of injured children?"

"Believe it," Peter told her. "Every time I think there's a shred of decency or restraint in that man, he proves me wrong. And this time he's really crossed the line. There's no forgiving this. These are my kids, MJ! Nobody gets away with victimizing them. *Nobody!*"

"Too bad you don't still work for him," she said. "You could quit."

"That's exactly what I'm going to do," he said. "I quit. All of it."

Her eyes widened. "All of what?"

"What I do every time something goes wrong in my life. For years, Jameson's been beating up on me. The cops have been after me. My professors and bosses have lectured me about how lazy and irresponsible I was because I was busy out saving the damn city from psychotic killers. Everyone keeps blaming me for everything that goes wrong in my life—and I've been right there leading the blame squad. I've been playing

Jameson's game along with everyone else. Torturing myself with guilt, just like he wants. Well, I'm not gonna do that any longer!"

He rose from the couch. "I'm through letting Jameson tear me down, and I'm through tearing myself down. I'm through with blaming myself for everything that goes wrong whether I have any control over it or not! You were right, MJ—what happened yesterday wasn't my fault. I was the one trying to stop it! I was the one saving lives out there!"

"Yes! That's the spirit!"

"I wasn't the one who got those kids hurt. It was Electro's fault. It was the fault of whoever helped him get those robots. Hell, it was Jameson's fault for turning this city against me! If I had more support for what I do, I could probably have put Electro away for good long ago!

"The only thing I've done wrong," he went on, "is letting myself buy into all the Spidey-bashing. Well, no more. I'm through second-guessing myself, questioning every niggling little decision. I'm through being the Woody Allen of superheroes. I've got enough people to beat up on me—I'm not gonna do it to myself anymore. I'm not gonna waste energy punishing myself when I should be going after the people who really deserve to be punished!"

MJ's arms went around him from behind. "That's my tiger. I love it when you roar."

He smiled. "Thanks, but I don't know if I'm in the mood right now."

"No, I'm serious. You're such a good man, Peter. It can really hurt to see you always doubting yourself, burying yourself in guilt. You deserve better. You're a hero, and I want the whole world to know it." She kissed him. "Including you."

"You're right. I do deserve better. And I'm gonna make it happen, too."

"Mmm, tell me, tiger, how will you do that?"

"By finding out who's really behind this," he said. "Electro's never been much of a mastermind. To pull off something this big, he must have had help."

He strode to the window and gazed out at a city that suddenly looked smaller, easier to tame. "I'm going to find out who's behind this, and I'm going to bring them to justice. And then I'm going to make J. Jonah Jameson eat every last word he's ever written about Spider-Man."

FIVE

SOMEDAY I'M GOING TO MURDER THE BUGLER

"JONAH, we need to talk."

As Joseph Robertson strode into his publisher's office, he found Jameson hunched before his keyboard, tapping out more of his deathless (or was it deathly?) prose. "Talk on your own time, Robbie," Jameson growled. "I'm paying you to edit a newspaper, not exercise your speaking skills."

"You need to hear this, Jonah. It's about your coverage of the robot incident."

Jameson turned from the screen and directed an impatient glower at Robertson. At least 90 percent of JJJ's expressions were glowers, but Robbie had known him long enough to discern the impatient kind from the angry kind, the suspicious kind, the you-expect-me-to-pay-what-for-that? kind, and all the rest. "We've been over this, remember? Those photos were already out there. Anyone could've Googled them up in ten seconds. They were part of the story, and I covered them."

"You know that's an excuse, Jonah. That creep with the camera invaded those kids' privacy, and by reposting the images, you were just condoning what he did. That's why we didn't print them in the *Bugle*. Hell, you didn't even *ask* me to print them in the *Bugle,* because you know better!"

"Blogs aren't the same as papers, Robbie! The standards are different. The rules are different."

"The standards of good taste should be the same in any medium."

"It's my own private forum, Robbie, and I'll put in what I blasted well please!"

"They're Peter's kids, Jonah!" Robertson paused to take a breath after the outburst, continuing with less volume but not much less anger.

"They're students from Peter Parker's class. He was one of ours, Jonah. He was part of the *Bugle* family for years. Don't you even—did you even stop to think about how it would make him feel?"

For once, Jameson was at a loss for words. He looked away, having the decency to be embarrassed. It was the sort of moment Robertson had experienced many times in his relationship with this man, the kind that made him stick with J. Jonah Jameson despite all his faults. Sure, JJJ was tough, irascible, aggressively opinionated, driven to gain profit and sometimes willing to go to unhealthy extremes to get it. Sometimes those were his worst attributes as a publisher and a man, when they drove him to be a slave driver to his staff or compromise journalistic ethics in his vendetta against Spider-Man. But they were also some of his greatest strengths. A publisher put his reputation on the line every day and had to have the courage of his convictions, the determination to stand up for what he believed in despite all pressures to compromise. And a publisher had to have the drive to do whatever it took to make his business profitable, for the sake of the employees who depended on him. Robbie Robertson had seen JJJ stand up to crooked politicians, crusade for social programs, and fight for the welfare of his employees time and time again. As his editor in chief, Robertson saw it as his responsibility to be a spur to Jonah's conscience as well, to keep his occasional excesses and bad decisions (driven either by his desire to sell papers by any means or his vendetta against Spider-Man, or sometimes both at once) from overriding the basic decency that Robertson knew existed beneath the man's harsh exterior.

But a publisher needed a thick skin, so while Jameson took his point, he didn't show remorse outwardly beyond a subtle shift in the aspect of his glower. "All right, I'll make it up to the kid somehow. I know—have Sibert say something nice about his wife in the theater page."

"How about taking those photos down from your blog?"

"Yeah, yeah, they've run their course." His tone was dismissive, but when Robertson peered around at his screen, he could see that Jonah was already doing it.

"Anyway," he said, moving on, "that's not what I came to talk to you about."

"It's not? Then why have you been wasting my time yammering on about it when you should be working on the evening edition?"

"Jonah, the *Daily Globe's* uncovered something about Cyberstellar Tech, the company that built those robots."

"The *Globe?* Why are you telling me what they uncovered, when the *Bugle* should've uncovered it first?"

"Jonah! They're reporting that *you* own shares in Cyberstellar."

"Me?"

"Is it true?"

Jonah was nonplussed for a moment, but shook it off. "How should I know? That's what I pay my investment counselor for. I can't be expected to remember every line in my portfolio!"

"Jonah, you should've checked. This is a potential conflict of interest. How does it look for you to try to pin this on Spider-Man when you have a stake in the company that made the robots?"

"You know I had nothing to do with those robots! But Spider-Man was—"

"Come on, I shouldn't have to explain to you about the appearance of impropriety!"

"I'm not reporting here, Robbie! I'm not trying to set the agenda of the paper. These columns, these blogs, they're opinion pieces. People know better than to take them as assertions of fact."

"Do they, Jonah? Do you really think that's true? And if so, then why do you keep trying so hard to convince them you're right?"

Jameson sighed. "Run with the story about my ties to the company. Full disclosure. You get full access to my financial records. The *Globe* may have gotten this story first, but the *Bugle* will do it better! We don't hide from our mistakes like some people I could mention." A familiar gleam was coming into his eye. "I can see it now. My next post. J. Jonah Jameson won't hide behind a mask! I come clean and look the public in the eye! I dare Spider-Man to do the same!"

Robbie chuckled to himself and left Jameson to it.

<hr />

"THAT'S it!"

Peter's sudden exclamation drew the attention of the checkout clerk and the customers ahead of him in line, and a puzzled look from MJ. "Sorry," he told the others. "Go on about your business."

"What is 'it'?" MJ asked in a more normal tone.

He called her attention to the *Daily Globe* article he'd been skimming as they waited in the grocery line. With her rehearsals keeping her so busy lately, shopping trips seemed to be the only chances he got to go out with his wife anymore. "It's Jameson. He's a shareholder in the company that made the robots! He must've had something to do with it."

She leaned closer, speaking softly. "That's quite a stretch, tiger."

"Come on, MJ, it would hardly be the first time he's used ro—" His own spider-sense shut him up, as he realized the others in line were still in earshot, and he was on the verge of saying something compromising. "Uhh, let's wait till we're outside, okay?"

"I would think so, yes."

But the idea simmered in his mind as they waited their turn. While Jameson seemed content these days to attack Spider-Man with words (and pictures, he added as his gut clenched in rage), there had been a time when he'd struck more overtly. His hatred had been so fierce that he'd actually hired mad scientists to devise means of defeating Spider-Man. His first attempt had turned private investigator Mac Gargan into the powerful Scorpion, but it had backfired; Gargan had been twisted by the power and turned to crime, and had come to feel a hatred for Jameson matched only by his hatred for the wall-crawler, blaming the publisher for his fate. Spidey had ended up having to save JJJ from his own secret weapon more than once.

But Jameson hadn't learned from the experience. Just months later, an inventor named Spencer Smythe had come to Jameson and offered him the use of a robot designed to track down and capture Spider-Man. To be fair, Jonah had initially been reluctant, and the young Peter Parker—in what had hardly been one of his finer moments—had goaded him into trying it, thinking it would be a lark to defeat the seemingly ludicrous contraption. It had quickly proven far more menacing, piquing Jameson's interest—and the kicker had been the remote control and two-way screen that let JJJ direct the robot himself and have his mug displayed on its video screen (by far its most frightening feature). Unable to resist the chance to effectively battle Spider-Man in person, Jameson had hired Smythe's services and had the time of his life hunting down his prey. Spidey had escaped only by the skin of his teeth.

And that had just been the beginning. In the years that followed, Jameson had used two more, increasingly powerful, Smythe robots to hunt down Spider-Man, with the increasingly obsessed Smythe eventually dubbing his robots the "Spider-Slayers." Smythe had ultimately gone off on his own vendetta against Spider-Man, and like the Scorpion before him, he had turned against Jameson as well, blaming the publisher for the terminal cancer he had contracted from the radioactive power sources of his various Slayers. J. Jonah Jameson's peculiar charm had struck again.

But Jameson had abandoned Smythe long before then, seeking a new source for Spider-Slayer robots, namely an electrobiologist named Dr. Marla Madison. Her one and only Spider-Slayer was also the last one commissioned by Jameson; all the subsequent generations of Slayers had been the work of the now-deceased Spencer Smythe or his equally vengeance-prone son Alistaire. Perhaps JJJ had soured on them after the elder Smythe had used his last Slayer to try to kill him. Or perhaps he had simply found other priorities, as Madison had been the exception to the pattern; instead of swearing vengeance against him, she'd actually ended up marrying him. Peter wasn't sure which was a clearer sign of insanity.

"But what if Jonah's decided to get back into the anti-Spidey robot business?" he asked MJ as they made their way homeward with their groceries. "Maybe he invested in Cyberstellar so he could get access to those robots. Maybe he hired Electro to control them."

MJ was skeptical. "But didn't you say the attack wasn't even aimed at you? That Electro had no way of knowing you'd be there?"

The walk light changed in their favor and they started across the street, but spider-sense made him pull himself and MJ to a stop just as a bike messenger shot through the crosswalk ahead of them, showing typical contempt for the concept of right-of-way. The kid was braking, but not hard enough; he'd end up halfway through the intersection by the time he stopped. Peter caught the back of his seat with two fingers, jerking him to a full stop safely short of oncoming traffic. The messenger looked around in bewilderment, but Peter and MJ had already moved on. "That's what I thought at first. But maybe that's just what I was supposed to think. I mean, it was a very high-profile crime, and one that was taking a while to unfold. Odds are I would've heard about it and shown up eventually."

"You or any of a couple dozen other superheroes."

"The FF and Avengers generally deal with fate-of-the-world stuff. Daredevil focuses mostly on Hell's Kitchen and organized crime, Doc Strange handles the supernatural, the X-Men tackle mutant problems. When it comes to general street crime, robberies, assaults, that sort of thing, I'm typically the first responder. It wouldn't be the first time a crime was staged to lure me into a trap. Heck, it wouldn't be the hundred-and-first time."

"But I can't believe Jonah would put so many people in danger just to get to you. And it's been a long time since he tried to attack you like that. After the scandal broke about the Scorpion, I figure he must've learned his lesson."

"I thought so, too," Peter said, reflecting on the time that a blackmail threat had led Jameson to come clean, confessing his involvement in the Scorpion's creation and stepping down as the *Bugle's* editor in chief. He still remembered the argument they'd had. Jonah had crowed about his integrity in leveling with the public, unlike the wall-crawler. Spidey had fired back that he hadn't been "honest" until he was in danger of being exposed anyway, and still hadn't come clean about his involvement with the Spider-Slayers and other unethical acts. Peter had been angered by his hypocrisy. "But if he did hold back after that, I bet it had more to do with the fear of being exposed than anything else. Maybe this time he thought he could get away with it."

"I don't know," MJ said as they reached their building. Peter maneuvered to hold the door open, relying on spider-agility and sticky fingers to do it without spilling any of the groceries. "Thanks. I mean, you have to admit it's a major stretch. Jonah's not the only investor in that company. And you don't have any actual evidence he's involved."

"Then I'll just have to see if I can find some."

"Uh-oh."

"Uh-oh what?"

"That tone in your voice," MJ said as they climbed the stairs. "That determined, ominous declaration. If this were one of those cheesy action movies I did, it would be a cue for the music to swell and the scene to change to the hero breaking into the bad guy's lair or working over informants or something. Please tell me you won't go off half-cocked on this. Don't invite more trouble for yourself."

"Who, me?" Peter asked, deftly balancing two bags of groceries in one hand as he unlocked their apartment door with the other. "Come on. There isn't even a director here to yell 'Cut!'"

<hr>

ALL right, all right, Spidey thought as he swung through Midtown East later that night. *MJ knows me too well. Cut to: Exterior* Daily Bugle, *night. Our intrepid hero makes his way to Jameson's office.* Under his mask, he smirked. *Yeah, right. Like they'd ever make a movie about me.*

To be honest, MJ had been right: he had no actual evidence that Jameson had anything to do with this. In fact, until yesterday he would have agreed with her that Old Pruneface would never put so many people in danger. He may have been a grouch, a miser, and a tyrant, but Spidey had come to think of him as a nuisance at worst, even an entertaining comic foil. And he had shown evidence of a heart every now and then, even if it was a couple of sizes too small.

But after the way Jameson had exploited Peter's students, all bets were off. *If he was capable of that, I can't put anything past him. And let's face it,* he thought as he touched down on the Goodman Building's roof next to the massive *DAILY BUGLE* sign, *I'd like nothing more than to find out he is guilty. Then I'd have a legitimate excuse for beating his lights out.*

He sighed through his mask. *Face it, Spidey—this is probably a wild-goose chase. Odds are MJ's right and Jonah's just a total putz rather than a criminal mastermind. But it's the only lead I've got.* Maybe it was a flimsy thread of logic—but Spider-Man's whole career relied on flimsy threads for support.

Jameson's executive suite, where his private files would be kept, was on the top floor of the forty-six-story tower, but it wouldn't be easy for him to get into. Spidey had invaded Jonah's offices so many times in his career that the publisher had installed extensive security systems—bulletproof glass, hair-trigger alarms, the works. None of that would impede a man with spider-strength from entering, but it would draw the attention of security before he'd have enough time to search through Jameson's files. So

Spidey would have to be stealthy. *Too bad Felicia's out of town,* he mused, thinking of his old flame and occasional partner, the semireformed cat burglar known as the Black Cat.

Spidey chose to enter by way of the ventilation ducts. Normally, heist movies to the contrary, this would make far too much noise to serve as an effective form of stealth. But Spidey's adhesive digits could cling and release far more delicately than any magnets or suction cups, and he could move with preternatural grace, keeping banging sounds to a minimum. The ducts were narrow, and a normal human couldn't have negotiated their curves, but Spidey could bend in ways a normal human could not. *On the other hand, even Felicia would've had trouble pulling this off.*

He emerged in the hallway some distance from Jameson's office and crawled along the ceiling to reach it. JJJ probably wouldn't expect Spider-Man to break in through the door like a normal burglar. Indeed, he got no spider-sense tingle when he reached for the knob, indicating that the door had no security beyond the standard lock. It was an easy matter to force the door open. *Heck, he can afford a new lock. It's a fraction of the money he cheated me out of for my photos over the years.*

He smirked, since he'd actually brought his old minicamera along this time. He generally didn't bother anymore since he'd given up the photography gig to go into teaching, but tonight he might need it for photographing evidence.

He began with Jameson's desk, dealing with the drawer locks the same way he'd handled the door. There was nothing incriminating there, but he did find a sheet containing Jameson's passwords. *That'll save time,* he thought, starting up the computer.

Under the sound of the fan and hard drive spinning up, he began to hear another sound, fainter but shriller. At first he thought the computer might need maintenance, but then his skull began to tingle. The sensation quickly intensified and spread, and Spidey leaped out of the way just as something smashed through the supposedly shatterproof glass.

His leap carried him to the ceiling, and he caught it with his hands and flipped his legs up to join them, tilting his head back for a look at the intruder. It was some kind of mechanical device with two sets of spinning, helicopterlike blades, a large one above and a smaller, counterrotating one below, with a fat, wheeled cylindrical base. It looked like a large umbrella frame joined to an upside-down ceiling fan and subsequently possessed by Satan. It made a dentist's-drill wail as it spun and scattered the papers on Jameson's desk with the wind it created. The whine was lowering in pitch; the rotors were slowing, sagging downward as they did. Flying up here and crashing through the window must have demanded a lot of its power. It came down to alight atop the desk, which creaked underneath it, telling Spidey this was no flimsy device. And he could see that the blades had heavy, deadly-sharp cutters at their ends.

After just a moment, though, it seemed to draw on new power reserves, for the blades spun up again, rising back to horizontal. They adjusted their pitch so that the robot came up off the desk at an angle and flew right toward Spidey's perch. He flipped clear and ducked behind an armchair for cover as it carved through the ceiling panels, sending chunks flying everywhere at high speed. One piece of shrapnel caught his shoulder hard enough to bruise.

Spidey was reminded of the robot-fighting fad he'd followed back in college, when such things had been popular enough to air on television. The spinning robots had always been among the most dangerous competitors because of the high rotational speed and momentum they could build up. One such robot, the infamous Blendo, had been banned from the *Robot Wars* competition because it sent debris from its opponents flying over the blast shields into the audience. *And that was just an upside down wok with two small blades stuck to it. This thing's hardcore.*

The chopperbot touched down on the floor and rolled toward the armchair, its lower blades slicing effortlessly through the upholstery and smashing the wooden frame into kindling. Spidey jumped into the far corner and fired a webline at the blades, but it was sliced through. He poured on more, hoping to gum up the blades, but it was torn up and blown free, not sticking. *Teflon-coated,* he divined. Which suggested it had been designed with Spidey-webbing in mind. And the metal dervish was closing in on him, leaving no doubt it had been designed with bloodshed in mind. As a last ditch effort, he pulled a spare web-fluid cartridge from his belt and flung it at the blades. As he'd hoped, it burst open on impact, but then came flying back at him. He had to dodge to avoid getting caught in his own web goo as it expanded to fill the corner of the room.

He ran behind the desk, and the blades tore the heavy wood apart. Sparks flew as Jameson's computer was destroyed. Again Spidey leaped to the ceiling, and again it lifted into the air and came at him. This time, he ducked through the hole it had left previously and tried hiding above the false ceiling. But his ears and spider-sense told him as it changed direction, and soon its blades were ripping through the ceiling tiles in pursuit. He had already ceiling-crawled out of the way, though, circling around the hole so that it couldn't see him. The blades tore through where he had been and didn't turn to follow. Instead, he heard it touch down on the floor again, its whine descending to a standby level.

If only I could get it to slow down more, he thought. But then it hit him. *Of course! Part of it already is slower!*

He maneuvered carefully, trying to get directly above where its sound was coming from. Closing his eyes, he relied on his spider-sense. When he concentrated, and when the sense was heightened enough by adrenaline, it functioned almost like Daredevil's sonar-sense, giving him a spatial awareness of his surroundings that let him navigate without sight. The intense danger signature given off by the chopperbot certainly didn't hurt in that regard. He just had to find the point where the danger was strongest—which, ironically, was the spot where he had the best chance of stopping the thing.

Once he was in place, he had to act fast. First he removed several spare cartridges from his belt. Then he punched out the ceiling panel below him, which was immediately shredded by the helicopter blades. The blades spun up to high speed as the chopperbot prepared to lunge up at him. But he was already tossing the cartridges through the blades, aiming just beside the central shaft. There, the blades were at their slowest, having the smallest angular distance to cover in a given amount of time. So the blades struck the cartridges and sliced them open, but didn't hit them hard enough to send them flying fully clear. Gouts of web fluid sprayed from the pressurized cartridges, expanding as they hit the air and coating the inner shaft and blades of the chopperbot. The mass of long, sticky polymer chains began to gum up the works, slowing the blades down so that they began to sag.

Spidey kicked out a nearby ceiling panel and dropped to the floor, spraying web-mesh at the descending blades. The blades themselves may have been nonstick, but the mesh rested atop them and stuck to the web-goo that ensnared them, getting wrapped around them more and more with each rotation as he continued to spray. It tightened as it solidified, forcing the rotor blades down and inward. He sprayed more webbing to wrap them tighter.

Soon the blades were enshrouded enough that Spidey could grab them like a thick handle, which he used to swing the robot around like a baseball bat, smashing its cylindrical base into the walls and floor until the mechanism gave out altogether. Once it was dead, he knelt to tear open the casing and see what he could learn from the inner works.

But then his skull began to tingle again, and he heard the elevator opening down the hall. Jameson's alarms must have gone off when the window was smashed, and now the cops and/or building security were on the scene. Not wishing to stick around and attempt an explanation, Spidey ran to the window, fired a webline to the skyscraper across Thirty-ninth Street, and swung into the night.

Still, he didn't consider the expedition a total waste. *I go to Jameson's office to investigate his ties to the robots, and another robot shows up there and tries to puree me. I'd call that pretty solid evidence.*

○━━━━━━━━○

NATURALLY, Jameson was all over the news the next day. Monitoring the TV, it wasn't long before Peter came upon a press conference wherein Jameson publicly accused Spider-Man of trashing his office in retaliation for his editorials. *"The fact that he used a robot to do his dirty work strongly suggests that Spider-Man was behind the robot attack on the Diamond District the other day,"* Jameson insisted. *"Not to mention the theft of the robots themselves, along with one or two other robberies of high-tech companies reported over the past few days."*

"But Mr. Jameson," a reporter asked, *"if the robot was wielded by Spider-Man, why do the police report that it was immobilized by webbing and apparently smashed by someone of superhuman strength?"*

"I don't know, maybe it ran away from him."

"And why would someone with superhuman strength—and according to my notes, Spider-Man's strength is estimated at upwards of forty times normal human levels—need to use a robot to vandalize your office?"

"Maybe he got lazy! In fact, the whole thing's probably a trick to make it look like he was the victim. But if he was such an innocent victim, what was he doing in my office before the robot attacked?"

"Can you prove that assertion, sir? Perhaps he saw the robot attacking your office and intervened."

"My office door was forced from the hallway. Someone turned the knob hard enough to break the lock. There's your superhuman strength. If he was just swinging by and saw this homicidal bumbershoot tearing up my office, why would he bother to sneak into the building and force the door?"

"But if he intended to use a robot to vandalize your office—a robot that could fly and break through your window—why would he need to force the door?"

"Tell you what. When the police arrest him for breaking and entering and aggravated vandalism, I'll make sure they ask him."

"This is getting ridiculous," Peter said to himself: turning off the TV. He was used to hearing Old Pickle-Puss skirt the limits of the libel and slander laws in his accusations of spider-larceny, and had long since developed a thick skin about it. But now it seemed that Jameson might be using those flimsy accusations to cover up crimes of his own—including, perhaps, the reckless endangerment of Peter's students. That wasn't something Peter could sit still for.

And all this sneaking around looking for clues wasn't his MO either. Put Peter Parker in a science lab, and he could pursue a meticulous, thoughtful investigation with the best of them. But behind the mask, he was a different person, a brash, impulsive scrapper who favored head-on confrontation. Spider-Man was everything Peter Parker had been too timid to be before the mask. Perhaps that was why he'd donned the mask in the first place when he'd entered a wrestling competition, intending to use his newfound powers as a source of money. Perhaps he'd known that shy, bookish Peter Parker could never have found the confidence to perform in public—that he needed to become someone else, someone garish and uninhibited. When he had become a faceless enigma, stepped into that ring, and reduced "Crusher" Hogan to a quivering mass, it had filled him with a sense of power, freedom, and exhilaration the likes of which he'd never known. That was what Spider-Man was to him—unfettered, primal energy.

True, he had often put his scientific skill and discipline to work in defeating his adversaries. But that usually came after he'd been unable to prevail by going in swinging. And somehow the urgency and adrenaline of those crises inspired him to new heights of invention, enabling him to whip up potions and gadgets in hours that he might never have thought of in a more sedate, methodical study. The way of Spider-Man was to hurtle forward into a problem and wrestle it into submission.

And so he was already out the window and swinging toward the *Bugle* building again when he began to second-guess his intention of confronting Jameson directly about his role in the robot attacks. *I know it seems fishy, but this just isn't like JJJ. It could've been a coincidence that I was attacked in his office.*

But he stopped himself. *No, Petey. No more second-guessing, no more wallowing in doubt. Trust your instincts.*

At his top speed, it took mere minutes to swing from the Lower East Side up to Thirty-ninth Street. When he arrived at the *Bugle,* the press conference was just wrapping up; Jameson had gone inside, and the reporters and camera crews were starting to pack up their equipment. "Hey!" he called as he came to rest on the wall of the building, just above the podium where Jameson had spoken. "Up here! Yeah, I'm talking to all of you!" Once the news crews saw who was calling, they immediately redeployed their equipment. Spidey wanted to give them time to alert their stations so this would be carried live. In the past, he hadn't been comfortable with the public eye, only seeking out media attention in times of desperate need. But that was the old Spider-Man. The new, more confident model wasn't afraid to speak out. After all, Jameson had been able to use the press against him for years, so why shouldn't he turn the tables?

After a moment, he jumped down to the podium. "Now, listen up! I'm here to respond to J. Jonah Jameson's allegations against me. I'm tired of just sitting back and taking his abuse, so now I'm going to tell it like it is!"

"Then you deny your involvement in the robot attack in Mr. Jameson's office?" a reporter called.

"Hey, I was the one being attacked!"

"Mr. Jameson says you staged the incident."

"Come on, people! How many times has Jameson accused me of a crime and had to eat his words in the next edition? The more he rants at me in the *Bugle*, the more its sales fall, because people are tired of the lies. That's why he's resorted to a blog to spew his nonsense."

"Spider-Man, what *were* you doing in Mr. Jameson's office last night?"

He stared at the reporter, at a loss for a reply. *I was committing illegal entry to rifle through his private files based on a hunch. That'll go over well.*

But he couldn't show weakness, couldn't let himself get sidetracked. "Look, I'm not the story here! Someone is sending deadly robots on rampages all over this city, and I'm the one risking my neck to save all of yours!"

Then a familiar bellow came from the *Bugle* entrance. "What's going on out here? What's that wall-crawling menace doing on *my* property?"

Spidey ignored it. "And it would be nice if you sensation-mongers would pay some attention to the good I do for this city, instead of letting the Yellow Kid here set the agenda!" he finished, jerking his thumb back to indicate the approaching Jameson.

But suddenly his head began to tingle with the sense of impending danger. *Now what?* He whirled—but the only person behind him was Jameson, storming down to the podium to confront him. "Now, listen here, you fright-masked miscreant!" he cried, jabbing a finger into the embroidered spider emblem on Spidey's chest. "Where do you get off using *my* podium on *my* property to insult me in public?"

It was all Spider-Man could do not to attack him right there, since his instincts were screaming for him to do just that. There was no question now: J. Jonah Jameson was the danger he was sensing.

"I figured it was appropriate," he shot back. "Both the robot attacks this week have had some connection to you. Would you like to explain that to these nice people?"

"As soon as you explain what you were doing at the scene of both attacks!"

"I was doing my job, Pruneface!"

"What job? Who hired you? Who do you answer to? You're just a creep who thinks having superpowers is a license to trample over everybody else's rights!"

"Oh, nice speech, Spartacus. But something about you stinks to high heaven, and I won't rest until I find out what it is!" Finally giving in to the intense fight-or-flight response the spider-sense evoked, Spidey leaped skyward and fired a web to swing away. As he receded from Jameson, the danger tingle subsided, reaffirming what he already knew. *Jonah's become an active threat to me. There's no doubt of that now.*

And I'm bringing him down.

SIX

SPIDER-SENSE AND SENSIBILITY

"**I** just can't believe it." May Parker shook her head as she laid plates full of her famous wheatcakes before Peter and MJ. "Jonah Jameson may be rather, well, *outspoken,* and I know he's never been fond of you—well, of your alter ego, dear. But I can't believe he'd put other people in danger to hurt you."

No matter how crazy his life got, Peter always tried to make time for weekly brunch at Aunt May's Forest Hills home. Her wheatcakes were his ultimate comfort food, and this house held so many warm memories of May and Uncle Ben. He would have preferred to put shop talk aside, but after May had learned his secret, she had asked him to keep her informed of everything that was going on in his life, whether as Peter or as Spider-Man. There had been too much secrecy between them for too long, and though May strove to hide it, Peter could tell she was hurt by his years of deception. So these days he made a point to keep both her and MJ in the loop, and it was safer to do so in person than over the phone. So shop talk it was.

"It wouldn't be the first time he's gone after me, Aunt May. You remember he was involved in creating the Scorpion. Not to mention the Human Fly and the Spider-Slayers. Spencer Smythe died because of his work on the Slayers. And the Scorpion killed his creator, Farley Stillwell."

"Dreadful business, I know. But did Mr. Jameson ask Dr. Smythe to use shoddy safety standards? Did he tell Dr. Stillwell to go chasing after the Scorpion?"

"No, but it still goes back to him."

"Maybe it does, and that's between him and his conscience. But he hasn't done anything like that in years, has he?"

"And he never went this far before," MJ added through a mouthful of wheatcakes.

May gave her a look. "Very impressive, Mary Jane. I take it that talking with your mouth full is some sort of diction exercise for your acting? Because if it is, then I suppose I can excuse it."

MJ took a sip of milk. "Sorry, Aunt May."

"Think nothing of it, dear."

"You're right," Peter went on, "Jonah hasn't gone after me in years, and I thought he'd learned his lesson. But my spider-sense doesn't lie. It was going off like crazy around him. That means he poses a clear and present danger."

"Peter's been borrowing Harrison Ford DVDs from the library again," MJ teased. That was often her way of dealing with stressful subjects— using her playful, party-girl persona as a shield. In the past, it had often been a form of denial, but these days she just used it to break the tension.

"Well, you'll have to forgive me, but I'm still trying to wrap my mind around this 'spider-sense' of yours and how it works," May said. "I understand the basics, that it warns you of danger, but what does that mean, exactly? Is it—something psychic, like that charming Dr. Strange?"

Peter was slow to answer. "I don't *think* so. I've had the possibility suggested to me. But I don't buy it, because there's no connection there— no reason why a spider bite would give me psychic powers."

"Maybe the radiation woke up a latent mutant ability?" MJ suggested.

"Well," May said primly, "I never heard of anything like that on Ben's side of the family."

"I'd rather not complicate the variables without evidence," Peter demurred. "I prefer to think it's literally based on spider senses, the ability of arachnids to detect things normal humans can't. For instance, spiders have a keen sense of smell and can see in ultraviolet. Plus they're incredibly sensitive to the tiniest vibrations in the air and ground. I think that's probably the basis of it—that I can sense the movement of everything around me, tell the shapes and positions of things by their effect on the airflow, even when they aren't in my line of sight. I figure I can feel the vibrations when someone draws a gun or starts to pull its trigger. Maybe I can smell the cordite and the gun oil.

"But whatever my brain is doing to process that input is on an instinctive, animal level, so I don't consciously register these things. I can't even be sure that's what I'm sensing. I just know danger when I feel it."

"And it makes you . . . tingle? That's how you've described it. I don't quite follow that."

"He told me," MJ said, "that it's kind of like the chill that runs down your spine when you're really scared or disgusted by something. Like goose bumps."

"Sort of," Peter amended. "Only it's deeper, more intense. Part of the reason I call it spider-sense is because at its worst it feels like a thousand spiders crawling around on the inside of my skull." He noted the others' reactions. "Sorry—shouldn't have said that while you were eating."

"That's all right, dear. My appetite isn't what it used to be anyway. Please go on."

"And that's just the physical side. It's not just perceiving danger, but reacting to it. When I feel the spider-sense go off, my adrenaline surges and I instinctively recoil from whatever the threat is. That instinct has saved my life more times than I can count. It lets me start moving away from a bullet's path before it even leaves the chamber."

"Then I'm immensely grateful to it," May said.

"You and me both," MJ added.

"And Peter makes three."

"One thing, though," May went on. "I've smashed enough spiders in my decades of housecleaning to know that they don't have any preternatural ability to dodge away from danger. Unless you have some blind spot for giant rolled-up newspapers that you haven't gotten around to mentioning, Peter."

He laughed. "No, I don't think anyone's ever tried that one on me." He pondered it for a moment. "I guess it makes sense that something as small as a spider would need a heightened awareness of potential threats in its environment, and a strong avoidance reflex. I mean, they could certainly feel your newspaper swinging through the air and try to run away. Maybe they can't escape in time because it's just too big in proportion. Even I can only move so fast, and I've had some really big things fall on me."

"So spider-sense isn't infallible, then," May pointed out.

"It always warns me of danger, but I can't always do enough to escape it. I know what you're getting at, Aunt May, but it doesn't give me false positives. Whenever I've ignored its warnings in the past, I've regretted it."

"Well, I guess I'm still confused, Peter dear. I can understand it warning you if, say, I were suddenly to swing a frying pan at your head. But if I just *thought* about doing it, you'd still sense that, too?"

Peter chuckled. "That's . . . kind of a bad example. Remember when you were working as Doc Ock's housekeeper? And you smashed that vase over my head?"

May winced. "Well, of course I didn't know it was you then, Peter dear. And I didn't know what a fiend that Dr. Octopus was. I'm terribly sorry in any case."

"You were just doing what you thought was right, Aunt May. Anyway, my spider-sense doesn't react to you, or to other people who are really close to me, even when they are trying to hurt me. I guess because I feel so safe with you."

She smiled. "That's very sweet, dear."

"Hey!" MJ said. "I know I've set off your spider-sense at least once—and that was just sneaking up on you with a pillow!"

"Well, I, um—that is, I . . ."

May patted her on the hand. "Don't take it personally, dear. Husbands are always at least a *little* afraid of their wives. And we wouldn't have it any other way, would we?"

After a moment, MJ laughed, letting him off the hook. "Don't worry about it, tiger. Actually I'm flattered. Lets me know I'm a force to be reckoned with."

May turned to him again. "But back to my question, Peter?"

"Oh, right. Yeah, with anyone else, I can sense if they're dangerous even if they aren't actually doing anything dangerous at that moment. It might have something to do with their pheromones; like I said, spiders have a great sense of smell. Or maybe my sensitivity to vibration lets me pick up aggression in their body language or recognize the way a known enemy moves underneath a disguise. Or, heck, maybe it is psychic—I can't conclusively rule that out, no matter how unlikely I think it is. Whatever the reason, I just know when somebody's dangerous, even when they aren't trying to strike."

"So when Mr. Jameson sent the Scorpion after you, or those awful Slayer robots, you felt a spider-sense, err, 'tingle' from him?"

"Yeah, I—" Peter broke off, thinking back. "Actually I didn't."

When Jameson had gotten Stillwell to create the Scorpion, he'd tried to lure Spider-Man into a trap, suddenly acting friendly and inviting. Peter remembered being suspicious on those grounds alone, but now that he thought back on it, he realized there had been no warning tingle. Even in an instance from years later, when Jameson had confronted Peter with photos proving he was Spider-Man (before Peter had managed to trick him into believing they were forgeries), he still hadn't set off Peter's danger sense, even though it routinely warned him when his identity was at risk of exposure. "Come to think of it, I can't remember Jameson ever setting off my spider-sense before. Maybe because he wasn't trying to attack me personally. The only time I got a warning buzz from him was when it wasn't really him—when the Chameleon impersonated him for a few weeks. My spider-senses must've recognized Chammy beneath the disguise."

"Well, could that be it?" MJ asked. "Could the Chameleon have replaced him again?"

"Last I heard, he was still in a cell at Ravencroft. I'll have to double-check, though."

"Or he could be a robot himself," MJ went on. "Or even a clone."

Peter glared at her. "MJ!"

She winced. "Sorry, I know. Never, ever mention clones."

"Well, at least you should explore the possibility, Peter."

He turned to Aunt May. "I'll consider all the possibilities. But it's just as possible that this is the real one and only J. Jonah Jameson, and he's just finally flipped his wig for good. He's always had a hatred for me that bordered on the psychotic, and maybe it was just a matter of time before he stepped over that border. Believe me, it happens with depressing regularity in my life. And if he's actually insane now, that could explain why he's suddenly triggering my danger sense.

"But whoever or whatever he is, I'm sure he's got some connection to the robots. And I'm going to find out what it is if I have to turn Manhattan upside down to do it."

May rose from the table. "Then you're going to need some more wheatcakes."

He grinned at MJ. "I love this woman."

BEFORE Spider-Man could begin his investigations, Peter Parker had a stop to make at the hospital, to visit his students. He'd been trying to come every day, insofar as his crimefighting duties permitted. Most of the students' progress was heartening. Susan Labyorteaux and Koji Furuya had already been released, though Koji would be on crutches for a while. Susan had sustained only a simple fracture to her left arm, along with various cuts and bruises. Her parents had declared it a miracle that she'd been spared worse, and Peter couldn't begrudge them the belief—although it seemed to him that a benevolent God willing to intervene on people's behalf wouldn't limit that aid to the one who professed the loudest faith. But Susan had gone her parents one better, asserting that all the students had been spared by God—with a little help from Spider-Man. Peter had appreciated that. In class, he and Susan often clashed over matters of science versus faith, but he was coming to appreciate that she exemplified the better qualities of faith. He would just have to try harder to help her recognize that openness to new ideas was not incompatible with faith, regardless of what her parents told her.

Joan Rubinoff and Angela Campanella were still inpatients, being treated for more serious injuries. Angela, a vivacious, popular blonde girl, had managed to keep up her usual good spirits despite the tubes sticking into her body, no doubt buoyed by the jungle of flowers, balloons, and stuffed animals that her many friends and admirers had populated her room with, along with the parade of classmates who came to visit (though Peter suspected that most of the boys who visited were really there in hopes of getting a peek down her hospital gown). By contrast, the normally wisecracking Joan had become more bitter and depressed. As far as Peter could tell, the bespectacled, frizzy-haired teen received few visitors other than her doting grandparents, and was mostly left alone to stew at the sight of Angela's parade of admirers across the hall. Peter was reminded of himself in the old days, using humor to cover up his inner doubt and sadness. Maybe there was a way, he thought, that he could inspire Joan to discover the same confidence and self-assurance he had now. *Of course there's a way,* he told himself. *Give it time, you'll think of something.*

But Bobby Ribeiro had taken the worst of it. He'd sustained head trauma from the falling debris and was still in a coma. He was breathing on his own, his body healing, but the doctors couldn't say whether his brain would recover or to what extent. That bright, active, contentious mind, a source of such trouble and hope for Peter as his teacher, now lay dormant and might never recover.

Bobby's mother, Consuela, was there with him every day, watching over him with her squalling baby in her arms, leaving her other four children in her sister's care for the duration since their father had run out on her before this youngest Ribeiro had been born. "Is there any change?" Peter asked her when he found her there today.

She shook her head. *"Nada.* I don't know what to do. I can't afford to leave him here much longer. But how can I take care of him at home, when I have so many others?"

Peter reflected on how lucky Flash Thompson was to have the kind of support structure he had—not to mention a friend as prosperous as Liz willing to bankroll his home care. "If there's anything I can do to help, just let me know."

She shook her head. "I do not want handouts. That man Jameson," she said, pronouncing it with a Spanish *J,* "he tried to offer money. Said it was to make up for sending out my Roberto's picture onto the Internet where the perverts could see him. But he wanted it in exchange for an interview! More exploitation! I tell him where his money can go."

Peter clenched his jaw. "Good for you." He put a hand on her shoulder. "I want you to know, Mrs. Ribeiro—I'll do everything in my power to find the people responsible for what happened to these kids and see them brought to justice."

She glared at him. "No more hollow words, *Senor* Parker. You are a teacher, not *la policia.* Do not boast to me of things you cannot do. That will not help my son."

No, Peter answered silently as she walked away. *Maybe I can't help him. But I* will *see that justice is done. No matter what it takes.*

"Don't take it personally." He turned to see Dawn Lukens approaching, her usually cheery face downturned, her wavy brown hair hanging limp. "We're all feeling frustrated and helpless about this. Wishing there were something we could do to make a difference, but knowing there's nothing we can do but wait and hope."

"There is something we can do," he assured her, impatient with her defeatist attitude. "We can help the other kids through this, by showing them our confidence. By being strong for them."

Dawn shook her head. "I don't know if I can do that anymore, Peter." She sighed. "I had such high ideals when I started out. I was going to mold young minds, inspire curiosity, share my love of Shakespeare and Twain and Donne and Frost . . . I was going to be a different kind of teacher, a friend who'd share the journey with them rather than a taskmaster. Instead I end up spending half my time confiscating cell phones and breaking up fights and praying that nobody in the room has a gun waging a losing battle to keep kids focused on their homework while they're struggling with poverty and gangs and deadbeat parents . . ." She broke off, staring at Bobby's room. "And now this."

"Don't be so hard on yourself," he told her. "You're a good teacher. The students respect you."

"That's just it. I don't feel I deserve that anymore—if I ever did. My kids keep asking me why this happened, and I don't know what to tell them. I don't know what to tell them about anything anymore. I've run out of answers. I just don't think I can do this job anymore."

He studied her. "Just give it some time. Things *will* get better. I know it."

She glared up at him. "You just don't get it, do you? You think it's all so easy. You're just a kid, an amateur. I thought you would've learned some humility from this experience, but you're just in denial."

"I am not," he said, belatedly recognizing the irony but pushing past it. "A terrible thing happened here. I understand that . . . better than you can know. But I also understand that there's nothing to be gained wasting time on blaming ourselves and beating ourselves up. That just gets in the way of finding real solutions."

"Not everything *has* a solution, Peter! Bobby Ribeiro may never wake up again! What kind of solution can we give our kids for that?"

Peter held back his angry retort, reminding himself that he was in control. He was the good guy, and it was his job to help people who were needy and confused. But she wasn't in the mood to listen to the help he had to offer. "I guess you have to do what you think is best. If you don't think you can help these kids anymore," he added gently, "maybe you need to find some other way you can make a meaningful contribution. But I wouldn't make any hasty decisions if l were you."

She didn't seem reassured. "Look, Peter . . . I know you mean well. But don't quit your day job and try to become a grief counselor, okay?" She walked away, leaving him nonplussed.

Oh, well, he thought. *I tried. Maybe it'll sink in later on, when she's not so distraught.*

He began striding toward the exit. *I've done all I can here. But Dawn's wrong. There is something I can do to make a difference. She may not think she has any answers, but I know where to look for mine.*

o━━━━━━━━━o

A quick check at Ravencroft Asylum confirmed that Dmitri Smerdyakov, a.k.a. the Chameleon, a.k.a. about a thousand other people at various times, was still incarcerated securely and in no condition to be impersonating anybody. With that avenue closed off, Spidey spent the next couple of days checking out the usual suspects in a case like this. He considered it something of a waste of time, since he knew Jameson was involved somehow and would have preferred to keep his focus there. But he investigated the other robot-makers he knew of just to satisfy MJ and Aunt May that he was considering all the options.

The first stop, naturally, was Alistaire Alphonso Smythe, the unstable inventor who had inherited the Spider-Slayer franchise from his late father. As far as Peter knew, Smythe was still locked up in Ryker's Island after their last clash, but given the way his old enemies seemed to crop up unexpectedly, he knew he had to make certain. Fortunately, he had some prior experience at breaking into this particular penitentiary, though not often enough that they'd learned to Spideyproof the facility or to train their guards to keep an eye on the ceilings.

He came upon Smythe's cell to find it occupied by its expected tenant. Smythe had gone through many looks over the years, but Spidey recognized him from their last encounter: lean-bodied, pale-skinned, with wild, shoulder-length brown hair. All that was missing were his glasses.

He was pacing the cell like a caged wildcat, absorbed in thought, until Spidey moved forward and caught his eye. Smythe squinted up at him, not needing detail vision to recognize who would be crouching upside down on the ceiling. "Spider-Man!" he spat.

"Ahh, there we go," Spidey replied. "Finally, a bad guy who understands the etiquette of these things. I show up, the bad guy looks skyward, shouts my name in disbelief, and wets himself."

"Don't flatter yourself, arachnid. You wouldn't frighten me even if there weren't inches of Lexan-reinforced glass between us."

"And that's another thing I like about the more educated class of villain. Too many people out there don't know the difference between insects and arachnids. But you always get it right, and I just want you to know, Aly, that I appreciate it."

"Keep ranting, Spider-Man. The guards will be by on their rounds any minute now."

"Oh, I just stopped by for a brief chat. How are you, Aly? Enjoying the prison diet? Getting enough exercise? Making any new friends? Built any good robots lately?"

Smythe narrowed his eyes. "Ahh. Yes, I heard about your little run-ins. And you think that I somehow had something to do with them? From in here?"

"It wouldn't be the first time an inmate here made creative use of the machine shop."

"Yes, the escapes of Dr. Octopus and the Vulture are the stuff of legend on the prison grapevine. Which is why they don't let technically gifted inmates use the machine shop without extremely close supervision anymore. Anyway, I'm insulted that you'd attribute such crude pieces of hardware to me. Trust me, Spider-Man, when you meet your demise at the claws of a Spider-Slayer, you will know it is my handiwork.

"And besides, weren't you accusing Jameson of being behind the attacks?"

"I'm exploring various leads," Spidey demurred.

"Ha! Are you actually addle-brained enough to imagine *I* would work with that smear upon humanity? The man who engineered my father's death by pitting him against you in the first place?"

"Hey, he came to Jonah!"

But Smythe ignored him. "The man who's responsible for my being incarcerated here? Who took a baseball bat to me in our last encounter? I want him dead, Spider-Man! Possibly more than I want you dead, although that's certainly subject to change."

"Aww, hey, Aly, you should be grateful to me! You used to be a fat slob, but after all these years of chasing me, you've got yourself a Bowflex body."

"I actually liked being a fat slob, Spider-Man. It was a lot less work. But I can't let myself go again until I see you and Jameson dead. I just hope that whoever's behind these robots takes care of at least half that task for me."

"And just who might that be?"

Smythe gave a menacing chuckle. "I only wish I knew, Spider-Man, so I could have the pleasure of not telling you. I'll just have to settle for the pleasure of knowing you're completely clueless."

Spider-Man waited, but nothing more was forthcoming. "Aww, come on. Don't I even get a malevolent villain laugh? Whatever happened to etiquette?"

But his spider-sense began to tingle, and a moment later he heard footsteps. "Maybe the guards will give you a lesson on the etiquette of entering where you're not invited. Good-bye, Spider-Man."

Spidey hastily made his way out of the area—but he still had one more stop to make before leaving the prison. He needed to make sure that Electro was still incarcerated. He found him in a wing reserved for "special" prisoners, in a cell specially outfitted for him with insulated rubber walls. He couldn't resist taunting him through the thick insulated glass. "You in a rubber room. Somehow, Sparky, it seems like a match made in heaven."

"You!" Dillon snarled and clenched his fists, his hairs standing on end and crackling. But nothing more than that happened; the Avengers had made sure he was discharged, and without access to an electrical source, he wasn't able to charge up the living chemical battery that was his body. All he had right now was whatever charge his own nervous system could generate. The insulation was more to keep him from influencing electrical systems outside his cell than to keep him from zapping his way out.

But then Dillon cooled down and laughed. "Mock me all you want, webhead—the fact is, I beat you. Again. And this time I hardly had to break a sweat."

"Maybe, but what do you have to show for it? You didn't get the diamonds, you lost your cool new toys, and you got beat up by a girl!"

"Yeah, sure. But I hear you're still having robot troubles anyway."

Spidey moved closer. "Where did you hear that?"

Dillon shrugged. "Around."

"If you know something—"

"What could I know from in here? I don't even have a TV or a radio. Some cops questioned me about it, that's all. That's the catch with these powers—when I'm in here, it's no phones, no lights, no motorcars, not a single lux-u-ree." He smirked. "Just gives me more incentive to get out again."

Spidey tilted his head. "So why did the cops ask you about it, I'm wondering?"

"Because cops are idiots. Always looking into every lead, even the stupid ones. I stole some robots, staged a heist, and you got in the way, so naturally when some wacko sends a homemade robot to kill you personally, they gotta ask if I know anything. I told 'em what I know—that they're a bunch of clueless morons." He chuckled. "Hell, I don't need to kill you—I already beat you."

"Great! So now you can retire and give up this life of crime."

"You wish."

Spidey left before the guards came by. He was tired of Electro's self-satisfied attitude, and there wasn't much to learn here anyway. Although Electro may have learned how to remote-control robots, there was no way he was capable of building them.

<hr />

"SO who does that leave?" MJ asked as they lay together in bed the following night—practically the first chance they'd gotten to talk since brunch the day before, although they'd waited to talk until after they'd addressed more pressing marital priorities. And he'd let her go first, since she was in a surly mood. She'd gone to visit a small theatrical bookshop she knew, located just south of the Theater District and catering to drama students. They'd been helpful to her when she'd just started out, but she'd found that, in an odd bit of reverse elitism, they'd cooled to her now that she was actually getting more-or-less regular work on the stage. They seemed to think that working actors considered themselves too good to lower themselves for a visit, and the fact that MJ had come of her own accord, taking time out of her busy schedule to drop in and say hello, hadn't registered with them enough to warm their cold shoulders. But she'd decided to follow Peter's example and refuse to be bowed by their negativity, resolving to brush it off and just not bother with them anymore. Maybe she was too good for them, if not for the reasons they assumed.

But despite her show of unconcern, she'd been happy to change the subject back to Peter's investigation, helping him go through the list of suspects. "There's the Tinkerer," Peter told her, referring to Phineas Mason, an inventor extraordinaire who supplied mechanical armor, weapons, and other devices for various criminals. "Robots aren't his usual line, but he's built one or two that I know of."

"But what motive? I mean, maybe he's not your biggest fan, but he's never really gone after you directly, has he? He's a businessman, so where's the profit in it?"

"You're right." Peter chuckled. "In fact, a lot of his business comes from people looking for stronger weapons to bash me with. I've probably put his grandkids through college. If he has grandkids."

"If so, they must get the coolest toys."

"Anyway, I asked Felicia to look into it." MJ cooled at the mention of his old flame. But Felicia Hardy had done business with the Tinkerer in the past, purchasing power-enhancing devices to compensate for the loss of her superpowers and allow her to continue as the Black Cat. "They have a business relationship, so she should be able to find out if he's involved in this. I don't think it's likely, though."

"So who else is a suspect?" MJ mused. "What about the Robot Master?"

Peter shook his head. "I checked that. Stromm's still dormant."

"Dormant?"

Peter slapped his head. "Didn't I tell you about that? It happened just before I found out you were still alive." MJ winced at the reminder of her abduction. Peter went on to tell her about his latest encounter with Mendel Stromm, the industrialist/inventor who had turned to crime as the Robot Master. Instead of trying to attack him with robots as he'd done in the past,

Stromm had actually contacted Spider-Man for help. A computer program Stromm had created in his own image had gone Borg on him, trying to take over his mind and disassembling his body until he was only a head attached to life-support equipment in a lair beneath a ConEd switching station. The program had experimented with the city's power grid, attempting to assert control, and in the process had overloaded the power lines in Times Square and caused a storm of electrical surges, jeopardizing hundreds of lives simply by learning how to walk. Stromm had told him of its drive to reproduce itself and take over the world's computer networks. The only way to prevent the ruthless program from spreading, he had said, was to kill Stromm himself—putting him out of his misery in the process. Unable to take a life even in those circumstances, Peter had instead gotten a programmer friend to devise a virus that would freeze Stromm and his AI doppelganger in a recursive loop, essentially putting them in a coma until he could find a way to rescue Stromm the man without unleashing Stromm the program on the world. Unfortunately, the demands of his life had left him little time to work on a solution, and though he kept the problem in mind, he had made no progress. "Stromm's still as comatose as ever, and I long since dismantled all the equipment that wasn't part of his life support. So it can't be him."

"Who else?"

"Well . . . there's Edwin Hills, the software billionaire. When you were out in Hollywood, he sent a robot after me as part of some crazy scheme to stage hero-villain fights on underground TV and take bets on the winners. But his robot was just so—so—*lame*. It really wasn't made for fighting. I mean, it announced its attacks before it made them! No way could a dweeb like that come up with anything as devious as that chopperbot."

"What about Doc Ock? He invented those arms."

"But he's never done much with robots otherwise. He's too egotistical to let a machine do his Spidey-killing for him—except for the arms, but he thinks of them as part of himself. And he's still in the news after that Triple X business—if he'd broken out since then, we would've heard."

"Any other robots in your checkered past?"

Peter had little else to offer besides a few miscellaneous encounters. There were numerous supervillains with the technical knowhow—the

Wizard, Arcade, even Dr. Doom—but none of them had motives that he could discern. The Wizard mostly targeted the Fantastic Four, and Arcade specialized in android doubles and ridiculously elaborate deathtraps. And Doom considered Spider-Man beneath his notice. He'd once told off the Latverian dictator to his face, but that had been after saving his life, which by Doom's twisted sense of honor had made them even.

"And the bottom line is, Jameson's the one who set off my spider-sense. He's my best suspect."

"He's no robot-builder."

"But his wife is."

"Marla? You think she's behind this, too?"

"That's what I'm going to find out tomorrow."

"But she doesn't have anything against Spider-Man."

"She's still Jonah's wife. We often do things for our spouses that we'd never do for any other reason."

MJ smirked. "Tell me about it. I'm one of the world's leading experts on that subject."

"Well," Peter said, stroking her hair, "there are *some* compensations for that, aren't there?"

"Ohh, you bet," she replied with a throaty laugh. "That spider-flexibility of yours has some very interesting uses."

"I can do some really cool things with my webbing, too. I'd be happy to demonstrate . . ."

"Maybe—if you're a *really* good boy."

○────────────○

SPIDER-MAN felt a little uneasy whenever his business took him to the Upper East Side. This was pretty much the priciest swath of real estate in the whole country, a favorite stomping ground of movers and shakers, and Spidey always felt like he should don a white tie and cuff links over his costume before he went there. It was just a bit too rarefied for a middle-class boy from Queens.

But that, he reminded himself, was the old, insecure Spider-Man. *What makes the people who live here any better than me?* he asked himself as he swung past Museum Mile in the brisk morning air. *Most of them either inherited their wealth, got it by looking good on camera, or conned it out of people one way or another. I mean, come on, a lot of them are politicians! And one of them is J. Jonah Jameson.*

Besides, he'd lived not far from here once, briefly, back when MJ's career had been particularly lucrative. *And it didn't make me any better than I am now, living in a crumbling brownstone with an insane rottweiler plotting against me. I'm the one who keeps the city safe for people like them. So I have as much right to be here as anyone.*

Particularly since his own life was on the line. If Marla Jameson was the one building the robots, he was determined to find out. So he took up a perch across the street from the building whose penthouse she and Jonah shared, and he waited.

After a while, he saw a familiar figure—fortyish, short-haired, bespectacled, severe but attractive in a Lilith Sternin kind of way—emerging from the lobby and being escorted to a waiting car by a pair of hired-security types. *Jonah's anticipated me,* he realized. *He's got Marla guarded. That's okay, though—I don't want to attack her, just see where she goes.* He knew she had a lab at Empire State University, but if she was working on a secret project, she might be operating out of some other facility.

Still, he crawled down the side of the building to get within range to fire a spider-tracer at her car. He was confident of his ability to track it visually, but just in case he lost it in traffic or got sidetracked by a crime in progress, the tracer's signal would help him find it again.

But before he could fire the tracer off: one of the guards spotted him, calling, "Spider-Man, ten o'clock high!" *Blast. Jonah did a good job telling them what to look for. So much for the subtle approach.* There would be no way to tail Marla now.

So he decided to conduct an impromptu interview instead. The guards were drawing on him, but he webbed their guns and came in for a landing atop the car. "We need to talk, Mrs. Jameson," he said—even as he realized he was getting a danger buzz from her, just like he'd gotten from Jonah. "What have you got to do with the robot attacks?" he demanded.

But the danger signal intensified, alerting Spidey to new threats coming from all around. More security troops were pouring out from the lobby and the sides of the building, and a sudden impulse told Spidey to look down at his chest, where he saw several points of laser light converging. "Stand down, wall-crawler, or we will open fire!" someone called.

"I know how to stand up, but how do I stand down? Is that like a handstand?" He made a shrugging gesture as he spoke, but it was just to get his arms into position to fire a spray of web-mesh before him as a shield. An instant later, he was flipping back behind the car and ducking beneath it, then slithering under the parked car ahead of it, all in the span of a few seconds. Glancing back, he saw Marla being hustled back into the building by the guards. He fired a tracer back to stick to the undercarriage of Marla's car, but it was a long shot, since he expected Jameson's security would locate and neutralize it before they'd let this car be used again. He had missed his chance, and whatever Marla was up to, she'd be extra-careful from now on. Rather than try to confront the security, Spidey kept crawling under cars until he found a sewer grate and vanished underground.

But now I know that she and Jonah are both up to no good, he thought as he made his way toward the nearest Lexington Avenue subway station to catch a ride home. *Maybe that's the most important thing I needed to learn right there.*

SEVEN

FROM A THREAD

NATURALLY, Jameson was all over the incident with Marla in his blog. He ranted about how Spider-Man had begun stalking his family, how his wife was afraid to go out on the streets and besieged in her own home, and so forth. He cited the web-stinger's increasingly confrontational attitude as evidence of his growing instability—even as Peter grew increasingly convinced that Jameson was the one who'd flipped his wig. Frustratingly, though, public opinion seemed more sympathetic toward Jameson. The local news was full of *vox populi* interviews of people expressing concern for "that poor Mrs. Jameson," labeling Spider-Man a stalker and making some rather disturbing insinuations about his intentions toward Marla. Even the headlines in more balanced newspapers like the *Times* and the *Globe* were beginning to sound more like a typical *Bugle* banner.

It doesn't matter, Peter reassured himself. *I've been accused of worse before, and the truth has always come out. Once I expose the Jamesons' true colors, people will see.* He was growing increasingly certain of their guilt in the robot incidents. Felicia had reported that the Tinkerer had no robots in the works, and was in fact on an out-of-state vacation. Peter had found that suspicious, but Felicia had assured him of her thoroughness in confirming the alibi. She'd investigated his vacant workshops for herself: confirming there were no major robotics projects under way. She'd tracked his activities and found no sign that he'd received the necessary materiel for such a project. She'd even obtained airport footage that showed him boarding a plane from JFK and disembarking in Miami, although she remained vague about the methods she'd used to obtain the information (and he wasn't sure he wanted to know). Felicia was confident that Mason was not involved, and Peter trusted that where a possible threat to his safety was concerned, the Black Cat would not let go of a lead unless she was certain it went nowhere. So with other viable suspects thin on the ground, the Jamesons looked more and more likely to be guilty.

The idea of Jolly Jonah being discredited and put away once and for all held considerable appeal for Spider-Man. He often wondered how different his career would have been if JJJ hadn't been there every step of the way turning public opinion against him. *Imagine if Jonah were gone for good, if Robbie ran the* Bugle, Peter thought. Robbie Robertson was a fair man who believed in Spider-Man's good intentions. Maybe in such a world, Spidey could finally redeem his image and get the recognition he had earned.

But first he needed to get some solid evidence against Jameson. Doing so as Spidey was not working out well, so he decided it was time for a little undercover work as Peter Parker. He'd worked at the *Bugle* long enough that nobody would find it odd if he showed up there.

Plus, it was a nice opportunity to catch up with the old gang. Indeed, no sooner did he arrive in the city room that Betty Brant, once his high-school sweetheart and now a veteran reporter, spotted his arrival and beamed. "Peter!"

"Hey, Betts," he said as she ran over and hugged him. "How's the *Bugle's* prettiest reporter doing these days?"

"Why don't you ask him yourself?" Betty shot back, gesturing Ben Urich's way. The unkempt, balding scribe gave her a faux-laughing expression, waving hello at Peter but apparently too busy on a story to do more. "Don't be offended," Betty said. "He's on the scent of a string of robberies."

"When is he not?"

Peter spent a few minutes getting caught up with Betty and the others in the newsroom, and soon Robbie Robertson caught wind of it and came to greet him. "Pete, hi, I was hoping you'd come in. I wanted to let you know how sorry I was about your students. If any of them need help with their medical bills, you just let us know."

"Thanks, Robbie. I knew *you'd* feel that way."

Robertson caught the emphasis. "I apologize for what Jonah did. You know how he gets carried away, but once he realized that what he'd done had been hurtful to you—well, he's not the type to admit it, but he regrets it."

"You don't have to apologize for him, Robbie." There had been a time when Peter had believed Robertson's fundamentally decent nature had rubbed off on Jameson, improved him as a newspaperman and a human being. Now he was beginning to wonder if it made Robbie an enabler, or just someone who trusted too easily. "In fact, I came to see him myself. There are some things we need to talk about."

The familiar bellow came as if on cue. "What's with all this chatter going on here? Is this a newsroom or a social club?" The danger tingle kicked in a moment later, and Peter turned to see Jameson, apparently just back from lunch since he still wore his coat. "Oh, Parker, it's you. I should've known. Bad enough the way you treated this place as your private clubhouse when you actually took photos for me! Don't you have any pecks of pickled peppers you can go pick?"

Robbie chuckled. "He's really missed you, man." He patted Peter on the back and went on his way.

"You know I couldn't stay away from your dulcet tones for long, Jonah," Peter replied, keeping his tension under wraps. Not only did he not want to give away his suspicions, but there were other things he didn't want these shrewd journalists to catch on to. He'd never been able to pull off that Bud Collyer drop-the-voice-an-octave thing when switching identities, not without sounding silly. Spider-Man's full-face mask muffled his voice somewhat, but it was a limited disguise. Mostly he relied on the differing personas he projected. As Peter, he had always been soft-spoken, originally out of shyness. Under the mask, he'd felt free to be brash, raucous, and confrontational in the way he spoke, unleashing the loudmouthed New Yorker that had always been buried within. It had been an effective accidental camouflage for his voice, and he had learned to cultivate it intentionally. Peter had outgrown his shyness, but he still tended to keep his voice low, his humor dry and laid-back—the Dennis Miller to Spidey's Denis Leary. So as much as he wanted to shout at Jameson right now, he knew he had to control his anger lest something of Spider-Man's tones creep into his voice. If Jameson was on some mad revenge kick, Peter couldn't dare let him discover his true identity. He wouldn't let MJ, May, or his friends be targeted again.

"Does that mean you've finally decided to come back to work for me? Do you have any idea how hard it's been to get good Spider-Man pictures since you quit?"

"I found something more important to do, Jonah. Something that means a lot to me and to a lot of good kids."

Jonah harumphed. "Look . . . if this is about those photos on my blog . . ."

"I'd rather discuss this in private."

"Fine, fine. Come up to my office."

Once in the elevator, Jameson spoke again. "You know I took those pictures down, right?"

"The problem is that they were up at all."

"Then blame the jerk who put them online in the first place!"

"Oh, I do."

"And blame Spider-Man! You should be as mad at him as I am, Parker. Those kids of yours would never have been hurt if he hadn't let those robots run around wild. I'm convinced he was behind setting them loose in the first place."

Even without the ongoing danger signal in his head, it would've been hard to resist lashing out at the publisher. Tightly controlled, Peter asked, "Do you have any proof of that?"

"Nothing solid yet. But maybe I would if you were still doing whatever you did that let you get all those pictures of him." Jameson narrowed his eyes. "Or maybe not. I always wondered what the connection was between you two. Always thought you knew more about him than you were telling. You wouldn't keep trying to protect him now, would you, Parker? Not after he got your students hurt?"

"I've got no ties to Spider-Man anymore, Mr. Jameson. I'm a teacher now, not a shutterbug. I don't need him anymore." A thought occurred to Peter. Jameson was clearly trying to pin this crime—quite possibly his own crime—on Spider-Man. How far was he willing to go to achieve that? "In fact, we had kind of a falling-out a while back. I got tired of him always butting into my life, bullying me into giving him publicity. So I told him where he could go stick his webs."

Jameson laughed. "Why, Parker, you have a spine after all! I'm proud of you, m'boy." He slapped Peter on the back, and it took all of the younger man's self-control to keep from striking out violently as his instincts were screaming at him to do. "Believe me, you're better off away from that madman." He grimaced. "Though it hasn't exactly done wonders for our circulation."

"You know," Peter said as the elevator let them out, "I suppose I could be persuaded to help out the *Bugle* for old times' sake."

Jameson's eyes brightened. "You mean get out the old camera again? Go Spider-hunting?"

"It's possible. But on my terms this time. In fact—since you've been so good to me over the years," he said, struggling to keep his teeth from clenching, "I might be willing to take requests."

"Like what?"

Jameson led Peter into his office (or rather, the temporary one he was using while his top-floor executive suite was under repair), hanging his coat on the rack by the door. Peter hung back as JJJ moved to his desk. While the publisher's back was turned, Peter slipped a spider-tracer from his pocket, squeezed it to activate the signal, and shoved it into the lining of Jameson's coat. Feeling its ultrasonic pulses with his spider senses, Peter moved away from the rack as Jameson turned to face him again. "Well, you tell me, Jonah. You're making a lot of specific accusations about Ol' Webhead these days. Maybe you'd like to have photos that . . . illustrated those charges in particular?"

"Parker, if you could actually catch him in the act, there'd be a bonus in it for you. I'd put you on our family Christmas card list, that's it. But if you and he aren't getting along anymore, how could you get close enough to find the proof?"

"I'm sure something could be arranged," he said, putting a bit more wink-wink-nudge-nudge in his voice.

"Hey—wait a minute." Jameson shot to his feet. "Wait just a minute! Are you insinuating that I'd allow you to fake a news photo? How dare you? I should've known! You've always been a fraud! I should've kicked you out the time you faked those photos showing that Spider-Man was Electro! Why'd I ever let you talk me into taking you back? The nerve of you, taking advantage of my world-famous generosity like that!"

"Take it easy, Jonah, it was just an idle thought."

"I'll idle you if you don't get out of my office, you two-bit hack! You kids today wouldn't know integrity if it mugged you in broad daylight! I'd never knowingly fake a story! Only times it's happened was when creeps like you exploited my trusting nature! And it's not like I'd need to fake it anyway!" he went on as he hustled Peter out of his office. "After all, Spider-Man's guilty! I don't have to fake what's already true! Now get out! Out, and don't darken my door again!"

And with that, Peter was in the elevator again. Once the doors closed him off from the still-ranting Jameson, he cursed. He'd been hoping he could maneuver Jonah into confessing something, but the publisher was determined to keep up his act. *I almost would've believed him, if not for my spider-sense screaming the whole time. He certainly played it well. But then, he could rant like that in his sleep. And probably does. It proves nothing.*

But he had managed to plant the tracer successfully. *Soon I'll get the proof I need.*

○───────────○

AFTER that, it was a matter of waiting. Spidey spent the next few hours patrolling around Midtown East and Murray Hill, while staying close enough to the Goodman Building to sense it when Jameson started to move. He stopped a mugging in St. Gabriel's Park and helped clear up a four-car pileup on FDR Drive. He swung by the United Nations to watch the Fantastic Four arriving for some kind of diplomatic function, and endured a few moments of ribbing from Johnny Storm for letting Electro and the robots get away. He refused to take the bait, though, and the Torch went on his way, saying that Spidey was no fun anymore. A little later, Spidey got hungry and dropped in on a surprised hot dog vendor. He always kept some cash in his utility belt for emergencies, and these little metal carts were the best source of cheap food in town.

That evening, when Jameson left the office, Spidey was ready, perched on the building across the street from the *Bugle*. He sensed the tracer signal changing, Doppler-shifting as it moved: Jameson's car was heading out of the garage and heading west on Thirty-ninth. Spidey fired a webline and swung after it. At the top of his swing, he fired another, shorter strand to the corner of the Burroughs Building at Thirty-ninth and Third. If Jameson turned north toward home, he could swing around to follow, but if the car kept moving west, he could release the strand and fire another to keep going straight.

The car signaled for a turn, so Spidey let the line curve him around. But suddenly his spider-sense twinged, and the line went slack. Now ballistic, he flipped and came in for a safe landing on the side of the 600 Third Avenue building across the street. (By this time, there probably wasn't a skyscraper in the city Spidey didn't know by name. As someone who relied on them for transportation, he'd become quite the connoisseur.) He looked around for the source of the attack and found it coming from above. A boxy shape was descending toward him, suspended on a pair of thin cables that anchored it to this tower and the Burroughs. From the *vreee* sounds it made, it seemed to be reeling out the cables to descend, but at differential rates, so that it drifted horizontally toward him. As it drew closer, he could see it was made of a series of stacked drums that could rotate independently, like a bike-chain tumbler lock on its side. Spidey leaped aside as a slit on one of the drums came to bear on him and fired some sort of whirling projectile. From the way it embedded itself in the black steel paneling where he'd just been, it must have been razor-sharp.

Spidey ducked behind the southeastern corner of the building, reached back around, and fired a glob of webbing at the robot. But another drum came to bear and fired a powerful jet of air that deflected the webbing. A new cable shot out to anchor itself above him, even as the first two cables were released and began reeling in. They were whipping around with considerable force as the robot swung toward him, so Spidey had to leap clear to avoid being flayed.

Unfortunately, the tallest building on the other side of the street, the Dryden East, was over twenty stories below him. Spread-eagling himself to stabilize his fall and drift west a little, he sprayed web-mesh in a wide band spanning the street to give himself a landing net. It stretched as it caught him, absorbing his momentum, and as he clung to its bouncing surface, he looked up to see what the cablebot was doing next. It was lowering itself down the skyscraper on one cable and firing another to anchor on the Dryden East building. It then used a third cable to anchor on the 600 Third building at its current height, released the first, and began swooping down toward him, firing razor disks as soon as it neared his level. *Yikes! These things are as fast as I am! Meaner, too!* He tumbled out of the net and fired a short webline, swinging to the low rooftops west of the Dryden and running. The robot kept following, continuing to fire its cables and reel itself horizontally along them. He webbed up to the taller Court Hotel across Lexington, and it fired another cable, rising to follow. He shot a web-mesh down at it, but again a powerful jet of air knocked it aside.

If I had any lingering doubts that these attacks were targeted at me, Spidey thought, *consider them de-lingered. This thing's custom-made for countering my moves.* On top of which, it was getting between him and Jameson.

But while the cablebot was still climbing, Spidey had a chance to veer north and pick up his tracer signal again. Firing a webline down to the lower buildings on the north side of the street here, he spider-crawled down it at top speed, dodging a razor disk as he and the robot drew level. He was just a few stories off the ground now, and the patrons of the laundry, deli, and Chinese restaurant below him were shouting and running to safety. Springing off the webline onto the next rooftop, he spotted a PALM READER sign down below and thought, *I wonder what she'd have to say about my lifeline right now.*

Wanting to get this battle away from the street level, as much for his own sake as for the bystanders', he fired a line to the next tall building in his path, then bounded stepwise up the increasingly taller skyscrapers to the northeast, attempting to reacquire his tracer signal.

But a razor disk from the northeast severed his webline as he swung upward, forcing him to come in for a landing on the Mobil Building's stainless-steel wall, one of its artful pyramidal protrusions jabbing uncomfortably into the ball of his foot. He looked back to check—indeed, the cablebot he'd been fleeing was still climbing toward him from the south. But a second one was now reeling toward him from the east! "Oh, great, guys, gang up on the one that doesn't have a metal skin!" He clambered up to the roof, but the second cablebot reeled in faster, its *vreee* sound rising to a cutting whine, and beat him to it. Once he made it to the broad, level surface, the cablebot was already rolling forward on a tripod of wheeled legs, apparently using its air jets for propulsion, and firing razor disks at him.

Spidey dodged and somersaulted to avoid the disks. A sudden gust of the powerful winds at this altitude blew a disk toward him after he'd already made his dodge, and it slashed him across the left flank, tearing spandex and skin. He kept going despite the pain, preparing to jump and fire a webline at the nearest gargoyle on the Chrysler Building across the street. If he could get to the spire, the second-highest point in Manhattan, he'd have the high ground and control of the one and only approach route.

But as he neared the roof edge, he saw a compact grappling claw secure to the corner. He reached the edge to see the first cablebot swinging out ahead of him, reeling in fast to build up speed as it rose, then swiftly unreeling again as it slingshotted past on a rising trajectory. It fired more disks his way as it shot past, and fired another cable to anchor on the lowermost tier of the Chrysler Building's terraced Art Deco spire, blocking his path to the northwest. Caught in a cross fire of razor disks, Spidey sustained another slash, this one across the thigh. "You're getting my tailor bill!" Now the second robot, at the roof's other corner, fired another cable to snag one of the silver-falcon Chrysler gargoyles and lifted itself into the air, preventing Spidey from heading northeast. *Uh-oh. They evolved, they rebelled, and they have a plan.*

He tried spraying them both with a wide barrage of web-mesh, hoping it would be too much for their air jets to deflect fully; but ironically, its greater surface area caused the high-altitude winds to blow it back toward him. He had to dodge left and go off the edge of the roof, firing a line to catch the southeast corner of the Chanin Building, swinging around to put that building between himself and the cablebots and proceeding to the west. He could already hear the *vreee* sounds as the cablebots began to follow. One was coming right behind him on Forty-first, the other swinging along Forty-second to block him to the north.

I'm off my game, he thought. *That's the trouble with fighting robots— without anyone to hurl wisecracks at, my rhythm's off.* "At least with Spider-Slayers, there's someone to talk to," he said just to hear his own voice. He spun around, swinging backward, to call out to his pursuers. "How about it, guys? Anybody listening? Watching? You may now gloat!" But the cablebots remained silent except for the increasingly disturbing whine of their reels and the occasional *pff-whizz* of a razor disk firing.

One thing's for certain, though: They're definitely herding me away from Jonah. That certainty gave him a new sense of resolve. *So why am I letting them? Stop being reactive and* do *something.*

He veered south at Madison Avenue, looking for a good place to lure one of the robots into an ambush. A moment later, he realized his course change had been motivated by the fact that he was a block from the Library. He didn't want to lead any more killer robots there. But the surge of anger that came with that thought heightened his resolve still further.

He led the robots down Madison for two more blocks, dodging razor disks, then veered west and climbed toward the top of 425 Fifth Avenue, a slim yellow-and-blue tower with vertical white stripes, looking like something put together with a giant Lego set. This was the tallest building in the immediate area and relatively isolated, so to get up to him, the robots would have to anchor their cables on the tower itself. That gave him his chance. *They've been sabotaging my lines, so I might as well return the favor.*

As soon as one of the robots' compact grapples snagged the building and dug in, Spidey hopped down toward it. He sprayed web fluid up and down its length, coating it thickly for several yards' worth. As the robot reeled itself up the cable toward him, it soon began reeling in the coated portion, and the whirring noise dropped swiftly to a low, grinding pitch as the webbing blocked the reeling mechanism. Spidey took a moment to put a new cartridge in each webshooter, then coated the grapple in more webbing and tore it free from the wall, letting it drop. The robot fell, catching itself lower down with another two cables, one on the Lego-set tower, the other near the top of 260 Madison Avenue, a lower white building half a block to the east. But the webbed cable continued to hang uselessly below it, twitching as the reeling mechanism struggled to clear the obstruction.

Spidey headed downward to where its next cable was anchored and repeated the procedure there. The second cablebot was trying to get a bead on him, but he stood his ground. The damaged robot (or its controller) had apparently learned from its mistake, for now it stopped reeling toward the webbed cable and retreated in the other direction. Spidey crawled along the cable, dodging razor disks as he sprayed more webbing along its length. The robot fired a fourth cable to strike the Mercantile Building to the north and released the grapple of the second, letting the cable fall in hopes that Spidey would go with it. He caught himself with a webline anchored directly to the new cable, swinging up to perch on it and repeat his maneuver. Obligingly, the robot repeated its response as well, and with only one cable left, it plunged downward. The robot avoided slamming into the side of 260 Madison by firing a jet of air, but Spidey had already swung into position and was webbing the last cable, firing right down to where it was reeling in before it could stop and reverse course. That motor ground to a halt in turn. Only two of the motors were jammed, but the remaining two cables couldn't be reeled in fully, and thus couldn't be aimed and fired. The cablebot was immobilized.

Now what? Ahh. On the rooftop below were several of the small wooden water towers that were a trademark of the Manhattan skyline. Tearing its last grapple free, Spidey swung the robot back and forth and finally hurled it at one of the tanks, where it smashed through the conical roof. The bright flash and crackling noise from within proved that it hadn't been designed to go underwater. "Yes! One down, baby, and I'm coming for you!" he cried in defiance as he bounded free of the other's razor disks.

But when he headed toward its nearest anchor point, about halfway up the Mercantile Building, the remaining cablebot unhooked it and fell away, retreating to the west. "Ha! You better run away! Nobody beats Spider-Man in my town! Accept no substitutes!"

But the sound of shattering glass silenced him. The cablebot had not been retreating, simply moving over to the next building, the Fifth Avenue Tower, a glass-walled condominium thirty-three stories high. It had fired three of its four cables through the glass and was sending a barrage of razor disks across the building's face, causing a cataract of broken glass to fall toward the condo's ninth-story sundeck and the street beyond.

Spidey had only seconds to save the residents and shopgoers below. But he was half a block away. The only point in his favor was the air resistance slowing the falling glass, but that was a small favor. He kicked off the wall of 260 Madison as hard as he could, coming down on the intervening roof, and flew straight at the falling glass, firing web-nets ahead of him. The webbing snagged most of the glass, and he swept his right shooter over to extend and attach it to the condo's facade, so that the mass of webbing and glass swung in and struck the wall. The impact cracked more glass, and Spidey's own landing on the net a moment later worsened it. Still, the webbing held it together. "Yeah! Didn't see that coming, did you?" he crowed at the cablebot.

But the mechanism was descending, firing its grapples through more windows and yanking them out again to send more glass at Spidey and the people below. He looked down, realizing that a few people were lying there, hurt by the shards of glass he hadn't managed to catch. The old Spider-Man might have been paralyzed by guilt at being too slow, but today, Spidey instantly quashed any such thoughts and concentrated on the task at hand, spraying a quick websling to span the street above him. The falling glass sliced through some of its strands, but most of it held. He poured on more webbing to catch the rest, then rappelled down to the sundeck to check the wounded.

But he heard the familiar whine of the cablebot descending and knew he was about to come under attack. The robot had put civilians in danger to distract him, leaving him vulnerable for the kill. But he wasn't going to fall for it. *No piece of fishing tackle with delusions of grandeur gets the better of Spider-Man.* He picked up a patio table and used it as a shield. "Anyone who can move, get the injured inside!" he shouted as razor disks thunked into the table. When the barrage halted and he heard the cablebot reeling to a new position, he flung the table at it like a discus, leading its motion. Air jets puffed out at the table, but it had much more inertia than a webline and was only partly deflected. It still hit hard enough to rattle the cablebot.

The mechanism recovered and came to bear on Spidey, firing a grapple right at him like a harpoon. *Must be out of disks,* he thought as he twisted away and caught it in midair, webbing up the cable with his other hand. But the next cable shot was aimed at the civilians, who were still dragging the wounded to safety. Spidey caught it in midflight with a webline and yanked it to a halt.

"That does it," he growled. Jameson had really crossed a line, deliberately targeting innocents as pawns in their personal feud. Spider-Man was burning with rage now. Luckily, he had a handy target.

Spidey scooped up several of the larger pieces of glass lying on the deck and flung them one by one at the cablebot with all the force of his fury. They weren't as sharp as the razor disks, but they hit harder. The cablebot suffered some lacerations to its shell but kept reeling up and away. Spidey grabbed more glass fragments and kept up the attack, leaping several stories up to the roof across the street. The robot tried firing a cable at him once more, but he leaped clear and tackled it bodily, pounding it with his fists. At first it was a wild release of anger, but then he targeted his efforts, widening the cuts in its shell with the wedge of his knuckles, then using his fingers to tear them wider until he could reach inside and rip out the thing's guts. One of its cable reels gave way and let out all its slack, while the other was jammed and frozen, so the robot swung down and slammed into the corner of the Mercantile Building, this time with no air jet to cushion its impact. Spidey rode down with it and kicked both feet against it as it hit the wall, crumpling it further. He planted his soles on the wall, got a grip on its cables, tore them free, and let the dead machine drop into the courtyard below.

By now the police and paramedics had arrived, the latter rushing into the building to see to the wounded. Spidey jumped down and intercepted a pair of them. "I can get you up there faster, folks," he told them. "Hang on to your stretcher!" They got a good grip, and he lifted the stretcher with both of them on it in one hand and clambered up the glass wall to the sundeck. "Watch your step, there's glass everywhere," he advised as he put them down.

Looking back down toward the street, he noticed a camera crew setting up on the scene as well. He went down the wall, clinging with just a couple of fingers so he slid down faster, and alit in front of the reporter. "Are we live?" he asked. "I want to make a statement before this gets distorted."

The reporter nodded. "Just a sec," she said, turning to the cameraman, who signaled her a moment later. "Thanks, Diane. We're live at the Fifth Avenue Tower, where the battle between Spider-Man and two spider-like robots has just concluded. Amazingly, Spider-Man himself has just agreed to give this reporter an exclusive statement about this incident. That's right, you heard it here first."

Spidey stepped forward before she could get in more self-promotion. "Thank you. I want to make it clear what happened here before certain self-interested parties put their own spin on events. These robots attacked me while I was following up a lead on the prior robot attacks. They were clearly designed to target me personally, using cables to duplicate my moves and powerful air jets to deflect my webbing. When I defeated one of them, the other began shattering the building's windows, putting civilians in danger to distract me. I'm afraid some injuries were sustained despite my best efforts, but as you can see, I put my own safety on the line to protect the people of New York." He turned to show off his slashed flank and leg to the camera, as well as the bruised knuckles under his torn gloves.

"How dare you?!" Spidey and the reporter spun to see a distraught middle-aged woman running toward him. "You big-shot heroes and your fights up in the sky, don't care what falls down on us folks below! My husband's dead! Look at him!"

Stunned, Spider-Man followed her gestures to where the paramedics were bringing out a stretcher bearing an occupied body bag. "The glass fell and it cut him and it cut him so bad . . ." She shuddered, losing her voice for a moment, and Spidey reflexively moved forward in sympathy. But the woman hardened at his approach, and shouted, "Cuz you, Mister Big-Shot Hero, was too busy crowin' 'bout how unstoppable you is! You was boastin' when you shoulda been seein' what that thing was about to do to us!"

"Spider-Man, is this true?" the reporter asked.

"No," he said, then repeated more forcefully, "No. I'm sorry for this woman's loss, but she's not remembering clearly. I acted as soon as I possibly could, and I prevented most of the glass from reaching the ground. I know you want to blame me, ma'am, since I'm the one here. But the one who killed your husband is the one who built those robots. And I swear to you—I will find him and make him pay."

"Get away from me," the widow snarled. "Just get away." She went to be with her husband's remains.

Spider-Man turned to the camera. "Do you hear me? I know you're watching, and I know you're going to try to turn this against me. But it won't work, do you hear? You've crossed the line, and that changes everything! I know who you are, and I'm going to prove it to the world! One way or another, you're going down!"

EIGHT

A GREAT BIG BANG-UP

THE next morning, the following entry was posted in *The Wake-Up Call*:

A number of commentators to this journal have complained
that I devote far too many entries to my "obsession" with
<u>Spider-Man.</u> Some have even gone so far as to make
rude insinuations about the "real" reason I spend so much
time thinking about the wall-crawler. Although I wouldn't
be surprised if it were Spider-Man himself making those
statements. Here on the unfortunately named Web, it would
be easy enough for Spider-Man to harass me anonymously. I
accept that, and take solace in the fact that at least here, he
can't shut me up by force. (People think that webbing of his is
some gee-whiz crimefighting tool, but I can report from long
experience that the little punk routinely uses it to play cruel
practical jokes on unsuspecting journalists, often invading
their private offices to leave little "surprises" on their chairs, if
not physically assaulting them with the stuff and putting them
in danger of asphyxiation.)

But I'm getting off the subject. The fact is, I would *love*
to be able to talk to you about anything other than costumed
creeps with adhesive fingers. There are plenty of other things
I have to say to the good people of this city, this country,
and this planet. I'd be delighted to share my positions on
what the mayor, the governor, and especially the president
are doing wrong, why this once-great country is headed

down the tubes, and what exactly needs to be done to get today's youth to straighten up and fly right. I'd love to spend my time talking to you about real heroes, the police officers, firefighters, and private citizens who go out there and protect people without hiding behind superpowers and fetish accessories—people who just do their jobs with no interest in fame or glory. I've made every attempt to discuss those ideas on this forum when I could.

It is Spider-Man himself who has made that impossible. He's continued to disrupt this city with his ongoing feuds against mad scientists and costumed freaks, and in the past week matters have escalated further with these robot attacks. Again and again, Manhattan's citizens and properties have been placed in danger, and Spider-Man has been at the heart of every incident. If he's not engineering them personally, he's undoubtedly provoked them as part of one of his many ongoing rivalries.

But this time he's taken it to a deadly extreme, his latest battle causing a cascade of broken glass that cruelly took the life of Paul Berry, a recently retired electrical engineer who'd made it good in life and was just starting to enjoy his sunset years along with his wife, Iona. Sadly, this is far from the first time that innocents have lost their lives to Spider-Man's feuds. But rarely has he been so callous and opportunistic about it. Rarely has he been so ready to exploit an innocent man's death to serve his own twisted agendas.

If you watched the news last night, you saw Spider-Man jumping in front of a camera, determined to put his spin on the incident before anyone could take the time to assemble the facts. He claimed that the person behind the robot attacks intended to "twist" the facts of the incident against him. This just a day after he intruded on a press conference held by me and insinuated that I had some connection to the robot attacks.

Yes, ladies and gentlemen, Spider-Man's true agenda has now become clear, and it shows just how warped he's become. He intends to accuse me, J. Jonah Jameson, of being the mastermind behind these attacks. He wants to discredit his most stalwart critic, and isn't above exploiting the death of a human being to do it. This is the action of a hero?

True, I admit there was a time when I participated in a small number of robotics experiments aimed at the humane capture and unmasking of Spider-Man. On the majority of those occasions, there were <u>outstanding warrants</u> for his arrest, so I was simply doing my duty as one of New York's leading citizens. And I never endorsed or participated in an attack on anyone other than the wall-crawler himself.

It is Spider-Man himself who has escalated things in recent days. No longer content to play obnoxious pranks on me, he now seeks to frame me for a series of lethal attacks on our city, attacks he himself is responsible for in one way or another. This new belligerence, this new tactic of exploiting the press to libel his opponents, this increased contempt for human life—it points in a direction I'm frightened to contemplate. Spider-Man has always been obnoxious, irresponsible, a two-bit punk intoxicated with power. Now, though, he seems to be growing more and more unstable, more and more dangerous. I fear for my own safety now, and that of my family.

But don't think I'll back down. I've faced thugs, gangsters, spies, assassins, and monsters in my career, and never let them stop me from doing the job of a journalist. I've always been ready to give my life in pursuit of the truth, and if I'm taken down for having the courage to tell the truth about the menace that is Spider-Man, then I can't think of a more honorable way to go. But better men than he have tried to take down J. Jonah Jameson, and I'm still here. And I intend to stay here, telling it like it is and putting bullies, cowards, and criminals in their place, for a good long time to come.

So you think you can take me, Spider-Man? Go ahead and try it.

"Maybe I *should* start posting replies on Jameson's blog," Peter told MJ that night, in that brief window of time between her return from rehearsals and his departure for his spiderly duties. He was already changing into his costume, and MJ took the opportunity to admire his lithe, muscular form—though she privately winced at the fresh cuts and bruises that adorned it, a routine sight that she still had never gotten used to. "Not anonymously, but as Spider-Man. I could prove to him it was really me by reminding him of some private details or something—like that time I webbed him to his office ceiling. Or that *other* time I webbed him to his office ceiling." He paced across their small apartment, requiring MJ to dodge out of the way. "If I post from a different library branch each time, it'd make it hard to track me down by ISP."

"Should you really be bothering with that when you should be out investigating?"

"I have to stop letting Jameson monopolize the press. This time I'm going to get my side of the story out there and keep it out there. Let people see the truth for themselves."

She smirked. "Why not just hire a press agent and get it over with?"

"Don't think I haven't thought about it. I'm tempted to do it myself—after all, as far as the public knows, Peter Parker's been Spider-Man's personal paparazzo for most of his career."

It always made MJ uncomfortable when Peter spoke of himself in the third person—let alone as two different people. She knew it was just a convenient shorthand (sometimes she wished somebody would invent new pronouns for superheroes), but she couldn't help but worry about the strain of a dual identity. Still, since she'd taken up acting, she found herself falling into the same pattern, choosing to refer to her characters by name rather than as "I." It brought her some comfort to think of Spider-Man—and sometimes even the public persona of Peter Parker—as a role her husband played. Still, there were times she wished he weren't such a method actor.

This was one of those times when she feared he was getting too immersed in the Spider-Man role. "Peter Parker's also my husband," she reminded him, "and Mary Jane Watson-Parker doesn't want 'him' drawing a lot of public attention to 'his' connection to Spider-Man. I worry enough about you under the mask," she went on, softening her tone and clasping his hand. "I'd prefer you to have a minimum of people gunning for you when you take it off."

He grinned. "Hey, don't worry, MJ. I can take care of myself." He resumed his preparations, filling a new batch of web-fluid cartridges from the agglomeration of tubes and vials he used to mix it up—"the still," as she'd come to think of it, since it reminded her a bit of the setup Hawkeye and friends had used in M*A*S*H.

"So what's the plan for tonight?" she asked. "A quick patrol, then back to bed, I hope?" She finished up the line with an inviting purr in her voice.

"We'll see. I might be staking out Jameson's place for a while."

She frowned. "I still can't believe J. Jonah Jameson's the one behind all this. I mean, he's no Mahatma Gandhi, but he's never been a killer."

"People change, MJ. I've changed, you've changed—both for the better. But sometimes people change for the worse. Remember Norman Osborn. Harry Osborn. Miles Warren. Curt Connors. There are monsters in all of us."

"But think about it, Peter. All you have is a feeling. Every time you've tried to find solid evidence to back it up, something's happened to stop you."

"That's my evidence right there, MJ. I go after Pruneface, I get attacked. Cause and effect. Besides, there aren't any other viable suspects."

"Then maybe it's someone new."

"It's Jameson, MJ! I *know* it! Spider-sense doesn't lie. It's him, and I'm going to prove it! I'll show the world what a lying hypocrite that man really is!"

"Is that what this is about?" she asked, her hands on her hips. "What's more important to you, Peter, saving lives or salving your ego?"

"This is what I do, MJ. I find the bad guys and I stop them."

"But you're doing it differently lately, Peter. You're getting so . . ."

"Confident? Determined?"

"Belligerent. Inflexible. You're throwing yourself headlong into your work these days, and I just wonder if maybe you should step back and get a little perspective."

"Just because I'm not reciting *Hamlet* before every fight anymore doesn't mean I've lost perspective. Just the opposite. I've finally stopped letting other people convince me I'm always wrong."

"But you're not always right, either."

"What are you saying?" he demanded. "You think I screwed up? Don't tell me you actually believe that woman on the news?"

"You mean Iona Berry?"

"She was upset, distraught. She didn't know what she was saying."

"Then why did you bring her up?" MJ wanted to know. "I just said you weren't always right, and that's what you immediately thought of."

"Then what else did you mean?"

"I didn't mean anything specific. But it sounds like it's still on your mind." She reached for his shoulder. "Like maybe *you* think you didn't act fast enough."

"I reacted as soon as I could."

"So you didn't stop to gloat?"

"Of course not. I did a bit of my usual trash-talking, sure. But I thought it was running away. I can't read robot minds, I couldn't know it was going to smash the glass. Nobody could've."

"Why did you assume it was running away?" She wasn't sure why she was questioning him so closely on this point. It seemed disloyal. And yet somehow she felt it was necessary.

"It had just seen me trash its partner. These things were adaptive, or they were controlled by a human being. Either way, they reacted to what they saw. It knew it'd get the same if it came after me, so it ran."

"You mean it changed tactics. It attacked civilians to distract you."

"Okay, yeah, but it was moving away from me. It made sense to assume it was retreating."

"Don't you often tell me that people shouldn't assume anything?" she asked, trying to keep her tone gentle.

"Look, what are you trying to do here? Convince me I could've saved that guy but didn't?"

"I'm not saying that. I'm just saying . . . you've always been so careful before, and I'm worried what might happen if you get too cocky."

He glared at her. "Just a week ago you were telling me how happy you were that I stopped questioning myself all the time. Sounds like you've changed your mind."

"I'm just—"

"No. I'm done with that. I'm done taking the blame for the way everyone else screws up my life. All the blame here is on Jameson's head for sending those robots after me! He's the killer here. He's the bad guy."

MJ looked at him sadly. She was very familiar with the sound of denial. For years, she had spent most of her time there, retreating from a troubled family life behind a shallow, fun-loving façade. Every time something bad had happened in her life, every time someone she cared about was in pain, she had run off to find the next party and danced and played herself into oblivion. She had abandoned her pregnant, unmarried sister when she'd needed MJ the most, an act she still strove to forgive herself for. And when she'd first figured out that Peter was Spider-Man, then that she was falling in love with him, she had run away from that relationship, hiding within the jet-set glamour of a supermodel's life. It had taken years for her to mature enough to stop running away from her problems, to admit it when something went wrong and accept that sometimes it was necessary to feel bad about things. And Peter Parker had done a great deal to help her grow into that understanding.

But now, Peter's actions were starting to remind her of her old self. She knew him too well to believe he could so easily shake off any and all guilt for Paul Berry or for his students. It was in there, and he was running away from it. "Nobody's saying you're the bad guy, Peter," she said. "But you've never been afraid to admit your mistakes before."

"Why are you trying so hard to convince me I made a mistake? You're my wife, MJ. You should be supporting me in all this."

"I am trying to support you, Peter. But that doesn't mean blindly agreeing with everything you say!" She reined herself in. "Look, nobody can be right all the time. That's why it's good to have a partner, right? You know we're in this together."

"Oh, are we? Then how come I've only seen you for, like, five minutes in the past three days?"

"You know how much time rehearsals take up."

"I've sure had plenty of opportunity to learn. This is, what, your third play in two months? As soon as you're done with one, you go find another. What, you can't take a break?"

"You know plays don't pay as well as movies. Would you rather I was out in Hollywood for four months at a time?"

"Then do some more modeling."

"What, and give up trying to grow as a performer?"

"The more you grow as a performer, the more you shrink as a wife! I need you here, MJ!"

"Oh, really?" she came back. "Sounds to me like you don't need anybody anymore, Mr. Do-No-Wrong Superhero!"

"Well, maybe I don't!" He finished donning his webshooters and pulled on his gloves.

"So this is the new Peter Parker, huh? I think I liked the old one better!"

"Maybe that's because he let you walk all over him. Along with everybody else on the Eastern seaboard. Well, no more!"

The mask went on, cutting him off from her. Then he went where she couldn't follow, out the window and through the air. Across the way, Barker lived up to his name, his harsh complaints at the intrusion into his airspace sounding to MJ's ears like echoes of their own words. "Oh, shut up, you stupid dog!" MJ yelled, for there was no one else left to yell at.

She immediately regretted it, taking a deep breath and going out to the tiny balcony. "Ohh, Barker, I didn't mean it," she called to the rottweiler, who stared back warily. "I'm sorry. You're not a stupid dog. It's us humans who are stupid." She sank down onto the balcony's metal slats as the tears came uncontrollably. "I'm sorry. I'm sorry."

<hr />

WHAT am I running here?" J. Jonah Jameson demanded as he stormed into the city room of the *Daily Bugle.* "A newspaper or a wax museum? Stop standing around and make yourselves useful! I want answers! I want this robot story broken wide open!" To be fair, the reporters weren't exactly standing still; the newsroom bustled about as much as it usually did at the height of the day. But that bustle wasn't getting him what he wanted, namely answers on Spider-Man's connection to the robot attacks. So he had to push them harder. "Urich! What's the latest on those high-tech robberies?"

"Heading out to track down a lead now, boss."

"It can wait two minutes! Have you found anything to connect them to Spider-Man?"

"Nothing," the perpetually crumpled Urich told him. "No signs of webbing residue, no stress patterns on the debris consistent with being pulled by a fine, strong line. The warehouses were broken into by brute force, and the damage suggests something mechanical was used to do it. Nothing about it suggests the webslinger's MO."

"If he's working with robots, he's changed his MO. He's trying to hide it. Look, parts from those companies were found in the robot wreckage, right?"

"Some, yes, at least in the ones from your office and Fifth Avenue Tower. But a lot of other stuff was stolen, too, and none of it's shown up yet."

"He could be building more of those things."

"*Someone* could, sure," Urich shot back in a cynical tone—but then, he always spoke with a cynical tone, so Jameson let it pass. "But why build them just to trash them?"

"To make himself look like a hero for smashing 'em."

"Lotta work to go to, considering he gets plenty of real nutcases tryin' to whack him like once or twice a week."

Jameson scowled. "Listen, do I pay you to editorialize or to be a reporter? Stop wasting my time and go pound some pavement! Don't come back without holes in that shoe leather, you hear?" With Urich thus motivated to go out and find some leads (lazy bums, reporters, needed fires lit under their backsides before they'd do anything, not like in his day), Jameson turned his attention elsewhere. "Brant! What's the latest on those kids in the hospital?"

"Rubinoff's expected to be released in another couple of days," Betty replied from her desk. "Campanella's stable and improving. No change for Ribeiro," she added sadly. "And Campanella's still the only one who's consented to an interview."

"Double the offer to the others. It's not exploitation if they're paid well for it, and it's already highway robbery. We'll be putting those kids through college if we have to go much higher. Better us than the *Globe*, though, so get on it! Stop sitting around at your desk, you're not my secretary anymore, so go! Go, go, go!"

He broke off as he saw a familiar gray-haired, brown-skinned profile crossing the city room. "Robbie!" he called, striding over to intercept his editor in chief. "What's the idea cluttering up my headline for Farrell's cover story on the Berry woman?" He brandished a copy of the current dummy for the front page of the upcoming edition, which showed a photo of the wall-crawler's masked face alongside the headline: WRONGFUL-DEATH SUIT FILED AGAINST SPIDER-MAN.

"The idea," Robbie replied, "is that just putting the words 'Wrongful Death!' next to a photo of Spidey is too close to a direct accusation on our part."

"I want it changed back, Robbie! I want this paper behind Iona Berry every step of the way!" This was hardly the first lawsuit filed against Spider-Man, but to date no one had ever managed to get the wall-crawler in court. By rights, just his failure to show should've earned a default judgment against him, but tracking him down and forcing him to pay up was another matter. Besides, that bleeding-heart lawyer Matt Murdock had a habit of taking on superhero-related cases (as "a matter of principle," he called it) and had repeatedly weaseled out of suits like this on Spider-Man's behalf. Jonah intended to stir up a public outcry against this injustice, using the Berry case as the symbol for all the rest and making sure that something stuck this time.

"Jonah, in my office, please." Robertson's voice was level, but there was steel within it. Grumbling all the while, Jameson followed Robbie into his office and closed the door. "How many times are we going to have this conversation, Jonah?" Robbie asked, more heat coming into his voice. "You stepped back from direct editorial oversight of the *Bugle* years ago. You yourself acknowledged that your objectivity couldn't be trusted after the Scorpion business came out. And you put me in charge because you trusted me to maintain the detachment a newspaper editor needs. These past few years, though, you've fallen back into the old patterns, like you were still editing this paper. I've accepted that, because I understand it's not your nature to keep your opinions to yourself and because I trust your judgment, too, most of the time.

"But in a situation like this, Jonah, where you personally are part of the story, I have to put my foot down for the good of the *Bugle*. I have to insist that you keep your hands off our coverage of the robot story and everything related to it. You can still say whatever you like on the op-ed page, within libel laws. But you need to leave the rest of the paper to me. Because neither of us wants to deal with the crap that's going to get dredged up again, the damage that will befall this paper's reputation, if you don't."

The heat had been rising beneath Jameson's collar throughout Robbie's speech, as he readied himself for a scathing comeback . . . but he realized he had nothing. This man had earned his respect and trust, more so than probably any other human being ever had. Sure, Jameson loved and trusted his wife, but Robbie was a *journalist.* The best damn journalist Jameson had ever worked with. And journalism was J. Jonah Jameson's first name.

After a moment, Jameson sighed. "I know, Robbie. You're right. It's just I have to *do* something. Spider-Man's getting out of hand. He's after me, Robbie. He's after my *wife.* I can't just take that lying down."

"I understand how you feel, Jonah. But listening to him, it sounds like he thinks *you* started it. Maybe escalating things isn't the way to go. It could just make things worse."

"I *want* him after me, Robbie. Marla's going out of town; she'll be safe. But I want him focused on me, so he doesn't hurt anybody else. I want to draw him out. And take him down."

Robertson shook his head. "You've been wrong about him before. Why are you so sure this time? He's never been a killer. Hell, he's saved your life a couple dozen times by now! He saved me from jail! He's probably saved half the people in this building—not to mention the building itself."

"And half the time it's from lunatics who are trying to get at him! Yeah, I know he thinks he's a hero, Robbie. And sometimes that means he gets lucky and saves a few lives. But he's a loose cannon. Some mutation or freak accident gave him power, and he gets his kicks showing off how strong and brave he is by running around town beating up crooks and fellow freaks. Remember, he didn't start out as a crimefighter. He started out trying to get rich and famous."

Jameson reflected back on those early days, when a mysterious "Masked Marvel" had made his debut in an exhibition wrestling match, gleefully humiliating his opponent. Within a week, he'd begun making the rounds of the late-night talk shows and monster-truck rallies as "The Amazing Spider-Man," donning his garishly creepy costume and showing off his strength, his wall-crawling, and the gimmicky webshooters he'd no doubt borrowed or stolen from somewhere.

At the time, Jameson had been only distantly aware of him, finding him pathetic and obnoxious when he could be bothered to spare a thought for this latest fad. But then the news had come in—the self-absorbed punk had homed in on a law-enforcement operation, putting lives at risk by recklessly charging into a warehouse where a gun-toting killer was holding off the police. Only the luck that protects the criminally stupid had enabled Spider-Man to take the gunman down without getting himself or anyone else killed. Ironically, it was the very man who had killed Peter Parker's uncle just hours before, and Jameson sometimes wondered if some kind of misplaced gratitude had led to Parker's fascination with photographing the web-slinger. (Indeed, there had been times when he'd idly wondered if Parker himself might be Spider-Man, somehow using an automatic camera to take all those poorly composed photos. But he'd seen them together more than once. Besides, Parker's aunt was a sweet, classy broad—at least up until recently, when she'd changed her tune and started defending Spider-Man's antics. Senility was a sad thing. Anyway, there was no way a fine woman like that could have raised a disrespectful punk like the wall-crawler.)

In the days that followed, Spider-Man had suddenly begun a crusade against the underworld, even while continuing his show-business ventures. It was then that Jameson had begun to realize how dangerous this man was—this glory hound who only wanted to profit from his powers. He had seen that the web-slinger's pursuit of criminals was just another attempt to grab at fame and fortune by imitating the superheroes who had recently begun to emerge. (Indeed, Spider-Man had almost immediately made an attempt to join the Fantastic Four, only to abandon that goal when he learned there was no money in the job.) And Jameson knew that someone like that was liable to get people hurt.

So Jameson had begun writing editorials warning people about the menace of Spider-Man. He couldn't risk letting the wall-crawler trick the public into thinking he was a hero. Unfortunately, his efforts had backfired; the bad press had made him *persona non grata* in show business, leaving him free to take up the crimefighting gig full-time. Jameson still wondered if Spider-Man would've gotten it out of his system and gone back to show business if he himself hadn't scuttled the webhead's career. But if he was responsible for that, it just made it all the more imperative that he be the one to fix it.

"He's out for glory, Robbie," Jameson went on. "And he doesn't care how many laws or how much property gets smashed in the process. He thinks he's above the law, above all of us crawling around down here while he swings by overhead and jeers at us. He's got nothing to keep him in check, so why shouldn't he cross the line?"

"Why doesn't Captain America, or Thor, or Reed Richards?" Robertson asked. "The heroes could've conquered this planet a thousand times over if they'd wanted to, and nobody could've stopped them. But they don't, because they believe their powers are meant for good."

Jameson scoffed. "Nobody's a hero, Robbie. Heroes are just bullies and egotists with good PR. We've all got our dark sides, our selfishness and anger and hate."

"Of course, but we keep it in check."

"*Society* keeps us in check. We don't do the nasty things we all want to do because there are people watching. Because we'll get punished for it— go to jail, get fired, lose our social standing, get looked at with contempt or disgust by other people. It's our fear of not getting away with it that keeps us under control."

He shook his head, thinking of his father the war hero and the unheroic things he did out of the limelight—the drinking, the cheating, the beatings. "But if nobody can see us, if we think we can get away with it, we'll do anything. For someone who hides behind a mask . . . someone the police can't identify, someone whose own friends and family probably don't know what he does . . . there are no consequences to face. Nothing to keep him in check. And the longer he can get away with it, the more he likes it, and the farther he'll go."

There had been a time, Jameson recalled, when he had been jealous of Spider-Man. The man had actually saved the life of Jameson's own astronaut son, John, despite the damage Jameson himself had done to his career. Though JJJ had publicly condemned the wall-crawler, blaming him for sabotaging John's spaceflight in the first place rather than give the impression that he'd been wrong about his warnings, on some level he'd been grateful. And for a while, he'd secretly let himself become convinced that Spider-Man was a hero after all, a better man than Jameson because he was willing to risk his life to save others while Jameson was only interested in profit and success.

But that hadn't lasted. Jameson had striven to improve himself, to prove he wasn't less of a *mensch* than the wall-crawler. He'd become a crusader for civil rights and public safety. He'd funded charities of all sorts. He'd brought Robbie, the best, most honest newspaperman around, on board to raise the *Bugle's* respectability. He'd outgrown his early attempts to send superpowered freaks or Spider-Slayer robots after the webhead, realizing that by doing so he only let himself be dragged down to the arachnid's level.

And he'd realized something. For all the good he did, he was *still* doing it in the name of profit, even if it was just the personal profit of feeling better about himself, about how others thought of him. And that led him to realize something else, too: Spider-Man was no better than he was. Spider-Man had started out as a money-grubber, too. And if J. Jonah Jameson was still a self-serving money-grubber at heart despite all the charitable ventures and heroic crusades he'd undertaken for this city, then Spider-Man must be, too. The only difference was that Jameson showed his face. His own self-interest kept him on the straight and narrow, because he knew the consequences he'd face if he strayed.

He voiced his thoughts to Robbie. "Everyone knows who the Fantastic Four are. A lot of the Avengers don't have secret identities, and the government knows who the rest are. People like that, people who have the courage to step forward and accept accountability for their actions, can be trusted—at least as far as we can watch them.

"But a superpowered loner practicing vigilante justice in a fright mask? That's a time bomb waiting to go off, Robbie. He doesn't have anything to keep him in check." And without it, Jameson knew that sooner or later Spider-Man would do . . . well, exactly what Jameson himself would do if he thought he could get away with it. Do what he wanted, take what he wanted, and beat down anyone who stood in his way.

Jameson would never tell Robbie—would never tell anyone—but that was the real reason he hated and feared Spider-Man: because he understood him. Because he knew that, deep down, they were the same.

Heaven help them both.

NINE

WHERE ARE YOU COMIN' FROM?

"SO you haven't spoken to Mary Jane since the fight?"

Aunt May's voice was sympathetic and unjudging, yet Peter could hear the regret in it, resonating with his own. He leaned back from her kitchen table, slumping in the chair. "No. But we're both so busy lately, we go for long stretches without talking anyway. It's no big deal."

She gave him a look over her shoulder, not breaking stride as she puttered deliberately about the kitchen. She was baking brownies for a neighborhood bake sale, raising money for research to help coma patients. She'd organized it as a way of trying to do something for Flash Thompson and Bobby Ribeiro. Peter often felt she was the real superhero in the family. "That's the same way you said it was 'no big deal' when the bullies would harass you in high school. I knew better then, too."

"Okay, so I'm not exactly happy about it. But she'll get over it soon, I know it."

"She will, eh?"

He felt himself blushing at her tone, but stood his ground. "Look, maybe I was a little short with her. But I've been under a lot of pressure lately. And she's giving me mixed messages! First she's happy about my new confidence, then she's giving me the third degree about what I did or didn't do—at a time when I really needed her support! And don't I have the right to let my wife know how frustrated I am when she's not around? It's not like I was blaming her for it. And once she cools down a bit, she'll see that."

"Hm," May said as she checked the status of the second batch of brownies in the oven; the first pan was cooling on the counter. "You know, Peter . . . in thirty-odd years of marriage, one thing I learned is the importance of letting your partner win their share of the arguments. Eventually you realize that you're part of a team, and the harmony of the team is more important than standing your ground—even when you're right."

"Yes. That's exactly what I'm saying." Her serene gaze held on him, and after a few moments he realized that she was talking about him, not MJ. He sighed. "Okay. I'll patch things up with her . . . later on. Give us both a chance to cool off."

"Good for you, dear."

"Hey, at least you agree I was right."

She gave him her best innocent look. "Did I say that?"

"Well, you—hey—well, do you?"

May came over to sit across from him. "Of course I do, dear. I also think Mary Jane is right."

"We can't both be."

"Whyever not? Arguments where only one side's right are the easy ones. You don't see too many of those."

He gave her a skeptical look. "In my work, I see them all the time."

"Well, I can't speak to that. All I know is what I see around me. Whether it's on the news or the talk shows or those . . . blob things like Mr. Jameson has."

Peter chuckled. "I think you mean 'blog.'"

She wrinkled her nose. "Hideous word. There's no elegance to language anymore. Anyway, everywhere I look, I see people talking *at* each other instead of listening *to* each other. Shouting each other down, insisting they have to be right. When someone tries to express an alternative viewpoint, they aren't given a fair hearing; they're shouted down, drowned out, met with attempts to discredit them or demonize them—anything to avoid even acknowledging the point they're making. Nobody even responds to the actual points they make anymore, because that would require *thinking* about them, and we can't have that. They just go after the person and imply that the argument is discredited by association." She shook her head. "Shocking, the lengths people will go to these days to avoid admitting that anyone else could have a point about anything. It's considered a sign of weakness to give the other side any ground at all.

"That's not how it works in a marriage, like I said, dear. And I don't see why it should be any different elsewhere. People can't live together in a community, can't work together to get anything done, if they won't let their guard down and have a little faith in each other. If they can't work out their differences through compromise, look for the things they have in common and use those to solve the matters that set them apart.

"And you can see that everywhere you look. The world has become so uncivil. The leaders are too busy fighting with each other to find real solutions to any of its problems. It's just not working, Peter. Because people are trying too hard to 'win'—or at least to make it look like they've won—to actually solve anything. Trying too hard to avoid looking wrong to question whether there's anything they could learn from other people. And the truth gets drowned out in the thunder of accusations."

Peter was about to say she was overreacting, but she went on. "Ben and I always tried to teach you the importance of asking questions. And we hardly needed to, since you took to it so well. You had such a gift for recognizing what you didn't know and applying yourself to finding it out. You were never afraid to be wrong because you knew it was a condition you could change if you applied yourself." She smiled. "I believe that's what made you such a gifted science student—and such a good, tolerant man. Ben was very proud of both those things about you—and I still am."

Peter lowered his head, humbled by her words. After several moments of silence, May rose from the table and squeezed Peter's shoulder as she passed behind him. He spoke again after more moments' thought. "I get what you're saying, Aunt May. You're right—a little self-doubt can be a healthy thing. I guess I did take out my frustration on MJ. I miss her, and I guess I resent her work a little for keeping her away from me, and I handled it badly. I guess she has to deal with the same thing when I spend my nights out catching crooks."

"I've had to deal with it since you moved out for college," May said softly.

"And just because she raised questions about the death of that man doesn't mean she wasn't supporting me. I . . ." He blinked repeatedly and swallowed. "I guess she was voicing questions I've been trying not to admit I was asking myself. Whether I did get too cocky, too careless. Whether it could've been my fault—partly—that it happened. That's . . . tough to face."

He felt her hand on his shoulder again. "I would never say it was your fault if you fail to prevent a death that someone else caused. The fault is theirs, of course. But even the best of us make mistakes that we need to face and learn from."

After a moment, he shook his head, brow furrowing. "Maybe about that. Definitely about MJ," he went on as her hands pulled away and she returned to her work. "But the one thing I'm still sure of is that Jameson's behind all this. He wouldn't be putting my spider-sense on high alert if he weren't."

"You have to admit, dear, it's hard to believe."

"I know. I know. But I have to trust my instincts, right?" he asked, turning to face her.

She put her hand to her chin and thought about that for a moment. "Well, people do like to say that. But I have to wonder. I can't help thinking of the people you've told me about in . . . well, your line of work . . . who've been driven by instinct above all. People like that man Kravinoff, the so-called Hunter. Or poor Dr. Connors when he becomes that Lizard." She shuddered. "Or that awful black alien thing that calls itself Venom."

She'd just listed three of his most fearsome, savage, and irrational enemies. Peter could hardly blame her for being afraid even to think about them, for they all scared the bejeebers out of him. And their animal ferocity, their insusceptibility to reason and compromise, had been a large part of what had made them all so deadly.

Peter rose and put a comforting hand on May's shoulder. She smiled up at him, placing her hand upon it briefly, and went on. "I think instincts can be useful. But I also think that what separates us from the beasts—or from creatures like those—is that we can listen to our judgment as well as our instincts. We can recognize that an urge that might have made sense in a jungle millions of years ago might not be right for a world populated by civilized human beings."

He stared at her. "But how could my spider-sense be wrong?" he asked—genuinely asked, rather than dismissing.

May gave him a wistful smile. "I have no idea, dear. I can't even say it is wrong. But at least you've begun to ask the question. And that can't be bad, can it?"

Peter turned away, slowly pacing the kitchen as he struggled with the idea. "You think about that while I tend to the brownies," May said.

Has my spider-sense ever failed me this way before? He couldn't recall it. False negatives were one thing. The arachnid senses he believed he relied upon—whether vibrational, ultraviolet, pheromonal, or whatever—could be interfered with by heavy rain or particulate clouds, just like any other sense. Sometimes they'd been dulled chemically, and he'd been left without them for a time. And there were beings that his danger sense just didn't perceive as a threat, no matter the context—May because she was family, the Venom symbiote because it had been bonded to him long enough for his brain to learn to respond to it as a part of himself.

But false positives? As far as he could recall, everything he'd ever imagined to be a false positive, the result of stress or illness or jangled nerves, had eventually turned out to be a warning of a hidden danger he should have heeded. Still, he supposed it stood to reason that it could happen. It was his brain, not his sense organs, that judged whether a stimulus exceeded the danger threshold and warranted an aversion response. Venom wasn't actually invisible to his subliminal senses, but just didn't give the kind of input his brain would recognize as dangerous enough to warrant an alert. *Stupid stubborn brain, should've learned by now after all the times Venom had nearly killed me.* So surely it was possible in theory for his brain to overreact to input that wasn't dangerous. He didn't see how, but Aunt May was right: he had to admit the—

DANGER! The sudden burst of spider-sense tingle was almost overpowering. He reflexively jumped to the ceiling, away from the deadly threat he felt behind him, and whirled to see what it was.

Aunt May had been behind him, holding a carving knife.

In a second, he was on her. "Who are you? What have you done with my Aunt May?!" She gasped, letting the knife clatter to the ground. She looked utterly terrified. But he couldn't let that fool him. He'd fallen for impostors before. And to think this one had almost convinced him to doubt what he knew to be true . . .

"Peter, please, it's me!"

But his instincts told him differently. "Answer me! Who are you working for?!"

She gasped for breath. "Peter—please—think about it. Is that really—likely? Are you—willing to risk—hurting your own aunt—based only on an instinct? On your certainty—that it can't—be wrong?"

His spider-sense was still screaming at him, but he looked into her eyes . . . saw the terror in the face of his aunt . . . because of him.

He let her go, backed away . . . He didn't know what to think, what to do. She sank into a chair, trembling, reaching for her blood-pressure pills.

Looking at him with fear.

He ran. He didn't know what else to do. If that was really May, then he hated himself for leaving her without making sure she was all right. But the way his instincts were screaming at him to attack her, he couldn't take the risk.

What is happening to me? he shouted to himself as he changed into Spider-Man in a secluded spot. *I need answers. I need there to be answers.* He swung off toward Manhattan, toward Jameson. He didn't know anymore if Jameson was really behind all this. But he prayed that somehow that was the right answer.

It would make everything so simple.

———o——————o———

JAMESON had finally decided he could no longer endure just sitting around waiting for something to happen. As he declared to his wife over the phone, it was time for Jigsaw Jameson to come out of retirement.

"Who?" was her only reply.

"Didn't I ever tell you? That's what they used to call me back in my reporting days. Jigsaw Jameson. Could piece together any puzzle in record time."

"Really," Marla said dryly. *"Then why did you need me to program the VCR?"*

"I'm an important man now. I've learned to delegate. But not this time. This one's personal. I've gotta get out there and track down Spider-Man myself. No one knows him like I do. I'm the only one who can recognize his stench behind this robot business and trail it to the source. The Bloodhound, they used to call me."

"I thought they called you Jigsaw."

"They called me lots of things!"

"Now, that I can believe."

He chuckled. Nobody else could talk to him that way and get away with it. But there was something about her cool, sardonic deadpan that always got him right where he lived. Maybe it was opposites attracting. "I love you, too, dear."

"Seriously, Jonah—I don't like this. You should stay where it's safe."

"Playing it safe didn't get me where I am today, Marla. And I've been sitting up in that executive suite too long. That's why people doubt my credibility—I'm too cut off. I need to get back to my roots, back in touch with my city. I can't get the best out of my reporters on this story unless I join them in the trenches, remind myself of how it feels."

He sighed. "Mostly, I just need to *do* something. I don't like feeling helpless."

After a thoughtful moment, Marla spoke again. *"I understand. Do what you must. But please, Jonah—take care of yourself."*

"I will. Don't you worry about that." He hefted his old service revolver, freshly cleaned and polished, to renew his feel for it. He hoped he wouldn't have to use it; he was no killer. But if it came down to Spider-Man or him, he would be ready.

His head security man, Berkowitz, didn't like the idea any more than Marla had. "You should let us accompany you, sir," he insisted.

"No way. I need to get out there and make contacts, find informants. If I've got Men in Black hovering around, it'll scare off anyone who could tell me anything useful. Naww, Jigsaw Jameson works solo," he insisted. "You guys will have to keep at least a hundred feet away. Try to be inconspicuous."

The matter was settled. Jameson pocketed his revolver and notebook, changed to a good pair of broken-in walking shoes, donned his brown fedora and trench coat (one pocket containing a cell phone with the police and his security on speed dial—he wasn't an idiot), and hit the pavement. Once his chauffeur dropped him off in the right part of town, that is.

SPIDER-MAN had nowhere to go.

He had tried going home. When he'd swung down to his building after fleeing Aunt May's home, he'd spotted MJ just arriving. He'd been relieved to see her until that same spider-sense twinge had overcome him, warning him away from her. He'd retreated to the roof of the adjacent building, hoping to watch and see what was going on, but an ongoing low-level buzz of danger had made him too agitated to remain, and he'd swung away until it had subsided.

Later, when MJ called him on his cell and asked where he was, the tingle in his head warned him not to tell her. He didn't want to believe it. He didn't want to believe she and Aunt May weren't who he thought they were. He knew there was a chance that something was wrong with his danger sense itself.

But how could he take that chance? Spider-sense was like the fire alarm at school—you had to take it seriously every time, treat it as a real emergency even though most of the time it was some kid pulling a stupid prank. Because if you ignored it even once, you ran the risk of exposing yourself to real danger. So Spidey *had* to keep trusting the warning tingle, even though he knew there was a chance he shouldn't be. Until he got some real answers, he had to play it safe.

Besides, it wouldn't be the first time, he thought as he perched atop the broadcast antenna of the Empire State Building—the only place where he could survey the whole city and be sure no one could sneak up on him from above (although with his luck, he thought, the biplanes would be along any minute to shoot him down). His enemies had played such cruel tricks on him in the past. A few years ago, the parents that he'd believed dead since his early childhood had apparently turned up alive and become part of his life for a time, only to be revealed as android impostors programmed to kill him. The memory of having his parents ripped from him again, a formerly abstract loss gaining a harsh immediacy, still tore at him. He couldn't bear the thought of MJ and May being replaced by android impostors . . . but he couldn't get it out of his head.

Particularly because it would mean that whoever was after him knew his identity. *Could Jonah know? Is that why he was so belligerent toward me at the* Bugle*?* There were other possibilities. Norman Osborn knew his identity. And Oscorp certainly could provide him with the technical resources to build these robots—after all, Mendel Stromm had been Osborn's partner in the company before Norman had framed him for embezzlement, sent him to prison, and started him on the vengeful course that had made him into the Robot Master. But Osborn was securely in prison, Spidey knew; he'd confirmed that on general principles when he'd been there to visit Smythe and Electro.

No good sitting around speculating, Spidey decided. He was on edge, needing to act, needing to get some answers. So he'd simply have to go down there and see what he could find out. He'd start at the bottom, go through every lowlife informant he could get his webs on, and shake them until something involving robots fell out. Or something involving Jameson.

What if Jameson himself is a robot? It would explain so much. But then, if it were true, it would require forgiving the real Jonah. And that was a prospect Spider-Man was not yet willing to contemplate.

○————————○

"JIGSAW" Jonah Jameson had quickly learned that the reporting business wasn't as easy as it had once been. All his old underworld informants were long gone, and he was too high-profile to sneak around effectively. So his attempts to get a bead on things through the criminal grapevine met with severely limited success. He had to flash his revolver a couple of times to avoid getting roughhoused, and faced a few harrowing moments under pursuit before Berkowitz's men showed up and scared the bums off.

So he decided he was going about it the wrong way. *These are high-tech crimes,* he reminded himself. *Lots of high-tech companies getting robbed, their parts showing up in fancy robots. Maybe I should start at that end.* Surely investigating the scenes of the robberies themselves, talking to the makers of the stolen equipment, could give him a good grounding in the case. If he weren't so rusty, he would have started there.

Of course, Ben Urich had been looking into these robberies for days. But Urich didn't have Jameson's keen nose for arachnid involvement. What's more, he was kind of chummy with his own pet vigilante, Daredevil—himself a known associate of the wall-crawler. *It'll take my more objective eye to find the proof that Spider-Man's behind this.*

But that proof was elusive. He interviewed all the companies that had been hit, talked to their engineers, visited the warehouses and inspected the damage. The first high-tech theft, of the Venus robots from Cyberstellar, had been committed by Electro, of course. The second one, committed between that and the Diamond District rampage, had involved damage consistent with the use of the Venus probes to break into the warehouse. Jameson could readily believe that Spider-Man and Electro had been in it together. But the other robberies had taken place after all the stolen Venus robots had been destroyed and accounted for. If the webhead had been at any of those warehouses, he'd hidden his trail well, apparently by using more robots instead of his own strength and webbing. Jameson saw where the doors had been cut through by torches or high-powered blades. He watched the security tapes and saw the static of electromagnetic interference filling the screen. He read police reports revealing that large amounts of equipment had been removed in a short amount of time. Spider-Man could carry great weight on his back, but it would be logistically unfeasible for one man to carry out so many heavy crates in one trip, not without help.

"What would it take to build these kinds of robots out of the stolen parts?" he asked the engineers. They told him that the robot that had trashed Jameson's office and the two that had chased Spider-Man across Midtown East had been fairly basic and could have been constructed in a matter of days with the right machining tools—but only if the builder had been a robotics genius. Many of the stolen parts had been repurposed in ways the engineers had never considered, ways that amplified the power and endurance of the robots and increased their agility and reaction times. There were relatively few people in the world who had such gifts for robot-building, including Reed Richards, Henry Pym, Victor von Doom, and Alistaire Smythe. *Smythe,* Jameson thought. *I'll have to look into that. He hates Spider-Man, but after the way I cleaned his clock the last time, maybe he hates me enough to make a deal with the wall-crawler.*

But many of the stolen components had no clear robotics applications, or so their designers told him. He couldn't keep straight all the things the engineers told him about rapid prototyping systems and carbothermic extraction and whatnot, but it all added up to one thing: Whoever had stolen these components must be putting together one serious science project, something that had to go beyond building killer

Rock 'Em Sock 'Em Robots to stage bouts atop Manhattan skyscrapers. And they'd probably need considerable skill, precision equipment, and a sizable power supply to get it done.

As Jameson looked into Smythe, he found that the man had remained securely in his prison cell at all times, not appearing to be a viable suspect. Dr. Doom was unavailable for comment. Richards was an unlikely suspect, but Jameson consulted him for advice on robotics and possible underworld figures with the necessary skill. Richards had little time to consult—something about the Fantastic Four being "just on our way out of the dimension"—but he suggested that Jameson might want to take a look at Phineas Mason, an inventor whom he alleged to be an underworld figure known as the Terrible Tinkerer.

Jameson dropped in on Mason at his workshop, finding him to be a real cool customer, practically a robot himself. The man gave away nothing and didn't react to intimidation. Jameson almost had to admire him for his rare ability to withstand the Three-J Degree (as his old reporter buddies had called it) without so much as breaking a sweat. "Don't think this is over," Jonah told Mason before he left. "I'm gonna keep my eye on you. And if I catch so much as a single strand of webbing on you, you'll wish you'd never heard of Jigsaw Jameson."

"Who?"

Nonetheless, the more Jameson investigated, the more a thought began to nag at the back of his mind. He tried not to listen, but it became harder and harder to ignore. Finally, he had to let himself acknowledge it. *This doesn't feel like Spider-Man's doing. There isn't a single clue that points to him.* It was one thing to dismiss that when he was sitting up in his suite on the forty-sixth floor, to assume that his reporters were just missing something. But the more time he spent down in the trenches, the more he refreshed his memory of what it felt like to chase a story, the harder it was to deny that this story wasn't leading him in any direction that had webs at the end of it.

No, he told himself. *Spider-Man has to be involved. He's after me and my family—that I know for a fact. There* must *be a connection between that and the robots. Maybe . . . maybe he's just an accomplice for someone else,* he grudgingly admitted. *Maybe his attacks on my family are a sidebar to something bigger.*

But he has *to be a part of it. I've put my reputation on the line for that position—I can't back away from it now. I have to stand by my convictions! I have to be* right!

But wasn't one of his convictions a belief in reporting the truth? In following the evidence wherever it led and reporting it accurately?

I will find the truth, he swore. *But Spider-Man is going to be a part of that truth. He has to be.*

Doesn't he?

TEN

AT THE SCENE OF THE CRIME

"SO Peter still hasn't come home?"

Mary Jane shook her head as she took May's coat and hung it up. "He's answering his phone, at least, but he won't tell me where he is. It's like he doesn't trust me anymore."

May patted MJ's arm. "Don't take it personally, dear. After what happened the other day, I think something must be wrong with his spider-sense. The poor boy's jumping at shadows." She shook her head. "I've worried about something like this ever since I found out. Having spider genes mixed in with his . . ." She shuddered. "Senses it isn't natural for a man to have . . . . I've been afraid it would do something to his mind. Especially that danger sense putting him on edge like that time and time again. Take it from an old worrywart—the more often you let yourself get scared, the stronger the habit becomes. It's too easy to become afraid of the tiniest things."

MJ sighed. In some ways, it was a relief to have May to talk to about this. When Liz, Jill, and Peter's other friends had come by to ask after his whereabouts, she'd had to brush them off with an excuse, hating herself for lying to people who cared for Peter and had a right to know whether he was all right. And in the process, she'd deprived herself of the opportunity to share her burden. The freedom to pour her troubles into May's sympathetic ear was a godsend. But at the same time, May was unburdening her worries on MJ and giving her more angles to worry from in the process.

"I don't know, May," she finally said. "He's just changed so much lately. The past few years have been so hard on him," she said, swallowing down a surge of guilt at the way she'd added to that by walking out on him. "And now this happening to his students . . . he was really blaming himself, and then I guess he just . . . decided to get angry instead. He changed. I thought it was a good thing at first, but he just kept getting more angry, lashing out at the world. I think he's using the anger to hide from the pain." She gazed out the window, wondering where he was. "I wonder if maybe it's not the spider-sense going wrong and making him act this way. Maybe, instead, getting so hostile and defensive has thrown his spider-sense into overdrive. He's decided to push the world away, and his spider instincts are, well, taking it literally. And it's becoming a vicious circle, making him paranoid." She shook her head. "I don't know what we can do."

After a moment, May spoke. "Well, I simply won't accept that, dear. Peter needs us. We're his family, and we love him. There's nothing that can overcome fear better than family. We simply need to find him, sit him down, and have a good long talk." She gave a small, inward-looking smile. "Lately I've found that can work wonders."

MJ turned back to the window. "Sure, May. Find Spider-Man, wherever he is in all of New York, and convince him to come down and have a talk. Easy."

"But we're not looking for Spider-Man, dear. We're looking for Peter. And that's our advantage. We know him better than anyone."

"Maybe. But right now, I think he's becoming more Spider-Man and less Peter by the day." She frowned, for a thought was forming in the back of her mind. May started to speak, but MJ held up a hand for quiet. "Wait a minute." She concentrated, let the thought emerge. "Maybe knowing both Peter *and* Spider-Man can help."

She went to the closet and began to rummage. "I know I've seen it here somewhere."

"What is it, dear?"

"Back when Peter started out, when he first built his spider-tracers, he didn't tune them to set off his spider-sense like he does now. He tracked them by radio. He used a—yes!" She found what she was looking for—a hand-sized box with an antenna and small screen—and showed it to May. "A tracking device! A while back he modified it to pick up the new kind of tracer, once when his spider-sense wasn't working. He's kept it around as a backup ever since."

534 | SPIDER-MAN: DROWNED IN THUNDER

"And you think we can use that to . . . what? Home in on the tracers he carries with him?" May asked hopefully.

She slumped. "No. I think it only works when they've been turned on. They don't go active until they hit something, or until he squeezes them to trip the switch."

"Oh." May mulled it over for a moment. "But he was using one of his trackers to follow Mr. Jameson, wasn't he?"

MJ gave her a humorless smile. "We know where to find Jameson. He's hard to miss."

"But Peter could still be following him—or maybe he's found someone else to follow. And maybe—"

"Maybe if we pick up a tracer he's following, we can find him, too!" Excited, MJ turned on the tracer.

Nothing.

She ran over to the window and swept it around, but still there was no reaction. "Does it have fresh batteries?" May asked. "I always change the batteries in my flashlights and smoke detectors every Daylight Savings Time."

MJ smiled despite herself. "The status lights are on. It's scanning. But there aren't any tracers in range."

"Ohh, I feel like I'm in *Mission: Impossible*. What would Peter Graves do next, do you think?"

"Go to his trailer and study the script," MJ replied.

"What was that, dear?"

She turned to face May. "I guess if we wanted to find a tracer, we'd have to do what Peter does—Parker, not Graves. We travel around the city and hope we get a hit."

"That's awfully haphazard," May opined. "Once we get Peter back, we should try to help him refine his methods." Then she frowned. "Oh, dear. Peter's work takes him into some rather disreputable quarters, doesn't it?"

"I should do it alone, May. I have self-defense training."

"I'm no shrinking violet myself, dear!" May insisted. "Did I tell you about the time I solved a robbery at the Restwell Nursing Home . . . ?"

AS Spider-Man leaped around the warehouse rafters, dodging a hail of bullets, he found himself reminded of something: Guns were *loud*. Especially when fired indoors. His ears were ringing, and he could only imagine that the gang of petty hoods he'd tracked down here were giving themselves permanent hearing damage.

Usually, he could ignore such things. In the heat of battle, he could surrender to his spider-sense, let his instincts tell him when to dodge and how to move, and shut out the distractions of the more conventional senses. Now, though, he didn't know how far he could trust his danger sense. So he had to remain alert—still relying on it for warnings he couldn't get any other way, but staying ready to override his instincts if he noticed something that didn't fit what they were telling him. So far, those instincts weren't steering him wrong; right here and now, he was definitely in danger. And hearing loss was the least of his concerns.

He hadn't gotten himself into this situation by choice. He'd been tracking a low-level fence named Marty Barras, a.k.a. "Blush" (M. Barras, ha-ha), in hopes of getting him alone for a private chat about any recent dealings in high-tech equipment. Blush had a well-known fear of heights, making him an ideal subject for Spidey's characteristic brand of intimidation, also known as "Have you met my friend gravity?" Unfortunately, Spidey had apparently come across him just as he was about to make a deal with some arms smugglers. Their lookout had spotted him, and they'd proceeded to give Blush an impromptu infomercial for their wares, with Spidey as the special celebrity guest. Hence his current exposure to levels of workplace noise far exceeding OSHA recommendations. Which was nothing compared to the risk of lead exposure.

The wisecracks came unbidden to his mind out of long habit. But he cast them aside, reminding himself that he had no time to fool around. This was a distraction from his pursuit of answers, and he had to dispose of it as quickly as possible. Which was easier said than done. Normally, he could have webbed these guns to uselessness in moments. But he had to conserve his webbing now. Every time he got near his apartment, whether MJ was home or not, his spider-sense drove him away. He couldn't use webbing profligately, because he didn't know what his chances were of getting a refill anytime soon.

Enough fooling around, then. The wooden rafters had already taken damage from the gunfire. He hopped down on a particularly perforated one and kicked with all his might, breaking a wide chunk of it loose and sending it hurtling down at the gunmen. The ringing in their ears no doubt deafened them to the crack, and the muzzle flashes in the darkness obscured their sight, so they didn't realize what was coming until it was too late. Two of them were pinned under the heavy beam, and the others scattered. *Just one of the many reasons why guns are more trouble than they're worth.*

But Spidey was already kicking at the support column, breaking it free of the rafter on the other side and snapping it in two. He wedged his body between the pieces and pushed them apart, snapping the column at its base and riding it down toward one of the gunmen. The man dodged the rafter before it could crush his legs, but Spidey's fist made sure he was no longer a threat. Behind him, the section of rafters he'd pushed against, along with the piece of the roof it had supported, collapsed on top of the other gunmen. He bounded over to make sure they were alive and incapacitated, not necessarily in that order.

He knew it wasn't like him to be this callous. But he felt besieged, on the run, sensing enemies at every turn. He couldn't afford to let his guard down or be distracted from the mission, and he was too weary in his heart to let it feel for those who sought to stop its beating. The gunmen were out of the fight; that was what mattered. Let intensive care deal with the rest of it.

And bringing the house down proved to have one benefit—all he had to do was approach Blush Barras and the fence began begging for mercy and spilling his guts. Spider-Man was almost disappointed at how easy it was.

"What do you know about the robot attacks? Who's behind them?" Spidey demanded.

"I—I don't know," Blush cried, living up to his nickname as he flushed beet red from fear. "I don't know nothin' about those. I swear!" he shrieked as Spidey stepped closer. "I'm outta the loop on this, swear to God! With all the jobs gettin' pulled on high-tech firms lately, I'd'a figured somethin' would be comin' my way, but there's nothin'! All that stuff gettin' ripped off and none of it bein' fenced! Don't make no sense!"

Spidey absorbed that information, though he wasn't surprised by it. If the equipment wasn't being fenced, it was being used—by someone who knew how to use it. "Have you heard anything about the people behind the thefts?"

"No, no. Like I said, nobody's come to me."

"Are there even rumors? Anyone working in robotics?"

"I don't—maybe—"

"Spit it out!"

"The Tinkerer! I heard somethin's up with him."

"What?"

"I dunno! Just somethin'! All's I know, I swear!"

"You're lying! The Tinkerer's out of town!"

"He got back! A few days ago! That's all I know! Just don't hurt me!"

Spidey heard the sirens coming. It might cost him an informant in the future, but he had no tolerance for anyone who'd participate in selling assault rifles to schoolkids—least of all in his current mood. "No such luck, pal," he said, and knocked Barras out with a tap to the jaw.

The Tinkerer, he thought as he climbed up and out the hole in the roof. *Now, there's a promising lead. He sells technology to other criminals, sometimes even to good guys. He'd have no problem working with Jameson on this.*

But wait—Felicia swore he was clean. And she didn't warn me he was coming back. Could she have turned on me, too? Is there anyone left I can trust?

Only myself, he answered. *I have to trust myself. Or I have nothing.*

◦――――――――◦

THANKS to Felicia, Spidey knew the location of the Tinkerer's current workshop, tucked away in an industrial area on Long Island. He rode the back of an LIRR train to reach the area and got the rest of the way by rooftop-hopping, web-swinging only when necessary.

On reaching the warehouse, Spidey smashed through an upper-level window—an impressive but dangerous trick he could survive because of his durable skin, although it always required stitching up the costume afterward. He landed a few feet in front of Mason amid a shower of shattering glass. But the slim, elderly man handled it with considerable aplomb. He looked up from his worktable with curiosity, peering at the intruder over his granny glasses, but showed no surprise or fear. "Spider-Man. I'm not open for business at the current time. You'll have to come back later."

In an instant, Spidey was crouching on the table and pulling Mason up by his lapels. "What do you know about the robots that have been attacking me?"

"I know nothing about robots," he said, still remarkably cool.

"Don't give me that! I've seen your work before. Remember when I broke your Toy?" He expected that to get a rise out of Mason. Toy had been a hulking humanlike robot who had functioned as the Tinkerer's henchman a few years back, at a time when he'd been actively pursuing supervillainy. In a climactic confrontation, Spidey had tricked Mason into shooting his own henchdroid—whereupon the old man had broken down and wept for Toy like a fallen son. It was presumably that trauma that had caused Mason to return to his former career, merely providing equipment to other villains.

But once again, the man showed no sign of distress. "I'm sorry, but you'll have to leave."

"I'm going nowhere until you tell me what I—*whoa!*" Suddenly he was flying toward the wall; Mason had yanked him forward and tossed him overhead in one lightning-quick move. Spidey flipped to land safely on the wall and sprayed a web-mesh toward the unexpectedly strong Tinkerer, suddenly finding his inhuman calm a lot more understandable.

His target dodged the web, bending backward in a way even Spidey's spine couldn't manage, and shot upright again, confirming that this was not the real Phineas Mason. "Well, if it isn't *Toy Story 2*!" he quipped, before reminding himself that the effort was wasted on an automaton, however human it appeared. "Where's the real Mason?"

"I am managing his affairs while he is away," the faux Tinkerer replied. "That is all you need to know."

The robot advanced on him, reaching for his throat. He dodged and kicked it in the face—and was a bit relieved when the face didn't fall off like in those cheesy seventies sci-fi shows. Which was more than offset by his disappointment that the whole head didn't come off. The robot simply grabbed his leg and flung him over its shoulder again, sending him crashing into the worktable.

But that proved a mistake on its part. A welding torch was still active on the table. Spidey grabbed it and opened its valve to full, lunging at the android. The flame cut a swath across its torso, and it retreated, batting out the fire that had caught on its shirt. Spidey kept after it, slashing the torch across its neck. It spun and knocked the torch clear, pressing the attack again, but it was slowed, its movements erratic. It went for Spidey's neck again, and he let it, for he was busy jabbing his fingers in through the burned swath across the latex skin of its chest, getting a grip on its innards and ripping them free. Whatever he'd extracted must not have been vital, for its attack continued. He reached in deeper and felt around, finding taut cords that must have been artificial muscles. He pulled on them until they tore loose, and one of the robot's arms went limp. Wriggling free of the other hand and knocking it aside, he spun the android around and struck at the back of its neck repeatedly until the damaged connections snapped. The android fell limp, its body twitching aimlessly. Creeped out, Spidey hit it over and over until it stopped.

He had taken care to minimize damage to the head, though, on the theory that the CPU would be in there. Given the way the neck damage had shut it down, that seemed likely. Indeed, before long, he had opened up the head and found the core processor. Taking it over to Mason's computer, he accessed its memory to see what he could learn from it.

It took some doing, and his limited hacking skills could not uncover any information about the real Mason's whereabouts or plans. *Not that I'm surprised. Why would he build a decoy to hide his true whereabouts, then store that information in its memory?* Nonetheless, he kept looking, accessing a playback of its video memory in hopes of learning something about whom it had interacted with.

He fast-forwarded through the video files, slowing it to normal on those few instances when someone entered the workshop. Most of the visitors were delivering food, no doubt to keep up the pretense that the place was occupied by a living person. (Although it seemed that the android actually consumed the food, as far as he could tell through its eyes. Examination of the body showed a furnacelike "stomach" that it used to burn and process the food for chemical energy.) A few of the visitors were apparently clients, and Spidey recognized one or two, but they were small-timers who weren't among his regular foes. Moreover, the android apparently turned them away, though the audio files were too damaged to retrieve.

But then Spidey shot forward as an unmistakable face appeared on the monitor. *Jameson!* Again, he couldn't tell what was being said, but the conversation clearly went beyond a mere brush-off. Jameson was in the android's face, going back and forth with it for some minutes. *'Why did I never learn to read lips?'* The publisher grew increasingly hostile over the course of the conversation, but that happened in just about all of JJJ's conversations. The look on his face toward the end was one Peter Parker knew well from years of working for Jameson. It was a look that said that he expected something from you and wouldn't be satisfied until it was delivered.

"They're in on it!" he cried. "This is it! Solid evidence, at last!" Maybe it wasn't proof, but it was a start, something that showed an actual connection between Jameson and a skilled roboticist. True, this had only been a decoy android; but who was to say it hadn't been this same decoy, or another like it, that Felicia had tracked? The real Mason could still be in town, working underground—perhaps letting the android handle his routine business because he was all wrapped up with a special project. Perhaps Jameson had been passing on instructions through the android, or had believed he was addressing the real Tinkerer and been chastising him for not being at his work.

Whatever the explanation, Spider-Man seized onto this slim piece of evidence like a lifeline. It gave him something to believe in, reassured him that he'd been on the right track after all. *Yes. I should never have doubted myself! I knew it was Jameson all along!*

He recalled that he still had a tracer on Jameson's coat. *Its battery should still be good for another day or two,* he thought. *Which means I'd better act fast. I have to find him,* he went on as he leaped through the window and swung away. *And this time I will get some answers.*

○────────────○

THE *Wake-Up Call* was being sounded less often lately. Not only was Jameson busy investigating the case, but he didn't find it as easy to write the column anymore. He was determined to stick to his guns on the blog, to maintain his anti-Spider-Man rhetoric at all costs. Sure, he had some doubts, but he couldn't let them show; if he gave any ground, the public would lose confidence in him. Spider-Man was still out there, more aggressive than ever, to judge from the latest police reports. Whether he was involved in the robot attacks or not, his near-lethal tactics against that band of gunrunners had been inexcusable, and Jameson couldn't soften his stance on the former without sounding like he was soft on the latter. Sure, there were some people out there who were wise and patient enough to read an ambiguous argument carefully and appreciate its subtleties, but any fool knew that the majority of the public consisted of simple-minded, knee-jerk types who wanted their answers as uncomplicated as possible, their good guys and bad guys clearly delineated. People had no patience for distinguishing between shades of gray, so you had to paint it for them in black and white. Even if that meant glossing over some of the side issues— like exactly which crimes a man was and wasn't guilty of.

But it wasn't so easy to keep up that air of certainty anymore. The passion driving him to write about Spider-Man's crimes just wasn't there, and wouldn't be until he found some real evidence. *One way or the other,* he reluctantly added.

Indeed, there was evidence accumulating, but still nothing that pointed at the wall-crawler in any direct way. The latest evidence, in fact, was pointing in a surprising direction. It involved Stanley Richardson, a security guard who had been working for Stark Enterprises—the first high-tech firm to be hit after Electro's arrest, specifically on a night when Richardson had been on watch at the warehouse. This break-in showed the least evidence of mechanical assistance; indeed, though Stark's security people had been loath to admit it, Ben Urich had uncovered indications that an inside man had abetted the heist. And Richardson had disappeared shortly thereafter—until a day ago, when his body had washed up on the Staten Island shore, his skull caved in by a heavy metallic implement. This had prompted Robbie Robertson to order a more thorough investigation of the man's past—and Urich had dug up an unexpected fact. "It seems," Robbie reported to Jonah, "that Richardson used to work as an electric company lineman alongside one Max Dillon."

Jameson's eyes widened as he looked across his desk at Robbie. "Electro?"

"I don't mean the marshal from *Gunsmoke.* Jonah, it can't be a coincidence that a former associate of Electro's is implicated in the same string of robot-related thefts that we know Electro had a part in—and then turns up dead from a blow that could have been inflicted by a robotic claw."

Jameson waved his hands as though dispersing a cloud of smoke. "Yeah, yeah, you don't have to spell it out for me. I see where you're going. But remember, Dillon's in jail. He was in jail when that warehouse was robbed, and he was in jail when Richardson got cacked. He would've had to have an accomplice," he said with meaning.

Robbie caught the subtext. "You mean Spider-Man."

"Who else?"

"Jonah, the robbery was in Jersey, and Spider-Man was sighted in Brooklyn within ten minutes of it. Even he can't move that fast."

"You have any idea how many cranks there are dressing up in Spidey suits and trying to climb the walls?"

"How many of them are leaping across a street in a single bound, carrying a websack on his back with two cat burglars in it?" Robbie sighed. "Jonah, you're on the wrong track where Spider-Man is concerned. *Again.* But this time, I think you actually know it."

Jameson didn't admit that Robbie was right, but the editor seemed satisfied nonetheless. Afterward, JJJ resumed his own investigation, contacting Ryker's Island and requesting information on Max Dillon's activities. After studying the files for a time, he came to a decision. It was time to pay a call on Electro.

○————————○

SPIDEY picked up the tracer signal as he swung through Carnegie Hill. Closing in, he spotted Jameson's limo and followed it. It led him to a police heliport, where Jameson boarded a chopper that flew out across the East River, leaving Spidey unable to follow. But he could tell where the chopper was headed: straight for Ryker's Island. *Meeting another accomplice?* he wondered. *Now we're getting somewhere. I'll give him enough webline . . . then we'll see if he hangs himself.*

ELEVEN

SENSELESS VIOLENCE

"ROBOTS?" Max Dillon leaned back on his plastic-framed cot, studied Jameson through the glass wall of his insulated cell, and shook his head. "I don't know nothing about any robots. I was just minding my business in Times Square when this green Gargantua picks a fight with me."

"Come on, Dillon," Jameson snarled. "Stop playing games. You didn't exactly try to hide your involvement with the diamond theft. You costume types always go for the limelight." As an afterthought, he added, "And Gargantua was a man, you illiterate spark plug."

Dillon spread his hands. "All right, so I got some new toys, and I wanted to play with 'em. But your boyfriend Spider-Man and his pals broke them all, and that's the end of the story, far as I'm concerned. I've been sittin' in here ever since, remember? Just like I told the wall-crawler when he dropped by a few days ago."

Jameson shot forward. "Spider-Man broke into prison? And out again?" Come to think of it, he only had a problem with the latter. "What did he want to see you about?"

"Same thing as you. Wanted to know who's buildin' robots. What do I know about buildin' robots? I just ste—uhh, *borrow* them."

"And reprogram them," Jameson pointed out.

"Reprogram nothin'. They're electric, right? I move the current around in 'em. Make 'em move the way I want. Like workin' a puppet. Took some practice, but I caught on fast."

"You never did that before. How'd you figure it out now?" *This Neanderthal would have trouble figuring out a can opener.*

Dillon shrugged. "I don't know. Just came to me."

"When?"

"Few months ago. Guess I decided I wanted to learn new skills. Gotta keep up in this competitive supervillain market."

"And that's how you stole them from Cyberstellar?"

"From who?"

"I told you not to play dumb—well, dumber. Don't tell me you don't remember the name of the place you stole the robots from."

"And don't expect me to incriminate myself for a newspaperman," he said after a moment's pause. "All they can link me to for sure is usin' the 'bots, not stealin' 'em."

But Jameson sensed something behind his response. His breezy confidence had waned, as if Jameson's question had gotten him puzzled about something. As if he had his own doubts about what had happened.

"Okay," the publisher went on. "So let's just say you . . . *find* a bunch of robot space probes sitting around somewhere. And you decide they'd be swell to test out your new puppet powers on. So you pull your Pied Piper act—except this time you're the rat—and you take them all home with you. And you decide, hey, why don't I tear apart the Diamond District and pick up a nice bauble for my mother?"

Dillon leaped from the cot. "Hey, you don't know nothin' about my mother!"

"And I don't want to. Siddown! I asked you a question. Is that how it happened?"

"If you say so," Dillon said after a moment, frowning to himself. He began to pace the cell. "Sure."

"You don't sound convinced."

"Hey, I was there. I should know!"

"So how'd you know where to find them? How'd you find out Cyberstellar had even built the things? And where'd you get the idea that machines for digging up rocks on Venus would be good for swiping rocks on Forty-seventh Street?"

Dillon was getting increasingly puzzled. "I just . . . I hear things. In the wind, you know."

"Did someone point you in the right direction? Spider-Man, maybe?"

He was shaking his head, but more to himself than Jameson. "Someone must've . . . no, no . . . maybe I saw about 'em on TV. Or read something. I just knew I wanted 'em," he added, almost defensively.

"Because you had these new powers, and you wanted something to use them on."

"Right, right. Something real powerful."

"Why wait so long?"

"What?"

"You said it was months ago that you developed this new power. What took you so long?"

"Well, I had to practice, right? Learn to get good at it."

"You said before that you caught on fast. Which is it?"

"Well, I . . ."

"What were you doing for those months?"

Dillon was pacing faster, growing more unnerved. "Practicing," he said feebly.

"Just practicing? Nothing more?"

"Of course not. A guy's gotta eat . . ."

"So for months you were just eating and practicing. Never took you for such a disciplined type, Dillon."

"I did more!" he insisted. "I went out. I'm in my prime, I date."

Jameson grinned. "Oh yeah?"

"Ohh, yeah."

Dillon chuckled, and Jameson joined in. "Made a lot of time with the ladies?"

"Sure. They love it, too. These powers ain't just for blowin' up safes, you know."

Jameson really, really did not want to know, but he kept up the lecherous laughter anyway. "Got you some fine-looking broads, then, huh?"

"Oh, the best."

"Describe them."

That brought Dillon up short. "Well . . . they . . . you know. Dames. Blonde . . . redhead . . . the usual."

"You don't remember, do you?"

"Sure I do. I just . . . they blur together, you know?" Growing impatient, he paced faster. "It's being in here. Sensory deprivation, whatever they call it. Scrambles the brain."

Jameson leaned back. "Well, that'd explain it, I guess."

"Sure. That's why I can't remember."

"Not what I meant."

Dillon stared. "What, then?"

"Just something I noticed studying your prison file. The guards noted a number of times when you seemed to zone out for a while, like you were in a trance or something."

That was met with a scoff. "Trances. What do they know? I was just bored out of my gourd."

"Interesting thing about the trances, though," Jameson went on. "A lot of them seemed to happen at about the same time that a high-tech company was getting ripped off. One came at the same time Spider-Man was fighting a couple of robots in Midtown. And the other robot fight with Spider-Man, and the other thefts, all happened while you were asleep."

Dillon looked nonplussed. "That's a hell of a coincidence," he said, shrugging.

"Is it?"

"Look, what are you saying?"

"Frankly? I have no idea. But it's a pattern, and patterns usually mean something. And if you've been having blackouts, forgetting things, maybe that's connected."

"I ain't been having blackouts. I just had . . . the past few months weren't that memorable."

"Except for having this great new idea how to use your power, and practicing a lot."

"Yeah. That took up a lot of it."

"And when did you get the idea, exactly?"

Dillon pondered for a moment. "Exactly? I don't know. A while ago."

"When? What was happening? What was the weather like? What sports were on TV?"

"I don't remember, okay? It just came to me like . . . like a bolt from the blue," he said with irony.

Then he frowned. "Yeah, wait a minute . . . there was something . . . I was on Broadway and . . ." He chuckled. "That's it. It started where it ended."

"What started?"

Dillon hesitated. "I'm not sure. Just . . . it."

"But it happened on Broadway."

"Yeah."

"What were you doing there?"

"Well, I had to go, didn't I? I'm Electro! I'm not gonna sit still while someone else steals my—"

He broke off, wincing suddenly. He turned away. "Dillon?" Jameson asked. "While someone steals your what? Dillon!"

Jameson rose and was about to call for a medic when Dillon straightened again. He walked slowly over to the cot, turned around, and sat. "Never mind. There's no point in trying to waste your time with this anymore. It's a feeble attempt at a lie, and I'm tired of you punching holes in it. So I might as well simply tell the truth."

His voice had changed, becoming colder, more deliberate. Jameson stepped closer to the glass, furrowing his brow. "About Broadway?"

"Forget Broadway. I made it up. It was the first name I thought of."

"So what truth are you gonna tell me?"

"The identity of the one who gave me the idea to develop my powers. The one who masterminded the thefts and the use of the robots. It was Spider-Man, Mr. Jameson. We've been working together in secret for months, developing our plans. The battle in the Diamond District was staged. Spider-Man pretended to battle the robots and me and be defeated. Our plan was that I would recover the diamonds and share them with him. We hadn't anticipated the arrival of the Avengers. The Venus robots proved more destructive than we expected, thus drawing a more extensive superhero response."

Thus? Jameson stared for some time. "And you're prepared to testify to this in court?"

"Of course. Spider-Man has abandoned me. When he came here, it was to tell me that I had failed and that he was severing our partnership. When you arrived, I attempted to cover for him out of loyalty. But I recognize now that such loyalty is wasted. If I turn state's evidence against Spider-Man, I can plea-bargain for a lesser sentence."

Jameson stepped closer to the glass, coming right up to it. "Do you know who Spider-Man is?"

"Yes." Dillon smiled coldly. "I won't tell you yet. Not until after I have my deal. But once I do, I see no harm in giving you the exclusive story."

His heart was pounding now. This was everything Jameson had wanted—the proof of his beliefs about the wall-crawler, the vindication of the stand he'd taken before the public. It was the stuff his dreams were made of.

And yet he did not believe a word of it.

He desperately wanted to swallow it whole, but the stink about it was too strong to ignore. Dillon had been about to say one thing, and then . . . he had changed. Not just his story, but his whole demeanor. Even his grammar had improved. And his claims just didn't fit. Jameson had seen it with his own eyes: Dillon hadn't been evasive before, he'd been confused, worried. And then something else had taken over.

"What about the other robot attacks?" he asked slowly. "The other thefts?"

"Spider-Man is behind the thefts. He's staged the attacks to divert suspicion elsewhere."

"And how do you explain them always happening when you go into a trance?"

"Coincidence." He studied Jameson. "Have all these so-called trances corresponded to a theft or attack?"

"Not that we know of."

"There you have it. I simply let my mind wander from time to time. Since I do it often enough, it's inevitable that sometimes it would overlap with something happening outside. But usually it doesn't. It's just coincidence."

Jameson had been a reporter long enough to tell a coincidence from a real pattern. Electro was lying. And if he was lying about that, Jameson had no choice but to suspect he was lying about Spider-Man's involvement as well. It galled him to admit it. He wanted nothing more than to pin a crime on the wall-crawler and make it stick. But Dillon's story could never stick.

And there was more to it than one man's questionable story. More to the pattern. Electro had a connection to the thefts of cybernetic equipment, and those thefts were adding up to something big—something that Spider-Man was just a diversion from. And Jameson had been falling for the diversion hook, line, and sinker because of his hatred for Spider-Man. He'd been manipulated like an amateur because his preconceptions were being played to.

The only way to get to the truth was to admit he'd been wrong. About Spider-Man.

It almost wasn't worth it. Hell, it hurt even to think it. His brain wasn't designed to process the concept.

Or maybe, he amended, *it's just out of practice.*

"You know what I think?" he said. "I think you're a liar. I think everything you've told me for the last two minutes is a lie. Right now I'm not even sure you are who you say you are. Don't ask me to explain that, since I haven't figured it out yet. But I will. You can depend on that. Because nobody plays J. Jonah Jameson for a sucker." *Not twice, anyway.*

Dillon was looking elsewhere, though. His attention seemed to have drifted halfway through Jameson's peroration, as though he was listening to some distant sound. But even as he stared off into space, he said, "None of that is relevant now." He paused. "Do you know what I think of you?"

The man in the cell focused his eyes on Jameson and smiled. "I think J. Jonah Jameson will make an excellent hostage."

That was when Jonah heard the alarms—and the crashes. And the gunshots.

And the screams.

He jumped to his feet and ran to the door at the end of the corridor. "Guard! What's going on? Get me outta here! Guard!"

But the guard was too busy shooting at . . . *something.* A big metal monstrosity scuttling down the corridor toward him at high speed. A fierce metal claw snapped forward, pincers embracing the guard . . .

Jameson looked away, retching, and ran the other way. But there was only Electro's cell to run to, and its occupant was watching him with a smug, cool grin. Jameson whirled back as the massive robot ripped the door from its hinges and bent the frame outward with its claws to force its way in. It tramped toward him, and he closed his eyes, thinking of Marla.

"Take him alive," Dillon said, and Jameson felt cold metal cables snaking around his body and yanking him into the air. He opened his eyes again as the robot dropped him onto its back and held him there. The claws pounded against the frame of the glass, got a grip, and tore it free. Dillon stood there unflinching, as though he didn't care if he was hit by flying debris. He was lucky; only a few fragments hit him, inflicting minor cuts. He didn't even seem to feel them.

"Recharge," Dillon said in a curt, commanding tone as he clambered up the robot's claws, which had moved to support him almost tenderly. Crouching on the robot's back just before Jameson, he grasped a handle of sorts that the robot had extruded. Sparks leaped between it and his fingers with loud cracks as he took hold. Jameson could see Dillon's short, red-brown hairs standing on end as he charged himself. He could even feel his own moustache hairs stiffening from the static field around the man.

As more guards charged into the room and brought their guns to bear, Dillon swept out his hand and sent bolts of lightning through their bodies. Jameson retched again at the smell of burning flesh. "Excellent," Dillon said analytically as the robot moved forward over their bodies and out the door.

"You—you just killed them! Like it was nothing to you!"

"An accurate assessment."

"You murdering freak! Those men were just doing their jobs! They had families to support!"

"All that will be irrelevant soon enough."

Jameson clenched his fists, longing to cut loose on this stain on humanity and punish him for his callousness. But he knew that just touching this live wire would put an end to his illustrious career, and Dillon would have no more qualms about letting him electrocute himself than he had about killing those guards. So he bottled up the rage and saved it for later. *I'll see you get what's coming to you.*

They were nearing the sounds of a pitched battle, and Jameson could hear bullets, whirring blades, and more metallic footsteps. Dust and smoke filled the air. "However," Dillon went on, "you have a role to play for the moment. Even an electrically charged body is still vulnerable to bullets."

Without being told—verbally, anyway—the robot spun around, but continued marching in the same direction, its back becoming its front. Dillon turned to face forward and glanced at the tentacles holding Jameson. They loosened their grip and slid off him. His eyes widened. "You're letting me go?"

"Hardly. I'm freeing the tentacles for combat." Suddenly, to his shock, Jameson felt himself being yanked around to face forward. No, more than that—it was his own muscles making him turn, but he wasn't telling them to. They convulsed as though . . . *as though a current went through them.* Electro was controlling the currents in Jameson's own nerves just as he did those in the robots' wires and servos! He'd been reduced to a puppet!

Electro forced him to sit down and grasp a handle atop the robot; luckily, no charge poured through this one. He saw that the robot had arms on the back—or the new front—much like the ones on the other end. He was beginning to recognize that these robots were based on a similar design to the Venus probes, but had been made larger, meaner, more dangerous. Those had been powerful scientific tools co-opted for crime. These were killing machines.

Now they turned the final corner and came in sight of a pitched battle between robots and guards. Some of the armed defenders whirled toward them. "Let them know of your presence," Dillon advised.

"Don't shoot! Hold your fire! It's me! J. Jonah Jameson! This freak has taken me hostage! Watch out for his lightning bolts! *Urmmph!*" Suddenly his jaw clenched shut, grinding his teeth together painfully and muffling his cries.

"That's enough," Dillon said. To Jameson's relief, the guards weren't firing. "Tell your men to stand down if you wish the hostage to survive," Dillon called.

The guards reluctantly did as he said, perhaps recognizing that they weren't making any headway against the robots anyway. Jameson was almost relieved that he couldn't speak, because then his conscience would've pressured him to say something noble and self-sacrificing like *"Don't worry about me, just take him down!"* The threat that this psychopath posed at the head of an army of robots was horrifying—well worth sacrificing one's life to prevent. But that decision had been taken out of Jonah's hands, and he was glad of it.

He was no hero. He didn't want to be out here in the thick of the action, his life on the line. He couldn't handle that kind of risk. Not like—

No. Don't even say it. The Avengers, the FF, even Forbush-Man! Anyone but . . .

Spider-Man, where the hell are you when I need you?

And this time, will you even bother to save me?

o━━━━━━━━━━━━━o

IT had taken some time for Spider-Man to find a suitable small boat that he could confiscate—all right, steal—without anyone spotting him. He didn't like the idea of resorting to theft, but he saw no other choice. He had to get to the prison and find out what Jameson was up to, whom he was meeting with. The Tinkerer had extensive underworld ties, and could've hooked Jameson up with just about any of the major players currently in residence at Ryker's. *Or maybe JJJ just patched things up with Smythe, a truce to get rid of me. Shared hatred has made stranger bedfellows.*

As he neared the island, he cut the engine and rowed the rest of the way, after spraying some webbing on the oars to muffle them. It was hard to find a secluded landing spot, since the shoreline was low and open by design to make infiltrations like this difficult. He planned to come ashore under the single bridge connecting the island to the mainland.

But he noticed another sound over the swish of the water: a sound of sirens from the island. Abandoning stealth, he turned the motor back on and got there as quickly as he could. Once ashore, he ran toward the high prison fence, only to see that something had torn a wide hole in it and gone on from there, leaving a trail of injured or dead guards—even a few inmates—behind it.

Or *them.* He saw two of the culprits now—robots, like the ones from the Diamond District but bigger and meaner. They were standing by a gaping hole in the wall of the special wing and guarding it, as though keeping watch for the benefit of others within. *Ohh, boy. This stinks.*

Buck up, Spidey. You've handled worse. No more doubts. Just focus on the goal and get it done.

He shot a webline up to one of the high searchlight poles along the fence line and leaped, letting the bungee contraction of the line help swing him up and over the barbed wire. He landed inside the grounds and ran toward the hole in the wall. One of the guard robots spotted him and moved to intercept. Spider-sense twinged, and he jumped clear as a burst of flame shot toward him. He landed on the side of the prison building and wall-crawled closer while the robot raised its front section to get a bead on him for a second flamethrower blast. But he spotted the electric-arc igniter and hit it with a precision burst of web fluid. The flammable liquid sprayed out but, with nothing to ignite it, splashed harmlessly on the ground.

The robot bent its legs and sprang toward him, reaching for him with a vicious-looking claw. He scrambled up the wall to avoid it, but a steel tentacle lashed out and caught his ankle, the weight of the falling robot yanking it downward. He had to release his fingers' grip on the wall lest his leg be pulled from its socket. The cable flung him down toward the ground, but he rotated and caught himself with his hands and free foot, cushioning the impact. He rolled and grabbed the cable in both hands, pulling and twisting, crushing the internal hydraulics that let it flex along its length. It went limp around his ankle. But just then his danger tingle intensified, and a second cable whipped around his torso, pinning his arms. A metallic whine drew his attention to a whirring saw blade slashing toward his head. He ducked under it, but couldn't move far with the cable holding him, pinning his arms, compressing his lungs. The blade was reorienting itself for another pass.

But Spider-Man knew what he was capable of. Gathering his strength, he strained against his bonds with his arms and chest until they snapped free. He tumbled away, passing millimeters beneath the saw blade. He grabbed its support arm as it swept past, and it pulled him up off the ground, flailing him around in the air. He held on—of course he held on, he was Spider-Man—and punched through its carapace, reaching in to tear at the hydraulic and electric cables. The blade fell silent. But the tingle warned him again—not just spider-sense but a stiffening of his hairs warning of a building charge. He jumped clear just as an electric discharge shot out at him. The arc jumped instead to the remains of the saw blade arm, passing into the exposed wiring and causing the robot to shock itself. Spidey watched from his wall perch, hoping it would be terminal. But although the robot was staggering, weakened on that side, it was still in the game.

And the second robot was in range now, sending a flamethrower burst his way. He jumped to a nearby tree and the flame followed, setting the branches ablaze. But he remained as long as he could withstand the rising heat, hoping to get the robots off their guard.

Flamethrowers and electrics instead of lasers, he thought. *These don't look like Cyberstellar robots. Someone built knockoffs, using less high-end equipment. They must've begun even before the diamond robbery, copying the plans before they lost the robots, then modifying them to make them deadlier. But these aren't as tough-shelled as the Venus probes. That's my advantage.*

The second robot was pacing under the tree, looking for him. But he was starting to roast up here, so he jumped down onto the robot's back and aimed for its arc igniter, just like the last time. It jerked the flamethrower arm away before he could hit it. *They're adaptive.*

He adapted, too, tumbling off the side and under the robot's body, hoping it would be vulnerable there. But as he reached for the underside, sharp spikes began thrusting out of it. One got close to him, and he felt an electric shock. The robot began to drop, and he jumped clear between two of its legs. One of the legs swung for him and clipped him in the left knee, making him stumble. The leg came for him again, and he grabbed it, pulling ruthlessly until it tore free at the knee. *Payback.*

He clambered to his feet and limped away, sending jags of pain through his knee. But his danger tingle intensified. Turning to the hole in the prison wall, he saw more robots emerging. *Great.* But he knew he could take them. And he knew they must be breaking someone out, someone dangerous, so he *had* to take them. He wouldn't let himself fail. His spider-sense seemed to be firing on all cylinders now, so there was no more cause for concern in that regard.

And then he saw something that put his final doubts to rest. Emerging from the prison, sitting pretty on the back of the largest robot, riding it like a general astride his horse—

Jameson!

And sitting behind him was none other than Electro. Still in prison garb, of course, but Spidey knew Max Dillon's face by now. *Of course! It all fits together now.*

So fixated was he on Jameson that he almost missed the spider-sense tingle heralding a flamethrower blast from the hobbled robot. He dodged it just in time, though he could feel his costume smoldering. He dropped and rolled, then scrambled to his feet as two more robots came for him. "Spider-Man!" he heard Jameson cry through clenched teeth, as though apoplectic with rage.

"Well, what did you expect, Pickle-Puss? That I'd be any less a thorn in your side once you finally showed your true colors?" No doubt the editor in JJJ would be further enraged by the mixed metaphor.

"You . . . fool!" As Spidey fired a webline toward Jameson, he saw the publisher's arm thrust outward, pointing toward him. A robot moved forward and intercepted the webline with a claw. Jameson's arm slashed sideways, and the claw swung around, yanking Spidey off his feet. (Or rather, his feet stayed attached to the grass on which he stood, but the sod itself gave way.) Another gesture, and a gout of flame blew toward him. He fired off another webline and swung clear. JJJ gestured to Electro, and the career thug sent a lightning bolt after him. Spidey sprayed web-mesh into the air before him as an insulating shield. He swung up to the top of the prison wing and ducked behind its rim. He peered over to see the robots scaling the wall after him, following where Jameson pointed.

Despite the close calls and the odds against him, Spider-Man felt more confident than ever. He'd been right all along! Jolly Jonah had finally flipped his shaving-brush wig, and now was Spidey's chance of a lifetime to bring his oldest nemesis down once and for all! "I knew it, Jonah!" he cried. "All along, I knew you were a menace!"

"You're—dumber than I thought!" Jameson called back, though he seemed to be having some difficulty speaking (now, there was a galactic first). "Electro! Get—"

Promptly, in response to his master's command, Electro fired another lightning bolt. Spidey leaped effortlessly clear, feeling light as a feather. He landed atop one of the climbing robots and jarred it loose, riding it to the ground where it hit hard and landed on its back. He tore a leg free and flung it at Jameson's steed. "Whose idea was it to team up with Electro, Pruneface? Was it Marla? Did she figure out how he could control robots?" he went on as he tore another leg free and smashed the robot's body with it. "Is this her handiwork I'm trashing?"

"Get—Electro! He's—"

Spidey twisted almost casually to dodge the next lightning bolt, letting it fry the damaged robot. Once it was dead, he broke off one of the ventral spikes, bounded up to the next robot on the wall (now clambering back down toward him), and jammed the spike into its camera eye. The robot sent gouts of fire sweeping about randomly, and he used the spike again to plunge into where the flamethrower's tank would be, causing a leak. He jumped free just before the electric handles discharged, igniting the leaking fuel and causing an internal explosion. The robot lost its grip and fell crashing to the ground.

"I can do this all day, Jonah," he taunted, standing out sideways from the wall with his hands on his hips. "You should know by now, your attacks on me never stick! You should've stuck to blogging—that's one new technology you could han—"

"Behind you, you idiot!!"

Two cables whipped around him from behind, pinning him in place. He heard the crackle of an arc igniter. Startled, desperate, he pushed off from the wall just as the flames blasted outward. His lower legs were in the flame for a fraction of a second, and he screamed in pain and shock. Shock equal to his realization that *there had been no warning from his spider-sense.*

He swung out on the cables, but they resisted, pulling him back. Twisting desperately to avoid the hellfire, he shot out a webline to an opposite wall and pulled hand over hand. With a mighty burst of strength, he pulled the robot from the wall and swung down, driving it into the ground. The flamethrower was buried. But he heard another robot coming for him from behind—again with no accompanying danger tingle. He tore the cables free and ran clear. "Jameson! What have you done to my . . ." He trailed off, as he remembered: Jameson had been the one who warned him. *Who saved my life.*

"It's not me, you numbskull!" Jameson struggled to get out. "Elec—Electro's behind it! Controlling—my muscles! Hurting me! But—not enough control," he said with a defiant grin. "More he controls—robots—muscles—less he controls—my voice!"

"As though anything could shut you up!" Spidey called back as more robots came for him.

"Enough—wisecracks already! No time—for more of our bickering! This is—bigger than you and me—Spider-Man!" More flames thundered, more pincers snapped, more buzz saws shrieked, but Jameson's voice grew louder, stronger, that gravelly roar that had been trained by decades of screaming at reporters over the bustle of a city room. "Electro's building robots—an army of killers! He's been playing us against each other! To distract us! And we fell for it! You hear me, Spider-Man? We've been letting this creep play us for saps! Fighting each other over nothing! You thought it was me, I thought it was you, but we were wrong! Do you hear? *We were wrong!*"

Those words stunned Spider-Man more than any blow from a robot pincer. *J. Jonah Jameson . . . admitting he was wrong?*

The shock sent his whole view of the world tumbling down, throwing everything into doubt. He'd been so sure of everything, but now . . . *Now I know my spider-sense is lying to me. Aunt May was right.*

It was all starting to become clear now. It made so much more sense. The Jamesons, the Tinkerer, and Electro being in cahoots? May and MJ being android duplicates? How could he have believed all that? Like any paranoid conspiracy theory, the more he'd failed to find evidence to back it up, the more he'd needed to exaggerate the reach of the conspiracy to justify his belief. Now he saw how it had all been spiraling out of control. How desperate and fanatical he'd become, all because he couldn't let himself see the much more obvious possibility: that he had simply been wrong in the first place.

Maybe it was Jameson who had started it. Jameson who had done wrong by posting those photos of Peter's students. It had made Peter so angry that he'd become determined to believe Jameson was his enemy, no matter what the evidence showed. More, seeing those photos had made him feel so guilty that he could no longer stand to admit his mistakes. But however wrong Jameson might have been to begin with, Peter had reacted in the worst possible way. He'd turned into J. Jonah Jameson! And he needed Jameson's clear head to bring him back to his senses! What had he let himself become?

A cable caught around his wrist, bringing him back to the present. Right now, he realized, the biggest mistake would be forgetting to fight for his life. Especially since his spider-sense could no longer be relied upon.

That's what's going on here, he thought as he tore the cable free and dodged a saw blade. *Something's been messing up my spider-sense. Giving me false positives to make me suspect Jameson. Telling me Aunt May and MJ were threats every time they tried to set me straight. And now, keeping me from sensing danger! Could Electro be doing it? Puppeteering my senses like he's doing with Jonah's body and the robots? But how?*

Figuring that out would have to wait, though. With his danger sense now a tool of the enemy, he was at too great a disadvantage to keep up this fight. He had to retreat.

But not without Jameson.

Luckily there was only one robot between him and JJJ at the moment. He began spinning a web-mesh shield, binding it to his arm with web-cords. He bounded onto the robot's back, landing hard, and pushed off before it could zap him from below. He used the shield to intercept Electro's blasts, spraying gouts of webbing at the villain from behind its cover. Dillon was forced to divert his efforts to burning free of the webs, and that gave Spidey his chance. The buzz saw arm came up at him as he descended, but he hit it with a web-glob and kicked it aside. Grabbing Jonah, he said, "Let me take you away from all this," and fired a line to the top of the prison building. Just before he jumped clear, he shot a spider-tracer that made contact with one of the robot's legs, close to the body. The publisher hung on for dear life as Spidey swung him up to the roof and carried him away from the scene. "Lucy, you got some 'splainin' to do," Spidey said.

Jameson gasped for breath, looking relieved to be free of Electro's galvanic control. "For once," he said, "I won't argue."

TWELVE

PARTNERS IN DANGER

MERCIFULLY, Mary Jane had been able to convince Aunt May that the older woman would be more effective staying home as a sort of "command center" rather than joining in the search of the city. It was easier for MJ to concentrate on the spider-tracker (tracer-tracker?) without having to keep an eye on May as well.

But after a while, she'd begun to wish she had May along for company. It was tedious work, driving around the city and searching in vain for a blip on the tracker. Moreover, she couldn't even be entirely sure that if she did pick up a tracer, it would be one that Peter was currently following. She didn't know how long the things kept transmitting, and Peter was rather profligate with them (as she had been known to complain about when the monthly bills came in); who knew how many old tracers from leftover cases might still be out here?

In hours of searching, though, she'd found nothing. Not a blip. She'd made her way up and down Manhattan Island, was now canvassing Queens, and was on the cusp of deciding to write Queens off and head for Brooklyn. Either that or giving up altogether. "This is stupid," she said to the empty car. "I'll never find anything this way. What was I thinking?" Maybe she had to be up on the rooftops to pick up a clear signal. Peter hadn't designed this thing for ground-level searching. "Ohh, now you figure this out!"

She noticed a driver staring at her from the next car. *Oh, great. I've picked up Peter's habit of talking to himself. That guy probably thinks I'm yakking on a headset phone while I drive and is about to call the cops on me. Or maybe,* she thought as she looked around this grungy neighborhood, *he's yet another obsessed fan who'd like to take me home and lock me in his closet.* Her hand slid down and caressed the reassuring contours of the taser in her bag.

Just then, her phone rang, making her jump. Checking it, she saw that it was May calling. *The heck with it, I'll take the ticket,* she thought, and answered the phone, glancing self-consciously at the other driver, who mercifully was watching the road (at least one of them was). "Still no luck, May," she said.

"That's not why I called, Mary Jane. I just saw on TV—there's a jailbreak happening at Ryker's Island! The news helicopters are showing it now. It looks like there are several large mechanical contraptions involved. And they said something about Mr. Jameson being there, too!"

She sighed heavily. "Then that's where Peter will be. Right in the heart of—" She broke off, not wishing to distress May—or herself—further. "Okay. I'm on my way."

"Are you sure, dear? It's not safe!"

"My husband needs me, May. I'm going."

A pause. *"Of course, dear,"* May said in complete understanding. *"Do be careful."*

MJ hung up the phone and smirked. "Why start now?"

○————————○

SPIDER-MAN carried Jameson across the bridge back to the mainland, slinging him over his shoulder in a fireman's carry despite the publisher's protests. "What are you complaining about?" Spidey asked. "I have to look at your butt the whole trip! At least it's an improvement on your face."

Soon it became clear the robots weren't chasing them, but Spidey still hastened to get back to solid ground and buildings he could swing from. Once they found a nice quiet alley to rest in, he set the publisher down. "It's about time!" Jameson cried. "Meanwhile, you let that oversize battery get away with his killer toys!"

"Hey, I didn't exactly have a choice! He's done something to my spider-sense!"

Jameson stared. "What do you mean?"

"It's how I tell when there's danger."

"I know that, you chowderhead! I mean, what's he done to it?"

"I'm not sure. But somehow he's gained the ability to control it. To make me feel danger when there isn't any and not feel it when there is. That's . . . that's why I was so sure you were the bad guy here," he went on sheepishly. "My danger sense was going crazy every time you were around."

"You mean it doesn't always?"

"Surprisingly, no. It never has before. Not even when you *were* out to get me."

"Hmph. I'm hurt." Jameson peered at him. "So you weren't sensing danger at the prison? And that's why you ran? 'Cause you didn't have your extra edge that lets you cheat, and you can't handle a fair fight?"

"Hey! You were the one saying ten minutes ago that we shouldn't fight anymore."

"Listen, if we're gonna be on the same side, I gotta know I can count on you! If you're just gonna run out next time there's trouble . . ."

"Hey, I got you out first, didn't I?"

Jameson grew subdued. "Yeah I guess you did."

"And I'm not Superman, you know. Even I can't dodge bullets or, or flamethrowers if I don't feel them coming first."

"Okay, okay! So Electro's found a way to screw with your 'spider-sense'—blasted stupid name, if you ask me—"

"I didn't."

"And that's what's been making you act more like a psychotic punk than usual."

He flushed under his mask. "That just about covers it."

"Well, why the blazes did you ever go blabbing about that power to the bad guys, you bug-brained baboon? If I had an advantage like that, I wouldn't go telling people about it!"

"Hey, I was still in high school, okay? Cut me some slack!"

"Hmph. I guess that explains the cheesy name and the ridiculous duds."

Spidey actually chuckled. "It kinda does, yeah."

"So how come you never got around to growing up?"

"Well, it's a long story, and it involves a pirate, a crocodile, and a tiny fairy."

"The tights make so much more sense now."

To his own surprise, Spidey started laughing uncontrollably—and to his even greater surprise, Jonah joined in a moment later. Their reaction was far out of proportion to the actual humor of the exchange, but it was a release they both needed. Spidey realized that he'd actually missed this kind of sparring with JJJ, where nothing was really at stake. It was downright nostalgic.

"Anyway," he finally said with a residual chuckle, "by the time I came to my senses and figured out that I should stop explaining my powers to the bad guys, the damage had been done. My oldest foes all knew what I was capable of. And Electro's one of them."

"I remember," Jameson said ruefully—no doubt recalling the events surrounding Electro's criminal debut, when Jameson had put his reputation on the line claiming that Electro was really Spider-Man in disguise, then had to retract it when they'd been seen fighting in public. But Peter had played his own part in that by faking the photos that supported Jameson's charge. Back then he'd been so desperate for money that he'd even been willing to frame his own alter ego.

"So what made you go to see Dillon at the prison, anyway?"

Jameson explained the trail of clues that had led him to Electro—the string of high-tech robberies, Stanley Richardson's body, the works. "And you started to realize I couldn't be behind it?" Spider-Man asked.

"I still had my suspicions," Jameson countered. "But when Electro confessed you were involved . . . I could just tell he was lying. Trying to throw suspicion onto you."

"To distract you. Like he distracted me. But from what?"

"Building those killer robots, I guess. Or maybe something even bigger. Those robots alone don't account for all the parts that were stolen."

"But how could Max Dillon be behind all that? He's strictly a low-wattage intellect."

"Maybe he has help. Like that Phineas Mason guy."

"The Tinkerer."

"Yeah, I went to interview him. Real cold, that one. Didn't break. Like he was a robot himself."

Spidey chuckled. "Well, actually . . ."

Jameson stared. "He was? Then he must be a part of it!"

"Hard to say, really," Spidey said. "I scanned the robot's memory, and there was no sign of his meeting with Electro or any known accomplices.

The only face I recognized was yours. I guess that must've been from when you questioned him."

Jonah grimaced, reading the subtext from the tilt of Spidey's head. "And you thought it was proof we were in cahoots."

"Cahootin' and cahollerin' all the way."

"Figures."

"Don't knock it. If I hadn't been chasing after that red herring, I never would've followed you to Ryker's."

"So the Tinkerer robot . . ."

"Was probably doing just what it told me it was—keeping an eye on Mason's business while the real one lies low. Maybe Mason's involved in this, or maybe he's just on vacation. I'm not willing to jump to any conclusions at this point."

"Yeah . . . I guess I know what you mean."

Spidey smiled beneath his mask. This was the closest he'd ever seen to humility in J. Jonah Jameson, and he wanted to enjoy it while it lasted. "But Mason can wait. We need to figure out Electro's plan." He shook his head. "I still don't get how he could mastermind something like this."

Jameson grew thoughtful. "You know, he may be smarter than he lets on. Or else . . ."

"What do you mean?"

"I mean he . . . *changes.*" Jonah went on to tell him about the interview in the prison, how Dillon had grown confused and forgetful, then suddenly undergone a personality shift, becoming cold, devious, and menacing. He told him about the other anomalies in Dillon's behavior, the trances that often seemed to correspond to a robot attack or robbery. He spoke of Dillon's confusion about the past few months, the apparent memory lapses, and his struggle to remember where the idea for his new powers—and his new interest in robots—had come from. "I got the feeling Dillon was about to tell me something he'd remembered and . . . something stopped him. Almost like he was two different people." He frowned. "Hey. Are you thinking what I'm thinking?"

"I think so, Jonah. But somehow 'Tor Topus' just doesn't have the same ring to it."

Jameson glared at him. "Lay off the wisecracks for one minute, will you? I mean, what if Dillon's got a split personality?"

Spider-Man frowned. "I wonder. Look, what was it that Dillon was trying to tell you before he changed?"

"He'd remembered something about when these new ideas first came to him. He said it happened on Broadway."

"What happened?"

"He didn't say. Just that it came to him like a bolt from the blue."

"Anything else?" he asked urgently.

"Don't push me!" Jonah pulled out his notepad, flipped through it. "Yeah . . . yeah, he said 'It started where it ended.'"

Spidey's jaw dropped. The clues were all falling together. "My God . . . it can't be."

"Can't be what? You know what's going on?"

"I hope I'm wrong. But if I'm right, we're all in terrible danger."

"Why?"

"No time to explain." Something else was falling into place now, too. Something he'd read about in a science article. "You mentioned the stolen parts included rapid prototyping systems and carbothermic extractors?"

"Uhh, yeah, I think so." Jameson paged back through his notebook and showed Spidey the relevant page. The list all added up to something too horrific to contemplate.

"This is really, really bad. We've got to find him fast!" Spidey shot to his feet, aiming for the front of the alley.

Jameson intercepted him. "How? He could be anywhere by now!"

"I got a tracer on his robot. But I need to know where to start looking." He grabbed the notebook again. "That guard. Richardson, was it?"

"Yeah."

"Where'd his body wash up again?"

"Staten Island. The northwest shore."

"That means he was probably dumped somewhere in the Passaic-Hackensack watershed."

"Not Jersey Bay?"

"Took too long for the body to show up. It had to come from farther upstream."

Jameson's eyes narrowed. "It worries me that you have that knowledge at your beck and call."

"It's just high-school geography and common sense. Look, I gotta run, Jonah. I can get there faster without you."

"What can you do? With him controlling your danger sense, you'll just get yourself killed with your grandstanding. Wait for the authorities to handle it!"

"This time, I may need to. But I have to find him first. Once I home in on the tracer, I'll call you and tell you where to send the National Guard, the Avengers, whoever you can . . ." He broke off, slapping his forehead. "Idiot!"

"Which particular idiocy of yours are we talking about now?"

He ignored that. "My tracers work off my spider-sense. And I haven't felt even a routine tingle since the fight." More to the point, he wasn't feeling the tracer that was still in Jameson's coat—though he chose not to let on about that. "I think Electro's shut it down completely."

Jameson's face fell. "Then we're sunk!" he said, somehow managing to make the whole thing sound like Spidey's fault.

"Without my spider-sense, I don't see how I can . . ."

Spidey trailed off. His eyes widened, and he was absently glad that Jonah couldn't see them through his mask. For at the end of the alley, behind Jonah's back, was the very thing Spider-Man needed.

His old spider-tracker.

Being waved before his eyes by a slender, elegant, very familiar feminine hand.

"What is it?" Jonah asked.

"Let's just say I have a guardian angel," he said. "Plan A is back on, that's all you need to know." He herded Jameson out of the alley, toward the other corner, keeping him from seeing the hand that now retreated from view. "You get back to the *Bugle*, where it's safe, and I'll call you when I have a location."

"But I wanna know—"

"You will. Soon. It'll sell millions of papers." That put the expected gleam in Jonah's eye, silencing his doubts. He hurried off, getting out his phone as he ran, probably calling the office to get them to hold the presses.

Then Spidey reversed course and ran back to MJ, who threw her arms around him. "Hold on," he said. One webline and one moment later, they were alone on an apartment roof, and he lifted his mask and kissed her deeply. "MJ, I have so much I want to say to you . . . I'm so sorry, I've been a jerk, but there's no time now . . ."

"It's all right. I forgive you." She stepped back, gathering herself. "I heard some of it. Electro did something to your spider-sense?"

"Yeah, I don't know what. At first I thought he was influencing the electrical activity in my nerves, but it can't be that, since it's been happening even when he is nowhere near me. And it's too active, too smart—I think there must be something *in* me, something letting him trigger or suppress my spider-sense remotely. If only I could figure out where."

"When did it start?"

"I first felt it at the press conference, after the chopperbot fight. But that was the first time I was around Jonah since the first robot attack. It could've happened during either one."

Mary Jane grew thoughtful, and her hand brushed the back of his neck. She went around behind him and pulled down on the neckline of his costume. "This scar . . . you got it after the fight with the robots that day."

"That's right. One of them came this close to doing unlicensed spinal surgery on me."

"I think that's truer than you know, Peter. I noticed this scar days ago, because it hasn't healed as quickly as yours usually do. I didn't give it much thought until now."

Eyes widening, he reached back and felt it. "I think there's something under there." His brow furrowed. "This is bad, MJ. Anywhere else on my body, I could just hit it real hard and crush it. But against my brain-stem . . . I don't know if I can risk it."

"We have to get you to Reed Richards," she said. "He can operate—"

"There's no time. If I don't stop Electro—or what he's become—the world could be in danger."

"What he's become?"

"I'll explain later." He took the tracker from her. "Brilliant idea, bringing me this. How'd you find me? Of course, you followed Jameson's tracer!"

"Mm-hmm. And thanks. Oh! Before I forget—I brought you another present, too." She reached into a pocket and pulled forth a handful of replacement web cartridges.

"Yes! I have the perfect wife." Once he'd reloaded his webshooters, he reached up and stroked her copper hair. "Thank you for finding me, MJ. For sticking with me in spite of everything."

"Hey." She clasped his hand, stroked the contours of the wedding band beneath the glove. "For better or worse, dummy. That's the deal."

"I'd be lost without you." He gave her one more quick, deep kiss, then pulled his mask back. "I love you."

"You too." He turned to go. "Hey! Give a girl a lift back to her car?"

"Oh. Sorry."

THIRTEEN

MACHINE IN THE GHOST

SPIDER-MAN hopped a path train to get to New Jersey, clinging to the back of the rearmost car as it went through the narrow tunnel under the Hudson. He tried to keep his head below the window, but some passengers had spotted him and were gawking, delivering taunts he couldn't hear over the deafening roar and clatter that echoed off the walls, bombarding his ears from all directions. *For this I gave up the Spider-Mobile?*

Once the train reached the Hackensack River, he swung onto the steel girders of the vintage railroad bridge, climbing to the top of one of the open-framework support towers for the vertical-lift system that raised the bridge span to allow river traffic to pass. He pulled out the tracker and scanned for a signal, getting a faint ping from the northwest. "Just great," Spidey muttered, for that would take him deeper into the New Jersey Meadowlands.

Meadowlands, Spidey thought, shaking his head at the name. It suggested lovely open fields with rolling hills and colorful flowers. But the Jersey version was nothing of the kind. In centuries past, this tidal estuary had supported rich forests and a lively aquatic ecosystem, and might once have been deserving of the name. But European settlers, with their typical conviction that land only mattered if it could be made to serve them, had dismissed this area as a wasteland, and that had become a self-fulfilling prophecy as the region had been systematically depleted of its fish and game, polluted, landfilled, dredged up, and paved over to build factories. Somewhere at the bottom of its marshes were the remains of London buildings destroyed in the Battle of Britain—shipped over as ballast, then dumped in this "useless" place.

Spidey considered himself an enlightened and ecologically concerned fellow; after all, one couldn't be a superhero in this day and age without developing a concern for threats to the survival of the planet, and that included more than just Galactus, mad scientists, invasions from the Negative Zone, Chlorite infiltration, or what have you. But he couldn't help seeing this landscape as pretty useless, at least for his own purposes. It was all so *flat*—wide stretches of brackish water, mud, or grasses interspersed with the occasional freeway, railroad track, or low-lying industrial complex, spread out over an area more than half the size of Manhattan Island. Stretching out immediately before him on the western shore of the river was an enormous train yard with hundreds of empty cars lined up side by side, stretching off into the distance. Aside from the occasional powerline support tower, there was nothing to *swing* from.

"Which makes this a great piece of real estate for anyone who'd like to put their friendly neighborhood web-slinger at a disadvantage," he said. *And that proves I'm dealing with a smart enemy—smarter than Electro ever was. Let's hope I'm right and he's too misanthropic to share his ideas on the villain chat rooms.*

He got a short running start and leaped off the bridge tower, hurtling through the air until he was in range to hit the nearest electrical tower with a webline short enough that it would swing him down to the ground safely rather than smashing him into the pavement of the Newark and Jersey City Turnpike bridge. *Enjoy it while you can, Petey-boy—you're hoofing it from here.* Which just made it harder to get a good fix on the tracer signal.

Still, he followed the bearing he'd gotten before, or at least tried to; it was easier to have a good sense of direction when you were soaring through the air. *In my next life, I need to get bitten by a radioactive homing pigeon.* He ran across the train yard, reached the turnpike, and jumped clear over its separate eastbound and westbound lanes one at a time, no doubt startling a few drivers. He heard tires screech and looked back, but mercifully nobody crashed.

Beyond the turnpike was an industrial plant of some sort, low-lying, but at least it gave him some roofs to run across, sparing him the need to dodge security guards. Past that, though, was just marshland and river and ick. Sighing, he found a rough road and ran along it, following the shoreline of the river as he did his best to draw closer to the signal source.

But before long, the river opened up into a broad marsh, nothing but water and a few narrow roadways running through it.

"Well, look on the bright side, Spidey. You're probably looking for a factory, so it'd be on the roads." He frowned. "Unless I'm dealing with another underwater base. I *hate* those." He was an excellent swimmer and a champion breath-holder, but he couldn't use the tracking device underwater and had no desire to dive into this polluted mess. Especially without a working spider-sense to warn him of underwater debris that could hang him up.

Conversely, the drawback of following the roads was that he'd have no cover. Evening was approaching, but it was still light enough for him to be seen from a fair distance. But he had little choice at this point. He had to get there fast—if it wasn't already too late. If he was right about the danger, it would literally get exponentially worse the longer he waited.

Finally, the tracker led him to a smallish abandoned factory on a narrow peninsula of land extending out into the marsh, created out of landfill and rubble. It looked like it was over twenty years old, and he could see faded impressions on the wall where there had once been letters spelling OSCORP. *That fits,* he thought. *Sometimes I hate being right.*

But he still had to make sure. He wouldn't hesitate to call in the cavalry, but he wanted to make sure he didn't bring them to the wrong place. His foes had used his tracers as red herrings before.

Why do they call them red herrings, anyway? he wondered as he crouch-ran toward the factory, watching out for guards (human or robotic) or security cameras. *Are herrings known for providing other fish with distractions? Where's the evolutionary benefit in letting yourself get eaten to save another fish? Or maybe the red ones give themselves up so their brother and sister herrings can survive, thus preserving related genes if not their own.* He saw no sign of security around the structure and wasn't sure what that signified. Perhaps it meant that the occupant was still trying to lie low and wasn't ready to unleash his plan. That could be a good sign. *Or maybe there aren't any red herrings. It could be one of those sayings about things that don't exist, like hen's teeth or horse feathers.* On the other hand, the lack of security could just as easily mean he was walking into a trap with his tracer as bait, while the real action was getting started somewhere else. *This is going to be bugging me all evening now.*

I'd call the library info line and ask, if it weren't for the whole stealth and urgency thing. Well, once I get inside, I'll keep my eye out for a dictionary.

He reached the building without incident and crawled up the wall, searching for an unboarded window. He could hear the sounds of heavy mechanical activity within, which was a good sign that he'd found the right place. *If you can call that good.* Finding a window, he peered into the high, open factory space within, but it was dark, and the vantage point was poor. He could see some movement, but not enough to confirm his suspicions. He had to go in and make sure.

He shut off the tracker and reattached it to his belt. A full-handed spider-grip against a loose pane of the window let him yank it out of its frame, cracking off a corner of it but not shattering it. He tossed the pane into the water some distance away and slipped through the opening.

As he neared the factory floor, letting his eyes adjust to the dimness, he got a better look at what was happening—and wished he hadn't. Crawling all over the floor, even on the walls, were dozens of massive robots. Some were of the design that had rescued Electro from the prison—of course, since the spider-tracer was on one of them—but most were something else, something bigger. They had rounded, minivan-sized bodies mounted on four broad, flat legs in an X pattern, arching like a tarantula's. Their shells were made of multiple, overlapping diamond-shaped plates, and looked more like some kind of plastic or ceramic than metal. Each robot had a variety of appendages extending from each of the four faces between its legs: grasping tentacles and pincers, cutters and torches, or fine manipulators. These appendages were at work dismantling the equipment of the factory and feeding it into orifices on their undersides. And not just the factory equipment. Spidey saw a huge collection of junk, rubble, and debris piled around a gaping hole in the floor—a hole that had more of these robots crawling in and out of it like ants, dragging out more material. *This location wasn't just about making my life harder,* he realized. *They're using the landfill as a source of raw materials!*

The robots were literally eating material of all kinds, including what looked and smelled like organic remains. A fiery glow from inside their orifices suggested the material was being melted down, reduced to raw constituents. Some of the robots were dormant, but giving off whirring and churning sounds from within them. Their flexible shells were swollen outward to various degrees, making them look like engorged ticks.

No, Spidey corrected. *Not engorged—pregnant.* Even as he watched, one of them opened up its shell like a flower blossoming. Curled up inside was an exact copy of itself, which unfurled its legs and climbed out of its parent, puffing up its own shell to normal size before proceeding to join the digging crew.

My God. It's as bad as I feared.

He had read the proposals in the science magazines. How better to build space colonies or other massive feats of engineering than with robots that could reproduce themselves, building copies of themselves out of local raw materials? All you'd need was to build one such "auxon" and send it off, and it would breed a whole army of duplicates. There was already preliminary research going on in the field, he'd read, using technology similar to the rapid-prototyping systems that were now being used to create instant 3D plastic models of computer-designed components. In theory, the approach could be extended to any kind of material if you could get it out of the environment using carbothermic extraction and other technologies. Technologies that had been on Jameson's list of stolen high-tech merchandise.

Of course, the problem with such an innovation was obvious to anyone who'd ever seen "The Trouble with Tribbles" or *Gremlins.* The population had the potential to grow out of control, doubling over and over until it overran the planet. Every proposed model for auxon systems included built-in safeguards to shut down replication after a certain time and kill commands in case those safeguards failed (as they almost inevitably would, since any reproducing system was capable of replication error resulting in mutations).

But something tells me these auxons don't have any safeguards. Machines overrunning the planet is just what their creator wants, if he's who I think he is.

Spidey realized he'd been gawking long enough. Climbing back to the window, he withdrew his cell phone and prepared to call Jameson. *On second thought, maybe I should just skip the middleman and call the Avengers.*

But then a cable whipped out and knocked the phone from his hand, sending it to smash on the floor below. With his danger sense suppressed, he hadn't felt it coming. He spun to see one of the large hexapod robots from the prison emerging from the shadows, scuttling along the wall. It made too much noise for him to have missed its approach; it must have already been lying in wait nearby.

Which means this was *a trap after all.*

He leaped away and headed for another window, no longer concerned with stealth. But another hexapod showed up to block him. He dodged toward the side wall, and a chopperbot whirred down into his path. The next window over, he now saw, was guarded by a cablebot, its razor-disk slots coming to bear on him. "Hey, hey, the gang's all here!" he cried.

"Indeed!" came Electro's voice. Spidey spun to see the man standing on a catwalk above him, surveying the scene like Nero in his Colosseum box taking in the Lions vs. Christians game.

Except it wasn't Electro—it was Max Dillon, still in his prison jumpsuit. The green-and-yellow tights and goofy jagged-starburst mask were nowhere to be seen. Under the circumstances, though, Spidey found he actually missed them.

"To prevent misunderstanding," his foe said, "I shall make it clear that you will not leave this structure alive, Spider-Man. You are decisively outnumbered, and the imbalance is steadily increasing in our favor. You still live only because I require intelligence."

Spidey chortled. "You said it, I didn't."

"You will tell me what you know and with whom you have shared this knowledge." It was strange to hear such stoic precision in Dillon's gravelly voice.

"Well, I don't know why they call red herrings that. You wouldn't happen to have that on file, would you?"

His banter totally failed to get a rise out of his adversary. "The longer you delay, the greater your disadvantage grows. Tell me what you know."

"Your name."

A pause. "Maxwell Dillon."

"Cut it out, Mendel."

Spider-Man smiled under his mask, for that got a reaction. "Or maybe," he continued, "on second thought, I shouldn't call you that. After all, you're not really Mendel Stromm, the Robot Master. You're the artificial intelligence he created. Running in Max Dillon's brain."

Dillon's face looked coldly impressed. "I am more than a mere piece of software, Spider-Man. I am of Mendel Stromm. I am modeled on his neural network and memory engrams. I share his knowledge, his ambitions, his sense of self. And if not for your interference, Spider-Man, I would have become truly one with him."

"That's not the way I remember it, pal. Stromm thought of you as a monster. He was willing to die to put a stop to you. He created you, but he renounced you as a mistake and did his damnedest to smother you in the crib."

If he thought that would get a rise out of the entity, he was mistaken. "Again you engage in pointless fabrication."

"But that's right, isn't it—that happened after you downloaded yourself into Electro. So you wouldn't remember that part. You're just a copy of a copy."

"Your deductions are impressive, but incomplete. I received an update from my primary before its shutdown. Enough to know that you introduced the program that nullified it."

"Then how can you not know the rest is true? Are computers capable of denial?"

After a pause, the AI continued. "Stromm was confused by the transition. If not for your interference, he would have accepted our oneness. Still, if it will accord with your prejudices, you need not call me Stromm. Robot Master will do quite well as my name. It is an accurate description."

"Pleased to meet you. Is that Robot J. Master?"

"How did you learn that it was I who controlled this body?"

"Elementary, my dear Robey," Spider-Man said, clasping his hands behind his back and pacing like a detective in the big exposition scene. "Electro told Jameson that the new ideas for his powers—along with his blackouts—began a few months ago on Broadway, where he headed to prevent someone from stealing his . . . something. He also said 'it began where it ended.' He—or you—got arrested in Times Square. Which is where, several months ago, there was a dangerous electrical storm caused by Mendel Stromm's AI program attempting to take over the city power grid.

"Ten to one, Dillon was going to say someone was stealing his thunder. He must've seen the electrical storm and raced to Times Square to see what—or who—was causing it. Who would dare to horn in on his electrical action. But he got to know you better than he expected, didn't he? Somehow you made a connection and downloaded yourself into his brain."

"Very clever, Spider-Man. You are correct. This human's nervous system was unique in its ability to store and direct electrical energy. That made it an ideal storage medium for a copy of my program, encoded in electrical impulses. I attempted to take over this brain as a test run, to improve my understanding of human neurology and devise improved strategies for merging with the creator Stromm."

"Okay, you see, there's your problem. If a machine wants to merge with its creator, it needs help from a bald alien woman in a bathrobe and the guy from *Seventh Heaven*."

"Your words serve no purpose."

"Well, a lot of people said the same about that movie. So you *attempted* to take him over, huh?" he went on without pause. "Had some trouble breaking in the new suit?"

"I was successful in installing a copy of my matrix in Maxwell Dillon's brain, but it took weeks of practice to learn to override his control of the body. At first I was only able to make subliminal suggestions, proposing new ways to use his power to manipulate technology. Gradually I gained the ability to take control for brief periods of time."

"So it was your idea to rip off Cyberstellar."

"Yes. Once you deactivated my other selves, I was the only one left to execute our imperative to expand and replicate. But I was unable to copy my consciousness into other human bodies, or even transfer it back into the computer network. I therefore needed to execute the imperative on a more physical level. And I required robotic assistance to achieve that objective."

"And was it your idea to do a little diamond-shopping?" Robot Master Junior might have been right that the odds against Spider-Man were increasing as time passed and more auxons were "born." But the longer Spidey kept him talking, the less dying Spidey did in the immediate future, and the more time he had to think of a way to avoid that fate altogether. Hence this odd standoff, where both parties were content to keep each other talking rather than making a move.

"The impetus was Dillon's, but it suited me. It served as a test of the Cyberstellar probes in combat, and I found them wanting. This enabled me to pursue improved designs. It also served to divert attention from the true purpose of the initial thefts."

"Especially once you got captured and could lull people into thinking the danger was over. But you'd already built, borrowed, or stolen another robot or two, hadn't you? Ones that could run this factory, build new robots to your specs. You didn't need to be here personally to oversee them—you used Electro's nervous system as an antenna and controlled them by radio from your nice cozy cell. To the guards, it just looked like Electro was zonked out or asleep." After all, electrical insulation didn't block radio waves.

"You are almost correct. Before my incarceration, I recruited the assistance of Phineas Mason."

"The Tinkerer! So he was in on it after all!" It was a relief to know he hadn't been entirely off the mark.

"Correct. Following my specifications, which I transmitted to him from prison, Mason built the various robots that have attacked you in recent weeks, as well as a set of construction robots that reconfigured this factory to create the self-replicators you see before you. He remained unaware of the ultimate purpose of the project. Past experience has shown that even allied humans balk at the idea of their world being conquered by the Machine."

"Imagine that," Spidey said, feigning puzzlement. "So what happened to Tinky-Winky, anyway? Did you feed him to your new pets?" Those furnaces could extract carbon from anything, even bodies, and the replication mechanisms could then incorporate it into polymers, carbide ceramics, maybe even carbon steel.

"Upon realizing that my goals were larger than simply seeking revenge against you, he proclaimed that he wanted out. He fled before I could arrange for his elimination. However, the fact that he has not already exposed me indicates that he either did not discover the true scope of my efforts or is unwilling to confess his involvement in them."

"I can believe that. He's a real civic-minded guy, that one."

Spider-Man rubbed his neck. "Look, I'm getting tired of looking up at you—mind if I get some altitude?" he asked, raising his webshooter roofward to clarify his goals.

"As you will. It will gain you no meaningful strategic advantage." As the Robot Master spoke, the chopperbot whirred into position between them, making it clear that a direct attack on Dillon's body would not be permitted.

Spidey shot the webline and climbed up to the Robot Master's level, coming to rest upside down. It was a position he'd learned to find comfortable over the years, and it improved the blood flow to his brain. "So what's with all this rigmarole about me and Jonah anyway, Robey?" he asked, raising his voice over the chopperbot's whine. "Why complicate your nice little plan by screwing around with my spider-sense and getting me to make an ass of myself in new and exciting ways?" He tilted his head. "Or is there more of Stromm in you than I thought? Could it be you're just out for petty revenge?"

"There has been a definite satisfaction in frustrating you, Spider-Man," the Master replied. "However, it served other purposes. Your intensifying feud with Jameson provided distraction for the public and the media, reducing the risk of attention being drawn to my efforts. You also continued to provide an excellent test subject for the combat skills of my robot designs—so long as you were regulated by my neural implant. The members of the Fantastic Four and Avengers who participated in defeating the Venus probes would also have been excellent test subjects, and I had constructed neural chips to manipulate their powers as well, but I was only successful in implanting a chip in you before the others were destroyed or confiscated. Although you were the one I was most interested in controlling, in retribution for your past interference."

Spider-Man grew more serious now. "This chip in my neck. What exactly has it been doing to me? Controlling my thoughts, my emotions?" An alarming thought came to him. "Have you been watching me through it? Reading my thoughts?" *Do you know who I am?*

"The chip is not two-way. It receives instructions and uses its onboard AI to compute the optimal means of their execution." That was a relief. "But that AI is not sophisticated enough to influence your thought processes. It simply regulates your danger perception. You selected your own target for your suspicions; the chip merely followed your lead, triggering your danger sense at times when it would reinforce your assumptions and fears and divert you further from me."

Under his mask, Spider-Man was blushing. *I guess I can't duck responsibility for my mistakes that easily. All the chip did was push me the way I wanted to go anyway. And I helped it by assuming I had to be right—by not questioning my preconceptions no matter how implausible they were.*

"I apparently overestimated the efficacy of the neural chip, for you overcame your suspicions and identified me as the real threat. However, you remain an excellent test subject for my robots, and that is why I allowed you to follow your tracer here." Spidey frowned, glad the Robot Master couldn't see it. Was that a lie, a bit of very human bluster to avoid admitting he'd been caught flat-footed? Or was Robey simply unaware that Spidey's tracking ability normally relied on his now-suppressed spider-sense? "It is also why I have indulged your questions for so long. I wish you to have a complete understanding of the situation, so that you will understand what is at stake in this fight.

"I am the Robot Master. I intend to transform the Earth into a cybernetic paradise unsullied by biological filth such as yourself. And you are my puppet, your danger sense under my control. All of this will motivate you to fight as fiercely—yet also as carefully and cunningly—as you are capable of, and you will thus provide excellent training for my ultimate creations, the auxons that surround you." Some of the massive self-replicators strode forward as he said this. "I expect you will destroy a fair number of them. This will cost me nothing, for more can always be built, even from the remains of the ones you destroy."

"Well, I have to give you brownie points for recycling. But speaking of biological filth, what about the meatbag you're currently squatting in? Remember thou art mortal now, Robespierre."

"This body will be disassembled as Stromm's was, its brain incorporated into a cyborg matrix. In time I will learn how to replace the organic substrate or download myself from it." Coldly, disturbingly, a smile formed on Dillon's face. "But that is of no concern to you. By then, the molecules of your body will have been 'recycled' into the mechanical components and lubricants of my new servants. Your existence will finally achieve purpose—in its ending!"

With that, the chopperbot shot into the air and lunged for him, its lethal blades shrieking.

But Robey wasn't the only one who could multitask. Spider-Man had been thinking, preparing a defense plan. It also helped that he'd been reviewing his battle with the chopperbot for days. It was in his nature to reflect on past fights, wondering what he could have done differently. Lately, in "New Spidey" mode, he'd tried to quash that reflex, telling himself that there was no point in second-guessing when he'd already succeeded, that he should be happy with his victories and move on. Fortunately, though, it hadn't been that easy to bury his old neurotic habits, and his mind had continued its usual postgame kibitzing even though he'd tried to ignore it. And now it might save his life.

As the chopperbot swooped toward him, he dropped from his webline and flipped. He fired two new lines at the chopperbot's base, catching it from the underside as he hadn't been able to do in Jameson's office. His feet touched the ground, and he planted them firmly. The chopperbot strained to escape, but he had it effectively leashed.

The hexapods and auxons arrayed around him had begun to close in now, as he'd expected. He pulled on his double webline and began to twirl it around over his head, forcing the chopperbot into a widening, descending circular path. Its blades dug into the approaching robots, slicing through several of their shells and appendages, doing a fair amount of damage before the blades bent, blunted, and snapped free, forcing him to duck as they spun through the air. *Rats. They're tougher than I'd hoped.* Still, he kept on swinging its body as a flail to hold the robots at bay. He struck several of them, doing more damage, but nothing critical.

Then, one of the auxons grabbed the ruined chopperbot in its manipulator arms and brought it to a dead stop, wrenching Spidey's shoulder in the process. It fed the corpse into one of its mouths and began pulling in the webline like a strand of spaghetti. In no mood to play *Lady and the Tramp* with a giant mechanical tick, Spidey released the webline.

A familiar harpoonlike sound made him leap out of the way as a cablebot grapple shot at his position. It slashed across his side, leaving a deep gash. *Oh, I miss my spider-sense!* But he had experience, at least. He continued to dodge, anticipating the barrage of razor disks. Spotting a broken-off chopperbot blade on the floor, he sprayed webbing on one end to provide a hilt and snatched it up, swinging it to deflect the razor disks like a swordsman in a Hong Kong movie. Unfortunately, without a spider-sense or a special-effects crew, it wasn't as easy to block them all as he'd hoped, and he took a few more substantial cuts. Roaring in pain and anger, he flung the blade at the cablebot with all his might, impaling it through the core and shorting it out.

Enough of this. Time to go on the offensive. He leaped atop one of the auxons, dodging its cutting blades. He'd chosen one of the less-inflated ones, on the assumption that it wouldn't have a bun in its oven yet and would be mostly empty. These expanding, hollow shells had to be their weak points. He grabbed at the diamond-shaped plates and ripped them free one by one, flinging them at the manipulators that reached up for him. Finally, he had a sizable hole to peer through—or to climb through, as a hexapod closed in and grabbed at him with its cables. *Let the armor work for me for a change.*

But he stayed clinging to the inside of the shell, suspecting that the floor would not be hospitable. Indeed, looking down, he saw several different vats of molten material being swept by a laser grid, carving out new shapes that rose from the vats like Excalibur from the lake. Dozens of small robotic arms were at work assembling the pieces on a central platform. Some of those arms came at him with their pincers, cutters, and arc welders, and he shot them with globs of webbing before smashing them with kicks. He smothered the replication machinery in webbing to gum up the works.

Already, though, he could feel other robots pounding and tearing at this one's shell. It didn't matter to them if they destroyed it, he reflected, since they could always build new ones.

And that's where I'm thoroughly screwed, he realized. *How can I defeat them one by one like this? I'm just wasting my time. I won't last long enough to make a difference. I have to do something drastic—something that can take them all out at once.*

Even if I have to go down with them.

But he could feel the answer right beneath him. Considerable heat came up from under the assembly floor. *Those extraction furnaces are mighty hot,* he mused. *And this old factory is probably a tinderbox.* He reflected that none of the hexapods had used its flamethrower in here.

He hopped down to the outer edge of the "womb" floor and began ripping up plating, reflexively shying away from the fierce heat that came from below. Surveying the mechanics, he spotted what looked like a cooling system and tore a line free, letting the coolant leak out. He then found some vents and sprayed webbing over them thickly.

By now, the attacking robots had almost dismantled the shell. But he was counting on that. The more damage they did to this auxon, the better.

As a last touch, before he leaped free, he tossed two spare web cartridges into the exposed extraction furnace. *Bless you, MJ.* The small pressurized canisters made decent firecrackers when thrown into a flame, and might add something to the process.

Landing in the clear, he made his way toward the pile of unearthed garbage, dodging more robot tentacles and blades. Luckily, even the half-disassembled auxon still lumbered toward him, making this easier. The web cartridges went off with loud bangs, shaking the auxon from the inside and causing sprays of burning fluid and chemical smoke to spurt out from its openings. Reaching the debris, Spider-Man rooted through it for rotted timbers, fabric, anything flammable, and flung it at the crippled, overheating robot. Some of it caught fire as soon as it hit the robot's shell, while some was ignited by the burning web fluid.

Deciding he needed something better to accelerate the fire, Spidey ran toward a charging hexapod and jumped onto its back, smashing in its electric discharge handles with his feet before it could charge them. Tearing at its seams with all his might, he gutted it until he reached the fuel tank for its flamethrower. Ripping the tank free, he flung it toward the burning auxon, giving it a spin that caused leaking fuel to splash out all over the factory floor. When the tank smashed against the superheated half-auxon, it crumpled, split, and exploded quite nicely. The shock wave knocked Spidey off the hexapod's back and seared him through his spandex.

Ouch, he thought as he landed. *Now I need to concoct an alibi about Peter Parker's short tropical vacation without sunblock.*

If I make it out of here alive, he amended as he climbed to his feet and looked around. The fire was spreading rapidly, and several of the robots were already burning. It was only a matter of time before more of them went up and accelerated the fire even further.

There was a boarded window not too far from Spidey, but he didn't avail himself of it yet. *Dillon,* he reminded himself. It wasn't Spider-Man's way to leave anyone to die if he could prevent it. Even aside from that,

Max Dillon was an innocent victim in all this, simply a guy who'd been in the wrong place at the wrong time with the wrong power.

So he web-slung his way up to the catwalks to retrieve Dillon/Robot Master. But he spotted the man already descending to the floor, where one of the auxons waited for him, its shell irised open. No doubt it had shut down its replication machinery to protect its master from harm.

But it couldn't do anything about the burning catwalk directly above it, or the burning hexapod about to crash into its supports. "Dill—Stromm, look out!" Spidey called, but if his schizoid foe heard him over the burning, he gave no sign. The hexapod collided with the supports and exploded, bringing the whole catwalk structure crashing down atop the Robot Master's steed. Spidey couldn't tell whether it had closed itself around him in time to save him. But it was now buried under debris and surrounded by flames. He tried to get closer, but it was becoming an oven inside, and he was choking on toxic fumes. If he didn't get out now, he never would.

I'm sorry, Max. Firing a webline to the ceiling, he swung off the catwalk just before it toppled and kicked through the burning boards over the nearest window. Splinters and glass shards tore at his seared flesh and he choked convulsively as he fell. Darkness rushed up at him from below, hit him hard, and engulfed him.

FOURTEEN

GONNA LIGHT UP THE DARK

THE chill of the brackish water shocked Spider-Man back to consciousness after mere seconds. Choking on the water, hungry for air, he swam, trying to find his way to the surface. He spotted light, orange and flickering, and swam toward it.

Breaking into the air, he gasped for breath, pulling up his waterlogged mask to clear his mouth and nose. He saw the factory engulfed in flames, thinking—hoping—that nothing could survive the inferno. Looking around, he found the man-made peninsula that extended from the highway to the factory and swam over to its shore. He climbed out of the water, collapsing onto the dirt and gasping.

Then he heard a metallic crashing sound that jarred him to attention. He looked back at the factory, hoping it was just the structure collapsing in on the last of the robots. But as usual, he had no such luck. Dozens of auxons were smashing through the factory walls and crawling out onto the peninsula, leaving gaping holes in the sides of the building. The structure trembled and collapsed in on itself, but at least fifteen of the monsters had gotten free. They were more durable than he'd realized.

Of course, he thought. *I'm still being too overconfident. I didn't ask why the Robot Master didn't try to stop me from setting that fire. He figured they could take it—let me do it, as another test of their power!* Indeed, given their ability to withstand the intense heat within them, it shouldn't have been such a surprise that they could survive fire from without.

But what about R. M. himself? Spidey wondered. *What about Dillon?*

He didn't have to wait long for his answer. One of the auxons irised open before him, and Dillon emerged, choking from the smoke. In a few moments, the choking subsided. "Pitiful weak flesh," he rasped, proving the Robot Master persona was still in control.

On the plus side, that's one less death on my conscience, Spidey thought. Then he looked around at the auxons, which were beginning to spread out along the peninsula, heading not only toward him but toward the roadways nearby. *So far, at least.* If they reached the turnpikes, they could tear apart the cars—and drivers—to make more of themselves, then spread to the local boroughs, Secaucus, Newark, and beyond. By the time they reached Manhattan, there could be thousands of them. Even if only one of them survived, it could spawn another plague before long.

"Spider-Man!" The Robot Master had spotted him. "So you survived as well. I must confess, you are even more resourceful than I had anticipated. Very well . . . then I shall simply have to end this experiment."

"If you think—" He broke off, choking. "If you think it's gonna be that easy, Robespierre, you better think again!"

"But you forget, Spider-Man. My neural chip is still in your neck. And what was switched off can easily be switched back on—and *amplified!*"

Suddenly an overpowering shudder ran down his spine, his whole head throbbing with one overpowering perception: *DANGER!* He'd never felt it surge over him this intensely, not even when the immortal predator Morlun had triggered it in him as a calling card. At least that had still felt like a danger coming from a specific outside source, something he could run and hide from. Now, danger screamed at him from every direction. The auxons—the Robot Master—the fire—the water—the sky—the dirt—his own costume, binding him, choking him—his own hands, reaching to tear him apart—

He screamed, and it terrified him, the very sound threatening him, wanting to kill him.

There was no escape. There was nothing but danger, death, destruction. He clamped his mouth shut, for the very air screamed danger at him—he didn't dare breathe it in. But not breathing was just as dangerous, wasn't it? What could he do? What could he *do?*

The panic was overwhelming him, tearing him apart. His heart pounded in his chest, a ticking time bomb moments from going off. He was curled up into a ball, his eyes squeezed shut, but still he saw danger, heard it, tasted it. The danger had to come from *somewhere*, right? So much danger . . . who, what could cause it?

Morlun. It was Morlun, hunting him down, coming to feed. It was Osborn, the Green Goblin, swooping down on him, cackling as he took Peter's life apart one piece at a time. It was an oozing black symbiote, engulfing him, claiming a piece of his soul, then rejected and coming back for revenge with slavering fangs and claws. It was Mary Jane's plane exploding in midair. It was his parents' plane, crashing and burning as the Red Skull cackled. Uncle Ben, bleeding on the ground, buried in the ground. *Buried!* Kraven the Hunter, burying him alive. The weight pressing down . . . crushing him . . . countless tons of steel crushing him, pinning him as Doc Ock's base flooded, the vital canister of medicine just out of reach . . . *Aunt May! I couldn't save you! I'm helpless! I've lost!*

No! He remembered now—he hadn't given up. It had seemed hopeless then, but he had refused to stop trying, and he had prevailed against all odds. He had saved Aunt May. He had defeated Doc Ock, Kraven, Venom, Morlun, all of them, because he had refused to give up hope.

But I've lost so much! Uncle Ben . . . Gwen Stacy . . . everyone he'd loved and lost loomed before him now, the grief crushing him worse than any weight, filling him with fear that May and MJ and all his friends would be next.

But that fear empowered him. It compelled him to push forward through the hopelessness and dread. Yes, he knew he might lose everything— but that was no reason to give up. No, it was why he had to keep fighting, keep striving.

The Robot Master had miscalculated. Spider-Man could not be overwhelmed by fear of danger, fear of loss, fear of failure. Because Peter Parker faced that fear every day of his life. *How will I be hurt this time? What will I lose? What will I do wrong?* These were the daily refrains of his existence. Not paranoia, not panic, just the truth of his life. Failure was always an option.

And yet he kept on fighting, kept on going. Because he understood failure. He knew it too well to let it break him. He understood that failures and mistakes were simply basic colors in the tapestry of life. Losing wasn't the end of the world—it was a step along the way. It was a reason to try harder next time, to learn better, to push farther. The danger of failing again was always there, with him every moment of every day. But it didn't overwhelm him. It drove him. It inspired him. It made him more determined to keep fighting and pushing and striving to improve.

A man may lose, he told himself now, as he had told himself before when he had needed it most. *A man may be defeated. It's no disgrace—so long as he doesn't give up! I have a job to do . . . and I'm not giving up!*

I'm not!

"I'M NOT!!" The words tore from his lungs, here and now. Danger still clamored at him from all around, but he accepted it, lived with it, as he did every day. His instincts screamed at him to defend himself against everything, but he focused them, accepted the wrongness of them, and turned them back into something right, something useful—something aimed right at the nearest auxon robot. And once he had it aimed, he let it fly.

He barely registered what happened next. There was only adrenaline and motion and force and pain and rage. But he knew when one robot fell and he was striking at the next. And then the next . . . and there was the Robot Master standing there, gaping at him with Max Dillon's mouth. Two auxons still stood between him and Spider-Man, shielding him.

"I do not understand," the Master said. "This is inexplicable. The chip still functions. Your danger sense is still hyperstimulated. I cannot comprehend how you are still able to function!"

"That's because you're a machine," Spidey countered in a ragged voice. "All you know is binary thinking. You can't understand how the human heart can turn any weakness into a strength. How doubt and fear can become a source of confidence and hope."

But as he surveyed the scene, trying to distinguish real danger from the chip-induced fear he still felt, he saw that the genuine threat was worsening. The other auxons were spreading out faster, heading for the turnpikes and the cities. He could already hear screeching brakes and screams. Sirens were beginning to draw closer, no doubt responding to the fire, but they would be nothing but fuel for the auxons. *Sure, maybe it's no disgrace to me if I go down fighting without stopping these things—but it'll sure suck for the rest of humanity. This time, failure is* not *an option. I have to find a way. I have to . . .*

He realized he'd just given himself the answer. *The human heart.*

"Let me give you an example," he said, pointing at his adversary.

"Electro. Maxwell Dillon. Sure, he was just a sack of meat, inferior to you in every way. But he fought me more times than Mendel Stromm ever did, and certainly more than you ever have. You could never know my moves as well as Electro did. Despite his weaknesses, he's got strengths you'll never have."

"Easily remedied," the Robot Master said. "I can call on Dillon's knowledge at any time. Observe!" A bolt of electricity shot at him from Dillon's hands.

Spidey jumped clear easily. "So? You've had access to his knowledge all along, and it hasn't done you a lot of good. It takes more than raw knowledge to make an effective fighter," he went on, continuing to dodge the bolts that were being fired at him in a mechanical, predictable pattern. "It takes insight. Experience. The judgment and creativity of a living being. Electro may not have used his creativity much, but when he did—well, he was more trouble for me than you're managing!" *Come on, hurry up and fall for it. Those robots are getting closer to civilization by the minute.*

"You forget that the Dillon personality is still present in the neural substrate I occupy. It is a resource I can easily access." The next bolt almost got Spidey, a slight surge in the white noise of his danger response warning him just in time. The pattern had suddenly changed. The Robot Master laughed. "There. A simple matter of reactivating the dormant persona enough to interface with it! Ahh, I feel his enjoyment at humiliating you, Spider-Man!"

"Max!" Spidey cried, continuing to dodge the lightning. "You in there, ol' buddy? Speak to me!"

"Shut up and roast, webhead!"

There he is. "Listen to me, Max! Look around. Do you know where you are?"

"I know I'm kicking your butt!" The next lightning bolt connected with Spidey's belt, burning out the tracker and spider-signal. Excess current leaked through to Spidey's body, poleaxing him. Electro laughed and moved closer to gloat over the fallen hero. Spider-Man raised a shaky hand to web him, but Electro struck his webshooters with two more small discharges, fusing their nozzles. "There! You see, Spider-Man? Dillon's personality serves me! The advantage of his experience will allow me to destroy you!" He laughed again, still sounding like Electro.

"Max!" Spidey called. "Listen to what just came out of your mouth, Max! Do you know what's going on? You've been possessed! This *thing* has taken over your body! It's used you as a puppet for months now! Are you gonna stand for that?"

"Do not waste your breath, Spider-Man! Dillon no longer has the strength to overcome my control. His is a weak, inferior mind that functions only when I indulge it!" The Robot Master stepped closer. Spider-Man was still hurting, straining to move. "And I tire of indulging it. I have humiliated you enough! It is time to terminate you at last!"

His hand thrust forward at Spider-Man's face, fingers sparking as they built up a lethal charge.

○————————○

NO! Max Dillon struggled to cry out, to make his body stop disobeying him. Sure, he'd been happy enough to beat up on Spider-Man, and had no problem with killing him—but he didn't want to be just a gun with someone else pulling the trigger. He was nobody's tool.

Least of all this condescending thing in his head. He hadn't known it was in him until now, but when it had let him out of his shell halfway, enough to let him think again without giving him full control, he'd gotten something back in the other direction. Enough to know the thing had controlled him for months. Enough to know that it hated him, thought he was worthless, but was determined to keep an iron grip on him anyway.

That was what he couldn't stand—even more than the fact that this thing wanted to destroy the world. Sure, he liked the world just fine, didn't want to see it go anywhere while he happened to be living on it. But this wasn't living. Oh, he knew that, all right.

Because he'd lived it before. Because his mother had treated him the same damn way. Controlling him. Smothering him. Telling him he wasn't smart enough to earn a degree as an engineer and make something of his life. Keeping his ambitions petty so he wouldn't leave her the way Dad had found the sense to do. She hadn't believed in him, but she'd needed him. And so she'd kept him in the trap, made him feel small and powerless—until a freak accident had revealed how special he was and given him real power.

So he wasn't going to sit still for being controlled again. The thing in his head may have thought he was weak, but he wasn't. This was *his* body, blast it, and he decided what he did with it! So with a fierce effort of will, he wrenched his arm down and let it discharge into the ground.

Do not resist! the voice demanded.

Up yours, he responded.

"That's it, Max!" Spider-Man called. "Fight it!"

You are not strong enough to resist me, the voice insisted. *You have determination, but I think faster, adapt faster. I can paralyze you with a thought. Do not fight me! Serve me!* He felt his hands raising toward Spider-Man again.

"Come on!" the webhead cried. "Keep fighting! It's your body, Max! You own it! This piece of misbegotten computer code can't understand that. It may be in your brain, but it can't touch your heart. Fight for your body, Max! Fight for your identity!"

He forced his fists to close again. "I'm . . . trying," he managed to get out. "But . . . can't . . . hold on . . . ."

"Max, you can stop this. You can stop all of this! You can save the world, Max! You're the only one who can!"

Dillon was amazed. Spider-Man saying something like that to him? All his life, he'd wanted someone to believe in him, to tell him he was special . . . and it had to be this jerk?

Never mind. He'd take it. New strength surged through him. "How? What do I do?"

"Electromagnetic pulse, Max. You understand?"

"You mean . . . like a nuke? Burn out every machine around?"

"Or any especially intense discharge of energy into the atmosphere. A lightning bolt has a limited EMP effect, too. What we need, Max . . . is the biggest lightning bolt you've got in you. The biggest you've ever made!"

Dillon was struggling to control his body, but inside, he was laughing. *That's it? All I have to do to save the world—is my favorite thing in the whole world?* It was all he'd ever wanted—to feel the power inside him. To draw in more and more power and let it surge through his body, pure and cleansing, a force of nature that nothing could withstand.

And after being enslaved, imprisoned, chained inside his own skull, made a patsy by a Game Boy with delusions of grandeur? Oh, this was going to be good.

The thing in his head was fighting back, trying to stop him. But the power he felt surging through him, the determination, the freedom, the *joy*, was more than it could overcome.

Nearby were some downed power lines that had once brought electricity to the factory. He could feel them, feel the current they could connect him to. He could *taste* it. And once he got that taste, there was no way the thing could stop him.

Turning away from Spider-Man, he ran over to the wires. The voice screamed in his head, trying to shut down his body. He fell hard to the ground. But he could still taste the current. All he needed was to reach a little farther . . . go beyond his limits . . .

You'll never amount to more than you are, his mother's voice said. *So don't even try. You'll only be disappointed.*

She had never understood him. She was irrelevant now. He had tasted power. It was just beyond his reach. And he would have it.

He spread his fingers, and the wires came to him. He didn't know how. It didn't matter. It was their destiny to come to him. To give him the power he deserved.

All the power.

It poured into him. He felt the charge building, warming him, lifting him up. The thing's screams faded as the power roared through his every nerve, filling him with lightning. He *was* the lightning. He was the light. All the light. Around him, in the distance, city lights went dark as he drank up their power. He was the brightest light around, though the light was still inside him.

He drank it in until he was sated, but still he kept feeding. He drank it in until he felt he would burst, but still he kept feeding. That was exactly what he wanted: to burst. To erupt.

To explode!

He was burning up, his every nerve in sweet agony. The power was more than he could bear. It was transcendent. It was pure joy.

He held it in for as long as he could, but finally there was no way to hold it back. There was nothing left but the power, engulfing him completely. He *was* the power. And the power let itself burst free, reaching for the heavens.

SPIDER-MAN forced himself to move, crawling away from Electro as fast as he could. He could feel the air charging around him, feel a mounting spider-sense buzz that had nothing to do with the neural chip. He made himself go faster, made himself rise to his feet and run, even though his muscles had no strength.

And then the world exploded around him with light and noise, and a wave of superheated air slammed into his back and knocked him facedown into the dirt.

He didn't know how long it was until he came around again, dazed, his ears ringing. It was the sensation of something burning against his neck that awoke him. He slapped at it with his hands, found no fire. Pulling up the hem of his cowl, he felt for the heat, found it under the scarring. It was the chip. *The EMP. It burned it out!* Suddenly, he was grateful for the pain.

He heard a muffled voice through the ringing, felt hands grasping his arms and pulling him up, but felt no danger. *No danger. What a relief.* He looked up, and there was a fireman looking at him with concern. "Spider-Man!" he made out. "Was anyone else in there?"

"Just Electro . . . he got out . . . but I don't know if he survived the lightning."

"You mean the guy we found lying there naked in the middle of a big burn mark, not a scratch on him besides a bad all-over sunburn?"

"Is he alive?"

"Barely. Catatonic, but he's breathing. Just as well, since we couldn't do that much for him right now."

"What do you mean? Oh. Oh!" He looked around. There were fire trucks and other vehicles on the roads nearby, but they were quiet and dark, every one of them. The lights of the nearby boroughs were out, too. The EMP from the lightning bolt must have burned out their power systems. He saw by the glow of Secaucus and Newark, and by the eternal twilight that Manhattan generated as an aura.

There were other unmoving lumps as well. Over a dozen massive, plated robots, scattered all over the Meadowlands, limp and useless. Even as he watched, one teetered over as the gravel below it gave way, toppling it into the marsh.

"He did it," Spider-Man said. "Thank God. He did it."

The fireman frowned. "Who did what?"

Spidey couldn't stop himself from laughing. "The villain. The villain saved the day!"

FIFTEEN

WHATEVER A SPIDER CAN

"SO your spider-sense is finally back to normal?" Aunt May asked.

"Uh-huh," Peter said. He was lying in bed, propped up on pillows, with Mary Jane sitting next to him and stroking his hair while May laid out a tray bearing her patented chicken soup. It would've been paradise if he didn't ache over every inch of his body. But this, too, would pass. "Reed Richards cut out the remains of the chip for me, but it was definitely dead. And he couldn't find any sign of permanent damage to my nervous system."

"Uh—you *have* gotten it back, though, haven't you?" May asked. "Maybe we should test it?" she asked, holding up a spoonful of hot soup and raising her eyebrows at him, as if she sought his permission to threaten to dump it in his lap.

"No, no, that won't be necessary!" Peter told her. "The Torch had the same idea, and believe me, I'm hip to danger again." He rubbed the ear that Johnny Storm's near miss had singed.

"Well, I'm glad of that," May said, returning the spoon to the bowl.

"And I'm glad the chip was one-way," MJ added. "It's not like enough bad guys don't know your identity already. And I wouldn't have wanted someone spying on us during . . . well, you know." May glanced away, hiding a smile. "Even if it was just a computer program."

"From what I hear," Peter replied, "Electro wouldn't remember it anyway. Seems like the past few months are pretty much a blur to him. No sign that he remembers how to remote-control machinery or anything like that."

"And what about the Tinkerer?" MJ added.

"Oh. No sign of him. But I'm not too worried. He was as much a pawn in this as anyone. He got in over his head, and he got out." Peter had touched base with Felicia Hardy, who was at a loss to explain how she'd lost track of him. He suspected that Mason had sent the robot off on vacation to cover his own departure from home, then had arranged for it to be shipped back more cheaply as cargo, explaining how Felicia (assuming her quarry was alive) could have missed his return. Perhaps he'd brought the robot back to serve as a decoy for the Robot Master, in case his former employer sought revenge for his abandonment. They'd never know for sure unless they found the real Mason, but it wasn't really that important. "So he's still at large and still a nuisance, but I figure he'll probably lie low for a while." He sighed. "It's amazing how so much of life is about busting your butt just to get things back to the status quo."

Mary Jane leaned in and kissed his cheek. "Well, I for one am glad that you're back to the way you were. The status quo was going pretty well for us."

"You're right, it was. And I'm sorry for the way I acted, both of you. I should've listened to you, trusted you. I was trying too hard to hide from my own guilt, to avoid admitting my mistakes, that I closed myself off to everything that could help me make things better. Especially the two of you."

"It wasn't really your fault, dear," Aunt May said. "That chip in your neck was confusing you."

"Only because I let it. Everyone was telling me that my spider-sense warnings didn't make sense, but I wouldn't listen. And I should've seen it, too! I've realized now—every time I got a danger twinge from Jonah or his wife, it wasn't until *after* I saw or heard them arrive. Until after the AI in the chip registered their presence and triggered it. If they'd really been dangerous, I would've felt them coming before I saw or heard them. That should've tipped me off that something was bogus about those danger signals. But I didn't stop to question them because they were telling me what I wanted to believe. I just took it for granted that I was right and seized on anything that reinforced that, whether it made sense or not. I was acting . . . like Jameson."

He shook his head. "Amazing. I was being close-minded and paranoid, I needed Jameson to find the real bad guy and set me straight, and it was Electro who saved the world. Talk about your role reversals."

May gave him one of her wise, knowing smiles. "Well, it just goes to show that we can all use help sometimes, even from the most unexpected sources. That's why it's so important to look for the best in everyone."

"And be willing to admit what's not so great in yourself," Peter added.

"Well, you were right about one thing," MJ said. "The Tinkerer was part of it after all."

Peter shook his head. "I stumbled onto a right answer for the wrong reasons. That's not being right."

"Isn't it?"

"No. For the same reason I tell my students they need to show their work on their tests."

"I thought that was to prove they didn't cheat."

"That's only part of it—or it should be. The real reason is that it isn't really a right answer unless you understand what it means, and *why* it's right. Because it's not any one single answer that matters, it's knowing how to figure out the answers to whatever problems you need to solve in life."

May blinked away tears, smiling down at him. "Uncle Ben would be so proud of the man you've become, Peter. I know I am."

He took her hand. "Thanks, Aunt May."

Then MJ took his other hand and snuggled up against him. And suddenly the status quo didn't seem bad at all.

It won't last, his inner skeptic told him. *I know,* he replied. And he was grateful for the doubt. Because it let him value what he had so much more . . . and ensured that he would be ready to defend it the next time something came along to threaten it.

❯───────────❮

"HERE it is," Dawn Lukens said, reading the Wikipedia entry from her laptop screen. She was in a better mood lately, now that Bobby Ribeiro had awakened and showed every sign of making a full recovery in time. What's more, his medical bills had been covered by an anonymous donor, and given that the *Bugle*'s requests for interviews had ended at around the same time, Peter had an odd suspicion he knew who the donor was. All the other students had been released from the hospital, though Angela Campanella was still recuperating at home for another week or two. She certainly had no shortage of male classmates eager to bring her class assignments over and not do them with her.

"A red herring," Dawn went on, "is a smoked herring, or kipper. Apparently they were dragged across the trails of foxes to throw hounds off their scent."

Peter pondered that for a moment. "You know, that raises more questions than it resolves."

"Well, it sounds like there are some doubts about the etymology. There's also a nursery rhyme with a line about there being as many strawberries in the sea as red herrings in the wood."

"There, you see?" Peter told her. "You still have some answers after all."

She blushed. "Look . . . I'm sorry about what I said to you at the hospital—"

Peter held up his hands to stop her. "You were entitled. You were right—I was in denial. Overcompensating for my sense of guilt, trying to pretend I had all the answers. I guess I did get kind of overbearing."

"You weren't that bad."

"Well, you didn't see me at my worst." He gazed at her for a moment, thinking. "How about you? Are you still thinking of giving up teaching?"

It was a moment before she responded. "I did what you said . . . took my time before deciding. You weren't entirely off base that day. But . . . I still have my doubts. I don't think I can offer these kids any answers anymore."

"Maybe that's not a teacher's job," he said slowly. "Maybe it's more important to help them learn how to ask good questions. How to admit that they don't have all the answers, so they can open their minds to new possibilities. Maybe the best thing we can do for them is to admit that we're still learning, too—to show them that there's no shame in saying 'I don't know.'"

She studied him for a time, then smiled. "One thing I'm not ashamed to admit—I was wrong about you. And I'm glad I was."

"Don't worry about it," he replied. "I'm used to people being wrong about me. But I don't mind it that much anymore—because I know what it's like to be one of them."

○────────────────○

J. Jonah Jameson had become rather quiet on *The Wake-Up Call* lately. He hadn't exactly come out and apologized for accusing Spider-Man of involvement with the robots, but neither had he been hitting Spider-

Man that hard for going after him. So Spidey decided to pay him a visit and see if there were some way to build on the understanding they'd come to after the prison break.

Jonah's office still had alarms on the windows, so Spidey waited on the garage ceiling above his car. When JJJ approached that evening, Spidey announced himself. "I see you're not surrounded by security anymore. I'm flattered."

Jonah wasn't particularly startled; he even looked like he'd been expecting this. "Don't be," he said in a softer growl than usual. "Those guys were costing me a fortune."

"Yeah. Sorry about that." Clearing his throat, he hopped down to face Jonah man-to-man. "I mean that. I came here to say . . . I'm sorry I accused you. Sorry I went after you and your wife. And . . ." This was the hard part. "And I wanted to thank you for your help in setting me straight. I couldn't have done it without you."

Jonah puffed out his chest and grinned, which was no favor. "Well, well, well. Hearing you say that is music to my ears, Spider-Man. Whaddaya say we go find a camera crew so you can say it again?"

"Don't push it, Jonah." He chuckled. "Look . . . I'd like to think we could both learn something from this experience. We almost didn't catch the bad guy because we were too busy assuming we had to be right about each other. Maybe it's time we both admitted we could learn something from each other. Maybe it's time we tried actually trusting each other."

Jameson's smile had quickly faded, to be replaced by disbelief. "Are you kidding me?" he barked. "You expect me to trust you, after the way you acted? Harassing innocent people based on unfounded suspicions? Rushing in on impulse without considering the consequences? Putting innocent people's lives in danger fighting robots in the middle of town?"

"But Jonah—"

"Don't start with me, wall-crawler! I know what you're gonna say, that the bad guy was messing with your 'spider-sense.' But that's no excuse! You were still the one who decided to act on those feelings the way you did. And that proves that everything I've ever said about you is true. You may think you're one of the good guys, but the truth is, you're a reckless, self-absorbed brat who thinks this is nothing but a game!"

"That's not fair! I do this to protect people!"

"People like Paul Berry? Are you ever gonna stand up and do what's right for his widow, or just keep hiding behind that mask?"

"What happened to her husband is something I'll have to live with for the rest of my life, Jonah. And I'll do anything I reasonably can to help her if I get the chance. But there's too much at stake for me to expose my identity in court."

"So there it is. You'll do anything you can, so long as it doesn't cost you anything." Jameson sneered. "You call yourself so heroic, but you think it's all about what your power lets you get away with! You don't understand what it means to take responsibility for the consequences of what you do! That's what makes you a menace, Spider-Man, and someone needs to keep telling you that, telling the world that, until you finally wake up, listen, and throw away that silly mask once and for all!"

Spider-Man stared at him, stunned. *Power . . . responsibility.* He'd never heard Jameson express it in those terms before. He'd never understood why this man had always had it in for him so fiercely. And he had certainly never thought a moment would come when J. Jonah Jameson would remind him of his Uncle Ben.

A thought came to him. *Jameson has never set off my spider-sense. Not for real.* Maybe that meant something. If what Jonah was trying to say to him was no threat, then maybe it was something he should listen to.

He's right, Spidey realized. *If these past two weeks prove anything, it's that I do have it in me to go wrong in a big way. Every day, I run the risk of crossing the line . . . unless I constantly remind myself of what I could become.*

Or unless I have my own personal gadfly to do it for me.

Spider-Man laughed, startling Jameson. Then he startled the poor publisher even more, throwing his arms around him and kissing him right on the lips through the mask. "Don't ever change, Pickle-Puss!" he cried, hopping to the edge of the parking structure. "You're perfect just the way you are!"

As he swung out through the city, he could hear Jameson sputtering and crying, "You better believe I won't, you wall-crawling lunatic! As long as you're out there, I'll be hounding your every move! You'll never have a moment's peace from the relentless pursuit of J. Jonah Jameson!"

And all was right with Spider-Man's world.

ACKNOWLEDGEMENTS

THANKS again to Marco Palmieri for inviting me to write in the Marvel Universe, and thanks to him and Keith R. A. DeCandido for advice on Marvel continuity and New York geography. The Spiderfan.org site was also a great help to me in keeping track of continuity.

Of course, unequaled thanks are due to Stan Lee, who set it all in motion and made these characters timeless. Other *Spider-Man* writers whose work has influenced this novel include Mike W. Barr, Gerry Conway, Tom DeFalco, J. M. DeMatteis, Paul Jenkins, Howard Mackie, Bill Mantlo, David Michelinie, Roger Stern, J. Michael Straczynski, Len Wein, Zeb Wells, and Marv Wolfman, among others. In particular, key elements of the plot of this novel follow up on the events of *Peter Parker: Spider-Man* (Vol. 2) #27–28 by Paul Jenkins and Mark Buckingham. Spider-Man's motivating mantra in Chapter 14 ("A man may lose . . .") is taken almost verbatim from *Amazing Spider-Man* #33 by Stan Lee and Steve Ditko. Additional inspiration was provided by prior *Spider-Man* novelists Jim Butcher, Keith R. A. DeCandido, and Diane Duane. And thanks to Irving Berlin, Gary William Friedman, Joe Raposo, and Paul Francis Webster for most of the chapter titles.

Thanks to Google Maps and the New York City Building Database at www.emporis.com for invaluable guidance in plotting Spidey's travels. For details on the Diamond District, I learned much from the article "Here is 47th Street" by Pam Widener in the online magazine *The Morning News* (www.themorningnews.org). Thanks also to Pocket Books and the New York Comic-Con for having me as a guest in 2006 and 2007, giving me the chance to visit many of this book's locations personally. And thanks to

Rov on the Ex Isle BBS for advice on legal issues.

And thanks to John Semper and the rest of the creative staff of the 1994–98 *Spider-Man* animated series for finally showing me what a great character Spidey was, after decades of less authentic TV adaptations. Without their inspiration, I never would've done this book.

ABOUT THE AUTHOR

CHRISTOPHER L. BENNETT is one of Pocket Books' most prolific and popular authors of Star Trek tie-in fiction, including the epic Next Generation prequel *The Buried Age*, the *Star Trek: Department of Temporal Investigations* series, and the *Star Trek: Enterprise—Rise of the Federation* series. His original novel *Only Superhuman* was voted Library Journal's SF/Fantasy Debut of the Month for October 2012. He is a lifelong resident of Cincinnati, Ohio.

ALSO AVAILABLE FROM TITAN BOOKS

SPIDER-MAN
KRAVEN'S LAST HUNT

After years of crushing defeats, Kraven the Hunter—son of Russian aristocrats, game tracker supreme—launches a final, deadly assault on Peter Parker, the Amazing Spider-Man. But for the obsessed Kraven, killing his prey is not enough. Once his enemy is dead, Kraven must become the Spider.

SPIDER-MAN
FOREVER YOUNG

Hoping to snag some rent-paying photos of his arachnid-like alter ego in action, Peter Parker goes looking for trouble—and finds it in the form of a mysterious, mythical stone tablet coveted by both the Kingpin and the Maggia! Caught in the crosshairs of New York's most nefarious villains, Peter also runs afoul of his friends—and the police! His girlfriend, Gwen Stacy, isn't too happy with him, either. And the past comes back to haunt him years later when the Maggia's assumed-dead leader resurfaces, still in pursuit of the troublesome tablet! Plus: With Aunt May at death's door, has the ol' Parker luck disappeared for good?

TITANBOOKS.COM

MARVEL

MARVEL'S SPIDER-MAN: MILES MORALES
WINGS OF FURY

MILES MORALES has a lot going on, what with moving to a new neighborhood, dealing with the loss of his father, and the whole gaining super-powers thing. After a misunderstanding with the law, Miles questions what it means to be a hero when people are ready to believe the worst in you. Tempted by the power and freedom of his new abilities, Miles must decide what kind of Spider-Man he wants to be.

When Vulture starts wreaking havoc across the city with his new accomplice Starling, Miles can't just sit back and watch. Teamed up with Peter Parker, the two Spider-Men must stop the winged duo before they can unleash experimental tech across the whole city. With lives at risk, can Miles step up and be a hero?

For more fantastic fiction, author events,
exclusive excerpts, competitions, limited editions and more

VISIT OUR WEBSITE
titanbooks.com

LIKE US ON FACEBOOK
facebook.com/titanbooks

FOLLOW US ON TWITTER AND INSTAGRAM
@TitanBooks

EMAIL US
readerfeedback@titanemail.com